SKETCHES OF IRISH CHARACTER

CHAWTON HOUSE LIBRARY SERIES:
WOMEN'S NOVELS

Series Editors: Stephen Bending
Stephen Bygrave

TITLES IN THIS SERIES

Forthcoming Titles

Mrs S. C. Hall,
Sketches of Irish Character

EDITED BY

Marion Durnin

Routledge
Taylor & Francis Group

LONDON AND NEW YORK

First published 2014 by Pickering & Chatto (Publishers) Limited

Published 2016 by Routledge
2 Park Square, Milton Park, Abingdon, Oxfordshire OX14 4RN
711 Third Avenue, New York, NY 10017, USA

First issued in paperback 2016

Routledge is an imprint of the Taylor & Francis Group, an informa business

BRITISH LIBRARY CATALOGUING IN PUBLICATION DATA

Hall, S. C., Mrs., 1800–1881 author.
Sketches of Irish Character. – (Chawton House library series. Women's novels)
1. Ireland – History – 19th century – Fiction. 2. Ireland – Social conditions
– 19th century – Fiction. 3. Ireland – Politics and government – 19th century
– Fiction.
I. Title II. Series III. Durnin, Marion, editor.
823.7-dc23

ISBN 13: 978-1-138-23548-9 (pbk)
ISBN 13: 978-1-8489-3390-3 (hbk)

Typeset by Pickering & Chatto (Publishers) Limited

CONTENTS

ACKNOWLEDGEMENTS

My thanks go to Jarlath Killeen and Eve Patten of Trinity College Dublin and to Margaret Kelleher of University College Dublin, who suggested the new edition. I am grateful to Stephen Bygrave and Stephen Bending, Chawton House Library Series Editors, for their encouragement and to Mark Pollard and Imogen Facey at Pickering & Chatto. Gillian Dow and all at Chawton House Library were a boon, ensuring that Chawton was a memorable haven in which to research during my Visiting Fellowship.

Others to whom I owe a debt of thanks are Owen and Maxine Durnin; the members of the Women's Studies Group 1558–1837 who have been a constant support, as has Sally Osborn with her editorial expertise and Brendan Durnin, ardent Francophile.

Finally, this book is dedicated to Kevin, *a chuisle mo chroí*; to the dear memory of both my mother Winifred, a fine Wexford woman, and my sister Deirdre, who was there at the beginning ... and to Niamh and Ruby, already well on the road to pedantry!

Ar scáth a chéile a mhaireann na daoine.

LIST OF FIGURES

INTRODUCTION

With the Catholic Emancipation Act of 1829 came the rejuvenation of Irish publishing as self-assured writers produced 'Trait upon Custom upon Legend upon Pastime of the Irish peasantry'.[1] Published and republished between 1829 and 1876, the early decades of the appearance of *Sketches of Irish Character* were troubled ones in Irish literary history. Overshadowed by memories of the French Revolution and the rebellion of 1798, the Irish publishing market was in the doldrums, divided along opposing political and religious lines, with publications from both sides overladen with religious propaganda. Class also counted; the peasantry could not afford to buy books whilst the ascendancy and aspiring classes preferred to appear *à la mode* by buying popular English or Scottish journals, such as *Blackwood's* or *Fraser's*.

Contrarily, the English periodical press was in its heyday. Complex factors fed an appetite for all manner of literature on Irish issues. Technological innovation enabled cheaper publications, as did reductions in tax and stamp duties, while rapid industrialization allowed easier travel. Social unrest in Ireland, following a slump in demand for arable products, and political agitation for Catholic Emancipation attracted much attention in the media, focusing a spotlight on Irish issues. Ireland as a backdrop was almost *de rigueur* in the novel, with Rochester sending Jane Eyre to find employment in Connemara.[2]

In her Introduction to the third revised edition of *Sketches of Irish Character* in 1844, Mrs Hall mentions straight away that her sketches are set in Bannow, 'my native' place'.[3] She points out that, in this neighbourhood where the days of her childhood were spent, 'there was, comparatively, none of the poverty and consequent wretchedness to be encountered unhappily elsewhere'.[4] In later life, surveying the past from her home in Addlestone, Surrey, Hall recalls her childhood in Bannow which made such an indelible impression on her. Her claim that the 'Firfield'[5] grass is not as green, as that which carpeted the meadows of Graige'[6] animates her declaration that 'this district of the County of Wexford is superior to any other part of the south of Ireland' and demonstrates an understandable bias to the locality of the baronies of Bargy and Forth which are especially fortunate; in their 'natural advantages'.[7] Such superiority arose, she tells us, because the inhabitants are chiefly, descendants of the Anglo-Norman settlers, who, in the reign of the second Henry, invaded and conquered – or rather subdued Ireland: and, until very recently they retained so much of their ancient customs and manners, as actually to speak a language unknown in other districts of the Kingdom. She declares that

> the people are to this day 'a peculiar people', and retain much of their English char-acter. This is apparent, not alone in the external aspect of the country – the skilfully farmed fields ... the well trimmed hedgerows ... The peasantry ... have an air of sturdy independence ... achieved by their own honest industry.[8]

This sense of Bannow being a special place is transferred to the people who inhabit it and both are inextricably linked with a notion of their being Irish, but in some way better because this 'Irishness' is measured against a template of Englishness. This is exemplified when Mrs Hall extols the beauty of Bannow:

> The neighbouring fields looked, indeed, beautiful; and the bright greenery extended, at either side, around the mill-stream; here and there a gnarled oak, or a gay thorn tree ... All of this 'formed a picture as calmly beautiful as even fruitful and merry England could supply.[9]

This serene image of the Bannow landscape occurs in the sketch 'Captain Andy', which recalls an event infamous in the records of the insurrection of 1798 – the firing of the barn at Scullabogue.[10] Yet, such 'calmly beautiful', idealized descrip-tions seem to have caught the imagination and attention of her readers above the stark, even Gothic observation such as is made later in the story:

> If there be a solitude like that of the sepulchre, it is the solitude of ruins: in mountain loneliness you may image an unpeopled world, fresh from God's own hand, pure, bright, and beautiful, as the new-born sun: but a moss-grown ruin, speaks powerfully, in its loneliness, of gone-by days, of bleached and marrowless bones.[11]

So, perhaps it should not seem unusual in the light of this growing interest in Irish locations, characters and themes that it occurred to Carter Hall, to encour-age his wife to follow him on the literary path. Carter describes the decision by Mrs Hall to write the sketches as a kind of epiphany. He describes how

> one evening she was telling me some anecdotes of her old Irish school-master, 'Master Ben'. Said I, "I wish you would write about that just as you tell it". She did so. I printed her story in *The Spirit and Manners of the Age*,[12] a monthly periodical I then edited, and from that day dates her career as an author.

Other tales of the friends and acquaintances of her childhood and girlhood fol-lowed. Eventually they were collected into a volume, entitled 'Sketches of Irish Character', and she became 'an author by profession'.[13]

The emergence of *Sketches* into the public sphere was not, however, as spontaneous as this anecdote might imply, and there is a complex history for almost every story that made it into the first volume. Moreover, despite the claims of both the Halls, 'Master Ben' was *not* the first story by Mrs Hall to have been published. When *Sketches of Irish Character* appeared, Mr and Mrs Hall were keen to suggest that Mrs Hall was a new writing talent, fresh to the market. However, under the pseudonym 'A. M. H.' Mrs Hall had already published 'The Murmurer Instructed: A Tale by A. M. H'. in *The Amulet: A Christian and Literary Remembrancer*[14], three years before the appearance in print of her *Sketches of Irish Character*. Moreover, 'The Gipsey Girl', which also bore her initials and writing style, appeared in the 1828 edition of *The Amulet*.[15] In the same magazine for 1829, reference was made to *The Amulet* and the editor and 'his ingenious lady', which Keane justly takes as further proof of Mrs Hall's pre-*Sketches* 'literary strivings'.[16] Moreover, Mrs Hall was appointed editor of the Christmas gift book, *The Juvenile Forget-me-not*, a role she fulfilled between 1829 and 1838 thus making her way in the sphere of journalism.

A point not previously noted is that Mrs Hall *also* published early stories under her husband's name, 'S. C. Hall', omitting the identifying 'Mrs'. *The Amulet* of 1829 contains stories titled 'The Fisherman', 'The Rose of Fennock Dale' and 'The Soldier's Wife', all attributed to 'S. C. Hall'. However in *The Mountain Daisy and other Stories* (1866),[17] published thirty-seven years later, these same stories appear, all attributed to the author of the volume by 'Mrs S. C. Hall'. Should any doubt remain that they are from her hand, Mrs Hall claims, in her introduction to this volume, that the publishers urged her to collect her '"waifs and strays" and place them before the public in a modern dress'.[18] By this, she does not mean that the stories have been appreciably altered, but that they were written 'so long ago, that a new race of readers have sprung up' which causes her to agree with her publishers that 'these old tales are as good as new'.[19] The existence of these earlier works make it even more perplexing that the Halls were so keen to give the impression that her *Sketches of Irish Character* was her first and almost casually produced work, when in fact she had been an aspiring and published writer for some time. This discovery prompts the suggestion that the Halls were sensitive to the commercial advantage to be gained by presenting Mrs Hall as a 'new' writer. She and her writing would thus be imbued with a freshness and vivacity that would be attractive to readers. This enthusiasm would hopefully then transmit to the 'new' form of stories emerging about the Irish. The combination of 'new writer' and 'new' kind of writing about the Irish peasantry could be judged a wily marketing ploy in which the combined novelty of author and subject matter might prove a winning combination in the competitive English marketplace.

Hall's stories published in *The Amulet* of 1830[20] align with the political and cultural ethos of that annual. Mrs Hall's Irish sketches, which were destined later for *Sketches of Irish Character*, 'Annie Leslie: an Irish Tale'[21] and 'We'll See About It'[22] embrace the theme of virtuous living overlaid with imperialist ideology expressing, as Seamus Deane explains, that 'it was very Irish to be irresponsible and very English to be responsible'.[23] In the first sketch, Annie Leslie is a 'flower of many lands', the offspring of an English father and a Scottish mother, with grandparents from Wales and 'beyant the salt sea' and she stands as a somewhat exotic hybrid imago awaiting metamorphosis into full Irishness.[24] This appears to be another gauche attempt by Mrs Hall to impregnate her stories with allegories of The Union, which she vehemently supports. The tropes of family and marriage are used to interrogate the notion of the English imperative to reform the Irish people in an age of imperial expansion.

In literature the frequent 'typing of Ireland as an alternately dependent or unruly daughter, sister, or wife' as a constant and reliable means of delineating 'Irish political incapacity'[25] is borne out in the story of 'Annie Leslie'. In the highly contrived unit that comprises Hall's Leslie family, all the countries of the Union of Great Britain and Ireland are represented in the English/Scottish/Welsh/Irish construct. The paterfamilias is Irish and holds sway over his daughter Annie's destiny. Annie's mother is Scottish and approves the union between Annie and Andrew Furlong, symbolic representatives respectively of Ireland and England. Annie's refusal to follow her (English) father's wish that she marry the publican, Andrew Furlong, takes on political and ideological currency. Annie's (Irish) sweetheart, James McCleary, describes Furlong as a 'lick-plate[26] to an unworthy member, who sould his country to the union and Lord Castlereagh'.[27] Thus, Annie symbolizes a recalcitrant Ireland, dragging her heels reluctantly on the matter of marriage or 'union' with Andrew Furlong (England) and she is rendered 'absolutely dumb' having shrunk with 'horror from his grasp'.[28]

Here Annie represents 'daughter Ireland' being pressured into a loveless and unwanted marriage by her anglicized suitor and English father. Annie is tempted with the blandishments of a limited freedom (a new jaunting-car) in which to drive to church 'as may suit your conscience'.[29] Annie's femininity, representative of Ireland, demonstrates the way in which gender may be used circuitously to articulate the unequal relationship between Ireland and England.

Ostensibly a story about a lover's tiff, Hall puts the case against the 'ill effects of the absentee system'.[30] She does not however recommend that the system be changed, merely calls for the return of the 'good' landlord to his estate. The deleterious effect of absenteeism on various sections of Irish society is borne out in the predicaments of the characters in 'Annie Leslie'. Hall attacks the injustices of the consequences of the absentee system, but not the root cause, colonization itself, with characters that teeter on the brink of stereotype. When Edgeworth treated the same subject in *Ennui* (1809) and *The Absentee* (1812), she threatened to turn 'potentially brilliant stories into treatises' by urging English landlords to return to their Irish estates. Hall, however, accentuates the Protestant code of hard work, virtuous living and redemption rather than addressing the deeper political question of colonial exploitation. In Annie's resolution to reform and not 'to coquet it again', Hall emphasizes the danger posed to society by women who threaten to disrupt the moral code through transgressive sexual behaviour and lack of restraint.[31] In the end, pious Protestant values are upheld.

Hall's sketches 'Master Ben', 'Independence' and 'Black Dennis' were tried first in another of Carter Hall's periodicals, *The Spirit and Manners of the Age*, 1829.[32] Hall's sketches fit well with the strong Evangelical bent of this embattled publication and she was keen to abstract and uphold those practical values of Evangelism suitable to an improvement philosophy. In her stories there are few problems that cannot be solved by good actions and adherence to the word of the Gospel and this is clear from her first published sketch, 'Master Ben'. The fashion for the pen-portrait sketch perhaps accounts for the popularity of 'Master Ben', whose portrayal ignited Mrs Hall's reputation. Strangely, the tragedy of the narrative, which reveals much of the lives of the peasantry, attracts scant attention. Underwriting this simple tale is the powerlessness of the peasants and the complaisance with which they accepted their lot. The story becomes autobiographical when 'Master Ben', the dominie, is hired to teach the young 'Miss Marie'. The character of the hedge schoolmaster Benjamin Rattin was based on Benjamin Radford, a teacher much respected in the area and known to correct the priest's bog Latin on occasion. Master Ben 'rose in estimation' in the locality when it became known that he had been chosen for the role of tutor to 'Miss Marie'. Similarly, 'Peggy the Fisher', 'Larry Moore', 'The Bannow Postman' and 'Old Frank' were characters formed from her childhood memories of the rich personalities that peopled her childhood days in Bannow.

So, having dipped her toe in the literary waters of the magazines with which her husband Carter was associated in the 1820s, fame came swiftly to Mrs Hall on the publication of her first edition of *Sketches of Irish Character* in 1829. The rapid loss of anonymity took her by surprise. She records 'how astonished I was to find myself 'famous' in the generous pages of the 'Literary Gazette' and occupying two columns of 'The Times!''.[33]

The sketches reveal the narrative voice of a woman with complex ties to both Irish and English culture at a crucial time in the history of both countries. Published in the same year as the passing of the Catholic Relief Act of 1829, *Sketches of Irish Character* was directed towards an exoteric English audience that might have been expected to find such writing provincial and naïve. Indeed, many reviewers regarded the work as 'thoroughly Irish', that is, 'with all the vivacity, blarney, blunders, pigs, and potatoes, of a Bannow cottage duly set forth'.[34]

In his essay, 'Mrs Hall's Ireland', Barry Sloan dubbed Mrs Hall 'the third significant female writer of Anglo-Irish fiction [after Maria Edgeworth and perhaps

Lady Morgan] in the first half of the nineteenth century'.[35] Mrs Hall's *Sketches of Irish Character* may now be considered a largely 'forgotten' work, where, once, she was a household name and *Sketches of Irish Character* so popular that jokes were made in the magazines about the number of its editions. Both W. M. Thackeray and Marguerite Power (Countess of Blessington) refer to Mrs Hall in terms that assume the reader's knowledge of Hall and her *Sketches*. In *Grace Cassidy: or, the Repealers*, Power's character Mrs Forrester recommends to Lady Oriel that

> [w]hen you visit Ireland, dear sister ... you will better be able to appreciate the truth and beauty of this lady's *Irish Sketches*; they are portraits from the life, and full of truth and beauty. The wife of one of my father's tenants, Grace Cassidy ... is just the heroine for the graphic pen of Mrs Hall, who alone could do her justice.[36]

Thackeray's casual mention of her in *The Irish Sketch Book* assumes the reader's prior familiarity with her writing.[37] The extent to which she was acknowledged as a kind of cultural 'celebrity' is evident in her appearance in 'The Gallery of Literary Characters' in *Fraser's Magazine*, (1836). Drawings of famous literary characters were accompanied by a pen-portrait, framed in the caustic prose of the magazine's director, William Maginn (1794–1842), and included eminent figures such as Goethe, Walter Scott, Thomas Moore and, in June 1836, Mrs Hall.

Mr and Mrs Hall were among the many artists and writers who followed the shift in political power from Dublin to Westminster. Among that 'absentee talent' were Daniel Maclise, John Banim and Lady Morgan; although Maria Edgeworth, born in Oxfordshire in 1768 crossed St. George's Channel in the opposite direction. Mrs Hall became an émigrée and moved to London aged fifteen, leaving the country house at Graige, near Bannow on the death of her grandmother. Samuel Carter Hall also found his way to England following his early life in Ireland; a move that saw him progress from parliamentary reporter to renowned editor.

The passing of the Act of Union in 1800 coincided with a steep rise in the output of antiquarian and other authors in the early decades of the nineteenth century. Writers began to regard themselves as distinctively Irish and this was reflected in the works they produced. There arose a 'glut in the market'[38] of fiction and the Irish output conveniently filled a coinciding niche in the English market. In tandem with this growth in published material, an obsessive interest developed in England about her Irish subjects. An appetite for ever more information about Ireland grew, whether this took the form of tales, sketches, scholarly works or parliamentary reports.[39] This interest may be attributed to the prior expansion in the popularity of antiquarianism in Ireland, concurrent with a similar phenomenon in England and on the Continent. Aspects of the peregrine and the Oriental, seen as exotic, led to a curiosity about 'Celtic' cultures, including Ireland. This interest may be traced to a gradual shift in consciousness among Ireland's social elite

between 1760 and 1890, during which time this group 'originally English in ethnic background, cultural outlook and political allegiance, redefined its self-image
and began to place itself under Gaelic auspices'.[40]

Thomas Crofton Croker (1798–1854), a friend of the Halls, is generally seen
as instrumental in a changed perception of Gaelic culture, from a 'written historical one' to the 'oral and contemporary';[41] the consequence of this being that
the Irish peasantry, previously seen as 'the sullen dregs of an old culture, full of
disaffection and hatred for their new rulers, gain cultural interest'. They come to
be viewed, in romantic, Grimm-like fashion, as the repository of quaint superstition and primordial folk and fairy tales'.[42] This taste for new renderings of the
life of the peasantry 'did much to de-historicize and de-politicize the image of
the Irish peasantry'. Their lives were no longer perceived to exist in a distinct
moment in history but 'rather in the timeless repository of a primeval, timeless
life ...'[43] Seamus Deane points out that

> from the 1820's, Ireland produced a sub-genre of memoirs, sketches, tales, legends,
> all of which were devoted to the recording of the hitherto occluded life of the Irish
> peasantry and many of which did so in an antiquarian spirit, setting down what they
> feared would be lost forever.

He counts among this type of work: Crofton Croker's *Fairy Legends and Traditions of the South of Ireland*, Eyre Evans Crowe's *Today in Ireland*, both of which
were published in 1825, Cesar Otway's 1827 work *Sketches of Ireland* and Mrs
Hall's first edition of *Sketches of Irish Character*.[44]

The reasons behind the proliferation of the literary sketch in the early decades
of the nineteenth century are complex. This was its heyday and the growth of its
popularity was fuelled by advances in print technology. As Onslow observes, the
reduction in punitive advertisement tax and stamp duty allowed new and interesting journals to flourish.[45] This growth in literary production grew alongside
a fresh curiosity about Ireland and the need to give an English readership what
it wanted. It was difficult to accommodate what Deane describes as the 'entity
'Ireland'' in the canon of traditional forms of literary representation and there
was a nostalgic desire to glimpse what Leerssen describes as the vanishing world
of 'the pleasant peasant', to recapture the past and to read stories about 'rustic,
ahistorical and apolitical community life, the idyllic view of Ireland as a mere
province or backwater where timeless quaint characters go about their humble
and picturesque ways'.[46] Importantly, these stories acted as a distraction from real
political issues and demand grew for information in varied forms, from sketches
to parliamentary reports from other colonial outposts, and it was argued that
these productions permitted English readers to themselves discern whether or
not their 'various possessions were peopled by rational and enlightened beings
or by barbarous and exotic savages'.[47] Consequently, the English reader could be

both mesmerized and distanced from the possible danger of encountering such 'savages' who were curtailed safely within the confines of 'the book'. Ireland was at this time a *terra incognita* to most across St. George's Channel. Ireland was 'unimaginably remote to some of its proprietors; if a few intrepid British souls set foot there for the odd vacation it was because, so Sir Jonah Barrington considered, the place was as exotically alien to them as Kamchatka'.[48]

Mrs Hall's choice of the sketch form and the people of Bannow, her native village in Co. Wexford, as her subject was innovative. Although it is probable that Hall was attracted to the sketch for the same reasons as Dickens and Thackeray, her work encountered the same problems as theirs. Although the villagers of Bannow were judged by Hall to be worthy subjects of her writing, they may not have been thought fit to occupy a central position in a sustained work of fiction, such as a novel. If this is the case, then her decision to employ the literary sketch is culturally and politically significant. Its use may have signalled the content of a 'sketch' as somewhat ephemeral and of passing interest; unworthy of being recorded for posterity. This left Hall open to accusations of stereotyping and W. B. Yeats criticized both Samuel Lover and Mrs Hall in this regard. Although acknowledging both writers as 'the driving forces of the literature of the time', Yeats believed that they did not take the populace seriously and imaged the country as a 'humorist's Arcadia'. Yeats does not accuse Hall and Lover of playing false in this, but charges that they 'merely magnified an irresponsible type, found oftenest among boatmen, carmen, and gentlemen's servants in the type of a whole nation'.[49] Rafroidi shades this comment by suggesting that the problem lay not so much in humorous or paternalistic portrayals of character, but that, as such, their dilemmas were 'the least likely to be directly attributed to economic, political or social causes'.[50] The sketch form, adopted by a member of the Anglo-Irish ascendancy, such as Mrs Hall, carried with it ideological associations of the artistic sketch, previously the domain of the eighteenth-century non-professional artist and dilettante, who also enjoyed a position of social superiority and power. The sketch form would therefore impose constraints upon the seriousness with which a writer's subject might be treated, the genre itself having historical associations via the artistic sketch with the amateur, the slight, the light, the unfinished. It might be that a writer such as Hall would choose the literary sketch over the more serious 'tale' or novel in order that matters of political and economic import and sensitivity might be glossed over and appear less prominent. It was her expressed aim to be 'of no party' as she saw in each 'much to praise and much to blame'; as Carter attests, 'she tried, as she did with her bonnet ribbons to blend the orange and the green'.[51] Despite this proclaimed neutrality, it would seem that the sketch form more easily allowed her to assume the 'neutral' stance of the observer whist all the while, her narrator was busy about her agenda of changing, remaking and reforming the Irish peasantry.

The Catholic Emancipation Act of 1829, the year *Sketches of Irish Character* was first published, brought new hope and resurgence to publishing in Ireland. This renaissance followed the years of stagnation since the Union of Great Britain and Ireland in 1800, when it was common for magazines to comment that 'a dreadful silence covers the land'.[52] In the eighteenth century, Dublin publishers had flourished, producing a record number of European novels at a competitive price, which allowed the reading public to buy cheap reprints. The industries of both publishing and printing suffered a decisive downturn with the introduction of the Copyright Act, which followed the Act of Union and rendered illegal the publication of pirated books. The period between 1800 and 1829 was 'an era of lassitude and aimlessness'[53] which resulted is the migration of talent to England where the situation was more optimistic. The growth in the periodical market there went hand-in-hand with a burgeoning interest in Ireland, an interest often satisfied by the inclusion of literary 'sketches' of Ireland in the periodical press. Both Anna Maria and Samuel Hall, who met and married in London having left Ireland, looked to the burgeoning English market for literary, editorial and financial success.

Political events were also a vital factor in a new interest in Irish affairs and the growth in political agitation led to a proliferation of media attention. The underlying fear that the Irish Catholic pressure for Emancipation would disrupt the Union fitted in with a view of Ireland as a 'squalid, fractious, brutalized nation' and, as Eagleton observes, created a vacuum into which such fears could be drawn. They could then be ameliorated in fiction and thus the danger of Irish strangeness and barbarity could be encapsulated and controlled.[54] The publicity that attended Daniel O'Connell's election in 1813 and his powerful personality in Parliamentary debate was a factor ensuring that 'Ireland became something of a fashionable topic for fiction'.[55] Since the success of Sydney Owenson's *Wild Irish Girl*[56] in 1806, it became almost *de rigueur* to provide at least an Irish backdrop to concerns not directly related to Ireland, though, paradoxically, the country could simultaneously be viewed as a 'locus at once of foreign and domestic revolution'.[57] Charlotte Brontë wrote 'An Adventure in Ireland' in 1829 and returns to the troubled relations between England and Ireland in both *Jane Eyre* (1847) and *Shirley* (1849).

An alleged lack of political bias was seen as an admirable quality in Hall's work. Indeed a recurring motif in commentaries on her ability to 'paint the nationalities of the peasantry and working-classes with a fidelity, to which are added touches of a more general nature ...'[58] The terms in which the opinions are couched announce a resolute if unconscious condescension by contributors who can state that

> though dwelling on the foibles of poor Pat, she makes him rather an object of sympathy than of ridicule ... while in all her writings we may observe a total absence of all appearance of that party prejudice which may too often be traced in writers on the subject of Ireland.

In 1829 when *Sketches of Irish Character* was first published, Mrs Hall implied that she was partly following in the footsteps of Mary Russell Mitford who enjoyed widespread success with her sketches of rural life in Berkshire with *Our Village* (1824–32). The realist model in fiction was still in flux at this time. As Killick points out, 'since the turn of the nineteenth century and the advent of the Waverley novels, the parameters for realism in fiction had shifted'.[59] The success of the historical novel had created a market for the type of naturalistic and descriptive style in which reality encompassed the present, but also the past and the future. What Mrs Hall admired in Mitford's work was her rendering of 'scenes taken from the life'.[60] But this 'life' was a fictive creation and Mitford's sketches 'work towards a particularly bourgeois, unashamedly sunny aesthetic of realism, rather than claiming to be concretely and unassailably real'.[61] Moreover, the reality of life in 'sunny Berkshire' was very different to that of Bannow; particularly the Bannow depicted not in the 'present' of 1829, the year *Sketches* was published, but projected nostalgically back to a way of life on the brink of extinction. The village of Bannow represented by Hall was set in the 1800s when memories of the rupture of the Rebellion of 1798 were still fresh in the minds of the inhabitants. Hall's attempt to represent the peasantry of her native village would inevitably be a different kind of fiction to that produced by Mitford. *Sketches of Irish Character* was published just as Maria Edgeworth was discovering that the disjunction of conditions in a post-Union Ireland rendered it impossible to continue to represent the same in her fiction. In choosing an intense study of one locality, Hall builds on, yet goes beyond, the regionalism initiated by Maria Edgeworth in *Castle Rackrent* (1800) and continued by Mary Leadbeater (1758–1826) in *Cottage Dialogues among the Irish Peasantry* (1811). The rise of evangelicalism was evident in the increasing moral inflection that characterized fiction and the periodical press. The improving virtues of practical Christianity were advocated by writers such as Hannah More. Dedicated periodicals of strongly Protestant religious bent, such as *The Iris* (1830–1), sprang up and fiction suitable for the tenor of these publications was in demand.

In form and content, the third, revised edition of *Sketches of Irish Character* differed from the more modest earlier productions, being larger in size, lavishly bound and illustrated. Hall was innovative in giving credit to the artists and engravers responsible. Their names and the title of each individual illustration are listed on the 'Contents' page, giving emphasis to their importance. Even more significant are the additions Hall made to the text in an attempt to integrate the five full plate portraits by Maclise. In their entertaining loveliness and flirtatiousness, it is pertinent to ask what these images do not show. In this, Hall wished to gain for her sketches the commercial success which illustration and embellishment had won for the annuals. Crucially, this undermining of the primacy of illustration over the written word raises the question of whether illustration reinforces meaning, subverts it or merely acts as decoration. Such an Ireland, populated by such engaging creatures would be a distraction from real political issues, but gives a reassuring glimpse of an Irish peasantry made to an orderly 'English' template rather than a place populated by the dirty and unruly.

Hall was much criticized for presenting caricatures of the Irish and of not truly understanding them. When it was suggested to William Carleton that his depictions of Irish peasant life were 'more reliable than those of Mrs S. C. Hall', he re-joined: 'Why, of course they are: did she ever live with the people as I did? Did she ever dance and fight with them as I did? Did she ever get drunk with them as I did?' To estimate the value of Hall's *Sketches of Irish Character* on such terms is to miss the point. Inevitably her writing is informed by her life as a member of the Protestant ascendancy class. The value of her writing lies precisely in the tension created by her 'inbetweeness'; by her formative years in Bannow, followed by marriage and life in London; by her Huguenot Protestant values informed by a solitary childhood as the pet of doting Irish Catholic servants; her formative years spent both as a nature-loving wanderer among the fields and coast of Bannow, to emigration, marriage and a life in journalism and authorship. Most importantly and, either ignored, unrecognized or misunderstood by her critics, Hall's very liminality leaches through the sketches to reveal the deep trauma felt by the Protestant ascendancy haunted by the rebellion of 1798. Far from being pretty tales of cottage girls and careless youths, they are riven with death, abandonment, orphanhood, even gothic strangeness, and bear witness to a way of life on the cusp of extinction.

Notes

1. B. Hayley, 'A Reading and Thinking Nation: Periodicals as the Voice of Nineteenth-Century Ireland', in B. Hayley and E. McKay (eds), *Three Hundred Years of Irish Periodicals* (Gigginstown: Lilliput Press, 1987), pp. 29–48.

2. C. Bell, [Charlotte Brontë], *Jane Eyre: An Autobiography* (Peterborough, Ontario: Broadview Press, 1999), p. 336.

3. Mrs S. C. Hall, *Sketches of Irish Character*, 3rd revsd edn, 2 vols (London: M. A. Nattali, 1844).

4. Ibid.

5. *Firfield*: The residence bought by the Halls in Addlestone, Surrey in 1849. Many celebrated friends visited to enjoy the Halls' hospitality and all were required to plant a fir tree to commemorate the occasion.

6. Mrs S. C. Hall, *Sketches of Irish Character*, 5th revsd edn (London: Chatto and Windus, *c*. 1876), p. vi.

7. Ibid., p. vi.

8. Ibid., p. vii.

9. Mrs S. C. Hall, *Sketches of Irish Character*, 1st edn, 2 vols (London: Frederick Westley and A. H. Davis, 1829), vol. 1, pp. 136–7.

10. See C. Tóibín, "New Ways of Killing Your Father': Review of *Paddy and Mr Punch: Connections in Irish and English History* by R. F. Foster', *London Review of Books*, 15:22

(1993), pp. 3–6, available online at http://www.lrb.co.uk./v15/n22/colm-toibin/new-ways-of-killing-your-father [accessed 15 May 2014].

11. Hall, *Sketches*, 1st edn, vol. 1, p. 155.
12. Mrs S. C. Hall, 'Master Ben', *Spirit and Manners of the Age: A Christian and Literary Miscellany*, New Series (London: Frederick Westley and A. H. Davis, 1829), vol. 11, pp. 35–41.
13. S. C. Hall, *Retrospect of a Long Life: From 1815 to 1883* (New York: Appleton, 1883), p. 551.
14. S. C. Hall (ed.), *The Amulet: A Christian and Literary Remembrancer* (London: W. Baines & Son, 1826), pp. 334–45.
15. S. C. Hall (ed.), *Amulet, or, Christian and Literary Remembrancer* (London: Baynes and Wightman & Cramp, 1828), pp. 91–105.
16. M. Keane, *Mrs S. C. Hall: A Literary Biography*, in Irish Literary Studies, 50 (Gerrards Cross: Colin Smythe, 1997), p. 26.
17. Mrs S. C. Hall, *The Mountain Daisy and Other Stories* (London: Nelson, 1866).
18. Ibid., p. vi.
19. Ibid., p. xvi.
20. S. C. Hall (ed.), *Amulet, or Christian and Literary Remembrancer*, (London: Frederick Westley and A. H. Davis, 1830).
21. Ibid., pp. 103–45.
22. Ibid., pp. 252–60.
23. S. Deane, *A Short History of Irish Literature* (London: Hutchinson, 1986).
24. Hall, *Amulet*, p. 103.
25. M. J. Corbett, *Allegories of Union in Irish and English Writing, 1790–1870: Politics, History, and the Family from Edgeworth to Arnold* (Cambridge: Cambridge University Press, 2000), p. 16.
26. *lick-plate*: a person who tries to gain favour by mean services. See W. Dickinson, *A Glossary of Words and Phrases Pertaining to the Dialect of Cumberland* (London: Pub. for the English Dialect Society by Trübner & co., 1878), p. 57.
27. Hall, *Sketches*, 3rd revsd edn, p. 251.
28. Ibid.
29. Mrs S. C Hall, *Sketches of Irish Character*, 2nd series (London: Frederick Westley & A. H. Davis, 1831), p. 70.
30. Hall, *Sketches*, 3rd revsd edn, p. 265.
31. Ibid., p. 264.
32. Hall, *Spirit and Manners of the Age*, New Series, vol. 11, pp. 35–41, 119–23 and 180–4
33. Hall, *Sketches* (c. 1876), p. xiv.
34. W. Maginn, '*Sketches of Irish Character* by Mrs S. C. Hall' *London Literary Gazette and Journal of Belles Lettres, Arts, Sciences, &c.*, 640 (25 April 1829), pp. 268–9, on p. 268.
35. B. Sloan, 'Mrs Hall's Ireland', *Eire-Ireland*, 19:3 (Autumn Issue, 1984), pp. 18–29, on p. 18.
36. M. G. Power (Countess of Blessington), 3 vols, *Grace Cassidy; or, The Repealers. A Novel*, vol. 2, pp. 228–9.
37. W. M. Thackeray, *The Works of William Makepeace Thackeray: The Irish Sketch Book and Critical Reviews*, 24 vols (London: Smith, Elder, 1879), vol. 18, p. 10.
38. This refers to a review in the *London Literary Gazette*; and *Journal of Belles lettres*, Arts, Sciences, &c., 737 (5 March 1831), p. 151, in which the writer compared the proliferation of Irish tales and legends to 'a glut of herrings in the market'.

39. W. E. Hall, *Dialogues in the Margin: A Study of the Dublin University Magazine* (London: Gerrards Cross, 2000), p. 22.

40. J. Leerssen, *Remembrance and Imagination: Patterns in the Historical and Literary Representation of Ireland in the Nineteenth Century*, in Critical Conditions: Field Day Essays and Monographs, 4 (Cork: Cork University Press, 1996), p. 11.

41. C. T. Croker, *Researches in the South of Ireland; Illustrative of the Scenery, Architectural Remains, and the Manners and Superstitions of the Peasantry with an Appendix Containing a Private Narrative of the Rebellion of 1798* (London: John Murray, 1824).

42. Leerssen, *Remembrance and Imagination*, p. 162.

43. Ibid., p. 163.

44. Deane, *A Short History of Irish Literature*, pp. 94–5.

45. B. Onslow, *Women of the Press in Nineteenth-Century Britain* (London: Palgrave, 2000), p. 9.

46. Leerssen, *Remembrance and Imagination*, p. 170.

47. W. E. Hall, *Dialogues in the Margin: A Study of the Dublin University Magazine* (Gerrards Cross: Colin Smythe, 2000), p. 22.

48. T. Eagleton, *Heathcliff and the Great Hunger: Studies in Irish Culture* (London: Verso, 1996), p. 127.

49. W. B. Yeats (ed.), *Fairy and Folk Tales of the Irish Peasantry* (London: Walter Scott Publishing Co., *c.* 1888), p. xv.

50. P. Rafroidi, *Irish Literature in English: The Romantic Period (1789–1850)*, 2 vols (New Jersey: Humanities Press, 1980), vol. 1, p. 185.

51. Hall, *Retrospect of a Long Life*, vol. 1, p. 483.

52. Hayley and McKay, *Three Hundred Years of Irish Periodicals*, p. 29.

53. T. Clyde, *Irish Literary Magazines: An Outline History and Descriptive Bibliography* (Dublin: Irish Academic Press, 2003), p. 15.

54. Eagleton, *Heathcliff and the Great Hunger*, p. 153.

55. J. Belanger, 'Some Preliminary Remarks on the Production and Reception of Fiction relating to Ireland, 1800–1829', *Cardiff Corvey: Reading the Romantic Text*, 4: 2 (May, 2000), p. 2, at http://www.cf.acc.uk [accessed 23 April 2014)].

56. S. Owenson (Lady Morgan), *The Wild Irish Girl: A National Tale*, 3 vols (London: R. Phillips, 1807).

57. N. J. Watson, *Revolution and the Form of the British Novel 1890–1825: Intercepted Letters, Interrupted Seductions*, (Oxford: Clarendon Press, 1994), p. 112.

58. Mrs. S. J. Hale and L. A. Godey, 'Illustrious Women of Our Time: Mrs. S. C. Hall', *Godey's Lady's Book*, 45 (August 1862), pp. 134–6, on p. 134.

59. T. Killick, *British Short Fiction in the Early Nineteenth Century: The Rise of the Tale* (Aldershot: Ashgate, 2008), p. 100.

60. Hall, *Sketches*, 1st edn, p. viii.

61. Ibid., p. 101.

SELECT BIBLIOGRAPHY

Butler, T. C., *A Parish and its People: History of Carrig-on-Bannow Parish* (Wellingtonbridge: Grantstown Priory, 1985).

Carlton, W., *Traits and Stories of the Irish Peasantry*, (Dublin: n. p., 1830).

Croker, C. T. *Researches in the South of Ireland; Illustrative of the Scenery, Architectural Remains, and the Manners and Superstitions of the Peasantry with an Appendix Containing a Private Narrative of the Rebellion of 1798* (London: John Murray, 1824).

Dunne, T., ed., *The Writer as Witness: Literature as Historical Evidence* (Cork: Cork University Press, 1987).

Eagleton, T., *Heathcliff and the Great Hunger: Studies in Irish Culture* (London: Verso, 1995).

Edgeworth, M., *The Absentee*, eds. W. J. McCormack and K. Walker (Oxford: Oxford University Press, 1988).

—, *Castle Rackrent: An Hibernian Tale, Taken from Facts and from the Manners of the Irish Squire Before the Year 1782,* 3rd ed. (London: J. Johnson, 1801).

Ferris, I., *The Romantic National Tale and the Question of Ireland* (Cambridge: Cambridge University Press, 2002).

Flanagan, T., *The Irish Novelists 1800–1850* (New York: Columbia University Press, 1959).

Foster, R. F., *Modern Ireland, 1600–1972* (1988: London: Penguin, 1989).

—, *Paddy and Mr. Punch: Connections in Irish and English History* (London: A. Lane, Penguin, 1993).

Gahan, D., *The People's Rising: Wexford 1798* (Dublin: Gill and Macmillan, 1995).

Hayley, B. *'Carlton's Traits and Stories' and the 19th Century Anglo-Irish Tradition: Irish Studies 12,* (Gerrards Cross: C. Smythe, 1983).

Hall, Mr and Mrs S. C., *Ireland, Its Scenery Character &c.*, new edn, 3 vols (London: Virtue, n. d.), vols 1 and 2.

Hall, Mrs S. C., *Lights and Shadows of Irish Life*, 3 vols (London: H. Colburn, 1838).

—, *Popular Tales of Irish Life and Character* (London: Simpkin, Marshall, Hamilton, Kent, 1856).

—, *Sketches of Irish Character*, 1st edn, 2 vols (London: Frederick Westley & A. H. Davis, 1829).

—, *Sketches of Irish Character*, 2nd edn, 2 vols (London: Frederick Westley & A. H. Davis, 1831).

—, *Sketches of Irish Character*, 2nd series (London: Frederick Westley & A. H. Davis, 1831).

—, *Sketches of Irish Character*, 3rd edn (London: How & Parsons, 1842).

—, *Sketches of Irish Character Illustrated Edition*, 3rd revsd edn (London: M. A. Nattali, 1844).

—, *Sketches of Irish Character: With Numerous Illustrations by the late Daniel Maclise, R.A., John Gilbert, W. Harvey, and G. Cruikshank*, 5th edn (London: J. Camden Hotten, *c.* 1876).

—, *Sketches of Irish Character: With Numerous Illustrations by Maclise, Gilbert, Harvey, and Cruikshank*, 5th revsd edn (London: Chatto and Windus, *c.* 1876)

—, *The Spirit and Manners of the Age*: *A Christian and Literary Miscellany, New Series*, 2 vols (London: Westley and Davis, 1829).

—, *Stories of the Irish Peasantry* (Edinburgh: Chambers, 1840).

—, *Tales of Irish Life and Character* (London & Edinburgh: Foulis, 1913).

—, *The Whiteboy: A Story of Ireland in 1822: Ireland from the Act of Union, 1900, to the Death of Parnell, 1881*, 2nd edn, 2 vols (London: Chapman and Hall, 1846), vol. 1.

Hall, S. C., *A Book of Memories of Great Man and Women of the Age, From Personal Acquaintance*, New Ed. (London: Virtue, 1876).

—, *Retrospect of a Long Life: from 1815 to 1883* (New York: Appleton, 1883).

Holden, M., *The Robber Freney: The Noblest Highwayman in Ireland* (Dublin: Mercier Press, 2009).

Hardy, P., ed., *Characteristic Sketches of Ireland and the Irish by Carleton, Lover, and Mrs. Hall* (Dublin: P. Hardy, 1840).

Keane, M., *Mrs. S. C. Hall: A Literary Biography* in Irish Literary Studies, 50 (Gerrards Cross: Colin Smythe, 1997).

Kiberd, D., *Inventing Ireland: The Literature of the Modern Nation* (London: Vintage, 1996).

Killick, T., *British Short Fiction in the Early Nineteenth Century: The Rise of the Tale* (Aldershot: Ashgate, 2008).

Leerssen, J., *Remembrance and Imagination: Patterns in the Historical and Literary Representation of Ireland in the Nineteenth Century* in Critical Conditions: Field Day Essays and Monographs, 4 (Cork: Cork University Press, 1996).

—, *Mere Irish and Fíor-Ghael: Studies in the Idea of Irish Nationality, its Development and Literary Expression Prior to the Nineteenth Century* in Critical Conditions: Field Day Essays and Monographs, 3 (Cork: Cork University Press, 1996).

R. Loeber and M. Loeber, *A Guide to Irish Fiction 1650–1900* (Dublin: Four Courts Press, 2006).

McManus, A., *The Irish Hedge School and its Books, 1693–1831* (Dublin: Four Courts Press, 2002).

Mitford, M. R., *Our Village: Sketches of Rural Character and Scenery*, 5 vols (London: n. p., 1824–32).

—, *Our Village: With an Introduction by Anne Thackeray Ritchie* (London: Macmillan, 1893).

Morgan, L., *The Life and Times of Salvator Rosa*, 2 vols (London: H. Colburn, 1824).

Musgrave, Sir R., *Memoirs of the Different Rebellions in Ireland from the Arrival of the English: Also a Particular Detail of that Which Broke out the XXIIID of May, MDCCXCVIII with the history of the Conspiracy which Preceded it. By Sir Richard Musgrave, Bar Member of the Late Irish Parliament*, 3rd edn, 2 vols (Dublin: R. Marchbank, 1802), vol. 1.

O'Dwyer, R. 'Women's Narratives 1800–1840', eds G. Meaney et al. *The Field Day Anthology of Irish Writing. Vol. 5.* (Cork: Cork University Press, 2002) pp. 833–93.

Owenson, S. (Lady Morgan), *The Wild Irish Girl: A National Tale* (Oxford: Oxford University Press, 1999).

Ritchie, L., *Ireland Picturesque & Romantic* (London: Longman, Rees, Orme, Brown, Green and Longman, 1837).

Sloan, B., *The Pioneers of Anglo-Irish Fiction 1800–1850* (Gerrards Cross: Colin Smythe, 1986).

Thackeray, W. M., *The Paris Sketch Book of Mr M. A. Titmarch and Eastern Sketches: A Journey from Cornhill to Cairo: The Irish Sketch Book and Character Sketches* (Boston, MA: Estes and Lauriat, 1884).

Trumpener, K., *Bardic Nationalism: The Romantic Novel and the British Empire* (Princeton, NJ: Princeton University Press, 1997).

Vallency, C., 'Memoir of the Language, Manners and Customs of an Anglo-Saxon Colony settled in the Baronies of Forth and Bargie, in the County of Wexford, Ireland in 1167, 1168 and 1169', *Transactions of the Royal Irish Academy*, 2 (1787–8), pp. 19–41.

Weston, N., *Daniel Maclise: Irish Artist in Victorian London* (Dublin: Four Courts Press, 2001).

Wolff, R. L., 'Introduction: The Irish Fiction of Anna Maria Hall (1800–1881)', in Mrs S. C. Hall, *The Whiteboy: A Story of Ireland in 1822: Ireland from the Act of Union, 1900, to the Death of Parnell, 1881*, 2nd edn, 2 vols (London: Chapman and Hall, 1846), vol. 1.

Woodham-Smith, C., *The Great Hunger: Ireland 1845–9* (London: Hamish Hamilton, 1962).

Yeats, W. B. (ed.), *Fairy and Folk Tales of the Irish Peasantry* (London: The Walter Scott Publishing Co., c.1888).

NOTE ON THE TEXT

Mrs S. C. Hall's successful first edition of *Sketches of Irish Character* of 1829 in two small volumes was dedicated in the introduction to Miss Mary Russell Mitford. The popularity of *Sketches* resulted in a second edition published in 1831. Containing the same introduction, this edition had a brief Advertisement, mentioning the success of the first edition and an article, 'The First Invasion of Ireland with some account of "The Irish Herculaneum"' by the Rev. Robert Walsh (see Textual Variants, pp. 437–85). These were the only additions to Hall's stories, which again took the peasantry of Bannow, Co. Wexford as their subject. Further success resulted in the publication of a second series of *Sketches*, also in 1831, which Hall inscribed to Maria Edgeworth. The second series comprised all new stories but still on her original innovative theme: the lives of the inhabitants of Bannow. In 1842 a third, illustrated edition inscribed to Thomas Boyse Esq. was published containing the same material as the previous editions of the first series (apart from 'Irish Settlers in an English Village', see Textual Variants, pp. 464–71) as well as a new Introduction and illustrations. The third, revised edition of 1844 is a re-issue of that of 1842, gathering in most of the stories of the first and second series with some new additions. It appeared in three different bindings:

- blue cloth, impressed with a harp in gold on the spine – the edition held at Chawton House Library, Hampshire;
- marbled boards and a leather spine; according to R. Loeber and M. Loeber, *A Guide to Irish Fiction 1650–1900* (Dublin: Four Courts Press, 2006), this binding also featured a frontispiece portrait of Mrs. Hall. The watercolour portrait by Maclise is held at Chertsey Museum, Surrey, close to the Hall's Surrey home of Firfield in Addlestone (see Figure 1, p. xxii);
- green cloth covers with a long High Cross and harp impressed in gold along the spine. The frontispiece illustrated portrait of Mrs Hall was painted by H. MacManus, *c.* 1836 and engraved by T. Ryall (see Figure 2, p. xxviii).

MRS S. C. HALL.

DRAWN BY DANIEL MACLISE. R.A.

IN 1830.

ENGRAVED BY LUMB STOCKS. R.A.

Figure 1: Engraving from the portrait of Mrs S. C. Hall around the time of her marriage, painted by Daniel Maclise. The original is held in Chertsey Museum, Surrey close to the Halls' home at 'Firfield', Addlestone where they moved from Kensington about 1849. It is a beguiling portrait of Hall, executed in quite a loose Romantic style; she is shown wearing a simple gown, without ornament and portrayed as a young woman unfettered by the constraints of society.

Emma Maria Hall [signature]

Figure 2: Engraving by T. Ryall from the portrait by Henry MacManus painted *c.* 1836. Mrs Hall holds in her hands, and thereby displays, *The Book of Gems*, written by her husband, S. C. Hall. In contrast to the previous portrait, she is represented as a respectable Victorian matron: sober, modest, orderly and controlled, with a more mature and professional demeanour.

After this third, revised edition came the fifth edition, *c.* 1876, which contained a new preface of dedication to Francis Bennoch and an Introduction to the third edition. Also estimated to have been published *c.* 1876, the fifth, revised edition contains 'A Rambling Introduction' (see Textual Variants, pp. 474–85). It contains a thirty-six page catalogue of books published by Chatto and Windus, dated November 1876, five years prior to the death of Mrs Hall on 30 January 1881. Posthumously, this edition was reissued as Mrs S. C. Hall, *Sketches of Irish Character* (London: Chatto and Windus, *c.* 1891). The sketches are followed by a thirty-two page catalogue advertising works published by Chatto and Windus, dated June 1891. American editions of *Sketches of Irish Character* were also published; Mrs S. C. Hall, *Sketches of Irish Character* (New York: J. & J. Harper, 1829); an illustrated edition: Mrs S. C. Hall, *Sketches of Irish Character* (New York: E. Ferrett and Co., 1845); an illustrated edition: Mrs S. C. Hall, *Sketches of Irish Character* (Philadelphia, PA: J. W. Moore, 1854); an illustrated edition with a Maclise portrait, 'Norah Clarey' impressed on the front cover, Mrs S. C. Hall, *Sketches of Irish Character* (Philadelphia, PA: D. McKay, n. d.); an edition 'illustrated with 93 engravings', sold by subscription only: Mrs S. C. Hall, *Sketches of Irish Character* (Philadelphia, PA: Union Publishing Company, 1868); an illustrated edition entitled *Wearing of the Green; or, Sketches of Irish Character* (Philadelphia: W. Flint, 1868) and two volumes with an Introduction by R. I. Wolff: Mrs S. C. Hall, *Sketches of Irish Character* (New York: Garland, 1979).

I have chosen as my copy text the 1844 third, revised edition, held at Chawton House Library. Materials omitted by Hall from this edition are included in the Textual Variants, alongside a short explanation of their context and relevance. I have intervened as little as possible in the texts. In keeping with the Chawton House Library Series house style, em-dashes have been replaced with en-dashes; double em-dashes with single em-dashes. I have silently corrected obvious typographical errors, while as far as possible retaining original punctuation and spelling. Internal page numbers in the original list of contents (pp. 5–6) refer to those of the third, revised edition of 1844 and, as such, do not correspond with the pagination of this Pickering & Chatto reset edition.

The following abbreviations are used to distinguish the different editions:
First edition, 1829: 1st edn
Second edition, 1831: 2nd edn
Second series, 1831: 2nd series
Third, illustrated edition, 1842: 3rd edn
Third, revised edition, 1844: 3rd revsd edn
Fifth edition, *c.* 1876: 5th edn
Fifth, revised edition, *c.* 1876: 5th revsd edn

NOTE ON THE ILLUSTRATIONS

On reading this lavishly embellished third, revised edition of *Sketches* it might be assumed that the illustrations had been specially commissioned for the work. However, it is interesting to note that the five striking full-plate portraits of women which dominate the work had previously been used to illustrate two volumes of Leitch Ritchie's *Heath's Picturesque Annual* of 1837 and 1838) and to discover that the five 'cottage girls' had an earlier publishing history. (See N. Weston, *Daniel Maclise: Irish Artist in Victorian London* (Dublin: Four Courts Press, 2001), p. 296). Ritchie (1800–65), a novelist and journalist, was commissioned to provide the letterpress for two series of books of travel between 1832–1845 and Daniel Maclise travelled with him drawing scenes and people on the spot.

The illustration 'Lilly O'Brien' which accompanies the sketch of that name portrays a young woman dressed in a hooded cloak of the type worn in Ireland in the nineteenth century. The iconography of a large rosary with crucifix identifies her with the Catholic religion and her attitude is one of prayerful devotion. This portrayal does not, however, marry with Hall's description of Lilly who is supposedly aged about thirteen with 'skin transparently white' and 'thick curls' of silky auburn'. The scene represented in the engraving offers no precise visualisation of the dramatic action of the story wherein Lilly bears little resemblance to the idealised Madonna-like woman depicted, apart from her donning a cloak to pursue her wayward cousin Edward. However, just at the close of the sketch, Hall inserts a another description of Lilly who, 'seeking to abstract herself from household cares and blessings, only that she may render grateful homage to her Creator – sits after evening vespers, with clasped hands and downcast eyes, her national hood shading, but not obscuring, the beauty of her pensive face...' (*Sketches*, 3rd revsd edn, p. 35). Heath had named this portrait 'The Irish Hood' and used it to explain the cloak, usually blue and universally worn by the women of Ireland, to his English readers.

Maclise's second full-page plate for *Sketches* is 'Mary Ryan's Daughter', engraved by Henry Robinson (bap. 1766–1871). Dressed in a patterned frock and dark cloak Mary carries two wicker baskets and gazes out of the picture space directly at the viewer. Due to an unsettling perspective contrast between girl and landscape, she appears a gigantic figure towering over a pass between two hills. Although Hall's description here matches the illustration, she does refer the reader directly to the artist's skill, breaking 'the willing suspension of disbelief' demanded by the narrative. Both reader and viewer are exhorted to admire the girl's dainty feet. What is absent from the text and the romanticized illustration is any sense that her unshod feet may be an indication of poverty. With this exiguity ignored, even idealised in the portrait, Hall underwrites acceptance of the *status quo*, thus removing any necessity to remedy what does, after all, not appear to exist. Portrait and text combine to mesmerise the reader into embracing the romantic picturesque.

Traditionally Ireland has been represented in art and literature by a woman; 'My Dark Rosaleen', 'Róisín Dubh' and 'Kathleen ní Houlihan'. This tradition is present in the Maclise portraits, particularly where the girl looms above the landscape; she becomes a symbol of Ireland and as such, the political implication of use of this portrait is crucial. 'Ireland' is become feminine, poor, naïve and *attractively* barefoot under the male gaze of England, the colonizer. When Ritchie previously used the engraving in *Heath's Picturesque Annual*, (L. Ritchie, *Ireland Picturesque and Romantic; with Drawings by D. M 'Clise, Esq. A. R. A. and T. Creswick, Esq.* (London: Longman, Orme, Brown, Green, and Longmans, 1838), p. 154), it bore the title 'Irish Market Girl'; a type, not an individual. Ritchie describes Mary Ryan's Daughter in terms of her physiognomy. She is 'a specimen of what in England would be a market girl' thus simultaneously reducing 'her' to anthropological type and demonstrating the colonial imperative of explaining the Irish to the English reader/viewer.

Maclise's portrait of 'Alice Mulvany' is placed at the opening of the third, revised edition of *Sketches* (although the original contents page states that it appears on page 161) and once again Maclise portrays a pretty young girl. On this occasion, Hall gives a full delineation in the text, almost guiding the reader's eye over this idealized and eroticised image as Alice throws off her mantle 'exhibiting her pretty figure to the best advantage' in order to 'jig it' with any boy that asked her in order to vex her boyfriend. Hall is critical of Alice's flirtatious ways which threaten to disrupt the harmony of a steady progress towards marriage and stability with her bachelor. Once again, Hall has altered her text to accommodate the addition of the Maclise portrait. Yet Hall chose this image for her collection and so, a point of instability is reached if an attempt is made to reconcile the opposing ideologies which underpin text and peritext. This instability may rest in the underlying 'unpalatable' truth that girls like Alice (whose characterisation may be 'read' as a representation of Ireland) may never learn to change their ways.

It is of note that in altering her text, Hall legitimated the primacy of illustration over text. If a comparison is made between the text of the sketch in both the unillustrated second edition and the illustrated third, revised edition, the second edition bears no description of Alice in her white jacket and buckled shoes as it appears in the third, revised edition. So, it becomes clear that Hall in this case, 'illustrated the illustration' of the third, revised edition by adding text appropriate to the engraving.

Ritchie, however, made very different use of the original of Maclise's pencil. In *Ireland Picturesque and Romantic*, the girl is not a native of Co. Wexford, but hails from Co. Galway. Ritchie describes his encounter with her thus:

'The young girl before us ... is dancing with soul and body. Her eyes, feet, and hair jig it at the same moment. Her hair, indeed, is rather out of bounds in its amusement, considering that it was actually combed in the morning – a discipline of extraordinary rarity ... She is herself Spanish all over, with a dash of indolent voluptuousness which proclaims her ancestry (L. Ritchie, *Ireland Picturesque and Romantic by Leitch Ritchie, Esq., With Twenty Engravings* (London: Longman, Rees, Orme, Brown, Green and Longman, 1837), pp. 190–1).

The tone of Ritchie's commentary on the painting is one of condescension and denigration by a detached and alienated observer. The image was collected by Ritchie as a 'type' and painted by Maclise in knowledge of that brief. It was then used by Hall to provide a near fit to her requirement for a representation that would appeal to her English readership.

Maclise's illustration 'Norah Clary' for the sketch 'The Wise Thought' presents a portrait of a young woman seated and holding a whistle to her mouth. Tendrils of dark hair escape from her mob cap. An ivy-clad arch frames her figure. Water falls into a large earthenware pitcher at her side. Attired in full shirt, with cloth pocket and scissors, she glances sideways at the viewer from beneath slightly hooded lids, as she plays a musical instrument.

Maclise portrays a girl, pretty and provocative whose interaction with the viewer is signified by a coy glance. The aims of Hall's improving discourse in this text is to ensure Norah marries her prosperous farmer and to advocate peace between her warring parents. Once again, the endeavour is to promote marriage and harmony as a resolution to conflict and a hedge against future instability. The image of yet another comely maiden with a roving eye provides an image that cuts against the import of the text. The political message inherent in the portrait seems at odds with the improving discourse promulgated in the text. The purpose of the image seems to be to provide the viewer with a pretty distraction or amusement. Yet tension is generated as the glance from the maiden seems at odds with the textual message of improvement; she has not been entirely won over. In this story, new to the third editions, Hall fits her text to the illustration as she describes Norah playing her 'Jew's harp', 'a merry maiden' of 'sweet seventeen'.

Ritchie named the illustration 'The Jew's Harp' – incidentally with no connection to Judaism. He used the illustration very differently; for Ritchie, it demonstrates the disappearance of the bards and their majestic harps, often set with silver and crystal, such as played by Brian Boroimh. He mourns their decline through the reign of Elizabeth, through Cromwell and William III as players 'became itinerant musicians playing for hire. Now,' Ritchie declares, 'we have only the cottage maid solacing her lonely house with the twang of the jew's-harp' (Ritchie, *Ireland Picturesque and Romantic*, 1837 edn, p. 77).

Maclise's final full-page illustration appears in Hall with the title 'Geraldine'. The image depicts a young woman praying before a framed image of the Madonna and Child. Her trailing hand loosely holds a rosary. The unsettling aspect of this illustration is the rather incongruous appearance of the woman. The overtly Catholic and church setting of the illustration seem slightly at odds with the revealing dress and somewhat eroticized depiction which appears to be presented in order to appeal to admirers of the female form.

Turning to the text of 'Geraldine', we find Hall directs the viewer immediately to the illustration, complimenting the artist at the same time. Once again, she 'intrudes' into the narrative, refusing to 'suspend disbelief' saying: 'Where my distinguished country man, Mr. Maclise, obtained the original of this portrait, I cannot tell; but it brought to my mind an incident that occurred to me a few summers ago, when visiting Honfleur'. Here, Hall acknowledges the 'earlier life' of the illustration and her further description of her eponymous character 'Geraldine' demonstrates that her text was written to fit the illustration. She describes her as 'kneeling before the pretty shrine of the Madonna, for hours together; her attitude one of perfect devotion; one small hand held the rosary, the other shaded her face; the cloak appeared abandoned to its own drapery – her hair fell, as you see, in the most *dégagé* undress (*Sketches*, 3rd revsd edn, p. 353). Once again we see Hall direct the eye of the viewer over the body of the person portrayed.

Ritchie used the same image in his volume of 1838 where it appears as Frontispiece under the title, 'A Lady at Prayers'. He writes that whilst in Limerick, he 'saw a much greater number of beautiful faces, in proportion to the size of the town, than is usual ...' He adds that the Catholic churches ... exhibit far more of the devotional picturesque than you find in most countries of the continent. He notes that while on the continent rich and poor intermingle in church, in Ireland there are galleries and below is reserved for the poor. 'Occasionally, however, a votary of a higher class is seen in the same devotional attitude. An instance of the latter is annexed produced by Mr. M'Clise.' (Ritchie, *Ireland Picturesque and Romantic*, 1838 edn, p. 199).

Ritchie demonstrates the twin Victorian obsessions; observation and physiognomy; he has spotted an unusual sub-species, and Maclise has captured the delineation with his pencil. This image he states is to be 'viewed by the English whom he declares, know as much of the Irish than they do of the Hottentots' (Ritchie, *Ireland Picturesque & Romantic*, p. 262) – more especially the English of those distinguished classes among which such books as mine chiefly circulate.'

In conclusion, it may be said that the illustration of texts and controversy thereon was nothing new. Dickens famously clashed with his illustrator Robert Seymour (1798–1836) on the issue of supremacy of illustration over text with tragic consequences. Pertinently, it would seem that Hall's inclusion of the Maclise portraits in *Sketches of Irish Character* was commercially driven and fuelled by the popular demand for images of women in the periodical press and the annuals. This demand was in turn facilitated by advances in print technology. Size also mattered. The Maclise portraits were the only full-page illustrations in a heavily illustrated work. As such, they dominate *Sketches* and appear to represent national character. Moreover, for the English reader, Catholicism was to be regarded with suspicion, if not fear, carrying with it the possible threat of Irish insurrection and instability.

ALICE MULVANY

SKETCHES

OF

IRISH CHARACTER:

BY MRS. S. C. HALL.

ILLUSTRATED EDITION.

LONDON:
M. A. NATTALI, 23, BEDFORD STREET,
COVENT GARDEN.
MDCCCXLIV.

INTRODUCTION.

THE Public having required a third Edition of these "SKETCHES OF IRISH CHARACTER," I have been called upon to prepare it – to revise the stories originally published, and to add several new; and the publishers have given to them the advantage of very beautiful illustrations.

The "Sketches" chiefly refer to one locality – the parish of Bannow, on the sea-coast of the County of Wexford – my native place, where the earlier years of my life were passed. The world has little interest in the personal feelings of a writer; but my readers will, I hope, permit me to say that my first impressions of Ireland were derived from the very favourable circumstances under which I was placed; for, in this neighbourhood, there was, comparatively, none of the poverty, and consequent wretchedness, to be encountered, unhappily, elsewhere. I have so frequently dwelt upon its almost exclusive privileges and peculiar features, in these "Sketches," as to render it unnecessary for me to preface them although, no doubt, the happy associations, connected with them, have made both appear brighter, in my eyes, than they may seem to others. It is certain, however, that this district of the County of Wexford is superior to any other part of the south of Ireland. Its landlord is not an absentee;[1] he is surrounded by an attached and a prosperous tenantry; the land is naturally rich, and facilities for improving it are many.

The Baronies of Bargy and Forth,[2] in the former of which Bannow is situated, are especially fortunate in possessing, to a very remarkable extent, all the moral, social, and natural advantages, which are to be found, although more limited, throughout the County. The inhabitants are, chiefly, descendants of the Anglo-Norman settlers, who, in the reign of the second Henry, invaded and conquered – or, rather subdued – Ireland; and, until very recently, they retained so much of their ancient customs and manners, as actually to speak a language unknown in other districts of the Kingdom.

The ruins of castles are so numerous, that, over a surface of about 40,000 acres, there stand the remains of fifty-nine; and the sites of many more can still be pointed out. The people are, to this day, "a peculiar people," and retain much of their English character. This is apparent, not alone in the external aspect of the country – in the skilfully farmed fields, the comparatively comfortable cottages, the barns attached to every farmyard, the well-trimmed hedgerows, stocked with other vegetables than potatoes; the peasantry are better clad than we have seen them elsewhere, and have an air of sturdy independence, which they really feel, and to which they are justly entitled, for it is achieved by their own honest industry.

In these "Sketches" I have aimed at a higher object than mere amusement, – desiring so to picture the Irish character, as to make it more justly appreciated, more rightly estimated, and more respected, in England; at the same time, I have studied – but I trust in a kindly and affectionate spirit – so to notice the errors and faults that prevail most among my countrymen and countrywomen, as to be of some use in inducing a removal of them. There are none powerless to effect good – except those who persuade themselves that attempts to produce it are hopeless. It has been my steady purpose, and zealous wish, to do justice to the many estimable qualities of the Irish peasantry, of whom it has been truly said, "their virtues are their own; but their vices have been forced upon them."

With these "Sketches" I was first introduced to the Public; I have since pro-duced other works, but none into which my heart so completely entered. They gave me, I presume to say, a place in public favour; – it has been my earnest and continued study to retain it.

Within a few years, the property upon which I lived has passed into other hands – from those, so near and so dear to me, who, in my time possessed it – I am happy to say, however, INTO GOOD HANDS; for the excellent and accom-plished gentleman to whom I have inscribed these "Sketches," while he is equally willing, is infinitely more powerful, to advance the moral and social welfare of the people committed to his charge.

CONTENTS, AND LIST OF ILLUSTRATIONS.

LILLY O'BRIEN.

LILLY O'BRIEN.

THE sweet Lilly of Bannow! – I shall never forget the morning I first saw her. Her aunt – who does not know her aunt, Mrs. Cassidy? – her aunt is positively the most delightful person in the whole parish. She is now a very old woman, but so "knowing" that she settles all debateable points that arise among good and bad housewives, from Mrs. Connor of the Hill, down to "Polly the Cadger," as to the proper mode of making mead, potato-cakes, and stirabout; and always decides who are the best spinners and knitters in the county; nay, her opinion, given after long deliberation, established the superiority of the barrel, over the hand, churn. There is, however, one disputed matter in the neighbourhood, even to this day. Mrs. Cassidy (it is very extraordinary, but who is without some weakness?) – Mrs. Cassidy will have it that a Quern – an obsolete hand-mill of stone, still patronised by "the ancient Irish" – grinds wheat better than a mill, and produces finer flour; she, therefore, abuses all mills, both of wind and water, and persists in grinding her own corn, as well as in making her own bread. By-the-bye, this very Quern was in great danger some time ago, when an antiquary, who had hunted hill and dale seeking for Danish or Roman relics (I forget which, but it is of little consequence), pounced upon it, declared it was a stone bowl of great antiquity, and that Mrs. Cassidy's maiden name, "Maura O'Brien," carved on it in Irish characters, proved it to have been used, either by Dane or Roman, in some religious ceremony, or Bacchanalian rite, I cannot take it on myself to say which: – but this I know, that the old gentleman was obstinate; had been accustomed to give large sums for ugly things of every description, and thought that Mrs. Cassidy could be induced to yield up her favourite for three guineas. He never was more mistaken in his life; nothing could have tempted Mrs. Cassidy to part with her dear Quern; so he left the neighbourhood, almost heart-broken with disappointment.

I respect the Quern myself, for it was the means of introducing me to the sweet Lilly. There, that little path, bordered with oxlips, primroses, and unobtrusive violets, –

"Whose deep blue eyes, Kiss'd by the breath of heaven, seem colour'd by its skies"[3] –

that path leads to Mrs. Cassidy's dwelling. You cannot see the cottage, it is perfectly hidden – absolutely wooded in; but it is a rare specimen of neatness. The farm-yard is stocked with ricks of corn, hay, and furze; with a puddle-like pond for ducks and geese, and a sty for a little grunting animal, who thinks it a very unjust sentence that consigns a free-born Irish pig to such confinement. How beautiful is the hawthorn hedge! – one sheet of snowy blossom – and such a row of bee-hives! – while the white walls of the cottage are gemmed over with the delicate green, half-budded, leaves of the noble rose-tree, that mounts even to the chimney-top; the bees will banquet rarely there, by-and-bye. A parlour in an Irish cabin! – yes, in good truth, and a very pretty one: the floor strewed with the ocean's own sparkling sand; pictures of, at all events, half the head saints of the calendar, in black frames, and bright green, scarlet, and orange draperies; a corner cupboard, displaying china and glass for use and show, the broken parts carefully turned to the wall; the inside of the chimney lined with square tiles of blue earthenware, and over it an ivory crucifix, and a small white chalice full of holy water; six high-backed chairs, like those called "education" of modern days; a well-polished round oak table, and a looking-glass of antique form, complete the furniture. The window – forget the window! – oh, that would be unpardonable! It consists of six unbroken panes of glass, and outlooks on such a scene as I have seldom witnessed. Let us open the lattice – what a gush of pure invigorating air! Behold and gaze—ay, first on the flower-bed that extends to where Mrs. Cassidy, with right good taste, has opened a view in the hawthorn hedge; then on, down that sloping meadow, dotted with sheep, and echoing the plaintive bleat of the young and tender lambs; on, on to the towering cliff, which sends, leaping over its blackened sides, a sparkling, foaming torrent, rapid as lightning, and flashing like congregated diamonds, for the sun's brightness is upon it, to the wide spreading sea, which reposes in its grandeur, like a sheet of molten silver. Yonder torrent is strangely beautiful. The rock from which it gushes is dark and frowning, not even a plant springing from its sterile bed; yet the pure water issues from it, full of light, life, and immortality, like the spirit from the Christian's clay. Dear Mrs. Cassidy loves the sea; her husband was owner and commander of a small trading vessel; and her happiest days were spent in coasting with him along the Irish, English, and Welsh shores. He died in his own comfortable home, and was quietly buried in Bannow church, leaving his widow (who, but for her rich brogue,[4] might, from her habits, have passed for an English woman) and one son, independent of the frowns or smiles of a capricious world. They had wherewithal to make them happy in their own sphere.

Edward was, even at two years old, an embryo sailor; a careless, openhearted boy, who loved everything ardently, but nothing long: except, indeed, his mother, who often regretted that his rambling disposition afforded her so little prospect of enjoyment in after life. She had a brother in the north of Ireland, who, dying, left an only child, our fair Lilly, lovely and desolate in a cold world; but Mrs. Cassidy would not suffer any of her kith or kin to want when she had "full and plinty;" and, accompanied by Edward, then a boy about fifteen, she journeyed to Tyrone, and returned to her cottage with the orphan girl. Soon after this circumstance (of which I was then ignorant), I paid the good lady a visit; and when the country topics, of setting hens,[5] feeding calves, and the dearness of provisions, were exhausted, I asked her if she still used her Quern?

"Is it the Quern? – and that I do, lady; just look at this! – (producing a very nice and snowy cake) – and, sure, bad manners to me for not axing ye to taste it, and my own gooseberry, before! Look at this, there's not a mill in the counthry could turn out such bread as that; and if ye like to see it at work, I've just lifted it under the thorn yonder, to the sunny side of the ditch, and been instructing a poor colleen, that the world 'ud be after hitting hard, because she'd no friends, never a one, barring me, if I hadn't brought her here to be like my own – and why not, sure, and she my brother's child? Well, I've been tacheing her how to use the Quern, as in duty bound; she's helpless as yet, but she shall soon know everything."

I followed Mrs. Cassidy into the garden, and, looking towards "the sunny side of the hedge," saw the child she had mentioned. She might then have been about thirteen; her figure was slight and bending as a willow wand, and the deep black of her low frock finely contrasted with a skin transparently white; her hair fell in thick curls over her neck and shoulders, and in the sunbeams looked like burnished gold; it was not red – oh, no! – but a pale, shining, and silky auburn. She was occupied in turning the Quern with one hand, and letting the grain drop from the other; when she looked towards us, and shook back the curls from her face, I thought I had never seen so sweet a countenance; her forehead was high and finely formed; but her soft blue eyes seemed better acquainted with tears than smiles: there was something even more than polite in her address – it possessed much of rustic dignity; and the tones of her voice were like those of a well-tuned instrument.

The cottage now possessed for me a charm that was irresistible: for, superior as the people of Bannow are to the general Irish community, nothing so pure as the Lilly had ever blossomed among us before.

Even the rude peasantry seemed to look on her as something far above them; and when, accompanied by her aunt and cousin, she passed up Carrick-hill on the Sabbath morning, to join in the prayers and receive the blessing of the priest, they all watched her footsteps, and declared that she appeared "a'most like a born jantlewoman" – no small praise from the poor Irish, who venerate high birth to an extraordinary degree. Lilly's time was not idly spent: Mrs. Cassidy resolved that she should know everything; and as her childish days had been occupied solely in the business of education – as she read correctly, and wrote intelligibly, it was time, the good lady thought, to teach her all manner of useful occupations;

consequently, spinning succeeded knitting, and then came marking,[6] shirt-making in all its divisions, namely, felling, stitching, button-holes, and sewing; then milking and churning; the best practical method of hatching and bringing up chickens, ducks, turkeys, geese, and even pea-fowl – two of the latter were, unfortunately for poor Lilly, given to her aunt just as she arrived at the cottage; then the never-ending boiling of eggs, and chopping of nettle-tops for the young turkeys, that they might put forth their red heads without danger of croup or pip;[7] then the calf, an obstinate orphan, had to be dosed with beaten eggs and new milk, because he would not feed as he ought; her cousin's and aunt's stockings regularly mended; and, worst of all, a dirty shoeless gipsy, the maid of all work to the establishment, was given to my sweet Lilly's superintendence: – to Lilly, who had never known a mother's care, had been a foolish father's idol, and who had no more method or management than a baby of five months old; however, her patience and gentleness worked wonders; from before sunrise she toiled and thought; and, at the end of six months, astonished even Mrs. Cassidy. The Quern never ground such fine flour, the poultry were never so well fattened, the needlework was never so neatly finished, and the cottage never so happy, as since Lilly had been its inmate! When the toils of the day were comparatively ended, and when the refreshing breezes of evening rambled among the sweet yet simple flowers that blossomed in the garden, Lilly loved to sit and read, and watch the blue waters; and, as the night advanced, gaze on the meek moon floating in her own heavens. She had now resided nearly three years at the cottage, and was, one fine summer evening, sitting under the old thorn tree; some grief must have been heavy at her heart, for tears, in the full moonlight, were trembling on her long eyelashes: – perhaps her aunt had been angry, or Edward had plagued her with too many of his never-ending errands.

"Well, cousin Lilly!" exclaimed a joyous voice, "I never saw such a queer girl as ye are; ye've been trotting, and mending, and bothering all day, and now, instead of a race, or a dance, or anything that way, there ye sit, with yer ould books, and yer blue eyes, that bate the world for beauty. Lilly, dear – tears! – as I stand here, you've been crying! What ails ye, Lilly? – what ails ye, I say? I take it very unkind of ye, Lilly," – and he sat down and took her hand with much affection – "I take it very unkind of ye to have any trouble unknown to me who loves ye (Lilly tried to withdraw her hand) as an own brother. Has mother vexed ye?"

"Oh, no!"

"Well, then, cheer up! Come, come! James Connor has lent us his barn to-night, and I met Kelly the piper going there, and there'll be a merry spree, and you must jig it with me, and Harry too, Lilly, dear; and mother'll be glad ye go. Come, sure ye're a blessing to the ground ye walk on. Come, put on yer pumps[8] and white stockings. The people say ye're proud, Lilly, but ye're not; though ye might be, for there's not one in the parish like ye"

Lilly's heart fluttered like a caged bird, as she did her cousin's bidding, and accompanied him to the barn, where the piper was blowing his best for the boys and girls, who footed gaily to their favourite jigs. The Irish, old and young, rich and poor, all love dancing; and although their national dance is rude and ungraceful, there is something heart-cheering in witnessing the hilarity with which it inspires them.

While Lilly and Edward were joining in the amusements of the evening, Mrs. Cassidy was sleeping or knitting at her kitchen fire, until disturbed by the raising of the latch, and the "God save all here!" of "Peggy the Fisher."

I wish I could bring Peggy "bodily "before you, for she is almost a nonde-script.[9] Her linsey-woolsey gown, pinned up behind, fully displayed her short scarlet petticoat, sky-blue stockings, and thick brogues; a green spotted kerchief tied over her cap – then a sun-burnt, smoke-dried, flatted straw hat – and the basket of fish resting "on a wisp o' hay," completed her head gear. Whenever I met her in my rambles, her clear, loud voice was always employed either in sing-ing the "Collen Rue,"[10] or repeating a prayer; indeed when she was tired of the one, she always returned to the other; and, stopping short the moment she saw me, she would commence with –

"Wisha[11] thin it's my heart bates double joy to see you this very minit. Will ye turn yer two good-looking eyes on thim beautiful fish, leaping alive out o' the basket, my jewil.[12] Och, it's thimselves are fresh, and it's they 'ud be proud if ye'd jist tell us what ye'd like, and then we'd let ye have it a dead bargain!"

Peggy was certainly the queen of manœuvring, and thought it "no harm in life to make an honest pinny out o' thim that could afford it;" but she had strong affections, keen perceptions, and much fidelity; her ostensible trade was selling fish, but there was more in her basket than met the eye – French silks, rich lace, or some drops of smuggled brandy for choice customers; and when the farmers' wives could not pay her in cash, they paid her in kind – meal, feathers, chickens, and even sucking-pigs, which Peggy disposed of with perfect ease, so extensive were her connexions. Then, she was the general matchmaker and match-breaker of the entire country. Those who could write confided to her their letters; those who could not, made her the messenger of sweet or bitter words as occasion required. And, to do Peggy justice, she has even refused money, ay, solid silver and gold, rather than prate of love affairs; for she pitied (to use her own words) "she pitied the young craturs in love; well remimbering how her own saft heart was broke, many's the day ago." Peggy lived anywhere – everywhere. There were few, married or single, who either had not needed, did not need, or might not need Peggy the Fisher's assistance; and the best bit and sup in the house were readily placed before her.

"Och, Peggy, honey!" exclaimed Mrs. Cassidy, "is that y'erself! – sure 'tis I'm glad to see ye, agra;[13] and what'll ye take? – a drop of tay, or a trifle o' whiskey to keep the could out o' y'er stomach; or may-be a bit to ate – there's lashings o' white bread, and sweet milk, and the freshest eggs ever was laid."

"Thank ye kindly, Mrs. Cassidy, ma'am; sure it's y'erself has full and plinty for a poor lone woman like myself. I'll take the laste taste in life o' whiskey – and may-be ye'd take a drop o' this, ma'am dear; a little corjial I has, to keep off the water flash," – continued she screwing up the corner of her left eye, and placing her basket on the table.

"Have ye got anything striking handsome under thim dirty sea-weeds and dawny shrimpeens, agra?" inquired Mrs. Cassidy.

"May-be I have so, my darlint, though it's little a poor lone cratur like me can afford to do these hard times; and the custom-officers, the thieving villains, in Waterford, Duncannon, and about there, they's grown so 'cute[14] that there's no ho[15] wid 'em now, at all, at all. There's a thing that's fit for Saint Patrick's mother anyhow," – displaying a green shawl with red roses on it – "there's a born beauty for ye! – and such natural flowers, the likes of it not to be met wid in a month o' Sundays – there's a beauty!"

"Sure I've the world and all o' shawls, Peggy, avourneen![16] – and any how that's not to my fancy. What 'ud ye be axing for that sky-blue silk handkerchief?"

"Is it that ye're after? It's the last I got o' the kind, and who 'ud I give a bargain to as soon as y'erself, Mrs. Cassidy, ma'am? – and ye shall have it for what it cost myself, and that's chape betwixt two sisters; it's ra'al Frinch, the beauty! – and it's wronging myself I am to give it for any sich money – dog chape, at six thirteens."

"Och, ye Tory," exclaimed Mrs. Cassidy: "six thirteens for that bit of a thing! Is that the way ye want to come over a poor widow, ye thief o' the world!"[17] and she avoided looking at the tempting article by fixing her eyes on her knitting, and working with double speed.

"Well, mistress dear, I never thought ye'd be so out of all rason," and Peggy half folded up the handkerchief. Mrs. Cassidy knitted on, and never even glanced at it.

"It's for Miss Lilly, I'm thinking, ye want it; and sure there's nothing in life would look so very nate on her milk-white skin as a sky-blue handkerchief – and so, ma'am, ye won't take it, and it killing chape?"

Mrs. Cassidy shook her head.

"Well, to be sure, for you I would do – so, there! (throwing it on the table) ye shall have it for five thirteens; and that's all as one as ruination to myself."

"I'll tell ye what, Peggy, a'coushla!"[18] and Mrs. Cassidy took off her spectacles, and looked at the kerchief attentively: "I'll tell ye what; it was four thirteens ye meant; and ye meant also to give Lilly two yards o' that narrow blue riband for knots, that ye promised her long agone."

"I own to the promise, as a body may say," responded Peggy; "I own to the promise; but as to the four thirteens for sich as that! – woman alive! – why –"

"Asy, asy, Peggy, honey, no harm in life!" interrupted Mrs. Cassidy, "take the blue rag, it's no consarn o' mine."

"Blue rag, indeed! – but" – after a pause – "it's no rag, Mrs Cassidy, ma'am, and there's no one knows that betther nor you that has all the wisdom in the whole counthry to y'erself; but howsomever, take it; sure I wouldn't disagree with an ould residenther,[19] for the vallee of a few brass fardins."

Mrs. Cassidy extracted from the depths of an almost unfathomable pocket, a long stocking slit like a purse in the centre seam, and tied with a portion of red tape at either end. From amid sundry crown, half-crown, "tin-pinny," and "five-pinny" pieces, the exact sum was selected, paid, and the kerchief deposited in an ancient cupboard that extended half the length of the kitchen, and frowned, in all the dignity of Jamaica mahogany, on the chairs, settle, and deal table.

"The boy and girl are out, I'm thinking," commenced Peggy, as she lit her cutty pipe, and placed herself comfortably in the chimney corner, to enjoy the bit of gossip, or, as well-bred people call it, "conversation," which the ladies, ay, and the lords of the creation, so dearly love.

"They're stept down to Connor's, to have a bit of a jig; I'm right glad to get Lilly out, she's so quiet and gentle, and cares as little for a dance, and less, by a dale, than I do!"

"Och, ma'am dear, that's wonderful, and she so young, and so perfect handsome! – and more thinks that same nor me."

"Who thinks so, Peggy?" inquired Mrs. Cassidy, anxiously.

"What! – ye don't know, may be? – Why thin I'll jist hould my tongue."

"Ye'll do no such thing, Peggy; sure the colleen is as the sight o' my eye – as dear to my heart as my own child, which I hope she'll be one o' these days, plase God; and I tould ye as good as that before now – the time, d'ye mind, I bought her the green silk spencer.[20] And why not? A'n't I rareing her up in all my own ways? – and isn't she o' my own blood? And Ned, the wild boy, that has full and plinty to keep him at home, if he'd jist mind the land a bit, and give over his sailing talk, 'ud make a fit husband for her; and thin I could make my sowl, and die asy in yon little room, betwixt my son and daughter. And I tell ye what, Peggy the Fisher, there's no use in any boy's casting an eye at my Lilly, for Ned's wife she shall be; and I, Maura Cassidy, say it – that was never gainsaid in a thing she took in her head, by man or mortal."

"Very well, my dear, very well, why!" ejaculated Peggy, as, gathering herself over the dying embers of the turf fire, with her elbows on her knees, she jogged slowly backward and forward, like the rocking motion of a cradle. They both remained silent for some time. But Mrs. Cassidy's curiosity, that unwearying feeling of woman's heart, neither slumbered nor slept; and, after waiting in vain for Peggy to recommence the conversation, she could contain no longer.

"Who was talking about Lilly's beauty, Peggy?"

"Oh, my dear, sure everybody talks of it; and why not?"

"Ay, but who in particular?"

"Och, agra! – no one to say particular – that is, very particular,"

"I'll tell you what, my good woman," said Mrs. Cassidy, rising from her seat, and fixing herself opposite the Fisher: "if I find out that you've been hearing or saying anything, or what is more, hiding anything from me, regarding my boy and girl, when I get you at the other side o' the door (for I wouldn't say an indacent thing in my own house), I'll jist civilly tell ye my mind, and ax ye to keep yer distance, and not to be meddling and making wid what doesn't consarn ye."

Peggy knocked the ashes out of her pipe, crammed her middle finger into it to ascertain that all was safe; and, putting it into her pocket, curtsied to Mrs. Cassidy, and spoke – "As to good woman, that's what I was niver called afore; and as to not hearing – would ye have me cork my ears whin I hard Ned and Harry Connor discoorsing about the girl, and I at the other side o' the hedge? Och, och! – to think I should iver be so put upon! But good night, good night to ye, Mistress Cassidy – cork my ears, agra! And now," she continued, as she hastily stepped over the threshold, "I'm at the other side the door, so say yer say."

Mrs, Cassidy's curiosity was more excited than ever; and her short-lived anger vanished as Peggy withdrew.

"Stop, Peggy! – don't, be so hot and so hasty; sure I spoke the word out o' the face[a], and meant no harm; come in, a'coushla; it's but nataral I'd be fiery about thim, and they my heart's treasures."

In three minutes they were as good friends as ever, and Peggy disclosed the secret, which, notwithstanding her apparent unwillingness, she came to the cottage to tell. "Ye mind the thorn hedge, where the knock slopes off; well, the day was hot, and I tired with the heat, and the basket, and one little thing or another; and so down I sits on the shady side, thinking o' nothin' at all, only the crows – the craturs flying to and fro, feeding the young rawpots that kicked up such a bobbery[21] in their nests wid the hunger; and of what the priest said from the altar agin smuggling, as if he was in right down arnest about it; and then it crassed my mind, to be sure, how hard it was for a poor lone body to make an honest bit o' bread these hard times, and the priest himself agin it; well, by an' by, who comes shtreelin' up the hill at my back, but your Ned and young Harry Connor; well, I was jist goin' to spake, but by grate good luck I held my wisht[b]; well, the first word I hears was from Ned's own mouth, and they were a good piece off at the time, too; 'She's always the same,' says he, 'always – sure I love her as my own sister.' Maybe more nor that,' says Harry, quite solid. 'Harry,' says Ned, solid like, too, 'don't go to the fair wid the joke; look, I'd suffer this arm to be burnt to the stump to do Lilly any good; heart frindship I have for her, and well she desarves it, but no heart love.' Wid that, my jewil! I thought Harry Connor 'ud have shook the hand bodily off Ned; and thin I hard Ned say as how he'd like a more dashinger girl for a wife nor his cousin; and thin agin he talked about travelling into foreign parts; and thin they comaraded how Ned 'ud bring them in company together as often as he could, and talked a dale o' the dance, and Ned said he never see the colleen yet he'd like to marry; and Harry's quite done over, for he swore he'd lay down his life for one look o' love from Lilly's eyes; and they kep' on talkin' and talkin', and I kep' creepin' an' creepin' alongside the ditch, till the road turned: – and ye know it was my duty to find the rights of it, and you consarned."

Mrs. Cassidy waxed very wroth[22] as Peggy's narrative drew towards a close; she had made up her mind that the cousins should be married, and thought she had managed the matter admirably. She was always praising Edward to Lilly, and Lilly to Edward; and it was quite impossible to think that two creatures so perfect (notwithstanding, it must be confessed, that her son often occasioned her much anxiety), and, in her opinion, so well suited to each other, should be constantly in each other's society without falling in love. Lilly's anxiety to promote her cousin's happiness, the perfect willingness with which she made all her industry, all her amusements, yield to his caprice, convinced Mrs. Cassidy that she would not oppose her wishes: and then came another puzzling consideration – Edward had always appeared so very fond of Lilly! The poor woman was fairly baffled; how she wished that Harry Connor was little, old, and withered as a cluricawn;[23] but, no, he was tall, handsome, and more gentle, more polished than her son. Ned was gay and careless as ever; his raven hair curled lightly over his finely formed head, and his hazel eyes, full of bright laughter, accorded well with the merry smile that played around his mouth. He was frank and generous, but he was also violent and capricious. Had Lilly not been so much with him, nay, perhaps, even had he not instinctively felt that his mother wished him to marry her, he would have fallen over head and ears in love, at once. He admired and respected Lilly, yet her quiet virtues were a silent reproach to his recklessness; and at heart he longed to sail on the blue waters, and visit other lands. Next to his mother and cousin in his regards, came Harry Connor; and Harry well deserved it. He was a most extraordinary Irishman; cautious and prudent, even when a youth, and gentle and constant. The second son of an opulent grazier, he had been educated for the priesthood, and would, no doubt, have been useful in his ministry, for he had kindly feelings towards all his fellow-creatures, but that the death of his elder brother made it necessary for him to assist his father and family in the management of the grass farm.

Poor Mrs. Cassidy! – do you not pity her? Mothers are the same, I believe, all the world over; and really it is a great shame that such an outcry should be raised against their innocent manœuvrings, though it must be confessed they are sometimes very annoying, and not unfrequently end in a manner little anticipated. Poor Mrs. Cassidy! After a few moments' cogitation, she was about to give vent to her anger, when the sweet voice of Lilly was heard, bidding "good night, and thank ye kindly," to – Harry Connor.

"Stay, stop, asy!" ejaculated Peggy, jumping up – " if that's Misther Harry, may-be (calling after him) ye'd jist give me, a poor cratur, a bit o' yer company down the lane, that I don't like to go alone: good night to ye kindly, and the blessing be about ye." And basket and all went off at a short trot – Peggy's peculiar gait.

"What ails ye, aunt dear?" affectionately inquired Lilly; for Mrs. Cassidy had not spoken.

"What ails *you,* girl alive – or dead – for ye're as white as a sheet – and where's Ned?"

"Ned went a piece of the way home with Katey Turner," replied Lilly, blushing, and tears gathering in her eyes at the same time.

"And you came a piece with Harry Connor?"

"I could not help it, aunt, dear," said Lilly, earnestly. "Sure, Ned ran off with Katey, and asked Harry to see me home."

"He did, did he? Why, then," cried the dame, rising in a great passion, "I'll soon tache him betther manners, the reprobate!"

"Oh, aunt, dear aunt!" – and poor Lilly threw her arms around Mrs. Cassidy's neck – "Oh, don't say a hard word to Ned – oh, may-be he couldn't help it!" and she burst into tears. "But don't, oh, don't, for the sake o' her that never angered ye, don't say a hard word to Ned."

"Ye're a good girl, I'll say that for you any how, my own colleen," said Mrs. Cassidy, kissing her fair forehead; "there, go to bed, my darlint; ye look very pale, a'n't ye well?"

"Yes, aunt, thank ye; but ye're not angry with Ned?'

"Well, well, go to bed, I'll not scold him much, avourneen?"

"Not at all, at all, my own dear aunt!"

"Well, there agra, you've begged him off; stay a minute, gramachree!"[24] – Lilly was just mounting the ladder which led to her small chamber: she returned. "I jist wanted my child to tell me why she calls me aunt, now, that used to call me mother when first she came to me. Lilly, darlint! Am I less a mother to ye now than I used to be?"

"Oh, no, no, no! – not that, dear a – mother," – she stammered out; and again her face and bosom were red – "not that!"

"What then, Lilly, love? I hope I'm yer frind, and ye ought to tell me."

"Oh, nuthin' at all – only Katey and the girls laughed when I called you mother, and said – "

"What did they say?"

"Oh, all a folly! – only they said – 'twas all a folly – they're very foolish, I'm sure."

"Well, but what was it, a'coushla?"

"Why, that there could be only three sorts of mothers – born mothers, and step-mothers – and, and – oh, it's all a folly – (poor Lilly covered her face with her shawl) – mothers-in-law."

Mrs. Cassidy replied not, but kissed her cheek, and then Lilly flew up the ladder – closed her door – after a pause, half opened it again, and without showing her face, said, "Remember, you promised not to be angry with Ned."

Lilly's feelings were both new and painful; she wept very bitterly, as she knelt at the side of her humble couch, and pressed her face to the coverlet; was it because her aunt was angry with Edward? No; for her anger was like the shower in April, ardent, but passing soon. Was she vexed at Edward's attention to Katey? She certainly thought he danced, laughed, and jested with her more than was necessary – but why unhappy at that? – Katey was her friend, Edward her cousin. When Harry pressed her hand with so much tenderness, at the cottage door, why did she shake it from him, and feel as if insulted? Lilly knew not her own heart, and wondered why she had spoken so sharply to poor Harry – Harry, who lent her books, and whose kindness was proverbial all over the parish. She was bewildered; all she knew was, that she was more unhappy than ever she had been in her life. She sat long, trying to collect her senses, and at last the rush-light sank into the socket of the white-ware candlestick; it had been her cousin's present. Then she again remembered that, although the moonbeams had long since began to peep through her little window, Edward was not returned; she opened the casement, which enclosed only two small panes of glass: the glorious prospect lay before her, and the watch-light gleamed brightly, over the dark blue waters, from the distant tower of Hook.[25] The weather had long been calm and clear, and the full-blown roses, that had never felt a rough blast, or a chilling shower, imparted their sweet fragrance to the midnight air; the path by which Edward would return crossed the meadow, and her heart bounded when his figure appeared hastily striding homewards. "I hope he did not see me," thought she, as she closed the window: "yet why? – sure he's my cousin." In a moment after the latch was lifted, and she distinctly heard her aunt say:

"A purty time o' night, indeed, for you to march home, Master Edward Cassidy! – and to lave me, a poor widow, and yer own mother, alone in this desolate hut."

"It's a comfortable hut, thin," replied Edward, laughing; "and how are ye lone, whin there's Lilly, and Ruth – the dirty sowl – and Bran, to say nothin' of ould puss, sitting so snug on the hearthstone?"

"How do you know Lilly's here? It's little ye care about her, or ye'd be far from letting that long gomersal[26] of a fellow, Harry Connor, see her home; and you flirting off with that jilting hussey, Katey Turner."

"Katey Turner's no jilt, or flirt either, but a tight, clane-skinned little girl; and Harry's no gomersal at all; but an honest fellow, that'll make a good husband for my handsome cousin, one o' these days – and not long neither. What a wedding we'll have, for sartin!"

Poor Lilly's heart sickened, and her head felt giddy, as she heard these words. She never intended listening, but her respiration was impeded in the deep anxiety with which she waited for, yet dreaded, her aunt's reply. Mrs. Cassidy was struggling for utterance; she had seldom, perhaps never, been so enraged. Ned's words, and perfect carelessness of manner, had almost maddened her.

"Look ye, Ned – Ned Cassidy!" said she, after a pause, during which Edward saw the storm gathering fiercely – " Look, I'd sooner see Lilly stretched on that table; ay, I'd sooner a hundred times, and a thousand to the back of it, keen at her berrin,'[27] than see her thrown away upon that ownshugh! She's for his betthers, though little they seem to think of it."

"Whew! whew! – is that what ye're after, mother dear? Well, then, now I'll jist tell ye the rights of it, and then we'll drop it forever, Amin. As to Lilly, a betther girl niver drew the breath o' life; and I regard and love her as a sister; but as to anything else, mother – I won't marry; I'll see the world. And, any how, she's not the patthern o' the wife I'd like."

Mrs. Cassidy clenched her fist, and, holding it close to her son's face, ejaculated – "Holy Mary! – ye born villain! – ye disobadient spalpeen![28] – ye limb o' Satan! – ye – ye – down upon yer bare knees, and ax my pardon for crassing me[a]; or, by the powers! I'll have father Mike[29] himself here to-morrow mornin', and marry ye out o' hand."

"I ax pardon for contradicting ye, mother; but ye'll do no sich thing. Say two more words like that, and the dawn o' day'll see me abord the good ship 'Mary,' that's lying off Hook-head, where they'd be main glad of a boy like me, as I heard to-night, to go a few voyages, and see the world."

"And is this the thanks I get for all my love, ye scoundrel; to fly in my face after that manner? Ye may trot off' as soon as ye plase; but the priest shall know yer doings, my boy. Och! ye ungrateful! – down this minit, as I tould ye; and, as God sees and hears me, ye shall be married to Lilly before to-morrow's sun sets!"

"I see, mother, ye don't mane to listen to rason; but one word for all: by the blessing o' God, I'll not marry Lilly; and I don't care that – (snapping his fingers) – for priest or minister."

"Take that, thin, for your comfort, and my heavy curse wid it!" And, enraged by her son's so wilfully destroying the hope that had latterly been the chief blessing of her life, in her fury she struck him a violent blow on the face. Poor Lilly rushed to her door; but her powers were paralysed. She could not undo the simple fastening, but clung to the window, that was close to it, for support. Edward spoke not; and his mother's arm sank by her side. Her rage was abating, when Edward, bursting with smothered anger, which he pent up with a strong effort, deliberately took his hat, walked to the door, and out, without uttering a single word. "Ned, Ned!" exclaimed Mrs. Cassidy; but Ned returned not. Lilly, pale and wild in her appearance, in a few moments was at her aunt's side. She had seen the desperate haste with which her cousin crossed the garden, trampling the flowers in his path; and, alarmed lest his passion should lead him to some dreadful act, she rushed down the stairs.

"Oh! to think," said she, "after yer promise, that ye should be so cruel to your own child, and all for one like me! Oh, if I'd ha' thought it, sure the grass shouldn't be wet under my feet before I'd be far from this house! Oh, call him back – call him back! – and I'll fly the place for ever!"

"He'll come back fast enough, I'll ingage," said the widow, "he's not sich a fool;" she opened the door, and saw in the moonlight his receding figure.

"He'll not, aunt. Oh, the blow! – the blow! – to think of your striking so high a spirit, and that 'Mary' lying off Hook-head, and the mate of her, Katey's uncle, putting his comether on Ned! Sure I saw it, only I never thought it 'ud come to this, at the weary dance to night."

"Indeed!" responded the mother, now really alive to the danger of losing her son. "Lilly, my darlint, you can save him; fly! – you can overtake him; there, he hasn't turned the knock yet; tell him he shall do as he plases; say, that I'll beg his pardon; only as he valees his mother's blessing, not to desart her in her ould age."

Lilly drew her cloak[30] over her head, and ran, as fast as her strength permitted, after her wayward cousin, whose firm, quick step, as he paced towards the main road, rendered the maiden's fleetness almost ineffectual: but at length she stood panting, almost fainting, at his side. It was then that a tide of conflicting feelings deprived her of utterance; for the first time, she felt herself a rejected, despised creature, and that by the being a thousand times dearer to her heart than life itself. When he knew that she had overheard the dreadful conversation in the cottage, what must he think of her? Modesty, the sweet blossom of purity, the mild glory of woman's life, had been outraged by her pursuing, even in such a cause, one who disdained her; and, as these ideas shot like fire through her brain, she caught at a tree for support, and murmured, "Holy Mary, direct thy child!" Edward spoke not, but looked on his cousin, with more of bitterness and scorn than of any other feeling. Twice she tried to speak, but vainly she unclosed her parched lips. "Ned," she at length articulated, "you are going, I know, to lave us; her, I mane, your mother; and you know, Ned, she has no hope but you. Oh, Ned! Ned! – in her old age do not fly her: think o' the time when she carried ye in sorrow and in bitter trouble – think – "

"Of the blow she gave me!" interrupted Edward, fiercely: "by all the holy saints, if a man, ay, my own father, had dealt so with me, I'd – I'd have knocked him down, and ground him into the hard earth!" And he stamped so violently, that poor Lilly was terrified at so sudden a burst of passion.

"Ned, you know you provoked her, and – "

"And so you, Lilly," he again interrupted, "you, with all yer modesty and quietness, *you* collogued against me too: and that's the upshot of your coming among us! Och! och! I thought ye had a more dacent spirit than to follow a boy to ax him to marry ye, and he yer cousin!" Lilly, roused by this unjust sarcasm, was collected in a moment; drawing her slight yet dignified figure to its full height, she shook back the beautiful hair that had clustered over her mournful countenance, and stood firm and erect, with the beams of the chaste full moon gleaming upon her uncovered head.

"Ye don't know me, then; and I have lived under the same roof with ye three years and more; but ye don't know me, Edward Cassidy: if, by axing the powerful king of England, who sits on his throne, to make me his queen, it could be done – the poor orphan girl would scorn it! Lilly O'Brien followed ye not for that. The grate God, that sees all hearts, knows that the words I spake are true. Never, till this woful night, did I think that yer mother wished me to be nearer to her than I am. Ye bitterly wronged me; but that's not what I came to say. I tell ye that yer mother begs ye to come back; and not to trust to the wild sea, when every comfort in life is for ye on land. She asks ye to forget; she even begs of ye, for Christ's sake, to forgive the blow; but stop, that's not all – I, the desolate orphan, who have, innocent-like, been the cause of all this misery – I beg of you, *you* that so insulted and wronged me – and I do to you what I never did to any yet, but my heavenly comforters – on my two knees, I beg ye to return. Edward Cassidy, ye shall see me no more. I have no other home, but I am young, and, for a poor girl, not ignorant, praise be to your mother for it. I will quit the house for ever; ay, before the sun rises. Do not let me feel that I have driven the fatherless boy to labour, may-be to ruin."

She raised her clasped hands as she spoke, and her eyes, filled with the pure light of virtue, met the wild gaze of her cousin.

"Lilly," he replied, raising her from the ground, and looking upon her more kindly, "things must go on as they are. What comfort would my mother – God help her! – have without you? I have been a trouble and a plague to her – but you have been like an own tender child, and smoothened every step. I'll go to sea for a while – it 'ill be long afore I can forget what she did to-night; whatever divil tempted us both to sich anger. I'll be well to do in the same ship wid Katey's uncle, and ye'll all be glad to see me, may-be, whin I come back. And Lilly, I ax yer pardon for saying the say I did of you; it wasn't from the heart, only the temper. I DO know ye betther; and my friend, Harry Connor, 'ill be a happy man yet, if ye'll only jist give him that young heart that's as innocent as a new-born babe. And now, God be wid ye! The 'Mary' may sail at day-brake for what I know to the contrary. God bless ye!"

The heedless youth hastened on.

"Oh, Ned, Ned! – and won't ye say a word, or even make a sign, that I may tell yer mother all is pace?" He stopped and waved his hat over his head, and the belting[31] of many foliage trees, that enclosed Mr. Herriott's estate, hid him from her sight. Tears came to her relief, and she felt happy that Edward did not suspect how dearly she loved him. She turned homeward with a sorrowing heart, and was proceeding slowly on, when Peggy the Fisher's little black dog, Coal (we beg his pardon for not mentioning the very busy, ugly little gentleman before), ran out of a break in the adjoining hedge, and renewed his acquaintance with Lilly, by jumping and whining in that peculiar tone which shows a more than friendly recognition. Lilly was astonished; but still more so when the flattened hat and round rosy face of Peggy appeared through the same opening.

"Why, then, Miss Lilly, dear, is it yer fetch?[32] – or where are ye moving along, like a fairy queen, in the green meadows by the moonlight? Ah, gramachree!" she continued, forcing her way through the hedge, "ye look like a spirit, sure enough! My poor colleen! Sorrow soon withers the likes o' you."

Lilly felt sadly mortified, for she had little doubt that Peggy had overheard the conversation between her and Edward. And, although "the Fisher" kept love secrets with extraordinary fidelity, yet she certainly did not wish to trust her.

"So he's gone, the obstinate mule! – but I ax yer pardon. I hard every word of it, over the place, just by accident, as a body may say; for you see, mavourneen,[33] I was waiting for a particklar frind that promised to meet me about a little bit o' business that can't just be done by daylight, on account of the law. Och! it's hard for a lone woman to get a bit o' dacent bread; and the free rovers[34] themselves are getting so 'cute that ther's no coming up to thim at all, at all; but I'm keeping ye here, and the poor woman 'ill be half mad till she hears tidings o' Ned, the boy. I'll walk a step wid ye, and be back time enough yet. God help me! I must travel to Hook and Ballyhack too, the morrow mornin'. Och! but it's hard to 'arn an honest pinny in this wicked world." And the lady smuggler crossed herself very devoutly.

"Hook! are ye going to Hook to-morrow mornin'?" inquired Lilly.

"Plase God, I'll do that same."

"Oh, Peggy, thin, it would be an act o' charity just to take Ned some o' his bits o' clothes and things; if he will go, sure he ought to go dacent; and I'll make up the bundle for him, and lave it under the black thorn, in an hour or two; for I'll try and get her to bed – the Lord console her! – and stale thim out like, for I know she'll be too angry to send him any comfort yet a bit, and the ship may sail before she comes to herself."

"Why, thin, that's wise and good, the colleen 'gra – but sure you're the last that ought to grieve after the boy; it 'ill be well for you, for sartin; the ould woman has all in her own power – and sure it's to the one that bides wid her she'll lave it. Mind yer hits, and –"

"What d'ye mane by spakeing to me after that fashion?" said Lilly, darting a look of anger on her companion, which, if Peggy could have seen, she must have felt. "How d'ye think I could get such bitter black blood in my veins, as to plan such divil's mischief as that! Keep that sort of advice for thim that 'ill put up with it; Lilly O'Brien scorns it."

"Hullabullo! there we go! Well, if ye're so wrapt up in thim that doesn't care a skreed for ye, why ye'd betther just go to the fairy woman and get a charm, and bring him back, my purty Miss."

"I'll tell ye what, Peggy – I don't meddle or make with anybody, and nobody need meddle or make with me; nobody can say agin my liking my cousin – and why not? My aunt meant all kindly to both; but the thorns are sown and grown; and sure it's heart sorrow to think o' his flitting from his own home; but if he was willin' this minute to take me afore the priest, d'ye think I'd have the hand and not the heart? Fairy woman, indeed! I've no belief in such nonsense."

"Oh, to hear how she spakes o' the good people, and the very spot we're in, may-be – Lord save us! – full o'thim! Well, there's the house – I'll take the bun-dle safe, agra." She stopped for a moment to watch Lilly enter the cottage, and then muttered: "I can't make her out; she's either a born natural,[35] or something much above the common."

Lilly O'Brien found it a painful duty to administer consolation, where she herself so much needed it; but, after all, continual employment is the best balm to the sorrowing mind. Save that her cheek was somewhat paler, and her gentle smiles less frequent, six months had made little change in my sweet Lilly's appear-ance. Not so was it, I am sorry to say, with Mrs. Cassidy, poor woman! she felt her son's desertion, as a mother only can feel; but still more she grieved, when week after week passed, and the Bannow postman brought no letter from the wander-ing boy. Post evenings found her at the end of the lane that led to her cottage, anxiously watching John Williams's approach. Still, no letter cheered her broken, restless spirit; though she would never confess that she wandered forth on this errand, every Monday and Friday found her on the same spot; and she was on those days more bustling and fidgety than usual. Sometimes she would abuse the absent one in no gentle terms; but Lilly never failed to remember some kind act of her cousin's, and her low musical voice, in the soft tones of unaffected feeling, was ever ready to plead for him. At other periods the widow would weep like a child over some little circumstance that brought Ned to her recollection. The flowers he planted blossomed – or the bee-hives he had watched wanted thatching – or the table he made lost its leg – or the pig wanted ringing.[36] Lilly never mentioned him, except when her aunt led to it; but her eyelid was often heavy with tears.

Luckily for all parties, an event occurred that fully employed, for the time, my worthy old friend's thoughts and actions.

The windmill, that, from the landlord's depending on the steward to get it repaired – from the steward's depending on the mason to see to it – from the mason's depending on the thatcher – the thatcher on the carpenter – the carpenter on somebody, or nobody, or anybody but himself (after the true Irish fashion) – the windmill, Mrs. Cassidy's particular aversion – the windmill! – that had suffered a paralysis for more than five years, although every body said how useful it could be made – the windmill was repaired, furnished with new wings, and commenced operations within the short space of three weeks, to the astonishment of the natives, who (I must confess it, however unwillingly) are like all their countrymen and women, the most procrastinating race on the face of the earth. Mrs. Cassidy was annoyed beyond measure. The Quern was kept in constant motion, and Lilly was left at home in "pace and quietness," while her aunt sidled from house to house, exhibiting specimens of the flour ground in her own cottage, and contrasting it with what she termed "the coorse trash o' branny stuff, made up o' what not, that comes out o' that grinder a' top o' the hill."

Mrs. Cassidy was from home; Lilly had finished her allotted portion of flour, and was quietly preparing the frugal supper, when our old acquaintance, Peggy the Fisher, and Peggy's little dog, Coal, entered the cottage. Lilly had never forgotten the low cunning the Fisher had evinced on the evening, every transaction of which she so perfectly – too perfectly – remembered; and her pale cheek flushed, and a shadow passed over her brow, as she returned the greeting of the village busybody.

"I'm not for staying; may-be I'm not over welcome, Miss Lilly – but never mind, agra! Whin people's angry wid people, and all for good advice, given from the heart, and wid good intintion, all through – why people must only put up wid it until oder people see the rights o' it. Well, my dear young cratur, it's little ye knows o' the world yet: ah! it's a bad world for a dacent poor lone woman to get a bit o' bread in. But sure you'll not be lone in it; I seen a handsome boy not tin minutes agone, that 'ud give his best eye – (and, troth,[37] it 'ud be hard to choose betwixt 'em) for one look of love from ye, as I hard him say, many's the day ago, with my own two ears."

"I am sorry for it, Peggy, if what you say is true; for no one in the wide world do I love, barring my own poor aunt."

"Asy, child! Sure I'm not axing ye any questions – only, it's long, maybe, since ye hard from beyant seas?"

"My aunt has never heard from Ned since he quitted," replied Lilly.

"Well, may-be, so best. No news is good news, they say."

"I hope so."

"Now, what 'ud ye say to a poor body that 'ud tell ye something?"

"I'm sure I don't know," said Lilly; "it would depend on what that something was."

"Well, thin, here it is;" and Peggy drew a dirty, sailor-like letter from her bosom, and placed it in Lilly's outstretched hand. "There, my colleen 'gra! – it's from Ned, sure enough; and for yerself. One who brought it tould me, for I've no larning; how should a lone cratur like me get it! but it's little ye'll like the news that's in it; and I don't know how the ould 'ooman 'ill like it, at all, at all." Lilly stood unable to inquire, unable to open the letter she had so long wished for. Peggy, with her usual sagacity, saw the dilemma, and, settling the basket on her head, departed, with "God be wid ye, mavourneen!" Lilly broke the wafer with trembling hand, and read as follows: –

"DEAR COUSIN,

"This comes hoping you and my mother is well, as I am at present – thanks be to God for the same! – and likes the sea; but the land, somehow, is a saferrer life; particular for a family man, as I am, having married out o' love, a girl I'm not ashamed of; an English born and bred, and well iddicated and mannered as need be for a boy like me. I'd have written afore, but didn't know how it 'ud end, as I was terrible in love. And now I ax my mother's blessing. And, Lilly dear, it's you that can get that for me; and I know ye'll do your best to make things comfortable. I'm sorry mother and I parted in anger; but it will be all for the best in regard of the wife. And I intind bringing her home to ye, and we'll all be happy thegither agin, plase God; and I'm determind my child sha'n't be an Englishman, so I mean my mother to be grandmother soon, and ax her to love Lucy – she's handsomer than her name, and had a good penny o' money too, only it's clane gone; things are dreadful dear here; and I know you'll love her, for you were always kind. And I beg you to write by return of post, and send a trifle o' money; as, for the credit o' my people, I'd like to return home dacent. Lucy joins me in love and duty; and trusting to yer good word, rests yer affictionate friend and cousin till death,

"E. CASSIDY."

Lilly sat long with her eyes fixed on the letter; she did not weep; but her cheek was ashy pale, and her eyes were swollen. Poor girl! – she had used her best efforts to root love from her heart, or to calm it into that friendship which she considered duty; yet the shock she received, when the full truth was known, that Edward was actually married, and returning with his wife to Bannow, was almost too great for her to bear. She read the letter over and over again; and at last sunk on her knees, earnestly imploring God to direct and keep her in the right way. She arose, strengthened and refreshed by the pious exercise, and her pure and noble mind saw at once the course that was to be pursued. Then she reflected on her plan. Her aunt, she knew, would be terribly enraged at his marrying at all. But an Englishwoman – a Protestant, most likely – it was dreadful!

"Lilly, my darlint, what are ye in such a study about?" said the old woman, as she entered. "I've good news for ye – that vagabone mill[38] – but save us! – why ye're like one struck! – has any thing turned contrary? It's not post-night, nor – what ails ye, child? Can't ye spake at onct?"[39]

"Sit down, aunt, dear; there's a letter from Ned, and he is alive and well."

"Thank God for all his mercies to me and mine! Well, child?"

"And he's tired o' the sea, and coming home; and sure ye'll resave[40] him kindly, aunt?"

"The cratur! and sure I will; why not? Sure it was only a boy's wildness after all. Resave him! after not setting my two eyes upon him for a whole tin months! Sure I will – and he'll like home all the bether! Och, I'm so happy!" The poor woman threw her arms around Lilly's neck, and kissed her affectionately. "But what makes ye look so grave, my own colleen, that'll be my raal –"

"Hush! whist! for God's sake, my dear, dear, dear, aunt!" And Lilly fell on her knees: "Aunt dear, the night you and Ned had the bitter battle, ye promised me ye would not vex him; yet ye did."

"Well, agra?"

"Well, ye say the same thing now; and yet, may-be, ye'd do the same thing agin for all that!"

"Well, Lilly, darlint, there's no dread in life of it now, I am so continted; but where's the letter? read me the letter – I knew he'd come back; I –"

"Aunt, I humbly ax yer pardon; have I, since Ned left ye, ever angered ye?"

"Never, my colleen."

"Then grant me this one prayer – may-be the last I'll ever ax ye, aunt! – swear, by this blessed book, never to reproach Ned with anything that is gone and past; but to take him to your own fond heart, and trate him as a son for ever,"

"It's a quare humour, my darlint, but I can't refuse ye anything to-night, I'm so happy; and the letther to you and all, as fitting!" She took the prayer-book in her hand – "To swear to forget all that's past is it, mavourneen? – and to trate him –"

"Say, him and his – him and his," interrupted Lilly, breathlessly.

"That I will," replied Mrs. Cassidy, "and with all the veins of my heart; to forget all that's past, and trate him and his with love and kindness to the end of my days."

She kissed the cross on the page of the prayer-book, after the manner of her religion, and was going to do the same to Lilly's fair forehead – when she ejaculated, "Thank God!" and fainted in her aunt's arms. She remained long insensible, and when the kind woman's efforts succeeded in restoring her, the first words the poor girl heard were – "that's my darlint child! – rouse up; there, lane your head on my shoulder; no wonder, agra! he'd think o' those curls, and that gentle face, and that sweet voice that falls upon the ear widout ever disturbing it! Oh, sure ye'll be my raal child! I see it all: fitting to be sure that the letther should be to you. Sure he could not but rimimber my darlint Lilly! Och, but I'm the happiest woman this minit in the big world, let t'other be who she will!"

A loud and heavy groan, as if the last effort of a bursting heart, which the maiden could not suppress, stayed the old woman's speech, and fixed her attention again on Lilly's ghastly features – "Tell me directly, this minit, my brother's own child – tell me, is there any thing in that letther you've not tould me, as you wish to be happy? Is Ned coming home?" Lilly moved her head in assent. "Is he well and happy?"

"Yes, aunt, yes."

"Then, in holy Peter's name, my lanna,[41] what is it ails ye? Sure I see long enough ago that ye loved him in yer heart's core; and now – praise be to God! – whin ye'll be married, and my heart at pace, ye're taking on as if the boy was kilt intirely! Sure, whin ye're married – "

"Aunt, for the blessed Virgin's sake, name that last no more, for it can't be!"

"Don't dare to tell me that, unless ye mane to start the life out o' me at onct! Lilly, Lilly! sure, girl, ye've not been listening to Harry, and promised unknowns't to me, out o' maidenly anger with Ned? If ye marry Harry Connor, Lilly, ye'll sup sorrow, for it's folly to talk, child – yer heart's not in it."

"I'll never marry either Ned or Harry, aunt, so don't mintion it."

"The girl's gone mad, clane mad," said Mrs. Cassidy, angrily. "Why, what's to put betwixt you and Ned now?"

"His wife!" replied Lilly, solemnly, and for the first time pronouncing the word which banished every lingering hope from her heart; "his lawful wife; who," she added, "though born in a far counthry, will make ye a good daughter and a loving when I lave ye."

It would be impossible to describe the terrific rage of Mrs. Cassidy, when informed of all the particulars; even her noble-minded niece suffered from it; for when, forgetful of her oath, she declared Ned and his heretic wife should never find refuge in her house, "Remember," Lilly would say, and, as she spoke, the large tears would shower down her cheeks – "you swore on the blessed book to forget the past, and trate *him* and *his* with kindness to the end of yer days." Then Mrs. Cassidy reproached Lilly with "colloguing"[42] against her; with "joining the whole world to make her desolate;" with "brakeing her ould heart," and "splitting it into smithereens."[43] Then she raved about Ned, and his strange wife, and concluded with – "I'll bet my life she's no betther nor she should be."

"Oh, aunt, how can ye say sich a word! D'ye think Ned 'ud be the boy to bring black shame to his mother's hearth-stone? Oh, no! Protestant she is – and English – and all that – but not bad; don't think that, any how."

"Well, any how, Lilly, if a boy sarved me as you've been sarved, I'd skiver[44] his heart to his backbone. I wish ye had a betther spirit in ye."

Lilly replied not, but heartily rejoiced when the good lady's anger and repinings were hushed in a sound sleep. She entered her own room, and counted over her savings, for Mrs. Cassidy had ever given more than supplied her wants. She had hoarded, not from selfishness, but from a feeling of generosity, that she might have the means of assisting some of her poorer neighbours; and this she had often done. With her hands, as well as with her money, had she bestowed cleanliness and comfort to many a neighbour's cottage. Her little store only amounted to three one pound notes, and a few shillings; the former she carefully wrapped up, and wrote as follows to her cousin: –

"Dear Ned,

"I could not ask yer mother to send you much money now, and I think she'd just as soon, when ye come, that ye didn't mention at all having resaved it, because it's so little, on account o' Lady-day[45] being nigh at hand, and the rent to make up, and money not plenty; and we'll be glad to get ye back, and the young woman that's my cousin now, too. My aunt's angry yet, but she'll soon come about. Let me know aforehand, the day we may expect ye; and, with prayers that heaven may rain down blessings on you and yours, I rest,

"Your sincere
"Well-wisher and cousin,
"Lilly O'Brien.

"Inside, three pounds."

The early grey of morning saw Lilly pattering along the sea-shore in search of Peggy the Fisher. This busy woman often lodged at a little cottage near the cliffs, that belonged to one Daniel McCleary, a man of doubtful character, as regarded the revenue. Lilly thought it not unlikely that Peggy would be there: so towards it she directed her steps. The sun had not even tinged the eastern clouds with his earliest rays, and the ocean rolled in heavy masses of leaden-coloured billows towards the shore, save where, here and there, amid the mistiness of morning, a fantastic rock, rooted in the "vasty deep,"[46] raised its dark head, prouder even than the proud waves that foamed for a moment angrily at its base, and then passed on. The cabin she sought was so miserable, that its mud walls and blackened thatch, overgrown with lichens and houseleek,[47] were hardly distinguishable from the long fern and bulrush that grew round it; it rested against (indeed, one of its sides was part of) a huge mound of mingled rock and yellow clay; and at spring-tides the sea advanced so very near, that the neighbours wondered Mc Cleary remained there. There were two paths approaching this hovel; one from the country across the marshy moor that stretched in front; the other from the cliffs which partly overshadowed it. Lilly pursued the latter, but was a good deal surprised at observing a very dark cloud of smoke issuing from an aper-

ture in the roof which constituted a chimney. She went on, looking at the smoke,
and endeavouring to guess its cause; when, suddenly, she felt her footing give way,
and almost at the same moment discovered she had fallen into an excavation, not
deep, but extensive. Before she had time to look around her, the exclamation of
"Tunder and turf! – what divil brought ye here?" from the lips of Peggy herself,
astonished Lilly beyond conception. Ere she could reply, three or four wild-look-
ing men, not one of whom she recognised, gathered round her: the red, flickering
light given by a peat and furze fire, and a few miserable candles, stuck without any
apparent fastening against the clayey walls; the heaps of grain piled to the very
roof; the blackened iron pots of all sizes; dirty tin machines, such as she had never
before seen; and, above all, the smell of turf and whisky, convinced poor Lilly that
she had tumbled into an illicit distillery, the existence of which, although within
half-a-mile of her own home, she had never suspected.

"Peg, ye ould cat, ye've sould the pass[48] on us!" exclaimed one of the men,
whose bare sinewy arms and glaring eye told both of strength and violence.

"Look out, Jack, for God's sake!" whispered another; "who knows but the
young one has a troop o' red-coats[49] at her heels!"

"Divil drive 'em!" said a ferocious looking fellow, with a pitchfork; "we're
done up fairly now, and there's nothin' for it but to skiver the both, and thin jist
trate 'em to a could bath this fine mornin'."

"What's the row?" inquired Daniel Mc Cleary himself, coming forward.
"Hey, powers above! ye ould traitor (turning to Peggy, who stood with her arms
folded, and managed to hold her tongue for a time), is it you that brought Miss
Lilly here? – we're ruinated. Och! Peggy, Peggy, to think ye'd turn informer!"

"Me – is it me? – ye lying vagabone! – Me? – ye desarve to be briled alive;
to be scalded to death in yer own potteen[50] 'ud be too dacent a death for ye. Me,
an informer! – the back o' my hand to ye, Dan Mc Cleary, for ever, Amin. As for
you, Mick Doole," and, as she spoke, she placed her arms a-kimbo, and advanced
to the knight of the pichfork: "you were niver good – egg nor bird – nor niver
will be, plase God. And as to skivering, Mick Doole, may-be ye'll be skivered or
worse, as nate as a Michaelmas goose, yer-self, afore long, only I scorn to talk o'
sich things. Paddy Leary! oh, it's you that's the brave[51] man; look out for the red-
coats; ah! ah! ah! fait, and it 'ud be good fun to see that innocent, young cratur
marching at the head of a rigiment, after yer bits o' stills, that, it's my thought, she
knew nothin' about till this blissid minit! Sure it's myself was struck, to see her
tumbling upon a hape o' barley, through the black roof, like a snowball. Spake
out, my lannan![52] Sure ye niver did that ye'd be ashamed to tell, and that's what
none here can say but yerself."

"Ay," added the first speaker, "we'll listen to rason."

"For the first time in yer life, thin," muttered Peggy.

"You gave me a letter last night," and Lilly turned to the Fisher as she spoke.

"True for ye, it was he," pointing to Mc Cleary, "brought it from Watherford."

"It required a quick answer. I couldn't get John Williams to take it, by rason he doesn't go till to-morrow; and I thought that you, Peggy, 'ud be on the trot somewhere near a post, so I wrote it last night, and thinking ye'd put up at Dan Cleary's, 'cause ye often do, I came early to try, for fear I'd miss of ye, and ill-luck sent me the cliff path, and all of a sudden I fell into this wild place; out o' which the Lord will, I hope, deliver the poor orphan in safety."

Lilly's tall, slight figure, and flowing hair, contrasted with the stout form of the Fisher, who stood a little in front; the rosary and a cross hanging from the arm which retained it's a-kimbo position; while the scarlet kerchief that confined her grizzled locks fell, like a cowl, from the back of her head, and fully exposed her large bronzed features, which showed in strong relief, as the light from the crackling fire flashed occasionally on them. Mick Doole, large and bony enough for one of the ancient inhabitants of the Giant's Causeway,[53] leaning on his pitchfork, and looking as if the roof rested upon his huge black head, towering over both Paddy Leary and Daniel, who, standing at either side of the colossus, formed another group; while some three or four beings, indescribable as to shape and features, because they were covered with dirt, and encompassed in an atmosphere of smoke and steam, filled up the back-ground.<retain hyphen>

"If ye came wid a letther, where is it?" inquired one of the party.

Lilly drew it from her bosom, and presented it to the querist. He turned it over and over, and then, observing quietly – "The smoke blinds me so, I can't read," – handed it to Daniel Mc Cleary.

"Well, that's good enough, too," said Peggy, "I niver hard tell yet of man or woman who could read widout knowing B from a bull's fut."[54]

"It's right enough after all," observed Daniel, "for I know this is for the boy I brought the letther from; not from him straight, only from one that knows him: there's something inside it?"

The idea that Mc Cleary might extract the money crossed Lilly's mind, but only for a moment, and she firmly replied, "Yes, three pounds."

"And I'm the one that'll put it safe into Taghmon, my jewel, afore twelve this blissed day," exclaimed Peggy, taking possession of the letter.

"Well, ye didn't go to come here as a spy, Miss Lilly, and I ax yer pardon for suspicting ye; but upon my troth it's dangerous, now ye know our sacret, to let ye go; who'll go bail[55] for ye?"

"I will," said Peggy.

"Your bail won't do, ye cross divil," replied Paddy Leary.

"Mine will, then," said a stout, middle-sized man, coming from amid the distant group; "I've been watching ye all this tin minutes, ye cowardly set – and it's no joke to be frightening the Bannow Lilly after that fashion, ye bag o' weasels! My colleen, never mind; ay, whin 'rattling Jimmy'[56] goes bail, who grumbles?" Certainly they all appeared quite satisfied. "Sure," he continued, "only you've no gumption,[a][57] ye'd know that the kind heart is niver mane: why, look at her, d'ye think sich as she 'ud condescind to inform on yer potteen? Ah! ye don't know her as I do."

"I never saw ye before," exclaimed Lilly.

"What, not the lame bocher,[b][58] that had lost the use of a leg, and was blind of an eye, all from lightning on the salt sea?" and he imitated the voice and halt of a beggar to perfection: "'twas a could night, but ye made me very comfortable, Miss Lilly; and don't ye remember the madman that frightened ye down the park, where ye were spreading the clothes to dry, last summer? I was sorry to frighten ye, dear; but fait, I couldn't help it, for we were wanting to get a little something, that same little sthill, past the park, and couldn't, for you; so I wint mad, and frightened ye; yet – God bless ye! – ye thought I looked hungry, and so ye brought out sich a dale o' food, and I laid it aside the hedge; but come along, the white rose can't blow 'mong the coorse weeds."

"Jim – Jim, ax her to promise on the book," said Paddy.

"Ax – not I: sure the honour's in her heart's blood." And so saying, "rattling Jimmy," the smuggler and the peep-o'-day-boy,[59] lifted Lilly kindly and respectfully out of Daniel Mc Cleary's black den.

"And now," said Peggy, "I'll finish my prayers."

A fortnight had nearly elapsed, and no letter arrived from Edward. Lilly most truly wished to leave the cottage, and urged every reason she could think of to be permitted so to do. "Miss Herriott was going for the winter to Dublin, and wanted a bettermost lady's maid, and a little time there would do her the world and all o' good;" or, "she had a bad cough, and it might go away if she went more up the country;" but the entreaties and tears of her aunt to whose very existence she seemed as necessary as the air she breathed, silenced her request; and she resolved to meet her relatives, however painful the meeting might be. "My aunt will get used to Lucy after a bit," thought she, "then I can go: and, any way, he doesn't know I ever loved him, and sure it's no sin, in the sight o' God, to love him as I have loved." And Lilly was right; there was no impurity in her affection. It was the feeling that seeks the good of its object, without any reference to self. She did not regret that Edward was happy with another; nor had she, towards his wife, one jealous or unkind thought. "And sure I shall rejoice to see him happy." This was her last idea, as she rested her head on her humble pillow; and yet the morning found it wet with tears; and then she knelt, and prayed to God to bless her aunt, and Edward, and his wife, and to direct her in all her paths.

"There's one wants to spake a word to ye, Miss Lilly, dear, jist down yonder," said Peggy the Fisher, as Lilly entered the garden, after breakfast, one morning.

"Who is it, Peggy?"

"Well, thin, it's jist Harry Connor, he's had a letter from Ned, and he wants to see ye on the strength of it." Peggy passed on her way, and Lilly proceeded to the spot the Fisher had pointed out. Harry Connor was there.

"I got word from yer cousin, Lilly," said Harry, "that him and his wife are at Ballyhack, and will be here to-morrow; and they'd have come before, but Lucy (I think he calls her) has been very ill from sea-sickness; and he begged me to tell ye so. Dear Lilly, I was glad of the opportunity; for there's no getting a sight o' ye; you're always at home, and even on Sundays yer aunt goes on the car to chapel, so one can't speak to ye. Oh, Lilly! Lilly! you were not always so distant – don't you remember when I used to sit of an evening in that garden, between you and Edward, reading, and you used to call me your master, and say the time passed so happily?" Tears gathered in Lilly's eyes, as she turned away her face; for she too, remembered those evenings. "Lilly," continued the young man, "have you heard anything against me? Your aunt always showed me the could shoulder; I don't blame her for that in past times; but now she would not, if you wished. Oh, do not say you cannot love me, Lilly! You have always shunned me when I wanted to spake about it; but tell me now, Lilly O'Brien! I will wait; I will do anything you wish – anything – only say, Lilly, that you do not hate me."

"No, Harry, I do not, indeed;" and she met his eye with steady firmness.

"Only one word more, and then," he continued, holding her struggling hand, "you may go. I will wait any time you please, only say that it shan't be in vain – that you will be my wife, and make one whose heart almost bursts at the thought of losing you – happy!"

"Harry I cannot desave ye," she replied, "nor would not, if I could. I know I've shunned ye; because I hoped that you would see why – to save us both all this heart-pain. I have always had rason to respect you – and I do: but love ye I never can; and I'll never marry the man I cannot love."

"Only one word," said Harry earnestly –" sure you'll hear me – you say you've a regard for me. Lilly, you go nowhere; you see no one. I do not speak of my being well to do in the world. But if ye were to let me near ye, to be with ye as I once was, in bygone days, the love might come. Oh, let me only try!"

"No, Harry, no, it would be useless; my heart here tells me so. You will find many fitter for ye, who can love ye as ye deserve. May the Almighty bless and watch over ye, Harry! And farewell." The young man still grasped her hand; and, as he gazed on her beautiful face, he felt that, if it were turned from him for ever, his sun of happiness was indeed set.

"Lilly, before ye go, hear my last resolve. If ye really cast me off, I, who love ye more than life – I, who, to see even the glimmer of the candle carried by this hand, have watched in rain and tempest under yon old tree – I will leave my father's home; and, for your sake, Lilly, I will take priest's vows, and forsake the world. Think well, Lilly O'Brien, if, from mere whim or maiden modesty, you would drive me to that."

"Harry, God forbid that you should ever do so! Ye would not be fit to sarve on the altar, if for anything like that ye went there. No, Harry, my heart must go with my hand. They're all I have to give, but they must go together: even you would despise, ay, hate that hand, if ye found, for lucre, it gave itself, when the betther part was wanting."

"Lilly, may-be ye love some one else? Oh! may-be I'm proud; but surely there's not a boy all round the country could win your heart."

"I do not love any one for marriage. So, onct more, God bless ye, Harry! – may ye be happy – happier," she muttered to herself, "happier than I shall ever be!"

Harry stood with his eyes fixed on the spot where Lilly had disappeared. His senses were bewildered; and it was not until a smart slap on the shoulder, and the voice of the everlasting Peggy, who appeared (one would almost believe, like Sir Boyle Roche's bird,[60] in two places at the same time) at his elbow, with her broad platter face, shaded by the fish basket – that he became fully sensible of the reality of his interview.

"Sure I tould ye ye'd get no good of the colleen; and if ye'd ha' mintioned the matther to me afore, I'd ha' tould ye the same thing, and may-be the rason too."

"I know," said Harry, musingly, "she does not love any one else,"

"Och, ye do, do ye? – humph, agra!"

"What do you mean, woman? Sure she told me she did not; and her lips never lied, nor never will."

"Asy! – the string o' my bades broke, and I was forced to stop to mend it jist behind that big bush o' furze. A poor creature like me can't afford to be buying bades every day. So, my dear – all accident (for I scorn a listener), I hard what she said – '*she loved no one for marriage.*' True for her; they talk a grate dale of her sinse; but it's poor sinse to go look for the snow that fell last winter. I'll tell ye what, as a dead sacret; – she loved the ground that her cousin walked on, more than all the gould that ever was in, or ever came out o' Indy. And she loves him still; ay, ye needn't look so strange; she loves him, but nothin' improper – I know that girl's heart as well as if I was inside of her – 'tis of the sort that doesn't stain, or spot; and now you'll see, her delight 'll be to tache his wife all the ould mistress's quare ways. And thin, whin she'll have made pace intirely among 'em, she'll stale off, like the mist up the mountain; and work (and well she knows how) for his sake that doesn't know she loves him. It's mighty fine to be so romantical all for pure love. God help us, poor women, we're all tinder! It was the way wid me, whin my bachelor[61] died – rest his sowl! – and that's the rason I'm a poor lone body now. Sure I sould the pig my mother left me, to pay the clargy, to get his sowl out o' purgatory; and wasn't it well for him to have it to depind on?"

Harry, heedless of Peggy's pathetic application of the apron to her eyes, turned towards his own home, "revolving sweet and bitter thoughts."[62] There is a delight imparted to every unsophisticated heart, by the contemplation of a noble or a virtuous action, that nothing else can give; and Harry's generous mind at once acknowledged Lilly's virtues: loving at first without knowing it; feeling it unrequited; and yet resolved to benefit its object to the sacrifice of every personal convenience and prospect in life.

The next day Edward and his bride arrived at the cottage. Mrs, Cassidy, in compliance with her oath, received them kindly. The mother's heart yearned towards her son; but poor Lucy saw the old woman entertained a strong prejudice against her.

The "kindly welcome," that murmured from Lilly's lips, sounded sweetly on the young stranger's ears; and, as fatigue compelled her to go to bed almost immediately, Lilly's gentle attentions were very delightful. The kind girl had displayed much taste and care in arranging their small sleeping room. Every article she could spare from her own chamber was added to its furniture. And when Lucy saw everything so clean and comfortable, she expressed both surprise and pleasure.

It was impossible not to love Lucy, when you looked at her; but it was somewhat doubtful if that sentiment would continue when you knew her. Her eyes were black, quick, and quite as likely to sparkle with anger as with pleasure. She was very *petite*, lively, thoughtless, and possessed precisely those acquirements that were useless in an Irish cottage. The daughter of a grocer in Plymouth, she had seen, fallen in love, ran away with, and married Edward in the short space of three weeks; and had not yet numbered sixteen years. Her youth pleaded strongly in her favour: but her extreme giddiness kept Lilly, the sweet, the patient Lilly, perpetually on the watch, lest she might do something to annoy her mother-in-law. It is true she quilled[63] Mrs. Cassidy's caps in so new and bewitching a style that everybody said Lucy made the good lady look ten years younger. She washed her old mode cloak in some stuff, of which whiskey and beer were the principal ingredients, and made it appear, to the astonishment of the whole parish, "bran new." Then she trimmed bonnets – one yard and a half of riband, managed by her, went as far as three and a quarter ('tis an absolute fact) with anybody else. She could work natural flowers upon gauze, and embroider the corners of pocket handkerchiefs. She could even get up fine linen:[64] but she could neither spin flax or wool, card,[65] or milk, or churn, or cram fowl,[66] or make butter, or a shirt or shift of any description: the worst of all was, she said, unfortunately, that she was certain no Christian body could eat bread made from the flour that was pounded out by those dirty stones; thus bringing Mrs. Cassidy's invaluable quern into contempt. Then it was quite impossible to keep her quiet; everything excited her risibility. One day, in particular, when the turkey-cock, affronted at Mrs. Cassidy's scarlet petticoat, which outvied his own red neck, picked unmercifully at her legs, Lucy only laughed, and never went to the rescue, which induced the old lady to say, that "Ned pretended to bring home a wife, but had only brought home a doll."

Lilly might be well called her guardian angel: when, like a school girl, she scampered over the fields, gathering flowers, or hunting every cock, hen, and chicken, over the potatoe ridges, Lilly followed to prevent her over-fatiguing herself, and to assist her home; then she would instruct her how to please her mother-in-law; and, if Mrs. Cassidy complained, Lilly had always some remark to soften down what was said. Her general apology was – "She's so young, but she'll soon be a mother, and then she'll get sense."

"I wonder Ned did not fall in love with you, Lilly," said Lucy, one day; "I'm sure you'd have made a better wife for him than ever I shall!" How poor Lilly blushed, and then turned pale; but Lucy heeded it not. "How industrious Ned grows! – well, they would not believe, in Plymouth, that he'd ever settle down into a farmer, but I'm sure he works in the fields from morning till night."

"People who are not rich must work, Lucy."

"Now, Lilly, that's a hit at me, who let you do everything; but do not look so angry with me, dearest Lilly; I beg pardon, you never hit at anybody. Oh! you are not like an Irishwoman!"

"Oh, Lucy, dear! – don't be after talking that way o' the country, afore my aunt, for it hurts her; and ye must remember how much she's thought of in the parish."

"Well, there, I'll be as good as gold – there;" and she sat down to work at some caps for a little stranger that was expected soon.

Edward was very affectionate to his young wife, although her heedlessness often annoyed him; but when he gazed on her fairy-like beauty, he forgave it.

The Protestant church was too far for her to walk; she would not go to mass, and her husband loved her too well to permit her to be teazed on the subject. Her mother-in-law, and even Lilly, were grieved at this, and lamented that she thought so little about serious things; however, Mrs. Cassidy always reconciled it to herself, by saying, "Niver mind, she'll be all the asier brought round to the right way, by-and-by." But, of all the amusements in which the thoughtless creature delighted, nothing pleased her so much as boating; if she could even get into a boat by herself, she would paddle it round the creeks, and into the bays, which in some places are overhung by scowling rocks, where the sea-birds nestle in safety.

"The potatoes are almost done, by their bubbling, I suppose, Lilly," said she one day, "so I'll go and meet Ned as he comes from the plough, and we shall be just in time for dinner;" and away she tripped, singing as blithely as a lark.

"She has a light heart," thought Lilly; "and why not? – mine is not as heavy as it used to be: well, thank God, it does make people happy to do their duty;"

and she assisted the little serving-girl in arranging all things in their kitchen – a task soon performed; the potatoes, laughing and smoking, were poured out on a clean home-bleached cloth, and the white noggins[67] frothed with fresh buttermilk of Lilly's own churning. Something prepared with extra care, for the delicate Englishwoman, was covered between two delf plates at the fire, and Mrs. Cassidy stood watching at the door, her hand lifted to her eyes, to shade them from the noon-day sun, while Lilly mixed some gooseberry wine with water and sugar for Lucy.

"Lilly, didn't ye say that Lucy went to meet Ned?"

"Yes, aunt."

"Well, here's Ned at the gate almost, and no sign o' Lucy."

"That's mighty strange," replied Lilly, advancing; "Ned, where's Lucy?"

"At her dinner, I suppose."

"Now, don't be so foolish, I'm sure she met ye."

"She did not, indeed, and I was longing to see her."

"It is some of her childish tricks," said Mrs. Cassidy.

"Her dinner 'll be stone could, though," said Lilly, looking out; "so I'll jist go see if I can meet her, and sit ye all down, or the pratees 'll not be fit to ate;" and she issued forth without further parley.

Ned did not sit down, although his mother urged him. "Her dinner has nothin' to do with yours, Ned; sure Lilly has something nice under the plate for her. No sign of her yet," she continued, after a pause; "sure she wouldn't be so foolish as to go to Tim Lavery's boat, for a bit of a spree; I caught her in it reading yesterday, but it was anchored safe, sure enough."

Ned made no reply, but followed the footsteps of his cousin; the field he had been ploughing was very near the beach; he hastily gained it, and his horror and dismay can be better conceived than expressed, when, gaining the cliff, the first object he beheld was Lilly, half in and half out of the water, dragging to shore the apparently lifeless body of his wife. When Lilly left the cottage, she first looked behind the large furze and hawthorn bushes near the field, and then the boat occurred to her; she sped to the sea, and saw it in shallow water, but upset, with Lucy clinging to the stern, faint and exhausted. To plunge into the water and bring her to land, was the work but of a moment, and done before Edward could descend the cliffs.

The thoughtless creature was soon conveyed home. Her nerves were quite shattered; she clung closely to Lilly's bosom, like a frightened child, and did not even return her husband's caresses. She was hardly laid on her bed, when shrieks of agony succeeded the half murmured words and sobbings of terror; and, after long and painful suffering, the being, who, not many hours before, had bounded in the full light and life of early youth, gave premature birth to a living child, and then yielded up her own existence. It was very sorrowful to mark the merry eyes closed for ever beneath their alabaster lids, and the long black lashes resting on her colourless cheeks.

Then came a long and loud debate between the Protestant and Catholic priests, as to who was to perform the last rites; as if the spirit's happiness depended on man's words repeated over inanimate clay. The widower roused himself from the lethargy that succeeds the first rush of impetuous grief, and said calmly, but firmly – "Plase your reverences, I'm a Catholic, and ever was and will be; but she that's gone from me was born a Protestant – married a Protestant – and, as she died one, so shall she be buried, and that's enough; and what's more, I promised her, when I didn't think that death and desolation would come at this time, that if the child was a girl it should go wid her, if a boy wid me. Now, gentlemen, I'm not a larned man, but my mind is, that a promise, to the dead or the living, is holy and firm in its natur'; and so, as I promised, it shall be. I couldn't look upon the babby's face for a king's ransom, nor do I know whether it be boy or girl; mother, say what is it?"

"A girl," replied Mrs. Cassidy.

"Well, may-be more betther; may-be you'd just baptize it, Mr. Barlow, and Lilly and my mother 'll stand for it; as my notion is it can't live – and why should it?"

But the little Lucy did live – thanks to Lilly's fostering care; and so fragile a thing it was, that even a rough kiss might have killed it. A nurse was immediately procured, and Lilly had the satisfaction of seeing all Mrs. Cassidy's solicitude directed towards the infant; nay she almost forgot the quern, and the only danger was that the child would be destroyed by kindness. There was, however, to Lilly's delicate mind, something most improper in her remaining in the same house with her cousin. He was again free; although she hoped that he did not suspect her love, yet he knew of his mother's old plan; he had once, in anger, reproached her as being accessary to it; and Lilly decided on leaving our village. Edward, since sorrow had laid her hand on him, was an altered man, and Mrs. Cassidy was enjoying a vigorous old age: so she could leave her, assured of happiness. It was a bitter trial to forsake her little godchild, yet she felt she owed a duty to herself. Mr. Herriott's family were again about to visit Dublin, and, without imparting her plan to any one, she offered her services to Miss Herriott. They were joyfully accepted; not without many expressions of wonder that "the Bannow Lilly," the flower of the whole country side, should leave a spot where she was so much beloved. Lilly pleaded a wish for improvement, and finally arranged to set off with Miss Herriott in three days. As she returned she heard Peggy's loud voice, singing her old favourite, "The Colleen Rue," just as she got to her favourite stanza –

> "I ranged through Asia – likewise Arabia,
> Through Penselvanie, a seeking for you;
> Through the burning region of the siege of Paris," –[68]

when she espied Lilly in her decent mourning habit.

"The blessing be about ye, my precious! – and may-be ye'd tell us where ye've been. Sorra[69] a bit o' news going now for a poor body."

"I've been up to Mrs. Herriott's, Peggy."

"Och! they're going to Dublin, all the way, on Tuesday. Sure that'll be the black journey for the poor, You needn't care, Miss Lilly; sure you've full and plinty, and an own fireside."

"I'm going as own maid with Miss Herriott, Peggy; – there's a small taste of news for yer comfort," continued Lilly, smiling – "and more, betokens, you've the first of it, for I've not tould my aunt yet."

"You going? Och, oh, oh! – don't be making yer fun of us after that fashion; we know betther nor that."

"It's quite true, for all ye may think, and so God be wid ye, Peggy! You and poor Coal will often cross my mind when I'm alone among strangers."

"Arrah, now, stop! – sure ye can't be in arnist. Sure there's not a living sowl in the parish but says you'll be married to Ned now; and at St. Pathrick's sure I hard 'em talking about it; and how Harry Connor's priested; sure he's Father Harry, for your sake."

"Peggy, I take shame to myself for harkening to your palaver for a moment; dacent talk ye have, and the young grass not green on *her* grave yet! Once more I say, God be wid ye." I have done right, thought she, but I shall not be able to make my dear aunt think so.

Poor Mrs. Cassidy scolded and cried with might and main; and Ned remonstrated, and even said that he took it very unkind of her to leave them, and, above all, the little thing, whose life she had saved. But Lilly was firm, and departed amid the reproaches and tears of her aunt, and the heartfelt regret of her neighbours.

How very irksome were her employments! – how did she shrink from the rude gaze of gentlemen and gentlemen's gentlemen, who, astonished at her full-blown beauty, paid homage by staring her out of countenance; and how often did she long for the quiet of the lowly cottage in the isolated village of Bannow! At first she imagined that city people must be very superior to country ones. But she soon grew tired of the pert flippancy and foolish airs of the servants whom she met; and by Miss Herriott's permission, retired, when unoccupied, to the solitude of her kind lady's dressing-room. She received letters once a month, generally, from her cousin. The two first, in addition to the necessary information, anxiously entreated her return, but latterly (for the stay of the family was prolonged, owing to Mrs. Herriott's illness) the subject was never mentioned; and the bitter feeling, that there no longer existed any one to love her, weighed heavily on her heart. Sixteen months had elapsed since Lucy's death; and Edward ever spoke of his child with all a father's fondness. Lilly longed to see it, but she had resolved on never again living with her aunt – and she remained firm to her resolution.

She had been dressing her young lady one morning, when, passing down stairs, the footman said – "There's one in the housekeeper's room that wants ye." She hardly entered when she was almost suffocated by the embraces of Mrs. Cassidy; and then she had to encounter the respectful but affectionate greetings of her cousin. Her aunt earnestly looked at her, would not sit down, but said – "Now, my darlint Lilly, it is much ye ought to thank me for this journey – in my ould age to take to the road agin; but ye see the rason is, that Ned is tired o' being bachelor, and he's going to change his condition, and jist wants to ax your advice and consint."

"Mine!"

"Now, mother dear, don't be mumming,"[70] said Ned: "Lilly, I come to ax ye to accept the hand of one who is unworthy to be yer husband, but yet would die to make you happy. Lilly, don't cast me off – for my mother's sake – for my own – for this one's sake;" – and he took from the arms of our old friend, Peggy the Fisher, a smiling, black-eyed little creature, who almost instantly nestled its curly pate in Lilly's bosom. "Sure ye can make us all happy, if ye like; and we'll be all in quiet Bannow agen. Say, Lilly! Oh, don't look so could on me!"

"Will ye hould your whisht, Ned!"[71] interrupted Peggy; "if ever I see'd anybody trated in that mismannerly fashion! Can't ye see wid half an eye that the cratur's as good as fainted, ye omathawn![72] No wonder, and ye both bellowering thegither. Ye don't know how to make a dacent proposhal; ye've frightened the grawl[73] betwixt ye – whisht, honey, whisht! (to the child) – there's a woman! – ay – come to your own Peggy, that's hushowed[74] ye oftin; and will agin, by the blessin' o' God."

Lilly, literally unable to stand, sank into the housekeeper's chair. Edward knelt at her side; and his mother, holding one of her hands to her heart, looked earnestly on her face, while Peggy, "hushowing" the child, was not an uninterested spectator.

"God knows," said the young woman, after a little time, "I did not expect this. Aunt, when I had no father to protect me – no mother to feel for me – you did both; you shared with me what you had; and, oh! what was more than all – while I ate o' yer bread, and drank o' yer cup, ye never made me feel that it was not my father's roof that sheltthered me. Ned, we grew together, and you were to me as a born brother. But ye wronged me, Ned, that night; the first time (and God, that hears me, knows it), the first time I ever guessed my aunt wished me to be nearer to her than her brother's child: that night, when, to prevint yer laving home, I proposed to quit for ever my only frind; when I did her bidding, an followed ye through the moonlight, to bring ye back to yer poor ould mother, ye cast a black word in my face, and ye said that I – I, Lilly O'Brien – was leagued agin ye – and that I followed ye to get a husband." She covered her face with her hands, and faintly continued, "I have never forgotten it; I have prayed to do so. No one ever knew it, but Peggy; she overheard it. Oh! it weighed here, at the very bottom of my heart, and when I slept it was wid me; it – "

"Oh, Lilly, how can ye take on so! – sure it was the bad temper that did it, and I didn't mane it. And sure you've proved since that it's little truth was in it; sure ye've been more like an angel than anything else; and sure when I ax yer pardon – "

"Stop, Ned, ye do *now*; but may-be, by an' by, ye might say the same thing agen; and if ye did it, and if we were married, I could never look up after!"

"Why, Lilly," said Mrs. Cassidy, "ye're making him out a fair black villain, after all yer goodness, to think he'd do the likes o' that – after yer coming over me, to take an oath *to resave him and his, as my own,* whin a word was only wanting to make me ban him for iver."

"And after her flying at me like a mad cat," echoed Peggy, "becase I gave her a bit of advice (for I was fairly bothered) to take care of a little property for herself."

"Ay, and all her attintion to the stranger," resumed Mrs. Cassidy.

"And her sinding him her own three pounds to bring him home," said Peggy.

"How do you know that?" inquired Lilly.

"Is it how I know it? Why, thin, I'll jist tell ye. I knew yer aunt hadn't a tester[a] [75] in the house, becase she'd given me every pinny to exchange for gould, that she might pay her rint in it – not in dirty paper – to plase the landlord."

"Yer good deeds are all known, Lilly. Oh, let me say *my* Lilly; sure ye'll forgive yer cousin. How can I admire ye as I ought? – don't shake yer head, Lilly, dear – but –"

The opening of the door prevented the conclusion of Edward's speech; and Miss Herriott entered, her face radiant with satisfaction, "So, Lilly, I am to lose you; nay, do not talk, girl, I know you love him; I knew it all along; Peggy told me all about it, at the end of the shrubbery, the night before we left Bannow; and my dress-maker has made the wedding-dress, because Edward Cassidy wrote to me, and asked my opinion and consent: which was fitting; and I assured him you had not been flirting with any one, and invited him and my old friend up to Dublin; as to you, Peggy, I never expected you, but you are not less welcome."

"Why, I thank ye, Miss, my lady; I jist came to see how ye all war, and to mind the child, and to look at the fine beautiful city, and the college, that bates the world for larning, as I have hard, and the ancient ould Parliament-house; and thin go back, and give rest to my bones among my own people; but I hope ye'll persuade Miss Lilly, my lady, for her own good; sure they love each other – and what more's wanting for happiness?"

"Ay, do, Miss, she'll do yer bidding, may-be; she's forgotten mine;" and tears rolled down the wrinkled cheeks of Mrs. Cassidy.

"Not so," replied Miss Herriott; and taking Lilly's hand, she placed it in Edward's; "and now," continued the amiable girl, "kneel for the blessing that ascends to the throne of the Almighty, like a sweet-smelling savour – the blessing of an honest parent." They dropped on their knees, and Mrs. Cassidy pressed them to her satisfied heart.

"And sure that's as good as a play," blubbered Peggy.

"Well, Peggy, you shall see a play if you please, to-morrow evening; but first I invite you to Lilly's wedding, which will take place to-morrow at four o'clock, in our great drawing-room, agreeably to the forms of the Catholic church, by a Catholic priest. Nay, Lilly, it is the last time I shall ever command you; so I bid you all farewell for the present." And the good, and kind, and generous young lady left them to their "own company:" which, it is scarcely necessary for me to say, was not very doleful or wretched; for although the heart of one of the party was too full for words, ample amends was made for her silence by the ever talkative Peggy.[a]

At three quarters of an hour past three (I love to be exact in these matters), Miss Herriott inspected her company in the back drawing-room. The arrangements for the ceremony highly amused her; first, Mrs. Cassidy, in an open rose-coloured poplin dress, as stiff as buckram, with tight sleeves reaching to the elbows, where they were met by white mittens, that had been the gift of Miss Herriott's grandmother, and which the old lady prized so highly that they had only twice seen the light in twenty years; a blue satin quilted petticoat, ditto, ditto; a white muslin apron flounced all round; high-heeled shoes, with massy[76] silver buckles; a clear kerchief, pinned in the fashion that used to be called "pigeon's craw,[77]" and a high-cauled cap, trimmed with rich lace, completed her costume. Peggy sported a large flowered chintz, whereon pink parrots, yellow goldfinches, and bunches of roses bigger than either goldfinch or parrot, clustered together in open defiance of nature and the arts; this was made after Mrs. Cassidy's pattern, and displayed to advantage a pea-green English stuff[78] petticoat, quilted in diamonds. There was little variation from Mrs. Cassidy's fashion in the other et ceteras, except that Peggy wore a flaming yellow silk shawl, with a blue border; that, to use her own expression, "matched everything."

Lilly looked beautiful – most beautiful. Miss Herriott dressed her as she pleased; in white – pure white; would not permit her to wear a cap, but let her hair curl after its own fashion, only confining it with a wreath of lilies of the valley.

There is no use in describing Edward's dress; all bridegrooms, I believe, wear blue coats with yellow buttons and white waistcoats. The little Lucy had a clean white frock, and a lobster's claw[79] to keep it quiet.

Oh! what a happy group of humble people were assembled in that gay drawing-room! Mrs. Cassidy – the desire of her heart gratified, the hope of years realized, the fervent and continual prayer answered – Mrs. Cassidy was, beyond doubt, the happiest of them all, as she sat, with her cheerful and grateful face, contemplating her "two children".[b]

"Ye're both too handsome and too good for me," whispered Ned, as he conducted Lilly to the great drawing-room, closely followed by her condescending bridemaid. Lilly courtesied as she entered, but did not look off the ground until an exclamation of surprise, from the bridegroom, roused her attention, and she saw – Harry Connor! – Father Harry! – ready to perform the marriage ceremony.

"It is even your old friend," said he, advancing: "Mr. Herriott, at my request, consented to my surprising you. Ned, when I give you this girl as your wife, I give you one whom no earthly feeling could tempt from the path of strict honour. She told me once that her hand should never go without her heart, and your being together proves you have it; a blessing will she be to thee, my early friend." A single tear glistened on his cheek as he pronounced the words that made them husband and wife: – it was a tear of which a seraph might not have been ashamed.[a]

Four years have passed since that happy marriage; and can you not tell who – seeking to abstract herself from household cares and blessings, only that she may render grateful homage to her Creator – sits after evening vespers, with clasped hands and downcast eyes, her national hood[80] shading, but not obscuring, the beauty of her pensive face, near yonder cottage, that looks so joyously in the setting sun[b] which sheds such glorious light over the ocean, that reflects every passing cloud upon its calm clear bosom? See her again, within the porch of her dwelling, where the flowers are blossoming; and where she has other blossoms than the flowers give. She is approaching the bloom of womanhood; yet grace is in all her movements. Her kerchief is carefully pinned across her bosom, and two or three rich auburn tresses that obstinately come forth, and will not be confined by the neat cap of snowy whiteness, move in the passing breeze; – that dark-eyed and dark-haired little girl, buoyant and animated, cannot be her child: yet it clings to her neck, and calls her "mother." There – the honest farmer, returning from his toil, is met by two almost infant prattlers; the youngest a perfect specimen of childish helplessness and beauty; – and, peering from the window, is the hardly altered face of – Mrs. Cassidy.

Oh, that voice! – it is Peggy's – old Peggy – as she is still called, "Peggy the Fisher." She has "a good penny o' money of her own," and sometimes visits around the neighbourhood; but she is so strongly attached to the family to whom the cottage belongs, that she almost resides there.

"Och, ye craturs, like fairy things, come in to the tay! – sure it's not fit for the likes o' ye to be muddling in the grass, even after yer daddy, ye born blossoms! – ye bames o' joy! – ye comforts o' the ould 'ooman's heart! – Come, all o' ye, to your own Peggy. Och! 'tis myself must set about, fair and asy, to make my sowl, and not be passing my time, like the flowers in May, wid the young blossoms of the BANNOW LILLY."

MARY RYAN'S DAUGHTER.

MARY RYAN'S DAUGHTER.

I NEVER saw any beauty in her – that's the truth" – exclaimed one of a group of females, who, lounging around a cottage door, were watching the progress of a young woman toiling slowly up a steep hill, and leading by the hand a very slight child. The cottage was in the valley – and the traveller must have passed the group – for, like the generality of Irish dwellings, it was on the road-side.

"I had the greatest mind in the world to ask her how she had the impudence to wear a bright *goold* ring on her wedding finger, as if she was an honest woman!" said another.

"And she asking with such mock modesty for a drink of water! I wonder how she relishes water after the fine wines she got used to," suggested a third.

"It was for all the world like a story written in a book," observed the first speaker; "how she left the Uphill farm (as good as seven years, come Easter), and no one ever knew exactly who she left it with – only guessing that it must be one of the *sporting squireens*,[81] that thronged the country about that time. Since the ould gentleman at the Hall died, and the place was pulled down, we have none of the kind going."

"Small loss," was the reply; "they were only good at divarshin – for themselves I mean; there was no use in them at all at all, for others."

"Did you see how white her hands were?" remarked another. "Well, I expect there will be murder of some sort done – for her father will never own her – and it's little she thinks there's a new mother to meet her. I hadn't the heart to tell her her own was dead! – bad as she is."

"Bad as who is?" exclaimed a clear, but aged voice. "Who is bad, girls, agra? It's a comfort to hear of bad people, so it is; it makes one say – 'Well, the saints be praised, I'm not as bad as *that,* any how.'"

"Oh, Daddy Denny, is it yourself that's in it? Oh, thin, that's luck!' they exclaimed together. "Think of that, now – and we never to see you coming, daddy, honey!"

"How could you see me coming," replied the stout beggarman, "when your backs were to me?"

"And that's true, Denny, dear! – but look, daddy, what do you see going up the hill?"

"Ay, wisha! – how do I know? – sure I'm sand blind, any way."[82]

"Don't bother us – your eye's as clear as a kitling's – who do you think it is?"[83]

"A woman, dear."

"Sure we know that – what else?"

"A child, my darling."

"What news you tell us – but who's the woman, and who's the child?"

"Ah, then, is it a witch ye think me? How can I tell?"

"Do you know Mister Phill Ryan, of the Uphill farm?"

"Do I know my right hand?"

"Did you know his wife?"

"The Lord be good to her! – Is it know her? – the holy saints make her bed in heaven; – I never say a prayer for myself without bringing her into it. Oh, she was the darling, with the open hand: there's few like her now by the road-side."

"Well, daddy, and you knew her daughter."

"I did, I did," replied the old man, with visible emotion: "I did – the poor darling – I did, God help me! she's heavier on my heart, this many a day, than all my sins – I often drame of her. Oh, Mary Ryan, dear, I wish you were as near all hearts as you are to mine!"

"She may be near enough to you, then, any time you like, for the future," replied one of the women, "for there she goes."

"Where, where?" inquired the beggar, eagerly: "Oh, as you hope for mercy, tell me where!"

"She's out of sight now," answered the first speaker: "but it was her you saw going up the hill."

"And did none of you tell her that her mother was dead?" inquired Denny.

"Why, then, what's come to you, daddy?" said the eldest: "my father would go mad if he thought we spoke to her."

"He'd do no such thing – he'd go with her himself sooner than she should go alone. Ah, girls! girls! one woman should never lean heavy on another: we should lave judgment to God, my darlings, and mind mercy, for we all want it, girls." The old man grasped his stick more firmly in his bony hand, and wiping the dew from his brow, which fatigue and emotion had brought there, he proceeded rapidly up the hill.

"Stop, daddy, stop, and have something to eat: – sure, the meal father promised you is ready – and you said you'd bring us word of Ellen Mullins's wedding, and what she'd on, and all."

"The next time, the next time," answered the old man, without turning back.

"And there's a drop of something in the black bottle," shouted another.

"Well!" exclaimed Stacey, the eldest of the sisters, "that bates all: I never knew daddy refuse the bit and the sup before! Mary Ryan always had the way of bewitching the men, though, to be sure, *now* she's both old and ugly."

"She's just your age," said Rose, the youngest girl.

"How do you know that?" was the query.

"Father said so."

"Father knows nothing about it," retorted the offended elder; but I must leave them to settle a question the most difficult to determine among either women or men, and proceed with my story. It is already known that Mary Ryan had left her father's house – but no one knew with whom – that she was returning with a child of her own, and ignorant of the fact that her mother was dead, and her father again married, and that there existed, at all events, one human being who felt interested in her fate – although he was only old Dennis, commonly called "Daddy Denny" – as notorious a beggarman as ever importuned upon the Irish highway. Daddy Denny had as many acquaintances in Waterford as Reginald's Tower,[84] and in Wexford, as the Bridge; but he only visited towns occasionally, loving better the by-roads, gentlemen's kitchens, and comfortable farm-houses of Wexford and Wicklow – feeling a particular interest in shipwrecks, and the waifs and strays appertaining thereunto; having an active mind and an active body, as far as walking was concerned; being a devout beadsman, a good story-teller, and well read in the domestic history of every house in what he called his three native counties – Waterford, Wexford, and Wicklow. His bold spirit, and reputation for sanctity, gave him an ascendancy over the poorer class, and his quaint good-humour caused him to be more than tolerated by the farmers and gentry.

"It's lead that's in my brogues this blessed day!" he said, aloud, as he mended his pace. "Holy Mary, speed me! Ah, yah, yah! I never think I'm growing old, barring when I have something good to do in a hurry – the poor girleen! – she little knows what I know;" and on he trudged, heartily and hastily, muttering every now and then, according to his custom, about what he thought, and praying for what he desired. Having reached the top of the hill which had been already climbed by Mary Ryan – for it was one of those small perpendicular ascents that are so common in the county of Wicklow – Daddy Denny saw, at a glance (notwithstanding his being "sand blind"), what was passing at the Uphill farm, which lay a very little to his left; indeed, if he had not seen, his attention would have been arrested by the voice of a woman in loud anger. A group of young alder trees overshadowed the dwelling, which partook more of the nature of a farm than a cabin: against one of these, which had been planted by her father at her birth, Mary Ryan – unable to support herself, was leaning, in hopeless anguish – uttering no word, shedding no tear – but listening, with opened eyes and gasping lips, to the vehement abuse poured upon her by her father's wife. Her child, a pallid, weary-looking little girl, of about six years old, was clinging to her dress, and her own younger sister – a woman in appearance, yet cowed into subjection by her step-mother – was standing half in, half out of, the door, not knowing how to act. Mrs. Ryan was one of a class by no means rare, who imagine that their own virtue is best evinced by condemning, with the utmost violence, every woman who has suffered under the supposition of swerving from the right path. She had known Mary in girlhood; she knew how beloved she had been by the mother to whom she had succeeded; she saw her changed, faded, and in despair; but, notwithstanding all this, the harsh tones of her voice mingled with the balmy breezes of a May evening: –

"Go back from where you came – Father, Moyra! deed, an it's himself that's in fine health, Lord be praised! – dacent man – and has enough to do to provide for dacent, well-behaved children, without having shame, and shame's daughter, to pick the potatoes God sends; for – oh, you brazen face! – take yer brat to yer mother's grave, and cry there!" Here Mary's sister interposed, but Daddy Denny could not hear the words. "If you touch her, or go near her, you shan't stay here, depend upon that!" exclaimed Mrs. Ryan.

"I'm yer father's wife, and I'll have none like her to curse our house; – if we're poor we're honest, not like other people."

"And who says she's not honest?" said the stout beggarman, interposing his portly person between Mrs. Ryan and the almost unconscious Mary. – "Who *dares* to say it? Fetch yer sister a drink of wather, to bring her to herself, Anty, this minute. I'm ashamed of yez all, so I am; I never heard tell of the like before, in my own three counties! Setting a case, she had been deluded – to shame I mean – did you never see a holy picture about a prodigal's return? Why, Mrs. Ryan, the print of it is hanging against yer own wall, the father houlding out his arms, and the calf – red and white, and fat – standing ready for killing; and yet ye see the craythur dying upon these stones, and don't lift her up! Ah, yah! Mary, mavourneen, asthore,[85] a machree! ye've supped sorrow sure enough, a lannan; but I know my own know, a'coushla: and I tell you," he continued, while, kneeling by Mary's side, he supported her on his arm – "I tell you, and call the Almighty, the blessed Virgin, and all the holy saints of heaven, to witness that she who rests on me now, in a dead faint – I tell you all – that, though foolish in what she did, she's freer from sin than e'er a one here, barring her own child – don't cry, my pet, your mammy's only in a faint, my bird. Here!" – he continued, as the farmer himself, unconscious of what was going on, leaped heavily over the ditch – "here! look here, sir, if you plaze; and may the Almighty, that stands the innocent's frind, turn yer heart to yer own flesh and blood!"

James Ryan walked to where his daughter was still supported by Dennis – his wife hung back, for she did not quite like to encounter the beggarman's eloquence, which was to the full as energetic as her own, when excited. Mary Ryan was very like her mother; and lying pale and speechless – without sense

or motion – the resemblance to her parent on her death-bed appealed so powerfully to his feelings, that he raised her in his arms, calling upon Dennis to
account for her appearance.

"I wonder at you, James!" said the wife; "don't you see it's Mary, whom you
often swore should never break the daylight at your door? I wonder at you,
Denny, to be taking advantage of the poor man's softness and innocence! Get
up, James; don't be demaning yourself to the like of *her,* before your honest wife
and children."

James Ryan looked bewildered; but, as he collected his scattered thoughts,
his horror of his daughter's sin overpowered every other feeling.

"And that's true," he said; "yet she's so like her mother – but it's true for all
that. She left us of her own accord; and the mother that bore her could find no
place but the grave to hide her sorrow in. She broke the heart of her own mother;
and, poor as I am, she was the first that ever brought shame on her name."

"Come away, come away, James," whispered her step-mother; – "come away,
and don't be letting yourself down with thinking of her."

"Let me alone, woman!" he exclaimed, rudely shaking off her hand: – "let me
alone, and do not turn your tongue on her – mind that. Go in, children; I swore
she should never darken my door; and she never shall!" He rose up, and walked
steadily towards his cottage; but, before he had time to enter it, the sturdy beggar
interposed.

"Look here, James Ryan," he said; "I tell you what I told her, who, I trust to the
Lord, is now in glory – I said to her, when that girl left your house, that sorrow
would follow her, but not shame; – I tell you, that she has never known a happy
hour since; but I tell you, besides, that she'll be righted yet; and that, though the
sunshine of her life be gone, you'll be proud of her – all of you – proud of her,
and proud of Mary Ryan's daughter. I tell *you* this – Mrs. Ryan, ma'am – because I
know you're of the sort that would give to get agin; and the time will come when
you'll be glad, may-be, to pick her potatoes, and winnow her corn; and I tell it to
you, Mister Ryan, because you're her father, and because the dread of her shame is
just now stronger in you than your natural love – that's why I do it."

"Hear the big beggarman!" exclaimed Mrs. Ryan.

"Hearing is all one ever got by being a beggarman from you, any way!" he
answered, sharply; "but it's the man of the house I'm speaking to; the father of
her who lies there suffering from another's sin, and not sinning herself."

"You speak like a book, Mister Denny, but it's no good to you," said Mrs.
Ryan; "don't look back at her, James, honey, though, sure enough, I wouldn't
be where I am but for her! If she hadn't broke her mother's heart, I'd never have
been so happy as to be your wife." Whether or not this artful piece of feminine
flattery succeeded, I cannot tell, but certainly James preceded his wife into the

house, and she shut the door, pulling the latch-string inside, to prevent it being opened.

"What'll I do with her at all!" soliloquised Denny, while surveying Mary Ryan and her daughter – "the foolish ould nagur, to be led that way by his young slut of a wife. She may have years of trial still, God help her! And where will she shelter? Rouse yerself, Mary, my own ould heart's darlint – rouse yerself. What's that you say? – that you murdered your mother, jewel? Faix, no, 'twas the will of God, avourneen – nothing passes his holy will – rouse, darling, and see if ould Daddy Dinny can't find you a night's lodging somewhere. Oh, the hearts of some fathers – and sisters too – to see how that young clip of a sister deserted her like the rest! Where will I take her too? I know," he said, after giving her head one of those earnest scratches which seem mysteriously to revive the Irish intellect – "I know! – ould Jenny Harper, the barony Forth woman, whose husband was killed in the mines, has a sore heart still, and that makes a feeling one."

And the daddy fussed and talked, and, at last, succeeded in rousing poor Mary into a flood of tears, while her child kept entreating her not to cry. Still the broken-hearted creature sat before her father's closed door moaning – "If he would only forgive me – only forgive me!" The night dews fell, and the moon rose; and, at last, the kind-hearted beggar persuaded her to accompany him to a cabin hard by, where she'd be sure of shelter. Silence not being one of his qualities, he muttered and jabbered all the way, like most great talkers, expecting no reply; and so busy was he with his own thoughts and opinions, that he did not hear the light foot of Anty Ryan, who flung her arms round her sister's neck, and was sobbing on her bosom. "Mary! it's your little sister that I am, and dare not speak to you before *her* – your *dawshy* Anty, agra! – don't take on too much about your mother; it was an inward complaint she had for ever so long – and sure, before the breath was out of her, she prayed for you with all her heart and soul – yes, she forgave you."

"But she thought me guilty?" inquired the poor creature, breathlessly.

"She forgave you, sister – I have no more to say; but here, don't be cast down here's a thrifle I saved – and that saving doesn't often trouble me – but I did save a few shillings, just for something – but I'd rather give it to you, my poor Mary; it's all I have. Well, if you won't have it, the child, God help it, will! I'm your aunt, honey; and, while you're Mary Ryan's daughter, I'll love you, my poor innocent baby: – there, God be with you! Daddy will tell me where you'll be. I must run back, for I pulled the loose stones from where the window's to be, to get out."

"Why, then, that's right!" exclaimed Denny; "and a good husband and soon to you, my brave hearty girl! That's the rale sort, mother's own child – success – and cross of Christ about us! that nothing may *cross* yer path worse than a beam of the May moon."

Mary Ryan and her daughter were, within an hour from that time, established, quite to Daddy Denny's satisfaction, in the cabin of the Widow Harper, a miserable dwelling composed of turf and loose stones, and consisting only of one room, but she had not forgotten the neat habits of her childhood; and, small and poor as it was, the floor was even and well swept; the chimney did not smoke: and the bed of dried heather was raised from the floor by some long boards, and covered by a patch quilt. The old woman showed every attention to her guests, boiled them some potatoes for supper, and afterwards bathing their feet in the potatoe water – taking care to throw it out when done with, that it might not be converted to any improper use by the fairies, who, it is said, have a great fancy for floating boats upon bath-water, and thereby sorely bewildering the imaginations of those who sleep, either in a cabin or a palace.

Denny betook himself to a neighbour's barn, as was his custom; and, when he reappeared in the morning, he found poor Mary Ryan suffering from the rapid approach of fever.

"I well know the sickness that's coming over her," said the widow; "and I'll tell you what, daddy, all I have to give her is the poor bed and the shelter – she's welcome to that – and I'll take a turn among my husband's people for a couple of weeks; I'll bring her little girl with me, if she'll come; and the neighbours won't let her want a mouthful through the window, quite convaynent. I can't stay within a mile of a fever myself, on account of a promise I made my mother – and she on her death-bed – never to do so: so that's all I can say, except may the Lord forgive unnatural relations!" The widow strove to prevail on the child to accompany her, but in vain; the little creature clung to her mother, importuning her with questions of when would she go home, which she had not the power to answer.

"God be with you, Mrs. Harper, ma'am," exclaimed Denny; "you've done a Christian turn; and if there's virtue in prayers, you shall have them, dear – maybe I won't pepper away at them for your sake!" and the widow cheerfully gave up her dwelling to the outcast from her own father's house.

"The neighbours" did watch – as they always do and the beggarman positively insisted upon having "a drop of wine, and a grain of tea," from the gentry, "for the sick woman, who had no one to look to her, only God, and the poor."

This was a common case enough, for, as I have often said, and am never tired of repeating, the Irish peasant is rich in the virtue of generosity; but the care and tenderness – the watchfulness of the child over the parent, were subjects of astonishment to all who knew it: – by day or night she never left her mother's presence – caring for her wants, and sitting quietly upon the ground in the light of day, or the darkness of night – her large lustrous eyes fixed upon the place where her mother lay. Anty Ryan, and Anty Ryan's sweetheart, had contributed largely to Mary's recovery, by bringing her those morsels of luxury which the rich do not value, and which were given to Anty by a kind lady for the purpose. The

watchful child knew who approached by the step, and her thin arm, and eager
hand, were immediately thrust through what the widow had pompously designated – "the window;" and the food placed in it, and hallowed by a blessing, was
immediately conveyed to her suffering parent. Mary recovered. Her mysterious
absence – the loudly repeated declarations of daddy (who either was, or seemed
to be, deep in her secrets), that she was innocent of shame – the harshness of
her father, the benevolence of the widow, and the extraordinary conduct of the
child, created and kept alive an interest in her fate, which operated in her favour.
When she was able to creep about in the sunshine, and enjoy the light breeze
that sports amid the woods and glens of all beautiful Wicklow, she was assailed
by numerous questions as to "Where she had been living?" "Who was she with?"
"Was she going back?" "Why did she leave?" and so forth. To all these questions
she meekly replied, "I cannot tell;" and though every one feared "she had been
very wicked," they felt for the poor, shadowy, worn-out creature, in whose behalf,
natural instinct seemed reversed; for, strangely enough, her little girl had grown
into her protector; and the mother looked to the child for her small store of
comfort. Wonders are wonders longer in the country than in the town; but Mary
Ryan continued to be regarded with sympathy long after astonishment as to her
whereabouts, and position, had ceased. Although three years had elapsed since
her reappearance, she still sheltered beneath the Widow Harper's roof, knitting
stockings of the finest wool, which were sought after by the visitors to "the Meeting of the Waters," and the immediate neighbourhood; and her daughter, who
had none of the mother's timidity in her composition, would offer them for sale.
She had become most useful to her mother; and the good widow, and Daddy
Denny, were perpetually on the watch to inform her *how* her zeal and activity
might be turned to the best account.

"Darling, dear! gather a handful of them flaggers[86] – the blossoms, I mean,
bind them with the fairy flax,[87] and be ready with yer courtesy at the Avoca
Hotel, and offer them to the ladies; the quality,[88] darling, will be soon astir to see
God's works below and above the earth; and sling a pair of the stockings on yer
arm: don't take any notice of me forenint the quality; it will do you no good to
be talking with the big beggarman – you're not begging, but selling, avourneen
– so you're above your poor daddy. Hould up yer head in the world, my girleen;
and, above all things, don't take common charity; if they give you a penny, have
something to give them for it: – never let any one have to say, you was a beggar,
avourneen! mind that." Or he would watch her going forth with a couple of baskets, into either of which she could have almost crept herself, her abundant hair
hanging over her fawn-like eyes, when not tossed by the breeze; her cloak, more
an incumbrance than a protection, tucked up by her arms; and her small bare
feet, beautiful in shape and proportion, rendering her appearance a picture worthy the painter's skill. "Ye're going after eggs, now, I'll go bail; and I heard them

say at the wooden bridge, that Mary Ryan's daughter's eggs were always fresh; and, better than that, the farmers would trust you to market their eggs sooner than many a grown woman; and, sure, that is a proud hearing for your mother;" and then the poor mother's eyes would fill with tears, and she would continue her monotonous occupation – knit, knit, knit for ever; walking, sitting, standing, "the needles" were never out of her hands. As the girl grew stronger, she would cut turf for their fire, and do so with an energy and determination that astonished every one.

"Ye're for the bog to-day, dear," the gaberlunzie[89] said); "and, by the blessing of God, it will not be *soft* weather; we had great prayers intirely last Sunday aginst wet – the poor man's foe; but, in troth, jewel, I don't like to see you working for evermore so cruel hard, and you so young!"

"Then come and help me, daddy," laughed the child.

"Ah, darling! I own to it – I'd do anything rather than work; it never came natural to me. Every one said I'd take to it as I grew ould and steady; but, jewel, I suppose I never did grow steady, for though I grow ould I like it less than ever. I used to herd sheep on the mountains, and used to lie and think how happy the sun, moon, and stars would be, travelling – it was their nature, you understand, as well as mine. It does not take much to keep an Irishman; the tongue in his head will do it, without his hands; though I don't travel much now – no, dear, I'll advise you, and think for you, *and watch for the time;* but as to working, it's too late in the day for me. Bedad![90] the Wicklow hills would shout with wonder, if they looked down on Daddy Denny clamping turf!"[91]

Sometimes Mary Ryan's daughter would encounter her grandfather, and then her eye would kindle, and her cheek flush; and she would spring out of his path with the fleetness of a wild roe. It is quite impossible to describe the tenderness and love she bore her mother; *she had no self but in her:* and the more feeble Mary Ryan became, the more devoted grew her child. Daddy Denny was the only one who knew what Mary's position really was; but he kept it a profound secret, never hinting but once, to the priest's housekeeper, as he was waiting to see his reverence, "that poor Mary Ryan was like Hagar and Abraham in the picture, only much worse trated."[92] Denny had great Scripture knowledge, in his own estimation, and was frequently known to argue thereon; and the poor people, not understanding what he said, came to the invariable conclusion that, in Denny's particular case, "the poverty had spiled a fine priest."

Days, weeks, months, and years, went by; and Mary Ryan's daughter was fast merging from the girl into the woman. She had gleaned a little learning from a hedge schoolmaster, one of the clever political old fellows, who, in bygone times, taught the "big boys" Law and Latin, Politics and the "Read-a-made-aisy,"[93] in the same breath. He usually got up, every day, such a scene as the following: – "Spell tyrant, James Sullivan. Now, Jimmy, hould up yer head like a man, to show ye defy it." "T-i – " "Och! murder, no. What spells Ty, besides T-i?" "T-n, sir." "Och! my, ye're only fit for a slave, Jimmy; I'm sorry for ye, your poor craythur. Try *your* tongue at it, little Neddy." – "T-y-r-a-n-t!" spells out the young rogue, his bare foot placed firmly on the damp floor, and his eyes sparkling with triumph.

"There's my haro![94] – take the top of the class. Oh! not the Latin class, my boy; you're not up to that, Neddy, yet – but above Jimmy Sullivan. Now for the meaning: who was a tyrant?"

"Naro,"[95] replies one. – "Queen Elizabeth,"[96] says another. – "Oliver Crummel,"[97] shouts a third. – "My daddy's landlord," observed Neddy, "when he turned us to the wide world to starve!"

"That's bould spoken," said the schoolmaster; "I see you understand the word, little Neddy."

"I have good right, sir," answered the child.

"Spell mother, girls," said the schoolmaster, who gave them, as he stated, "word about," and managed to appropriate domestic phrases to the female class, "I'm not in two syllables yet, sir," said Mary Ryan's daughter, upon whom the schoolmaster's eye fell.

"M-u-d – " began one of the class. – "No, that won't do. Sure you ought all to be able to spell it; for sorra a one that does not know what it is to have a good mother, barring one or two. Mary Wright, poor child! your mother's in heaven since the day she gave you to a broken-hearted world; and, indeed yours" – and again his eye fell on Mary Ryan's daughter – "never did much for you – so I'll excuse you."

"If you please, sir," said the girl, growing very red, "I'll not be excused for that reason: my mother did the best she could for me;" and – she burst into tears – and then as suddenly checked her emotion, and spelt the cherished word correctly.

"From that hour she became the old man's beloved pupil; and he suffered her to come without any payment, or at any hour she could; and often would she enter his lowly dwelling at night, with a long piece of bog-wood, or a farthing candle, and crouch at his feet – conning, from borrowed and half torn books, the lesson which he not only heard, but assisted her to learn – dismissing her with the invariable assurance that "she would be a bright girl yet."

Daddy Denny greatly encouraged this love of learning. He brought her a slate from Wexford, and books from both Arklow and Waterford – one being the "Seven Champions," and the other "Cinderella." "Learning," he would tell her, "is better than house and land, they say; but I'm sure it's better with the house and land than without it. Who knows what will turn up yet, if the Lord only spares poor daddy – till – the time comes? That's all I pray for, jewel: and I take care of myself, and all for you; though the Lord he knows it's a great loss to me – the wearing brogues I mean – to keep the could from my chest; – for, when I attend the coaches, the vagabone beggars set the quality again me, shouting, 'What does he want? – look at his brogues;' and then they call me 'brogey;' and all because I want to live for your sake, agra! – for I'm almost kilt walking the world for divarshin, until it has turned into hard labour on me. I wish we could rouse your mother, Peggy, honey; but she's sat under the trouble so long, that I'm thinking she'll a'most miss it, when it goes. Ah, yah! – well, it is a weary world – a long, weary road, to travel from one's birth to one's death: – an unbareable road, if a poor sinner dare say so – *only for what it leads to* – the heavenly Jerusalem. Oh! that's great glory to think on; and them that raise their eyes to that, won't faint with the length of the way. It raises a poor man's heart to think that a Lazarus like myself may lay in some great saint's bosom. Well, dear, you're growing to be a'most a woman, Peggy; and don't keep company with any of the boys about the place – sorra a one of them fit for *you*. I hope you haven't got a sweetheart in your sweet head, jewel? – it's mighty inconvenient – and – "

"Oh, daddy! if I do get such a thing into my head, it's you that will put it there, and so I'll tell mother: – and have you seen my hen, with eleven chickens at her foot? Mother minds them; and the poor widow has taken ever such pains at the needles, and we're going to be rich, sure enough – so I'll hold my head as high as you please, for I've got two silver testers in my pocket; and I'll give one to you, Denny, who have been my best friend."

The old man took the little coin, and deposited it in one of his numerous pockets, muttering – "I'll fasten it on my *bades*, God bless her, for a mimorial."

"There's one thing I often want to speak about, but can't, never, *to her*" said the girl, "because it almost kills her. Do *you* know anything of my old home and my father?"

"Whisht, a'coushla! how should I know anything? You never saw me there."

"No, never – I wish I could forget it, but. I can't. I remember my mother catching me out of my sleep, and flying from the house like mad; – and mind, too, the oaths and the curses that followed us. Oh! then, I was glad to keep wandering anywhere from him."

"Whisht, avoumeen! it's foolish to give sorrow a tongue. What do I know about such things? Hould up yer head – sing at your work – say your prayers mind – your mother – and, as the schoolmaster says, Mary Ryan's daughter will be a bright girl yet."

Two months after this little scene had passed, the widow, on waking in the morning, found that Mary Ryan was up before her: – this was something new. Peggy, indeed, was always a-foot early – the first to rise, on the town-land; but Mary was feeble, and seldom awoke until long after the lark had finished his matins. For a moment the widow thought the girl had grown careless; the few sods of turf necessary for boiling potatoes were there, and the three-legged pot was hanging over them; but the fire, so seldom extinguished in an Irish cabin, was out; and the kitten, singed by the turf ashes from black to red, was seated on the stone, guiltless of pur or gambol, and looking as sullen as possible.

"Where are they, pusheen?" said the widow, who would rather talk to a kitten than remain silent. "Is Peggy gone after some quality speciments for the bride and groom at the wooden bridge? – but where's Mary Ryan? Ah! then, don't be winkin' that way, but tell us the news."

"Pusheen" seemed as perplexed as her mistress, and said so in her own way, uttering an abrupt mew, and then humping her back with a dissatisfied air. The morning advanced, but no Mary returned; no Peggy, with careful step and thoughtful face, swept the floor that day, or fed the hens, who looked about, as if in astonishment at not receiving their usual attention: her three books were on the poor dresser; but her bonnet and shawl, and her mother's cloak, were gone. Before night, Mrs. Harper had inquired of every neighbour if they had seen her friends? No one had seen them: but a "wise woman," who had been called in the middle of the night to attend a farmer's wife, had met two women and a man, as she jogged double on the farmer's horse, and was fully convinced that the youngest was Mary Ryan's daughter. The country people were both astonished and alarmed at this mysterious disappearance; and her father, who had maintained his harsh conduct towards them, relented, when it was too late, and endeavoured to trace them in every way. At one time he thought they were in Enniscorthy;[98] – at another, in Bray;[99] – but still he found them not. Some called to their remembrance that they had seen Daddy Denny and Mary Ryan in close conversation several times, and on several days previous to her disappearance; – but then, as the bluff old beadsman was in the confidence of half the women of the parish, nothing strange was thought of it at the time.

Mrs. Harper was in a state of distraction, and declared to every one, she would travel the world until she found them. They had replaced what was lost to her, in a great degree; and while the helpless nature of poor Mary worked upon her affections, the steady industry and activity of the daughter commanded her respect.

It was perfectly true that the beggarman had brought information to Mary Ryan and her daughter, by which they were induced to leave the roof that had so long sheltered them.

"All I've got to say to you, jewel, agra!" he said, when arranging how they were to "steal away" from Mrs. Harper, "is, tell no news, give no information to any one; – now, just mind that: – and then we can let them know about it when the end comes; there's no use in rising a talk, dear – it's just like rising a fog, which bothers all who have any call to it. Avourneen, there's a tower of strength and a rock of wisdom in a silent tongue! I blaze out a good dale, dear, myself; but one can say a power of words, without any maning, and that's the way I manage the country; and, faix, many a legislature, which manes a law maker, ma'am, would give his two born eyes for that same sacret. Ah-yah-wisha! he's a wake-minded man that can't keep his own counsel."

By the time the morning dawned, and Mrs. Harper awoke, the trio were far on their journey, and in a different direction from any it was imagined they had taken. – They agreed to keep off the high road as much as possible. It was strange to observe how Denny's mendicant propensities, and his kind heart, were at variance when they reached the pretty village of Newtown-Mount Kennedy: the Wexford coach was just passing through, and it was evident the Daddy longed to prosecute his usual attack upon the pockets of the passengers; yet he was loath to forsake his companions for the purpose, and consoled himself with rejoicing that the clumsy efforts of the clamorous crew had not procured them a single penny.

"Ah!" he exclaimed, "it's wonderful hard to soften some people's hearts: they have no feelin' in them for the poor. I've heard a gentleman swear he wouldn't give a beggar-woman a farthing, barring she had some fun in her, and, at the same time, she had a matter of six soft children starving to death in the sight of her eyes – it's hard to make fun out of starving children! The insides and the outsides must have different tratement altogether. You may pass a joke with the outsides, and touch them up with a story betwixt times; but seeing that it's mostly ladies and gentlemen that's insides, they must be handled like a nest of young thrushes; no matter how ould they are, the ladies I mean, – a blessing on their beauty will smoothen all the frowns away. I remember once, a very stately one – and frosty-faced she was an ould residenter upon the earth, sure enough: – well, one poor innocent young woman held up her baby to her, and bid her think of her own little grandchildren at home. Och! that turned her to hard vinegar! Another prayed the Lord might make her bed in heaven. Well, that's foolish, for people that are rich and ould don't like to think of their end – not a halfpenny did they get; but, at last, 'Sweet lady,' I says, 'I'm thinking of the little sixpence you gave me, two years ago, and God bless you for it.' 'That's a lie,' she says, 'for I never gave a beggar a sixpence in all my life.' 'Didn't ye, dear!' I says, 'well, then, it must have been Lady Mary, the beauty of the county, and it's no wonder I'd make the mistake, for you're as like as two peas in a pod.' I saw the corners of her mouth move; and she gives me a penny! If ye see a raw college boy, with a goold band to his cap, sure he wants to be thought in the military line; and ye're safe in calling him 'handsome captain,' or 'noble major.' I've known a shopboy have the same dress outside on a week's holiday to his people; there's no harm in mistaking every spalpeen you meet for a gentleman – though," added Denny, thoughtfully, "it's not pleasant to be degrading one's self, if one could help it. When ye see a lady, with little children about her, *praise* the children; and if they're as ugly as frogs, lay on them all kind of angels; and if they're roaring wicked, with ill-temper, call them 'little lambs;' then, if she has any motherly feeling about her, you're sure of a tester: if ye see a couple mighty loving together, ye may bless the lady's sweet face; but it's hardly sure, for, bedad! the young men think as much of their own beauty – and may-be it's nothing you'll get for your trouble: it's asy enough to work the money out of any pocket, if ye can understand the *nature* of the body that carries it – that's where the knowledge is wanting. Foreigners are mighty soft at first; and there used to be grate trade intirely at the Pigeon house, and about there – women with twins – as near to match as they could get 'em – widows – deserted wives, and fatherless children – lame men, blind men, and the falling sickness; but that's over long ago: in the heart of the war I made a purty penny myself, as a wounded soldier, with a plate in my head and a bad leg – anything for a bit of bread! Sure the half of us would work if we could get it; and the Lord above knows that the lies we tould *for variety,* weren't worse than the truth; – that the plain, hard, griping starvation was with us at home and abroad, by night and by day; – that was true, any how; but people had heard of it so often, they did not like to be bothered with it; so, after all's said and done, it was against that we strove – God help us and forgive us the inventions – starvation makes one's wits bright, bedad! I was so thin, one or two of the hard summers, that if it wasn't that I had the wit to put stones in my wallet, I'd have been blown away."

I wish I had space to recount all Daddy Denny's stories. Some of them could not fail to make you weep; and his transitions from humour to pathos were truly characteristic of his calling. There are many who cannot fail to remember this energetic, yet lazy personage, who latterly begged from habit, rather than necessity; and who was at all times trusty, and trusted by many of his superiors, particularly in the time of "the troubles," when, I have been told, he was in the prime of life, and rendered humane assistance to whoever needed it.

The wanderers had journeyed for nearly a week, when, on the evening of the fifth day – "Do you know where you are, Peggy?" inquired Mary Ryan of her daughter. "I think I do," replied the girl; "I think I know the turn of that river – I think – yes, I do know those trees: that's just the way the crows used to be flying, with the same noise – yes, mother – though I never looked from this hill before, I know that big brick house, and the gate that I used to be climbing, but never could swing on. Och!" she added, with an involuntary shudder, "I hope we ain't going to live there again."

"Whisht, honey! whisht!" ejaculated the beggarman; "wishing is a mighty foolish thing for those who put their trust in God. Sure everything will turn out well to those that have faith, dear, – if not well for this world – well for the next. I'll go now and hear the news, and you can sit here with yer mother till I'm back, a'coushla," and away went Denny at his own particular and professional trot.

Peggy found a "dry ditch" for her mother to rest on; and having rolled her own shawl into a "soft sate," she made her sit upon it, placing herself higher up, so that her mother's head rested in her lap. The worn-out woman did not speak a word for more than an hour; but the large tears kept rolling from her eyes, while her daughter murmured, every now and then, "Mother, avourneen! don't take on so – mother, darlin', you're wearin' out my heart – mother, honey, trust in the Lord. Oh, what will I do at all! and no one near me – she'll die here with the fair trouble o' mind."

"Trouble is a long time killin', or I'd have been dead long ago," replied her mother, to whom the shedding of tears had been a relief – "but I'm easier now, God be praised; and Peggy, the time is come for me, your mother, to humble myself to tell you, my born child, the whole truth."

"Don't distress yerself, darlin' mother! don't, I know all I want to know," replied the girl, with a trembling voice; "where's the good of going it over?"

"You know nothing, Peggy – how should you?"

"Oh, bad news travels with hare's feet," she answered; "but don't, mother, I'd be happier not to hear it from your own self; because I'll be still thinking, maybe, the half was lies."

"Peggy, honey, in sight of his house and under the blessed canopy of heaven – and knowing the Almighty's eyes are on me – as sure as all this, so surely am I your father's wife!" The girl, at first, made no reply, but clasped her hands around her parent's neck, and, at last, said: – "An' why didn't, you tell me this before? sure if it was a secret, not to take away my shame would I own it – only just for inward satisfaction to myself."

"Why you never let on to me you were reproached with it, my darling."

"No, mother – how could I? sure it isn't easing my own heart by chilling yours I'd be! but what does it signify? I'm able for the world now! I can look an honest woman's daughter in the face; – oh, mother, jewel, and I to doubt you!"

"You must hold your tongue still, Peggy, until I give you leave to speak. Your father, dear, was above me, and I'd never have known him, but for his coming about our place in the shooting season. My father and mother had fixed on one in my own line of life for me, and I knew I'd be forced to marry him if I stayed at home; and all the time my heart's whole love was with your father. I tried to hide this from my father and mother, as well as from the young man I loved; but, och, hone! I blinded my parents, but not my lover. I was proud of his love – he was so above me – and he said he was proud of my beauty! Well, dear, I agreed to leave my parents, as he promised to marry me; but as he was entirely dependent on his father, he book-swore me to keep it secret from man and mortal till his father's death. I was satisfied, and went with him one Sunday evening – to return no more: he eased my heart with a marriage; but there was only us two by, and the priest, if he was a priest, who said the words For the first few months he was very kind; and though I was under the heaviest shadow that can fall on a woman, still I was his wife, and I bowed down under it, thankful to look at him – to hear him speak; though his words became mixed with bitterness, still the voice was his. You were born; and what was such joy to me, was sorrow to him: his father, he said, grew frightened for fear he should marry me; and, instead of being allowed to sit at his table, he sent me to the kitchen, there to bear the insults of an old bad woman, whose daughter had formerly filled my place. Oh, my darling child! may the Lord preserve you from the double death of finding out, bit by bit, that what you loved was beyond hate. Still, I clung to him; I longed to go home, and then thought how I had no home: my mother was kind, but I had a hard father. I thought, may-be, that, being his wife, God might turn his heart; and I told him so, once. – Oh! the cruelty of that laugh, when he answered that I was a fool, and dared me to find a witness for what had passed between us. As long as I thought to do him good, it was well enough; but I roused against this, and he turned us from his door with curses and blows – blows, darlin', that fell only on me. I thought to tell his father the truth; but even if I hadn't taken the oath, sure it would hurt him, and not have served you, for I wouldn't be believed: since then, darlin', he openly married one of his own rank, for his father died."

"And why did we come here, mother, darlin'; and what has Daddy Denny to do with us?" asked Peggy,

"There's no time to tell that," interrupted the beggar, who had approached without being observed – "no time; the breath's in him still, and the use he made of it for the last twenty minutes is to rave about you; and my heart aches for the poor lady who is patient as a lamb, and begs, for God's sake, to bring any one that will ease his mind –"

"Then you were sent for, mother, dear?" inquired the poor girl, while assisting her to rise. "Yes, dear; Daddy contrived to get a friend of his own into the place, and when your father got this mortal sickness, he brought me to be near, thinking that, at the least, he might do us justice."

The three hurried to the house, which was full of lamentation – people running backward and forward, crying and howling "for the master." The priest, who had administered "the last rites," was standing near the door, reproving the more noisy. Dennis advanced to his reverence, and falling on his knees to crave his blessing, which was quickly granted – told him that "the woman his honour wanted to see was come!" "Then you have had a hand in this?" said the priest – "but so best, Denny; if you never do worse, the next penance I give you – (and I gave you *one,* I remember, about six years ago) – I will not put you to much trouble: let the woman come in?"

When Mary entered the chamber of death, the last throes of dissolving nature were convulsing the frame of the dying man! She staggered towards the bed – from which the lady he had married, had been forcibly removed – and, falling on her knees, clasped and kissed his clammy hand. He rallied, and recognised her; he felt her hand, finger by finger, and when *he touched the ring* he half rose up – stammered "Mary" – fell back – and his spirit departed. The poor woman forgot everything save the love of her early days: she uttered no complaint of his cruelty and injustice, but she wept bitterly. Not so Dennis; he had expected that wrong would have been made right – and he followed "his reverence" out of the house; when every beggar in the district crowded into it, expecting the tobacco and whisky, besides other good cheer, which in these days accompanied the funerals of all classes. Whatever his conversation with the priest may have been, it was known only to themselves, but it had the effect of sending Denny back to the house, where he mingled among the crowd, seeking Mary Ryan, or her daughter, and hoping they might not have left the house. At last one of the servants told him, that the woman the "poor master called for," had fallen in a fit, that she had carried her to a loft, and that, for her part, she didn't think she'd live. "And the girl?" She knew nothing about her, except that she had set a strange girl in a back house to mind the boilings, or there'd be nothing for the people to eat, – the dwelling was so "throng," and would be worse as the night drew on. She locked her in, and wouldn't have thought of her for another hour or two, but for him. Dennis reconnoitred through a window, and, finding that the unwilling watcher was Mary's daughter, accomplished her liberation; and having first charged her, on no account – no matter what indignity she or her mother suffered, to leave the place until he told them they might do so, he sent her in search of Mary Ryan. After much delay and many repulses, Peggy succeeded: it was a miserable loft, in a distant part of the rambling building, where she had been carried; the slates were off in many places, and the wind rushed through the shadowy laths, tumbling, at every fresh gust, some lump of mortar, or clattering tile. As the night advanced, the voices of intoxicated persons, mingled into one great discordant noise, ascended to where the heart-broken girl was chafing her mother's hands; while she laid across her feet to impart a portion of her young warmth to her parent's weary limbs. She had arranged some old curtains that had been thrown into a corner to decay, into a tolerably comfortable bed, and moistened her lips with some milk which the servant had given her for herself: her consolation was, that *there* they were left to themselves; and, from behind a parapet, she could see all that passed in the courtyard. The moon rose to its full height, and the shadows it threw upon the floor were, she thought, very terrible. Once a huge cat peered down upon her from a rafter, and then scampered away, while bits of the old roof tumbled on all sides. She was shivering from head to foot, and the old damp hangings she threw over her shoulders, seemed to make her still more cold; but her mother slept, breathing as gently as a sleeping child – *that,* at least, was a consolation; if it had not increased her loneliness the more, it would indeed have made her heart beat with thankfulness and joy. She knelt softly down by her mother's side, and, after repeating her prayers, she enumerated to herself every instance she had ever heard of GOD's watchful care by night, as well as by day; this strengthened and refreshed her; and yet every cloud that passed athwart the moon, and so caused a partial eclipse to the small, shivering, chilly light, which flickered through the apertures, made her repeat the words more fervently: sometimes she would fix her eyes on a bright solitary star, and then turn them on her mother, who looked, in the dim uncertain light, so deathly pale, that the girl would hold in her own breath to listen for the manifestation that she was still in life. Suddenly she was roused from a nodding sleep, by the fall of a stone, or brick, which rattled into the room, followed by a heavy grunting sort of noise, as of a person breathing hard after violent exertion. A shriek quivered on her lip, but she repressed it, and immediately felt the wisdom of having done so. "Peg – Peggy, avourneen," puffed a well-known voice, "don't be frightened, darlin' – it's me, a'coushla machree – ould Daddy Denny – wait till I catch my breath, which is flying from me like widgeon from a gun – och, hone! – I'm too ould for climbing, and couldn't have reached you at all, but for the tough bames of the stable, and a ladder, dear, that Peter Mullowny's hould-ing. I've got the girl of the house, dear, to forget where yez are – and so keep quiet till ye're wanted, jewel; and here's more than you'll ait, I know, for the three days of the wake – or drink aither, – fresh mate, and white bread *of your own* – father's, I mane; for, poor man – God be good to him – he's to the fore still, and a fine wake as ever I was at, lashings of everything, more especially people; the lady has a fine spirit in her – an' – but, faix, dear, my head's bothered somehow, and the moon's turning round on me, so the Lord be wid yez – I needn't bid ye take care of yer mother – for sure it's Mary Ryan's daughter ye are – and pray for yer sinful soul – I mean my – hould hard and fast, Peter, dear – for somehow both myself and the ladder's mighty unsteady."

"The girl of the house" did, to all appearance, forget Mary Ryan and her daughter; but some one, every morning, placed a full measure of milk at the rough door of the loft – a measure so full, that, after both had partaken abun-dantly thereof, they had enough to cause the great cat, which had so frightened Mary, to pur and look as contented and cheerful as became the solidity and respectability of his ancient race. Still, these three days and nights passed in all the aching anxiety of knowing nothing – and hoping and fearing all things. At last the wild, yet solemn pageantry was over. The hearse, the mourners, the priests, the people, departed. Mary Ryan watched from the broken roof, the road it took – the same road she and her child had traversed in years long ago: – *they* had returned; but *he* who drove them to despair would return no more. Holy masses were said for the repose of his soul that day, but none prayed as fervently for his eternal repose as she whose heart he had crushed almost to bursting.

Peggy wept and prayed from sympathy with her mother, but she could hardly keep down the spirit of strong indignation that was roused by a full sense of the injustice they had sustained; and no Hart ever panted for the water-brooks more than did hers for liberty.

Before the funeral was completely out of sight, the only noise that broke upon the stillness of the house was the rough shutting-to of doors, and the echo of footsteps; at last "the girl of the house" made her appearance, and beckoning them to follow down a half ladder, half stair, conducted them to a large parlour, from which the remnants of the entertainment had been hastily removed, and thrust them, with very little ceremony, and sundry mutterings of "being bothered with the like," into a sort of ante-room to which it led. The door hung loosely on its hinges, and remained unclosed. Presently, a pale, gentle looking woman entered the room, and her widow's dress made Mary's heart beat more quickly; she was followed by others, who had returned from the funeral, and, in a short time, the party were placed round the table, the priest being seated at the widow's right hand, while the attorney of the next town intimated his intention of reading the will of his "late friend."

He read and read; but all that Mary Ryan and her daughter could comprehend was, that he read the same thing over and over again. At last – was it – could it be possible – were they awake? Was it reality? Could he who had that day entered the cold and silent grave – could *he* have made such a confession? "Mary Ryan – his own lawful wife!" and such and such lands to pass to her and her child! – "*thereby hoping to make atonement for his sins.*" Peggy felt her mother sinking, and clasped her in her arms; after this all was confusion: the lady who had been so grossly deceived was carried from the room totally insensible; her brother, roused at such indignity, declared the man must have been out of his senses, and that there was no proof; and while the attorney avowed the man's perfect sanity, the priest said that, without, of course, violating the sacredness of the confessional, there *was* proof, – and Daddy Denny was brought forward, who declared he had witnessed the marriage, by means anything but straightforward certainly; and of this fact even Mary Ryan was not aware until that moment Daddy Denny was very unwilling to be cross-questioned on the subject, but was obliged to submit; and certainly the evidence was very clear, even according to his own showing – that he had been courting a "responsible woman" – the servant to the "couple beggar" – who performed the hasty ceremony, and that she had "put him in press," in a corner cupboard, to be out of the way, from whence he saw Mary married. After all, the woman jilted him; and, at any other time, his bitterness on the subject would have created much amusement. Mary and her daughter had come forth in the *mêlée,* and if a doubt had existed of the nobleness of Mary's nature, it would have vanished before the earnestness she evinced that nothing might be done to hurt the poor lady's feelings.

Daddy Denny always stoutly denied that he knew the contents of the will – how should he? – his anxiety to keep Mary and her daughter in the house, being (I quote his own words) "intirely from a drame he had." Be that as it may; – Peggy, or, as she was called on the evening of her changed fortunes, *Miss* Margaret, is living still, and often speaks to him she loves best in all the world – her husband – of the enduring patience and virtue of her mother, who lived meekly and prosperously during the remainder of her few years, and died soon after her daughter became a wife.

What a privilege it is to know a person unspoiled by prosperity! – Mary's daughter is one of these. I have sat with her, upon her mother's grave, and heard her story, of which I am the faithful chronicler; and at that time the beggarman – then hale and hearty as a frosty day – stood beside us; since then *he* has fallen asleep; but I well remember the proud expression of his bright face, as he asked me what I thought of Mary Ryan's daughter?

THE BANNOW POSTMAN.

"He's taking his own time this evening, I'll say that; for the sun's as good as set, and no signs of him yet. Can you spy him out?"

"No, colleen; how d'ye think my ould eyes could see him whin yours can't? But, Anty, honey, ye're mighty unasy about the postman; dy'e expict a new riban', or a piece o' tape, or some sugar-candy, or – a love letther, Anty? Oh! Anty, Anty! – don't blush after that fashion; ould as my eyes are, I can see yer rosy cheek getting quite scarlet,"

"I'll tell ye what, Grey Lambert," replied the lassie to the old man, who was literally leaning on "the top of his staff," under the shadow of the walls of a singularly fine and perfect castle of ancient days; "I'll jist tell ye, it 'll be long enough before I'll come to see ye agin, out o' pure good-natur, in yer unchristian-like ould place, if ye talk afther that fashion to a young cratur like me, that niver turned to the like; d'ye think I've no dacency? Sure ye're ould enough to forget love letthers, any way."

"That's true, Anty; an ould man of three score and sixteen hasn't much to do wid what are called love letthers; but, may-be there's a differ betwixt love letthers and letthers o' love; and sure there's one still that sinds that last to his poor grandfather; and from beyant the salt seas too."

"Well, 'tis a comfort, sure enough; but I often wonder that ye a'n't affeard to stay in such a place as this, widout anything wid ye, but Bang, the baste, that's almost as ould as yerself – poor Bang!" And Bang pushed his nose into Anty's hand.

There was something picturesque in the appearance of the pair, who awaited the postman's coming – for such was really the case; the young maiden expected a lover's letter; the aged man hoped for a remembering token from a solitary descendant. "Grey Lambert," as he was called, had taken up his abode in a corner of the castle under whose shadow they stood – the castle of Coolhull[100] – and no entreaty could induce him to leave the lonely dwelling. He was a singular, but a very fine-looking, person; wore neither hat nor cap; never cut either his beard or hair, which were purely, perfectly, white, and flowed over his shoulders, and down his breast, even below a leather girdle that encircled his coarse frieze wrapping coat; his feet were bare; his forehead high and bald; his dress clean, betokening singularity but not poverty; and he had been a traveller in his youth – a sailor – a soldier – some said a pirate; but that, I firmly assert, never could have been the case, for Lambert was the gentlest of old men; children and animals (who seem to have an instinctive dread of bad people) all loved him; and on Sunday evenings the village urchins, and their little cur dogs, visited him in his castle, or sat at his feet on the green sward, while he recounted tales and adventures of other lands.

Anty was a merry, laughing, blue-eyed lass, somewhat short, and without one good feature in her face; yet the gipsy was esteemed pretty. It was really very provoking – she was anything but pretty, and yet it was absolutely impossible to look on her face and think so; she had such coaxing smiles, and that heartfelt charm – a sweet, low voice – "an excellent thing in woman;"[101] and so many "ah, do's," and "ah, dont's;" and a trick of blushing – and blushes stealing over a pure white skin, are, it must be confessed, very agreeable things indeed to look upon; then there was a cheerfulness, a joyousness about her, perfectly irresistible; at wake or pattern[102] she had all the best boys at her command, and how she laughed at them! But I may affirm – now that she is not before me – the little hussy was anything but pretty.

Bang was certainly a venerable relic of canine antiquity – tall and grey, haughty and stately, of royal Danish descent, and his courtesies had an air of kingly condescension; when he noticed even the bettermost dogs of the parish, there was so much aristrocratic bearing about the dignified brute, that they, one and all, shrunk from his approach. But he was faithful to his master – night and day by his side: and always paid particular attention to Anastasia Mc Queen, who, strange to say, was a very frequent visitor at the dilapidated castle; nay, was almost daily seen trudging towards it; – her short scarlet cloak meeting the broad hem of her blue stuff petticoat, while the hood only half covered a profusion of deep nut-brown hair, (I feel it here a duty to my country peasant girls to say, that they generally have long and most luxuriant tresses, and, womanlike, are not a little proud of them); and, from her well-turned, but red arm, usually hung a basket, containing such presents as a Bannow maiden could present; dried fish, fresh cockles, delicate butter, barley or oaten cakes, thin and curling, or new laid eggs. She certainly paid very great attention to the old man, and he was much attached to his lively visitor.

"May-be it's long since ye heard from young Pat Lambert?" she inquired, after caressing Bang.

"True, love, dear; it seems long to one like me – a poor ould, very ould, man; may be he's forgotten his grandfather."

"No, *that* he's never done, I'm sartin sure; he's as thrue-hearted a boy as iver crossed the sea; that I know, and I take it very unkind o' ye to say he'd forget you."

"Well, Anty, whin I write agin I'll tell him that there's some don't forget *him,* any way."

"Oh!" said Anty, blushing in good earnest, "ye need not say that; sure in a Christian country, everybody remimbers their neighbour. – How beautiful the sea looks, as if there niver was an end to it!"

"How beautiful the sea looks!" repeated Grey Lambert, smiling and shaking his head at the same time: "Well, Anty, I see ye're an admirer o' the beauties of natur. The sea is ever beautiful to my thinking; whin the great waves foam and lash the shore, and whin they toss big ships, such as you niver saw, up and down without any trouble in life – then 'tis beautiful, and whin it sleeps under the setting sunbames, as it does now, it is beautiful. How well ye see the entrance into Watherford harbour from where ye stand! – though a score o' miles and more from ye. Well, I love this ould castle for the prospect; but it's a grand place, and I niver could think to live anywhere else, now. The thickness of the walls might be one of the world's wonders; then the gometry staircase,[103] and the curious writing on the hard stones that nobody iver understood yet; and the grate oak bames. The jewil of a castle, ye are, my darlint! – to think how bravely ye stood against ould Oliver, the black villain! Och! many a brave heart – many a bright eye – many a smile dancing like the sunbames on the sea, has been in ye, whin ye stood with yer high walls and turrets in the morning light; but now yer're ould, and even yer stones look withered, and the cow and the wild goat shelter where princes stood; and the owl screams where the harp sounded; and I, a poor worm of the earth, live to see it, whin their noble bones make part of the sod I stand on!"

Lambert's apostrophe to his beloved castle was lost on Anty, who eagerly exclaimed, "There he is! – there he is! Now I'll run and meet him, and see if he has got a letther for you." Away she flew, swift as an arrow, to meet John Williams, postman, and, it may be truly said, carrier, to the united parishes of Bannow, Kilkaven, and Duncormuck,[104] for above thirty years. Even in these isolated spots people cannot do without news; it is almost necessary to existence. Twice each week John Williams still journeys to the nearest post-town, and conveys "the leading journal of Europe," the Fashionable Post, the Wexford and Waterford Papers, and others, to the news-loving inhabitants. Honest John is a heedless, good-tempered fellow; but a very jewel of a postman. He had been originally engaged only as a circulating medium for letters from Wexford to Bannow; but he was either bribed, or coaxed, or both, into executing commissions for everybody who had commissions to execute. John Williams's list was regularly made out; and ribands, tea, candles, sugar, books, paper, music, gowns, and even caps, garnished his Rosinante[105] – for when his orders were many, John was obliged to take his steed; not that he ever ventured to ride the poor lame beast, whom he could out-tire at any time; but he walked in a companionable manner with it, in and out of Wexford; and, in truth their caparisons[106] were most extraordinary.

When Anty met him, his loose drab coat was hardly secured by a solitary button, and his leather bags dangled over his shoulders; his "cawbeen"[107] on one side of his grey shaggy head, his scratch wig[108] on the other, and his "doodeen"[109] serving a double purpose – keeping his nose warm, and exhilarating his spirits; the poor horse, more fatigued than its wiry conductor, eyeing the green straggling hedgerows, and the close turf, and loitering to catch a mouthful as he passed. At either side his neck hung two blue bandboxes,[110] filled, doubtless, with multifarious finery; while a coil of thick cable, like a huge Boa, passed over his head, and held, suspended, ten or twelve flats of cork, bespoke by the captain of a coal vessel lying at Bannow quay – three new kites, four skipping ropes, ten tops, two bags of marbles, a dozen slates (for Master Ben), a pair of pole screens[111] (for the lady at the big house), and some blankets; all, of course, so carelessly papered, that they had more than half escaped from their confinement.

"Good even', and God save ye, Mister John!" quoth the breathless lass. The postman was never given to much speaking, and nodded. "May-be ye wouldn't have a bit of a letther for Grey Lambert?" John stopped, and so did the horse; while John took from his bag a long, narrow, dirty-looking letther – presented it – replaced his bag, and journeyed on. Anty stopped, and looked after him; "John, John, I want to speak to ye." John again stopped. "I wanted to ask ye, if so be that ye found – I mean met – a – a – I thought, maybe, ye might have – ah, John! ye know what – for poor Anty?" John took the pipe from his mouth, and simply said:

"May-be ye'd tell a body who likes plain spakeing what ye're after?"

"Well, thin, John, have ye a letther for me?"

"Yes: why didn't ye ask me that a while ago, and not give me the throuble of taking off my bag twice?"

"Why didn't ye give it me, and I to the fore? Sure ye knew ye had it."

"Why, look ye, Anty Mc Queen, I have been thirty years a postman; and I have always done what the back of the letter tould me; and see, the direction on it is – 'Anty Mc Queen, Hill Side, Bannow, County of Wexford, Ireland – postpaid – to the care of John Williams, Bannow postman; to be kept till called for.' Sure it was no business o' mine to give it ye till ye called for it, or, what I consider the same thing, asked for it."

Anty took the letter, and, placing it in her bosom, turned towards the old castle, to give to Grey Lambert his epistle. John pursued his path, until he arrived at the village Public.[112] There, what a crowd awaited his coming! "John, what's the news?" – "John, the paper." – "John – oh, John, don't mind 'em, but give me my cap! I hope it isn't in that bandbox that's had the dance in the mud. There – John, honey – don't 'squeege' it so! – sure no cap can stand a 'squeeging!' " – "John, is my bonnet come? Och! meal-a-murder![113] what made Miss Lerady put an

Orange riban' in my beautiful English straw?" "John, I hope ye didn't forget the tobaccy?" – "John, agra – the two ounces o' green tay for my granny." – "John, my twinty-four marbles." – "John, och, John! sure it's not come to that wid ye, that ye'd forget the green silk handkerchief!" – "John," said a fine-looking fellow, pushing through the circle, "John, did ye get the thing I tould ye of?" John winked; and from his waistcoat pocket drew forth a very little parcel, wrapped up in white paper. The young man took it, smiled, and soon after there was a bustle at the far window; for the parcel contained a plain gold ring, which the saucy youth was endeavouring to try on the finger of pretty Letty, the gentle daughter of mine host of the "Public." – "John, any letthers for me?" inquired the bustling man of the big shop – "One, Darby, very like a bill." – "Humph!" said Darby. – "Did ye bring the doctor's stuff for father?" asked Minny Corish. – "Och! murder-in-Irish! sure ye're not afther forgetting the five yards o' red stuff," exclaimed no less a person than Mrs. Cassidy herself, "and I wanting to quilt it for a petticoat, to keep my ould bones from freezing!" – "John," said a village lounger, who expected nothing, and yet wanted to say something – "John, why d'ye wear yer wig over yer hair?" "Why," replied John, dryly, "sure ye wouldn't have me wear my hair over my wig." – "John, I take shame that I didn't offer ye this afore," and the landlord presented a large glass of whisky to the postman, who drank it off, remarking afterwards – "thrue Parliament, to be sure," which raised a general laugh. – "Come, John, ye're enough to set a body mad," said fussy Tom Tennison, who was ever in a bustle about something or other, "Master Ben has been here more than an hour, waiting to rade us the news, and there ye stand, taking the things out as asy as—; can't ye give us the paper?" "No – I say, no – not till it's yer turn, Mister Fussy; take the patthern o' yer manners from Mister Ben; see how quiet he stands, as the song says – 'tall and straight as a popilar tree;'[114] and two of his bran new slates cracked by that devil of a horse. Arrah, don't be bothering me, all o' ye; ye forget, so ye do, that I have five or six places to go to yet; if ye taze me afther this fashion, hang me, but ye must get another postman; the moment ye see me, ye're like a pack o' Curnol Piggot's[115] hounds in full cry, afther a hare; can't ye larn patience? sure every body knows it's a vartue."

John's next resting-place was the Parsonage; such a lovely spot – just what a parsonage ought to be; only look, is it not perfectly delicious? That softly swelling meadow, over which the evening mist is stealing, paled off from the mossy lawn that fays and fairies might delight to revel on; the lowly, yet elegantly-thatched, cottage; the green-house, the flower-borders – did you ever see such splendid flowers? – there – such balsams[116] – such peonies – such a myrtle – such roses! roses red, white, pure white, the maiden's blush, the damask, and the many-coloured Lancaster, not rivalling each other, but uniting to charm sight and smell by their combined beauty and fragrance. Ah! there is Marianne amongst the lilies, fit model for a sculptor, alike lovely in person and mind. And the eldest, Henrietta, noble and dignified, though very different from Marianne; conscious of her magnificent beauty, yet condescending and benevolent to the poorest peasant. Then, Ellen the youngest; not the handsomest, but certainly the most useful; a perfect Goody Two-shoes, with more wisdom at fifteen than most women at fifty. The postman is to them all a most welcome visitor. "Oh, John, is it you? Do give me papa's and mamma's letters." "Oh, don't, Marianne!" said the young Ellen; "don't take them all yourself; do let me have the newspapers, at least, to give papa." "John," inquired Hetta, "the netting-silk,[117] and the silver bodkin – I hope you have chosen a nice one – and the two skipping ropes, for my sisters; – thank you." "All right, I hope, Miss." "Thank you, all quite right; will you come up and take something, John?" "No, Miss, I humbly thank ye, all the same." "John, tell me – have you got a letter for poor Mrs. Clavery?" "Yes, Miss." "Ah, now I *am* happy; poor woman, she will be so delighted!"

"There," thought John to himself, as he passed on – "there, that is what I call the true breed of the gentry. Such a born beauty as that to think of a poor sorrow-struck woman! Ah, the thick blood without any puddle, for ever! – that's the sort that warms the heart."

Mrs. Clavery's story will be best told in her own words, as she herself related it to the family at the Parsonage, a few months before John brought her the letter that made Miss Henrietta so happy.

One tranquil evening in autumn, a pale, delicate young woman rested her hand on the gate that opened to the green sloping lawn which fronted the Parsonage-house; uncertain whether or not she might venture to raise the latch, she gazed wistfully on the group of children who were playing on the green. Although in the veriest garb of misery, there was nothing of the common beggar in her appearance; and the two little ones, who clung to her tattered cloak, were better covered than their mother. She carried, on her back, a young sickly-looking infant, and its weak cries arrested the attention of the good pastor's youngest daughter, who bade her enter, in that gentle tone which speaks of hope and comfort to the breaking heart. How much is in a kindly voice! When the woman had partaken of food and rest, and remained a few days at the Parsonage, she thus told her tale: –

"May God reward ye! – for ye have fed the hungry, and ye have clothed the naked, and ye have spoken hope to her that thought of it no more; and ye have looked like heaven's own angels on one who had forgot the sight o' smiles. May God's fresh blessing be about ye! – may ye never want! But a poor woman's prayer is nothing; only I am certain sure the Almighty will grant ye a long life, and a happy death, for yer kindness to one who was lone and desolate in a could world. It's little matter where one like me was born, only I came of dacent honest people, and it could not be said that any one belonging to me or mine ever wronged man or mortal; the boys were brave and just – the girls well-looking and virtuous: – seven of us under one roof; but there was full and plinty of everything – more especially love, that sweetens all. Well, I married; and I may say a more sober, industrious boy never broke the world's bread than my Thomas – *my Thomas!* I ask yer pardon, ladies; but my heart swells when I think that may-be he's gone to the God who gave him to me, first for a blessing, then for a heart-trial.'

The poor woman wept; and the father of the family she was addressing, adopting the figurative language which the Irish so well understand, observed, "The gardener prunes the vine even to bleeding, and suffers the bramble to grow its own way."[118]

"That's true; thank ye, sir, for that sweet word of comfort," she replied, smiling faintly: "it's happy to think of God's care – the only care that's over the poor, though it seems ungrateful to say that to those who are so extraordinary kind to me. Well, we had a clane cabin – a milk-white cow – a trifle of poultry – two or three pigs – indeed, every comfort in life, according to our station, and thankful we were for them. Time passed as happy as heart could wish, and one babe came, and another; but the eldest now was the third then, for it pleased God to take the two first in a fever; and bad, sure enough, was the trouble, for my husband took it, and there he lay, off and on, for as good as four months; and then the rint got behindhand, and we were forced to sell the cow: one would think the baste had knowledge, for when she was going off to the fair (and, by the same token,[119] it was my brother-in-law's sister's son that druv her), she turned back and mowed; ay, as natural as a child that was quitting the mother. Well; we never could rise the price of a cow agin, and that was a sore loss to us, for God sent two young ones the next time, and betwixt the both I could niver get a minit to do the bit o' spinning or knitting that the landlord's wife expected as a yearly compliment. She was not a born lady; and they're the worst to the poor. Musharoon gentry! that spring up and buy land, hand over head, from the raale sort, that are left, in the long run, without cross or coin to bless themselves with; all owing to their generosity. Well, to make up for that, I was forced to give up some of my best hens, as duty fowl, to the lady, on account that she praised their handsome toppings. That wasn't all; – the pigs got the measles; and we might have sould them to advantage, but my husband says, says he, 'Mary, we have had disease and death in our own house; and don't let us be the manes o' selling unwholesome mate, upon no account – becase it brings ill health, and we to answer for it, when no-thin' will be to the fore but the honest deeds and the roguish ones, straight aginst each other, and no one to judge them but the Almighty – the ONE who knows the rights of all;' – that was true for him. Well; we might have got up agin, for my poor Thomas worked like any negur[120] to the full; but just after we had sowed our little field of wheat (it was almost at the corner of the landlord's park, and we depinded on it for the next gale day),[121] nothing could sarve the landlord but he must take it out of our hands, without any notice, to plant trees upon. I went to my lady, and, to soften her like, took what was left of my poor fowl – the cock and all – as a present; she accepted them very genteelly, to be sure, and promised we should have another field, and compensation money. We waited, and waited, but no sign of it; at last my husband made bould to go to the landlord himself, and tould him all that had passed between the lady and me. 'Don't bother me, man,' was the answer he made; 'compensation, indeed! – what compensation am I to have for being out of my rent so long, the time ye were sick, and ye without a lase? And I am sartain my wife never promised anything of the sort to the woman.' 'I ask yer pardon, sir,' replied Thomas, civil, of course – for Thomas was always civil to rich or poor; 'but she did, for my Mary tould me.' 'She tould ye a lie, then,' said the landlord; and my husband fired up. 'Sir,' said he, 'if ye were my equal you dar'n't say the likes o' that of my Mary, for though she's not of gentle blood, she's no liar!' Then the landlord called my husband an impudent blackguard;[122] and Thomas made answer, that he, being a gentleman, might call him what he pleased; but that none should say that of his wife that she did not desarve: however, the upshot of the thing was, that we got warning to quit all of a suddent; but there was no help for it; as the neighbours said – true for them – that Thomas was by no manes so strong a man as before the feaver; and the steward found out some stranger who offered money down on the nail for the land, that we had in such prime order. Every one cried shame on the landlord, but sure there's no justice for the poor! 'Twas a sorrowful parting, for somehow a body gets fond of the bits of trees even, that grow up under their own eye; and I was near my lying-in, and the troubles came all at once, and all we could get to shelter us was a damp hole of a place. My husband got plenty of work; and though it wasn't in natur not to lament by-gone comforts, yet sure the love was to the good, firm – ay, firmer than ever – and no blight was on our name, nor isn't to this day – thank God for it! – for nobody breathing can say, Thomas, or Mary, Clavery, ye owe me the value of a thraneen. Oh! but that's a fine thing and a cheering after all! Well, the change of air, and the fretting, and one thing or other, made me very weakly; and we lost the fellow twin to this one; it was happy for the darlint – but it was heart-scalding to see it peeking and peeking – wastin' and wastin', and to want the drop of wine, or the morsel of mate, that might keep it to be a blessing to its parent's grey hairs. It was then, just after my child's death, that, to drive the sorrow from his heart, Thomas took a little to the drop; and yet he wasn't like other men, that grow cross and fractious – he was always gentle to me and the young ones; but in the end it ruined us, as it does all who have any call to it – for he was as fine a young man, though I say it, as ye could see in a day's walk – standing six feet two, in his stocking vamps,[123] and admired for his beauty; and he went to the next town to sell my little spinning, that I had done to keep the dacent stitch on the childer; and, as was fated, I suppose, who should ' be there but a recruiting sargent – and when the drink's in, the wit's out, and he listed – listed![124] – And the parting – oh! but I thought the life would lave me

– sure I followed him to the place of embarkment, and there they druv me from him; and I stood on the sea-shore, and saw him on the deck of that black ship, his arms crossed over his breast like one melancholy mad; and it was long before I believed he was really gone – gone – gone; and that there was no voice to cheer me – for *these* did nothing but cry for food: it was wicked, but I wished to die, for my heart felt breaking. The little left me was soon gone; I was among strangers – I could not bear to go to my own people or place, because I was more like a shame, and my spirit was too high to be looked down on. I have travelled from parish to parish, doing a bit of work of any kind when I could get it, and trusting to good Christians to give something to the desolate children when all else failed."

"Have you never heard from your husband?"

"Oh, sir, he sends his letters to Watherford, to the care of one I know, but I cannot often hear, the distance is so great."

"Did he not forward you money?"

"Three pounds; but we owed thirty shillings of it, betwixt rent for the last hole we lived in, and two or three other matters. I was overjoyed to be able to send the money, for the debts lay heavy on my heart; and, to be sure, the children wanted many a little thing, and the remainder soon went."

The good pastor and his family were deeply interested in Mary Clavery's simple tale; and, on further inquiry, its truth was fully established. It was also found that her husband was in a regiment then at Jamaica, commanded by the clergyman's brother, a gallant and distinguished officer. The story circulated very quickly, in a neighbourhood where every little circumstance is an event; and, to the credit of my favourite Bannow, be it known that, on the very same Sabbath morning, in the Protestant church and Catholic chapel, a collection was made for the benefit of the distressed family. Another week saw Mary and her children in quiet possession of a small two-roomed cabin; the parish minister and parish priest conversing at the door, as to the best manner of procuring the industrious woman continued employment; and the three young ladies busily engaged in arranging new noggins and plates, and all manner of cottage furniture, to their own sweet taste. Then, Farmer Corish gave Mrs. Clavery a sack of potatoes – Master Ben engaged to "teach" the children for nothing – Mrs. Cassidy sent, as her offering, a fine fat little pig – Mrs. Corish presented a motherly, well educated goose, capable of bringing up a numerous family respectably – good Mr. Rooney, as considerate and worthy an old bachelor as ever lived (how angry I am with *good* men for being old bachelors!) sent her a setting hen and seven eggs; – in short, the little cottage and garden were stocked so quickly, and yet so well, and the poor woman was so grateful, that she could hardly believe the reality of what had occurred. Her kind friends at the Parsonage, however, saw that something more was wanting to make their *protégé* perfectly happy. What that was, need I tell? – my lady readers have surely guessed it already, and even the gentlemen may have found it out. The clergyman, without acquainting Mrs. Clavery, had written to his brother, mentioning all the particulars, and begging Thomas's discharge; the last post had brought him a letter, stating that his request was granted.

But the three graces[125] (as my young friends of the Parsonage were always called) denied themselves the pleasure of communicating the joyful tidings; leaving the expected letter from Thomas Clavery himself to tell the news. They could not, however, forego the gratification of witnessing the joy the cottagers would feel when the information was communicated, that the husband and the father was on his homeward journey, and they hastily followed the postman to Mary's abode.

John's next resting-place was at an old weather-beaten but spacious mansion, somewhat out of the Bannow district, and close on the beach. It belonged to a gentleman whose health obliged him to reside for a time on the continent, but who had lent his house to his relative, Sir James Horatio Banks, M. P., for the summer, as the sea-bathing is very good all along the Wexford coast: consequently, Sir James Horatio, his lady, and all his little ones and servants, were, fortunately, only birds of passage – I beg that this fact may be clearly understood, as I would on no account have the family confounded with our own dear resident gentry. Sir James Horatio Banks, M.P., was a great[126] man in his own way, and a strange way it was. Anything but a spendthrift, in the usual acceptation of the word, and yet in perpetual embarrassments; for he was always at law; – never, to do him justice, missed an opportunity of litigation, whether for a thousand pounds or a thousand pence – an estate or an acre. Long Chancery suits[127] were his delight, and he anticipated Term[128] with absolute rapture. Most people complain of the law's delays. Not so Sir James Horatio Banks. He was always anxious to retard its decisions; so much so that he was once designated, in open court, "a filthy pebble in the wheel of justice."[129] He stood a contested election, or, rather, Lady Banks got him through it, and triumphantly *speechified* on the hustings; but the many thousands expended on that memorable occasion, would have broken his heart to a certainty – if, fortunately, three fresh lawsuits had not thence arisen to console him. It was some comfort to the Irish to discover that his mother had been a native of Wales; for he was very mean in his household expenses; which they asserted, could not have been the case, had he been "raale Irish." In truth he had a miserly aspect; a thin spare body, covered with a parchment-like skin, a rattish expression of countenance, and little peering grey eyes that seemed eternally seeking for flaws in everything. He used to ride a bony black horse, and always wore overgrown jack-boots, a threadbare long coat, a flapped hat – that sometimes answered the purpose of an umbrella – and invariably fastened a pair of horse-pistols to the pommel of his saddle. One of our Bannow poets made the following rhyme on the worthy member, and contrived, in a crowd, to tie them to the tail of his horse. – How he mourned that he could never discover the author! –

"The Divil Sir Jimmy to Parliament sint;
To plaze his master, Sir Jimmy he wint,
On his ould black horse, that look'd like a hack;
Success! cried the boys; may ye niver come back!"[130]

Indeed, the peculiarities of the family afforded much amusement to the neighbourhood where they resided for a time. Lady Banks was the very opposite of
her husband; possessed, as a brother sportsman once said of her, "blood, bone,
and beauty;" wore a scarlet riding habit; hunted in grand style – was always in
at the death; sung songs after supper – loved claret; never scrupled at an oath;
called Sir James "her little man," – always saw the horses fed; obliged her girls to
stand fire – her boys to go barefoot to make them hardy; and obtained for herself,
amongst the country people, the universal *sobriquet*[131] of "Man Jack." Perhaps all
these eccentricities might have been forgiven had she possessed the kindly feelings
of her sex, for she was young and handsome; but she was neither an affectionate
mother nor a sincere friend; she loved to dash and to astonish, and left a family of
beautiful children to the management of a French lady's maid and head groom.

The postman's arrival was a matter of great importance to the household, as
Sir James always expected letters, and the family had many wants to be supplied.
Ma'm'selle Madeline had descended to the servants' hall to await John's coming,
and two or three of the younger children accompanied her: on a table, in the
centre of the apartment, Miss Julia, a lovely girl of five years old, was dancing a
jig to the great amusement of two or three men servants, who sung St. Patrick's
Day to "plaze the jewil;" Carlos and Henry, two younger urchins, were riding a
magnificent Newfoundland dog; the groom and the footman were playing cards
at a small side-table near the fire; and near it was a jug of whisky punch, to which
the butler, housekeeper, and coachman frequently resorted. Ma'm'selle Madeline
looked contemptuously on them all, until roused from her reverie by the butler's
inquiring "if Miss Maddy wouldn't taste a drop of the genuine – betther, ten to
one, nor all the wine that iver sailed out of France?" "Non, Merçie, bien, tank
you, Monsieur – ver oblige, mais – but I ha' de horreur great to your ponch.
Faugh! – excuse moi – 'tis von great bad shmell. – Faugh!" – and the lady's maid
refreshed her nose with "Eau de Luce,"[132] much to the amusement of the servants, "Oh, John! – welcome John!" "Oh, Monsieur John, you not be come at
last." "John, the rings for the pigs." John here, John there, John everywhere, as
usual; at length, the papers and letters were piled on the table, and Ma'm'selle
Madeline had received, and disappeared with, her band-boxes. "Larry," said the
butler to the footman, "take up the papers – why don't ye?" "Let them wait till
I've looked at them myself," replied Larry; "I want to see what news from the
Curragh,[133] as my lady has a heavy bet on Captain Lofty's sorrel coult." "Any
news of the law business?" inquired the steward. "How do I know, or what do
I care!" replied Larry:" what does it signify whether law actions are gained or

not? – don't we all know what comes over the divil's back must go under –"
"Dacency!" screamed the cook. "All I know," observed the steward, "is –"

"I'll tell ye what, boys," said John Williams, "ye'd betther mind yer business,
and take the letthers up, out of hand; for Sir James and my lady both saw me
coming down the avenue."

"Och, murder, John! – why didn't ye tell me so before? – by the powers, 'Man
Jack' 'll bate my brains out!" and the footman hurried off amid the laughter of
his fellow-servants.

"Any news, Sir James?" inquired the lady, as she tried on a new velvet hunting-cap.

"Yes, my dear, I've just received the bills for my last suit in the King's Bench."

"You lost the cause, I think."

"Yes, owing to the hurry that Counsellor Playdil was in; – never can take his
time about anything."

"What's the damage?"

Poor Sir James groaned. "It will stand me in, one way or other, eighteen hundred and thirty-seven pounds, fourteen shillings, and threepence farthing."

"The devil it will!" exclaimed the lady, laying down the hunting-cap: "I wonder, Sir James, you don't at once take my advice; have done with the law, and the
torment of it. I'll bet ten to one you'd be as happy again. Oh, if you had my spirit!"

Sir James thought, perhaps, that she had enough for both: a pause ensued,
and at length the M. P. began – "My dear Lady Banks, do you know that Major
McLaughlin's filly has won the cup."

"Then I'm in for a cool hundred, that's certain, or else there's some foul play.
Curse me, though," continued the lady, "but I'll find it out! – a colt like Lofty's!
– such a chest – such action – such limbs! Why, Mc Laughlin's was no more to
be compared to it – but it's all your fault, Sir James – I never have my own way; I
ought to have been on the race-ground; but here you would stick and vegetate like
a cabbage; except, indeed, in Term time; you don't care what's spent on law-suits."

" 'Sdeath,[134] Madam, were it not for the law we should be ruined, your extravagance is such – you never ask the price of anything; – hadn't I to go to law with
your habit-maker for his overcharges?"

"Oh, yes! – and to pay three-and-thirty pounds more than the original bill."

"Well, but *still I had the law,* and I showed the fellow I could not be imposed
upon. Oh, Lady Banks, Lady Banks! I wish you were less extravagant; we must
retrench. Do you know, were I not a Member of Parliament I should be in a jail;
think of that, Lady Banks! – in a jail!"

"Well, and have you not to thank me for your election? – who in their senses
would have sent *you,* little man, to be a representative, if it hadn't been for my
canvassing? The House would be half memberless, if only those sat there who
paid their debts!" – and she laughed loudly. "Your law tells you that the M. P. is a

cloak against bailiffs! *Vive le plaisir*! Why, you don't expect me to turn mourner, and spend my allowance only – like a school-girl; a woman of my spirit! *Pardonnez moi!*" She was leaving her husband surrounded by letters, all demanding money, when some idea or sensation occurred, that stopped her on the threshold. "Sir James, Madeline tells me that Caroletta is ill; perhaps the child wants change of air; she grows fast – is getting quite womanly; you had better send her to your sister at Portarlington for a time; I have not a moment to attend to it, but as she is your pet I thought I would mention it." The lady went to look after horses, and the gentleman (who certainly loved his family), to inquire after his eldest child, whom he well knew not to be her mother's favourite, because she was growing so tall and handsome that the vainglorious woman dreaded a rival.

By the time our useful postman had completed his rounds, for he had much to do after he had left the Honourable Member's house, the moon was high in the heavens, and John and his steed had ensured sound slumbers by active exertion. There were many, however, who woke, and some who wept, while the stars sparkled in the blue sky, and the unruffled ocean murmured along the shore. How different is night in the country from night in town! Oh, for my native hills by moonlight! – the very breeze tells of repose, and the lone and beautiful clouds, passing so silently along the heavens, that they –

"——————————— seem to be
Fair islands in a dark blue sea,
Which human eyes at eve behold;
But only then, unseen by day,
Their shores and mountains all of gold."[135]

At the Parsonage the three sisters were chattering, as only girls can chatter, arranging further plans to benefit the poor and needy; and even while their hearts were uplifted to the Giver of all good, they sank into the sweet slumbers of innocence.

A trembling light, that issued from Mrs. Clavery's window, showed she was still awake. Seated by the bed-side, where her three little ones, their arms twined around each other, slept the refreshing sleep of childhood, she read, for the last time that night, the lines which her husband's hand had traced; and feeling how sweet it was to have near her anything that came from a beloved object, placed the letter under her pillow, and then, while earnest, silent tears coursed each other down her cheeks, prayed that an all-directing Providence would guide her husband in safety over the wide waste of waters.

Lady Banks had just finished her last song, after supper, which was loudly applauded by the very mixed company that sat around the board, while her husband looked gloomy enough at the foot of the table, meditating on his long debts and neglected daughter.

Our old friend, "Grey Lambert," and his faithful Bang, were soundly sleeping in the castle, while the breeze that moaned along the decaying walls was to them as a sweet and soothing lullaby.

Anty Mc Queen – poor Anty! – she slumbered not. Her father's cottage was on the hill side, and a very neat cabin it was; well filled, too, with children of all ages and sizes, from Anty, the eldest, who, in her own opinion, was quite old enough to be married, down to a fat rosy "lump of a boy," who, although hardly able to crawl, fought manfully with the pig for every potatoe it took into its mouth. The household, with the exception of Anty, were all fast asleep, and, from the nature of her dress (according to the fashionable acceptance of the word, she might have been called full dressed), it would seem she had been in bed; however, there she sat over the dying embers of the fire – an end of candle stuck in a scooped potatoe, that served as a candlestick – and an open letter in her hand, which she turned one way, and then another, without being able to understand a single word of its contents.

Poor Anty! – it was only when she had received from the postman the long-expected epistle, that it occurred to her that she was utterly unable to peruse it. Indeed, she could hardly decipher print. But as to writing – she never had a pen in her hand in her life. Had she been inclined to make confidants of her father and mother, she would have been precisely in the same dilemma, for they were equally ignorant; and bitterly did she regret the obstinacy of her disposi-tion, which prevented her hearkening to Master Ben, when he counselled her to become a scholar. Grey Lambert, she knew, would at once have read every word of it, "for he had grate larning;" but, unfortunately, as her sweetheart was no other than his grandson, she did not exactly wish him to have so much subject-matter to jest her about. She had taken the letter to Mary-the-Mant,[136] who, next to Peggy the Fisher, perhaps knew more about the love affairs of the neighbourhood than any body else; but Mary-the-Mant was not at home – gone to Waterford – would not be back for three days! Master Ben then occurred to her. But, no! – she could not bear him to read it for her; not that he would laugh; but he would feel no interest, and perhaps find fault, with the skill of a practised critic, and condemn the spelling and diction of her beloved letter with-out mercy. What could she do? Letty Connor – she was well educated; but then she had been a sort of rival of hers, and she did not wish her to know anything at all about the matter. John Williams? No; he would make fun of her in his own quiet, sly way. What should she do? – There she sat over the fire, twisting and turning the manuscript, that looked, to tell the truth, like a collection of strange hieroglyphics, more than anything else; and, after much consideration, Anty resolved on two things: one, even to take the letter to Grey Lambert (for waiting three entire days for Mary-the-Mant was out of the question), and get him to read it. The other was to offer herself again as a pupil to Master Ben, and get herself taught writing "out of hand" – all in a minute – and surprise her lover (who was a wonderful scholar entirely) with her acquirements.

The next morning Anty arrived at Coolhull before Lambert had finished his prayers; for, on peeping through a large slit in the door, she saw the old man on his knees before a crucifix, at the farther end of the great hall – Bang sitting by his side, while the bright red light of morning streamed through one of the broken windows, and rested on their heads. Her visit was immediately noticed by the faithful dog, whose scent, or ear, soon discovered that she was outside. He walked steadily to the time-worn door, and laying his long nose on the ground, sniffed loudly three or four times, and moved his tail slowly, in token of recognition, as she entered. The young girl busied herself in lighting the fire, and settling the few rude articles of furniture, according to her own taste, until Grey Lambert's orisons were finished. When he arose from his knees, she knelt and asked his blessing.

"Well, Anty, what's come to ye, my child, to be two good miles from your own home, and it not six o'clock yet? ye weren't heavy for sleep this morning, I'm sartin; is there anything the matter at home, mavourneen, for something strange must have brought ye? Come, don't look so shy; what is it ails the colleen? – have ye lost yer tongue? – fait, agra! it's bad indeed wid ye, if that's gone. "Anty shook her head. "Well, I'll sit down here, and wait till ye choose to spake, and not spind any more o' my breath on ye; for, to tell God's truth, I've not much to spare; only I can't think what's over the girl." – Lambert sat down; and after a considerable pause, during which Anty twisted and untwisted the corner of her apron with admirable perseverance, she drew the letter from its hiding-place, and, turning away her blushing face as she spoke, said, with considerable hesitation –

"Ye funned me about a letther last night, sure I couldn't help it if the boy chose to write. It's no faut o' mine. I didn't put any comether in life upon him; and more betokens, I wouldn't have troubled ye to rade it for me if I could rade it myself; and sure, Grey Lambert, I didn't desave ye by no manner of manes; for I knew ye mistrusted we were almost keeping company afore Pat took the turn for going to sea."

"Well, Anty, ye mane to be Grey Lambert's grand-daughter; whisht now! – I'll rade the letther."

"My Dear Anty,

"I do hope that these few lines will meet acceptance and true love from you, for ye haven't forgot the fippinny-bit; the half of it, and the long curl, are next my bateing heart this minit, and sure it's in the core of it they should be, if I had any way to get them there; but it's all the same. I'm unasy in my mind about two things – my poor ould ancient gran'fader, and your little innocent flirtish ways. Ah, Anty! sure there's all the boys on land that you used to taze the life o' me about. And ye think it no harm to laugh wid 'em now; but it wouldn't be the same if we were married. – Ye'd behave yourself, thin, Anty. And that and my ould ancient gran'fader has made up my mind. – And the thoughts of it has prevented my spending. – And I'm coming home, plaze God, only don't tell the ould man, nor Bang, the baste, becase I mane every mother's sowl o' ye much joy. – And I've bought such a beautiful gown-piece[137] for the wedding. Only, to my thinking, Anty, nothing can make ye handsomer than ye are. And many charmers I have seen, but none like my Bannow girl. And Jim the boatswain has made a song upon ye, according to my telling, and every varse ends wid –

> 'Anty, the darlint of the land,
> Is still her Paddy's pride.'[138]

Oh, it's a dale a finer song than 'Colleen das Crutheen Amo,'[139] as you'll say whin ye hear it, which 'll be very soon afther you, and my ould ancient gran'fader, gets the letthers. And there's another boy travelling home to Bannow, by the name of Thomas Clavery, a late soldier, but discharged – an honest, dacent craythur as ever drew breath, and doating alive upon the wife and the grawls. Be faithful to him that's faithful to you, 'true as the needle to the poll.' – God's blessing be about ye, prays, my dear Anty,

"Your most affectionate lover,
"(Husband soon) till death,
"PATRICK LAMBERT."

Grey Lambert folded up the epistle, and returned it to its rightful owner; the old man did not jest upon its contents, but, rising from his seat, laid his hand on Anty's head, and, in a deep but solemn voice, said –

"So, colleen, the promise has passed betwixt ye, that in God's eye is as binding on ye as if the blessed Pope had joined yer hands in his holy temple at Rome. I knew ye had a kindness for each other, from many little things, more especially from the way Pat always mintioned ye in his letthers; but I didn't think ye were contracted, or else, Anty, who I love (and good right I have to love ye, as my own child), I would have talked more seriously to ye about the little flirting ways yer true love mintions. Anty, look up in the ould man's face, and tell him, did ye ever think – think solidly – what was required of woman in marriage?" There was that in Grey Lambert's manner which conquered levity, and the young girl looked up with the expression of countenance which replied "No." "Few craturs at yer age do," he continued: "and what I say to you, ye young wild flower, sweet and spotless as ye are, I will say to him, and more too, for ye are far faithfuller in yer naturs than us. Ah, Anty! it's asy enough to be true to the young heart's first love, whin all is full of hope; but, in my early days, I have seen affection that seemed as strong as life, and then, a breath, or a word, or a look, may-be, has begun unkindness, and that has increased, until, at last, bitther scorn, ay, and black hatred, grew, where there had been nothing but love and smiles. And women have much to bear, Anty; for it's little men heed an unkind word, unjustly spoken, may-be, and yet to be borne, almost as if it was dear or darlint – which is the hardest word I hope ever to hear Patrick make use of to you. But, my girl, when ye knew of the promise, it wasn't quite right of ye to skit, and laugh, and dance, as if ye were free."

"I'm sure, Grey Lambert," interrupted Anty, half crying, "ye've no rason to turn on me, after that fashion, for I meant no harm, and nothing in life would ever make me jilty."[140]

"Asy, agra, till I tell ye a little story to divart ye a bit, and it's all thrue, and I know ye'll find out my maning, for ye're 'cute enough." And Anty listened very attentively, pulling first one and then the other of "Bang, the baste's" ears, which he bore patiently, not even increasing her perplexity by moving his head from off her lap.

"In the ancient times, when flowers, and trees, and fairies were on spakeing terms, and all friendly together; one fine summer's day the sun shone out on a beautiful garden, where there war all sorts of plants that ye could mintion; and a lovely but giddy fairy went sporting about from one to the other (although no one could see her, because of the sunlight), as gay as the morning lark; then says the fairy to the rose – 'Rose, if the sun was clouded, and the storm came on, would ye shelter and love me still?' 'Do ye doubt me?' says the rose, and reddened up with anger. – 'Lily,' says the fairy to another love, 'if the sun was clouded, and a storm came on, would ye shelter and love me still?' 'Oh! do you think I could change?' says the lily, and she grew still paler with sorrow. – 'Tulip,' said the fairy, 'if the sun was clouded, and a storm came on, would ye shelter and love me still?' 'Upon my word!' said the tulip, making a very gentleman-like bow, 'ye're the very first lady that ever doubted my constancy;' so the fairy sported on, joyful to think of her kind and blooming friends. She revelled away for a time, and then she thought on the pale blue violet that was almost kivered with its broad green leaves; and, although it was an ould comrade, she might have forgotten it, had it not been for the sweet scent that came up from the modest flower. 'Oh, violet!' said the fairy, 'if the sun was clouded, and a storm came on, would ye shelter and love me still?' And the violet made answer – 'Ye have known me long, sweet fairy; and in the first spring-time, when there were few other flowers, ye used to shelter from the could blast under my leaves; now ve've almost forgotten me – but let it pass – try my truth – if ever you should meet misfortune – I say nothing.' Well, the fairy skitted at that, and clapped her silvery wings, and whisked, singing, off on a sunbame; but she was hardly gone, when a black cloud grew up out of the north, all in a minit, and the light was shrouded, and the rain fell in slashings, like hail, and away flies the fairy to her friend the rose. – 'Now, Rose,' says she, 'the rain is come, so shelter and love me still.' 'I can hardly shelter my own buds,' says the rose, 'but the lily has a deep cup.' Well, the poor little fairy's wings were almost wet, but she got to the lily. 'Lily,' says she, ' the storm is come, so shelter and love me still.' 'I am sorry,' says the lily,' but if I were to open my cup, the rain would bate in like fun, and my seed would be kil't entirely – the tulip has long leaves.' Well, the fairy was down-hearted enough, but she went to the tulip, who she always thought a sweet-spoken gentleman. He certainly did not look as bright as he had done in the sun, but she waved her little wand, and 'Tulip,' said she, 'the rain and the storm are come, and I am very weary, but you will shelter and love me still.' 'Begone!' says the tulip; 'be off!' says he; 'a pretty pickle I'd be in if I let every wandering scamper come about me.' – Well, by this time, she was very tired, and her wings hung dripping at her back – wet indeed – but there was no help for it, and, laneing on her pretty silver wand, she limped off to the violet; and the darlint little flower, with its blue eye, that's as clear as a kitten's, saw her coming, and never a word she spoke, but opened her broad green leaves, and took the wild wandering craythur to her bosom, and dried her wings, and breathed the sweetest parfumes over her, and sheltered her until the storm was clane gone. Then the humble violet spoke, and said – 'Fairy Queen, it is bad to flirt with many, for the love of one true heart is enough for earthly woman, or fairy spirit; the ould and humble love is better than the gay compliments of a world of flowers, for *it* will last, when the others pass.' And the fairy knew that it was true for the blue violet; and she contented herself ever after, and built her downy bower under the wide-spreading violet leaves, that sheltered her from the rude winter's wind and the hot summer's sun; and to this very day the fairies love the violet beds."

Anty smiled, and suffered Bang's ears to escape, when the story was finished. Grey Lambert smiled also, and, as she was departing, inquired if her parents knew of the contract? She frankly replied in the negative; and the old man accompanied the little gipsy to her father's cabin, where the news was joyfully received. Everybody liked Patrick; and, moreover, every body suspected that in some sly corner the old man had wherewithal to make a plentiful wedding.

Nothing happened to prevent matters coming to a happy termination. Thomas Clavery and Patrick Lambert returned on the same day. The gown-piece was declared to be an "uncommon beauty," even by Mrs. Cassidy; and a time was fixed for the wedding: – but where do you suppose it was celebrated? In no other place, I assure you, than in Grey Lambert's old castle.

"It's a fancy, I know," said he, "and a strange one, but I can't help it; the bride and bridegroom can trot off to their nate little cabin, that's all ready for them, and that I defy any one to say wants a single thing; and it will make me happy to know that once more laughter and music will visit the ancient castle of Coolhull."

Such a wedding was never seen in the country from that day to this; it was a most wonderful wedding! More than fifty long torches, of bog-wood, were stuck up and down in the walls, and the ivy and wild plants formed a singular but not un pleasing contrast to the grey stones and flaring lights. – One end of the dilapidated hall was reserved for dancing; and there, on a throne of turf, sat the immortal Kelly; a deep jug of whisky punch close to his footstool, and he "blowing away for the dear life" on his pipes. At the other end was a long table, formed of deal spars – covered with such cloths, plates, dishes, glasses, noggins, jugs, and sundries, as the neighbouring farmhouses could lend – placed on stones and turfs, sufficiently elevated. What a supper! – rounds of beef – turkey – geese – such profusion! – the "wedding of Ballyporeen"[141] was nothing to it! And when the cake was fairly cut, Father Mike's perquisites were many, for Grey Lambert, whose reported wealth was no jest, laid down a golden guinea on the plate. He had bidden many of the neighbouring gentry to the marriage, and, as the old man was much respected, and the arrangements very singular, there were few apologies. The great hall was, at an early hour, nearly filled with motley company; ladies and gentlemen, farmers and farmers' wives, "boys and girls" of all ranks, in their Sunday gear, and with happy joyous faces; some whispering so closely that Father Mike was led to believe a few more weddings would take place before Lent; then the Babelish noises! – Kelly's pipes – merry laughter – loud tongues. The clergyman and the parish priest sat at the same table; and it must be confessed that neither Ude's nor Kitchener's sauces[142] were wanting to make the feast palatable.

Grey Lambert danced most merrily with the young ladies from the Parsonage, and "bate them off the flure," at the Irish jig. The bride looked provokingly pretty and mischievous; and the boatswain, who came from Waterford to the ceremony, sung not only –

> "Anty, the darlint of the land,
> Is still her Paddy's pride!" –

but composed extemporaneous verses on the occasion, which were received with much applause.

Was that all? No; in the far corner sat Thomas and Mary Clavery!

John Williams, whose dislike to conversation disappeared in a very odd way, probably owing to his continued potations, annoyed Anty continually by calling her "Mrs. Lambert;" and the old man kept up the joke, somewhat unmercifully, by now and then reminding her of the past – "Sure I'll not come to see ye in yer unchristian-like place, if ye talk after that fashion to a young cratur like me!"

As his company departed, he conducted them with the air of a prince to the grate gate; and Father Mike, after he had earnestly prayed that his full blessing might rest on them all, declared he had never been at so happy a wedding.

I am not prepared to state whether or not Anty learned writing, for she was able to prevail upon Patrick to "give up the sea," and content himself with the occasional management of a fishing boat; consequently, she was not likely, in the whole course of her life, to receive another letter. She remembered the fairy tale, and, to the credit of the sex be it spoken, left off "her flirting ways." Grey Lambert is still in possession of the old castle and extraordinary health; and John Williams may carry this tale to "mine old home," in his capacity as THE BANNOW POSTMAN.[a]

"WE'LL SEE ABOUT IT."

"WE'LL see about it!" From that simple sentence has arisen more evil to Ireland than any person, ignorant of the strange union of impetuosity and procrastination my countrymen exhibit, could well believe. They are sufficiently prompt and energetic where their feelings are concerned, but in matters of business, they almost invariably prefer *seeing about,* to DOING.

I shall not find it difficult to illustrate this observation: – from the many examples of its truth, in high and in low life, I select Philip Garraty.

Philip, and Philip's wife, and Philip's children, and all the house of Garraty, are employed from morning till night in *seeing about* everything, and, consequently, in *doing* nothing. There is Philip – a tall, handsome, good-humoured fellow, of about five-and-thirty, with broad, lazy-looking shoulders, and a smile perpetually lurking about his mouth, or in his bright hazel eyes, the picture of indolence and kindly feeling. There he is, leaning over what was once a five-barred gate, and leads to the hag-yard;[143] his blue worsted[144] stockings full of holes, which "the suggan,"[145] twisted half-way up the well-formed leg, fails to conceal; while his brogues (to use his own words), if they do let the water in, let it out again. With what unstudied elegance does he roll that knotted twine, and then unrol it; varying his occupation by kicking the stones that once formed a wall, into the stagnant pool, scarcely big enough for full-grown ducks to sail in.

But let us take a survey of the premises.

The dwelling house is a long rambling abode, much larger than the generality of those that fall to the lot of small Irish farmers; for Philip rents a respectable farm, and ought to be "well to do in the world." The dwelling looks very comfortless, notwithstanding: part of the thatch is much decayed, and the rank weeds and damp moss nearly cover it; the door-posts are only united to the wall by a few scattered portions of clay and stone, and the door itself is hanging but by one hinge; the window-frames shake in the passing wind, and some of the compartments are stuffed with the crown of a hat, or a "lock of straw;"[146] very unsightly objects. At the opposite side of the swamp is the hag-yard gate, where a broken line of alternate palings and wall betokens that it had been formerly fenced in; the commodious barn is almost roofless, and the other sheds pretty much in the same condition; the pig-sty is deserted by the grubbing lady and her grunting progeny, who are too fond of an occasional repast in the once-cultivated garden to remain in their proper abode; the listless turkeys, and contented, half-fatted geese, live at large and on the public; but the turkeys, with all their shyness and modesty, have the best of it, for they mount the ill-built stacks, and select the grain *à plaisir.*

"Give you good morrow, Mr. Philip; we have had showery weather lately."

"Och! all manner o' joy to ye my lady! – and sure ye'll walk in, and sit down; my woman will be proud to see ye. I'm sartin we'll have the rain soon agin, for it's everywhere, like bad luck; and my throat's sore with hurishing thim pigs out o' the garden – sorra a thing can I do all day for watching thim."

"Why do you not mend the door of the sty?"

"True for ye, ma'am dear; so I would if I had the nails; and I've been threat'ning to step down to Mickey Bow, the smith, to ask him to *see about it.*"

"I hear you've had a fine crop of wheat, Philip."

"Thank God for all things! You may say that; we had, my lady, a fine crop; but I have always the height of ill luck somehow; upon my sowkins[147] (and that's the hardest oath I ever swear), the turkeys have had the most of it: but I mean to *see about* setting it up safe, to-morrow."

"But, Philip, I thought you had sold the wheat, standing."

"It was all as one as sould; only it's a bad world, ma'am dear, and I've no luck. Says the steward to me, says he, I like to do things like a man of business; so, Mister Garraty, just draw up a bit of an agreement that you deliver over the wheat field to me, on sich a day, standing as it is, for sich a sum; and I'll sign it for ye, and thin there can be no mistake – only let me have it by this day week. Well, to be sure, I came home full o' my good luck, and I tould the wife; and, on the strength of it, she must have a new gown. And sure, says she, Miss Hennessv is just come from Dublin, wid a shop-full of goods; and, on account that she's my brother's sister-in-law's first cousin, she'll let me have the first sight o' the things, and I can take my pick, and we'll have plinty of time to *see about* the agreement to-morrow. Well, I don't know how it was, but the next day we had no paper, nor ink, nor pens in the house; I meant to send the gossoon to Miss Hennessy's for all – but forgot the pens. So, when I was *seeing about* the 'greement, I bethought of the ould gander; and while I was pulling as beautiful a pen as ever ye laid yer two eyes upon, out of his wing, he tattered my hand with his bill in such a manner that sorra a pen I could hould for three days. Well, at last I wrote it out like print, and takes it myself to the steward. – Good evening to you, Mr. Garraty, says he. Good evening kindly, sir, says I; I've got the 'greement here, sir, says I, pulling it out, as I thought – but I only cotcht the paper it was wrapt in, to keep it from the dirt of the tobacco, that was loose in my pocket for want of a box; so I turned out what little bits o' things I had in it, and there was a grate hole that ye might drive all the parish rats through, at the bottom, which the wife promised to *see about* mending, as good as six months before. Well, I saw the sneer on his ugly mouth (for he's an Englishman), and I turned it off with a laugh, and said air holes were comfortable in hot weather, and sich-like jokes, and that I'd go home and make another 'greement. 'Greement! for what? – says he, laying down his grate outlandish pipe. Whew! may-be ye don't know, says I. Not I, says he. The wheat-field, says I. Why, says he, didn't I tell you then, that you must bring the 'greement to me by that day week? – and that was (by the same token pulling a red memorandum book out of his pocket), let me see – exactly this day three weeks. Do you think Mr. Garraty, he goes on, that I was going to wait upon you? I don't lose my papers in the Irish fashion. Well, that last set me up – and I had the ill luck to knock him down; and, the coward, what does he do but takes the law o' me – and I was cast, and lost the sale of the wheat, and was ordered to pay ever so much money: well, I didn't care to pay it then, but gave an engagement; and I meant to *see about it* – but forgot; and, all in a jiffy, came a thing they call an execution – and, to stop the cant,[a][148] I was forced to borrow money from that tame negur, the exciseman – and it's a terrible case to be paying *interest* for it *still*."

"But, Philip, you might give up or dispose of part of your farm. I know you could get a good sum of money for that rich meadow by the river."

"True for ye, ma'am dear, and I've been *seeing about it* for a long time, but somehow *I have no luck*. Just as ye came up, I was thinking to myself that the gale-day is passed, and all one as before; yarra a pin's worth have I for the rint; and the landlord wants it as bad as I do, though it's a shame to say that of a gintleman; for, jist as he was *seeing about* some old custodium, or something of the sort, that had been hanging over the estate ever since he came to it, the sheriff's officers put *executioners* in the house; and I am sartin he'll be racking me for the money; indeed, the ould huntsman tould me as much: but I must *see about it,* not indeed that it's much good, for I've no luck."

"Let me beg of you, Philip, not to take such an idea into your head; do not lose a moment; you will be utterly ruined if you do. Why not apply to your father-in-law? – he is able to assist you; for at present you only suffer from temporary embarrassment."

"True for ye, my lady; and, by the blessing of God, I'll *see about it*."

"Then go directly, Philip."

"Directly! I can't, ma'am dear, on account of the pigs; and sorra a one I have but myself to keep them out of the cabbages; for I let the woman and the grawls go to the pattern at Killaun; it's little pleasure they see, the craturs!"

"But your wife did not hear the huntsman's story?"

"Och! ay, did she; but unless she could give me a sheaf o' bank notes, where would be the good of her staying? – but I'll *see about it*."

"Immediately, then, Philip; think of the ruin that may come – nay, that must come, if you neglect this matter: your wife, too – your family reduced from comfort to starvation – your home desolate – "

"Asy, my lady! – don't be after breaking my heart intirely; thank God, I have seven as fine flahulagh[149] children as ever peeled pratee, and all under twelve years ould; and sure I'd lay down my life tin times over for every one o' them: and to-morrow for sartin – no – to-morrow – the hurling; I can't to-morrow; but the day after, if I'm a living man, *I'll see about it.*"

Poor Philip! his kindly feelings were valueless, because of his unfortunate habit. Would that this were the only example I could produce of the ill effects of that dangerous little sentence – *"I'll see about it!"* Oh, that the sons and daughters of the fairest island that ever heaved its green bosom above the surface of the ocean, would arise and *be doing* what is to be done, and never again rest contented with "SEEING ABOUT IT!"

THE LAST OF THE LINE.

IT was on a tranquil evening, in the sweet summer month of June, that a lady of no ordinary appearance sat at an open casement of many-coloured glass, and overlooked a wild, but singularly beautiful, country. From the window, a flight of steep stone steps led to a narrow terrace, that, in former times, had been carefully guarded by high parapets of rudely-carved granite; but they had fallen to decay, and lay in mouldering heaps on the shrubby bank, which ran almost perpendicularly to a rapid stream that danced like a sunny spirit through the green meadows, dotted and animated with sheep and their sportive lambs. In the distance, rude and rugged mountains towered in native dignity, "high in air,"[150] their grim and sterile appearance forming an extraordinary, but not unpleasing, contrast to the pure and happy-looking valley at their base, where, however, a few dingy peasant-cottages lay thinly scattered, injuring, rather than enlivening, a scene that nature had done much to adorn, and man nothing to preserve. Half way up the nearest mountain, a little chapel, dedicated to "our Lady of Grace,"[151] hung, like a wren's nest, on what seemed a point of rock; but even its rustic cross was invisible from the antique casement. Often and anxiously did the lady watch the distant figures who trod the hill-side towards the holy place, to perform some act of penance or devotion.

It was impossible to look at that interesting woman without affection; one might have almost thought her destined –

"To come like truth, and disappear like dreams."[152]

Though she was young, there was much of the dignity of silent sorrow in her aspect; and it was difficult to converse with her, without feeling her influence, – not to overpower, but to soften. Her form was slight, but rounded to the most perfect symmetry, and an extraordinary quantity of hair, black as the raven's wing, was braided, somewhat after the fashion of other lands, over a high and well-formed brow; although, such was the style of the time, she wore no head-dress, except what nature had bestowed; a golden rosary, and cross of the same metal, gemmed with many precious jewels, hung over a harp-stand of antique workmanship; a few of the strings of the harp were broken, and a pile of richly-bound music gave no token of being often disturbed. Silken Ottomans, gilded vases, fresh gathered flowers, and a long embroidered sofa, filled up, almost to crowding, the small apartment. In a little recess, opposite the window, a child's couch was fitted with much taste and care; the hangings were of blue damask, curiously inwrought with silver, such as the nuns in France and Flanders[153] delight to emboss: there was also a loose coverlet of the same material, and a tasseled oblong cushion at either end. I have said that the lady was seated at the casement; sometimes she pressed her small white fingers to her brow, and then passed them over its rounded surface, as if to dispel, by that simple movement, thoughts, "the unbidden guests of anxious hours;"[154] – but still it was only for a moment her gaze was turned from her best treasure, her only child; her eye followed it as, in its nurse's arms, it enjoyed the evening breeze that played amid its light and clustering hair; the baby had blue eyes and a fair skin; and if it sometimes, in the infantine seriousness that passed as airy shadows over a smiling landscape, resembled its mother, now, as it laughed and shouted, in broken accents, "Mamma! mamma!" she thought how like its father it spoke and looked. Clavis Abbey – as the strange mixture of ancient and modern building, inhabited by the household of Sir John Clavis, was called – was wisely situated. The monks of old always chose happily for their monasteries; the sites of their ruined aisles tell of the good taste, as well as good sense, of their projectors. Hill, wood, and water, were ever in their neighbourhood, and the red deer and salmon were always near, to contribute to their repast.

But the fair possessions had, nearly two centuries before our tale commences, passed from the hands of holy Mother Church. The marvellous tale of its exchange of masters is still often repeated, and always credited; it is said and believed that the stream, which runs through the valley I have described, is, every midsummer-night, of a deep red hue, in mysterious commemoration of the massacre of the priests of that abbey, which took place as late as the Elizabethan reign. Certain it is that the projector of such indiscriminate slaughter never reaped the rich harvest he anticipated; for, unable from severe illness to visit the court of the maiden queen, he despatched his son's tutor on the mission, with communications of the services he had rendered to the state, and a petition for a grant of the lands he had rescued from "popery." The tutor, however, made himself so agreeable to the royal lady, that she either was, or affected to be, severely angered by the unnecessary effusion of blood; and, so far from approving, testified her displeasure, and bestowed the fair lands of the murdered monks upon Oliver Clavis, the false, but handsome, accessary of the priest-slayer. But no family could take possession of consecrated ground in Ireland, without falling under the ban of both church and people; and, notwithstanding the bland and liberal conduct of the new owner of the estate, then called Clavis Abbey, Oliver lived and died unpopular. Tradition says that none of the heirs male of the family ever departed peaceably in their beds, and much learned and unlearned lore is still extant upon the subject.

Somewhat about the year 1782, Sir John Clavis entered upon his title and property, in consequence of the sudden demise of his father, Sir Henry, who was drowned on a moonshiny night, when the air and the sea were calm, and he was returning from an excursion to one of those fairy islands that at once beautify and render dangerous the Irish coast. The people who accompanied him, on that last day of his existence, say that he had been in unusual health and spirits during the morning, and had fished, and sung, and drank as usual – that as the night advanced he became reserved and gloomy, and, as they neared the coast, insisted on taking the helm – that suddenly yielding the guidance of his little vessel, he sprang overboard – that immediately the crew crowded to save him, but a black cloud descended on the waters, and hid his form from their eyes, and it was not until the boat[a] had driven an entire mile (as well as they could calculate) from the spot, they were enabled to behold the sea and the sky. Some laughed, some surmised, but many credited the tale: for superstition had hardly, at that period, resigned any of her strong holds; and the peasantry, to this day, believe that Sir Henry Clavis acted under the influence of a spirit-guide, that had lured him to sudden death, conformably with the old prophecy –

> "The party shall fail by Clavis led,
> And none of the name shall die in their bed."

Sir John had just completed his college course when he was called upon to support the honours of his house and name. At Trinity[155] he was considered more as an amiable gentlemanly young man, than an *esprit fort,*[156] or one likely to lead in public life. At that period the college lads were a very different set of youths from what they are at present. The rude but generous hospitality, the thoughtless daring, the angry politics, the feudal feeling, that characterized the gentry of the time, were not likely to send forth subjects submissive to college rule; and the citizens of Dublin were too often insulted and aggrieved by the insolent aristocratic airs of unfledged boys, ripe for mischief, who, half in earnest, half in jest, sported with their comforts, and often with their lives. Party feeling, also, ran (as unhappily *there* it always does) to a dreadful height; and the young baronet, whose father had invariably drank "The Glorious Memory,"[157] and "Protestant Ascendancy," every day after dinner, was frequently called upon to defend or support his party, although he invariably declared that as yet he was of none – that he must wait to make up his mind, &c. &c. It must be confessed that this extraordinary irresolution, at such a period, was more the effect of constitutional apathy than of reflection; he had a good deal of the consciousness of birth and wealth about him, but he disliked either mental or bodily exertion. As an only child, he had suffered nothing like contradiction: and had he horsewhipped and abused his servants (when at the age of twelve, he sported two of his own racers at the Curragh of Kildare), instead of speaking to them as fellow-creatures in a mild and kindly voice, it would have elicited no rebuke from his father, who secretly regretted that the youth was neither likely to become a five-bottle man, a staunch Orangeman,[158] nor a Member of Parliament – the only three things he considered worth living for.

The young baronet never could have resolved upon visiting the Continent – an exploit he had long talked of – but that an anticipated general election frightened him away, as he would certainly, if at home, have been expected to offer himself as a candidate, and make speeches. He hated trouble, and of the two exertions chose the least – committed his affairs, for twelve calendar months to the management of Denny Dacey, his nurse's son, who had acted satisfactorily, as steward, since the second childhood of the old and respected man who had for sixty years filled the situation; and left the Abbey, attended by only two servants and one travelling carriage. This was a matter of surprise and conversation to many, more particularly as Sir Henry and his neighbour, Mr. Dorncliff, a Cromwellian settler, had arranged that their children should be united, when of sufficient age. Miss Dorncliff was handsome, and an heiress, and, it was said, in no degree averse to the union; they had been companions in childhood, but the lady, it would appear, was of too unromantic a disposition to remove the young baronet's indifference. As his carriage rolled passed the avenue that led to her dwelling, he merely leaned forward, and cast a fleeting glance towards the house. Where he met, and to what precise circumstance he owed the possession of so lovely a wife as the lady I have endeavoured to describe, is still a mystery; his business-letters conveyed no intelligence of his marriage; nor was it until the arrival of gay furniture, from a fashionable Dublin upholsterer, that the idea of such an event occurred to the inhabitants of Clavis.

When the baronet returned, and announced, as his lady, her who leaned upon his arm; when the domestics received her with that warm-hearted and affectionate respect for which Irish servants are so justly celebrated; and when the rumour went abroad that Sir John Clavis had married a Spanish lady, a Catholic, and "one who had little more English than a Kerry-man," great was the consternation, and many and various the conjectures. "What will become of the 'Protestant Ascendancy,' and the 'Glorious and Immortal Memory,' now that a popish mistress is come to Clavis?" said one party. "Some chance of luck and grace turning to the ould Abbey, now that the right sort's in it," observed the other. Not a few affirmed that the lady had absconded from a convent; others asserted that she was picked off, with a few other survivors, from a wrecked vessel in the Mediterranean; those who had not seen her whispered that she was no better than she should be; but Miss Dorncliff – who, at first, perhaps, to show she was heart-whole, and afterwards from real regard, was often Lady Clavis's guest – generously declared that she was the most charming woman she had ever met, that she was highly accomplished, and, although a Catholic and a Spaniard, anything but a bigot.

Her want of knowledge of the language, when she arrived, prevented her joining in conversation either with those who visited her, or those at whose houses she was received. Perfectly unconscious of the rules and etiquette of society in our colder regions, she was sure to commit some grievous fault in the arrangement of her guests, which invariably threw her husband into an ill temper, that, after the honeymoon was over, he seldom thought it necessary to conceal. Sir John had shaken off a good deal of his *ennui* by journeying; and when be came home he no longer stood on neutral ground, but suffered the excitement of politics to take the place of that which is the accompaniment of travelling. He had now discovered that, for the honour of the house, it was necessary he should adopt his father's side of the question; and accordingly the gardener was ordered to fill the flower-beds with orange lilies, and the hangings of the spare rooms were garnished with orange bindings. Unfortunately, the members of an Orange Lodge were invited to dine at the Abbey, and Lady Clavis positively refused to wear their colour, in any way, *because* she considered it as the symbol of persecution to the Catholic religion, of which she was a devout and faithful member. When her husband, after much contention, gave up the point, she ordered a green velvet dress for the occasion, embroidered with golden shamrocks; she did this with a view to gratify him, never imagining that the colour which emblems the beauty and fertility of Ireland, *could* be obnoxious to any body of Irishmen. What, then, was her astonishment, when he, whom she had been so anxious to please, expressed a most angry opinion of her costume – which occasioned a flood of tears from one party, and from the other, an over hastily expressed desire that, as she could never understand the customs of the country, she would give up trying to do so. Matrimonial disputes are dreadfully uninteresting in the recital, – not entertaining as are lovers' quarrels, simply because there is no danger of a heart-breaking separation arising from them; it is only the two engaged in those unhappy differences that can understand their bitterness; the world has, for them, but little sympathy. Enough, then be it, that the innocent green velvet was the commencement of much real disagreement: the lady insisting that she had the dress made as a compliment to his party: the gentleman protesting that it could not be so, as green was always opposed to orange. This he repeated over and over again, without troubling himself to inquire whether his wife understood him or not. Many an unpleasantness grew out of this trifle, that continued silently, like the single drop of rain, to wear the rock of domestic happiness. Sir John persevered in drinking deeply of the bitter cup of politics, that universal destroyer of society and kindly feeling. He soon discovered, or imagined he had discovered, how perfectly a continental education unfits the most amiable woman in the world for the society and habits of our islands; and the very efforts Lady Clavis made to appear cheerful, were silent reproaches to him for not endeavouring to make her so; they had, however, still one feeling in common – affection for their child.

While the mistress of Clavis Abbey was engaged in watching every movement of her beloved daughter, as the nurse paced slowly beneath her turret-window, the baronet was sitting *tête-à-tête* with no other than Denny Dacey, who, from being what in England is termed bailiff to the estate, had risen to the rank of agent, under the title, as his correspondents set forth, of "Dionysius Dacey, Esq." &c. &c. How this person ever acquired the influence he possessed over his patron, must now remain a mystery: it is to be supposed that he insinuated himself into his good graces, as a weasel does into a rabbit-burrow, by various twists and windings, of which nobler animals are incapable. It was no secret in the county that, although Sir John's political apathy no longer existed, he had not acquired the active habits that are so especially necessary where a gentleman's affairs are embarrassed, and where nothing but good sense and steady economy, can retrieve them. During the young baronet's residence abroad, Dacey had exceedingly prospered; and though one or two shrewd landholders suspected he used means, not consistent with his employer's interests, to obtain both influence and wealth, there was so much plausibility about the man, that the most watchful could bring nothing home to him; his bearing was blunt and open; he affected honesty, but his look belied the utterance of his tongue, for his eye lacked the expression of truth, and, instead of looking forth straightly from beneath its pent-house lid, was everlastingly twisting into corners – with cat-like quickness, watching a fitting opportunity, when those with whom he conversed were busied about other matters, to scan and observe their countenances. It has been to me an entertaining, though often an unpleasing, study, to attend to the varied expressions conveyed by the mere action of the eye, almost without reference to the other features; and I would avoid, as I would a poisoned adder, the person whose eye quivers or looks down.

The two *friends* (such is the usual term given to those who eat meat at the same board) were seated at either end of a somewhat long table, on which were piled papers of various dates and dimensions: a huge bowl of punch had been nearly emptied of its contents, and the baronet did not appear particularly fit for business. He leaned listlessly on the table, as if in reverie, and it was only Dacey's voice that roused him from his reflections.

"But, my dear Sir John," he commenced, with his peculiar drawl, while his eye was fixed on the punch-ladle: "My dear Sir John, 'pon my sowl it weighs upon my conscience, so it does, to be managing here, and you to the fore, with such a fine head and so much cleverness (a sly glance to see how the flattery took); 'tis a shame you don't turn to it yourself, for by-'n-by you'll, may-be, find things worse nor you think 'em, as I have told you before, God knows – "

"And will my looking over these cursed papers make things better? It is positively enough to set me mad – just at a time too, when our grand county meeting is coming on, and the general election, and so much exertion expected from me; and the house will be full of English company from the castle,[159] and Lady C. has not an idea how English people should be entertained."

"But sure Miss Dorncliff is coming to stop with my lady while they stay."

"Very true; she is a capital, good-natured girl, 'faith, and much better looking than she was eight years ago, when I left Ireland. Oh dear! I wonder young men of fortune marry, Dacey!"

"Sir John, it is very necessary."

"Well, well, I suppose it is, but say no more about it; there are enough of disagreeable subjects on the table already." The baronet looked upon the pile of papers, and the agent glanced keenly up, but his eye was quickly withdrawn.

"My lady was in a convent, I believe, Sir John?"

"Ay; it was a fine exploit to get her out of it. Well, poor thing, she trusted to my honour, and was not deceived."

"Of course you were married by a priest?" (This was said cautiously.)

"To be sure we were, and by a jovial fellow too; he went with me to the convent-wall, and performed the ceremony at the foot of a beautiful old cross, by the way side, as the moon was sailing over our heads, and the orange trees were showering perfume around us. Poor Madelina!" he continued, almost involuntarily, "I found the withered orange-blossoms, which that night I bound upon her maiden brow, encased in a casket, with the hair of our child, only this morning."

"You had the ceremony repeated on your arrival in England?" inquired Dacey.

Sir John Clavis fixed his eyes upon the reptile, and, in a sterner tone of voice than was his wont, in his turn became the querist.

"Why do you ask?"

"For no reason, only that if you had a son it would be well to see that the marriage was firm and legal."

"Thank you," replied the baronet, drily, "there is not much chance of that being the case; and if there was – "

A long pause followed the last sentence, which neither seemed inclined to disturb. Dacey gathered the papers towards him, and, pulling his spectacles from his forehead to his nose, occupied himself in sorting and placing them in separate piles; every five or ten minutes a heavy sigh escaped from his lips, the last of which was so audible, that Sir John exclaimed, "What the devil, man alive, do you growl for in that manner? – one would think that you expected the ghost of your uncle, the priest, to start forth from the papers, and upbraid you with your apostacy!"

"Sorra a *ghost* at all, then, Sir John, among the papers; only the *reality* of botherin' debts, custodiums, thrown-up leases on account of the rackrent, and the Lord knows what!"

"And whose fault is it?" replied the gentleman, angrily; "*did I not leave it all to your management?* The property *was* a good property, and why should it not continue so? I'm sure I can't think how the money goes; to do Lady C. justice, she spends nothing."

"There's the hounds, the hunters, and five grooms, of one sort or other, Sir John; to say nothing of town houses, and carriages, and – "

"My father always had the same establishment," interrupted Sir John, "and never kept an agent to overlook matters either."

"More's the pity!" ejaculated the manager (the exclamation might have been taken in two ways).

"There's no manner of use in my keeping *you,* if I am to be pestered with these eternal accounts – accounts – accounts – morning, noon, and night. The simple fact is," continued Sir John, rising from his seat, "the simple fact is, money I want, and money I must have. After flying to the Continent to avoid an election, I find that now, at this particular crisis, I cannot help running into the very strait I endeavoured to steer clear of. My friends say it is necessary, and would even subscribe (if I permitted) to return me free of expense; that I will never do – so money, Dacey, money I *must* have, that's certain."

"It's easy say money," retorted the agent; "will you sell, Sir John?"

"What?" interrogated the baronet.

"There's the Corner estate, that long strip, close by Ballyraggan; your cousin Corney of the hill has long had an eye to it, and would lay down something handsome."

"You poor, pitiful scoundrel!" exclaimed Sir John, "do you think it's come to *that,* for me to sell *land,* like a huckster! – and to Corney too, a fellow that gathers inches off every estate, as a magpie picks fi'pennies! – a fellow who, basely born, and basely bred, has, nevertheless, managed to accumulate wealth like a pawnbroker, on the miseries of others! I know he has had an eye on that property these eight years, but look – sooner than *he* should have it, I'll beg my bread – I'll sell the estate to a stranger to prevent the possibility of his ever possessing an acre of the land."

"Please yerself, sir," replied the manager, sweeping some of the papers into a wide-mouthed canvass sack which he drew from under his chair. "Here's Mr. Damask's, the upholsterer's, letter – swears, if he's not paid, he'll clap on an execution like lightning; it's as good as 2,500*l.* now, with costs."

"Fire and fury!" exclaimed the baronet, who, his apathy once shaken off, became terrible in his violence; "do you want to drive me mad?"

"Then I'll say nothing of Mr. Barry Mahon's little letter," continued the man of business, quietly, "who writes, that as you've decided on *standing,* in opposition to him, he'll trouble you for the money he lent you as good as four years ago, to complete some purchase or another; it ends very civilly though, by saying that it's only the knowledge that a gentleman like you will be a formidable adversary, which obliges him to strain every nerve to make his own step firm."

"A blight upon him and his civility!"

"Then here is – ." Mr. Dacey was prevented from finishing his sentence, by Sir John's striking the table so violently with his clenched hand, that the very punch-bowl trembled, and the agent ejaculated, "Lord, save us!"

"Look here!" said the baronet, "you have, *I know* – means, somehow or other, of raising money when you like; find me the sum of ten thousand pounds by this day week, and that very estate, so coveted by my cousin Corney, shall be yours for ever, at a peppercorn rent, provided the matter be kept secret; mind, *provided it be kept secret,* and you bind yourself never to let a twig of it into Corney's possession."

"It's easy to keep secret a thing that never happens," observed Dacey, rolling the cord of the bag between his finger and thumb; "is it me get money when I like? – and I obliged to go at credit even for these brogues on my feet!" – and he put forth a topped boot, well-polished and shining, as he spoke.

"The Corner estate, as it is called," repeated Sir John.

"At a peppercorn rent," pondered Dacey; "if a body could any way make up the money, I'd do a dale to oblige you, sir; and, though I've neither cross nor coin to bless myself with, to be sure I know them that has, who, may-he, for a valuable consideration, might – though I don't know – the little estate – eh! – ten thousand – it's badly worth that, Sir John, unless, indeed, you'd throw the fourteen acres of pasture by the loch into it."

"Well!" exclaimed the indolent baronet, though perfectly conscious that the land was worth double the sum; "we'll talk about that, provided you insure me the money; and now gather your parchments, and vanish; I've had enough of arithmetic to last me for some months – and, Dacey!"

"Yes, sir."

"*After* the election, I will really look into matters myself; but, at present, when the good of my country is at stake – when we are threatened with invasion from without, and rebellion from within – the man must be basely selfish who thinks of self. – Oh, Dacey! did you see the Madeira safely into the cellar?"

"Yes, Sir John."

"Good night, Dacey! – there – good night – you won't forget – ten thousand – hard gold – none of your flimsy paper – the Corner estate."

"And the pasture."

"There, good night," repeated the baronet, as the wily agent bowed himself out of the apartment. Sir John Clavis rose from his seat, and threw open the window which was directly under the turret that formed the boudoir of his Spanish wife; indeed, it was the sound of her guitar that had drawn him to it; and he recognised a favourite seguidilla,[160] to which he had written words; he remembered having taught her to repeat them; and the full rich voice that had given them so much beauty – if in that twilight hour it sounded less melodious – had never fallen upon his ear so full of tenderness; its simple burthen –

"Sweet olive-groves of Spain,"[161]

brought the remembrance of what Madelina was to him, in the days when he playfully chid the mispronunciation of his poetry; and as the prospect of receiving the ten thousand, and not being plagued about money matters, had somewhat softened his temper (the idea that he was diminishing his property had no share whatever in his thoughts – possessing, as he did, the dangerous – nay, fatal, faculty of looking *only* on to-day), he thought, I say, of his wife, with more complacency than he had done since the affair of the green velvet. He was pleased when he heard Miss Dorncliff (of whose arrival he was unconscious) urge her to repeat the strain. She commenced, but at a line which he well remembered –

"I know no blessing but thy smile."[162]

Her voice faltered, and the next moment he heard her friend chiding away her tears; his first impulse was to proceed to her apartment, and inquire their cause; but then he hated scenes; and vanity or curiosity, or both, prompted him to remain; and the broken dialogue which followed, happily for the repose of his soul, roused, in his wife's cause, the best feelings of his heart. Many were the affectionate expressions lavished by Miss Dorncliff on her friend, and many the entreaties that she would cease to agitate herself upon what, she insisted, was a surmise without foundation.

"You would not say so," replied Madelina, "if you had seen his attentions, his tenderness, on the Continent – or heard his repeated promises that my religion should be held sacred; the little silver shrine, that my sainted mother so often knelt to, I have been obliged to remove, even from this chamber, which it is mockery to call my own; and though I cannot understand all he says – and though his eye is bright, and his lip smiles, sometimes, yet he never looks upon me as he used; *to me his countenance is sadly changed.*"

"I'll tell you what, my dear," replied her friend, taking advantage of a pause in her complaint, "adopt the course I should have taken, if my good father's scheme had, unfortunately for me, been carried into effect. Assert your own dignity; if he looks as cold as snow, do you look as cold as ice – if he stamps, do you storm

– if he orders, do you counter-order – if he says, 'I will,' do you say, 'you shan't.' My life on it! – such conduct for one week would bring him sighing to your feet. Here you sit, with your baby, which if he had the common feelings of a man, he would worship you for presenting to him – "

"Stop, my dear Margaret," said Lady Clavis; "do him not injustice; he loves his child as fondly us father ever loved a child; he has not changed to it – "

"*Yet,*" interrupted, in her turn, the indignant Margaret, "he has not changed *yet,* but who can tell how soon he may? The man who would change to *you* must be base indeed."

"He is not base," replied the wife, in a sweet, low tone, which penetrated into the inmost recesses of Sir John's heart, "not base, only weak; he is surrounded by a parcel of flatterers, many of whom hate me because of my religion, and others for reasons which I cannot define; but look, Margaret, were he to treat me as a dog, were he to spurn me from him, and trample me to dust, even that dust would rise to heaven's own gate to ask for blessings on his head."

"She is an angel after all!" thought Sir John.

"You are a fool, my dear!" both thought and exclaimed Miss Dorncliff; "and I only wish I were big enough to throw him over the terrace of this old musty place, and I would soon choose you a husband worthy of your love."

"Upon my word, I am much obliged to you, Miss Minx!" murmured the baronet, as he cautiously closed the window, resolving to turn over a new leaf, and station himself, for the remainder of the evening, in his wife's dressing-room. He could not avoid thinking, as he passed through the winding corridors and up the stair-cases, "a very pretty wife I should have had, if it had been as my worthy agent seems to think it might be even now. The fellow means well, but he is mistaken; I should not have been able to call my life my own – the termagant! Thank goodness, I escaped her! I never valued my blessing before!"

He met his child in the lobby, and took the laughing cherub from the nurse's to his own arms. As he prepared to enter, "You may go down, Mary," he said, seeing the maid waiting to receive the child. "I will take Miss Madeline in myself."

How easily can a man make the woman who truly loves him, happy! It was enough for lady Clavis that her husband was at her side – enough that he smiled upon her – enough that he called her "darling:" although it would have been better for them both, had she possessed the strength of mind to entitle her to the name of "friend," the most sacred, yet the most abused, of all endearing terms. Miss Dorncliff exulted in her happiness, though her more cool and deliberate temperament led her to believe that Sir John's "love-fit," as she termed it in her own mind, would not be of long duration. She little knew the service she had rendered Lady Clavis by her somewhat intemperate advice; nor the dread of the baronet lest any portion of that advice should be followed by his gentle wife.

As Mary Conway, Madelina's nurse, descended to the vestibule, she heard a voice, whose sound was familiar to her ear, repeat her name two or three times, and in various tones; she lingered for a moment, and then, as if gladly remembering that her infant charge was committed to its parent's care, turned into an abrupt passage, leading from the great hall to one of the archways, where dews and damps mouldered from day to day upon the massive walls.

"What are ye afther wantin' now, Mister Benjy?" she inquired, as the outline of her lover's (for there is no use in concealing the fact) figure became visible to her laughing eyes.

"Nothing particular, that is to say very particular," replied the youth, who was no other than Dacey's nephew; "only I'm going a journey to night, and I thought I'd be all the betther for your God speed, or, may-be, a bit of prayer to the saints you think so much of."

"A journey – where to?" inquired Mary, with a palpitating heart.

"Why, thin, just to Dublin, Mary, honey. And it's glad enough I'd be to get out of this murderin' grand ould place only just for one single thing."

"And might a body know what that is?" again inquired the maiden.

"Honour bright, Mary, because I shan't see yer sweet smilin' face for many a long day, may-be; for uncle says he's a dale o' business to transact in Dublin, and that he'll be wanting me to look afther it; indeed, I'm thinkin' that he has a notion we're keeping company, and don't over like it; though, Mary, darlin', it's more nor he can do to put between us."

Mary covered her face with her hand, and, though no sigh or sound escaped her lips, tears bedewed her cheeks. She was nothing more nor less than a frank-hearted, good-natured girl, with only three or, perhaps, four definite ideas in her pretty round head – the first of which was decided love for her mistress, and her mistress's child – a great portion of affection for Benjamin Dacey – and no small regard for finery, in all its branches and bearings; she consequently had not a multiplicity of objects to divide her attention, which was therefore steadily devoted to the service of her three or four several propensities. The idea of her lover's being sent away, and to Dublin too, overwhelmed her with grief, to which she would have given more audible vent, but that Benjamin had unwittingly observed, his "uncle didn't over like his keeping company with her," which aroused the maiden's pride; she therefore said, "that, indeed, Mr. Dacey ought to remimber when he once held two or three acres of land under her father," and that, "though she was at the Abbey, she was far from being a *rale sarvant*; she took care of Miss Maddy more from pure love nor anything else. May-be, it was Mister Benjy himself that wanted to be off the promise – if so, she was willing and ready," &c. &c. But, in fact, these lovers' quarrels are the same in all cases; I could give a recipe by which people might quarrel, *agreeably*, ten times a week on an average – only, as love would be the principal ingredient in *my* prescription,

I fear the misunderstandings would be too soon understood for your genuine downright-in-earnest quarrellers. I must not tarry with those young people, during their parting scene, but only recount that "Mary," as she afterwards expressed it, "got a dale out of Benjy, which no one should be the wiser for; only her heart was fairly crushed – thinkin' what a misfortune it was to a boy like him to have such an uncle;" even this she only communicated to her particular friend and companion, Patty Grace.

When the expected company arrived from Dublin, – from "the Castle," as it has been familiarly termed for ages – it was evident that Sir John had nerved his mind to some great undertaking to which he was secretly urged by Dennis Dacey. Indeed, the particular party which had once been led by his father, were anxious he should tread in the same steps, and they again regretted that his union with a Catholic was likely to cool his ardour in "the good cause:"[163] they, however, did their best to urge him forward – and "the glorious and immortal memory" was drank so often after dinner, that those who sacrificed to the sentiment had neither glorious nor inglorious memory left. The humble parish priest never joined in these revels; and when Dacey, in Lady Clavis's presence, hinted at this circumstance, and had, moreover, the audacity to assert that his absence was a tacit acknowledgment of disloyalty, the lady roused herself in defence of her ancient friend, and told the agent that, if religion was a proof of loyalty, he must be the worst of traitors, for he was a renegade from the faith of his fathers, and had changed for the love of filthy lucre. Dacey trembled and turned pale: but as he quitted the apartment he muttered a deep and bitter curse against the lady of Clavis Abbey. Not only had "the little estate" been secretly transferred to Dacey, along with the fourteen acres of pasture, and the ten thousand pounds paid for present relief, but other sums must, at this crisis, be advanced to relieve the necessities of the proprietor, and other lands sacrificed to feed the rapacity of the agent. Mr. Barry Mahon resolved to stand as the people's champion, and already were the addresses of the several candidates duly printed in the county papers. The Abbey became such a scene of interminable bustle and confusion, as the day for the commencement of the election approached, that it would be difficult to convey an idea of the strange persons and objects which crowded on each other. To Mary Conway's great delight, Benjamin unexpectedly returned; and, from the manner in which his uncle received him, it might be supposed that he was not particularly pleased at the circumstance; he, however, carved out for him the task of managing (dare I say bribing?) a few refractory freeholders at some distance; but the young man did not depart until he had whispered some words of moment into his true love's ear. The same evening, when Mary was undressing the little Madeline, Lady Clavis entered the room, happy to escape from a tumult she could hardly understand.

"I'm so glad yer honourable ladyship's come in," said the girl; "I wanted so much to know what you'd have packed up to take into town to-morrow, my lady – as, in coorse, you mean to go with his honour to see the election and all that?"

"Indeed, Mary," replied Lady Clavis, "I have no such intention; I shall be but too glad to escape the bustle of it here – and I should be only in the way, Sir John says."

"Och, my grief! does his honour, the masther, say that? But, no matter, Madam, dear; for the love o' God, as ye value yer own honour, and the honour of this sweet babby, go! – go, for God's sake! – or you'll be sorry for it, – mark my words!"

Lady Clavis was astonished at the girl's vehement manner and gestures, but still she remained firm to her purpose. She was suffering acutely from mental anxiety and bodily exertion; and as Sir John had continued to treat her with great kindness, she was anxious to shew how willingly she would yield to his wishes – even where they were opposed to her own. But Mary was not to be thus satisfied. She "hushowed" her little charge to sleep, and descended to the lobby that led to her master's study. She paused for a few moments at the entrance, and inclined her head so as to catch any sound that might pass along, having ascertained that persons were speaking within. I cannot avoid lamenting that she was led away, by what might be called "natural curiosity," to draw near – very near; so near that her ear covered the key-hole – and listen – systematically listen – to whatever conversation was going on. She might have remained some fifteen minutes, in no very comfortable attitude, when she suddenly started up; but had hardly receded three steps from the door, when it was opened, and the round, vulgar face of Dacey appeared, carefully prying into the darkness. Mary saw she could not escape unnoticed, so, with ready wit, she inquired, "Oh, Misther Dacey, have you seen my lady's Finny? I've been huntin' all the evenin' after the ugly baste, and can get neither tale nor tidings of it? – Finny! – Finny! – Finny!"

"Can ye see in the dark, like the cats, Miss Mary, with yer fine red topknot?" said Dacey, earnestly.

"Troth, ye may ask that," she replied, "for my candle went out."

"And where's the candlestick, Miss Mary?" persisted the keen querist.

"No wonder ye'd inquire, but sorra one have we been able to lay hands on these three weeks, for the shoals o' company, so I just used the same candlestick my father and your father, Misther Dacey, war best acquainted with – my fingers, why! – Finny! – Finny! – Finny!"

She was receding, calling the dog at the same time; when Dacey, whose ire was roused, followed her nearly to the end, and said, "You'd better not turn yer tongue against my family, Miss Impudence, for ye're mighty anxious to get into it, I'm thinkin'."

"Not into your family, Misther Dacey," retorted Mary, proudly. "Anxious, indeed! I don't deny that Benjy and I have been keepin' company, though my true belief is, he's no nevvy[164] of yours. Ye'd think little of *adoptin'* any man's child or property either."

"Hah!" he exclaimed, seizing her arm, and pressing it firmly, "is that the news ye're afther? – ye'd better – " but the girl prevented his finishing his threat by screaming "Murder!" so loudly, that Sir John Clavis rushed out, with a candle in his hand, to inquire into the nature of the disturbance.

Dacey looked extremely foolish, while Mary lifted her apron to her eyes, and, with well-feigned tears, declared, "It's a shame – and I'll tell my lady, so I will, that when I was looking for little Finny, he came out of your honour's study to kiss me, yer honour – a dacent girl like me – I'll tell my lady, so I will. Finny! – Finny! – Finny!" And off she marched triumphantly, leaving Dacey to explain his equivocal situation as he best could.

The night had become dark and stormy, and when Mary put her head from under the archway, before-mentioned, large drops of rain were drifted on her face. She hastily folded her grey mantle round her, and stepping from parapet to parapet of the ancient enclosure, gained a particular elevation that overlooked the entire country. Here she paused for a moment, and then pushed into the brushwood that covered the slope leading to the meadows. Having reached the stream, that partook of the agitation of the evening gale, she seemed puzzled how to make her passage good; but her perplexity was not of long duration, although the stepping-stones were perfectly covered by the swollen waters. She seated herself on the wet grass, took off her shoes and stockings, and, folding her clothes round her, prepared to cross the river. – Having achieved her purpose, after much buffeting with both wind and water, she re-adjusted her dress, and proceeded on her way so intently, and with so much resolution, that I doubt[165] if she would have stayed her course had she even met the bogle that frightened the good Shepherd of Ettrick – [166]

> "Its face was black as Briant coal,
>   Its nose was o' the whunstane;
> Its mou' was like a borel-hole –
>   That puffed out fire and brimstane."[167]

Regardless of banshees, cluricauns,[168] or any of the fairy tribe, Mary pressed earnestly forward till she arrived opposite a small gate that opened into an extensive park; the lock was out of repair, so that she had but to apply her finger underneath, and push the bolt back. She only paused to inhale a long breath, and flew onward across the yielding grass, startling birds and herded deer from their early slumbers: this continued fleetness soon brought her opposite the gate of a noble modern mansion, but she preferred entering through a little postern-door, to ascending the stone steps.

"Where's her honour?" she inquired of an old serving-man, astonished at her untimely visit.

"Lord, Mary! you've frightened the senses out o' me."

"Why, then it's myself is glad to hear it."

"Why so, Mary?"

"Because it's the first time I've heard of yer havin' any in, – but where's the lady?"

"Umph," replied the old servant, evidently annoyed, "find out!" and, turning on his heel, he was leaving the offended damsel alone, when she snatched the candle that maintained a very equivocal equilibrium in his hand, and ran up the back staircase.

"That one has the impudence of the ould boy in her, and makes as free in this house as if it was her own," he observed.

She tapped gently at the door of a small apartment, and a clear-toned voice responded, "Come in." In another moment Mary was in Miss Dorncliff's presence. She advanced, making a courtesy at every second step, until she stood opposite the young lady, who regarded her with much surprise.

"Why, Mary, is your mistress ill – or has anything happened to little Madeline?"

"No, God be thanked! – nothin' – to say nothin' – yet," replied the girl, laying her hand on the back of a chair for support, for she had traversed nearly five Irish miles in less than an hour.

"Sit down, sit down, my good girl," said the lady, kindly; "and, as soon as you can, tell me what has agitated you thus."

"Thank you, my lady – sure ye said that just like herself that's the angel intirely, if ever there was one, God knows! – and God counsel her, and you, my lady; for she won't be said or led by me, and more's the pity!"

"You speak of your mistress, Mary, I suppose," interrupted Miss Dorncliff, "but do come to the point at once, for I am all anxiety."

"I can't make a long story short, Madam, particular when my heart's all in it – but as fast as I can, I'll riddle it all out, for sure my heart's burstin' to tell it." The lady assumed the attitude of a patient listener, and Mary, again drawing a long breath, and pulling first one and then another of her red but taper fingers, commenced the disclosure of her mystery.

"Ye remember, when her ladyship first came over, the bobbery and the work there was about her; and the people – the protestant people (savin' yer favour – all but yerself) saying this, that, and t'other about her, as if she wasn't what she ought to be. Well, to my knowledge and belief, the one who kept this stirrin' was no other than that ould vagabond – that the beams of God's own sun and moon 'ud scorn to rest upon (savin' yer presence, for mentionin' him before ye) – ould Dacey; because ye're sensible[a] he's *a turn-coat* in the first place – and my lady is so steady to her duty, that it was ever and always puttin' him to shame; and then to be sure my lady, seein', I suppose, that in foreign parts the poor are all *negres*, God save us! (may-be black bodies too) my lady was high to him – she has a high way with her, I grant, and sure so has the lilies, though they're so sweet and gentle when you come to know them – well, for *that* he hated her; and I'm sure it's more to get at the way of punishing her, than even securin' the property, that he's been goin' on as he has lately –"

"Securing what property? – going on how?" eagerly demanded Miss Dorncliff.

"Let me tell ye my own way, Miss, agra! or I can't go on: besides, how would ye get at the rights of it, if ye didn't hear it from the beginnin'?"

Miss Dorncliff resumed her patient attitude.

"Ye see ould Dacey knows what he's afther, and Sir John has a way of his own of never seein' to anything – gentleman-like – though I can't but think it a bad fashion; and while he was away, there was a dale of plundering roguery goin' on; and when he came home, sure the agent managed to keep him employed gettin' presentments, and entertainin', an' making speeches about, pathriotism, and all that (I've been tould he's a powerful fine speaker, though I can't say I ever heard him) – and ever divartin' him with sich things, till the right time, when he turned, my dear! as quick as a merryman,[169] and bothered him with debts and accounts. Now the masther, bein' a classical scholar (as I've heard tell), didn't by coorse like the figures, which are only common larnin'; and the ould one played his cards so well, that he made him hate the sight of a bill, or a figure; till at last Sir John said, 'Manage it all yourself,' which he was glad to get the wind of the word to do, though all the time he was purtendin' he wanted the masther to look to it himself – the thief o' the world! As well as I can come at it, Madam (Miss, I ax yer pardon), Sir John agreed to let Dacey have pieces of estates, on the sly, for ready money, at half their valee–agreein' that Dacey should keep it to himself; for the pride, ye see, wouldn't let him own it; and the ould one, 'cute like, got sich another rogue as himself, in Dublin, to go somethin' in it. You're *sinsible*, Miss, my lady? Bein' not a well larned girl, never having got beyant my *read-a-me-daisy*,[170] I can't understand the rights of it, only that these two was cochering[171] together, and procurin' money – for what I know, *unlawful* money – from foreign parts, and gettin' bit by bit of the poor masther's property from him, and tyin' him down, as Benjy said."

"As who said?" interrupted Miss Dorncliff.

"Why Benjy said so," stammered forth the girl, confused at committing her lover's name.

"Then Benjy, as you call him, was your informant as to these pretty villanous plots, I suppose?" interrogated the lady.

"I didn't say *that*, Miss Dorncliff: sure a body may make a remark, as the poor boy did, when they *hear* a thing, without being the one to *tell* it?" retorted the girl, keenly looking into her face; and the lady, wisely, seeing that Mary was now put on the *qui vive*[172] to prevent her lover being suspected as the informer, merely replied, "Go on."

"Ye've put me out ever so many times! but all I've got to say's asy said now; it isn't enough for that ould devil's pippin[173] that he has *custotied*, or some sich thing, the whole land, so as to make the noble gentleman all as one as a genteel beggar, but now that the election is come on, and Sir John goin' to stand for the county and all – what d'ye think, but he's laid a plan to get the poor gentleman into W—, to give the word to some thraythors of vagabonds, and get him arrested and shamed fore'nent[174] the whole county, unless – (oh, the black villain!) – unless – (the sneakin' ditch-hopper!) – unless – (oh, indeed I can't say it, for the chokin' of my throat!) – unless he puts away his darlin' wife – who can be made out not his wife, on account of the religion, as I'm creditably informed; and that, if he doesn't give in to this, he'll expose him in the face of the people, which I know the masther 'ud rather die than stand. Well, Miss, ye see, he's got Sir John to promise intirely that he'll not take my lady with him, because she's delicate like; and he persuaded masther she'd be in the way. And I want her to go – for look," continued Mary, giving full scope to the action and energy of her country, "if she was *with* him, he couldn't desart her, and look in her sweet patient face, and her two darlint eyes, that send the bames of true and pure love right to his soul; he couldn't look at *that*, ma'am dear, and consent to stick a knife in her heart, and send the blessin' of the poor, the light of one's eyes – *the fond craythur that* trusted him, as if she was a thing of shame, abroad into the *could, could,* world! – but – " and here the poor girl's voice sank from the highest tones of hope, to the low and feeble ones of uncertainty – "if she's *not* with him, and that villain at his shoulder – and the disgrace – and lose the election – and all that; and if he agrees – plinty o' money – and the seat – and every thing smooth, and keep him more than half or whole mad, betwixt the fame and the whisky! – it 'ill be all over with my poor lady! – Oh, she little thinks! – this blessed night – she'll lay down her head and die!" Mary hid her face in her hands, and sobbed bitterly.

"My poor friend! – my dear Madelina!" exclaimed Miss Dorncliff, as she hastily passed up and down the apartment; "how worthy of a better fate! – Mary, there is no use of your denying it; Benjy *has* given you this information, and he *must* give it publicly."

"D'ye want ruin on him too?" returned the subdued girl; "sure he's above a trade, and has been brought up like a born gentleman to do nothin'; – and, even if he had a mind, how can he turn agin the ould villain, his uncle, when sorra a penny he'd have in the world, and doesn't know how to make one?"

"Look," said the lady; "if Benjamin will bring forward such proof of trickery as can force conviction on Sir John's mind, *I* will settle upon him a sufficiency for life; and there," she continued, throwing her purse into Mary's lap, "is the earnest of my promise." For a moment, the girl forgot her mistress's interest in her own, as she eyed the glittering treasure; but soon she reverted to what, with true Irish fidelity, was nearest her heart.

"My lady, you'll come to her now, and persuade the masther to take her, and make out something to oblige him to take her. Och! my heart never warmed to ye as much as it does at this minute! – for they said –." She stopped before the conclusion of the sentence.

"What did they say, Mary?" inquired Miss Dorncliff.

"That you, my lady – only I'm loath to repeat a lie – that, may-be, you'd marry the masther, if he'd put away his wife."

Miss Dorncliff's face and forehead crimsoned to the deepest dye at this villanous insinuation. "Me!" she ejaculated, as if to herself, "Me! – the base-born churls! But I will save *her*, come what may. Mary," she continued, after a pause, "Mary, do not say a word of your having been here – mind, not a syllable. You will see me in the morning."

"Before masther goes?" inquired Mary.

"No, but soon – immediately after. Fear not, my good girl, your mistress shall be safely cared for."

"May the holy Mother, whether ye've faith in her or no, preserve ye from harm, and may heaven be yer bed at last!" replied Mary, clasping her hands, and looking most affectionately at Miss Dorncliff; "and a good night, and a fresh blessin' to ye every mornin' that ye see day-light!"

When Miss Dorncliff was again alone, she resolved her plans as she paced along her chamber. For the last three years she had had the sole management and control of her father's affairs, whose age had, in a great degree, swallowed up his mind; and a large property was also at her sole command, which she had already inherited from her uncle. That night she neither slumbered nor slept; repose came not to her body or her spirit; and, from the highest window of the dwelling, she watched until she saw Sir John's equipage, with his troop of noisy retainers, pass the great gate on its way to W—. She then ordered her own carriage, and in a little time was at Clavis Abbey. The first person she inquired for was Mary, and doubtless she derived some information from her, for they were long together. She then proceeded to Lady Clavis's dressing-room, and found her in tears.

"I cannot tell why," she said, "but I feel a sad anticipation of evil hanging over me. It was so strange, John kissed me this morning when he thought I was asleep; and, do you know, he attempted to kneel at Madelina's cradle, but he rushed, like a madman, from the room, despite my efforts to recall him."

"We must follow him, then," observed Miss Dorncliff, assuming an air of gaiety, – "we must follow him; I want most sadly to go to the election – my presence will cheer on my own tenants to his service; and there is no saying but that some of them, were I not on the spot, might dare to think for themselves. Besides, I can only go under the protection of a matron, you know. No interruption – I must be obeyed; we will set off this afternoon, so as to hear his maiden speech from the hustings."

Lady Clavis offered a very weak opposition to what her heart longed to engage in, and they arrived in W— at about half-past ten at night. The little Madelina was left in Mary's care at the Abbey.

There was no difficulty in finding the inn, or, as it was called, hotel, where the Orange member put up; for he had steadily refused going to the house of either of his constituents.

The waiters immediately recognised Lady Clavis, and, with many bows, conducted her into the passage, which was empty at the time, though the sounds of music, singing, and loud debate, were clearly distinguished by the ladies, even before they alighted from their carriage.

"You can shew us to a sitting-room, where we can wait till Sir John is disengaged. We wish to surprise him," said Miss Dorncliff.

"I can't tell him ye're here just now, my lady," replied the man, "for Mr. Dacey said they war not to be disturbed; and there's two gentlemen, I'm thinkin' from Dublin, besides two or three others, waitin' to get speakin' with him. And it's myself don't know where to put yer ladyships, barrin' ye'll go into a purty tidy room jist off where his honour's settlin' a little affair of business with Mr. Dacey. Sure, if I'd known you war comin', it's the great grand committee-place I'd have had readied out for ye."

"Be firm and cautious now, my dear friend, for the hour of trial is come," observed Miss Dorncliff, in French, as she pressed her friend's arm closely to her heart; – "the men from Dublin, and all: we have just arrived in the right time – depend upon it, all will be well."

The waiter stared with stupid astonishment, and said, "May-be ye'd have the goodness, my lady, not to speak out much, as Sir John's at business in the next room, and he mightn't like to be disturbed; it 'ill do to tell him by-'n by, won't it, my lady? But what'll you please to take?"

"Nothing – nothing now," replied Miss Dorncliff; for Lady Clavis appeared incapable of either mental or bodily exertion. Her friend had revealed to her a considerable portion of her plans and anxieties during their brief journey, and her elegant but weak mind, unable to arrive at any conclusion, remained in a state of passive obedience.

Communicating with the next apartment was a small door, which hung very loosely on its hinges; the cracks and chinks were many; and through the principal one Miss Dorncliff saw Sir John sitting at a table, his face buried in his hands; while Dacey, whose head was approached close to his, was talking in a low, eager tone – so low that only broken syllables reached her ear.

At last Sir John removed his hands, and, lifting his eyes slowly, while his pale and sunken features expressed the painful struggles he endured, said, "It must not be, Dacey; do you think I want to ensure damnation to my soul? What possible difference can it make to you, that you thus stipulate for her destruction? Men are seldom so desperately wicked without a motive."

"Hasn't she scorned me, and ordered me out of the room as if I was a neagre?[175] – hasn't she treated me with the contempt which a man never forgives? – hasn't she – but the short and the long of it is, Sir John, that you know my determination: disgrace her, or disgrace yourself! – disclaim your marriage, or go to jail! – to jail, instead of to parliament! – to the jail, where Mr. Mahon can point, as he passes it, at the last of the house of Clavis! There's the pen and the ink; I don't force ye – do as ye please – it's no business of mine." The fellow pushed some parchments and papers towards the unfortunate baronet, and gathered unto himself a pile of rouleaus[176] that were filled with gold, while his eyes gloated and glared on the agonized face of his *patron*! "Sure, there's no harm in life in keeping a foreigner like her," continued the brute; "many has done the same, and will again. Send her back to the 'olive-groves of Spain,'[177] she's so fond of singing about, and –"

"Peace, miscreant!" roared Sir John, in a voice of thunder, quite forgetting the time and place.

"Whisht!" exclaimed the coward, "never call names so loud – you know I'm yer best friend. If these sheriff's officers hear ye, it will be high mass with us all!"

The baronet sank back in a state of stupefaction, and the agent advanced towards him, pen in hand. Almost mechanically Sir John took the little instrument in his fingers – its point touched the paper – even the letter J was traced, when Miss Dorncliff pushed strongly against the door; and, in the same instant, both Sir John and Dacey were trembling in her presence. For some moments, all parties remained silent – gazing at each other with such varied expression as would be difficult to describe. With the politeness with which Nature has endowed every Irishman, from the prince to the peasant, both pushed seats towards the young heiress, which she declined; at last Sir John inquired, as the pen dropped from his fingers, "to what circumstance they were indebted for the honour of her visit?"

"I came, Sir John," she replied – and the first sentence was uttered in a trembling voice, which gained strength as she proceeded, "I came to save the HUSBAND of my friend, Lady Clavis, from destruction!"

Sir John's pride mounted, as he replied stiffly and formally, "that he was not aware to what Miss Dorncliff could allude."

"This, Sir John," she continued, heedless of his interruption, "is a bad time for compliments; you were about to sign a paper repudiating your wife, in order that that *bad* man might relieve your present necessities, and save you from arrest. I cannot now bring forward the proofs that I possess, of his villanies, and the various arts he has used to dupe your understanding, while he ruined your property. I pledge my word to do so; and to redeem all, even the *little Corner estate* from his clutches, if, instead of signing *his* paper, you will sign *mine* – and, to relieve your present embarrassment, I will tell down guinea for guinea of the money you are to receive from that person! Need I say more? – Need I urge the love you have tried? – Need I ask if you will consign your child to shame? – Need I –"

She was interrupted by a loud and piercing shriek from Lady Clavis, as with one strong effort she rushed from the outer room, and threw herself into her husband's arms. He was so unprepared, so astonished, that he did not appear able to support her, and she sank gradually on her knees – her hands clasped – her hair falling in heavy masses over her neck and shoulders – and her eyes shining with unnatural brightness, from amid the bursting tears that flowed incessantly down her cheeks. It is impossible to describe the mingled look of hope and anxiety with which she regarded Sir John. Miss Dorncliff advanced to her side; and, as her tall, commanding figure towered over the bending form of her friend, she laid her hand on the baronet's arm, and, in a low, impressive tone, said, "*Can you look upon and crush her?*" The appeal was decisive. He pressed his wife convulsively to his bosom, and it is no disgrace to his manhood to confess that his tears mingled with hers.

"This is all mighty fine," at length exclaimed Dacey, whose vulgar perplexity was beginning to subside into assurance, "but I don't understand it."

"And who supposed that the wallowing swine comprehended the sweetness of the ringdove's note?" replied Miss Dorncliff, casting upon him a withering look of contempt and scorn.

"I don't deserve that from you, Miss," said the savage, interpreting the expression of her countenance, "for I meant to help you to a husband."

"Sir John Clavis – I call upon you to turn that man out of the room!" replied the lady; "let him and his gold vanish; – and trust for this night to the agency of your wife's friend!"

Bitter and deep were the curses he muttered, while depositing the coin in his leathern wallet; he would have formed no unapt representation of Satan preparing baits for sin – but foiled even in this effort.

"I recommend you, Dacey, to be silent," said the baronet.

"But others won't be so," growled forth the menial, as he retired. He had hardly closed the door, when he remembered the papers and parchments he had left on the table, and returned with a view of securing them. Miss Dorncliff had anticipated the movement, and, placing her hand firmly on the documents, signified so decidedly her intention of not suffering their removal, that, baffled at all points, he finally withdrew. He could hardly have reached the hall, when the officers, who had been waiting outside, made their appearance, in no very gentle manner, to make good their seizure. This, however, Miss Dorncliff prevented, by paying the amount demanded, and the room was soon cleared of such graceless company.

"Now, then," said the generous girl, looking round her with a happy and cheerful countenance, "now, Sir John, *my* document must be signed. I claim *that* as my reward. My own lawyer will settle other matters at some future date, but that *must* be done before I either slumber or sleep – the physician demands her fee."

The baronet seized the pen, which, a short time before, he had taken to perform a very different office, and affixed his name to the paper she presented. After placing it within her bosom, she remained sometime silent, while the vacillating man was endeavouring to explain his conduct to his wife, who, loving much, forgave all.

"It is well," thought Miss Dorncliff, "that such men should be wedded to such gentle women. My affection would always expire with my esteem; but now, she loves and believes, as if he had never been about to ruin her reputation, and to stigmatize for ever their innocent child! There must be something mysterious in this love, which I cannot comprehend." She could, however, comprehend the heights and depths of the noblest friendship. Her sleep that night was light and refreshing; and it was not till the morning was far advanced, that the shouts and bustle of an Irish election woke her to consciousness and activity.

It is not to be supposed that Dacey's bad but enterprising spirit would rest composedly, under detection and consequent exposure. He conjectured, truly, that Miss Dorncliff, through some means, which at present he could only suspect, had obtained information of his intentions, and was prepared to render null and void his basely-earned bargains and nefarious schemes. He was aware that, until the election was over, no investigation could be systematically gone into; and he hit upon a cold and villanous design to prevent the inquiry he had so much reason to dread. He knew well the character of the opposing candidate – a fearless, careless, man – vigorous and imprudent –

————————"Jealous of honour,
Sudden and quick in quarrel;"[178]

who had fought more duels than any man in the county; and was as often called "Bullet Mahon," as "Barry Mahon." He existed only in an atmosphere of democracy; and his hot, impatient aspect, firm tread, blustering voice, and arrogant familiarity, formed a very striking contrast to the polished, weak, but gentlemanly, bearing of Sir John Clavis. It was not at all unlikely that a quarrel would ensue, before the termination of the election, and many had even betted upon it. With the generality of Irishmen, it would have been unavoidable. But, though Sir John had never shown the white feather, he was a decidedly peaceable man – and was known to be so. Dacey, however, resolved not to trust to chance in the matter, and, on the morning of the second day, he was closeted with Mahon for nearly an hour. When the candidates appeared on the ill-constructed hustings, to greet their respective constituents, it appeared evident that Mahon was overboiling with rage at some known or supposed injury. Sir John's address was mild, and more than usually facetious – a style better understood and appreciated in England than in the sister island; he alluded to, without exulting at, the favourable state of the poll; and, after a short and cheering exhortation to his friends, resumed his seat.

When Mahon prepared to address the crowd, he swung his body uneasily from side to side, looking, when wrapt up in his huge white coat, as the personi-fication of those unhappy polar bears who suffer confinement in our menageries. At last, elevating his right arm, as if threatening total annihilation to all who even differed from him in opinion, he began one of those inflammatory addresses that have been followed up by so many second-rate agitators in modern times; he talked of the distresses of the people, until those who had just eaten a hearty din-ner imagined they were literally starving – and assured them so often that they were in a debased state of bondage, that at last they fancied they were sinking under their fetters' weight. "I would have you beware," he said, exerting to their utmost power his stentorian lungs, "I would have you *all*, green as well as orange, beware of those who would purchase your votes by bribery! If a man gives a bribe, he will take one! – and I wonder my opponent is not ashamed – *I say, ashamed* – to show his face here, after the conduct he has practised in private!"

Sir John Clavis called upon Mr. Mahon to explain.

Mr. Barry Mahon said he did not come there to *explain* – he came to speak – and speak he would – *no descendant of an impostor* should put him down – if Sir John Clavis wished for explanation, he could seek it elsewhere – if he did not do so, he was a COWARD!

The language had grown too violent, or, as the interfering parties called it, "too warm," even for an Irish election: and the friends of both candidates endeav-oured to put an end to it, or, at all events, to conclude it in another place. As Mr. Mahon refused to make any apology, or even give any explanation, it became necessary, according to the received and approved code of honour, for Sir John Clavis to send a message to the gentleman who had so grossly insulted him.

It was sent, but Clavis so worded it as to leave the matter open to apology. This, however, was not taken advantage of, and a "meeting" for the next morning was, of course, agreed upon.

Since their reconciliation, poor Lady Clavis had been suffering severely from agitation; her mind and body had received a severe shock; and though the happy termination, through her friend's kind sacrifice, had set her trembling heart at ease, her health had not yet mastered the struggle; she had been confined to her chamber, unceasingly attended by Miss Dorncliff.

About seven o'clock in the evening of the distressing quarrel between the candidates, Lady Clavis had just requested her friend to open the window, that she might feel the breath of heaven on her fevered cheek, even for a few moments; her fine dark eyes were fixed on the setting of a rich autumnal sun, which shed its glories over the scattered houses, and converted them into dwellings of molten gold. She was reclining on a couch formed of the high-backed chairs of the rude apartment, and, as her husband entered, she greeted him with inquiries as to the state of the poll. Miss Dorncliff thought within herself, that he looked pale and agitated, but did not allude to the circumstance. He was hardly seated, when a servant placed a note in Lady Clavis's hand; she just broke the wafer, and, glancing at the contents, burst into tears; Sir John perused it with almost the same agitation; and the intelligence it conveyed was well calculated to excite sorrow, for it said that the little Madelina had been taken dangerously ill, and Mary Conway, the writer, entreated Lady Clavis, "for God's sake, to come home, if she wished to see her child alive." The mother lost no time in her preparations; she thought not of herself; and to Sir John, under existing circumstances, her departure was a relief: he kissed and handed her into the carriage; the door was shut, and the coachman preparing to drive off, when Sir John called to him to stop. The evening sun had set, and the night wind was blowing sharply in the faces of the horses; the baronet pushed the footman away, and, unfastening the door, let the steps down, so that he could kneel upon them.

"Madelina," he said, in a low, agitated tone, and in her own dear native tongue – "Madelina, do you *from your heart* forgive me, for the unkindness I have shown – for the injury which, under the influence of a villain, I would have done you, and our innocent child?"

"My soul's life," she replied, "why do you ask? I cannot think of you and injury at the same time; *from my heart*, I have forgiven you." She bent her head forward to kiss her husband, and the wind blew one of the long locks of her raven hair across his face – he seized upon it as a treasure.

"I must keep this to wear next my heart till –" "we meet again," he would have added, but the sentence remained unfinished, while he severed the ringlet from the rest; he then extended his hand to Miss Dorncliff, and continued, even in a more broken tone, "You have been her friend, as well as my preserver – I *commit* her to your care!"

"How kind and affectionate he has grown!" observed Lady Clavis, as the carriage drove on; "when this dreadful election is over, and our darling recovered, we shall be *so* happy! – and to you, my dear, dear friend – my more than sister – I owe all this; his first love was not so sweet to me as his returning affection;"

and, overcome with many contending feelings, the gentle creature sank into a troubled sleep.

The calm was but the prelude to a storm. How often, when our hopes are highest, and our certainties of happiness seem firmest, is the thunder-cloud gathering over us that will soon ruin both! Even at the very moment when the wife had the surest confidence in days of enjoyment and repose to come, and the friend was luxuriating over the consciousness of a good deed done, they were on the very brink of a precipice, from which there was, alas! no retreat. Alas! still more, that a vile hand should have had the power to force them over it. But thus it is –

> "————Sorrow and guilt,
> Like two old pilgrims guised, but quick and keen
> Of vision, evermore plod round the world,
> To spy out pleasant spots, and loving hearts;
> And never lack a villain's ready hand
> To work their purpose on them."[179]

The roads were heavy, and the lumbering carriage and fatted horses little accustomed to hasty journeyings; they had proceeded at the rate of three miles, or three miles and a half, the hour, and were within five miles of the Abbey, when their progress was arrested by a figure on horseback seizing the reins, and commanding them to stop. "God be thanked for his mercy," ejaculated a well-known voice;" by his blessin' it 'ill not be too late, and he may be saved yet."

"Who saved? – what do you mean, Mary?" eagerly demanded Miss Dorncliff, for Lady Clavis was not sufficiently collected to make any inquiry, and only looked wildly from the carriage-window.

"The masther! the masther! – turn the horses' heads, Leary, as ye value salvation, or the priest's blessin'!"

"Explain first, Mary, for this is madness," replied Miss Dorncliff; "where – how is the child?"

"Here," she replied, unfolding her cloak, and placing the smiling cherub on its mother's lap. "I knew misthress 'ud never believe it was alive and well, when I hard o' the trick just to get ye all out o' the way, my lady – and you too, Miss, who unriddled so much before, that he thought you'd be at it again – the villain! The short an' the long of it is, that ould rascal tould some lies to the other mimber as wants to be, and, on the strength of them lies, him, the other man, insulted masther forenent the people; and they'd a row; and the upshot of it is that they're to fight a jewil to-morrow morning – Lord save us! – like Turks or Frenchmen; and 'twas he wrote the note – as one let on to me, who rode a good horse to tell it – and, troth, grass didn't grow under my feet either. But turn, turn! – we'll may-be get a help of horses on the road; I'll gallop on and have 'em ready, though it's as much as we can to reach town by daylight."

The servants urged the jaded animals to their utmost speed; and prayers mingled with the tears of Lady Clavis shed, as she pressed her child to her bosom. Miss Dorncliff endeavoured to give what she did not possess – hope. She knew that Barry Mahon's bullet was unerring; and, from time to time, she let down the front glass to cheer forward the anxious coachman. The horses Mary procured on the road were more a hinderance than a help, so restive and ignorant were they as to carriage-harness. Never did culprits, who watch for, yet dread, the coming day, feel more bitterly than they did when the first thin stream of light appeared on the horizon; the stars, one by one, faded from their gaze; and at last the spire of the church of W— appeared like a dark speck on the clearing sky.

"Forward, forward, my good Leary!" said Miss Dorncliff; "there's the church-steeple – hasten now, and reward shall not be wanting."

"It isn't the reward – it's the masther I'm thinking of," replied the faithful fellow. "If we had the luck to be on the Dublin road itself, there'd be some chance of help; but here –" He groaned audibly, and by words of encouragement, and a more liberal application of the whip, forced the horses into something like a trot.

"I can see the masts of the vessels that are lying in the harbour," exclaimed Mary; "for God's sake, hasten, Leary!"

"I may as well throw down the reins," replied Leary; "they can only crawl; this one's sides are cut with the whip, and that one's fallen lame too!"

"I could walk faster than the horses can go now," said Miss Dorncliff.

"And so could I, and *we will* walk," replied Lady Clavis, rousing all her energies.

"Do, do, my dearest friend," retorted Miss Dorncliff, "for I see figures on the bridge that cannot be mistaken; and if we could only get there in time, all could be explained."

Lady Clavis sprung from the carriage with a promptness that astonished her friend. She folded her child closely to her bosom, and took the path, across some meadows, which led, by a nearer way than the carriage-road, to the field that, for centuries, had been the duellist's meeting-place. The agony of her mind may be imagined, but cannot be described. There was her husband – every step rendered him more visible – she pressed onward – and her child was rocked by the panting of her bosom. The ground is measured – she flew without disturbing the dew that trembled on the grass – repeatedly she raised and waved her arm, eager to arrest attention – in vain!

Man to man stood opposed – not in spirited combat, but with cold murdering designs on each other. She screamed loud and fearfully, and her scream was answered by a fiendish laugh, which seemed to proceed from the hollow of a blighted tree that stood in her pathway: as she passed it, the bad face of Dacey glared upon her with bitter exultation. She shrank involuntary from his ken, and the report of a pistol struck upon her ear with appalling distinctness; it was followed by another, and the next minute saw her kneeling by the side of him whom she had loved with all the fervour of the glowing south, and all the fidelity of our colder climes; the innocent child crept from her arms over his bosom, and pressed her little lips to those of her dead father. Lady Clavis motioned off the people, who wished to remove the body, and, with fearful calmness, unbuttoned the bosom of his shirt, and looked intently on the wound and the oozing blood. She attempted to unfasten it still more, but started back as if some new horror had been displayed, when the tress of hair he had severed from her head the night before, appeared literally resting on his heart. Tears did not dim her eyes, which became fixed and motionless; and her whole figure assumed a frightful rigidity. The scene was even too much for Ellen Dorncliff's firmness: she fainted while endeavouring to take the child from the remains of its ill-starred parent.

"IT'S THE LAST OF THE LINE, sure enough!' exclaimed an old keener,[180] who had watched the melancholy proceeding; "for a girl, and such a girl, if report says true, has no hoult on the land; ill got – ill gone!"

My tale is told, and many will recognize it as *over true*. Lady Clavis's intellect never recovered the shock it received, and some years afterwards she died in a convent in Catalonia. The property of Clavis passed into other hands; and those who obtained it were generous and honourable enough to settle upon Lady Clavis and her child a larger income than they would have been entitled to, had there even been *legal* proof of the marriage, which, it was generally supposed, could not be obtained, or Miss Dorncliff would have procured it. So perfect, however, was the evidence she had collected of Dacey's villany, that he was never suffered to enjoy his ill-gotten wealth. I remember him in extreme old age – a hated, mischievous, drivelling idiot. Mary and Benjy were "as happy," to use the tale-telling phrase, "as the days were long;" and Miss Dorncliff – who was a living refutation of all the scandal ever heaped upon that most maligned class of persons called old maids – received, in her declining age, more than even a child's attention from Madelina Clavis.

THE WOOING AND WEDDING.

IT was a rich and glowing evening, in the budding and blossoming month of May – the sun was setting with calm magnificence over a cultivated and beautiful country, and there was nothing to obstruct the view of his farewell glory, except the high and verdant trees, whose leaves were hardly moved by the passing zephyr. No one could enjoy so happy a scene more fervently than Helen Gardiner – Helen, the most lovely lass in the whole country – purely and truly lovely was she; so delicate, so graceful – the gracefulness of nature. It was very strange, and I never could account for it, but Helen was decidedly not a coquette;[181] how she came to avoid it I know not; it is a fault that pretty women almost universally fall into. Yet there she was, the second daughter of an opulent farmer, in her twentieth year – a belle and a beauty; and, most certainly, she never flirted one single bit in her whole life – good-tempered and affable withal – active in her domestic duties – exquisitely neat in her person (the sure index of a well-regulated mind), and exact in the performance of her duty. I have said she was lovely, and it is most true; but she was very pale – it was seldom, indeed, that the faintest colour tinted her fair cheek; her hair was of a deep chestnut, plainly braided across a well-formed forehead, and confined in a large knot, or sometimes plait, at the back of her head; her eyes were decidedly beautiful, like two large dewy violets – and such eyelashes! – fancy her other features as harmonizing with her placid character – and fancy also a dignified figure, and then exert your imagination to finish the picture, and behold our rustic favourite, on such an evening as I have described, sitting at the door of a happy, well-wooded cottage in Somersetshire, sometimes looking up from her occupation (which by the way, was trimming a neat straw bonnet with plain green riband), to glance at the glorious sky, or, more frequently, watching a long green lane which led to the house, and in which nothing very interesting appeared to an ordinary observer. It would seem that not many visitors came up that lonely footway, for the little path was nearly overgrown by long grass. Yet, true it is, that Helen watched it, and true, also, that when the sound of two cheerful voices rang upon her ear, she looked no more, but most assiduously pinned on the strings, arranged the simple bow, and concluded, just as two men emerged from under the overhanging trees, by running an obstinate corking-pin[182] into her finger.

"Helen, why, Helen?" exclaimed the elder, who was her father; "here's your old friend, Mr. Connor – to be sure, we are all glad to see him."

Helen extended her hand to the younger of the party, and her eyes spoke the welcome which her tongue refused. She led the way into her cottage; her father and the stranger followed. The two men were odd contrasts: – Gardiner was a perfect picture of an English yeoman, habited in a clean white "frock;" his round and florid countenance proclaiming peace, plenty, and much prudence; and his hair which, unthinned by time, fell over his movable and wrinkled brow, was slightly touched by gone-by years. "Mr. Connor" (or as he was called in his own land, for he was a *rale* Emeralder[183] – "Mark, the traveller"), was a fine, handsome fellow, gifted by nature with an animated, expressive countenance, and manners far above his situation in life; there was a mingling both of wildness and tenderness in his voice and address; and his garments, of the blended costume of both countries, had a picturesque appearance to English eyes. He could never be reconciled to smock-frocks, to which all the Irish peasantry have a decided antipathy; but he had discarded knee-breeches and woollen stockings, and wore trowsers, which certainly looked better with his long blue coat; his scarlet waistcoat was "spick and span new," his yellow silk neckerchief tied loosely, so as to display his fine throat, and his smart hat so much on one side of his thickly-curling hair, that it seemed almost doubtful if it could retain its position. "Mark, the traveller," was the eldest son of a respectable cattle-dealer, and frequently visited England to dispose of live stock, whether pigs, cows, or sheep, which, of course, he could sell more cheaply than English farmers could rear them. He had long known Helen and her father, and had loved the former with fervour and constancy. She loved him, too, silently and unchangingly; the gracefulness of his manners first attracted her attention and she saw – or what, even with a sensible girl in love, is pretty much the same thing – she fancied she saw good and noble qualities to justify her attachment. Those quiet, pensive sort of girls, have always ten times the feeling and romance of your sparkling, giddy gipsies; and, notwithstanding that Helen discharged all her duties as usual, and no common observer could have perceived any alteration, yet her heart often wandered over the salt sea, beat at the sound of the Irish brogue, and silently inquired if, indeed, the natives of the green island could be uncivilized savages? She had, moreover, a very strong passion for *green*, and it was actually whispered that she wore in her bosom, a shamrock brooch, carefully concealed by the folds of her clear white kerchief. Her elder sister had been a wife, a mother, and a widow, within twelve months, and resided with her father and Helen; they might truly be called a united, contented family; perhaps Helen was somewhat more than contented, as she prepared the simple supper for their visitor, who had been some days expected, and who sat in their neat little parlour, at the open case-ment, into which early roses, and the slender Persian lilac, were flinging perfume and beauty; the honest farmer puffing away at his long white pipe, as he leaned half out of the painted window sill.

"I'm thinking, Mr. Connor, ye don't use such long pipes as these 'uns, in your country!" said the yeoman, after a pause.

"Ye may say that, sure enough; – we brake them off close to the bowl – and thin it comes hot and strong to us."

"Ye're very fond of things hot and strong in that place, Mister Connor; but I'll do you the justice to say, I never saw you in liquor all my life, though I have known you now more than six years."

"Nor never will, sir, I hope and trust. I never had a fancy for it, nor my father before me, which was a powerful blessing to the entire family, seeing it kept us out o' harm's way."

"I knew I had something particular to speak to you about," resumed the old man. "Do you remember the last lot of pigs you sold me?"

"May-be I don't."

"That means I do, I take it, in English. Well, perhaps you recollect one with a black head – a long-bodied animal – strangely made about the shoulders."

"Ough, an' it's I remember it, the quare baste! good rason have I; with its wigly-wagly tail, and the skreetches of it. Sure, because ye were my friend, I warned ye to have nothing to say to her; and you ('cause, ye mind, ye said when she was broadened out, she would make good bacon) took a great fancy to her, and so I let you have her, a dead bargain."

"Bargain, indeed! she would eat nothing we could give her, and, knowing she was Irish, Helen picked the potatoes, mealy[184] ones, and –"

Here Mark cast a look of indignation at his host, and exclaimed –

"Well, that bates Bannaher![185] Miss Helen, who's more like an angel than a woman, pick potatoes for an unmannerly sort of a pig; a *Connaught pig*, too, that *could* have no sort of manners! Sure I ought to have tould ye, sir, the Connaught chaps (the pigs I mane) 'll never eat *boiled* potatoes – the unmannerly toads, it's just like them. Well, to make up for his ignorance, take yer pick out of the drove for nothing, and welcome, to-morrow, and I'll go bail not a Connaught pig is in the lot – not a squeak did they give, getting on board, only all quiet and civil as princes."

"Thank ye, that's honest, and more than honest," replied the farmer. "I have no objection to an abatement – that's all fair; but to take the pig for nothing is what I won't do; for ye see fair is fair, all the world over."

"You'll do what I say, master, because ye're an old friend; and be in no trouble on account of the cost, for I have had a powerful dale of luck lately. My mother's uncle, in America, is dead, and left a dale more behind than 'ill bury him; a good seventy a-piece to the three of us – and so, before I came this turn to England, I took a neat bit of ground on my own account; and have as pretty a house on it as any in the county, for the size of it; three nice rooms, with a door in the middle, and a loft; it was built for a steward's lodge; and a bawn[186] at the back, with every convenience; and when I was on the move, I left ten pounds o' the money with Matty, my youngest brother, to have the room off the kitchen boarded for a parlour, for I mean to have it the very morral[187] of an English cottage, as I mean – if – if – I – can – to have an English – girl for a – a – wife."

"Well done, well said, Mister Connor; but who do you think would go over with you to that unchristian country, where –"

"I ax yer pardon, sir, ye're under a mistake; there are as good Christians, and Protestant Christians, too, in Ireland as in England – (I mean no offence) – and with such as fills that purse (and he drew from his bosom a long leather bag, and flung it on the table), and such a boy as myself, an English girl may be had, Mister Gardiner; though (he added, in a subdued tone) the one my heart is set upon is not to be bought with silver or gould."

"Not bought with silver or gold, Mr. Mark! Well, hang it, that's more than I'd say to any of the sex."

"You wrong them, then, sir; – money's a powerful thing – but look, there's some of them (one that I know of in partickler), so pure somehow – like a lily, for all the world – that a heavy sorrow would crush, or the least thing in life spot; and nothing could buy the love of *that* heart, because, as well as I can make it out, it has more of heaven than earth about it."

"No one can make you Irishmen out," retorted the farmer, laughing: "but may I ask *who* this lily – this delicate flower is?"

"Is it who it is?" replied Mark: "why, then, no one but yer own daughter, Helen Gardiner by name, and an angel by nature; and now the murder's out," he continued, "and my heart's a dale lighter."

The worthy yeoman put down his pipe, and looked at Mark Connor with a sort of stupid astonishment; he was a keen, sensible man, shrewd and knowing in matters concerning wheat, rye, oats, and all manner of grain; the best judge of horse-flesh in the whole county; and such a cricketer! such an eye! – could get six, or, perhaps, seven notches at one hit, and was, even then, a first-rate bowler: had, moreover, an uncontaminated affection for youthful sports, marbles, ball, humming and spinning tops; and would leave his pipe, at anytime, for a game of blind-man's-buff; yet it was certainly true that the idea of Mark Connor's aspiring to the station of his son-in-law never once entered the honest farmer's head. "My Helen! Well, Mister Connor, every father, that is, every man who has the feelings of a father, must feel as a compliment an offer – I mean such as yours – and I take it very sensible that you have mentioned the matter to me first, Mister Mark, because, of course, I must know best. As to Helen, poor girl, she has never thought about anything of the sort; and, indeed, Mister Connor, although

I highly respect you, and knew your father in the Bristol Market, an honest man (though an Irishman) as any in England, and know you to be a Protestant, and all, yet I must say my girl is very dear to me, and I should not like to trust – I mean, not like her to leave Old England."

Mark Connor was not much discomfited by these observations; he pushed his hair back from his forehead, and paused a moment or two; during the interval the farmer resumed his pipe, and puffed, and puffed.

"You were quite right, farmer," resumed the lover, after a pause, "quite right in supposing that I had never mentioned matrimony to Miss Helen, but ye see I mentioned –"

"What?"

"Why, it came quite natural like, the least taste of love; and she never gainsaid me, though she listened like any lamb."

"Indeed," said Mr. Gardiner, "you must give me leave to – almost doubt you. Now," he continued, seeing that Mark's face assumed a glowing aspect, "no anger, no getting into a passion for nothing – let us understand each other. Helen is my child; I love her more than any other living thing, and have done so ever since she, my wife, whom she is so like, was taken from this home to one she was better suited for. She was – " John Bull's heart, whatever its casket may be, retains the stamp of early affection longer than any other heart in the world, and the feelings of the honest farmer sent some big tears to his eyes, when he remembered her who had possessed his perfect love for more than thirty years. "Forgive me: if you love Helen, you can forgive me, for still mourning one my dear girl so closely resembles. It is not natural, Mister Connor, that I should like my child to leave me, particularly to go to a country of which I have been told so much evil; and, had Helen never heard of this, I certainly should not have told her: I know she regards you as a friend – but love, believe me, is out of the question; however, I will this moment speak to her, and – but I will first speak to her on the subject."

The farmer bustled out of the room, and summoned Helen into the little apartment which she called her own; it was a neat, delicate lodgment, fit resting-place for such a maiden. The walls were of snowy whiteness; a large looking-glass, in a plain black frame, surmounted the chimney, on which were placed sundry little rural figures, in variegated china. A deer, a fawn, a trim girl, with her milking-pail – (the pail, by the way, green, and the tree which overshadowed, a bright blue, but that was of little consequence) – then a shepherd with a smart pink hat, with a purple flageolet, and two hornless goats, one minus three legs – then the pretty pictures! – the neat sampler with its border of blue strawberries, and yellow roses – "Helen Gardiner, aged ten years," in double-cross stitch at the bottom: the bed, with its white cotton hangings, its pretty patched quilt, all diamonds, corner-pieces, and striped bordering, harmonizing wonderfully well after all. The simple toilet with its snowy covering – and the glistening cherry-tree wardrobe – putting to shame French polish, and Neapolitan varnish, by its brightness. On one of the two rush-bottomed chairs Mr. Gardiner seated himself, and drew the other closer to him, which Helen was directed to occupy. Helen trembled much at first, but still more, when her father somewhat abruptly inquired, if Mr. Connor had ever asked her to marry him?

"No, father," was her immediate reply – given, nevertheless, in a tremulous voice, while busily occupied in rolling up the end of her band, which, by the way, was green also.

"Nor ever talked to you of love?"

"Love, father?"

"Yes, love, I suppose you call it."

"No – that is, not much, father."

"Well, I am glad he has not spoken much on the subject, Helen; for, indeed, it would grieve me to see you married to an Irishman, however worthy he might be. So, my dear, I will tell Connor at once that he must give it up, as – as – it is the better way, I assure you."

"Dear father," exclaimed Helen, grasping his hand, as he rose from his seat; "you do not, cannot mean what you say; indeed you must not – it would – make me so – very –"

"What, child?"

"Oh, dear father, after the encouragement – indeed you must not –"

"Here's a coil! – must not – encouragement – and all that. Why, Mary, Mary, I say –"

Helen's widowed sister entered.

"Did you know of this pretty piece of work – your sister's listening to love-tales, and giving encouragement to a man, an Irishman too, without my knowledge?"

"I knew, sir, certainly, that Helen was attached to Mark Connor, and Mark Connor to her, and it was impossible to suppose that you did not know it also; for you may remember how much they have been together, and you never prevented it."

"How did I suppose they were to fall in love? – Helen, who was so strict, not like other girls! Surely she refused Alexander Brownrig – a man that half the girls in the parish are after."

"I am sure," interrupted Mary, "it was Mark Connor who drove Brownrig out of her head."

"I wish he had been driving his own pigs, then," responded the father; "but there, Helen, there – since you choose to fall in love without my consent, I suppose my consent is not necessary for your marriage – there, let go my hand."

She did let go his hand, for the unkindness he expressed had such an effect on her gentle spirit that she fainted on the floor, before her sister or father could support her: the revolution in her parent's feelings was instantaneous; he pressed his lips to her pale forehead, bestowed on her all the endearing epithets he could think of, and finally called in Mark to help to revive her: both father and lover knelt at her bed-side, while her sister chaffed her temples with such refreshing stimulants as the cottage afforded. When she opened her eyes, they rested upon the two beings she loved most, and the colour flashed over her pallid features, as words of sweet import broke upon her ear.

"I won't refuse either consent or blessing, my own Helen, but you ought to have told me you loved –"

"Hush! dear, dear father!" cried the blushing girl, as she raised herself on the simple couch; "do both go away, and I shall be better, quite well, in the morning."

"What piece of finery is this?" said the father, picking off the coverlet the identical shamrock brooch which I before hinted at.

"Oh, nothing, only – a – a – "

"A little token I gave her," said Mark, smiling, "though I never knew she wore it before."

"She always wore it," observed her sister, "except when you came; I'm sure, father, you might have seen it, confining the folds of her neckerchief."

Notwithstanding the different feelings of the little party who assembled around the plain supper-table of Farmer Gardiner on that memorable evening, they might all have been pronounced happy. Helen and Mark were perfectly so; the old man had resolved to make the best of the matter, and was also pleased and flattered by his intended son-in-law expressing his hopes that he would come over to them and lay out their farm upon the most approved English principles. The youthful widow, the light of whose existence had been so dimmed by the loss of the partner her heart had chosen in all the purity of its first affection, looked upon her sister, and the smile struggled with the unbidden tear, as she pressed her own little one to her heart.

The next day it was very evident that something was going forward of a particular nature in the cottage; a great part of the early morning was spent in consultation with Julia Mailing, the little London dressmaker, who sported a French hat and French curls[188] – "only just come up;" – and then an adjournment to the village shop; and, in the afternoon, Mark Connor and Mr. Gardiner, mounted upon their trusty nags, set off to Bristol, both looking full of business, and then came a cutting and snipping of book-muslin and sundry prints, and glimpses of white satin riband, and – but it is unnecessary to dwell upon the preparations; my readers must know already that nothing but a wedding is anticipated; and a wedding surely it was, though not conducted after the bridegroom's notions of the parade essential on such an occasion. Helen, to be sure, looked most beautiful – every body (that is every body who saw her) said she looked more beautiful than any woman in the world ever looked before, but Mark complained sadly that there were not people enough, nor dancing enough; and then Helen did not appear to be half joyous enough; and when, as the ceremony was concluded, he pressed her to his bosom, and called her "wife!" he was somewhat mortified to find her warm and glowing cheek wet with many tears; he could not understand, when he was literally half mad with joy, what could make her sad, for he knew she loved him; and he thought to himself that had his wedding been in Ireland, instead of in England, there would have been more mirth, and more music, and Helen would have been more cheerful; as it was, she would neither sing, dance, nor speak. She sat like a beautiful marble statue between her father and her husband; and, but for the flush that passed occasionally over her calm face, she had little of a living being about her. Mark loved, and, like all Irishmen, gloried in making a bustle about it; he could not fancy a wedding without much rioting: his gentle bride loved also; though it was not given to him to comprehend the depth or the delicacy of her untainted affection.

But we will, if you please, leave the bride and bridegroom to make their arrangements, and conduct their leave taking, after the most approved fashion, rejoining them in Ireland, on their landing in the village of Ballyhack! – Ballyhack! – the dirtiest town – indeed, the only dirty town – of our county; the very emporium of lean pigs, bad butter, and unclad beggars!

Helen had, therefore, an ill example of Ireland, and certainly did think it must be a wretched country; but, when ascending the hill that opens a view of Lord Templemore's house on one side, and the beautiful scenery around Dunbrody Abbey[189] on the other, she changed her opinion, and expressed her delight at the improving prospect. "Och! wait till we get home, Helen! and though you musn't think to find all like in England, yet you'll soon be able to make it so." This was easier said than done. Poor Helen! – silently and patiently did she toil; and, to do Mark justice, he aided all her undertakings, in open defiance of the sneers of the entire parish, with very few exceptions. Helen's calmness was called pride, and her exact neatness was a positive reproof to the slovenly habits of the uncultivated peasantry; and here I think it right to mention, lest there should be any mistake about the matter, that she was not fortunate enough at that time to be a resident exactly in Bannow. Mark had wisely taken his cottage as a good space from his mother's dwelling, for he knew that the friendship of relatives, brought up so differently, increases with distance. They resided in the vicinity of the "Seven Castles of Clonmines"[190] – a remarkable, and peculiarly interesting locality on the other side of "the Scar"[191] – dim records of a gone-by history – early structures raised by the first English conquerors, to keep the possessions they had gained by the sword, and control the "mere Irish."[192] Matty, his younger brother, was often with them, and he improved much by the wise precepts and uniformly good example of his new sister; but Helen's greatest torment was a fault-finding, pains-taking (as far as making mischief went) old maid, the chronicle, and scandalous magazine of the county. Nobody liked her, and every body tolerated her, for the simple reason why every gossip finds a welcome – because she was full, brimfull, of news and scandal. The parish had a little occasional rest when "Judy Maggs," as she was called, pursued her vocation of carder,[193] and wandered from county to county in search of employment; but, unfortunately, her only brother died at sea, and left her in possession of "a good penny o' money," so that, at the period to which I allude, she might be considered only as an amateur carder. She was chiefly occupied in investigating and meddling in everybody's business, within five miles of her dwelling; not that she objected to long journeys: she has gone three times in a week to Waterford, a distance of seventeen miles, to find if Katey Turner's gown really cost two shillings and eight-pence per yard; and no one can deny that she was not well repaid for her trouble, when she ascertained it to be an absolute fact, that the little gipsy got it a dead bargain at two and six. She went messages for every one, from those of the squire's house, to the mud cabin of blind Peggy O'Rooney! Nothing came amiss to her in that way; she might be termed, in the exercise of walking, a most wonderful woman, a universal carrier, from a whisper to an "established fact."

"Why, then, Mrs. Connor, ma'am," said she, one morning, addressing Helen, who, as usual, was setting her house in order, "will ye be afther telling us what the young masther is ploughing the ould wheat-field for?"

"To sow flax in, Judy."

"That's English, asthore! – sure, poorer land nor that 'ud do for flax – where did he larn to throw flax into sich rich soil?"

"In the Netherlands, I have heard, they never sow flax except in good soil; and you know the best linen comes from that country."

"I ax your pardon civilly, Mrs. Connor, ma'am – as *if I* didn't know all relating to the seed, breed, and generation of all the flax in the world wide! Oh! wirrasthrew![194] – to even that to me! – the Nitherlands! what is they to the North,[195] in regard o' linen-makin'!"

Gentle Helen Connor had enough to do to appease the angry dame, who, as a professional carder, was thought omnipotent in all flax questions; and she had at length got her into good humour, when Mark's brother, unfortunately, entered, and introduced a new subject of contention.

"Now that the reaping is over, Matty," said Helen, "I hope you will bind and stook the crop at once, not leave it on the ledge, as you did last year – I think it will rain – at all events it may; and it is better to be on the safe side."

"Bind and stook the *crap*,[196] afore a body has time to turn round!" exclaimed Judy – "Och hone![197] that's another English fashion, I suppose – or, may-be, it's from the Niverlands![198] – wouldn't to-morrow, or the day afther, do for that? I'll go bail for the weather – sorra a good in doing things in a hurry!"

Helen made no further remark, and Matty promised, in open defiance of Judy Maggs, to see that the corn was bound and stooked immediately. "But what I came in for, principally, Helen," said he, "was to tell you that the pig is laid out ready for burning in the barn."

"Burning in the barn!" echoed Judy, starting from her seat: "and are pigs so plinty with ye, that ye mean to burn 'em, and so many poor crathurs starving? Och, that I should live to see such fashions! Good mornin'! – good mornin' to ye, Mistress Mark Connor! – and God sind ye better sense, and a little more Christianity! – burn a pig! Och, my grief!" – Judy Maggs stood no further question, but trotted off, eager to communicate to her neighbours the melancholy intelligence, that Mark Connor's English wife "wint so far with her notions as to make *fire-wood*, of a pig!" On her journey, it was her misfortune, or rather, considering her love of tattle, her good fortune, to encounter Mister Blaney O'Doole, the parish carpenter, who was seated on the car that, turned on end, served as a gate to stop the gap leading to the short cut to old Mrs. Connor's dwelling. Blaney was a short, thick-set man, who, all over the world, would be recognised as a real Emeralder. "Good morrow, Mr. Blaney," said she. "Good morrow to ye, kindly, ma'am," said he. "What's stopping ye, sir?" said she. "Why, thin I'll tell ye, ma'am, dear, if ye'll give me time," said he, "but it's yerself was always the devil afther the news – though sorra a much's stirrin' – but I'm waitin' to take the stone out o' my brogue, that 'ud never ha' got there, only for the bla'gardly[199] way they made the new road. What could the country expect from the presintment overseer, and he a Connaught man? Didn't I see him with the sight o' my eyes, after bargaining with Tim Dacey to take tinpence a day, and a shilling allowed by the county (and paid too) – didn't I see him give poor Tim the full hire with one hand, and take back the odd pence (that weren't pence but pounds) with the other! so that, if called, he could make oath, with a *safe conscience*, that he ped the whole." "That's a good story, faith!" replied Judy, laughing, and losing all feeling of the roguery of the transaction in the amusement occasioned by its cleverness, – "but hardly as smart as one that *I had the sight* of my eyes for, up in the county Kilkenny, as good as tin years agone, – when a man – a *gentleman*, they called him – got a presintment to mend a piece of a road; and what does he, but lays the notes down along – along – iver so far on the bare ground of the highway, and then picks them up – claps thim into his pocket – walks off to the nixt grand jury – and makes affidavit, that 'he *laid* the money *out upon the road*.' – But is it manners to ax where 'ud ye be going wid yer bag full o' tools?"

"I'm jist stepping down to Mark Connor's, to get the *morral* of a new barrow with two wheels, that he wants made, and that he says is powerful good for all sorts and manner o' work. I wonder he didn't get it done of iron, like the cart he brought over, which cost him a good five guineas, and I could ha' made him one of wood twice as big for three."

"Of iron, agra!" repeated Judy.

"Ay, astore!" replied the carpenter, "and so much wood in the country; wasn't it a sin? How grand he is, to be sure, as if the sort o' cars his neighbours have wasn't good enough for him!"

"Thrue for ye – that's a thrue word; – but I could tell ye more than that; pigs are so plenty with them, that his fine English madam of a wife, at this very minute, is burnin' a pig in the barn."

It was now the carpenter's turn to be astonished.

"Burnin' a pig! – O thin, for what?"

"For what!" said Judy, a little puzzled; "why thin it's myself that can't tell exactly," she replied; "only for sport, as I could make out, or for firewood, may-be!"

"Holy Mother!" ejaculated the astonished man of chips, and wended on his way; while Judy called after him, "Find out for me the good o' burnin' a pig."

The evening of this day was a very pleasant and cheerful one in Mark Connor's kitchen. A neat white cloth was spread on a clean deal table; there was a small square carpet laid over the centre of the floor; and the tin and copper vessels on and under the dresser were brightly burnished; the fire certainly appeared almost as if made on the hearth, but, in fact, it was burning in a very low grate, that had both hobs and a trivet; and at each side of the capacious chimney were stuffed settles, neatly made and comfortable. On one of these, Mark was stretched at full length; the other was occupied by Matty and Blaney O'Doole; and Helen was endeavouring to convince a wild, but good-humoured looking, serving girl, that a gridiron[200] ought to be kept clean, and was much fitter to do a pork griskin[201] on, that was crying, like Kilkenny fowls, "Come, eat me – come, eat me," than the kitchen tongs that the lassie had extended on the fire for the purpose, although the gridiron was just as easy to get at.

The cloth, as I have said, was laid, and the supper in active preparation, when in walked old Mrs. Connor. Now, let people be ever so much inclined to find fault – let them be ever in so bad a humour, there is something almost irresistibly soothing in a group of smiling, happy faces, and a well-regulated apartment. I care not whether it be in a palace or a cottage; a wooden chair may be as well placed as one of gold and damask; and if a youth is wooingly disposed towards any damsel, as he values his happiness, let him follow my advice; – call on the lady when she least expects him, and take note of the appearance of all that is under her control. Observe if the shoes fit neatly – if the gloves are clean, and the hair well polished. And I would forgive a man for breaking off an engagement, if he discovered a greasy novel hid away under the cushion of a sofa, or a hole in the garniture of the prettiest foot in the world. Slovenliness will be ever avoided by a well regulated mind, as would a pestilence. A woman cannot be always what is called *dressed*, particularly one in middling or humble life, where her duty, and, it is consequently to be hoped, her pleasure, lie in superintending and assisting in all domestic matters; but she may be always neat – well appointed. And as certainly as a virtuous woman is a crown of glory to her husband, so surely is a slovenly one a crown of thorns. Now, having given what is seldom attended to, gratuitous advice, I must proceed to say, that old Mrs. Connor was never particularly sweet or gentle in her temper, and, as she entered the cottage, according to the Irish phrase, Mark wondered "what was in his mother's nose now." When, however, Helen took the great corking-pin out of her mother-in-law's cloak (which, by the way, for want of a string, had torn a large rent in the cloth), and, placing her gently on the easy settle (a luxury perfectly unknown in the generality of Irish cabins), gazed sweetly and calmly in her cranky face, and inquired affectionately after her health, the old lady softened a little, and looked around with a less dissatisfied countenance.

"Just in time, mother," said Mark, "just in time to share our supper; indeed, Helen had laid by something nice for ye, which Matty was to take over to-morrow; but make yerself comfortable; and, though it's been a busy day with us all, yet we're no ways in confusion." The old lady had not time to reply, when there was a smart knock at the door, and Mark's cheerful voice gave the usual invitation, "Come in, and kindly welcome;" our old friend Judy Maggs appeared immediately, and a sort of interchanging glance passed between the two ancient dames.

"Sure it's glad I am o' shelter," said Judy, taking off her new beaver hat, and carefully wiping it with the tail of her gown.

"Ye don't mane to say it's rainin'?" retorted Blaney O'Doole.

"Pepperin' like fun," replied Judy, "and so suddent too!"

"Och, my grief! – and all my little handful o' barley, that I had the ill-luck to rape as good as a week agone, upon the ledge."[202]

"Ours is safe," exclaimed Matty, joyfully, "thanks to Helen for it – for Mark hasn't time to look to everything – and sure I'd ha' never heeded it, but for her." Helen smiled at her good-natured brother, and it was observed that Judy looked particularly confused.

"Mark," said Blaney, "did ye hear what a shockin' misfortune happened Mr. Clancy? – sure his crap o' flax was no crap at all, afther his takin' three years' lase of Stoney Knock, thinkin' 'twould do well enough for flax; and the agint won't let him oft his bargain."

"Serve him right, I told him how 'twould be," replied Mark; "poor land never gave out a good crop yet – jist like people expecting to fatten pigs upon green food. I wish your sister Mary was over here, Helen, to teach us how to fatten them her way."

"One 'ud think yer father's son ought to know how to fatten pigs better than any one, and he bred, born, and reared, among them," observed Mrs. Connor. Poor Helen, for the life of her, could not comprehend Irish metaphor; and she repeated, with a flushed cheek, "Mark's father born and reared among pigs! – surely you mistake!"

"No mistake in life, Helen; sure, there's myself and his sons to the fore, who are proud to own it." Helen looked to her husband for an explanation, but he only laughed.

"I don't understand Irish," replied Helen, smiling in her turn, "and I think I make many mistakes for that reason."

"I'll niver stand to hear any one abuse my English," said Mrs. Connor, angrily; "and, Mark, if you can stand to see me turned on afther that fashion, by yer wife, I'll not – that's all."

"Nor I, neither," added the woman of many professions.

"Helen! my Helen, abuse you, mother! – Helen! – she never abused either you or any one else; the fact is, she does not understand your *Irish,* and *you* don't understand her *English*—"

"Mark," interrupted Mrs. Connor, rising hastily, and looking very angry and grand, while Judy Maggs, whose figure was little and rotund, crouched close beneath the shadow of her elbow, "Mark, I'm a plain-spoken Irishwoman, and your natural mother, and I feel it my duty to tell ye that I don't like yer goings on; I'd scorn to say a thing behind yer back, for I'm neither a flea, a fly, nor a Connaught man, but I tell you to your face that I do *not* like yer outlandish ways. Now, Helen, I don't want to make ye cry, girl; and ye needn't interrupt me, Mark, for I'll say my say, and be done wid it. In the first place, Helen, it was not manners, the day my brother Hacket called on you, out o' civility, on his way from the fair, for you to mix wather wid the drop o' whisky ye handed him; and, whin he drank the trashy stuff, ye had'nt the dacency to fill him another sup, but says, '*Will* you take a little more? – may-be, ye'd rather not?' – Was that the way (I'd lave it to judge and jury) to trate a relation?"

"Mother," said Helen, "it was not that; but indeed Mr. Hacket had taken enough before he came here, and I didn't like –"

"That's more of it," interrupted the old lady; "I say nothin' agin his being a little merry now and thin, but to talk of his havin' taken *enough!* Oh, to think of that bein' evened to a brother o' mine! – but wait; it's only to-day I heard that you, Mark, had sint for Jimmy Smith, the mason, to make a back door to yer house. What need has any dacent quiet family like yours, of a back door? Sure, there's no rogues among ye, that ye need a back door to escape through?"

"You don't understand, mother," said Mark.

"I don't want to understand," replied the old woman, who had talked herself into a belief of all she uttered; "I want to spake my mind, and to put a stop to yer *improvements,* as ye call 'em. I wonder ye wouldn't have more pathriotism than to be bringin' foreign ways into the country! – I'll say nothin' to ye about the iron car – Lord save us! – iron! – and so much wood to be had for a song! – nor the barrow with two wheels! – though my wonder is, where or how ye can put two wheels under a barrow; nor about iron cornstands – and stones to be got for nothin'; – but I don't see why there should be such a set-out o' tins shinin' about the kitchen; in my time, two or three things sarved for all – and why not? – but it's my duty I'm doin', and—"

"Don't forget the pig," whispered the curious and impatient Judy, raising herself on tiptoe to Mrs. Connor's ear; – the old lady seized the idea with avidity: "But, may-be, as I understand nothin'," said she, ironically, "ye'd have the goodness to Irish me the English of 'burnin' pigs?'"

"Burning pigs!" echoed Helen.

"Burning pigs!" repeated Mark.

"Ay, burnin' pigs! – makin' fire-wood of them!"

"I never heard of the like even!" replied Mark, "not in all my travels."

"Oh, the lies and wickedness of the world!" exclaimed Judy, clasping her hands together, and turning up her eyes; "and it done here this very day!"

"It's you that's telling lies, Miss Maggs!" exclaimed Mark, eager to vent the anger which had been for some time accumulating; "it's you that's telling lies, and well I know that ye're the mother of lies, and the counthry will never have rest or peace, till you, and the likes of ye, are out of it."

"Hould yer tongue, Mark!" exclaimed Mrs. Connor, "for it's the truth Judy's tellin'. Speak up, Judy, didn't ye see Matty and Helen both set fire to a live pig?"

Helen looked perfectly astonished, while Matty swore and protested that he had never done, or even thought of, such a thing in his whole life: the wind changed, and Judy, who (owing, it is to be presumed, to the imaginative organ being frequently called into action, and, consequently, acquiring considerable vigour), having certainly enlarged the report, after the fashion of all approved story-tellers; Judy found it somewhat awkward to be brought to *facts;* and, as a *dernier ressort,*[203] denied having ever used the word "*live.*" Old Mrs. Connor continued positive in her first assertion; and, at all events, after much bitter bandying of many words, the scene closed, upon old Mrs. Connor and Judy Maggs quitting Mark's cottage, at variance with its inmates and each other; while poor Helen, leaning her head against the wall, was weeping bitterly, and even Mark appeared worried and out of temper.

Mark Connor was anything but weak; and yet, being seriously angry with his mother, and the gossiping sisterhood in general, he did not kiss the tears from Helen's cheek, his customary mode of chasing the sorrowing tokens away, but in no very gentle tone said, "Ye'd better leave off crying, Helen; – women's tongues and women's tears are always ready when not wanted."

"I seldom trouble you with my tears, Mark," replied Helen, perhaps a little, *leetle,* pettishly.

"You've seldom reason, Helen."

"I am not saying I have."

"But I say you have not."

Helen was silent – unjustly so, perhaps – but it was a slight indication of woman's temper, and Mark was in no humour to put up with it.

"I say you have not, nor never have had since you have been my wife."

The remembrance of his mother's rudeness, and Judy Maggs' vulgarity, was fresh upon her mind, and she ejaculated –

"Mark! Mark! how can you say so?"

"Oh, very well!" replied the husband, "very well! I suppose the first tale you tell your father, and he coming over next week, will be – 'how ill I have used you!'"

Helen was again silent, and her calm features assumed somewhat the expression of sulkiness.

"Do you mean to tell your father that I have used you ill?" reiterated Mark, raising his voice at the same time.

Helen's tears flowed afresh, and she sobbed, "You never did till now."

It was very unfortunate for both Mark and Helen that others were witnesses to this first difference; for had they been alone, Mark's pride, and Helen's too, would have given way; but, as it was, neither would make the first advance towards reconciliation, and Mark swore a wicked oath, consigning all women to the care of a certain unmentionable black gentleman; and ended his pretty speech by muttering certain words; their import being that he wished he had never married an Englishwoman. This was the unkindest cut of all. Helen, now really angry with her husband, and justly hurt at his unkindness, left the kitchen with the air of an offended princess, and the cooking to the little serving maiden, who performed it most sadly. "I'll not stay supper, thankee, Mark," said Blaney O'Doole, who had wisely forborne all interference in a most *un*Irish way, rising as he spoke, and stroking his "*cawbeen*" with the open palm of his hand, "I'll not stay supper, I thankee kindly, all the same, but I'll go home; only, Mark, if I had swore that way at Misthress Blaney O'Doole, my wife, you know, I wouldn't be in a whole skin now, that's all; good night, and God be wid ye!"

"I'll go to bed, Mark." said Matty, "I'm very tired; only, Mark; asthore! don't be hard upon Helen; sure, ye know, the English are finer-like than us, and I saw her lip shake when you swore so at her; and, indeed, I can't help thinkin' our place a dale nicer than any one else's; she does bother about it to be sure, and is horrid partiklar, but she's gentle-hearted, and gave me such a beautiful green silk Barcelona[204] for Sunday, and says she'll give me a silver watch whin I'm fifteen; – don't be cruel, Mark; do you know that when I'm a man, I'll marry an Englishwoman!" And off went Matty, but not to bed: he left his brother sitting stubbornly at supper, his elbows resting on the table, and his face resting on his hands. "He's in one of his sulks," thought the good-natured boy, as he stole round the gable end of the house to his sister-in-law's bed-room window, "and, if they're long coming, they are desperate long goin'! I'll see if I can't coax Helen to go and make it up with him; and I'll find some way to punish that meddlesome ould woman – for it was all of her that my mother was stirred up for a battle to-night – as if Mark hadn't a right to his own way!" These thoughts brought Matty Connor to the little window that was curtained on the outside by the leaves of some fine geraniums, Helen's own particular plants; he peeped through the foliage, and saw Helen, her eyes still red with weeping, turning over the leaves of the small bible (it had been her father's parting gift), as she sat at the little neat dressing-table.

"Helen! Helen!" said he softly, "Helen, avourneen! don't fret, dear, but jist make friends with Mark; the natur' of us Irish, you know, is hasty and hot; but sure, Mark loves ye (and good reason he has) more than his heart's blood, and it's proud he is to have an English wife; sure it was only this mornin' he owned so, and he guidin' the plough; when Mister Rooney, the man with the big farm, said that this house was a pattern to the country-side, 'It's my wife I may thank for it,' made answer my brother, as well he might."

"For your mother to accuse me of burning a live pig!" said Helen, indignantly.

"Helen, dear! I know what that was owin' to; that blunderin', ould, wizzen-faced, go-by-the-ground,[205] Judy Maggs, who, whin I tould ye the pig was ready for burnin' in the barn (meanin', you know, that it was ready to have the hair singed off, the Hampshire way, for bacon, instead of bein' scalded our way), was all in a fuss to know what I was afther: I was in no way inclined to gratify her curiosity; don't you mind, I mean rimimber, what a lantin' puff[206] she set off in this very mornin' about it."

Helen sighed, and thought, as everybody else thinks who attempts to improve Ireland, that the *beginning* is difficult, if not dangerous – *c'est le premier pas qui coute.*[207] "But you ll make it up with Mark, Helen; poor fellow! there he is sitting by himself, and the fire out, and Biddy spoilt the supper entirely – sorra a bit he's eat."

"Not eat any supper!" repeated Helen, slowly looking up.

"Not as much as 'ud fill a mite's eye! – and Helen," added the cunning rogue, "he had a hard day's work, and wasn't over well."

Helen turned over the leaves of the little book, then closed and pushed it gently from her.

"Good night, dear Matty – don't forget your prayers – good night."

Matty had an intuitive knowledge of woman's heart, which it puzzles many a philosopher to acquire, so he only murmured – a "God bless you!" and withdrew, thinking slyly to himself, "that 'ill bring her round, any way."

Soon, very soon after, a small, gentle hand lifted the latch of the kitchen door; presently, Helen's face appeared at the opening, sweet, but serious. Mark pretended to be both deaf and blind – he still retained his position – and, though she advanced into the kitchen, he moved not. Helen's pride and her affection wrestled for a moment within her, *but the woman triumphed;*[208] she threw her arms around his neck, and looked affectionately in his face; – it was enough – "there was naebody by"[209] so Mark compromised his dignity, and the past was forgotten. I do believe this was the last, as I know it to have been the first, quarrel that followed Mark Connor's wooing and wedding. It was a long time before Judy Maggs found out the real meaning of Helen's burning the pig; and, indeed, she would never have been perfectly enlightened on the subject, but for Helen's good nature, who sent her a portion of the "burnt" flitch,[210] as a make-up for Mark's bluntness, he having forbidden her the house; a course that all who loved peace speedily adopted likewise. The most obstinate disciples of old customs in time saw the advantage of Mark's farming improvements; his flax was the finest in the country; his corn was always stacked in time; his bacon the best ever tasted; and even his mother confessed the superiority of the two-wheeled barrow. The back door, I fear, was always regarded as a sad innovation, notwithstanding the proof of its being the means of keeping the front one clean. Helen's housekeeping, even, after a long, trial received its due meed[211] of praise, though I fear that her husband's family was the last to award it; – the "cry of the country"[212] obliged them to do so at length, and then, as Mark himself said, "The deuce[213] thank them for it." He was wise in suffering, after that night, no interference; and the greatest triumph Helen experienced was when old Mrs. Connor not only requested her receipt to make a plum-pudding, but actually begged her to go to her house to make it – a tacit acknowledgment of her superiority.

About four years after her marriage, when her father came to see her for the second time, as he walked down the garden to her little flower knot, for which he had brought some rare bulbs, and held her little boy (a rosy, "potato-faced" fellow) by the hand – who amused himself by breaking his grandfather's pipe into short pieces, an operation that was not perceived by either grandpapa or mother – the following conversation took place between them: –

"I confess, Helen, I feared you would never be as happy as you appear. I never doubted Mark's kindness – but really the people are so careless—"

"Yet good-natured," said Helen, smiling,

"So insincere,"

"Not so, father; they always *mean* to perform what they promise; but they are, I confess, too apt to promise beyond their *means.*"

"So passionate."

"But so forgiving."

"So extravagant."

"So very hospitable."

"So averse to English settlers."

"About as much as we are to Irish ones."

"Averse to improvement, then."

"Not when convinced in what improvement consists."

"Helen, do you know it is very hard to convince an Irishman; he has so many quips, and cranks, and puzzling sayings, and would prefer being reduced to expedient, to attaining anything by straightforward means – provided it was not too troublesome."

"There is truth in all that," replied Helen, thoughtfully, "and no good will ever be effected by flying in the face of their prejudices; they are a people that must be led, not driven. Preconceived ideas cannot be hammered out of their heads – but they may be directed to other objects; though you cannot stop the source of a river, you may turn its course; – but yonder is Mark's uncle, Mr. Hacket, coming to see you. I must not forget to *give* him a bumper of whisky; not *ask* him 'Would he rather not?' which once got me into a terrible scrape. Dear father, farewell for a little time; and, if nothing else reconciles you to Ireland, remember it was Mark's wooing, and the wedding which followed, that made your Helen happy."

JACK THE SHRIMP

SOME ten or fifteen years ago there lived, in the neighbourhood of Bannow, a long, lean, solitary man, known by no other appellation, that ever I heard of, than that of "Jack the Shrimp." He was a wild, desolate looking creature; black, lank hair fell over his face and shoulders, and either rested in straight lines on his pale, hollow cheeks, or waved gloomily in the passing breeze; his eyes were deep-set and dark; and there was something almost mysterious in his deportment. Some persons imagined him to be an idiot; but others, who knew Jack better, asserted that his intellects were of a superior order; however, as few enjoyed the privilege of his acquaintance, the former opinion prevailed. Jack could be found everywhere, except in a dwelling-house; he had a singular antipathy to dry or sheltered abodes, and never appeared at home except when on the rocky sea-shore, scrambling up the cliffs, or, in clear weather, looking out for the scattered vessels that passed into Waterford harbour. Nobody seemed to know how he came to our isolated neighbourhood; his first appearance had created a good deal of village gossip, but that had gone by, and his gentle and kindly manner endeared him to the peasantry: the affectionate greeting of "God save ye!" – "God save ye kindly!" was frequently exchanged between the solitary shrimp-gatherer (for such was Jack's ostensible employment), and the merry "boys and girls," who, at all seasons, collect sea-weed, and burn it into *kelp,* on the sea-shore. Often have I seen him in the early morning, at low water, his bare, lank legs tramping over the moist sand, or midway in the rippling wave; his pole, some six feet long – the net full of shrimps at one end, and the heavy hook at the other, balancing it over one shoulder – while from the opposite were suspended two wicker-baskets, frequently filled with lobsters, or smaller shell fish, which he contrived to hook out of their holes with extraordinary dexterity. The sole companion of his rambles was a little, black, – I really know not what to call it, so as to distinguish its peculiar tribe, but it may be sufficient to state that it was a black, ugly dog, who, by way of economy, usually walked upon three legs, partly blind, and, like its master, lonely in its habits, and shy in its demeanour. This animal, who, appropriately enough, answered to the name of Crab, was the means of my introduction to its taciturn lord. Even in childhood I was devotedly attached to the sea; somewhat amphibious – fond, when I dared, of getting off my shoes and stockings, and dabbling in the fairy pools which the receding ocean left in the hollow clefts of the rocks; and fonder still of chasing the waves as they rolled along the sloping beach. My affection for this dangerous amusement was so well known, that I was never permitted to go to the strand, although it was considerably within a mile of our house, unattended by an old, steady dependent of the family, Nelly Parrell by name, who was entrusted with the care of all the young folk in the country on their sea-side excursions. But there was another companion who loved to be with me – my noble favourite, Neptune, a tall, stately, Newfoundland dog, thoughtful and sagacious. It was not to be supposed that so high-born an animal would condescend to associate with a low-bred tyke;[214] and no mark of recognition, that ever I perceived, passed between him and Crab, any more than between myself and the shrimp-gatherer, who, I dare say, thought a noisy, laughing girl of ten, a sad disturber of his solitude. One morning, during spring tide, having just bathed, I had quitted the box to take my accustomed stroll along the shore; when, on a rock, a considerable distance from land, and which the inflowing rapid waves were covering fast, I saw and heard poor Crab in evident distress: the fact was, that part of his master's tackle wanted some alteration; and Jack, forgetting it was spring tide, had placed his lobster-baskets on a high rock, and directed his dog to watch them until his return from the village; Crab would not desert his trust, and to save him appeared impossible, even to his master, who had just descended the cliffs, as the intermediate waters became deep and dangerous. I never saw any man in greater agony than Jack on this occasion; repeatedly did he call to the faithful animal – yet it would not quit the spot. Neptune was never particularly quick; but, when he did comprehend, he was prompt in doing all things for the best; suddenly he understood the entire matter, plunged fearlessly among the waves, and soon returned, bearing Crab, between his teeth, to the shore; not content with this exploit, he twice re-entered, and brought the baskets to the feet of the grateful man of shrimps. I do believe the poor fellow would, to use his own words, at the moment, have walked "barefoot to Jericho, to serve me or mine."[215] He snatched the dripping animal to his bosom, and, amongst other endearing epithets, called it his only friend. Ever after, Jack and I were intimate acquaintances: not so Neptune and the black cur: the latter never forgot his obligations; but Neptune only returned the humble caresses of the little creature by a slight movement of his stately tail, or a casting down of his small dark eye, as well as to say, "I see you!"

Still there was something about "Jack the Shrimp," I, notwithstanding my most persevering curiosity, could never make out; his mornings, from the earliest dawn, in fair or foul weather, were employed in catching the unwary fish; at mid-day he attended his several customers, and in the evenings he again repaired to his haunts among the wild birds, and amid the ocean spray: his general place of repose was a hollow rock, called the OTTER'S-HOLE;[216] and there he used to eat his lonely meal, and share his straw bed, at night, with his faithful dog. I saw him one morning, as usual, poking after shrimps, and was struck by the anxiety and energy of his movements; notwithstanding his seeming employment, he was intensely watching every sail that appeared on the blue waters: when he saw me, he rapidly approached.

"The top of the morning to ye, young lady, and may every sunrise increase yer happiness!"

"Thank ye, Jack; have you caught many shrimps this morning?"

"Yarra no, my lannan – sorra a many. – Ye wouldn't have much company at the big house to-day?"

"I believe we expect some friends."

"Ye wouldn't know their names?" ho inquired, looking at me, while his sunken eyes sparkled with feelings which I could not understand.

"Some, Jack, I know – Mr. Amble, and Mr. Cawthorne, and Father Mike, and the rector."

"Any of the red-coat officers from Duncannon,[217] agra?"

"Not that I know of."

"Are you sure?" he continued, peering earnestly into my face; "ye wouldn't, sure ye wouldn't, tell a lie to poor ould Jack, Miss, darlint, – you, whom he'd go tin pilgrimages to sarve, if he were to die to-morrow – you, who have so often spoke kindly to him when yer voice fell on his ear like the song of a mermaid – sure you wouldn't desave me, *mavoureen!*"

"Indeed, Jack, there is no reason to deceive you on the subject – the matter cannot concern you; but, to make your mind perfectly easy, I will ask the house-keeper; she knows who are expected, and I will let you know when you bring the lobsters to the house."

"God bless ye, and God help yer innocent head! – sure dy'e think I'm such an ould fool entirely as to be bothering myself about what's no business of mine? – may-be, like the rest, ye think me a *natural?*"

His lip curled in bitter scorn as he uttered the last sentence, and his eyes grew brightly dark under the shadows of his beetle brows. After a moment's pause, he continued, "Ax the master himself, dear – ax the master if any of the officers are to be wid ye: the housekeeper won't know – that she won't; just ax the master who's to dine wid ye to-day, particular about the officers; – but don't, Miss, dar-lint, don't say I bid ye; ye don't know what harm might come of it, if ye did – it might cost me my life; besides, it would demean ye to turn *informer.* Now, Miss, machree, – young as ye are, ye're the only one about the big house I'd trust with that; and so God be wid ye, I *depind* on your honour." I was ten years old, and it was a glorious thing to think that a secret (although I hardly knew in what the secret consisted), was in my keeping, and it was still more glorious to be told that my honour was depended on. Jack was, moreover, a favourite with the household, and I had never been forbidden to speak to him. Grandmamma and mamma, were, I knew, busied with the housekeeper in the preparation of jellies and pasties, in the manufacture of which, adhering to the fashion of the good old times, they themselves assisted, at those periods of bustle and confusion in country-houses called company-days. I was consequently aware that I should hardly see them until dressed for the drawing-room. During my conversation with Jack, my biped attendant, Nelly Parrell, had been busily employed in packing up my bathing-dress, and locking "the box;" so she knew nothing of Jack's anxiety. I saw the old man watch me attentively, until I ascended the upper cliff on my way home, and then he returned to his occupation. I did not fail to ask my grandfather, at the breakfast table, if he expected any of the officers from Duncannon to dinner, that day? The kind man laid down "the Waterford Chronicle,"[218] which he was perusing, and, smiling one of those sweet and playful smiles that tell, more than words can do, of peace and cheerfulness, inquired, in his turn, if "my head was beginning to think about officers already?" I was old enough to blush at this, but returned to my point, and was told that none had been invited. Soon after, I saw Jack, and little Crab, the one striding, the other trotting, down the avenue; as he passed the open casement he stopped, and I told him that grandpapa did not expect any of the Duncannon officers: the old man crossed his forehead, and muttered – as he reverently bowed, and passed to the kitchen offices – "May heaven be yer bed at the last, and may ye niver know either sin or sorrow."

Poor Jack! I have often since thought of his benediction. Dinner was at last over, and dessert fairly placed upon the table, when horses' feet were heard clattering into the court-yard; and, in a few seconds, the servant announced the captain of the detachment of a regiment then quartered at Duncannon; a gentleman who accompanied him, but who was not announced, entered at the same time; he was a gigantic, gloomy, harsh-looking man; and when the servant retired, the officer introduced him as Mr. Loffont, the new chief of the Fetherd and Duncannon police. This man was universally disliked in the country, and Captain Gore knew it well; he, in some measure, apologized for the intrusion of both, by stating he had been that morning called upon, by Mr. Loffont, to give assistance to the police in a rencontre with the smugglers, which was that night expected on our side the coast; this was, I believe, unwelcome intelligence to all, but to none more than myself; an undefined dread of some evil that might happen to my poor friend, the shrimp-gatherer, took possession of my mind; and, to the astonishment of my good grandmother, even my strawberries were untasted. I have since learned that, when the ladies withdrew, Captain Gore informed the company that he expected some of his men to meet them at the termination of our oak belting: and, he added, "he was convinced Mr. Herriott would render every assistance to the king's servants in such a cause." Mr. Herriott was peaceably inclined, and only agreed to go to the beach with the soldiers, because he thought it likely he might act as a mediator between the parties. Well do I remember the breathless anxiety with which I watched for his passing through the entrance-hall, for I longed to speak to him – but it was useless; he did not come out till near midnight, and then he was surrounded by gentlemen, who whispered in an under-tone; at last, with a palpitating heart, I heard the old butler ordered to bring the long double-barrelled gun. The company departed, and I seated myself in the nursery window, which overlooked the beautiful plantations, and the distant sea that was tranquilly reposing in the beams of the full moon.

Slowly and stealthily did the party proceed to the shore; and they stole in silence, and in safety, upon the unfortunate smugglers, who were, at the time, landing their cargo at the entrance to the OTTER'S-HOLE. A few peasants were waiting, with empty cars, to convey away their purchases; and the gang was, evidently, unprepared for the attack; neither party, however, wanted courage; and they fought, man to man, with desperate resolution. Loffont was foremost in the fray; youth, age, and manhood alike felt the overpowering force of his muscular arm, or the unerring ball of his pistol. Silently and darkly did he fight, more like a destroying spirit than a mortal man. At length, in the midst of a combat that had given him more than usual trouble, for he had engaged with a young and daring antagonist, he was arrested by a harsh, growling voice, like the deep but murmured anger of an African lion; and his arm was grasped by long bony fingers, that seemed the outcasts of the grave. "And you're here! – you, who crushed my brave, my eldest boy; who seduced, from her innocent home, my Kathleen – my daughter – my dear, dear girl; – you, who drove us to wandering and want! Stand back, James – drop yer hoult of my only living child, ye hell-fiend!" continued the agonized old man, as he shook the huge frame of Loffont, even as a willow-wand; "once before, when my other boy was murdered, I struggled with ye for his life, and ye cast me from ye, as an ould tree: – but now!" – his eyes glared fearfully upon his victim, and, for a moment, smugglers and soldiers remained silent and motionless. Loffont trembled in every limb; he felt as if his hour was come, and, turning from the shrimp-gatherer, he said, "Pass on, John Doherty; enough of your blood is already on my head." The old man replied not, but closed upon the revenue-officer. Long and desperate was the struggle – hand to hand, foot to foot – until, as they neared the overhanging edge of the precipitous cliff, the shrimp-gatherer grappled the throat of his adversary; one step more – and both went crashing against the pointed rocks, until the deep, heavy splash in the ocean announced that the contest was over.

Speedy relief was afforded, and they were both dragged out of the water, still clasped, as in the death-struggle! Loffont, his harsh and demon-like features blackened and swollen by suffocation, was indeed a corpse; and although Doherty was living, and in full possession of his faculties, it was evident his spirit was on the wing. Still did he grasp his antagonist's throat; and, even when besought by my grandfather to relax his hold, he raised himself slowly on his elbow, and turned a steady gaze upon the features of one he had hated even unto death. His son knelt by his side, his heart full, almost to bursting. In the meantime, the contest between the soldiery and the people was renewed, and every inch of cliff vigorously disputed.

"James," said the dying man, as his glazed eye followed the bloody contest, upon which the full moon cast her bright and tranquil beams – "James – the boat – the boat – gain the ship! My murdered children now can rest in their graves – their murderer is punished."

"Jack," interrupted the kind-hearted gentleman, "for God's sake, think of the few moments you have to live – think of where you are going."

"Ay, sir, if God would spare me to make my soul, now I might think and pray to him; – but before – could I think of any but *them* who are in heaven? Now God – God have mercy on a poor sinful man!" His hands were clenched in prayer, when a loud shout from the peasantry, which was repeated by a thousand echoes along the rocky shore, announced that they had beaten their opponents fairly off; the old man started – waved his hands wildly over his head, as in triumph – fell back – and expired on his son's bosom.

The smugglers escaped to the vessel, and the youth bore off to it the dead body of his father. The ship's crew and the peasantry disappeared, as if by magic, carrying with them as much of the brandy and tobacco as had been landed, for they knew that the police would shortly return with a reinforcement; and in one or two moments Mr. Herriott found himself alone with the corpse of Loffont, on the wild sea shore; – not quite alone, I should say; the dog of the shrimp-gatherer, poor Crab, came smelling to the strand where his master's body had lain, raised his little voice in weak and pitiful howlings to the receding barque, and finally laid himself down at the feet of the watchful Neptune, who had never deserted his master's side. From that hour, the noble animal became the protector of the low-born cur – never suffering him to receive either insult or injury.

The body of the wretched Loffont, who had met with so shocking a death, was conveyed to our house; it was buried – but few attended the funeral, which in Ireland is always a mark of disrespect. It was not to be wondered at, for the history of poor Jack became generally known: he had once a home, and all the joys which home can give; – a wife, two sons, and one lovely daughter, the pride of her father's life, and of her native village. She was seduced by Loffont, under the promise of honourable union – but she could not survive her disgrace – her heart broke! She was found, one morning, a stiffened corpse at her father's door, with a snow-shroud for her covering, and the cold ice of December for her bed. Then it was that her mother quietly and calmly laid down and died; the fountain of her tears had dried – her heart withered within her bosom.

The husband and father, thus rendered wild and desolate, became a man of desperate fortunes, and swore that nothing but blood should wash out the memory of his daughter's shame. He joined a party of smugglers, with his eldest boy, whom, in an engagement with the police, he saw shot and stabbed by the same hand that had brought sin and death to his once happy dwelling. He was himself so much injured in this engagement, as to be unable to remain at sea; so he wandered along the sea-shore, watching the movements of the officers stationed on the preventive service, and directing those of the smuggling vessel in which his younger son had embarked. This will account for the great anxiety he had manifested to ascertain who was to dine at our house on that eventful day – dreading, doubtless, that the officers were on the lookout for the expected ship. He could not have known that Loffont was so near his usual haunts; for he would have stopped at nothing to shed his blood.

* * * * * *

This story was brought to my remembrance, many years afterwards, when I visited the old churchyard of Bannow, in which the remains of that," bad man" were interred. The church is of very remote antiquity, and it overlooks a singular scene – the "Irish Herculaneum"[219] – a town buried beneath the sand. In the interior, among broken walls, are the remains of several tombs, which retain abundant evidence of "long-ago magnificence" – sculptured slabs and stone coffins; and among them arc monuments to the memory of the good, and upright, and benevolent – of, comparatively, yesterday. To me the spot is sacred; it contains the ashes of nearly all my relatives and friends.

Alas! if, in early life, we revisit the scenes of our childhood, where shall we look for those who are dear to our hearts and memories? In the churchyard!

The grave of Loffont, to which my story has reference – rather than to those of characters far opposite – was pointed out to me by the widow Parrell – my old bathing-woman – as one upon which, for a long time, "grass would not grow." "I've seen," she said, "many a fine funeral within these ancient walls: I remember that of the ould Master of Graige House;[220] and well I mind your own grandmother's – the heavens be her bed! And the hundreds that followed her, though an Englishwoman, to her grave – the hundreds! besides three priests, and three ministers; and then her husband! And beautiful are the words he had carved upon that square flat tomb, to her memory; then the ould lady, his sister, all in the same big vault – ah, yah! – the fine place went into other hands; and, if it was to pass, sure, better relations and neighbours than strangers – the old name reigns over it again – the old stock, still! – Wisha! wisha!" she exclaimed, rubbing her finger across her sallow brow, and then plucking tufts of maiden hair[221] out of the old walls; – "it bothers one to think how often that tomb has been opened! – Well, the Lord above grant it may not be opened for a very long time." When I was young, I took great delight in wandering about these old tombs; and, even when Loffont was killed, I remember I'd as soon go into a graveyard, as into a flower-garden. "Death seems so far off then, that it's no trouble to think of it – it's like the wave we see rolling betwixt the two Keeroes:[222] we never heed its size till it's almost at the shore; but now, I don't care if I never cross the walls – barring to look at that tomb of ould French[223] – that's a consolation – a hundred and forty years is on the tomb – more says it's a hundred and four, but I don't see why a body mayn't as well live to be the one as the other." The poor woman seemed to derive consolation from this reflection, and added, "What a pity it was that Jack the Shrimp died so soon! he'd be sure to have made ould bones, and had a fine funeral if he'd only have waited for it, as he might, and no harm." Many stories she told me of those who lie beneath that green turf; and now, she herself rests there – one of the last who, in her lifetime, companioned poor Jack the Shrimp.

HOSPITALITY.

"HOSPITALITY – no formality – there you'll ever see:"[224] – so runneth the old song. Quite true – true to the very letter; and there was not a more hospitable house, in the province of Leinster, than Barrytown.[225] "Kindly welcome" was visibly expressed by every countenance, and all things bore the stamp of – "Hospitality!" The master was large; the house was large; the trees were large; the entrance-gates were large: the servants were large; all the domestic animals were large; the worthy owner's heart was large – and so was his purse. He was cheerful and happy; his house, particularly in the shooting or summer season, was always full of company, more numerous than select, but all resolved to enjoy themselves, and Mr. Barry, their worthy host, determined to promote their enjoyment. I have said his house was large – it was almost magnificent. It stood on a gentle declivity, and commanded a pleasing, though not very extensive, prospect; the entrance-hall was lofty and wide; the walls well garnished with fowling-pieces,[226] fishing-rods, and, at the farthermost end, the antediluvian horns of a monstrous elk, which spread even to the ceiling's height. Of this extraordinary production of nature Mr. Barry[227] was very proud, and boldly challenged the Dublin Museum to produce its equal. The pavement of the hall was formed of beautiful Kilkenny marble; its polish certainly had departed, yet the rich and varied veins were distinctly visible. Dogs of various sizes – from the stately Dane, the graceful staghound, the shaggy Newfoundland – to the fawning spaniel, the little rat-catching, black-muzzled terrier, and the sleepy, silky Blenheim[228] – considered the hall as their own exclusive property, yet lived on terms of perfect good fellowship with a Killarney eagle, a Scotch raven, and a beautiful Angola cat,[229] who shared the same territory, the latter, indeed, looked upon a deer-skin-covered couch as dedicated to her sole use and benefit.

The great dining-room was worthy of such an entrance; it was wainscoted with black oak, and, at the top of the apartment, the extreme darkness of the wood threw into strong relief the massive sideboard, with its highly-wrought, antique plate. The dining-table rested on enormous pillars, and bore evident marks of having seen good service in convivial times; the chairs were high-backed and richly carved, cushioned with crimson damask; and the large wine-coolers and plate-buckets were rimmed and hooped with silver. "The family canvas,"[230] in heavy framework, smiled or frowned along the walls, just as they ought to smile or frown; and represented, to say the truth, a grim, clumsy-looking set of personages; even the pastoral young lady, who was playing on a pipe – the sheep (I suppose they were sheep) looking tearfully in her face – her well-powdered hair graced by a celestial blue riband: even she, the beauty of the party, squinted most frightfully. But the good Mr. Barry had a profound veneration for them all, so we will leave them without further comment. The curtains and carpet had seen their best days, and Mr. Barry had been talking about purchasing new for the last ten years; nevertheless, the old remained, and certainly looked very venerable. The withdrawing-room, or, as the "master" called it, the ladies' proper apartment, held a motley assemblage of new and old furniture; a splendid rosewood piano was placed next to a towering old triangular flower-stand, with monkey heads, and scallop shells at the corners, but which, nevertheless, served as a "what-not."[231] Silken Ottomans[232] reclined, in eastern luxury, near to less elegant, but more sedate, hard-stuffed sofas; and a lumbering old arm-chair, covered with cream-coloured embroidered satin, the cushion fringed and tasseled with gold, stood to the right of the fireplace; a small stool, garnished after the same antique fashion, and a little table inlaid with silver, which appeared hardly able to support an old family Bible, with studded clasps, were placed beside it.

The interesting occupier of the arm-chair was no less a person than Lady Florence Barry, the mother of the hospitable master. I never saw so beautiful a relic of female nobility; when I remember her, she was verging on her ninetieth birthday; – her figure delicate and much bent; her eye black as jet, small, and sparkling, fringed by brows and lashes which time had rendered perfectly white. Her features had been handsome, but at such an age were much wrinkled, and her own hair, straightly combed from under the high lappet cap,[233] added to her venerable appearance. The dress she wore was always of the most valuable black Genoa velvet or satin, made after the olden mode, with deep ruffles of Mecklin or Brussels lace, and a small cloak of rich black silk, fastened at the breast with a diamond brooch. The old lady was very deaf, but her sight was perfect; and when she received her son's guests, she did it with so much grace, so much dignity, that it could never be forgotten. Perhaps the affectionate respect and attention manifested by Mr. Barry to his mother was the most delightful trait in his character. "She brought noble blood and a princely dower to my father," he would say, "and made him a true and loving wife to the end of his days; and when, in the full bloom of womanhood, she became husbandless, for my sake she remained so. Can I honour her too much?"

Mr. Barry had nothing in particular to distinguish him from "the raale true-born gintry." He had a fair and open brow, that unerring index to a noble soul, and a manly expression of countenance; but he had more of his father's heedlessness than of his mother's penetration, and, at sixty-two, knew less of "the world" than most of our fashionables after they have been "a winter in London."

The domestics of Barrytown had grown grey in their services – in verity, all things in the house were "of a piece" except the visitors; they ruined the *harmony* of the picture, while they gave spirit and variety to the *colouring.*

The month was June, which is more like May in England, for our skies shed many tears, even in the summer time; as usual, the coach-houses and stables were crowded; the former with gigs,[234] "suicides,"[235] and jaunting-cars,[236] outside and in; and the latter with all manner of ponies and horses. The servants' hall, too, was full, and a "shake-down" had been ordered even in Mr. Barry's own study, a gloomy, dusty place, almost untidy enough to be the *studio* of a literary man – that odious receptacle for books and spiders; when old Mary said to old Mabby – long Mabby, as she was generally called: –

"Mabby, honey, my drame's out – for, upon my conscience, if yon, on the broken-down-looking jingle of a jaunting-car, isn't Miss Spinner, and her ould trunk; and her ould maid that's as bothering a'most as her divil of a mistress. Och! it wasn't for nothing I dramed of a blue-bottle fly upon master's nose, buz, buz, about like a mill-wheel! – the jazey![237] – there she is, as yellow as a Yarrow blossom."[238]

"Why, thin, it's herself sure enough," responded Mabby; "and if she had stayed in Dublin, 'mong the larned people she's always talking about, none of us would have asked what kept her. Och, it's as true as I'm standin' here, she's got a new wig!"

"New, nonsense!" said Molly, "it's only fresh grased. I'll not go look after her things; – a month won't excuse her out of this, and no mortal ever saw cross or coin afther her yet. Where'll she sleep? Sure there's two in a bed all over the house, barrin' master's. Mabby, count how many there is in now;

I'll tell thim over – the best first: – Mr. Altern, his two hunters, and the groom, to say nothin' of the dogs; but he's a generous gintleman, and the groom's a hearty boy."

"That's four," said Mabby.

"Och, you born sinner!" replied Molly, "sure it's not going to count the Christians with the bastes, ye are?"

"Tell over the Christians, thin."

"Well, thin, that's two. Miss Raymond – in raale goodness she ought to go for two, the jewil!"

"Three."

"Mrs. Croydon, Miss Lilly, Miss Livy, the footman (bad cess[239] to that fellow! – the concealed walk of him is parfectly sickening, coming over us wid his Dublin airs), and my lady's maid, to be sure."

"You've forgot Mr. Wortley."

"Why, thin, I oughtn't to do that, for he never forgets anybody – he's both rich and kind; although he's an Englishman, I'd go from this to Bargy on my bare hands and feet to do a good turn for that gintleman – there isn't one in the house (of the visitors I mane) I'd do a civility for so soon, only Miss Raymond. What a pity it is that young lady hasn't some yellow guineas of her own! Mr. Wortley is mighty sweet upon her, I think. Och, then, 'tis herself, the darlint, 'ud make the nice wife for him! – but the English, the poor, narrow-minded craturs, are all for the money, you know."

"Well, Mabby, any way, that's nine. Miss Spinner and her follower, sure!"

"Eleven."

"That foolish-looking clip of a boy, that looks mighty like a gauger,[240] and his comrade that hunts among the ould places for curosities, and their outlandish man, Friday, as I hard Miss Raymond call him."

"Fourteen – and no bad increase to a family that always, when by itself, sits down twenty to dinner, counting the parlour, servants' hall, and second table, not to reckon the weeders[241] and the gossoons;[242] to be sure, the bit they ate is never missed; how could it, from a gintleman like our master? – the blessing be about him! My honoured mistress smiled as I passed her in the corridory to-day; well, she is very ould – and yet so cheerful; and, though she's little, there's a state-liness about her that always made me the smallest taste in life afeard; but she was wonderful good in her time, and master dotes down upon her."

After this dialogue, the two old housemaids departed, mutually determining to avoid Miss Spinner, who seemed to be the terror of the establishment.

In the drawing-room, the greater part of the visitors were assembled, awaiting the ringing of the dressing-bell. Lady Florence, as usual, in her cream-coloured cushioned chair, reading her Bible; Miss Raymond sketching flowers from nature – white and blue peas, and a china rose;[243] Mr. Wortley, neither absolutely sitting nor lounging, on one of the old-fashioned sofas, was apparently engaged in looking over a large rolled map; Mrs. Croydon, netting; Miss Livy, and Miss Letty, the one attitudinising, and winding a skein of silk – which the other held so as to display her little white hands to advantage; when, at length, Miss Letty broke silence by asking –

"La, ma'! – who do you think is come?"

"How should I know, child?" replied her mother, looking up from her net-ting; "our party is so very pleasant" – and she smiled a gracious smile on all around – "that I can hardly wish it increased."

Mr. Wortley smiled also, but it was a different sort of smile.

"Guess, Livy."

"I never guess right, Mr. – Mr. – "

"It is not a Mr. at all."

"I wonder you guess at Misters," said ma', with an aside drawing-down of the brow; "I am sure, my love, *you* care so little about gentlemen – at least, so I used to hear at the Castle, where my little Olivia thought fit to be so frigid; I wonder, child, you mention *Misters*."

The young lady, who was not as accomplished a manœuvrer as her mamma, saw she had done wrong, although she did not exactly know how to amend her error, and wisely held her tongue.

"Guess, Gertrude," recommenced Miss Letitia, "Gertrude Raymond, can't you guess? – well, then, I will tell you – Miss Spinner."

"Oh, mercy!" screamed Miss Olivia and her mamma, "that blue!²⁴⁴ Oh, Miss Raymond! – Oh, Mr. Wortley! – oh! what will poor Mr. Altern say! Mr. Barry asked her once, and she makes it a general invitation! – oh, I shall be afraid to open my lips! – sha'n't you, Gertrude?"

"No," replied Gertrude, laughing.

"Oh! you arc so wise, Miss Raymond," said Miss Letitia, "that you are not afraid of anybody! – I dare say you would not mind a bit being in company with Sir Walter Scott, or Lady Morgan, or Doctor Johnson!"

"Hush, my dear!" interrupted Mrs. Croydon, who, it must be confessed, had enough to do to keep the levity of one daughter, and the ignorance of the other, within bounds; "Hush! – you know Miss Raymond has had many advantages, and she is *older* than you – so she has less reason to fear clever people; but you are such a nervous little darling!" – And mamma, in patting the "little darling's" cheek, managed to give it (unperceived by the *rich* Mr. Wortley) a little pinch, which said, as plainly as pinch could say, "Hold your tongue!"

"Nobody has any reason to fear *really* clever people," said Mr. Wortley, rising from the sofa, and joining, for the first time, in the conversation, if so it might be called; "and certainly not Miss Raymond," he continued, bowing to Gertrude; who immediately bent more closely over her drawing than was at all necessary, for be it known that she had very good sight.

"There's a compliment from the sober Mr. Wortley!" laughed Olivia; "who ever heard of such a thing before?"

"It would be impossible to compliment Miss Olivia Croydon," replied the gentleman; "her beauty is so universally acknowledged that it needs not my poor commendation." The silly girl looked pleased at extorted flattery.

Mrs. Croydon was the widow of a general officer, and, in twenty years' campaigning, had seen a good deal of "the world." She was a pretty and a vain woman. As her husband fell in love with her at a garrison ball, and as she calculated on a similar destiny for her daughters, she resolved on adding to their beauty every accomplishment under the sun, as they were nearly portionless. What hosts of masters! Painting on velvet, japanning,²⁴⁵ oriental tinting, music, dancing, singing, fencing, riding, French – everything in the world, except the solid usefulness of *education*. Accomplished they certainly were, but not educated.

Alas! how many lovely women shed tears of bitterness – when the flush of youth and fashion has passed, never to return – over hours spent in the acquirement of frivolous accomplishments, which, if occupied in the improvement of qualities that shed a halo, and diffuse a perfume, over home – woman's best and brightest earthly dominion – would have made them useful and beloved, even to the end of their days.

Mrs Croydon "carried on the war," as Mr. Altern used to say, "most famously." She had good connexions; and, as her daughters' education, to use her own words, "was completed under first-rate masters," she resolved to devote herself to her friends, and let her house in Dublin, except for three months in the year, when it was absolutely indispensable that she should attend the Castle festivities, "for her daughters' sake – heigho! – she had no taste, now, for the world's pleasures!" – Nevertheless, many suspected that she would not have objected to become Lady of Barrytown – a thing by no means likely, as Mr. Barry looked upon her in no other light than as the widow of his old friend.

Mr. Wortley, also, was an object of much interest to the lady. He admired beauty – so Miss Olivia was instructed to play off her best looks and best airs. He admired music – and Miss Letitia sung, until he was tired, all the cavatinas[246] that Mozart and Rossini ever composed. Fine girls and fine singers often go too far, and "overshoot the mark;" they are perpetually assaulting your eyes or your ears, until both ache even to weariness. Nothing unconnected with intellect can please long; we soon grow weary of scentless flowers, and senseless beauties. At all events, the ladies deserved some praise, for their perseverance in the siege – although their efforts were somewhat like those of three nautilus[247] storming Gibraltar.[248]

Gertrude Raymond was a being of a very different order. Her figure was large – more dignified than elegant; her features when tranquil, had an expression of hauteur; her brow was lofty and expanded; her eyes, deep and well set; her skin, nearly olive; her hair rivaled the raven's wing; her cheek was, in general, colourless, except when her feelings were excited, and then the rich blood glowed through the dark surface with the deep colouring of the damask rose, the eyes brightened, and the generally placid Gertrude Raymond burst upon you in all the magnificence of beauty! Born of a noble but decayed family, and left an orphan at three years old, this high-minded young woman was adopted by an elderly maiden relative, the only one who retained wealth and influence. Gertrude, of course, had numerous enemies – for no other reason than that she came between certain persons who entertained certain views on a certain property. Wherever there is a "long-tailed family"[249] there is much grappling and intrigue to know who holds the best cards. Miss Raymond had of course observed the various schemes pursued by her cousins, but with no other emotion than that of pity. She pursued a course of undeviating rectitude, in opposition to their petty manœuvrings. Her aged friend was a woman whose temper had been soured by much early misfortune; and Miss Raymond bore her caprices from grateful, not from interested feelings.

When Gertrude had attained her seventeenth year, Miss, or, as she was usually called, Mrs. Dorrington, resolved to leave her country house, near Bar-rytown, and reside for a time in Bath. The principal object of this change she declared, was her anxiety that Miss Raymond should receive all the advantages of finishing-masters, and polished English society, as she would inherit the greater part of her fortune. It is impossible to conceive anything like the sensa-tion this avowal excited! An earthquake was nothing to it! All the cousins to the fourteenth remove, were in dreadful consternation; public and private commit-tees assembled; and all minor jealousies were, for a time, forgotten, in order that the common enemy – poor Gertrude! – might be dispossessed of the stronghold she held in her rich relative's good opinion.

"It is quite bad enough," said one, "to have her put over all our heads, and she very little nearer the old lady than ourselves; but to leave the country and go off, like a duchess, to Bath, and be pampered up, is too much entirely." "It's enough to break a heart of stone," said another, "to see her riding here and riding there, in the carriage, and looking so mealy mouthed all the time; and her kindness to the poor – all put on to gain popularity." They plotted and plotted, and, planned and planned, but to no purpose; go the old lady would, and go she did. In vain did the enemy declare their deep sorrow at parting, for a time, with their beloved Mrs. Dorrington, and their dear "Miss Gurry;" in vain did they offer, either singly, or in a body (forty-five of them, at the very least), to accompany their sweet friends to Bath, or all over the world, at any personal sacrifice, rather than suffer them to go alone amongst strangers. Mrs. Dorrington thanked them for their atten-tion, and abruptly replied, that two thousand per annum made a home of any hotel in England, and friends of all strangers; and that she was able to take care of Gertrude, and Gertrude was able to take care of her. The poor of the neighbour-hood sorrowed sincerely after their young benefactress. Mr. Barry knew more of Miss Raymond's charities than any other person, for she never failed to send him, from Bath, little sums of money, and presents for her poor pensioners. Mrs. Dor-rington was quite right in her estimation of society; she had soon plenty of *friends* at Bath, and Miss Raymond's attractions drew many admirers to their house.

It is a difficult thing to find an Irish agent who performs his duty like an English one; a circumstance, perhaps, more to be attributed to want of busi-ness-knowledge than want of inclination. Mrs. Dorrington's remittances were delayed beyond all bearing; and after "absenteeing" for some time, she surprised Gertrude one morning by informing her that she had made up her mind to go over to Ireland for a fortnight or three weeks, and look into her own affairs that wanted arranging. "It will astonish them all," she continued, "to see the old woman looking so well; and, as you have so often promised Mrs. Ackland to spend a little time with her at Clifton, we will separate there; and I will not be absent more than three weeks. I shall certainly never suffer you to revisit Ireland, until you are married in that sphere of life which your birth, and the property *I have left you*, entitles you to."

Gertrude had not permitted any opportunity to pass, that enabled her to say a few words in favour of her relatives; for *self* was never uppermost in her mind. But Mrs. Dorrington's reserved, and even austere manners to her dearest earthly tie, were seldom even so bland as to permit such observations. Gertrude accompanied her friend to Clifton, and saw her departure with sincere sorrow; she yearned to behold the green hills of her country, and the dear companions of her childhood: but Mrs. Dorrington's fiat was not to be disputed. The first letter she received contained a long description of the bad management that had occurred during her absence, and her resolve to set all to rights before she returned to England. The next was filled with details of sundry arrangements; and then came a long silence. No letters; post succeeded post; no intelligence. At length came a letter from Mr. Barry: Mrs. Dorrington, he informed her, was seriously ill, and begged she would come over immediately. No packet sailed that day: the next brought another account – her friend was dead. The shock was more than she could bear; and when she arose from a couch of suffering and sorrow, several letters were presented to her by the lady of the house. The two principal were – one from her old and steady friend, Mr. Barry, entreating, if she knew of the existence of a will, to see to it at once, as the heir-at-law had already taken possession of the property on the presumption that no document existed leaving any provision at all for her: – the other from the heir himself, desiring that all the letters, papers, and personal property of "the late Miss Dorrington, (how that cold sentence wounded!) should be forthwith delivered to Mr. Scrapthorne, Attorney-at-law, Back Lane, Bristol; who was empowered to take possession of the same.

> "From, Madam, yours,
> "Thomas Dorrington."

The very abject, who, but six months before, had requested "the always kind interference of his friend (whom he was proud to call relative), Miss Raymond, with that most respected lady, Mrs. Dorrington, to beg he might have forty acres of the upper farm, now out of lease, on fair terms, and a loan of thirty pounds to help to stock it

> "From your humble servant to command,
> "And most faithful cousin,
> "Thomas Dorrington."

Poor Gertrude! – the ingratitude manifested by the last epistle – for she had procured the man sixty pounds, and obtained his other request – aroused all her energies, and diligent search was made for a will; but no document, even alluding to one, could be discovered. Every body felt for "poor Miss Raymond." "Such a melancholy change!" "Pity she was not married before!" "Hard fate!" "Very distressing!" Some asked her "to spend a few days until she fixed upon her future plans;" others extended their invitation to an entire month; but Lady Florence Barry, albeit unused to letter-writing, added the following postscript to her son's letter, which was despatched when all hopes of finding a will were abandoned: – "I am old, Gertrude; my hand trembles, and my eyes are dim; but my heart is warm, warmer towards you now than in your sunnier days. Come to us – be to us as a child, and your society will bestow a blessing which we will endeavour to repay."

Gertrude's reply to this generous offer was at once simple and dignified.

"It is not," she said, "that I do not value your kindness, dear and beloved friends, above every earthly blessing, but I cannot live *dependant* even on you. I have accepted a situation as governess in Lady B—'s family, and I will endeavour to do my duty in that sphere of life unto which it hath pleased God to call me. Believe me, the change must serve; I almost think I was too uplifted. I have now put my trust in God, who will do what seemeth best unto him. To-morrow I leave this place, its false and glittering friends, to enter on my new duties in London. I am promised a month's holiday, and, if I can summon fortitude to visit Ireland, I will see you then. I hear the new possessor has sold all off, even the ornaments of the old mansion; – that is heart-rending. But, worst of all, my poor pensioners! – however, I shall be able to spare them something out of my earnings – *my* earnings; let me not be unthankful; I remember, with gratitude, that my education has saved me from the bitterness of *dependance*."

In a decent, solitary cabin, on the Dorrington estate, resided nurse Keefe, so called from having "fostered" Miss Raymond. She was considered by her neighbours "a remarkable well-bred, dacent woman;" and, when Gertrude left Ireland, the faithful creature would have accompanied "her foster-child," had it not been that her husband was in ill health, and demanded all her attention; he died about six weeks before Mrs. Dorrington, but nurse had made up her mind to return with the lady to England; her sudden death, of course, prevented it, and nurse Keefe awaited "her dear child's coming home to take possession of her own;" mourned for the dead, and rejoiced in her young lady's prospects almost at the same moment. When she heard that the property was going into other hands, nothing could exceed her grief; she was almost frantic, and abused the heir-at-law in no measured terms, declaring that he had made away with the will, and all were thieves and rogues. Mr. Barry assured her he was using his exertions to induce Miss Raymond to reside with his mother; and that information afforded her some little comfort; but when she found that her nursling was going as governess to a family, the poor creature's misery was truly distressing. She returned to her cottage with a breaking heart, and did not even go to Barrytown to inquire after "Miss Gurry" for three weeks. When she again made her appearance there, she astounded Mr. Barry with the information that she had "canted all her bits o' things," had drawn what money she had saved up in the bank out of it, given up her farm, and was absolutely setting off to London to see "her child," as she generally called her. "I'm not going to be a burthen, sir," she said to Mr. Barry, when he pointed out to the affectionate creature the folly of her journey. "I have as good as a hundred-and-twinty pounds, solid gould and silver, that's not mine, but her's, now she happens to want it – mores the pity! Sure it was by sarving her I got it, which makes it her's whin she's distressed, (that I should live to see it!) if not in law, any how in justice, which is the best law, without any manner of doubt. So I'll jist take it her myself, to save postage; and I'm stout and strong, and able to get up fine linen, and clearstarch, with any she in the kingdom of England; and sure she'll be able to get me plinty of work; and that trifle can lay in the London Bank for her, whin she wants any little thing, as sure she must; and I'll be near her to keep her from being put upon, by them English. And, God be praised! I'm able to stand up for her still, and make her sensible of the honour she's doing them by staying there at all. And now my blessing, and the blessing of the poor, be about yer honour! You'll not see me until I can't be of any use to Miss Raymond – the angel!"

So nurse Keefe journeyed to London; and, at last, found herself at Hyde Park Corner, quite bewildered by the crowd and noise, and endeavouring to make her way to Grosvenor-place. Her quaint appearance attracted attention, as she passed along. Short black silk cloak – white dimity petticoat – shoes and silver buckles – small black "mode" bonnet, hardly shading her round good-natured face, were singular gear, even in London; and her rich brogue, whenever she inquired, "if any one could tell her, where Lady B—'s, and her young lady's house, was, in Grosvenor-place," caused a universal laugh, which she did not at all relish. She stood at the corner opposite Hyde Park, gazing wildly about, resolved not to ask any more questions, when a gentleman good-naturedly inquired, "if she was looking for any particular house."

"Is it looking! – troth, and I am, sir, till I'm blind and stupid, and can see nothing – God help me! – with the noise and the people, skrimitching and fighting; they may hould their tongues about the wild Irish; the English here, I'm sure, are all mad; but as ye're so kind, and, no doubt, knowledgable, maybe you could tell me the way to one Lady B—'s, and my young lady's, who live somewhere hereabouts in Grosvenor-place."

"Lady B—'s!" repeated the stranger; "I am going there, and you may follow me, if you please." The gentleman walked on, and the delighted nurse breathlessly addressed him: –

"Ah, then, sir, every joy in heaven to ye! – and sure ye know my young lady?"

"I have not that pleasure."

"I ax yer pardon, but ye said ye knew Lady B—"

"I do."

"Well, yer honour, sure my young lady stops with her."

"No young lady, that I know of, lives there, except – oh, I have heard of a young Irish lady, a governess, I believe; but, of course, she is not seen."

"Not seen!" repeated nurse, who had no idea that Miss Raymond could be excluded from any society: "is she sick, sir?"

"Not that I know of; but I suppose she is in the nursery, or study, or somewhere with the children."

This information could not be borne silently, and she told the gentleman the history of her "young lady," with so much earnestness that, although he was much interested, he heartily wished himself housed; for nurse Keefe's eloquence attracted a crowd. As they ascended the steps of Lady B—'s residence, Gertrude and her pupils were descending. The poor creature sprang forward, fell on her knees, and grasped Miss Raymond's dress, unable, fortunately, from her violent agitation, to utter a sentence. The face of an old friend is more delightful than sunshine in winter. Gertrude raised the aged woman to her bosom; and, heedless of the presence of strangers, burst into tears. When, after the lapse of an hour, nurse Keefe and Miss Raymond were seated in the study appropriated to Gertrude's use, the faithful creature opened her simple plan to her foster child, and endeavoured to impress on her mind that the money she had brought, carefully wrapped in an old stocking, belonged to Gertrude. Much did the good nurse regret that she could not make "her darlint" understand this; and Miss Raymond, in her turn, laboured as fruitlessly to convince her that she was perfectly happy, and treated quite as she ought to be.

"I can't believe it – I can't believe it, Miss, machree! – How could I, whin that fine-spoken young gentleman tould me he never set eyes upon you, although he came often to the house? D'ye think I've no sense? – or that I'm out an' out a fool? – Sure it's well I remember, after yer angel of a mother died, whin ye came to be Mrs, Dorrington's child (who had no *born* child, on account she was an ould maid), that I used to have to bring ye into the grand parlour as good as tin times a day, in order that they might all admire yer beauty; and lords and ladies, and even mimbers of Parliament, fighting like cat an' dog for the first kiss, and I fighting to keep them from dragging the head off o' ye. And now to be in a bit of an English lady's family, as a sort of a – Oh! ullagone! ullagone![250] – my poor ould heart 'ill split!"

Gertrude had some difficulty in pacifying her; convincing was out of the question. "Well, may-be so, my dear. – Happy! – I can't understand it; may-be so!"

The next thing was to provide a lodging for nurse Keefe; and, as she soon placed what she called Miss Raymond's "trifle o' money" in a banker's hands, she became anxious for employment. Lady B., who was really kind and amiable, was highly pleased with the poor woman's generous feelings, and, in less than a month, the good nurse had more clearstarching and "fine-plaiting"[251] than she could manage. Thus, to use her own words, "the money powered in upon her." She visited Gertrude once or twice a week, and never came empty-handed; nuts, oranges, and cakes, were her general presents; but sometimes she added pieces of gay riband, and two or three yards of lace. The person who gave her most employment, and paid her best, was her kind conductor when she first visited Grosvenor-plaee. The gentleman knew something of the neighbourhood where Miss Raymond had resided, for Mr. Barry and his father had been college friends at Oxford, and he often chatted with nurse Keefe when she brought home shirts and cravats ("that would bate the snow for whiteness") to his lodgings in St. James's-street, and highly gratified her by the information that, as he occasionally joined Lady B.'s family circle, – he had sometimes the pleasure of seeing Miss Raymond. She was a little mortified that he did not praise her young lady, as she thought everybody ought to do, but consoled herself by muttering, as she went home – "Well, it's mighty quare, but these Englishmen are afeard of wearing out their tongues; who knows, for all that, but, may-be, he's like the countryman's goose, that thought all the more for not spaking."

Mr. Wortley, for it was the self-same gentleman, did think much on every subject, but, latterly, more of Gertrude than of any other: he had not seen her often, but he had heard of her a great deal. Lady B. spoke of Miss Raymond in the highest terms, and the children manifested the strongest attachment towards their "dear, kind governess." "She is always so dignified and correct," said her ladyship; "and is never out of temper," said little Jessica; "and although she is sometimes melancholy," added Miss Clorinda, the eldest of the children, "which is not to be wondered at, because once she had almost – almost as much money as mamma, yet she smiles away her sorrows so sweetly, and sings for us of an evening, as well – indeed, quite as well – as Miss Stephens, and very like her, too, the ballads that make one weep." "Dear mamma," said Charles, a rosy boy of seven years old, "do coax Miss Raymond to drink tea in the drawing-room with us to-night; she will never come when there's company; but Mr. Wortley, you know, is an old friend, and nobody; – and then she will sing for us; – do, mamma." The request was readily granted, and he ran off with a message from mamma, begging Miss Raymond would that evening take tea in the drawing-room. He stopped at the door, and said playfully to Mr. Wortley, who had been some time in the rooom, "Mind, I heard you say to papa, the other day, that you wanted a wife; – now, you shan't have my Miss Raymond, for she shall be my wife, when I'm a man."

"Dignified and correct – never out of temper – with much reason to be sorrowful, and yet chasing it away, even to the gratifying of childhood; and singing – I never, never heard any woman sing with half so much feeling. What an admirable wife she would make!" So soliloquized Mr. Wortley when he left the family party one evening; and, of course, came to the resolution of knowing more of this "very interesting and superior woman." That, however, was not easily accomplished; the education of Lady B.'s children occupied all Gertrude's time; and even if the duties of her situation had not prevented it, she had so recently smarted from fashionable fickleness, that she was not at all inclined to stake even an hour's happiness upon it again. When Mr. Wortley met her, his very anxiety to render himself agreeable made him awkward. He experienced, however, some alarm, when he found that Gertrude Raymond was going to spend two entire months at Barrytown, during Lady B.'s intended tour on the Continent; and thought he would speak to her at once as well as be could; but a little reflection convinced him that this would be the most effectual way to obtain a decided refusal, as he could have yet made no progress in her affections, and he knew her mind was too noble to calculate merely upon worldly advantages in a matrimonial connexion. After much pro and con, he resolved to speak to Lady B. on the subject, and, without waiting for his curricle[252] walked quickly towards Grosvenor-place. When he arrived, he was informed that Miss Raymond, attended by nurse Keefe and Lady B.'s own footman, had just departed for Ireland; and that Lady B. was completing her arrangements previous to her Continental tour. He felt at once a strong inclination to visit Ireland. "Every man of liberal feeling should make the tour of the sister Isle – he wondered he had never thought of it before; the Lakes of Killarney were celebrated all over the world – the Giant's Causeway, too, one of the most wonderful works of nature – the County Wicklow – the Vale of Avoca[253] – (he repeated Moore's lines to the beautiful valley, with absolute enthusiasm).[254] Besides, there was his father's old college friend, Mr. Barry; he had seen him in England during his parent's lifetime, and knew he would be so glad to receive him – dear old gentleman! – how delightful to talk with him of his father! It was, really, very ungrateful not to have visited him before; and, now that London was quite empty (the carriages were jostling at every corner), he must go to the country – and he would go to Ireland." Accordingly he wrote immediately to Mr. Barry, informed him of his anxiety to pay his respects to his father's old friend, and explore the beauties of a country he had heard so much of; hoped he should not inconvenience Mr. B. – would await his answer at Milford; and concluded by saying that he earnestly requested he would not mention his intended visit to any one, except Lady Florence, as he had a particular – very particular reason, indeed – for not wishing it mentioned, which he would hereafter explain.

There is a sort of freemasonry in goodness, that none but the good can understand. Mr. Barry, very soon after Mr. Wortley's arrival, both knew and approved
of his manly and disinterested attachment to his young friend; sincerely rejoiced
at the prospect of wealth and happiness that was brightening before her; and only
dreaded lest Gertrude's high feelings would prevent her being dependant (as she
would call it) even on a husband. The manœuvrings of Mrs. C. and Co. entertained him much; and, after dinner, on the evening of the day that the "blue lady"
arrived, as the gentlemen entered the drawingroom, Mr. Barry and Mr. Wortley
paused, and whispered to each other the same words, "How superior is she to all
around her!" Certainly the contrast between Gertrude and Miss Spinner was very
ludicrous; – the real information of the one, and assumed learning of the other,
reminded one of Florian's [255]beautiful fable, *Le Rossignol et le Prince:*[256]

> "Les sots savent tons se produire;
> Le mérite se cache, il faut l'aller trouver."[257]

One was as presuming as the sparrows; the other as retiring as the nightingale.

"Now, re-e ly," commenced the learned lady, "now, re-e-ly (she was ambitious of the English accent) I am so glad you are come; gentlemen, I contest for
woman's talent, but I lowly bend to the magnificent intellect of the creation's
lords – although, it must be confessed, you are not 'melting as a lover's prayer,' as
Hughes[258] beautifully expresses it; and though, sometimes, 'ye are more changea-
ble than Proteus,'[259] yet are ye 'glorious as Mars,'[260] and 'luminous as stars!' There,"
said the lady, making a low courtesy, "is rhyme and reason, which I consider the
perfection of oratory!"

Miss Livy and Miss Letty laughed; Gertrude smiled, and the gentlemen
could scarcely keep their countenances in proper form. Mr. Altern, the rattling
foxhunter, complimented the lady on her eloquence, which was, he said, "as
good as a play;" and seated himself by her side, to draw her out; – there was
little occasion for it, for when once a woman gets a taste for display, it is like
the overflowing of the Nile, which no earthly barrier can withstand; I fear me,
however, it does not fertilize like that river. When the tea equipage was removed,
Miss Spinner proposed "that they should busy themselves in some intellectual
exercise. "I am sure," she continued, "Miss Raymond, who has so long enjoyed
the enlightening beams of London society, will second this motion; and, indeed,
I wished particularly to ask her, if she had seen any of the celebrated characters
– the lions of the day?"

"Yes, I have, I believe, seen many of them."

"Oh, how I envy you! Perhaps you attended the celebrated Dr. Townsend's[261]
lectures, on the use and abuse of the steam-engine; – of course you recollect
Darwin's beautiful lines: –

'Fresh, through a thousand pipes, the wave distils,
And thirsty cities drink the exuberant rills.'"[262]

Gertrude confessed she had not attended the lectures.

"What a pity! I think I saw your daughters, Mrs. Croydon, in that sweet fellow's botanical studio, at the Rotunda – I forget his name – Rose – Rosacynth![263] – do you recollect his delightful, and exquisitely touching, description of the papilionaceous tribe?[264] – and his hortus siccus?[265] – so talented and classical! – to poetize the loves of the flowers like Moore's loves of the angels!"[266]

"Oh, yes!" replied both young ladies, "we all remember Mr. Rosacynth; we attended his lectures, and all such things, before our education was finished. I suppose, Gertrude, you will make Lady B.'s daughters, *your pupils*, do so, when they are old enough?"

"Young ladies," replied Mr. Barry, quietly, "I believe Miss Raymond will soon devote her exclusive attention to one pupil – at least, I know one who would give – "

"Dear sir," said poor Gertrude, springing up, "do, do hold – peace, for pity's sake!"

"Bless me, what's the matter?" inquired old Lady Florence; the Croydons exchanged glances; Mr. Wortley stooped to look for his handkerchief, which was in his hand; and Mr. Altern gave a long *whew*. The silence showed symptoms of continuance, which, nevertheless, the foxhunter at length broke. "I hope you don't patronise the three B's that presides over conversazioni?"[267]

"What are they?" laughed Mr. Barry.

"Blue stockings,[268] blue milk,[269] and blue looks."

"Sir – Mr. Altern," said Miss Spinner, indignantly, "I am sorry for you! You have no more taste for the beauties of literature – to think or speak so becomes a Goth, a Vandal,[270] or – a foxhunter !"

"Whew! – dear madam, don't plunge so; a joke's a joke – though, 'faith, there's some truth in it. I was inveigled, once, to one of their conversazioni; what a pucker[271] they were in! – worse than a pack of hounds in full cry, but not half the spirit or harmony, for they were all after different game; some shooting, some coursing, some angling, some (old ones too) ogling – they seemed to me to neglect no sort of business, except eating; and that was not their fault, for they had nothing to eat, save trumpery biscuits[272] and half-starved sandwiches; my Sly would swallow plates and all, in a moment – coffee, and *eau sucres*,[273] and such poison! – oh, what is it to a baron of beef and a foaming tankard, or a smoking jug of whisky-punch?"

"But, sir," said Gertrude, kindly, for she saw Miss Spinner was annoyed, "surely people do not assemble merely to eat and drink; as intellectual beings, we have higher objects in society, and –"

"I'll tell you what," said the honest, but unpolished squire, "you are much too pretty for one of the sisterhood."

"Sir, I thank you," and Miss Spinner arose and courtesied low – very low – to Mr. Altern.

"Miss Olivia," said Mr. Wortley, eager to avert the coming storm, "do, pray, favour us with that beautiful cavatina of Rossini's – we all like music."

Miss Livy did not need a second request; and, for some time, she was listened to with much attention. At last, Miss Spinner became tired of silence, and, gliding up to Mr. Barry, said, "that as Mr. — (she forgot the name) had gone off that morning in search of Roman pavements, and broken vessels, pipes, and interesting relics of the olden time, and had not yet returned to illumine their orbit by his brilliant discoveries, she had a few little curiosities in her bureau, up-stairs, that might afford amusement – she would bring them down while they were singing." The lady soon imported various packages, boxes, and bags, placed them on the sofa, piled up on her right hand and on her left, and looked not unlike a venerable mummy encompassed by Egyptian relics. She exhibited her specimens of conchology; mineralogy; her little electrifying machine;[274] her figure from the inquisition at Goa;[275] a snuff box that Buonaparte had – looked at; a lock of hair, cut from the tail of Marie Antoinette's favourite lap-dog; a bit of Pope's willow;[276] a leaf of Shakspeare's mulberry tree; a petrified toe of St. Peter, which was classically labelled – "*Digitus de Sancto Pietro!*"[277] – and many other equally valuable relics. The young people grouped around her, and she was unusually elaborate and eloquent in her descriptions; nay, she even repeated an extemporaneous poem she had made upon herself on a misty morning.

Gertrude and Mr. Wortley were standing near each other, when Miss Spinner pulled various old-fashioned boxes from a yellow silk bag. "I purchased these very interesting relics of antiquity at a receptacle for old furniture – vulgo,[278] a broker's shop; it is very obscure; I fancy there is part of this strange-looking box unopened, it appears so thick and clumsy – perhaps the fastening is concealed by some spring; it has hitherto baffled my utmost ingenuity, and I hardly thought the man would sell it without examination."

"I ought to know it," said Gertrude; "it belonged, I am certain, to my dear old friend's cabinet." She took it, and touched a spring that was concealed by a small stud; the bottom opened, and discovered, tightly pressed in, a folded parchment.

Mr. Barry seized it, hastily unfastened the riband which tied it, and exclaimed, "Gracious Providence! – the Will! – the Will! – the Will! She was neither forgetful nor unjust. Mr. Wortley, I give you joy; – she'll have you now, because she'll be almost as rich as yourself; joy – joy! Oh, I'm so happy! – quite right! – 'all my personal and estated property too,' – my dear Miss Spinner, you are the sweetest being on earth – 'to Gertrude Raymond, – just as it should be!"

"Dear – dearest Gertrude!" exclaimed Mr. Wortley; but Gertrude had fainted on his shoulder; and salts, eau-de-luce,[279] de Cologne,[280][281] de Mille-fleurs, were abundantly supplied by the young ladies, who hardly understood the matter, but knew that all was in delightful bustle, or, as Miss Spinner said, "soft confusion – rosy terror!"

When Gertrude had recovered, and time was afforded for deliberate investigation, Mr. Barry read the will aloud. Mrs. Dorrington had left her entire property to Miss Raymond, subject to some life annuities, either to old and faithful servants, or poor relatives. Amongst other paragraphs contained in it was the following: – "And whereas, I have good and substantial reasons for believing that Thomas Dorrington (who is, unfortunately, by the will of God, my nearest relative) is a double-dealing craven and a heartless man; seeing that, like the fabled Janus,[282] he carries two faces, I leave him to be provided for by Gertrude Raymond, convinced that she, of her generosity, will do more for him, in consideration of his family, than my love of justice would permit me, knowing his duplicity as I do; – I leave him to her mercy."

"It is singular," observed Mr. Barry, "that my old friend should so studiously have concealed all information on the subject of her will from us; to execute it with her own hand, and never mention its existence. She was a good lawyer, however, for it is duly witnessed; but where shall we find those people? – this document has been nearly four years in existence. 'Patrick Muller,' the old butler, he is dead; 'Frank Hayward,' and 'Jane Miller,' have you any idea where they are, Gertrude?"

"Frank Hayward married Jane immediately on our going to Bath, and my dear relative, you know, sir, never retained married servants; but she procured them confidential situations in Sir Thomas Harrowby's family. They have been ever since on the Continent; I believe they are now at Rome."

"How very fortunate," said Miss Spinner, "that I happened to purchase the box! My dear Miss Raymond, I give you much joy."

"Oh, so do we all!" said Mrs, Croydon; somewhat awkwardly, however, for Mr. Wortley's exclamation had convinced her, that her daughters' beauty and accomplishments had been displayed in vain; and that, even when portion-less, and a governess, Gertrude Raymond, notwithstanding her want of tact, advanced age (twenty-two), and what Mrs. C. always termed "very plain appearance," had conquered, what she considered, "a man worth looking after," because he had five thousand a-year!

"Gertrude," said Lady Florence, who, by the assistance of her ear-trumpet, heard and understood all that had occurred – "my dear Gertrude, your old friend rejoices for you. Nearly a century has passed over this grey head, and those who number only half my days, must experience much of joy and sorrow; yet this is one of the happiest hours I have ever known. I sorrowed, bitterly sorrowed, when you, of ancient family, and mind capable of adding lustre to the highest rank, became a labourer for independence. Yet, Gertrude, I loved you more and more; for even the pittance you worked for, you divided with the poor and the afflicted. Nay, child, I will speak; I do not often praise; but you deserve more than I can give. – Never did you utter unkindness towards those who had dashed your cup of happiness to the earth, even as it had touched your lips. Never did you suffer the breath of slander to dim *her* memory, from whom you had a right to expect so much; for you were unto her as a dear and tender child. I know the heart has ties stronger than those of kindred, but you had claims from both these sources."

"My dear Lady Florence," interrupted Gertrude, much affected, "you over-rate – I knew my friend too well to imagine, even, that she would forget me; I should have been base if I could for a moment have believed it!"

"Your trials are now passed," resumed the old lady; "the wind of adversity separates the chaff from the wheat. You have learned to value *the world's* friend-ship. And when I remember the virtues that characterized your amiable and excellent parents, the words of this holy book press upon my memory – 'I have been young, and now am old, yet saw I never the righteous forsaken, nor his seed begging their bread.'"[283]

"Hang me!" said Mr. Altern, after a pause, "but it's worth riding a steeple-chase, to come in for all this."

"It would make a delightful tale, if well wrought up," interrupted Miss Spin-ner, "quite good enough for – perhaps not for Blackwood,[284] but for something else, particularly if it ends, as I presume, with a – a – spare my blushes!"

A sunny Sabbath morning succeeded this happy *dénouement*,[285] and the finding of the will was noised all over the parish. The most busy agent on this occasion was nurse Keefe, who went to first mass, expressly for the purpose of telling, "how my young lady will have her right, and the bad breed 'll be forced to fly the country; and more will be happy than me – the fine English gintleman, that many was afther, the silly crathurs! as if it would be any good for them to put themselves equal to my young lady, with the raale gintleman who had sich beautiful estates, and sich a power of money, and a raale castle, built on a gould mine (as I hard tell); and whin he wants, he has nothin' to do but say to one of his men, 'James, go down and bring me up a bucket of gould;' and to another, 'Charles, my boy, go down and bring me up a bucket of silver.'"

The peasantry, who most cordially hated "the new man," rejoiced very sin-cerely at the intelligence. "Thos. Dorrington, Esq." was neither fitted by nature nor education to occupy the station in society to which his wealth had raised him. He was what the poor termed "a hard man;" – let the land to the high-est bidder, without any regard to the oldest tenant; and distrained[286] for rent whenever it was not paid to the hour. Such a person was not likely to obtain popularity; and his low habits effectually prevented his associating with the gen-try on equal terms.

"Well, bad as he is, Mistress Keefe," said Paddy Magin, "he didn't spirit away the Will, which for sartin I thought he did, for he always had the look of a dirty turn."

"Well, I set it down to that too, Paddy; and it's well for him he didn't. I'll stop myself, after grate mass,[287] jist to see my young lady go to church, and pass the mock[288] people on the road."

"Success to ye for ever, Mistress, honey! – and I'll gather the boys, and we'll have a shout for the young lady, and a groan for the by-gones, that 'll shiver[289] the mountains in no time; – it's a pity it's Sunday, or we'd have a bonfire."

"Ay, Paddy, we'll have that same whin she's set up safe and sound in her own house; I don't think they'll have the face to dispute the will."

Paddy did "gather the boys," and a glorious shout and a deafening groan they gave.

"Thos. Dorrington, Esq.," affected at first to disbelieve the existence of the will; but he secretly procured what money he could from the tenants, and, deserting his unfortunate wife, whom he had long treated with brutal indifference, fled to America, and left them to the mercy of one who loved mercy. The reader will easily imagine that every difficulty in the way of a – a – the event, at the allusion to which Miss Spinner blushed, was by this fortunate circumstance removed; that the good Gertrude had now no scruples to overcome; and that no barrier existed to the completion of the perfect happiness, to which she was so fully and so justly entitled: –

"Heaven doth with us as we with torches do;
Not light them for ourselves; for if her virtues
Had not gone forth of her, 'twere all alike
As if she had them not."[290]

Barrytown never was so full of company as about three months after Miss Spinner's box had been found to contain so valuable a parchment; "shakedowns" in every room; open house, sheep and oxen roasted whole, barrels of ale and whisky, fiddlers and pipers; Lady Brilliant and suite;[291] nurse Keefe, deputy mistress of kitchen ceremonies; Miss Spinner, in a white satin hat, looped up with roses *à la pastorelle*,[292] and a *real* new wig; Mrs. Croydon and her daughters (poor spite!) "so particularly engaged that they could not do themselves the honour from which they expected so much happiness – but wished the bride, and bridegroom, more than a thousand blessings." Barrytown was always noted for its hospitality; for the poor, as well as the rich sheltered under its roof, and the generous master afforded relief to all who really wanted it. But when Gertrude Raymond was married to Alfred Wortley, everybody wondered where, even in Barrytown, such crowds could have been packed. Lady Florence Barry, who had not been outside her own avenue gate for twenty years, accompanied the bride; and Mr. Barry gave her away. More people could not have been at a priest's funeral than assembled on this memorable occasion –

> "When the wrong was made right,
> And the dark light,"

as Miss Spinner quoted it; and the "might and right" were exemplified for many years by the inhabitants of Barrytown and Mount Gertrude (as Lady Florence called Mrs. Dorrington's old residence).

> "Hospitality,
> No formality,"

became the motto of both houses, which were conducted on the same plan, except, indeed, that the great hall at Wortley-mount was garnished with merry, laughing children, instead of dogs, eagles, cats, and ravens.

"TAKE IT EASY."

"ALL ye can do with him, Aileen, when he gets into those humours, is – to take it asy."

"Take it *asy*, indeed!" repeated the pretty bride, with a toss of her head, and a curl of her lip; "it's asy to say, take it asy. I'm sure if I had thought Mark was so passionate, I'd have married Mike!"

"But Mike was mighty dark," replied old Aunt Alice, with a mysterious shake of her head.

"Well, so he was: but then I might have had Matthew."

"Ah! ah!" laughed old Alice; "he was the worst bird of the nest! Look, ye can wind Mark round yer finger, as I wind this worsted thread – if ye'll only *take it asy*."

"Oh! I wish – I wish I had known, before, that men were so ill-contrived! I'd have died sooner than have married," sobbed Aileen; who, to confess the truth, had been so much petted by the neighbours, on account of her beauty, that it would have required a large proportion of love, and a moderate allowance of wisdom, to change the village coquette into a sober wife – I say a large proportion of love: "Wit," to quote the old adage, "may win a man," *but wit never kept one:* unless a woman cultivate the affections, even more than knowledge, she will never secure a husband's heart. It is to this cultivation, indeed, that women owe – and to which, only, they ought to owe – their influence; and the neglect of which inevitably engenders that mutual distrust which can end only in misery.

"Ah, whisht! avourneen!" said Alice, "sure I told ye all along. 'Mark,' says I, 'is all fire and tow[293] – but it's out in a minute; Mike is *dark*, and deep as the bay of Dublin; and Matthew is all to the bad intirely.' You've got the best of the three. And ye can manage him just as the south wind, that's blowing now – God bless it! – manages the thistle-down that's floating through the air, if *ye'll take it asy*."

At first, Aileen pouted, then she sat down to her wheel – was too much out of temper to do what she was doing, well – broke her thread – pushed it from her – took up her knitting – dropped the stitches – shook the needles – and, of course, dropped some more.

"*Take it asy*," said aunt Alice, looking at her, over her spectacles.

Aileen flung the knitting away, clasped her arms round her aunt's neck, rested her head on her bosom, and wept outright.

"Let's go into the garden, sit under the ould lime tree, and watch the bees that are near swarming," observed aunt Alice, "and we'll talk yer trouble over, avourneen. It's very sorry I am to see ye taking on so, for a thrifle, at the first going off. But you'll know better by-'n-by, when real troubles come."

Poor Aileen, like all young people, thought her troubles were very real, but she held her peace; until, observing the bees more than usually busy, she muttered, "I wonder, aunt, you don't tell the bees to take it asy."

"So I would, dear, if I saw them quarrelling; but they are too wise to quarrel among themselves, whatever they do with *furriners*. They fly together, live together, sing together, work together, and have but the one object and aim in life; ah, then, many's the good lesson we may learn from the bees, besides that which teaches us to bring all that's good and useful to our own homes." The old woman paused; and then added, "Sit ye down here, my child, and listen to what I'm going to tell ye. Ye know well, avourneen, I was lawfully married, first, by ould Father John, to Richard Mulvaney – my heart's first love he was; heaven be his bed this blessed day, and grant we may meet above the world and its real troubles! Aileen, it was, indeed, a trouble to see my brave, young, handsome husband, dragged out of the blue waters of the Shannon; to find that, when I called, he could not answer; when I wept, he could not comfort; that my cheek rested for hours on his lips, and he did not kiss it; and that never more, in this world, would I hear his sweet and loving voice!"

Fourscore years and five had passed over the head of that woman: and her age was as beautiful, according to its beauty, as had been her youth. She had been married three times; yet her eyes filled with tears at the remembrance of the love and sorrow of her early days, and it was some time before she could continue.

"Well, dear, one day, Richard and I had some little tiff, and I said more than I ought to have said. And it was by the same token, a fine midsummer morning; I strayed out to our garden, and picked up a shiny snail; and as I looked at the snail, I remembered how, the last midsummer day, I had put just such another between two plates, and sat for an hour by the rising sun, with the forefinger of my left hand crossed over the forefinger of my right hand; and then, as thrue as life, when I lifted the plate, the thing had marked as purty an R, and a piece of as beautiful an M, as the schoolmaster himself could write, upon the plate; and I cried to remember how glad I was then, and how sad now; and, at last, I cried myself to sleep. Alanna machree! I was little more than a child, – not all out sixteen. Well, dear, in my drame, I suppose I must call it, I saw the beautifulest fairy (the Lord save us!) – the very handsomest of the good people that ever the eyes of woman looked upon, – a little deeshy-dawshy[294] craythur, footing it away, all round the blossom of a snow-white lily; now twisting round upon the tip of her tiny toe; then, as if she was joining hands round, down the middle and up again, to the tune of the 'Rakes of Mallow.'"[295]

"The 'Rakes of Mallow!'" exclaimed Aileen.

"The 'Rakes of Mallow!'" repeated Alice, solemnly; "I heard it as plain as I hear the rising march of the bees at this blessed minute. Well, of a suddent, she made a spring, and stood upright as a dart upon the green and goolden crown, in the very midst of the flower, and pushed back her ringlets, and settled her dress at a pocket looking-glass, not so big as a midge's wing; then, all in a minute she looked at me, and said, 'I don't like the sight of a wet eye; – what ails ye, young woman?'

"Well, to be sure, my heart came to my lips; but I had too much manners not to answer the great lady; and, 'Madam,' says I, 'my eyes would be as dry, though not as bright as yer honour's, if it was'nt for my husband, my lady, who wants to have a way and a will of his own.'

"'It's the way with all the men, my own husband into the bargain,' says the queen, for she was no less; 'and there's no use fighting for the upper hand,' says the queen, 'for both the law and the prophets are against us in that; and if it comes to open war,' says the queen, 'we get the worst of it: if your husband falls into a bad temper, or a queer temper, – if he is cross, or unkind, or odd – take it asy,' says the queen, 'even if he does not come round at once. This quiet way of yours will put you in his heart, or him at your feet (which is pretty much the same thing) at last: gentleness does wonders for us women, in Fairy-land. You could hardly believe what power it has; it's a weapon of great strength entirely, in the hands of a purty woman – and you are very purty for a mortal,' says she again, looking at me through the eye of a heart's-ease,[296] which she wore about her neck for a quizzing-glass.[297]

"'I thank you, my sweet and beautiful lady,' says I, 'for your compliment.' 'Ah! ah!' and she laughed, and her laugh was full of joy and hope, like the music of the priest's own silver bell. 'It's no harm,' she continued, 'if now and then you give him a taste of that which makes your eyes so bright, and your cheeks so red, just now.

"'What's that, Madam?' says I.

"'Flattery,' says she. 'Make a man, be he fairy, or be he mortal, pleased with himself, and he is sure to be pleased with you.' And then she laughed again. 'Whatever he says or does,' says her majesty, while she was getting into a goolden saddle, a horseback[298] on a great dragon-fly, dressed in a beautiful jacket and gown of green velvet, with a silver riding-whip in her hand, 'take it asy,' says she; and I heard her laugh and sing when she was out of sight, and her sweet voice shook a shower of white rose-leaves, from a bush, on my face. And when I awoke, I saw the wisdom of her words, and I kept them close in my own bosom; and often, when I'd be just going to make a sharp answer to him I loved, for all that, above the world, I'd think of the fairy's word, and the evil would pass from my heart and lips without a sound – no one the worse for it, and I all the better. And sure Richard used to say I was like an angel to him. Poor fellow! he was soon to be taught the differ, for the angels took him from me in earnest!

"After a couple of years I married again. I've no reason to fault the second I had; though he was not gentle, like him who sighed out his soul in the blue waters: he was dark, and would not tell what offended him. Well, I'd have given the world to have had some one to whom I could make a clean breast; but I had none; and, somehow, I again sat in the same spot, at the same time – again slept – and again saw the same one of the good people. I did not think her honour was as gay as she had been, and I wondered in my heart if she, too, had taken a second husband; it would not have been manners for me to spake first, but she was as free as ever.

"'Well,' she says, looking at me very solid-like, 'you've tried another; but though you have not forgotten my advice, you do not follow it.'

"'Oh, my lady, plase yer majesty,' says I, 'the tempers of the two do so differ!' and I thought with the words my heart would break: for the moment poor Richard's humour was out, it was off; but James would sulk and sulk, like a bramble under the shade of an oak: and the fairy read my thoughts as if they were an open ballad. 'This one is dark, my lady, and gets into the sulks, and is one that I can't manage, good or bad; not all as one as it was with my first husband, plase yer majesty; for when we had a tiff, it was soon over – God help me, so it used to be; but this one sits in a corner, and never speaks a word, not even to the cat.'

"'Ah,' said she, 'they are different: but the rule holds good – gentle and simple – hot and cold – old and young – you must take them asy, or you'll never be asy yourself. Let a passionate temper cool; don't blow upon it – a breath may ruffle a lake, and kindle a fire. Let a sulky temper alone, it is a standing pool; the more it is stirred, the more it will offend.' I try to talk her fine English, Aileen, but it bothers me," continued old Alice. "Well, the end of it was, that she finished as before, by telling me to *take it asy;* which, after that, I did; and I must say that James's last breath was spent in blessing me. Well, dear, Miles Pendergrast was rich, and I was poor; he wanted a mother for five children, and a servant for himself; and he took me. This was the worst case of the three. There was a great deal of love – young – fresh – heart-sweet love to the first; and more than is going, in general, to the second: but, oh, my grief! there was *none* to the third. Oh, but marriage to a woman without love! what is it? Where love is, it is even pleasant to bear a harsh word, or an unkind look – a satisfaction that you can show your love, by turning bitter to sweet. Service is no service then – his voice is your music – his word yer law – his very shadow on the ground yer brightest sunshine!"

"Aunt," said Aileen, "you did not think that with the first, at the time, or you would not have wanted the good people's advice."

"True for ye, avourneen; we never value the sunbeams so much as in the dark of the moonless night; we never value a friend's advice until he is beyond our reach; we never prize the husband's love, or the mother's care, until the grave has closed over them; and when we seek them there, the grass that we weep over is green, the mallow and the dock have covered the cross or the headstone, and the red earthworms we have disturbed bring us no message."

"I don't want to hear any more, aunt," said Aileen, pained by the picture her aunt had drawn; "now I'll own to the first of the quarrel, and the last word of it, if Mark will confess to the middle."

"Let a quarrel alone, when once it's over," interrupted her aunt. "A quarrel, darlint, is like buttermilk – when once it is out of the churn, the more you shake it, the more sour it grows."

"And must I say nothing when he comes home?"

"Oh, yes, say, 'Mark, my heart's delight!' "

"Oh, aunt, that would never do!"

"Well, if ye're ashamed to say what you feel, a smile and a kiss will do as well. And a smile and a kiss will work wonders, darling, if the heart goes with them; but if they are only given because they're dutiful gifts, ah! they fall like a snow wreath upon the spring-flower, chilling and crushing, instead of warming and cheering. Not but duty's a fine thing; but it's dark and heavy to a married woman when there is no back of love to it."

"Did the fairy queen give you the same advice the third time?" said the bride, blushing like Aurora at Alice's counsel; "for I suppose you saw her the third time – "

"I must say, achora,[299] she wasn't so civil to me the last time, as she was the first and second," answered the old dame, bridling. "She tould me I wasn't as purty as I used to be – that was true enough, to be sure, only one never likes to hear it; she tould me that, when the bloom of a woman's cheek fades, the bloom of her heart ought to increase; she talked a deal, that I did not quite understand, about men making laws and breaking them; and how every one has a thorn of some kind or other to bear with; she tould me how hard it was to find three roses in a garden all of the same shape, colour, and scent, and how could I expect three good husbands? She said that, as I had borne my crown, I must bear my cross; she was hard enough upon me; but the winding-up of her advice to me, in all my troubles, – was to take it asy; she said she had been married herself more than five hundred years."

"The ould craythur! And to talk of your not being so purty as you were!" said Aileen.

"Hush avourneen! Sure they have the use of the May-dew[300] before it falls, and the colour of the lilies and the roses before it's folded in the tender buds; and can steal the notes out of the birds' throats while they sleep."

"And still," exclaimed Aileen, half pouting, "the best advice they can give to a married woman, under all her trouble, is – to take it asy!"

"It's a sensible saying, if properly thought of," said old Alice, "and will bring peace, if not love, at the last. If we can't get rid of our troubles, it's wise to TAKE THEM ASY."

PETER THE PROPHET.

"Don't talk to me, Paddy Mulvany – don't talk to me! – where's the use of your talking, chitter-chatter, chitter-chatter, like a nest of magpies? Don't I know what I know? – Improvements, indeed! – answer me this: am not I fifty-two years and three months old – and having a fine memory, as well as much foresight – thanks be to God for the same – don't I recollect as good as fifty years? And what then? Why this; that all the trading-boats landed, on that out shore, safe and sound, whatever was wanted. – Don't tell me of the place being inconvanient, Paddy Mulvany: it's no such thing. In a peaceable village, building a quay to land coal! As if the people can't burn turf as their grandfathers did afore them! And timber! – won't wattles do for the cabins as well as ever? But mark the upshot of this – every potato, every grain of corn, 'll be bought up, and sent out of the country, when the English boats come in, and we shall all be starved; and neither man, woman, nor child, will be left alive to tell the story."

"Why, thin, Mister Peter, sure it's yerself that sees the sunny side of a thing; ye've a mighty cheering way wid ye, ever and always," said Paddy Mulvany, looking archly at his companion.

Sunny side! – Why, there's no sunny side, man alive, to see. When Wellington Bridge[301] was built over the Scar, and sure they were talking of that bridge more than a hundred years before it was begun; – no good will come of it, says I, and I was right; it has now been built three years, and no road made to it yet; and, by the same token, it's cracked in the middle; I knew no good would come of it. Oh, what sarvice that money would have done the neighbours, if it had been properly laid out!"

"Troth, Master Peter, you may say that – that is, I suppose, if you had had the management of it; but, any how, the quay 'll be built in spite o' ye; for it's an English gentleman that has taken it in hand; and, bless ye, although I know ye kept a creditable shop in the town o' Ross, you have no notion how quick they get things done in England. Sure I see it all whin I used to take Mister Nick Lett's pigs to Bristol fair; ye'd hardly credit it, but I have seen an entire street of houses built up, plastered, painted, papered – great, big houses – and the people ateing, drinking, and sleeping in thim, comfortable as anything all in one week. Bless ye, they go about things, and finish them out of hand in a jiffy!"

"So much the worse – so much the worse, Paddy Mulvany; no good can come of that; but I suppose, as you say an Englishman has taken it in hand, the quay will be built. Ye're all mad, I believe, barring myself; I see how it will end; but you mark my words, Paddy Mulvany, no good will come of it. I'll just step over to see what they're after yonder; so good-bye, Paddy – remember my words!"

"God be wid ye, Master Peter. Hulloo! I forgot to tell you that Friar Mulloy's brown nag pitched him into a ditch, and Mister Hollin's chimbly took fire on account of the new English way of sweeping; they put a goose at the top of the chimbly,[302] and let it fly down."

"There, didn't I say so?" replied the little man, stopping and looking as pleased as Punch at the narrative of accidents. "Sure, I told Friar Mulloy, 'that nag 'll brake yer reverence's neck,' said I – I knew it; mark my words: and as to the chimbly, – sure, I guessed that, though I said nothin' about it."

"Why, thin, ye're a quare little animal of a Christian, and ye believe every word I said, ye little fool of a thing!" continued Paddy, as he looked after Master Peter Callaghan, *alias*, "Peter the Prophet," *alias*, "Peter the Croaker;" "and it's a dale more ye think of yerself than anybody thinks of ye; so much the better; one madman in the parish is enough. But yon chap's not to say clane mad, only a little touched, and mighty puffed out, thinking he's got more in his brain-box than any other body in the whole kingdom – priests and bishops into the bargain. God forgive us all our sins!"

And Paddy went off in an opposite direction from Peter the Prophet, who journeyed towards the intended quay. Peter was a slight, stiff, pertinacious, pragmatic old bachelor – sour as a crab-apple, and obstinate as a mule; he had realized a small independence, and invariably passed his summer months at Bannow, having taken it into his head that sea air did him much good; he was a source of great amusement to the peasantry, who named him "Peter the Prophet," from his habit of prognosticating; others called him "Peter the Croaker," for he always prophesied evil. Paddy Mulvany was a very different person – a cheerful, careless Irishman, whom the farmers held in constant request, as a drover. The most wealthy considered themselves fortunate in securing Paddy's services, when cattle were to be sent to England or Wales. In matters of business, Paddy's word was his bond; and, although he could neither read nor write, his accounts were always "fractionally" correct, and he made most extraordinary sales for his employers; he had not even his national fault, the love of whisky; but I confess that he sometimes indulged in most marvellous stories, and often quizzed without mercy. He took especial delight in tormenting Master Peter, and it was perfectly astonishing how "the Prophet" could ever have believed a word that Paddy Mulvany uttered. He spoke the truth, however, in saying that an English gentleman was going to build a quay in Bannow harbour; no spot could be better suited for the purpose than that so judiciously fixed upon; it was well sheltered, and beautifully situated, with sufficient water to float a thirty-ton sloop, even when the tide was out – the road which led to it was a succession of hill and dale, at one side shadowed by trees, while the view, on the other, passed over sunny fields and little cottages, and was terminated in the distance by the sea – the boundless sea, forming innumerable creeks and bays along the coast. The little island opposite was enlivened by a cheerful-looking farm-house, while a few relics of some old castles, o'er parts of which –

"The plough had passed, or weeds had grown,"[303]

served as a relief to the sameness of the view, and afforded subject for meditation: on the land side, high hills rose above the valley in rude magnificence, their heathy hue broken by patches of cultivation; and, indeed, nowhere could a more interesting spot be found, than the one selected by the English gentleman, Mr. Townsend, for the long-projected quay. I lament, for the sake of Peter the Prophet's reputation, to be compelled to state that all things went on prosperously at the new building; and even the gentry were astonished at the rapidity with which the work proceeded; each man had his allotted portion, and the wages were paid every Saturday evening, precisely as the clock struck six. To the quay were added stores and a salt manufactory; and, before a twelvemonth had elapsed, all was finished – properly finished, plastered, and pointed; the windows were even and set – the slates regularly pegged – the tiles all of a size – and the buildings had a neat and business-like appearance.

Peter the Prophet and Paddy Mulvany met at nearly the same place where they had separated about a year before, and both turned their steps towards the new quay.

"It's a fine sunny day – God bless it! – Mister Peter, and I suppose ye're going to the new quay to see the fun; it was, I must say, very generous of Mr. Townsend to give us a let-out;[304] all the top of the gintry are to have a grand entertainment – a cold *collution*[305] they call it – up stairs in the stores; and below there's a piper – and who knows what! – and the atin' and the drinkin' in lashins – and the two sloops, that are after comin' in with the timber and coal, have such gay streamers out as it's quite charmin' to see."

"I don't see anything charming in it, Paddy Mulvany – charming in a coloured rag flying, red and blue, like a turkey-cock! – and as to the entertainment – mark my words, no good will come of it. What are entertainments of all kinds but empty puff – 'vain show,'[306] as the poet says? – but you have no taste for poetry. No; few have; I had, however – but I gave it up – I had a turn for the grocery business, and poetry; but no man can be great in two things – so I fixed on the former."

"That was a mercy, Mister Peter, for somehow, although I am but an ignorant man, seeing I don't know B from a buttercup, yet I think yer poetry wouldn't have sould as well as yer tea and sugar."

"Humph!" replied the Prophet: "I see, Paddy, that long red house is to be let, and the owner's off to America; there – my words always come true; no good will come of that man, says I, and so it was."

"Why, I knew no good could come of him myself," replied Paddy; "who ever saw a good end come to any one that was hard to the poor? – besides being unjust, didn't he write a will, and make his dead uncle put his name on it, by houlding the corpse's hand? and then he swore he had life in him at the time – and troth, so he had, for he put a live worm in the dead man's mouth – the baste!"

"That's one of your stories, Paddy; like what you tould me, long ago, about Friar Mulloy's brown nag, and Mr. Hollin's chimbly; there goes the friar; that's not a nag, but a fine hunter he's on now; I suppose that's the one Paul Doolan gave him for marrying him to that foolish bit of a widow; he's a holy man, with-out doubt: – but mark my words, that beast will break his neck, it's so spirity!"

"As to the worm, ye may believe it or not, as you plase, Mister Peter, but it's as true as the sun above us; and as to Friar Mulloy, sure all the world knows he's a holy man, and a good; never a cratur passes his door without the bit and the sup, barring the gauger – the blackguard! – that tuck his potteen, and kilt his ilegant little bit of a mare. Oh! wisha! every day's bad luck to him for that same!"

"Is it true that your niece, Alice, is going to be married to Corry Howlan? She's a sweet pretty girl, but – "

"Now, Mister Peter, or Peter the Prophet, or whatever other name you may have, I'll just trouble ye to hould yer tongue about Alice and Corry; not that I care a toss-up (with all due respect) for yer prophecies, although ye want every-body to believe ye've the second sight, like a Highlander; but ye see, as they are to be married, it's unlucky to have any ill laid out for them; and as to the girl, God's blessing be about her! she's the light of my eyes, and the joy of my heart, every day and hour of her life, the jewil."

Peter looked annoyed at hearing his prophetic powers called in question, but he deemed it safer to hold his peace for a time; at all events, until they came in view of the new quay.

Along a green, shady lane, which led to the centre of that day's attraction, two people were walking, or rather strolling, very different in appearance from Paddy and Peter. – A lively, lovely girl, with roguish, hazel eyes – not the soft sleeping eye of that bewitching colour, but a round, brilliant little orb, now twinkling, now dazzling, now half shut, not unfrequently stealing under its pent-house lid to "the far corner," and peeping slyly about, for fun or mischief; the nose of this little personage was, moreover, *retroussée*[307] – an unerring token of much spirit, and, if vexed, not a little spite. But it was the glittering fairness of this fairy creature which, united to the pure glow of health and cheerfulness, completed her fascination, and made Alice Mulvany the most perfect bit of Nature's colouring I ever had the good fortune to behold. Her companion, Corry Howlan, could not have been mistaken as belonging to any country, principality or power, but the green little island. How often have I been both amused and mortified at hearing my English friends exclaim, whenever a particularly miserable, dirty, round-faced person met their view, "Oh, how like an Irishman!" – "quite impossible to mistake that *creature* for anything but an Irishman!" Trust me, those know little of our peasantry who judge of them from bricklayers' labourers, superannuated watchmen, and Covent-garden basket-women. Corry Howlan was a good specimen of our small farmers, and I will sketch him for your amusement, gentle reader, as he loitered down that green lane with his merry companion: – height, six feet, or nearly so – an air of easy confidence, and every limb well proportioned; face, oval; teeth, white and even; nose, undefined as to aquiline, Grecian, snub, or Roman, but, nevertheless, highly respectable; eyes, large, *bien foncée*,[308] and expressive; brow, open – shaded with rich, curling, brown hair; the dress, as usual on holiday occasions – red waistcoat, blue coat, knee-breeches, white stockings, neat, black, Spanish leather shoes – shirt-collar thrown back, *à-la-Byron*,[309] loosely confined at the base by a green silk neckerchief, – a "bran new beaver," placed on one side the head in a knowing position, and a stick, not dignified enough to be designated as "shilalah,"[310] nor slight enough to be called "switch." There are many likenesses which, though correct as to shape and feature, fail in expression; and so it is in the present instance. I cannot paint the affectionate feelings portrayed in the young man's face, when his eyes rested on the careless, thoughtless girl who tripped at his side, as giddy as the gay butterfly that wavered from the perfumed meadow-sweet to the beautiful but scentless convolvulus, whose long, twirling stems were supported, at either side their path, by black thorn or greeny furze. One of the most beautiful features in an Irish landscape is the quantity of small singing-birds which animate every brake and bush. As they paced along, the young folk disturbed either the soaring lark, the merry stone-chatter, the gay goldfinch, the tiny wren, the linnet, bunting, or yellow-hammer; when they approached the thicker coverts, a jetty blackbird, or timid partridge, would rustle for a moment amid the leaves, and then dart across their path, swift as an arrow.

"The poor, harmless birdeens!" said Corry; "Alice, do you know, I never could hurt one of thim small things."

"Well, nor I, Corry," replied the little lass, "particularly the robin red-breast, that has got, you know, the blessed Virgin's own Son's blood upon it; for when the Saviour was crucified, the poor bird was heart-sorry, and away it flew round the cross, and over the cross, bemoaning all the time; and whin the cruel Jew-man pierced his holy side, some of the blood flew on the cratur's breast, and then it never stopped until it nested in the holy Virgin's bosom; and, to be sure, she knew the blood, and the faithfulness of the robin, and she blessed it, and settled it so, that every red-breast has the mark of the holy blood to this very day."

"You've a good memory, Ally; I hope you'll think of everything as clear as that; and, above all, don't forget what you more than half – indeed, as good as whole – promised me last night at yer uncle's door, and I laning aginst the post."

"I'm sure, Corry, I've not the laste thought of anything; – was it about Paddy Clarey's white mare that broke into uncle's clover-field?" And Alice stooped to gather a wild polyanthus, whose blossomy coronal pushed its way over some cuckoo-bells[311] and crawling "Robin-run-the-hedge."[312]

"Ye're the devil's teazer, Ally, darling! – ye haven't yer little cocked-up nose for nothing."

"Well, if I'm the devil's teazer, you own yerself the devil; and as to my nose, there are plenty to admire it without you."

"Sure it's I that do admire it, and what's more, love it, and its owner; but, Alice, last night, don't you remember, when the moonbames fell on your sweet face, and whin ye turned away, even from that weak light, to hide yer blushes – (that ye did not need, on account that ye're too handsome, even without them) – and whin I held yer hand, and did what I'm sartin no man living would dare to do but myself – kissed it, with warm love, and yet with as much respect as if it had been a queen's: – do you remember – oh, I know you do! – that whin, not only I, but yer uncle, begged ye to fix the day, ye whispered – oh! it was so low, so sweet – sweeter, Alice, than ever I heard even your own sweet voice before! – 'to-morrow I will tell?' – that, that was all you said; that sweet 'to-morrow.' Alice, I have thought on it ever since. You will not disappoint me. We can't fail to be happy; and all so smiling: yer uncle, who loves me next to his own; my mother, who dotes upon ye – how could she help it? – a nate farm; and this morning I've been after a milch white cow,[313] for the sake of the luck – such a one isn't in the whole bar'ny[314] – and I've bought it too, and we'll look at it this evening after a bit o' dance at the new quay. I didn't mane to tell ye yet, but somehow I can't keep anything from ye that would give ye satisfaction. And now, darlint! – Ally, my own Ally – the day, the day!" The young man took the maiden's hand within his, and was about to press it to his lips, when, instigated by a sudden fit of caprice, she jerked it from him, and averting her head, to hide the self-satisfied smile which played over her countenance, replied:

"You need not make so free, *sir;* I said that, jist to please uncle. I can do no such thing; and I hate white cows."

Corry had been long enough a lover to have suffered from those little whimsical tricks which, poor as well as rich, Misses practise for their own amusement, and their lovers' mortification, I must confess, I am often amused at the discomfiture the lords of the creation experience upon such occasions; they twist and writhe so much under their sufferings, like eels trying to get out of their skin;

anxious to show off in all their native dignity, yet fearing to offend the slippery fair one, who, for all her teazing, would not lose the "tasseled gentil"[315] for worlds. Then, after marriage, the noble Sir beginning to think it is *his* turn to show off, grows capricious; and then some old bachelor uncle, or brother, tough and crusty, and perpendicular as a church-steeple, gives the bridegroom his "word of advice, to put his feet in his shoes, keep her nose to the grinding-stone, support the dignity of his sex, keep his own secrets," &c. And the bride has her "female friends;" old maiden aunts, who hate "male creatures," and beg their "dear niece to have a will and a way of her own, and be mistress in her own house;" and poor relations, anxious that the lady should have a private purse, that stumbling-block to domestic happiness: – "so disagreeable to go to a husband for every shilling," – "no need to inform a man of all things," – "never suffer a husband to know how much you love him." And if these counsellors are attended to, the cat-and-dog warfare commences, and the "I will," and "I won't," – "You shall," "I shan't," – "Sir," – "Madam," – all which terminates with the mutual exclamation – "Would to heaven we had never been married!"

Now a little harmless teazing does no harm in the world: where "bear and forbear" is moderately attended to, it gives a zest, a spirit to existence; and where there is much and pure affection –

> "The short passing anger but serves to awaken
> Fresh beauties, like flowers that are sweetest when shaken."[316]

Not that I mean to say Alice was right in asserting "she hated white cows," which was a decided story. No Irish girl or woman yet ever hated a white cow; the thing is impossible – quite. Every body, who knows anything, knows that a white cow is as good as the priest's blessing, or holy water, in the house of the early wed; and it was much too saucy a thing to say: but her nose was up, and her tongue went as nimbly as a greyhound's foot.

"Well, Alice," replied Corry, who, as I said before, often suffered from his love's whimseys – "I'm perfectly astonished at yer not liking the white cow that I bought to plase ye; but, whin ye see her, I know ye'll admire her, beyant – "

"Ye need not have troubled yerself to buy the cow, Mr. Corry, for *me;* for may-be I'll never own her," interrupted Alice.

"Ye're not going to be jilty after yer promise, and yer uncle to the fore, Alice," said Corry, who loved her too well to have the wedding jested about.

"I gave no promise to be bothered wid ye; and, whether I did or no, I'll change my mind if I like, myself."

"Is that the pattern of yer honour, Miss Alice Mulvany?" inquired the young man, much annoyed.

"Mind yer own business, if ye plase, Mr. Cornelius Howlan, and I'll mind mine. I've bothered him fairly," she muttered to herself, "I knew I'd get a rise out of him."

"May-be, Miss Alice, ye'd rather have my room than my company?"

"There's no manner o' doubt of it."

"May-be, Miss Mulvany, ye'd wish me to take my lave?"

"Ye have the lave, so now take yerself off," she replied, very sharply.

The young man looked earnestly in her face, and said, in his usual affection-ate tone, "Dear Alice, let us be friends – dear Alice – you can't, can't really mean to quarrel with your Corry – dear – "

"Don't dear Alice me, sir, after that fashion! Don't dare to dear Alice me! – what do ye mean? After callin' me jilty, and all manner o' names, to be coming 'dear Alice' over me! – no, sir; and I tell ye my mind, Mister Cornelius Howlan, I hate you as well as the white cow, and I won't dance a step with ye, nor spake a word more to ye, this blessed day, Amen! – and if ye take my advice, ye'll be off with yerself!"

Alice, after this pretty piece of eloquence, tossed her little head, pressed her lips firmly together, and walked sturdily towards the main road. Corry did all he could to make her laugh or speak – but no; she was as obstinate as a mule. He gathered wild flowers, and stuck them in her hat – she flung them from her; he told his drollest stories; then he reasoned with her; then, in his fine, rich voice, he sung her favourite airs; – and the only wonder is, that she managed to hold her tongue so long – she afterwards confessed it was sore at the tip from inaction. – At last, quite wearied by her stubbornness, Corry said, as they drew near the new quay, "Now look, Alice, I'll not taze ye with spaking any more, this day; but, may-be, before night comes, you'll be sorry for this fit of the dumps."

What a cheerful, noisy assemblage! A pattern! – a pattern was nothing to it. There was the clear sea, and the small waves running little races on the firm strand; the two brigs, the largest ever seen close to the shore in that part of the world, drawn up to the quay, which was crowded by the gentry and bettermost farmers' wives and daughters, with the piper at one end, and the fiddler at the other, both playing the same tune, of which little could be heard for the shout-ing, the laughing, and the chattering; then the windows of the stores were all open, and such of the ladies as did not like to encounter the heat of the sun, tempered even as it was by the refreshing sea-breeze, were seated on high, enjoy-ing the noise and bustle; while the large rooms beneath sent forth such clouds of savoury perfumes as told of roast and boiled, pickled and preserved, besides spicery and cates,[317] that would do honour to an aldermanic assembly. Then the machines, employed to convey the company invited from various parts of the country, were amazingly curious: one or two carriages of ancient days; some few gigs; jaunting cars, under all their classifications – the double, the inside, the outside; then the common car "made comfortable," for the more homely, first filled with straw, then a feather-bed covered with that destroyer of time, calico, and taste – a patch quilt. I have seen five dames, strange as it may seem, in such a conveyance; two seated next the horse's tail, partly on the shafts of the car, two in the middle of the feather-bed (no bad seat that), and one cross-ways at the bottom; this unfortunate is always obliged to hold fast with both hands, for a sudden jerk would inevitably dislodge the most ponderous. So they reached our pretty quay of Bannow, situated in a district for which commerce ought to do much more than it has done; although our harbour is not a good one for large vessels, it is "elegant" for small craft. The place is very picturesque. Directly opposite is the village of Fethard,[318] a corruption of "Fought-hard;" so called, it is said, because here occurred the first battle between the Anglo-Normans and the "mere Irish," immediately after the arrival of the former upon the soil, of which they subsequently became possessors. One of the earliest castles of the invaders still exists – a picturesque ruin. A few miles inland is "Tintern Abbey,"[319] now a modern residence, but once a famous monastic institution; where, it is reported, and universally believed, the spirits of the murdered monks still take their solemn walk, yearly, on the eve of the anniversary of All-Saints. Overlooking the quay is the old church of Bannow; and still nearer to it are the remains of one of the old square towers, of which the followers of Strongbow[320] erected so many in all parts of our country. The whole neighbourhood is, indeed, deeply interesting to the historian and the antiquarian. But to my story.

The sailors mixed with the rustic groups, congregated under several awnings that stretched along the strand, and enjoyed the eagerness shown by the untravelled peasantry to inspect the wonders of their barques, which were cleaned and trimmed gaily out for the purpose of exhibition. The most interesting of all the sights, however, was a black cabin-boy;[321] scarcely any one, in Bannow, had ever seen a negro, and the poor little fellow was subjected to all manner of inspection; the old women were for washing and scraping him, to see if he could be brought to a "dacent colour;" the young ones appeared terrified; and Peter the Prophet, after much critical examination, declared "that no good could come of bringing such outlandish things among Christians."

"Ally, my dear," said Paddy Mulvany to his niece, "what ails ye, that ye look so solid? – come, you and Corry are ilegant hands at the jig, and ye must both put the best foot foremost to-night, 'cause of the gintry."

"I'll not dance a step this night, uncle, with Corry!" she replied, heartily sick of her resolve, but mistaking obstinacy for firmness: "I won't do it, because I said I wouldn't; and, for the matter of that, he doesn't want me to – he's been flirting away this half-hour with Ellen Muccleworth."

"He's been doing no such thing, my dear; I've been watching ye both; you won't spake to him, and yet ye ixpict him to sit at yer elbow, putting up with yer snouting – for what? I'll go bail ye don't know yerself. It's well, pretty Alice, I'm not yer bachelor; I'd lave ye to get rid of yer humours as ye could, my jewel." So saying, Paddy Mulvany turned on his heels; tears filled the fine eyes of Alice, but she remained obstinate as ever; and, when Corry danced with Ellen, she really believed herself a much injured, insulted little maiden.

"I don't care," said she to herself – "I'll not sit quiet to please him – I'll jig it with the very next boy that asks me." And so she did; throwing off her mantle; folding her gay kerchief over her head and neck; and exhibiting her pretty figure to the best advantage, in her loose "jacket" of white, bordered with muslin; while her buckled shoes marvellously set off her small feet. "The next boy that asked her," was no other than handsome Horatio Laverton, the mate of the timber vessel; and Corry had the mortification of seeing that Alice danced to perfection, and of hearing such expressions of approbation from the surrounding company, as – "illegantly danced!" – "Success!" – "Well, in all my time, I niver saw so sweet a couple on the flure." "Corry, ye're bate out by the English boy – clane bate – and at the jig too." "Hurra! – there's a fling; well, that *is* dancing!" Then Alice figured in a three-handed reel, with the mate and her rival, Ellen, and, certainly, she had the advantage there; for Ellen was pronounced as "not fit to hould a candle to her." Yet, as the evening waned on, Alice's bad spirits increased, and even the attentions of the handsome Horatio Laverton failed to reconcile her to the reproaches of that little, silent, yet powerful, monitor within her own bosom. As the moon rose slowly over the waters, she remembered that she had been more happy at her uncle's door, with no eye upon her but her lover's, than she was at that moment, walking up and down the pier, with an almost stranger, and listening to so much praise that she began to doubt she could deserve it: still she remained obstinate.

"We will make friends to-morrow," said she to herself; and, as she stood leaning on handsome Horatio Laverton's arm, looking towards the little island of Bannow, Corry and her uncle came on the pier. She saw, in a moment, that her lover had taken too much whisky-punch, and this reminded her that he had broken a promise he had made her the preceding evening. She forgot how she had acted herself; and, when Corry good-humouredly spoke to her, turned away, curled up her nose, and replied not.

"I am glad to find, Alice," he said, "that you like the smell of tar better than that of whisky." This remark was only noticed by the little nose mounting still higher; but the sailor immediately replied:

"I suppose Mister Irishman, the young lady may like what she chooses."

Corry, hot, hasty, and rapid, was nothing loath to answer; but Paddy Mulvany interfered immediately.

"Mister mate – that young lady, as you are so civil as to call her, is my niece, and, moreover, engaged to that young man; some tiff came betwixt them this morning, but it'll blow off, only I'm sorry my eldest brother's child should act so flirty a part. Come, you two shake hands; sure we ought all to be glad of the strangers who will bring, not only plenty, but peace, to our strand." The young men shook hands, and Paddy Mulvany placed his niece's arm within his, and whispered that it was time to go home.

"What do you think of our pier and harbour?" inquired Corry of the mate.

"It's nicely suited for trade," replied the sailor, "and the little island opposite, shelters it from the nor'-west wind. I'll try and swim to that spot to-morrow morning; though, if I can do it, I suppose I'm the only one in the country could; it's a long stretch."

"It's a good swim for sartain, but I'd do it as easy as kiss my hand – clothes and all, this minute, with all the ease in life."

"Well, that's good, faith! – now, do you expect me to believe that? Why I'd bet ye a gallon of stiff grog ye'd founder before ye'd get half way."

"Done."

"Done."

"Done and done's enough betwixt us two at any time, and so here goes, clothes and all, excepting coat and shoes."

"What are ye after, Corry?" inquired Paddy Mulvany, seeing him taking off his coat.

"Going to swim to the island for a small taste of a wager; this gentleman says, though he's a seafaring man, it's impossible; so I'm jist going to show him the differ, for the honour of ould Ireland; I'm no fresh water rat, to fear a ducking in the brine – here goes!"

Whenever a true-born Patlander[322] meditates a dashing exploit, it is for the honour of "ould Ireland"; and many of Corry's friends, heedless of the consequence, cheered him to the undertaking. Paddy expostulated; but the voice of the thoughtless is always loud; his reasonings were not heard.

"What! – strike a bet to an Englishman? – a bet mus'nt be broken."

"But I say it must and shall," said Paddy, "he's not in a fit state to swim; put on your coat, Corry; here's Ally will ax you not to go."

"Will she?" exclaimed Corry; "if she does, I'll give it up – pay the grog; and that's more than I'd do for any man, woman, or child, barring herself."

"Alice," said her uncle, in an under-tone, "Alice, for the love of God, ax him not to go; as sure as ye're alive some harm 'll happen to him."

"I don't care," replied the sulky beauty.

Corry heard the words. "You don't care, Alice; – now here goes in earnest!" and he sprang off the pier into the ocean. Alice flew to the spot, and ejaculated, "Dear Corry!" – but it was too late. "I knew the tide would be over strong," exclaimed Mulvany; "and so much whisky!"

"By George, he's doing it nobly!" said the Englishman.

"Ould Ireland for ever!" shouted the peasants. Paddy knew well that the attempt was highly dangerous; he had often seen Cornelius swim, and perceived the difference now. Without uttering a sentence, he jumped from the pier to the deck of the nearest vessel, then dropped into a little boat that was along-side, which was quickly unmoored, and, seizing the oars, tacked after his young friend. This was the work of a moment, and one of the English sailors observed –

"I say, who'd ha' thought that yon old fresh-water chap could have slipped that craft off so nimbly?"

It was one of the clearest evenings that ever beamed out of the heavens; the moon had risen up an unclouded sky; the waters reflected the "night's fair queen," and the little twinkling stars, in its clear blue bosom. The island may be some-what more than an Irish mile from the pier, and the efforts Corry made to gain it were distinctly visible; but the eddy near the distant shore was very strong. As there were many jutting crags that intercepted the even flowing of the tide, Paddy Mulvany did not follow in the exact track, but kept to the right of Corry; Alice stood on the pier in breathless anxiety; and that feeling was increased to one of indescribable agony, when she heard the mate exclaim, "Good God! – sure it can't be! – yes, the current – he's struggling! as I hope to be saved, he's gone down!" The crowd now pressed forward to the end of the pier. Stoutly did Mulvany try to tack his boat so as to gain the drowning man; but, unfortunately, she stuck upon a sand bank, and there was no time to disengage her; he, therefore, relinquished the oars, and plunged into the sea. By this time Corry had risen; but before his friend reached him he had again disappeared. One loud, long shriek of agony drew the attention of the spectators for a moment, to the land; it was Corry's aged, wid-owed mother: she rushed fearfully along the quay, exclaiming, "My boy – my boy! – my blessed boy!" It was with difficulty she was restrained from casting herself into the waters; her eyes fixed on Alice, and she said, in a tone between bitterness and affection, "Ally, Ally! – why did ye let him go?"

Mulvany had watched the moment for Corry's rising, and "treaded the water," while he seized him by the collar, so as to prevent the possibility of grap-pling. Instead of the exertion he expected, he was much horrified to find the poor fellow apparently a motionless corpse; and, when he placed him in the boat, no symptom of lingering life was manifested. A loud shout from the shore told, plainly, how sincerely the people rejoiced in what they considered the suc-cess of Mulvany's exertions. Alice and Corry's mother rushed into each other's arms, tremblingly awaiting the arrival of the boat; but it is quite impossible to describe what followed, when the wet and senseless form of the beloved of their hearts was laid on the strand.

One in the crowd tried to soothe the wild grief of Alice. "Asy, asy, dear! sure it's God's will!" She turned towards the man who had spoken, and pointed to the body; then, with the action of frenzy, shook the pale hand, shrieking, "Corry, oh, Corry, dear! – why won't ye wake? Oh, wake, wake! 'tis I that ask it!" and the unhappy girl fell senseless on the bosom of him she had dearly loved. The noise roused the mother, who had been wiping off the chill damp from her son's forehead; – her sorrow "was too deep for tears." "I tell ye, Alice, he's dead!" she murmured, when the girl's lament broke upon her ear, "and will never wake again!" She bent over him, while her hand rested on his ashy brow, and muttered, unconscious of the presence of strangers, "You were a good son, agra! – the green plant of the desert. How like his father he is now, whin I saw him last – jist before they put him in the could grave, in the morning of his days – dead – dead – "

"My good woman," said the captain of the vessel, pushing through the crowd, "it is impossible that such a strong, fine fellow as that, could be smothered, in so short a time, by a mere mouthful of salt water; come, my hearties, lend a hand, and haul him on board; there's hot water, and stoves, and every convenience, and it won't be the first time we brought a lad to life after a ducking!" The old woman looked earnestly in his face, and clasping her hands, faintly articulated, "Life – to life! God's blessing! – life – life!" – and accompanied the kind-hearted Englishman.

At any other time, the Irish would have strenuously exerted themselves to prevent the interference of the English about "death consarns;" but the captain's kind manner, and Mr. Townsend's going on board, silenced all their scruples. Paddy Mulvany, also, followed, supporting his niece, whose youthful feelings rebounded at the prospect of Corry's recovery. As Paddy was stepping on board, some one pulled his sleeve, and the ominous face of "Peter the Prophet," popped over his shoulder.

"I just wanted to remind you, Paddy Mulvany, that I tould ye no good would come of the new quay; you'll just please to remember, Paddy Mulvany – "

Paddy turned full on him – "Ye ill-looking, croaking, money-making, ould vagabond, if I catch yer wizen raven-face within tin yards of me or mine, either in town or country, I'll just give ye the finish – and here's the beginning!"

The drover made a blow at Mister Peter, which, if it had arrived at its destination, would have silenced his prognostication for a time; but he had wisely retreated, and ever afterwards kept the other side of the road when he espied Paddy's figure approaching.

The efforts of the English crew were successful; and the next morning a group of three – no – *four*, passed up the green lane, where the birds were singing, and the flowers blossoming, as sweetly as on the past evening.

An old woman could hardly be said to be in the advance, so closely did she keep, and so often did she turn back to look upon the party of three, who filled up the pathway. A young man, exceedingly pale, was in the centre, and he derived support and happiness from those on whom he leant. The girl was delicate to look upon, and the tear-drop glittered in her eye, even when the pale youth gazed upon her with looks of unspeakable affection. His hand lay, but could hardly be said to lean, upon her fairy arm; while his companion, on the other side, had enough to sustain.

Alice became a reformed flirt; and, although she never quite conquered her love for ingeniously tormenting, yet did she conquer her obstinacy, and declare unqualified approbation of the white cow. – I cannot say so much for Peter, who continues to prognosticate, after his old fashion, and bitterly complains that a prophet hath no honour in his own land.[323]

KATE CONNOR.

"Trust me, your Lordship's opinion is unfounded," said the Lady Helen Graves; and, as the noble girl uttered the words, her eye brightened, and her cheek flushed with a better feeling than high-born "fashionables" generally deem necessary.

"Indeed!" exclaimed the Earl, looking up at the animated features of his goddaughter, "and how comes my pretty Helen to know aught of the matter? – methinks she has learned more than the mysteries of harp and lute, or the soft tones of the Italian and Spanish tongues. Come," he continued, "sit down on this soft Ottoman, and prove the negative to my assertion – that the Irish act only from impulse, not from principle."

"How long can an impulse last?" inquired the lady, as she seated herself at her godfather's feet, just where he wished, playfully resting her rosy cheek on his hand, as she inquired – "tell me, first, how long an impulse can last?"

"It is only a momentary feeling, my love; although acting upon it may embitter a long life."

"But an impulse cannot last for a month, can it? Then I am quite safe; and now your Lordship must listen to a true tale, and must suffer me to tell it in my own way, *brogue* and all; and, moreover, must have patience. It is about a peasant maiden, whom I dearly love – ay, and respect, too, and whenever I think of sweet 'Kate Connor,' I bless God that the aristocracy of virtue (if I dare use such a phrase) may be found, in all its lustre, in an Irish cabin.

"It was on one of the most chilly of all November days, the streets and houses filled with fog, and the few stragglers in the square, in their dark clothes, looking like dirty demons in a smoky pantomime, that papa and myself, at that *outré*[324] season, when everybody is out of town, arrived here, from Brighton; he had been summoned on business, and I preferred accompanying him to remaining on the coast alone. 'Not at home to any one,' were the orders issued when we sat down to dinner. The cloth had been removed, and papa was occupying himself in looking over some papers; from his occasional frown I fancied they were not of the most agreeable nature; at last I went to my harp, and played one of the airs of my country, of which I knew he was particularly fond. He soon left his seat, and, kissing my forehead with much tenderness, said, 'That strain is too melancholy for me just now, Helen, for I have received no very pleasant news from my Irish agent.' I expressed my sincere sorrow at the circumstance, and ventured to make some inquiries as to the intelligence that had arrived. 'I cannot understand it,' he said; 'when we resided there, it was only from the papers that I heard of the – dreadful murders, horrible outrages, and malicious burnings. All around us was peace and tranquillity; my rents were as punctually paid as in England; for in both countries a tenant, yes, and a good tenant, too, may be sometimes in arrear. I made allowance for the national character of the people; and, while I admired the contented and happy faces that smiled as joyously over potatoes and milk as if the board had been covered with a feast of venison, I endeavoured to make them *desire* more, and then sought to attach them to me by supplying their new wants.'

"'And, dear sir, you succeeded,' I said; 'never were hearts more grateful – never were tears more sincere, than theirs, when we left them to the care of that disagreeable, ill-looking agent.'

"'Hold, Lady Mal-a-pert!'[325] interrupted my father sternly; '*I* selected Mr. O'Brien: *you* can know nothing of his qualifications. I believe him to be an upright, but, I fear me, a stern man; and I apprehend he has been made the tool of a party '

"'Dear papa, I wish you would again visit the old castle. A winter among my native mountains would afford me more pure gratification than the most successful season in London.' My father smiled, and shook his head. 'The rents are now so difficult to collect, that I fear –' he paused, and then added abruptly, 'it is very extraordinary, often as I mention it to O'Brien, that I can receive no information as to the Connors. You have written frequently to your poor nurse, and she must have received the letters – I sent them over with my own, and *they* have been acknowledged!' He had scarcely finished this sentence, when we heard the porter in loud remonstrance with a female, who was endeavouring to force her way through the hall. I half opened the library-door, where we were sitting, to ascertain the cause of the interruption. 'Ah, then, sure, ye wouldn't have the heart to turn a poor crathur from the doore – that's come sich a way jist to spake tin words to his Lordship's glory! And don't tell me that my Lady Hilin wouldn't see me, and she to the fore.' It was enough; I knew the voice of my nurse's daughter; and would, I do think, have kissed her with all my heart, but she fell on her knees, and, clasping my hand firmly between hers, exclaimed, while the tears rolled down her cheeks, and sobs almost choked her utterance – 'Holy Mary! Thank God! – 'Tis herself, sure! – though so beautiful! – and no ways proud! – and I will have justice!' And then, in a subdued voice, she added – 'Praise to the Lord! – his care niver left me; and I could die contint this minute – only for you, mother, dear! – yerself only – and –' Our powdered knaves, I perceived, smiled, and sneered, when they saw Kate Connor seated that evening by my side – and my father (heaven bless him for it!) opposite to us in his great arm-chair, listening to the story that Kate had to unfold.

"'Whin ye's left us, we all said that the winter was come in arnest, and that the summer was gone for ever. Well, my Lord, we struv to plase the agint, why not? – sure he was the master ye set over us! – but it doesn't become the likes o' me, nor wouldn't be manners, to turn my tongue agin him, and he made as good as a gintleman, to be sure, by yer Lordship's notice – which the whole counthry knew he was not afore, either by birth or breeding. Well, my lady – sure if ye put a sod o' turf – saving yer presence – in a goold dish, it's only a turf still; and he must ha' been Ould Nick's born child (Lord save us!) when yer honour's smile couldn't brighten him! And it's the truth I'm telling, and no lie; – first of all, the allowance to my mother was stopped for damage the pig did to the new hedges; and then we were forced to give our best fowl as a *compliment* to Mr. O'Brien – because the goat (and the crathur without a tooth!) they said, skinned the trees; then the priest, (yer Lordship *minds* Father Lavery) and the agint quarrelled, and so – out o' spite – he set up a school, and would make all the childer go to larn there; and thin the priest hindered[326] – and to be sure we *stud* by the church – and so there was nothin' but fighting; and the boys gave over work, seeing that the tip-tops didn't care how things went – only abusing each other. But it isn't that, I should be bothering yer kind honours wid. My brother, near two years agone, picked up wid the hoith[327] of bad company – God knows how! and got above us all – so grand-like – wearing a new coat, and a watch, and a jewil ring! – so, whin *he got the time o' day in his pocket*, he wouldn't look at the same side of the way we wint; well, dear lady, this struck to my mother's heart – yet it was only the beginning of trouble – he was found in the dead o' night – (continued poor Kate, her voice trembling) – but ye hard it all – 'twas in the papers – and he was sint beyant seas. Och! many's the night we have spint crying to think of that shame – or, on our bare bended knees, praying that God might turn his heart. Well, my lady, upon that, Mr. O'Brien made no more ado, but said we were a seditious family, and that he had yer Lordship's warrant to turn us out; and that the cabin – the nate little cabin ye gave to my mother – was to go to the guager.'[328]

"'He did not dare to say that!' interrupted my father, proudly; 'he did not dare to use my name to a falsehood!'

"'The word – the very word I spoke!' exclaimed Kate. 'Mother, says I, his Lordship would niver take back, for the sin of the son, what he gave to the mother! Sure it was hard upon her grey hairs to see her own boy brought to shame, without being turned out of her little place, whin the snow was on the ground – in the could night, whin no one was stirring to say, God save ye. I remember it well; he would not suffer us to take so much as a blanket, because the bits o' things were to be canted next morning, to pay the rint of a field which my brother took, but never worked; my poor mother cried like a baby; and, *hap-*

ping[329] the ould grey cat, that your ladyship gave her for a token, when it was a small kit, in her apron, we set off, as well as we could, for Mrs. Mahony's farm. It was more than two miles from us – and the snow drifted – and, och! but sorrow *wakens* a body! – and my mother foundered like, and couldn't walk; so I covered her over, to wait till she rested a bit – and sure your token, my lady – the cat ye gave her – kept her warm, for the baste had the sinse a'most of a Christian. Well, I was praying to God to direct us for the best (but, may-be, I'm tiring your honours), whin, as if from heaven, up drives Barney, and – '

"'Who is *Barney*, Kate?'"

"I wish, my dear Lord, you could have seen Kate Connor when I asked that question; the way-worn girl looked absolutely beautiful; I must tell you that she had exchanged, by my desire, her tattered gown and travel-stained habiliments, for a smart dress of my waiting-maid's, which, if it were not correctly put on, looked, to my taste, all the better. Her face was pale, but her fine, dark, intelligent eyes gave it much and varied expression; her beautiful hair – even Lafont's trim cap[330] could not keep it within proper bounds – influenced, probably, by former habits, came straying (or, as she would call it, *shtreeling*) down her neck, and her mobile mouth was garnished with teeth which many a duchess would envy; she was sitting on a low seat, her crossed hands resting on her knees, and was going through her narrative in as straightforward a manner as could be expected; but my unfortunate question as to the identity of Barney, put her out; – face, fore-head, neck, were crimsoned in an instant; papa turned away his head to smile, and I blushed from pure sympathy.

"'Barney – is Barney – Mahony – my lady,' she replied, at length, rolling up Lafont's flounce in lieu of her apron – 'and a great true friend of – of – my mother's –'

"'And of *yours*, also, I suspect, Kate,' said my father.

"'We were neighbours' childer, plase your honourable Lordship, and only natural if we had a – friendly –'

"'Love for each other,' said my lordly papa; for once condescending to banter.

"'It would be far from the likes o' me to contradict yer honour,' she stammered forth, at length.

"'Go on with your story,' said I, gravely.

"'I'm thinking my Lord, and my lady, I left off in the snow – oh, no! – *he* was come up with the car: – well, to be sure, he took us to his mother's house, and, och! my lady, but it's in the walls o' the poor cabins ye find hearts! – not that I'm down-running the gintry, who, to be sure, know better manners – but it's a great blessing to the traveller to have a warm fire, and dry lodging, and share of whatever's going – *all for the love of God* – and *céad míle fáilte*[331] with it! Well, to be sure, they never looked to our property; and Barney thought to persuade me to make my mother his mother, and never heeded the disgrace that had come to the family: and, knowing his heart was set upon me, his mother did the same, and my own mother, too – the crathur! – wanted me settled; well – they all cried, and wished it done off at once, and it was a sore trial that. Barney, says I, let go my hand; hould yer whisht, all o' ye, for the Blessed Virgin's sake, and don't be making me mad intirely; – and I seemed to gain strength, though my heart was bursting. Look! (says I) bitter wrong has been done us; but no matter, I know our honourable landlord had neither act nor part in it – how could he? – and my mind misgives that my lady has often written to you, mother, for it isn't in her to forget ould frinds; but I'll tell ye what I'll do, there's nobody we know barring his riverence, and the schoolmaster, could tell the rights of it to his honour's glory upon paper: his riverence wouldn't meddle nor make in it, and the schoolmaster's a frind of the agent's; so ye see, dears, I'll jist go fair and asy off to London myself, and see his Lordship, an' make him *sinsible*. And, before I could say my say, they all – all but Barney, set up sich a scornful laugh at me as never was heard. She's mad! says one; she's a fool! says another; where's the money to pay your expinses? says a third; and how could ye find your way, that doesn't know a step o' the road, even to Dublin? says a fourth. Well, I waited till they were all done, and then took the thing quietly. I don't think, says I, there's either madness or follow in trying to get one's own again; as to the money, it's but little of that I want, for I've the use of my limbs and can walk, and it 'll go hard if one of ye won't lend me a pound, or, may-be, thirty shillings, and no one shall ever lose by Kate Connor, to the value of a brass farthing; and as to not knowing the road, sure I've a tongue in my head; and if I hadn't, the great God, that taches the innocent swallows their way over the salt seas, will do as much for a poor girl who puts all her trust in Him. My heart's against it, said Barney, but she's in the right; – and then he wanted to persuade me to go before the priest with him; but no, says I, I'll niver do that till I find justice; I'll niver bring both shame and poverty to an honest boy's hearth-stone. I'll not be tiring your noble honours any longer wid the sorrow, and all that, whin I left them; they'd have forced me to take more than the thirty shillings – God knows how they raised that same! – but I thought it enough; and, by the time I reached Dublin, there was eight of it gone; small way the rest lasted; and I was ill three days, from the sea, in Liverpool. Oh! when I got a good piece of the way – when my bits o' rags were all sold – my feet bare and bleeding, and the doors of the sweet white cottages shut against me, and I was tould to go to my parish, – then, then I felt that I was in the land of the could-hearted stranger! Och! the English are a fine, honest people, but no ways tinder; well, my Lord, the hardest temptation I had at all (and here Lady Helen looked up into her god-father's face, with a supplicating eye, and pressed her small white hand affectionately upon his arm, as if to rivet his most earnest attention) was whin I was sitting crying by the road-side, for I was tired and hungry, and who, of all the birds in the air, drives up in a sort of a cart, but Mister O'Hay, the great pig marchant, from a mile beyant our place; well, to be sure, it was he wasn't surprised when he seen me! Come back with me Kate, honey! – says he; I'm going straight home and I'll free your journey; whin ye return, I'll let the boy, *ye know*, have a nate little cabin I've got to let, for (he was plaised to say) you desarve it. But I thought I'd parsevere to the end, so (God bless him for it!) he had only tin shillings – seeing he was to receive the money for the pigs he had sould at the next town – but what he had he gave me; that brought me the rest of the journey; and if I hadn't much comfort by the way, sure I had hope, and that's God's own blessing to the sorrowful; and now, here I am, asking justice, in the name of the widow and the orphin, that have been wronged by that black-hearted man; and, sure as there's light in heaven, in his garden the nettle and the hemlock will soon grow, in place of the sweet roses; and whin he lies in his bed – in his dying bed, the just and holy God –.' My father here interposed, and in a calm, firm voice reminded her that, before him, she must not indulge in invective. 'I humbly ask your honour's pardon,' said the poor girl, I lave it all now just to God and yer honour; and shame upon me that forgot to power upon *you*, my lady, the blessings that the ould mother of me sint ye – full and plinty may ye ever know! – said she from her heart, the cratur! – may the sun niver be too hot, or the snow too could for ye! – may ye live in honour, and die in happiness, and, in the ind, may heaven be yer bed!'

"You may guess how happy the poor girl became, when sheltered under our roof; for the confiding hope, so powerful with those of her country, was strong within her, and she had succeeded in assuring herself that at length she would obtain justice.

"And now, my dear Lord," continued the Lady Helen, "tell me, if a fair English maiden, with soft blue eyes, and delicate accent, had thus suffered; if driven from her beloved home, with a helpless parent, she had refused the hand of the man she loved, because she would not bring poverty to his dwelling if she had undertaken a journey to a foreign land, suffered scorn and starvation – been tempted to return, but, until her object was accomplished, until justice was done to her parent, resisted that temptation – would you say she acted from *impulse*, or from *principle?*"

"I say," replied the old gentleman, answering his god-daughter's winning smile, "that you are a saucy gipsy to catch me in this way. Fine times, indeed, when a pretty lass of eighteen talks down a man of sixty! But tell me the result."

"Well, now you must hear the sequel to my story; for it is only half finished; and I assure you the best half is to come: –

"Instead of returning to Brighton, my father, without apprizing our *worthy* agent, in three days arranged for our visiting dear Ireland! Only think, how delightful! – so romantic, and so useful, too! Kate – you cannot imagine how lovely she looked; she quite eclipsed Lafont! Then her exclamations of delight were so new, so curious – nothing so original to be met with, even at the *soirées*[332] of the literati. There you may watch for a month without hearing a single thing worth remembering; but Kate's remarks were so shrewd, so mixed with observation and simplicity, that every idea was worth noting. I was so pleased with the prospect of the meeting – the discomfiture of the agent – the joy of the lovers, and the wedding – (all stories that end properly, end in that way, you know) – that I did not even request to spend a day in Bath. We hired a carriage in Dublin, and, just on the verge of papa's estate, saw Mr. O'Brien, his hands in his pockets, his fuzzy red hair sticking out all round his dandy hat, like a burning furze-bush, and his vulgar, ugly face as dirty as if it had not been washed for a month. He was lording it over some half-naked creatures, who were breaking stones, but who, despite his presence, ceased working, as the carriage approached. 'There's himself,' muttered Kate. We stopped – and I shall never forget the appalled look of O'Brien, when my father put his head out of the window – (Cruikshank should have seen it).[333] He could not utter a single sentence. Many of the poor men, also, recognised us, and, as we nodded and spoke to some we recognised among them, they shouted so loudly, for fair joy, that the horses galloped on, not, however, before the triumphant Katherine, almost throwing herself out of the window, exclaimed, 'And I'm here, Mr. O'Brien, in the same coach wid my Lord and my Lady, and now we'll have justice!' at which my father was very angry, and I was equally delighted. Two 'weeny' children met us at the entrance to the cottage – Barney's cottage; their healthy cheeks contrasted with the wretchedness of their attire; and told my father, at once, the condition to which his negligence had reduced my poor nurse – for the children were hers. I will show them to you, one of these days, a *leetle* better dressed. It was worth a king's ransom to see the happiness of the united families of the Connors and Mahonys; the grey cat, even, purred with satisfaction: – then, such a wedding! Only fancy, my dear Lord, my being bridesmaid! – dancing an Irish jig on an earthen floor! Ye exquisites and exclusives! – how would ye receive the Lady Helen Graves, if this were known at Almack's?[334] – From what my father saw and heard, when he used his own eyes and ears for the purpose, he resolved to reside, six months out of the twelve, at Castle Graves. You can scarcely imagine how well we get on; the people are, sometimes, a little obstinate, in the matter of smoke, and, now and then, an odd dunghill, too near the door; and, as they love liberty themselves, do not much like to confine their pigs. But these are only trifles. I have my own school, on my own plan, which I will explain to you another time, and now will only tell you that it is visited by both clergyman and priest; and I only wish that all our *absentees* would follow our example, and then, my dear god-papa, THE IRISH WOULD HAVE GOOD IMPULSES, AND ACT UPON RIGHT PRINCIPLES."

FATHER MIKE.

"Heaven defend us! – did ye ever hear sich a storm? – and the snow's as good as knee-deep this blessed minit, in the yard; it's hard to say whether sleet, snow, or hail, is the bittherest, for they are all drifting together, and always in a body's face. Martin, is there no sign of his reverence yet?"

Martin, who had been industriously stuffing some straw into his huge brogue, and Molly M'Clathery, who had made the inquiry, rose at the same moment, opened the window-shutter, looked forth upon the night, and listened, in hopes to hear the wonted tokens of the priest's return.

In the kitchen of old Father Mike, the usual "family circle" had assembled, of which Molly and Martin formed a principal part. The house stood on a bleak hill-side, exposed to the full rush of the sea blast, without a tree to shelter either dwelling, barn, or hayrick. On such a night, its exterior presented anything but a comfortable appearance; it was an ill-built, slated house, flanked by thatched offices, which formed a sort of triangle, at the smallest point of which a wide gate stood, or rather hung, almost always open; to say the truth, it was only supported by one hinge, the other never having been repaired since the county member's carriage frightened it to pieces, when he visited the worthy priest, a month or two before the last general election; although Father Mike had, a thousand times, directed Martin to get it mended, and Martin had as often replied, "Yes, plase yer reverence, *I'll see about it.*"

At the back of the house nearly an acre of land was enclosed, as "a garden;" but the good priest cared little for vegetables, and less for flowers; and it was, of course, overrun with luxuriant weeds, insolently triumphant, in the summer time, over the fair, but dwindling rose, or timid lily, that still existed, but looked as if they pined and mourned at the waste around them. The inside of the dwelling was rambling and inconvenient; it had a dark entrance-hall, or passage, a kitchen, a parlour, a cellar, on the ground floor: while a sort of ladder staircase led to the upper chambers. The kitchen was the general family room, the parlour being reserved for company, and kept in tolerable order by the priest's niece, a dark-eyed little lass of sixteen.

Martin and Molly had resumed their seats on a black oak settle, that occupied one side of the large open chimney: Molly, of spindle-like stiffness, her lean
figure and scraggy neck supporting a face "broad as a Munster potato," while her
wide mouth, and long, sharp teeth, betokened her passion for talking and eating:
Martin, whose shaggy elf-locks clustered thickly over a well-formed forehead,
and deep-set but bright grey eyes, resembled, very much resembled, a *cluricawn* –
that particularly civil, wily, sharp-sighted Irish fairy; Martin Finchley was almost
as little, quite as knowing, quite as clever, and by trade a brogue maker, to which
fraternity all cluricawns belong; yet the straw peeped forth from his brogues!
Ah! but Martin was a genius – knew more of every body and everything than
any man in the county, sung a good song, told a good story, brought home the
cows, fed the pigs, minded the horse, and performed many domestic offices in
the priest's establishment, yet found time to learn all the news, and nurse half the
children in the parish. Molly and he had lived fifteen years with Father Mike,
and had never passed a day, during that period, without quarrelling, to the great
amusement of Dora Hay, the priest's little niece, who was now kneeling at the
other side of the fire, her wheel laid aside, while she carefully administered some
warm milk to a young lamb that had suffered much from the heavy snow. Two
large dogs, a cat, and a half-grown kitten, shared also the wide hearthstone, and
enjoyed the bright, cheerful light of a turf and wood fire. On an old-fashioned
table, partially covered with a half-bleached cloth, was spread the priest's supper;
a large round of salted beef, a silver pint mug, with an inscription somewhat
worn by time, an unbroken cake of griddle bread, with a "pat" of fresh butter
on a wooden platter, and two old bottles, containing something much stronger
than water. An antique arm-chair, with an embroidered but much soiled cushion, was placed opposite the massive silver-handled knife and fork; all awaiting
his reverence's coming. From the rafters of this wild looking apartment hung
various portions of dried meat, fish, and pigs' heads, the latter looking ghastly
enough in the flickering light. The dresser, which, as usual in Irish kitchens,
extended the whole length of the room, made a display of rich china, yellow delf,
wooden noggins, dim brass, and old, but chased-silver candlesticks. A long deal
"losset,"[335] filled to overflowing with meal and flour, was (if I may use the expression) united to the wall by a heap of potatoes, on which a boy, or "runner," was
sleeping as soundly as if he had been pillowed on down; a large herring barrel, a
keg of whisky on a stand, to "be handy like," and a firkin of butter occupied the
spaces along the wall of the apartment.

Still the storm continued. The fire was again heaped, and yet the master was
absent.

"Miss Dora, my darlint," said Molly M'Clathery, after a very long pause, "go
to bed, agra, yer eyes are heavy for sleep, and no wonder, for it's a'most elivin by
the ould clock. Martin, I thought ye were to get the clock settled, but it 'll be like

the gate widout the hinge, and the windy widout the glass, and the mare's leg; to say nothing of the wine last summer, that worked itself to vinegar, for want of a bung. His reverence is a dale too quiet for all of ye. Whin Jacky the tinker was married – (sure, may-be, I don't remember it!) – he comes here, and talks his reverence over not to ax the money for the wedding until the nixt time he was wanting. Well, at the first christening my chap had the same story, and so on, putting his reverence off, from that to the next, and the next, and the next, and so on, till the seventh brat came. Well, that was all well, as a body may say; and at last his reverence, knowing he was getting powers of money, jist mintioned the ould score: – five shillings for the wedding, and then six christenings at a thirteen[336] and a tester each. And, what does the spalpeen? – as keen as the north wind: 'Oh, very well,' says he, 'as yer reverence plazes, only there's Friar Kannett christens for half-price, and the protestant minister for nothing, and one's as good as another.' And, to be sure, to save the soul of the grawl, his reverence gives up intirely, and makes the thing a holy Catholic, out and out at once, for nothing."

"Will ye hould yer clack,[337] Molly! What do I care about Jacky the tinker? and as to the wine, it was as much your fault, and more, than mine. And for the mare's leg, how the plague could I hinder her breaking it if she liked, and I three mile off at the same time? But I won't be spinding my breath on ye; only – bad luck to all famales!"

"Thank you, Martin," said Miss Dora, who had really been half asleep, her small foot resting on the step of the wheel, and the thread hanging on her finger, while her head fell carelessly on her delicate shoulder.

"I humbly ax yer pardon, Miss Dory; I didn't mane you to hear that, it was only the like o' she I meant, that can never let well enough alone, but's evermore naggin', naggin', naggin', at a body, like a swaddling pracher."[338]

"Martin, I'll tell ye what it is – give us none o' yer impudence – for I haven't been Father Mike's housekeeper, or Miss Dora's nurse, for fifteen years, to stand talk from a man, much less from you, ye dawshy clodhopper!"[339]

"Stop, Molly!" interrupted Dora; "stop; you are sometimes a little cross; and it is too late to quarrel to-night, I wish you would go to bed; and I will wait up for my uncle."

"Och, no, my dear – and lave you by yerself in this big kitchen! Save us! – d'ye hear how that boy is snoring? Dick! Dick! – wake up, I say; what does his reverence give ye mate, drink, and clothing for? – is it to lie there snoring, as comfortable, on thim illegant pratees, as the king on his throne, when yer master, a holy man like him, is out in the could snow?"

"Sure, ye may let the boy alone, he's doin' no harm; he's not wanted till his reverence comes home, and then I'll wake him, to hould the light for the horse to the stable."

"He shall wake now; one idle body's enough in the house, Martin Finchley;" and in her own way she proceeded to effect her purpose. Dick roared lustily at the blow which reached him, while Martin very quietly observed, "Now she's upturned everything, may-be she'll be asy herself." And so she was, for, kneeling with her face to the wall, she commenced gabbling over her prayers, "to keep her employed," as she said, till his reverence came in. Dora, to beguile the time, entered into conversation with Martin.

"Martin, was there any news stirring this morning?"

"Nothing worth much, Miss; it's very dead for news now, on account that Mary-the-Mant's gone to Waxford, and Mrs. Murphy (oh, what a fine-spoken woman that is!) has just got two young ones that keeps her widin; – and the poor widdy Mooney is out o' sorts: I wish ye'd jist say a kind word for her, the cratur, to his reverence, Miss, dear – may-be, the morrow, whin he's takin' his punch afther dinner; – sure he spoke to her from the altar last Sunday, on account of her havin' tasted something besides new milk in the mornin' – poor thing! She has a wake head, and a warm heart, and a nimble tongue (not that she's by any manner o' manes as fine-spoken a woman as Mrs. Murphy – far from it), but, any way, she's almost ashamed to let the bames o' day see her face; sure she can't help her wake head, the sowl! – and she'll niver recover – barring you spake the soft word for a poor distressed neighbour."

"Oh, Martin, you know she is always tipsy."

"Oh, no, 'pon my conscience, Miss, she niver takes more nor a noggin afore breakfast, and, any way, she can't help it – it's the natur o' the cratur. Oh, do spake the good word!"

"Martin, did Lavery get the saddle back?"

"Och, thin, I know I had somethin' to tell ye; ay, sure enough, it came of itself, seemingly; sated quiet and civil at the door this mornin'; and it's Friar Donovan Jack Lavery may thank for that; for Jack complained it to him, how he lost his beautiful saddle as good as new, for his father bought it a little afore he died, and 'tis not much above ten years agone, and what signifies the few times it was crossed, an' it a Dublin saddle! So Friar Donovan, like a good Christian, didn't wish the poor man to be at the loss of the saddle, and so, says he, an' he praching for Father Clancy in the chapel of Rathangan,[340] says he (he's a power-ful man), says he – I know the boy that stole that saddle (as well he might, for I knew him myself,) and what's more, says he, if he that has it does not return it to honest Jack Lavery afore to-morrow night, he'll be riding upon that same saddle through –; I ax yer pardon, it's not fit for a young lady to hear; only it's the devil's coort he meant, and said it out plump and plain in the face of the congregation – he'll be riding through the very hot place afore this day week, says he, if he doesn't return it immediately; and sure enough Jack has got the saddle, for it was sated quietly down at his own door the next mornin' early."

"Well, Martin, I am glad of it. Any more news?"

"O, nothin' particular; only ye hard, no doubt, how discontented Father O'Shea (God be good to him!) was, at being buried in the black North, whin his own people had sich comfortable lodging in their own place, and how he came to his brother Mick, the farmer; and Mick, says he, how d'ye think I can lie asy in the wet, could, damp hole they put me in, and all my people so snug in their own place; take me up, says he – (och, Molly, ye need not stare, for it's as thrue as the beads in yer hand!) – take me up, says he, and put me in warm berring-ground;[341] for if ye don't I'll give ye no pace, and ye'll have no luck – to lave your brother, and he a priest, in such a sitiation! Stale me away, says he. Now, to be sure, the brother knew that it was far from right to take a priest from the berring-ground of his flock, where he was placed so proper, facing his congregation 'ginst the day of judgment. Nevertheless, what must be must be – so they stole him off in the dead o' the night, and settled him comfortable in the ould church-yard yonder, in the middle of his own people; it cost a power o' money – but niver mind, he's asy now.

"I dare say," continued Martin, after a long pause, "it was jist sich a night as this that the bitter desolation came upon the ancient, fine, ould town of Bannow; for, no doubt, Miss Dory, you that has such larning knows that there's an entire town under thim sand-hills.[342] The sea rushed in one night, and all the craturs o' sinners asleep, quite innocent-like, were kilt and spilt. And when the sea went back to its own place – bad luck to it! – the storm came, and the sand heaped in mountains over the dead town; and, barring the church, that was on a high hill, every living house was kivered over, only one chimbly, that used to return a borough member, before the Union[343] and Lord Castlereagh,[344] and the likes o' thim, murdered ould Ireland intirely."

"But the proof, Martin, the proof!" inquired Dora, laughing.[a]

"Is it proof ye're wanting, my darlint Miss? why, isn't the town to the fore, underground? – and isn't there, in Waxford city, the book to prove that as good as six streets, in the ould town of Bannow, paid cess, and tithe, and tolls? – and the cockle-strand, where the girleens are picking cockles? sure that's a proof; for it's out o' that the sand come. The gintry talk of digging it up, and unkivering the sunk houses; but those that have money don't care, and those that have not – why, they can't, ye know. Ye've seen the curious font inside the church; the rain water that falls in it is holy of itself – Lord save us! Father Grashby, ye know, said it was a shame to lave such a beautiful cut stone in an ould church; and so, without saying so much as 'by yer lave' to priest or minister, he claps the blessed relic in his own new chapel, tin miles off, as quiet as anything. To be sure, ye mind, whin the whole parish cried shame – and such a hulla-boo-loo as there was! – the women skreetching for the dear life, and saying (true for 'em) that the luck was gone for iver and iver from us: but the very nixt night – (now, ma'am, don't be always skitting that way: I ax yer pardon, but it's not what I'd expect from the likes o' you, to trate holy things so; and what I'm telling is as true as gospel – I'd take my bible oath of it!) – the very nixt night such a storm as you niver heard, nor any one else; and a bur-r-r, boo-ooo-b-o-o-o, through the air; and the font went over the house-tops, and the trees, like a shot, whirring and bubbling, and bright as a star, and lit all along through the sky by the dazzling candles of the good people before and behind, shouting, chirming,[345] and making such sweet music, through the whirlwind – and fair and softly, they niver stopped till they placed the font in its ould place, and whir and away the charmers, to their homes in the blue-bells, and the rose-buds, and the wather-foam – "

"Lord save us!" ejaculated Molly, and muttered her prayers faster than ever. A long pause ensued, and, half asleep, Dora inquired if there had been a dance at the public that evening?

"Sorra a one," replied Martin, "whin I came away. I just looked in a minit; Phil Waddy, and yer cousin Brian, and one or two more, were there; and, by the same token, Raking Phil has a wicked look about the eyes when he's crossed."

"I never saw him look wicked," replied Dora quickly. "He always looked so kind and good-tempered, and –"

A loud knocking prevented Dora's finishing the sentence. Shag and his companion gave each one bark, and then ran wagging their tails to the door.

All were on their feet in a moment. Before Martin could hold the bridle rein, Father Mike (for it was the long expected priest) had dismounted, and with unwonted alacrity entered the kitchen, without the usual salutation of "God save all here!"

"Dear uncle," said Dora, taking his hand as he sat down, "let me take off this coat; what is the matter? – sure something has happened ye; speak, my dear uncle!" and the affectionate girl unbuttoned the collar; then, suddenly starting back, exclaimed, "Good God! here is blood, wet blood, upon yer cravat! – dear, dear uncle, you are hurt – hurt!" and poor Dora, who did not possess much mental or bodily strength, nearly fainted on her uncle's arm. The old priest kissed her forehead, but it was some moments before he could reply. At length he said: –

"It is nothing, child; a mere nothing! – the bough of a tree, broken by the storm, might have scratched me here as it fell;" and he pointed to his throat, where more collected witnesses would easily have perceived a broken bough could not have harmed him; it satisfied, however, the innocent Dora, and the stupid Molly: and in a few minutes the priest was seated at the table.

"You don't eat, sir," said Dora; "you have, perhaps, supped at Mr. Herriott's, or at one of the farmers'."

"No, my dear."

"Then you do not like the beef."

"Thank God, child, it is very good."

"Well, let me make you some punch, nice whisky-punch; here's hot water, sugar – white sugar – all ye want; and, ye know, I'm a capital hand."

"I know ye're as dear to me, Dory, as ever born child was to father or mother. Make what ye please for yer old uncle. Molly, you and the boys may go to bed; I shan't be long, and it's Tuesday mornin' by this time."

"Hadn't Miss betther go to bed?" inquired Molly; "sure I'll sit up and do whatever's wanted wid all pleasure, as in duty bound, plase yer reverence."

"No, Molly, do you go." Molly retired, and, after a short pause, Father Mike spoke: "Dory, dear! – have ye said yer prayers to-night?"

"No, sir."

"Kneel down, then, love, at my knee, as ye've done, off and on, since my poor sister died – and that's more than fourteen years ago; ye'll be seventeen yer next birthday."

Dora smiled, and knelt as she was desired.

"Stop! – before you begin, child, take an *obligation* on yourself, to answer truly to every word I question, when ye've done; there, don't blush so; my sister's child, I know, has nothing to hide from her confessor and friend."

Dora prayed in tremulous accents, and, perhaps, she never looked so lovely as at that moment; her brown hair – long, thick, and somewhat curled – hung over but did not conceal, the expression of her upturned face; her eyes were half closed, and the lids were beautifully fringed with dark lashes; her complexion, though somewhat embrowned, was delicate, and the lower part of her face, particularly her quivering lip, expressed feelings as yet undefined, but powerful: the priest's arms were crossed on his bosom; and when his eyes rested on the child of his adoption, his lips moved with the increased earnestness of heartfelt prayer.

"Now, Dora, sit down; not on that low seat – ye're always crouching at my feet like a frightened hare; when Philip Waddy was here, yesterday morning, what did he say to you? – keep yer hand from yer face, and answer me!"

"Say, uncle?"

"Yes, child, say."

"Why, he said that it was a very fair morning."

"Anything else?"

"Oh, yes! he asked me if I was to be at Mary Gaharty's wedding next week, and – and – if – it was a very foolish question, uncle – "

"Well, dear, what was it?"

"Why, only – if – I'd like to be at my own wedding?"

"Well, and what did ye say?"

"I said – nothing, sir."

"Did he not ask ye anything else?"

"Only if I loved my cousin Brian better than him."

"And what did you reply?"

"Oh," said Dora, smiling, "I said I loved Brian ten times better; and he got quite angry."

"Indeed! and is it true, Dora, that you love Brian the best?"

The girl spread her hands over her face, and even her throat coloured deeply, as she murmured – "No."

"Dora," said Father Mike, "it is very unlikely that you will ever see Philip Waddy again; but if you should – " and his small grey eye, kindled by some hidden fire, as he spoke, looked dazzling]y bright, as it sparkled from under his dark brows, – "if you should see him, as you value my last blessing, as you value my last *curse*, shun him, fly from him, look not on him; the thunder of God will pursue, and overtake him, for he is – "

"Remember!" exclaimed a voice, both loud and deep.

The priest started from his seat; with one arm folded the terrified girl to his bosom, and, with the other, seized the knife that lay upon the table before him. Within the apartment, all was still as the grave, except the large dog, who sprang to the half-closed shutter, but neither growled nor barked. The priest placed Dora on the chair from which he had risen, advanced to the window with a firm step, carefully bolted it, and then returned to where his niece, the victim of many contending feelings, retained a perfect consciousness of all that passed, but was nearly deprived of reason by extreme terror.

She was, at length, roused by her uncle's affectionate kindness, and retired to her chamber, where a passionate burst of tears relieved her. Young, inexperienced, and perfectly ignorant of the world's ways, Dora Hay might have been truly called the child of nature; she had lost her mother at the moment she entered into existence, and her uncle adopted the friendless infant, (her father had died some months before), and poured on it the affections of a heart that yearned for an object on whom it could bestow especial love. Dora, certainly, deserved all he could give, for never was child more devotedly attached to parent than she was to her uncle; when he was at home, she followed his footsteps, listened to his words, and treasured up his instruction with the greatest eagerness and attention; and, when absent, she thought only of what she could do to promote his happiness on his return. He was, indeed, her sole teacher, and, as he had received the advantages of a more polished education than falls to the lot of the priesthood generally, having resided at Paris during the old *régime*,[346] his niece had the full benefit of all his advantages; – although, it must be confessed, he was not very competent to give lessons in the usual female acquirements. He instructed her in French; nature directed her how to sing, and that most sweetly, the wild airs of her native land; every Irish girl dances intuitively; and Martin taught her all the legends, and interested her in all the superstitions, of the country. Thus, the young maiden might have been pronounced accomplished, by more fastidious judges than Father Mike's flock. Still, it must be confessed, Dora had great faults; next to her uncle's opinion, she thought her own better than any other; and, like most girls, was vain of her beauty. The farmer's daughters she deemed too ignorant to be her companions; and the young ladies in her immediate neighbourhood, to say the truth, were somewhat (I am sorry for it, but it is true, nevertheless) haughty, so that Dora had no friend of her own sex; but she had what, perhaps, she thought better – two lovers – her distant cousin, Brian, and Raking Phil Waddy. Brian was a steady well-principled youth, of a slight and rather genteel appearance – gentle withal, except when influenced by the destructive spirit that has been one of the sorest curses on the land; then he was rash and unguarded; he had served his apprenticeship to a humble surveyor, near the priest's, and was about to commence business for himself. Any young man might have loved Dora for her own sake; but, as she was considered "a fortune," she would no doubt be sought by many. "Raking Phil Waddy" was the third son of a half gentleman – a noxious species, almost peculiar to Ireland; these *half* gentry are *whole* idle, and, on the strength of their relationship to some rich family, or on the prospect of, at some future period, being rich themselves, they exist without any visible means of support, except what they "genteelly" beg: not that they are ill dressed, or ill fed, far from it; they go from house to house, relying upon the hospitality of the owners, and always manage to claim relationship with the opulent, who, "for the sake of the family," will not suffer them to wear a shabby appearance. The females of this species make excellent toadies, and the males, chorus laughs; they draw corks, tell lies, smuggle occasionally, thrash bailiffs, seduce innocent girls, and end their lives generally (for the system cannot always last) either in New South Wales, or in a jail. Phil's father, *as yet*, had done neither; he dwelt some eight miles from Father Mike's, with his wife, who had, at one time, possessed both money and beauty, but was now *passée*,[347] in a tumble-down house by the wayside, where the nettle and the thistle strove for mastery, fit emblems of the bitterness and neglect that existed in the uncomfortable dwelling. Mr. and Mrs. Waddy agreed but upon one subject, namely, that, as they were well connected, it was quite impossible to put their sons (fortunately, there were no daughters) to any business, and that, as they were nice looking lads they might visit from one house to another, until they obtained commissions either in the navy or in the army. They were received by a good many respectable families, but there was a cloud, a something, inexpressible, yet felt, that hung over their characters, more particularly that of Philip; although he seemed a rattling lively fellow, gifted with much talent, and foremost with the jest. A relative wished him to study the law, and placed him with a very eminent solicitor in Dublin; he returned, soon after, to his father's house – no one knew why; but the shadow had deepened over him. In person he was not so stout as he was muscular; his hair was light, his forehead well proportioned, his lip smiling, his eye, in unguarded moments, like a cat's – fierce and prowling. Dora's fortune attracted his attention; as to love, he knew it not; the word flew often from his lip, but it sprung not from his heart; he had read of a new philosophy, too, and because he was quick-sighted enough to discern the errors of Catholicism, he grasped at the belief that there was no religion that ought to interfere between his passions and their gratification. The spring budded, the summer glowed, the autumn yielded her fruit, and the winter – the seasons' night – afforded leisure for reflection; yet Philip heeded neither their beauty nor their usefulness, for he had said in his heart – "There is no God!" He was too cunning to give utterance to these thoughts, and made even Father Mike believe that he would soon settle down into a steady man; he visited frequently at his house, as he said, to benefit by his instruction. The priest, however, perceived Dora's kindly feelings towards him, and was not inclined to encourage them: Brian, he knew, was much more likely to make her lastingly happy, from the correctness and uniformity of his conduct.

On the morning of the day we have just recorded, Father Mike was pacing leisurely along the high road leading to Ross, when his kinsman, Brian, met him, with the salutation:

"I was just stepping down to ye, sir, to speak a word that's very heavy at my heart. You know that ever since *she* was a child, you've said, I might wear her if I could win her, when she grew up; but there's no chance of it as long as that rattling fellow, Phil, with his coaxing words, and his learning, and his fine clothes, is at her side; and I just wanted to ask yer reverence if I might take upon me to tell him to keep his distance, and then I should have some chance."

"Who are you speaking of, Brian?"

"Oh, ye know very well; who but my – I wish ye'd marry us out of hand, and let her be, indeed, *my* dear little Dora. Sure she could lead me with a halter o' snow."

"There are two words to that; or, indeed, I may say, but one, and that's her's, for mine you have, and my heart along with it. As to Philip, he is a wild, rattling boy, and a strange, but he would not do an unhandsome turn for a king's ransom; only, to be sure, girls do fancy odd chaps sometimes, and I'll just tell him my mind."

"For the love of God, leave me to do that, sir," said Brian, earnestly, "don't meddle nor make with him; neither half nor whole lawyers are good for much, and I'll speak to him myself."

"Well done, Brian, my boy!" replied Father Mike, laughing. "So you think yourself more fit to deal with a bit of a lawyer – you, who are only two-and-twenty – than an old, sober fellow, who has seen summers threescore-and-two pass over his grey head. Ay, the old story, youth and inexperience *versus* age and wisdom!" The priest laughed again, and Brian, with a serious aspect, laid his hand on the bridle-rein, and said: –

"Sir, there's more about that fellow than you believe. As I'm a living soul, he meddles and makes with more than concerns him."

"There again, now! – ye think yerself sharper than me, just because ye're a little jealous of Philip. Ah! when I was young, before I was priested, I was like you; but now – there's Philip, I declare! – don't look so like a thunder-storm, Brian."

"I will see you to night, sir, at eight, if you will be at home," replied the young man, hastily; "good-bye." He was going to cut into a path which crossed some pasture-land, when Father Mike, in an authoritative tone, ordered him to stop, and not to run as if "ould Nick was at his heels." Accordingly, Brian met Phil with ill-concealed dislike: while Philip smiled with gracious sweetness, inquired kindly after Dora, and, with an unconstrained and even careless manner, gave the "farewell kindly," and passed on.

"That fellow's a match for the 'devil and Lord Castlereagh,'" muttered Brian; "but for all that I'll be a match for *him,* clever as he is. I'm just thinking, yer reverence," he commenced, after a short pause, "that that chap's never without his fowling-piece lately; sure the sporting season's over."

"I'll tell ye what, Brian, I'll not listen to anything you have to say in your present humour; come over this evening, and we'll both talk it out. There, don't torment me now with your nonsense; go your ways, and let me be at peace, though you can't be so yourself, or I'll tell Dora what a discontented temper you possess." So saying, the priest rode on, and, after the lapse of a few moments, Brian proceeded homewards.

The evening advanced very slowly, in the lover's opinion; and when he left his office and arrived at Carrick, on his way to Father Mike's, he found it was only five o'clock. Martin, whom he had met, told him that Miss Dora was up the village, and he stationed himself in the window of the public-house, thinking she would pass that way, and that he could walk home with her. At last a neighbour induced him to take one, only one, glass of whisky, "to keep up his heart;" and then, another prevailed on him to take part of a tumbler of "real Cork," that wouldn't hurt a new-born baby, and was as mild as new milk; and after that poor Brian needed no further pressing. "Let the devil in, and he'll keep the castle;" and so it was. Glass succeeded glass, and at last, when Brian was more than half tipsy, Philip Waddy entered. He appeared in high spirits, and drew near the place where Brian and his friends were sitting. Brian at first resolved to hold his peace, and keep his thoughts to himself, but some remarks that Waddy made annoyed him, and, with the restless feeling of drunkenness, he seemed anxious to engage in a quarrel. Philip, on the contrary, appeared wishful to avoid it; and their companions, Irish-like, always anxious for "a row," thought him by far too peaceable.

"Come, my boys," said Waddy, "I'll give ye something to drink upon; here goes! Oh! I bar water, it shall be the pure whisky; what, Brian! – you must drink it – fill, fill!"

"I won't," replied Brian, "I have just taken enough, and there is nothing, as Father Mike says, so much to be thought of in a young man as – sobriety."

A loud laugh followed this speech, and Philip continued: –

"Never mind – up, boys, that won't flinch from a glass, or the health of a pretty girl. Now with three-times-three, as they used to say in our Dublin club – long life, health, and beauty for ever to Dora O'Hay!"

In an instant Brian sprang from his seat, his cheek flushing, while he hastily inquired, what right Phil Waddy had to name Dora O'Hay after that fashion?

"Now, Brian, my boy, keep cool; I suppose I've a right to name a girl I love, and one who I've positive proof doesn't hate me, when and where I please; so take it asy."

"Ye lie!" said Brian, fiercely; "ye've no proof that she loves ye – ye're a false liar!"

Phil was not brave, but he made a show of courage, advanced towards Brian with his fists clenched, and then backed, observing, "If ye weren't her cousin, by the powers I'd tear ye limb from limb!"

"I'll tell ye what, Phil Waddy, ye think yerself a gentleman; gentleman, indeed! the sweepings o' the gentry! – and ye think people are afraid of ye; but ye're mistaken; and I'll tell ye what ye are – and these honest men to the fore! – ye're no better than a well-dressed beggar; and when ye hear the dinner-bell ring at the grand houses, in ye go, and then sit at the foot o' the table, and eat and drink what ye'd scorn to work for. But it's not the worst; I could say *that* of you, Phil Waddy, that would place ye as high as the gallows-top, if ye were as grand as Colclough,[348] and make ye a thing that the crow and the raven would turn from, for sure natur would tell them that even yer corpse was poisoned with the badness o' yer shrivelled heart! – only mind the old vault in Dane's Castle,[349] and who ye met there, and what ye said last Monday was a week! But never heed turning pale, I'd scorn to be an informer; only, as to Dora O'Hay, I warn ye – lave her; the vulture and the wood-quest[350] 'ud be bad companions."

So saying, Brian strode out of the public-house, and Waddy made no attempt to follow. If Brian's threat had moved him, he concealed it effectually from his half-drunken companions, although some of them afterwards pretended to remember, when the occurrences of that evening were referred to, that Waddy's eyes glared fearfully, and that his lips quivered. Again they drank of the liquid fire, and none of the party were able to call to mind at what hour, exactly, Waddy departed; long, certainly, he did not remain. The snow was falling thickly around him, but it had not obliterated the foot-marks of one who wended a somewhat unsteady pace towards the priest's dwelling on the hill. Near the village there were many prints on the whitened surface; but, as the lights twinkled more faintly in the cottage windows, there was but one track distinguishable by the light of a moon somewhat obscured by white but opaque clouds. Waddy kept on the trail like a bloodhound; his gun was slung across his shoulder, and in his right hand he carried a stout stick: the shadow of a huge black thorn-tree crossed his path; he stopped, sprang amid its branches, and bore down a thick and knotted bough; hastily he tore off the slighter twigs, and, flinging his former staff over the hedge, firmly grasped the one he had just gathered. The next shadow he perceived was moving onwards, and his speed increased – as he thought to himself – "I was right; I knew there was some one in the under-vault; and, from its size, there could have been but *one!*" – and the murmur of a low, but fiend-like laugh mingled with the whistling wind: and then he thought, "Fool, fool, fool, not to keep his own counsel!" Brian heard not the footstep – it fell lightly; his thoughts were with Dora; they were seated, in fancy, at the priest's cheerful fire, and he almost imagined he could hear the soft music of her evening song, at the very moment when the murderous club was raised for his destruction; hard, hard it fell, and the heart was aroused from its trance, and the body was grovelling in the snow; harder, and yet more hard; and then the crackling sound of the crushed skull-bones, and the warm oozing and outpouring of the red blood, on the fair white robe that covered the earth! Then, as the murderer, like a second Cain, stood over the prostrate dead, came the hasty trampling of a horse, and Father Mike issued from a grove of tall fir-trees that joined the road, and scowled on the black deed – the first within man's memory that had ever been perpetrated there. In an instant, before Waddy could move hand or foot, the priest sprang off his horse, and grappled with him; the moon shone brightly forth, as if to show the unequal struggle, for the aged man was overpowered, and his throat was pressed, for a time, almost to suffocation: the fiend, however, relaxed his hold, and spoke:

"You are there, and you see what I have done. Why didn't ye pass on, or what devil brought ye to yer own death? No – hear me out; stir hand or foot, and this ends ye!" and he drew a pistol from his bosom. "Ah, ah! I'm not priest-ridden, and think as little of one sort of earth as of another. Only look ye, Father Mike, in Counsellor Finlon's desk (and a superstitious old dog he was), were the papers that, if shown, would have hung you out and out, many's the day ago; you know for what – for in yer young days ye were bitter enough against government. Well, it's good to have more pocket pistols than one; so I took them, and a few others that might stand me at a pinch, and would never be missed now, as the matter's as good as forgotten; and so ye see, holy father, you tell, and hang me; and I tell, and hang you! It 'ud be easier to settle ye here, but I don't care to do that; so if you'll let me alone, I'll let you alone: there, jog off; but mark – there are those in the next barony that, if a finger is raised against me, don't care a traneen[351] for priests, bishops, cardinals, or pope. Never mind – no nostrum of yours can make that feel again!" – and he pushed his foot against the stiffening body of poor Brian, over which Father Mike had stooped – "so much for your immortality!"

The murderer did not utter another word, but turned into the little wood that skirted the road.

Father Mike deliberately mounted his horse, and paced slowly homeward; the horrid events that pressed upon his brain almost deprived him of reason.

Brian dead – Waddy, the murderer – the struggle – the papers. He writhed under the powerful coil of the serpent he had fostered and befriended. In this state of mental wretchedness, uncertain how to act, he arrived at his house.

Let us leave this fearful incident of our tale for a while, to relate a few of the circumstances that led to the dreadful occurrence which, for the first time within the memory of man, had laid an indelible stain on the parish of Bannow.

The fact was, before the Irish reign of terror of 1798, Father Mike, like many of the Romish[352] clergy, had entered into a clandestine correspondence with foreign powers; this had been suspected, and after the rebellion he was arraigned on the charge of high treason. Proof, however, was wanting; and it was believed that Counsellor Finlon, who conducted the prosecution, had been induced to suppress the principal evidence against him; this, however, was merely suspicion. Father Mike was acquitted, returned to his parish much wiser than he had left it, and afterwards showed his good sense by never meddling in politics; and, as party feeling died away, the charge was almost forgotten.

It has been seen that poor Brian was justified in thinking so ill of Waddy; but he was most imprudent in applying his information as he did. The horror which the lower and middling class of Irish have of delivering any one up to the violated laws of their country, is a fearful source of evil; indeed, in the most civilized parts of the island, this feeling still exists. An old ruin, called Dane's Castle, was on the estate of a gentleman in the neighbourhood, and, as it was crumbling fast to decay, he wished to have it pulled down. Brian, who, in his capacity of surveyor – architect, or, more properly speaking, a country union of both, had been engaged to build and repair some offices about his house – was directed to examine the stones of the castle, and inform him if they could be usefully employed in the new building. The relic of olden times was far from any dwelling, and even the few cattle that used to shelter beneath its walls had lately deserted it. Some scattered brushwood grew around it, and the strong ivy might be said to repay its former support by keeping the mouldering fragments together. Evening was closing when Brian went to inspect it; he thought it almost too late to observe the ruin distinctly, but then it was a "good step to go and come;" and, after examining the outer stones, he descended into a little cell, or cave, which, tradition said, had been the abode of a pious monk many centuries ago; the grey twilight stole tremblingly through the various apertures in the decayed wall and stony ceiling, and the surveyor was on the point of clambering up, when Waddy's voice struck upon his ear; he could not be said to suspect anything, yet he stood motionless, and heard him in earnest conversation with a stranger, one not of the province of Leinster.

"They can't have got scent of me," said Philip, "it's morally impossible; however, it 'll be a lesson to the rest not to be lettin' their land to new tenants."

"I think," replied the other, "we could have warned them off, only ye advised the burnin'; and to be sure there was nothin' else for it, when once the robbery was finished, for they all knew us. How were ye ever back in time?"

"Oh, the mare's worth a million! – she's prime. 'Tisn't the first time, nor won't be the last, I made my neighbour's horse do the turn: and the best of it is, when Sam Corish found her warm in the mornin', he sets off to the wise man for a charm; and there's a horse-shoe nailed to the door; for he swears the fairies are after Black Bess!"

"Well, Phil, ye're strong and hearty. I own the job was almost too much for me: I can't bear finishing the innocent women and childer."

"Oh, I thought ye'd better sense than that! Sure it puts 'em out of pain. But what I wanted to say most to you is, how we're to manage when this place comes down – (there 'ud be fine pickings in the house that owns it, but I'll have no hand in anything so near home); you know this is a very convenient place to stow any little thing the Roving Jenny puts in, till we send it off. Bridge's chamber's too exposed; this is far from the sea to be sure, yet it is lonely; – however, we'll talk more about it; there's nothing hid away now, and that sop of a fellow, Brian, 'll be looking here for the sake of the stones, to-morrow, I suppose. However, you step to the Public, and hear the news – they're almost tired of talking of the burning in the county Waterford."

Even when the echo of their footsteps died away, Brian could hardly believe the reality of what he had heard, and he resolved to keep it to himself until a fit opportunity occurred of mentioning it to his father confessor, and asking his advice. His imprudence at the public-house cost him his life, for Philip was assured that he knew his secret.

When Father Mike returned to his home, after the dreadful scene he had witnessed, he was followed in the distance by the murderer, who, although he thought the priest sufficiently in his power, feared that something might induce him to deliver him up to justice. The glimmering light from the kitchen-window attracted his attention, and he carefully watched the movements within, until the moment when Father Mike was about to speak of him, in the presence of Dora. He remained outside the house, like a prowling wolf, after the shutter had been fastened, and at length saw a single ray stream from Dora's window; the demoniac thought flashed across his brain that, if he could speak to the innocent and affectionate girl, he might win her to his purpose, and thus have a double hold on the priest. The window almost rested on the top of a sloping roof, and was easy of access: he crept up the thatch, and through the uncurtained lattice saw Dora sitting on the side of her small, low bed, her head resting on her hand, her whole appearance betokening much and bitter sorrow. He tapped at the window, and she looked towards it, but with a bewildered ken, as if she hardly comprehended what it meant.

"Dora, dear Dora, hush! Sure ye know me, love? I just want to speak one word to you; there, don't be frightened – why should ye? – just open the window for one little minute."

Dora moved towards it, her whole frame violently agitated; she tried to speak, but the words died on her lip, and she motioned him to begone.

"No, love, no; not till ye have heard me. Sure I'm yer sweetheart, and will be yer husband in spite of them all; and now every one's asleep, there's no harm in your speaking to one you love."

She drew still nearer the window, but utterance was denied her, and again she moved her hand for him to depart.

"Undo the fastening, love," he repeated; but still she motioned him away. "Then," said he, "as I must speak to you, you force me to this!" and, urged by every bad and unmanly passion, he, by one strong effort, burst open the casement. Dora gave a faint scream, and fell on the floor; he was in the act of entering, when little Martin appeared at the chamber-door, and presented to his breast a double-barrelled gun that was nearly as long as the room.

"I ax yer pardon, Mister Phil; but I can't help it; it comes quite nataral-like to purtect a woman; and I'll just take lave to say that ye choose a mighty quare time for visiting, particular whin there's no one to resave ye – for Miss there looks as dead as a door-nail.[353] Hulloo – hulloo – hulloo – oo – o! all o' ye!" and he sung out a tally-ho. "Here's housebreaking, and fire, and Miss Dory dead! – If ye stir hand or fut, Misther Phil (I'm heart-sorry for ye, but it's thrue as that I'm little Martin) – if ye stir hand or fut, ye're gone – gone, hot-trot to the devil!"

At this moment Father Mike rushed into the apartment; enraged at seeing his niece, to all appearance dead on the floor, and Waddy half in at the window, forgetful of all circumstances connected with himself, he articulated, in a voice rendered hoarse by violent feeling – "Seize – seize him, Martin! – *he is a murderer!*" By this time Dick, and another "working-boy," who lived in the house, had entered; – the wretched man made an effort to escape, by drawing back from the window. Martin, however, resolved he should not get off so easily, and discharged his gun; the fire took effect, and Philip rolled off the building over which he had climbed, but a few minutes before, in perfect strength and fiend-like vigour.

Martin looked out of the window after him, and quietly said, "He's only a taste hurt – not kilt outright: we'll step down and pick him up, and then yer reverence 'll tell us what to do wid him; there, Miss Dora's a-coming to herself, the darlint! God presarves his own!"

On examination, Philip was discovered to have been badly wounded in the shoulder; he would not suffer any dressing to be applied, but sat, the picture of sullen crime and obstinacy, in the kitchen, which filled by degrees with the neighbouring peasantry. He neither spoke nor moved; when the priest addressed him he smiled – such a smile! – not like those of other days.

It may be here necessary to state, that when Father Mike left his niece in her little chamber, he went to the ladder-stair which led to Martin's dormitory, and called to him to arise. In a moment Martin was with his master; and the priest hastily told him that murder had been committed in the neighbourhood – that as he was coming home he had witnessed it; at the same time carefully concealing that Waddy was the perpetrator of so foul a deed; he directed him to arouse the farming boys, and bring the body to the house. Martin obeyed, wisely thinking that he ought to take the gun; and while in the act of loading it, Dora's faint scream broke upon his ear.

When the bustle had subsided a little, the two young men, accompanied by three or four of the peasants, went to seek for the body of poor Brian. Martin alone remained – his long gun resting on his knees, and his eye steadily fixed on Philip.

The remains of the murdered youth were brought in. As they passed Waddy, many believed they bled afresh; he started from his seat, and one thrill of human feeling seemed to rush through his frame. He gazed for an instant, and then covered his face with his hands. They laid the corpse on the long table, where, not two hours before, the priest's supper had rested; and deep groans, and bitter sobs, echoed through the humble room. The murderer sat apart, his wound still bleeding, while all looked upon him as a being accursed.

The early morning saw the culprit in the hands of justice. When he was led forth, manacled, to the car that was to convey him to Wexford jail, he turned to Father Mike, and, showing his wrists, said, in a deep under-tone, "This is the liberty you promised!"

"I – I – " replied the priest, "I promised you no liberty. I confess I deserved what followed. You intimidated me by your threat, at the very moment when self ought to have been a secondary consideration; but God is wise – he would not suffer the murderer to escape, and I am punished for my weakness. But you must have been worse than devil, at such a moment, to think of harming that spotless child; repent, there is yet time – repent; although there can be no deeper hell than your own heart!"

He answered not; the car and escort pursued their way amid the execrations of the peasantry.

The wake took place as usual, and great was the assemblage; but the untimely death of the young man shed a gloom over it, which neither "tay, whisky, snuff, nor tobacco," could dissipate. The best "keeners" were collected, but their hired cries were not heeded. Many sincere tears were shed for poor Brian, and his good qualities were amply praised. "Och, sorra o' my heart!" sobbed out Molly, "to think the beautiful corpse he'd ha' made, if he'd been let alone!"

"Is that yer trouble?" replied Martin, who was engaged in making a "cauldron" of hot whisky-punch; "why then, Molly – only ye haven't much mother-wit[354] to yer own share – I think it's a different thing to that ye ought to say."

"What 'ud you say, wise man Martin?" inquired one of the company.

"Why, thin, I'd jist say, that it's not much matter how a corpse looks, so what was once inside was beautiful and in the thrue way."

Towards morning, when the principal number of people had departed, and only six or eight aged women remained in the apartment with the body, Dora Hay opened the chamber-door to ascertain that all was quiet; and, throwing the coverlet over her as a mantle, descended to the "wake-room," Her mind had been shaken, yet at that moment her purpose was nerved for temporary exertion, and she clearly comprehended what she was about to undertake. When she opened the door, her ghastly and unexpected appearance terrified the women, and they crowded together. She advanced to the table on which the corpse lay, fully dressed, according to the custom of the country. The mangled head was covered, and she did not attempt to disturb the cloth, but took one of the hands in hers. She recoiled from the first touch, and the icy chill of death appeared to have been communicated to her. For some moments she stood motionless as chiseled marble: again she took the hand, and, slowly bending on her knees, just touched it with her lips; she continued kneeling for about five minutes, with head elevated, and lips moving as if in prayer; but no sound escaped them. Slowly she crossed herself; and, pressing the little crucifix, that was suspended from her neck, to her heart, with the same quiet step returned to her apartment.

The funeral was not only numerously, but respectably, attended, for rich and poor lamented Brian's untimely end: and I have before said, that Father Mike was universally esteemed.

There was an old, miserable-looking hag that resided over the Scar (an inlet of the sea that separates Bannow from an adjoining parish), and near the ruins of the Seven Castles of Clonmines. This wretched object, had she lived a hundred years ago, would most certainly have been burned as a witch; as it was, she was regarded both with dislike and terror by old and young. Squalid in her appearance, her rags fluttering in every passing blast, she sat, during the funeral, on one of the high tombstones that "mark the lowly dead." As the crowd passed from the churchyard, she singled out Martin, and beckoned him to her. Martin was not at all flattered by the distinction; but, too superstitious not to attend her command, immediately obeyed.

"God save ye kindly, Mrs. Madge! – I'm glad to see ye."

"That's a lie, Martin Finchley, and ye know it is; there's no one glad to see me – no one cares if the earth opened and swallowed ould Madge! But that's not what I wanted to spake about. Man alive! – if indeed ye be a man – don't stand cronauning[355] there, but come close – closer to me!" And she stretched forth her bare, bony arm, and, grasping little Martin's shoulder with her long, claw-like fingers, drew him towards her, as a cat pulls out a mouse to execution. "Ye know the Seven Castles o' Clonmines; well, the one next the wather, where there are such broad, flat stones, ye'll see one bigger nor the rest; there, under that you will find what consarns Father Mike 'bove the world, if ye'll take the throuble to find it. It's for the sake of the dark-eyed girl, that's often done me a kind turn, though she's not long for this world, for her yarn is spun. There, go yer ways; only, hark ye, mind whin ye go to the place, or, may-be, ye'll meet with more company than ye'd bargain for."

Martin loved his master too well not to risk even his life for him if it were necessary; but he felt delighted when he was fairly out of Mag's sight. Perfectly unconscious of what could "consarn Father Mike 'bove the world," he concealed himself among the ruins of Clonmines, until the evening closed; he then removed the large flat stone she had described, and dug like a rabbit for some time, amongst the rubbish, before he discovered anything. At last he found a small bundle of papers, tied with red tape, and then a small parcel. He was proceeding in his search, when he thought he heard a rustling on the pebbly shore, as if some one was approaching; and, securing what he had found, he hastily got behind a projecting buttress of one of the castles. His conjectures were right, for a man immediately turned the corner of a little bay, and proceeded direct to the flat stone which Martin had not time to replace. The Irish dumb show is very expressive, and the gestures of the disappointed seeker were strongly indicative of rage and disappointment. The man at last went away; and Martin, who, to use his own expression, had "lain snug," proceeded home with his prize. Arrived at Father Mike's, he waited quietly in the chimney-corner until the priest was disengaged; and then went into the little parlour, and, locking the door, crept round the room, spying and peeping about, as if the wall had ears. The priest, accustomed to Martin's eccentricities, did not pay much attention to his movements; for, truth to say, he was discussing his tumbler of whisky-punch – it was not as palatable as usual, for Dora had not compounded it. Martin at last approached the great chair, and gently pulled the sleeve of his coat; Father Mike turned round, and awaited an explanation. Martin presented the packet.

Father Mike put on his spectacles, untied the fastening, and, to his no small astonishment, found various memoranda concerning circumstances long past, which at once convinced him that he had actually in his possession the papers to which the villain Waddy had alluded. The parcel contained also a few small articles of plate, and some letters that mysteriously alluded to dark and bloody deeds which either had been, or were to be, perpetrated. Martin detailed, in his own way, the manner in which he obtained them; and Father Mike had no doubt that they were to have been made use of to his injury by some of Waddy's associates.

Every effort was made to induce Waddy to disclose his crimes, but in vain. He remained cool and collected; civil, but sarcastic, to those who approached him; and appeared to summon all his faculties for the purpose of banishing every relic of human feeling from his breast. When his mother visited his cell, he received her kindly, but betrayed no emotion, although she wept upon his shoulder until the fountain of her tears seemed dried up.

As the assizes drew near, rumour became more busy than ever, and crimes were imputed to the wretched man, of which it is more than probable he had never been guilty. The day of trial came, and Father Mike was summoned to give evidence against the murderer, who had refused all spiritual aid, and would converse neither with priest nor minister.

The crowd, assembled outside the court-house of the county town, was greater than had ever been collected on any former occasion. In Ireland, the feelings of the lower order of people are usually enlisted in favour of a prisoner, for they appear to think that all who come under the arm of the law are victims. But it was not so in Waddy's case; he had murdered the kinsman of a priest, and had attempted to violate the sanctity of a priest's house, which is considered as holy as the altar; the bitterest execrations were, therefore, uttered against him.

Father Mike was making his way through the motley throng, when a low, murmuring growl ran along the people, and various exclamations of – "Oh, the murdering reprobate!" – "Oh, to think of it!" – "Oh, it is impossible he could be guilty of it!" – struck upon the priest's ear; and he soon learnt that Waddy had anticipated the sentence of the law, and strangled himself in prison.

* * * * * *

The spring had passed, and the summer – the sunny summer – was nearly at its height, when the priest one evening entered his little parlour, and called his niece to him. She was engaged at her wheel, the only employment to which she attended; it appeared to give her occupation without the effort of thinking, and she turned it mechanically from morning until night.

"Dora," said the kind old man, as she entered, "Dora, will you take a walk to the village, or up the hill? – you have not been out since Sunday."

"Yes, uncle."

"Dora, stay one moment: do not break my heart; it is old now, and has known much sorrow – much sorrow have I known in this world, Dora; but, child, the bitterest of all my afflictions would be to see you – you, whom my heart so joyed in – pine away, and leave me. And, oh!" continued the weeping old man, as he fell upon his knees, "oh! with more than enough – with plenty, plenty to my portion, of this world's good – oh, Heavenly Father! hast thou willed that I, an old, grey, time-worn man, should outlive all that are dear to me, and that strangers should close my eyes?"

Dora also knelt, calmly and deliberately, by her uncle, and looked steadily in his face. He was much agitated; and there was something about her countenance that betokened returning feeling and interest.

"Sure, Dora," he proceeded, after a pause, "sure you can unburthen your mind to me! Even your duties to God have all been neglected – you have not been to the confessional since – "

"Stop, stop! I well remember since when," she interrupted, hastily – "too well! I have been wrong, I know; but all in this world has appeared to me so changing, so wicked, so uncertain! May-be, dear uncle, my head has not been right – everything seems changed."

"Am I changed, Dory?"

"Oh, no, no, no!" – and tears, that sweet relief to the overcharged bosom, gushed from her eyes, as she threw her arms, with the affection of former days, round her uncle's neck. "I have not cried this long, long time; and now I am better – my head is not so heavy – and I will tell you now, dear uncle, all that has passed in my mind. Brian – poor Brian! – I did not think of him as he thought of me; and the black wickedness of that bad man, whose smile wiled[356] away my thoughts! – but when I saw Brian's corpse, I knelt and made a vow that I would go into a convent, and lead a holy life, for his sake whom I did not value as I ought. Uncle dear, I am not what I was, and every day that delays me from a holy life, adds to the sin of a broken oath."

The poor priest was bewildered – almost distracted: to yield up, even to the church, the fair girl whom he had expected to be the blessing of his old age, was a trial for which he was unprepared, and which he had not strength to meet. It was some time before he spoke, and his words were then scarcely articulate.

"Dear Dora, I am punished! I gave you the love that belonged to the Almighty; and now you leave me in age and helplessness."

The next morning, Father Mike mounted his faithful steed, and, at an early hour, was on the high road to his bishop's house, having resolved to tell him the whole story, and to act according to his advice. The bishop felt much for his old friend, and observed, that Dora could easily be absolved from her oath, by the church. But her uncle knew that she would persevere, with a sort of insanity, in her determination so to devote herself. Nevertheless, the bishop thought he would converse with her, and see if any plan could be arranged that might render Father Mike and his niece at peace in their once happy home. He accompanied the priest to his dwelling, and felt convinced, after a brief conversation with Dora, that her mind had become weak and wandering; however, he succeeded in persuading her that she could perform her vow, and still remain with her uncle, as "it was not likely he could live long."

"My dear child," said the bishop, "it would be almost killing him if you were to leave him now; but put on the dress of the holy Ursulines[357] – the order of which you intend to become, I hope, a worthy member – perform its penances and prayers, and keep apart from the world in your uncle's house: you will make him happy; and be a blessing to that good man, whose hairs would go down with sorrow to the grave, if you deserted him in his old age."

Dora has now been some years truly a "blessing" to her uncle and the neighbouring poor; but it is difficult to determine whether or not her intellects are gaining strength, as she holds no converse with any one except Father Mike. She passes from cottage to cottage, the ministering angel of peace to the afflicted: neither joy, nor, it would seem, sorrow, have marked her pale, marble-like countenance; and little Martin, who wears like a Turkey carpet, often observes, as she passes, with slow but noiseless step, along the old kitchen –

"To think of that banshee-looking cratur being the dancing, singing fairy – light of eye – light of foot – light of heart – until that horrid night of blood and sin that brought desolation even to the house of FATHER MIKE!"[a]

LARRY MOORE.

"THINK of to-morrow!" – that is what few Irish peasants ever do, with a view of providing for it: at least few with whom I have had opportunities of being acquainted. They will think of anything – of everything, but that. There is Larry Moore, for example: – who, that has ever visited my own pastoral village of Bannow, is unacquainted with Larry, the Bannow boatman – the invaluable Larry – who, tipsy or sober, asleep or awake, rows his boat with undeviating power and precision? – He, alas! is a strong proof of the truth of my observation. Look at him on a fine sunny day in June. The cliffs that skirt the shore, where his boat is moored, are crowned with wild furze; while here and there, a tuft of white or yellow broom, sprouting a little above the bluish green of its prickly neighbour, waves its blossoms, and flings its fragrance to the passing breeze. Down to the very edge of the rippling waves is almost one unbroken bed of purple thyme, glowing and beautiful; – and there Larry's goat, with her two sportive kids – sly, cunning rogues! – find rich pasture – now nibbling the broom-blossoms, now sporting amid the furze, and making the scenery re-echo with their musical bleating. The little island opposite, Larry considers his own particular property; not that a single sod of its bright greenery belongs to him – but, to use his own words, "Sure it's all as one my own – don't I see it – don't I walk upon it – and the very water that it's set in is my own; for sorra a one can put *foot* on it widout me and 'the coble,'[358] that have been hand and glove as good as forty years." But look, I pray you, upon Larry: – there he lies stretched in the sunlight, at full length, on the firm sand, like a man-porpoise – sometimes on his back – then slowly turning on his side – but his most usual attitude is a sort of reclining position against that flat grey stone, just at high-water mark; he selects it as his constant resting place, because (again to use his own words) "the tide, bad cess to it! was apt to come fast in upon a body, and there was a dale of throuble in moving; but even if one chanced to fall asleep, sorra a morsel of harm the salt water could do ye on the grey stone, where a living merwoman sat every new-year's night combing her black hair, and making beautiful music to the wild waves, who, consequently, trated her sate wid grate respict – why not?" There then, is Larry – his chest leaning on the mermaid's stone, as we call it – his long, bare legs stretched out behind, kicking, occasionally, as a gad-fly[359] or merry-hopper, skips about what it naturally considers lawful prey: – his lower garments have evidently once been trowsers – blue trowsers; but as Larry, when in motion, is amphibious, they have experienced the decaying effects of salt water, and now only descend to the knee, where they terminate in unequal fringes. Indeed, his frieze jacket is no great things, being much rubbed at the elbows – and no wonder; for Larry, when awake, is ever employed, either in pelting the sea gulls (who, to confess the truth, treat him with very little respect), rowing his boat, or watching the circles formed on the surface of the calm waters by the large or small pebbles he throws into it; and as Larry, of course, rests his elbow on the rocks, while performing these exploits, the sleeves must wear, for frieze is not "impenetrable stuff."[360] His hat is a natural curiosity, composed of sun-burned straw, banded by a misshapen sea-ribbon, and garnished by "delisk,"[361] red and green, his "cutty pipe" stuck through a slit in the brim, which bends it directly over the left eye, and keeps it "quite handy widout any trouble." His bushy, reddish hair persists in obstinately pushing its way out of every hole in his extraordinary hat, or clusters strangely over his Herculean[362] shoulders, and a low-furrowed brow, very unpromising to the eye of the phrenologist: – in truth, Larry has somewhat of a dogged expression of countenance, which is relieved, at times, by the humorous twinkle of his little grey eyes, pretty much in the manner that a star or two illume the dreary blank of a cloudy November night. The most conspicuous part of his attire, however, is an undressed wide leather belt, that passes over one shoulder and then under another strap of the same material that encircles his waist; from this depends a rough wooden case, containing his whisky-bottle; a long, narrow knife; pieces of rope, of varied length and thickness; and a pouch which contains the money he earns at his "vocation."

Our portrait of him is sketched on the beach directly under the old churchyard of Bannow – upon the roof of one of the houses, it may be, for scores of them are buried beneath the sand; and the chimney of the ancient town-hall still exists, a mass of coarse mason-work among the graves. The surrounding scenery is more interesting, perhaps, than beautiful; though, to me, there is the beauty of association in every object within ken. But the curiosity, even of a stranger, may be excited by the distant promontory of Bag-an-bun,[363] where –

"Irelonde was lost and won,"

seen to great advantage from this particular spot. We may not moralize, however; our intention is to converse with Larry.

"Good morrow, Larry!"

"Good morrow kindly, my lady! may-be ye're going across?"

"No, thank ye, Larry; – but there's a silver sixpence for good luck."

"Ough! God's blessing be about ye! – I said so to my woman this morning, and she bothering the sowl out o' me for money, as if I could make myself into silver, let alone brass: – asy, says I, what trouble ye take! sure we had a good dinner yesterday; and more by tokens, the grawls were so plased wid the mate – the craturs! – sorra a morsel o' pratee they'd put into their mouths; – and we'll have as good a one to-day."

"The ferry is absolutely filled with fish, Larry, if you would only take the trouble to catch it!"

"Is it fish? Ough! sorra fancy I have for fasting-mate – besides, it's mighty watery, and a dale of trouble to catch. A grate baste of a cod lept into my boat yesterday, and I lying just here, and the boat close up: I thought it would ha' sted asy while I hollooed to Tom, who was near breaking his neck after the samphire for the quality, the gomersal! – but, my jewil! it was whip and away wid it all in a minit – back to the water. – Small loss!"

"But, Larry, it would have made an excellent dinner."

"Sure I'm after telling yer ladyship that we had a rale mate dinner, by grate good luck, yesterday."

"But to-day, by your own confession, you had nothing."

"Sure you've just given me sixpence."

"But suppose I had not!"

"Where's the good of thinking that, now?"

"Oh, Larry, I'm afraid you never think of *to-morrow!*"

"There's not a man in the whole parish of Bannow thinks more of it than I do," responded Larry, raising himself up; "and, to prove it to ye, madam dear, we'll have a wet night – I see the sign of it, for all the sun's so bright, both in the air and the water."

"Then, Larry, take my advice; go home and mend the great hole that is in the thatch of your cabin."

"Is it the hole? – where's the good of losing time about it now, when the weather's so fine?"

"But when the rain comes?"

"Lord bless ye, my lady! sure I can't hinder the rain! and sure it's fitter for me to stand under the roof in a dry spot, than to go out in the *teams*[364] to stop up a taste of a hole. Sorra a drop comes through it in *dry weather.*"

"Larry, you truly need not waste so much time; it is ten chances to one if you get a single fare to-day; – and here you stay doing nothing. You might usefully employ yourself, by a little foresight."

"Would ye have me desert my trust? Sure I must mind the boat. But, God bless ye, ma'am darlint! don't be so hard intirely upon me; for I get a dale o' blame I don't by no manner of means desarve. My wife turns at me as wicked as a weazel, becase I gave my consint to our Nancy's marrying Matty Keogh; and she says they were bad to come together on account that they hadn't enough to pay the priest; and the end of it is, that the girl and a grand-child are come back upon us; and the husband is off – God knows where!"

"I'm sorry to hear that, Larry; but your son James, by this time, must be able to assist you."

"There it is again, my lady! James was never very bright – and his mother was always at him, plaguing his life out to go to Mister Ben's school, and saying a dale about the time to come; but I didn't care to bother the cratur; and I'm sorry to say he's turned out rather obstinate – and even the priest says it's becase I never think of *to-morrow*."

"I am glad to find the priest is of my opinion: but, tell me, have you fatted the pig Mr. Herriott gave you?"

"Oh! my bitter curse (axing yer pardon, my lady) be upon all the pigs in and out of Ireland! That pig has been the ruin of me; it has such a taste for eating young ducks as never was in the world; and I always tether him by the leg when I'm going out; but he's so 'cute now, he cuts the tether."

"Why not confine him in a sty? – you are close to the quarry, and could build one in half an hour."

"Is it a sty for the likes of him! cock him up wid a sty! Och, Musha! Musha![365] the tether keeps him asy for the day."

"But not for the *morrow*, Larry."

"Now ye're at me agin! – you that always stood my friend. Meal-a-murder! if there isn't Rashleigh Jones making signs for the boat! Oh! ye're in a hurry, are ye? – well, ye must wait till yer hurry is over; I'm not going to hurry myself, wid sixpence in my pocket, for priest or minister."

"But the more you earn the better, Larry."

"Sure I've enough for to-day."

"But not for *to-morrow*, Larry."

"True for ye, ma'am dear; though people take a dale o' trouble, I'm thinking, when they've full and plenty at the same time; and I don't like bothering about it then. Sure, I see ye plain enough, Master Rashleigh. God help me! I broke the oar yesterday, and never thought to get it mended; and my head's splitting open with the pain – I took a drop too much last night, and that makes me fit for nothing – "

"On the *morrow*, Larry."

"Faith! ma'am dear, you're too bad. Oh dear! if I had the sense to set the lobster-pots last night, what a power I'd ha' caught! – they're dancing the hays[366] merrily down there, the cowardly blackguards! but I didn't think – "

"Of the *morrow*, Larry."

"Oh, then, let me alone, lady dear! What will I do wid the oar! Jim Connor gave me a beautiful piece of strong rope yesterday, but I didn't want it; and – I believe one of the childer got hold of it – I didn't think – "

"Of the *morrow*, Larry."

"By dad, I have it! – I can poke the coble on with this ould pitchfork; there's not much good in it; but never heed – it's the master's, and he's too much of a jentleman to mind trifles; though I'm thinking times a'n't as good wid him now as they used to be; for Barney Clarey tould Nelly Parrell, who tould Tom Lavery, who tould it out forenint me, and a dale more genteel men, who were taking a drop o' comfort at St. Patrick's, as how they bottle the whisky, and salt the mate, at the big house; and if that isn't a bad sign, I don't know what is; – though we may thank the English housekeeper for it, I'm thinking – wid her beaver bonnet, and her yellow silk shawl, that my wife (who knows the differ) says, after all, is only calico-cotton."

"What do you mean by bottling the whisky and salting the meat, Larry?"

"Now, don't be coming over us after that fashion; may-be ye don't know, indeed? Sure the right way, my lady, is to have the whisky on draught! and then it's so refreshing, of a hot summer's day, to take a good hearty swig; and in winter – by the powers! ma'am, honey, let me just take the liberty of advising you never to desart the whisky; it 'll always keep the could out of yer heart, and the trouble from yer eye. Sure the clargy take to it, and lawyers take to it, far before new milk; and his holiness the pope – God bless him! – to say nothing of the king (who is the first king of *hearts we* ever had), who drinks nothing but Innishown[367] – which, to my taste, hasn't half the fire of the rale potteen. It's next to a deadly sin to bottle whisky in a jentleman's house; – and, as to salting mate; – sure the ould ancient Irish fashion – the fashion of the good ould times – is just to kill the baste, and thin hang it by the legs in a convanient place; and every one can take a part of what they like best."

"But do you know that the English think of *to-morrow*, Larry?"

"Ay, the tame negres! that's the way they get rich, and sniff at the world, my jewil; and they no oulder in it than Henry the Second;[368] for sure, if there had been English before his time, it's long sorry they'd ha' been to let Ireland so long alone."

"Do you think so, indeed, Larry ?"

"I'll prove it to you, my lady, if ye'll jist wait till I bring over that impatient chap, Rashleigh Jones, who's ever running after the day, as if he hadn't a bit to eat: – there, d'ye see him? – he's dancing mad – he may just as well take it asy. It's such as him give people the feaver. There's that devil of a goat grinning at me; sorra a drop of milk can we get from her, for she won't stand quiet for a body to catch her; and my wife's not able, and I'm not willing, to go capering over the cliffs. Never mind!"

At last Larry and his boat are off, by the assistance of the pitchfork, and most certainly he does not hurry himself; but where is Rashleigh going to? As I live! he has got into Mr. Dorkin's pleasure-boat, that has just turned the corner of the island, and will be at this side before Larry gets to the other. Larry will not easily pardon this encroachment; not because of the money, but because of his privilege. I have heard it rumoured that, if Larry does not become more active, he will lose his situation; but I cannot believe it: he is, when fairly on the water, the most careful boatman in the county; and permit me to mention, in *sotto voce,*[369] that his master could not possibly dismiss him on the charge of heedlessness, because he himself once possessed *unencumbered* property[370] by field and flood, wooded hills, verdant vales, and pure gushing rivers. Those fair heritages are, however, passing into the hands of other proprietors; and the hair of the generous, good-natured landlord has become white, and sorrow has furrowed his brow, long before sixty summers have glowed upon his head. His children, too, do not hold that station in society to which their birth entitles them; and, latterly, he has not been so often on the grand jury, nor at the new member's dinners. The poor love him as well as ever; but the rich have neglected, in a great degree, his always hospitable board. The parish priest told me, in confidence, that all the change originated in our excellent friend's never thinking of TO-MORROW.

KELLY THE PIPER.

"Judy – Judy Kelly – Judy! – will ye give us no breakfast to-day – and the sun splitting the trees these two hours? – and the pig itself – the cratur – skreetching alive wid the hunger?"

"Och, it's true for ye, Mick, honey! – true for ye – and the pratees are almost done – and yon's Ellen. She carries the pitcher so lightly, that it's little milk she's got from the big house, this fine harvest morning."

And Mistress Kelly "hourisht"[371] the pig out of the cabin – placed three noggins on an old table that she pulled from a dark corner (there was but one window in the room, and that was stuffed with the Piper's coat, in lieu of glass), wiped the aforesaid table with the corner of her "praskeen,"[a][372] and, from another corner, lifted the kish,[373] that served to wash, strain, and "dish" the potatoes, feed the pig, or rock the child, as occasion might require.

Judy Kelly was certainly one of the worst specimens of an Irish woman I had ever the duty of inspecting. She never washed her face except on Sundays; and then it always gave her so bad a cold in her head – on account (to use her own words) "of the tinderness of her skin" – that she was obliged to cure it with liberal draughts of whisky – the effects of which rendered Judy (at other times a peaceable woman) the veriest scold in Bannow. Poor Kelly always anticipated this storm, and on Sunday evenings mounted his miserable donkey – miscalled Dumpling (a name, however, which might have been appropriate before he took service with his present master), and, with pipes under arm, posted to St. Patrick – the most respectable "sheebeen[374] shop" on the moor – and finished the night, sometimes with a comfortable nap by the road-side, or on a sand-bank. The most delightful sleep he ever had was one night when Dumpling, being, I suppose, tipsy, like her master, fell, ascending a nice muddy hill, and, unable to rise, remained on her knees, until Pat Furlong discovered them both early on Monday morning; Kelly loudly snoring, the glorious sun casting a flood of light over a visage thin, yellow, and ghastly – except a long, pointed, crimson nose, with a peculiar twist at the end, which assumed a richer colouring, shading to the very tip in deep and glowing purple; the bagpipes still tightly grasped under the "professor's" arm.

The family of this village musician was managed like many Irish families – that is, not managed at all; indeed the habits of the parents precluded even the possibility of the children's improvement in any way; they moved about, a miscellaneous mass of brown-red flesh, white teeth, bushy elf locks, which rarely submitted to the discipline of a comb, and party-coloured rags; yet were, nevertheless, cheerful, strong, and healthy. Clooney evinced much musical talent, which served as an excuse for idleness, uniform and premeditated. Molly was the best jigger for ten miles round; and Ellen would have been a pretty, roley-poley, industrious gipsy, if she had not been born to the lazy inheritance of the Kelly household; as it was, she did more than all the brats put together; and as her little bare feet puddled through the extraordinary black mud, which formed a standing pool around the stately dunghill that graced the door, she was welcomed by her father's salutation – "The top o' the morning to my colleen! – little to fill the noggins ye've got wid ye; well, niver mind, clane water's wholesome, and lighter for the stomach, may-be, nor milk; any way, the pratees are laughing,[375] and I must make haste for once: where's Molly?"

"She's just stept out to look after her pumps for the pathern,[376] but niver heed, we'll not wait," replied Mrs. Kelly, pouring the potatoes into the kish.

"It's little use, thin, mother honey, ther'll be for pumps, or pipes, or shillalahs, this harvest; for there's black news for the boys and girls, and it's myself was sorry to hear it; – there's to be no pathern."

"No pathern!" screamed Mrs. Kelly, letting half the potatoes fall on the floor, to the advantage of the pig, who entered at the lucky moment, and made good use of his time; while Kelly stood with open mouth, ready to receive the one he had dexterously peeled with his thumb-nail; – poor man, he was petrified; the pattern, where, man and boy, he had played, drank, and quarrelled, in St. Mary's honour, for thirty years; the pattern, with its line of "tints," covered with blankets, quilts, and quilted petticoats, its stalls glittering with gingerbread husbands and wives for half the country; the pattern, where his seat, a whisky barrel, was placed under a noble elm, in the middle of the firm greensward, where the belles and beaux of the neighbouring hills had footed gaily, if not gracefully, to "Moll Row," "Darby Kelly," or "St. Patrick's Day,"[377] until the morning peeped on their revellings, for more than a double century!

"It's impossible, ye little, lying hussy! – who dare stop the pathern? – the pathern, is it, in honour of the holy Vargin; for what 'ud they stop it? – there niver was even a bit of a ruction at the pathern o' Bannow, since the world was a world; ye wicked limb, tell me this moment who tould ye this news?"

Ellen looked at her father, and knowing it was a word and a blow with him when he was in a passion, meekly replied – that Pat Kenessy, the land-lord of "St. Patrick," had been turned off the pattern field, when in the act of striking the tent poles, to be ready for the next day, by Mister Lamb, the 'Squire's Scotch steward; and that Mister Lamb had informed Kenessy that his master would not permit any pattern to be held on his estate, as it only drew together a parcel of vagabonds, occasioned idleness and quarrels among men and women, and flirtation and courtship among girls and boys; and that a constable was ready to take the first man to Wexford jail who pitched a tent.

Poor Kelly! – at first he would not believe it; but some of the neighbours confirmed the information, and soon a council assembled in his cabin, to consider what measures ought to be adopted; the peasantry could not bear to give up quietly the only amusement they enjoyed during the year.

"That's what comes o' the 'Squire's living so long in England," said Blind Barry; "I thought little good it would end in, when he said, t'other day, that my cabin must be whitewashed every six months."

"He threatened to turn my dunghill into the ditch," cried the wrathful Piper – "but if he dares to lay his finger on it – "

"Don't fear," said Mickey the tailor, who possessed great reputation, both as a wit and a sage, and who did not enter regularly into the conference, but stood leaning against the door-post – "don't fear; great men don't like to dirty their fingers with trifles."

"It's long afore his uncle would have done so; but the good ould times is past, and there's no frinds for poor Ireland now," sighed Paddy Lumley, an old, white-headed man, more than eighty years of age.

"It's hard, very hard though," continued Kelly; "he knows well enough that the trifle I gets at the pathern, for my bits o' music, is all I have in the wide world to depind on for the rint; and sure it's little I picks up the counthry round to keep the skreeds[378] on the woman and childer – God help thim! – to say nothin' o' the atin' and the drinkin'; but niver mind; if there's no pathern, my curse be upon him and his! – may the grass, and the nettle, and the –"

"Asy, asy, Kelly!" cried the tailor – "asy, take it asy; can't ye think – never despair, says I; and so I said to Jim Holloway whin his wife died; never despair, says I; he took my advice, and married agin in three weeks. Why won't one field do ye instead of another? Can't ye borrow another place for the day, man alive?"

"Did ye ever hear such gumshogue!"[379] cried Blind Barry – "who'd gainsay the 'Squire, d'ye think? Which of his tinants would say ay to his nay, and have a turn-out, or a double rint, for their punishment?"

"Barry, will ye whisht! Listen to me, Kelly, and we'll have the pathern yet. Clane yerself, and go up to the big house to Mister Herriott; he's an ould residenter, and has a heart to feel for and a hand to relieve, the poor man's sorrow; let him know the rights of it, and, I'll go bail, he'll lend you some field of his own. And as to the 'Squire, you know he does not care a brass farthin' for him, on account of the half-acre field they two went to law about; I hear say it cost them, one way or t'other, a clear seven hundred; and the field itself not worth a traneen; but that's neither here nor there."

"Mick," said Kelly, "you have it! – by the powers, I'll go off straight; to be sure, if we have a pathern it's little matter where, excipt that it's pleasure for the girls to dance on the same sod their mothers danced afore them; but niver mind – won't some o' ye come to back me?"

"No occasion in life for that; but we'll go wid ye to the gate, and hear the luck when ye come out."

Kelly was soon ready, and set off on the embassy in high spirits: as they journeyed, they talked over the matter more at length, suggested a variety of fields and meadows, and told the story to all they met. The Irish, careless of their time, are ever ready to "tell or hear some new thing;" and Kelly's train became almost a troop, before it arrived at the hill which overlooked Mr. Herriott's small but beautiful domain.

It was, indeed, very beautiful: the old mansion, with its tall white chimneys, bursting from a thick grove of many-coloured foliage that, early in August, was deepening into the brown of autumn; the long, straight line of trees that marked the avenue, and the bright blue sea at the distance, reflecting a cloudless sky; the hill, sloping gradually down to the back of the house, which, though not exactly a common, was rendered nearly so by the kindness of its possessor, who gave grass to half the lazy cows and troublesome pigs in the parish.

"We can see the sign of the Welsh coast, the day's so clear," said Mick.

"The dickons[380] drive it back, say I! – the Welsh and English are all foreigners alike; and it's o' them all the bother comes," retorted Kelly.

"How dark the mountain of Forth[381] looks! Do you remimber once when it looked bright, Jim?" said Hurling Jack to a tall, powerful man, who strode foremost, of the party.

"Do I not! The red-coats were in the hollow, and the boys on the hill; they covered it like a swarm o' bees. Och! if we had but attacked thim as I wanted, not a mother's son would have lived to tell the story; but they got to the whisky and the pipes, and the reinforcement came up, and it was all over. Kelly, I remember you were blind with the drink, and yet ye kept on playing for the dear life –

> "We'll down wid the orange, and up wid the green,
> Success to the croppies wherever they're seen!'"[382]

"Whisht, Jim, whisht!" cried Kelly, looking about quite frightened; "how do you know who's listening? – and, as I'm a sinner, yon's the master down in the glin, looking as mild as new milk."

"How can ye tell how he looks, and his back to ye, ye nataral[a]?" slyly inquired the tailor; "but I'm sorry he is there, for I thought we might have taken the short cut through the round meadow."

"We may do that still," replied Kelly, "for his honour's too much the jentle-man to look back whin once on the road; and there's others know that as well as me, I'm thinking; for I see Biddy Colfer turning her two-year-ould calf in, through the gap; well that bates all – and she only a Kerry woman!"

Kelly and his friends were, in some measure, disappointed. They certainly took the short cut, and his honour did not look back, but he did as bad; he seated himself deliberately on the wheel of a car that was turned upside down in the ditch-side, and answered all the purposes of gate and turnstile; whistled two rambling spaniels to his side, to share the caresses so liberally bestowed on Neptune, a huge Newfoundland dog, who disdained frolic and fun of all descrip-tion, and looked up in Mr. Herriott's face, with an owl-like gravity, that made it doubtful whether his steadiness proceeded from sagacity or stupidity. As the crowd advanced, he drew still closer to his master's side, and in low, sullen growls expressed much displeasure at so ill-dressed a troop approaching the avenue.

"We are in for it," whispered Kelly, in a low voice, "so we may as well put a bould face on it at once, and spake altogether."

In another moment Mr. Herriott was surrounded by the bareheaded com-pany; Kelly, and Mickey the tailor, a little in advance.

"Every blessing in life on yer honour! – and proud are we all to see yer hon-our looking so fresh and bravely this fine morning."

"Kelly, is it you? – and Mick? – and – why, what earthly business brings such a gang of you here? Have I not warned you, over and over again, not to make your confounded paths across the clover field? – And I see half the barley is destroyed before the sickle can be put to it, from your everlasting trespasses."

"Is it? Oh, then, more's the pity, to say nothin' o' the shame!" exclaimed the Piper, looking very sorrowful; "but we had no intintion in life to trespass; only we saw yer honour from the top o' the hill, and as we had a little business wid yer honour, to save time, and not to trouble ye at the house, we thought it best to take to the path. We've not done a taste of harm, yer honour."

"Well, Kelly, do not do so again; it sets a bad example, and destroys the fields. (Neptune, down, sir!) But what's your business? – another disagreement with your worthy lady? – or a quarrel? – or a –"

"Nothin' at all, at all, of that sort, sir; it's far worse nor that, yer honour, long life to ye! It's all o' the pathern; a burning sin, and a shame, and a disgrace to the whole town and counthry: the likes of it was niver heard since the world was born!"

"Is that the way to discoorse a jentleman?" interrupted Mick; "how can his honour understand ye? – ye're for all the world like a born nataral;" and he pushed the diminished Piper back, and, advancing one foot forward com-menced his oration, at the same time rubbing the brim of his hat with much dexterity – "To-morrow as is well known to yer honour, being a raale scholar, and a born jentleman – not like some neighbours, who have a power o' money and nothing else – will be (crossing himself) the blessed day of our Lady, and always the pathern day of the parishes of Kilkaven and Bannow. Now yer honour minds[a] the little square field at the foot o' the hill – always, in the memory o' man, called the pathern field; well, it has plased t'other 'Squire – not that I'd iver think of turning my tongue aginst the gintry, the raale gintry, yer honour, (bowing low to Mr. Herriott) – has thought fit to forbid the pathern, and to threaten to sind the first man caught pitching a tint-pole on his land, by a constable to Wexford jail."

Mr. Herriott possessed a kind and benevolent temper; he loved to see the peasantry happy in their own way, and spent his fortune on his estate, anxious, both by precept and example, to instruct and serve his tenantry; but he had a decided, old-fashioned, Irish hatred of jails, constables, lawyers, soldiers, &c.; and often did he glory in the fact, that neither soldier, constable, lawyer, physician, nor water-guard,[383] were within twelve miles of his mansion. "The rich 'Squire," as he was called, was a very good man as times went, but so fond of carrying everything with a high hand, that the benefits he conferred on the poor (and they were many) were seldom received with gratitude, because he made little allowance for the customs or foibles of those among whom he dwelt. Moreover, he loved soldiers, talked of establishing a land and water-guard, and a dispensary, in the parish; all good things, but yet decidedly opposed to the views of his more gentle and amiable neighbour.

"Indeed, a constable!"

"Ay, yer honour, to a paceable parish."

"You have been, and are, a peaceable set of men, considering you are Irish," added Mr. Herriott, smiling; "and certainly I believe no one here had anything to do with that uufortunate riot at Duncormuck, where poor Murtough was killed."

"No, no, yer honour," they loudly and unitedly replied; one, in a low voice, added, "He was only a Connaught man after all!"

"I should be sorry, indeed, if the Bannow boys wanted either soldiers or constables to keep them in order; but I do not see how I can interfere. I cannot oblige Mr. Desmond to lend you the field."

"No; but your honour could give us the loan of one of yer own to keep our pathern in; and long may yer honour reign over us."

"Amin!" said Kelly.

"One of my own? I do not think I could do that," replied Mr. Herriott; "the fields that join the road are surrounded by a bounds-ditch,[384] and young plantations; and as to those in the centre of the domain – impossible, quite."

"No harm would happen to the trees," replied Kelly, "but it would be very inconvanient, no doubt. So I was jist thinking, if yer honour would have no objection, the place forenent the grate gate would be quite the thing; and I'll go bail that they'll all walk as if 'twas on eggs they were threading,[385] and neither gate nor green will resave the laste damage in life."

"Very well," said Mr. Herriott, "remember you are security for the good conduct of your friends."

"Oh! every blissing attind yer honour, and the mistress, and all the good family! – hurrah, boys! we've gained the day," cried the triumphant Piper, capering about and snapping his fingers; "we'll jig it, and paceably too; no quieter lads in the counthry: if that ould scoundrel, Tim Mc Shane, and his fiddle, comes within a mile o' me, by the powers I'll –"

"Stop, stop, my good fellow," said Mr. Herriott, "peace; no disturbance: the slightest fray, and, depend upon it, I will set my face against fairs and patterns for the next ten years."

"Oh! God bless yer honour! I'll take an oath against fighting and whisky, if yer honour wishes, with heart's delight."

"Never mind; if you swore against it in one parish, you would take it in another; that would be pretty much the same thing, I fancy; there, go the road way, and now no more talk this morning," continued the kind man, as he rose from his seat; "I will walk up with the ladies, and see that you are all quiet and steady, to-morrow evening."

"Long lifes," "powers o' blessings," "stores o' good luck," were bestowed upon "him and his," and the parties pursued their separate paths.

"The great gate" terminated the long straight avenue before mentioned, where, sheltered by some five or six noble beech and horse chesnut trees, and peeping from amidst a profusion of sweet-brier and wild roses, stood a little lodge, meek and lowly as a hedge primrose, with two lattice windows, and a slated roof – that unusual covering of Irish houses.

The interior of this pretty cot was more interesting even than its outward seeming; within, sat an old female spinning, her white hair turned up in front, a clean kerchief pinned over her cap, and knotted under her chin, and a short red cloak, fastened by a broad black riband; her face was thickly wrinkled, perhaps by age, perhaps by sorrow. When erect, her figure must have been tall and imposing; and long, bony fingers, and sinewy arms, told of strength and exertion. At her feet was sitting, on what the Irish peasantry call a "boss," a very slight girl, with a quantity of light hair, shading a face of almost unearthly paleness; she was carding flax, and laying it, in flakes, on a clean table at her side. The maiden, as she conversed with the aged crone, raised her large blue eyes to her withered face, and gazed on it with as much affection as if it possessed the most fascinating beauty; while the woman's harsh voice softened when she spoke to a being evidently so dear to the best feelings of her heart.

"Oh, blessed be the day, or rather the night, whin I saw ye first, mavourneen! – for you are the blessin' o' my life, and what was sorrow to you, was joy to me."

"Joy to me, nurse, not sorrow; for, if I lost one parent, I found another in you."

"A poor parent, my darlint May, but a fond; – however, God's will be done; ould Nelly Clarey's heart is not could yet."

Old Nelly Clarey, in her early days, had been a bathing woman, and, accustomed to the sea from infancy, had become almost amphibious; her fearless disposition induced the ladies who visited the beautiful banks of Bannow, in summer, to rely solely on her guidance; and, moreover, she could row a boat as well as any man in the country. There are a pair of green islands, about three miles from the borough of Ballytigue, called the "Keeroes," where, in summer, a few starved sheep, or one or two goats, wander over about an acre of moss and weeds. In spring tides and stormy weather these rocks are very dangerous to vessels whose pilots are not fully acquainted with the channel; and a winter seldom passed without some shipwreck occurring either on or near them. A dark, squally morning succeeded a fearful night of storm, about fifteen years before the period of my story. The hovel she then lived in was so near the beach, that even the rippling of the summer surge cheered the loneliness of her dwelling; but, on the occasion to which I refer, it was not the "soft music of the waters" that roused her from her bed; but the often repeated boom, sounding above the tempest, which she well knew to be the minute-gun of distress from some perishing vessel.

The early dawn beheld her wandering among rocks, accessible only to the sea-birds and herself. She clambered the highest point, and extended her gaze over the ocean, which still angrily chafed and growled along the shore. Beyond the breakers, the surface was somewhat smooth; but little was seen to mark where the islands rested, save the white and sparkling foam, dashing and glittering in the early light, finely contrasted with the deep colouring of the sky and water. Nelly still gazed, and now shaded her eyes with her hand, for she thought she discovered something like a motionless mast amongst the distant breakers. She was confirmed in this opinion by observing several floating spars and casks rapidly borne towards the main land. On descending to the beach, she found many of the neighbours anxiously watching the approach of what they considered lawful plunder.

"The wreck is between the Keeroes, Jack," said Nelly to a rough, shaggy-looking man, who, half in and half out of the water, was straining every nerve to haul in a cask, in danger of dashing against a huge dark mass of rock, that jutted into the sea.

"And what's it to you or me, ould girl? – 'twould be fitter for you to be in your bed, than down on the wild shore, with yer whity-brown hair streaming about yer shoulders. Ye look for all the world like a witch!"

"It's you, and the likes of ye," she replied, "that bring disgrace upon poor Ireland. Phil Doran's boat has passed through breakers worse nor these, and it shall go out, or I'll know the rason why; and so many poor strangers, may-be, dying at this blessed moment on thim islands!"

"It's few'll go wid ye, then," replied the man, as he grappled with the cask; and, pulling it in, added, "if it's strangers ye're thinking of, there's one come already," pointing to a heap of sea-weed – "his bed is soft enough, at any rate. The ould fool," he continued, as Nelly strided towards the spot, "she'll take more trouble about that sinseless corpse than she would to look after the bits o' Godsinds the wild waters bring us."

Nelly found the body of a youth, apparently about eighteen, nearly embedded in sea-weed. She disentangled it with speed and tenderness, carried it up the cliffs, dripping as it was, with perfect ease, and laid it out before the turf fire in her humble hut. One of the arms was broken, and sorely mangled; and the bitten lip and extended eyelids plainly told that the youth had wrestled daringly with death.

"Ye'll no more gladden your mother's heart, or bring joy to your father's home," sighed the excellent creature, when perfectly convinced that restoratives were useless. "God comfort the mother that bore ye! – for ye were brave and handsome, and, may-be, the pride o' more hearts than one."

As the morning advanced, tokens of extensive shipwreck crowded the beach, and many respectable inhabitants assembled, to prevent plunder. The surf still ran so high, that Nelly's pleadings were disregarded. Although the mast of the lost vessel was now distinctly seen, the hardiest boatman would not venture out to the Keeroes.

"I cannot call ye Irishmen," said she, after using many fruitless arguments to urge her neighbours to attempt the passage; "vile Cromellians are ye all, wid not a drop of true Milesian[386] blood in yer shrivelled veins!"

The evening sun had cast a deep red light over the ocean, whose waters were less disturbed than they had been at noon; and the moon rose, with calm majesty, over the subsiding waves – attended by her train of silent, but sparkling handmaids, scattering light and brilliancy over her path.

Nelly could not sleep; again she clambered the "black rock," and scared the sea-gull from its nest – anxious to ascertain, although almost beyond human ken, if any living object remained on the Keeroes, now more distinctly visible. As her eye wandered along the shore, it rested on Phil Doran's boat, which had been drawn up on the shingles; her mind was, at once, made up to a daring enterprise. No village clock tolled the knell of the departing hours, but she knew it must be near midnight. She returned to her cabin, wrapt a long cloak around her, and secured a bottle of spirits in the hood. A few minutes found her on the strand; the oars were in the strong, but rude fishing-boat, and she soon drew it to the water. When in the act of pushing off, a head appeared, from behind one of the rocks, and a voice exclaimed – "Botheration to ye, on what fool's journey are ye now? It's myself believes ye've doings with the ould one, for there's no rest for a body near ye, day nor night."

"Come, Jack," replied the woman, convinced that assistance would be useful, "it's calm enough now, and ye may find something on thim islands you'd like to have. I cannot rest in pace, while I think there may be a living thing on the rocks."

The love of plunder, and the love of enterprise, the latter, perhaps, inspired by the whisky he had drank during the day, urged Jack to accompany the woman. As they approached the Keeroes, their little bark leaped lightly over the billows, and Nelly, like others of her sex, gloried in her opinion being correct, for the mast, and part of the rigging of the vessel, still adhered to the wreck, and, absolutely, hung over the largest island.

Jack commenced prowling for plunder; Nelly could not perceive a single body on the shore. At length she discovered, midway the mast, something like a female figure, so securely fastened, that even the waters must fail to disentangle the cords and scarfs, with which the hands of affection had secured it to what appeared the last refuge.

"It's a faymale, at all events," said Jack, when Nelly succeeded in fixing his attention. "I'm sartin it's a faymale; so here goes! – bad as ye think me – bad as, may-be, I am – Jack Connor never did a bad turn to the women."

He managed to get to the mast, cut the braces, and lower the corpse (for so it was), still enveloped in many shawls, into Nelly's arms.

"She's gone, as well as the boy ye picked up this morning, Nelly," he exclaimed.

"God, in his mercy, save us all!" she exclaimed, falling on her knees, "God, in his mercy, save us! Her stiff arms are locked over a living baby, and its little head is on her bare bosom!"

It was even so. The lady was dead; her weak frame had been unable to retain life amid so many horrors! and her spirit could not long have lingered behind HIS, whose last efforts were exerted to preserve the objects of his purest affections, when to others, "all earth was but one thought – and that was – death!"

Jack – croppy,[387] smuggler, wrecker, poacher, white-boy,[388] rogue, and rapparee,[389] as he either was, or had been – Jack Connor (I wish to do everybody justice) placed the unfortunate lady carefully in the boat, took off his jacket, which he added as another covering to the still living infant; and, without plundering a single article, or uttering a single sentence, rowed steadily to the shore. As he carried the body up the cliffs, the morning light was stealing over the now calm ocean. "Nelly," said he, as he rested the burden on her bed – "Nelly, I'll never gainsay ye again; if I'd done yer bidding yesterday, that cratur would be a living woman now."

Nelly's courage and humanity gained for her high approbation. The vessel was ascertained to have been a Chinese trader, on her homeward passage; but of the crew, or passengers, none remained, except the infant the bathing-woman had so heroically rescued.

Mr. Herriott persuaded Nelly, for the sake of her adopted child, to take up her abode at the avenue lodge. The babe was called May, and much did Nelly complain of what she termed a "heathen name." But Mr. Herriott convinced her it was right, as the letters M. A. Y. were wrought in a bracelet found on her mother's wrist. No inquiries had ever been made about the little stranger, and her story was seldom thought of; but she was very different from the peasant children; not so fond of play, and always sweetly serious. She heard the intelligence that the pattern was to be celebrated outside the great gates, with more fear than pleasure, and could hardly understand why Miss Kelly so gloried in her father's having gained the day. Old Nelly "stood up" for Mr. Herriott's ascendancy, with true clan-like feeling; not that she cared for the pattern, but she hated soldiers, and constables, and lawyers, and water-guards, because she knew "the master" hated them; and so, in honour of the pattern victory, she told May that she should cut as good a figure as any of them – and better too, for the matter of that; there was a long, narrow scarf, that had belonged to her mother (heaven rest her soul!) and she should wear it as a sash, and she should dance, too –

"I do not care for dancing, dear nurse," observed the pale girl; "my heart's not in it: but I'll do my best to plase you; and I dare say it will be a merry pathern."

And so it was. Such a pattern! – such a sight of tents had never been seen by the oldest man in the parish, except at the fair of Ballynasloe,[390] which, as Kelly said, he had never seen, but only heard of! Such a "power" of people! There was the old Lord of Carrick, as he was called – the most respectable butcher for ten miles round, with his bob-wig over his grey hair, all on one side, from joy and whisky. There was Mickey the tailor, with his seven sons; such fine boys, not one of them under six feet, and the youngest only one-and-twenty. There was Pat Kenessy's tent, with a green flag flowing without, and whisky "gilloure"[391] flowing within. There was Mary-the-Mant, in a "bran new gown;" and the five Misses Kenessy, with every earthly and heavenly colour on them, except orange. Then the Corishes – the never-ending Corishes! – Pat Corish and his childer; Jim Corish, and his childer; Tom Corish and his childer; Mat Corish and his childer – not a quiet English family of three or four young ones each; but ten or fourteen romping rogues, boys and girls, with stentorian lungs, and herculean fists. And who would be cruel enough to interrupt their amusements, of hurling, jumping, eating, drinking, dancing, and fighting, in pattern time – while their parents were employed, generally speaking, pretty much in the same way?*ᵃ

---

*   If my accomplished countryman, Mr. Maclise,[392] met in the County of Wexford the subject he has so admirably pictured, and which stands at the head of this story, it must have been at Taghmon – Taghmon, cheerless, boisterous, and dirty, even in these days of temperance and whitewash. Well might Kelly the Piper say that, "though the Taghmon girls were the dickons at the single and double fling, they hadn't a taste of the Bannow modesty."

"The grate tint" was reserved for dancing, when the "quality" came; and often did Kelly parade around it, to see that all was right; and many a longing look was cast down the avenue, to watch if the gentry were approaching.

"The great bell did not ring for dinner as early as usual," said Nelly Clarey to her adopted, as she placed the last pin in her sash, and arranged the flapping bows to her own peculiar taste. "I don't want you to go amongst them yet, till the quality come; but stay," she continued, "let me try;" and she opened a little box, that contained a chain, three rings, and a small, but curiously wrought, bracelet – "stay; these were your poor mother's, and beautiful she looked, and quiet – when I took them off, and swore to keep thim for you, my darlint, and niver to let poverty part thim from me. But it's little poverty I've known, thank God; and blessings on him and his that presarved us from it." During this speech, Nelly had tried first one, then the other, of the rings on May's fingers. "They're all too small for ye; well, sure enough, *she* had the sweetest little hand I ever saw. The fastening of the chain's not good, or ye might wear that; but what's to hinder ye putting on the bracelet? – ye cannot lose it. M.A.Y. – it was yer father's and mother's hair that formed thim letters, I'll ingage." May gazed upon it, and teardrops gathered on her long eyelashes.

"My child – almost my own child," – said the affectionate Nelly, "why do ye cry? – you are always sad when others are merry. Ah, May, May; you'd forget – look! – there's Mr. Herriott, and the mistress, and the young lady, and the strange dark gentleman – master's ould frind they say – at the gate; and you not fit to be seen; there – stand asy, and wash your eyes. I'll attind their honours; and in five minutes ye'll look my queen agin."

Kelly and some of his train stood outside the gate ready to receive "the gintry;" and way was soon made for them to pass along the line of tents. The bustling and skirmishing instantly ceased. The men held their hats in their hands, and the women rose and courtesied respectfully, as Mr. Herriott and his family proceeded, while many a heartfelt blessing followed their footsteps.

Perhaps the most perfect happiness in the world is that which a good Irish landlord enjoys, when his tenantry are really devoted to his service; because their devotion is manifested by those external signs which can only emanate from an enthusiastic temperament. "How well his honour looks! – sure it's a blessing to see him; and the mistress so queen-like, and yet so humble, with her kind smile, and asking after the childer, so motherly."

"Who's the stranger?"

"From foreign parts, I b'lieve, by his dark skin."

"Very like: in all yer born days, did ye ever see anything like the state Kelly takes on himself? to be sure he's o' very dacent people, and the best piper in the whole barony; but there's rason in all things, and there 'll be a power of gintry in the pathern before night. Mr. Cormack and the ladies, Mr. Jocelyn, and Mr. Lambton, and, may-be, they won't put up wid Kelly's talk, like the rest."

"Never heed; sure, they all know his ways; but come," and the oldest crone of the assembly rose off a seat, where four or five, "withered and wild in their attire,"[393] had been sitting smoking their "doo-deens," and making observations on everybody, under the shadow of one of the great trees. "Come, they're crowding into the tint, and we'll be all behind, like the cow's tail, if we don't make haste."

Kelly had taken his seat, or, rather, erected his throne, on the top of one of the largest casks that could be procured in the parish; and on forms,[394] at each side of the musician, were seated the "gentlefolk;" – a small space between – and men, women, and children, crouched or stood, as they best could manage, leaving sufficient room for the dancers; for which purpose, certainly, not much was required, as either reel or jig can be performed on a good-sized door, always taken off its hinges, and laid on "the sod" for the purpose.

The wide entrance to the tent was crowded with a mass of laughing Irish faces beaming with joy.

Paddy Madder – who but Paddy Madder was fit to open the ball? Paddy, the oldest man in the parish, and, in his youth, it was said (for none remembered it), the finest dancer ever seen in all Ireland. Paddy acquitted himself nobly, considering that he had numbered eighty and two years; and Mr. Herriott placed the old man by his side, and heard, with delight, of the youthful feats which age so dearly loves to dwell upon.

Miss Kelly next dropped her bob courtesy to young Tom Corish; who, after "covering the buckle"[395] to admiration, and beating his partner at the "high-land fling," made "a remarkable genteel bow" to poor May, heedless of the smiles and approbation pert Jane Roche bestowed on his performance. May was not at all flattered by the distinction, and clung to her nurse's side, until desired, in an authoritative tone, by Kelly, to "step out, and not look so sheepish." May danced, I must confess, very badly, but she looked very lovely; timidity and exercise gave a colour to her cheek which it seldom possessed, and her light, sylph-like form, graced by the flowing sash, formed a strange contrast to the almost gigantic figure of her partner.

"Who is that girl?" inquired the strange gentleman of Mr. Herriott.

"I cannot tell you WHO she is, but she has been nursed by a very deserving woman, who attends our gate lodge."

"Indeed."

The gentleman again looked at her. As May continued, she forgot she was the object of general attention, and danced with more spirit. The stranger rose from his seat, and appeared to watch her movements with extraordinary anxiety.

"It is strange," said he to Mr. Herriott, "but that child is singularly like one whom I loved more than any earthly being; – my sister Anna."

"Indeed; I never saw her; – but you often mentioned her to me when we were schoolfellows; do you remember saying how much you should like me for a brother-in law?"

"Boyhood's imaginings, my dear friend. She returned to her family at Calcutta, when her education was completed, and married a young merchant, her inferior in rank – but I knew she was happy, and forgave it – poor Anna! She accompanied him to China, and, if their traffic succeeded, they were to have voyaged to England. I found they embarked on board a vessel for the purpose, but – "

"Shame upon ye!" exclaimed Tom Corish, loud enough to interrupt the narrative Mr. Herriott was so earnestly attending to; "ye know his honour does not dance, May, but it's only manners for ye to ax his honour's frind to take a step, now that you've bate me clane off, lazy as you wint about it."

Poor May made her courtesy, all panting and blushing as she was, and, without saying a word, or looking up, extended her hand to lead him to "the floor;" but she uttered a piercing shriek, when, seizing her arm with a powerful grasp, the stranger half dragged – half carried her, to the entrance of the tent; there he tenderly supported the frightened girl, but still held the arm she had extended to him with unrelaxing firmness; while his eyes wandered from her face to the golden bracelet which her nurse had clasped. The peasantry were perfectly unable to comprehend the matter. Kelly descended from his throne; and Nelly Clarey looked quite thunderstruck. She was, however, the first to recover her surprise.

"What do you mean by glowering that way on my child?"

"*Your* child, woman! Herriott, you said she was not hers; you said you could not say who she was. Speak, I entreat, for mercy speak, and tell me how that bracelet came – who gave it her?"

"Nobody gave it her," replied Nelly, "I myself took it off her mother's arm – God rest her soul! – the very morning that Jack Connor and I picked thim both out of the salt shrouds. The waves were her early cradle, poor thing!"

"How long since?"

"Oh, for the matter o' that, it will be fifteen years, come next Candlemas."[396]

The strange gentleman let the braceleted wrist drop, and folded the trembling May to his bosom.

"She is my sister's child," said he, when he could speak, "and henceforth mine."

Mr. Herriott suggested the propriety of their going into the lodge. Poor Nelly followed the gentry, keeping close to her adopted, muttering, "I have lost her now, any how." The rings and the chains were produced; but the strongest witness was the bracelet; M.A.Y. were the united initials of May's father and mother; and a spring, under the clasp, which had escaped observation, discovered a miniature of Mr. Monnett (the strange gentleman), which he had himself given to his beloved sister, as a token of affection, on her leaving Calcutta.

"So ye're a lady after all, by fortune as well as birth," said Nelly, looking affectionately at May, "and I must call ye Miss; and ye'll be no more near me; and no more shall I hear yer sweet voice in the soft summer evenings, calling to me from the wood, or reading to me whin the snow hangs the trees with white, like cherry blossoms; and the place will miss ye; and I shall be left desolate in my old age. But ye'll think of me; think of yer poor nurse, Nelly, who, on her bare knees" – and as she knelt she extended her clasped hands to heaven – "prays that the tears o' sorrow may niver dim yer eye; that the blush o' shame may niver paint yer cheek; that the blessings of the poor may strew the sweetest summer flowers in yer path; and that a long life and a happy death may be yer blessing; and after," continued she, solemnly, "in heaven – in the presence of the Father and his holy saints, may the poor Bannow woman see ye a bright angel of glory!"

May flung herself on her nurse's bosom; and Mr. Monnett assured them he hoped they would never separate; "for I think, Nelly," said he, "May looks so delicate that she will need your kind care wherever she goes; and she would be unworthy of my affection if she wished to leave you." Consequently, there was not a single sorrowful heart among the population, rich and poor, of "the united parishes of Bannow and Kilkaven."

"Any body might see," exclaimed Kelly, half an hour afterwards, when May appeared at the gate, for a moment, to receive the congratulations of her former companions, leaning on the one side on her uncle, and on the other, on her nurse – "any body might see that she had always the gentle drop in her; and I tould you so, Miss Jinny, my lady," continued he, sneeringly, to Jane Roche, who had always treated poor May with contempt, and looked somewhat disconcerted at her sudden elevation; "fine feathers don't always make fine birds." Miss Jenny, however, had one consolation; hereafter, a powerful rival would be removed out of the way.

"Kelly," said Mr. Herriott, "but for you this discovery would not have been made; for there would have been no pattern; therefore, my boys, crown him king of pipers, patterns, and whisky; and plenty of that, and good Irish roast beef, shall you have, and a glorious supper outside these gates – peace – plenty – and whisky!"

"King Kelly for ever, and long life to the May!" cried Mickey the tailor; and they chaired or rather shouldered, Kelly round the green; and poured a noggin of pure whisky over his head, which made him as good a king as the best of them (they said); and the Piper composed a jig, extempore, that beat jig Polthouge, aud all the jigs ever made before or since, clean out of the field, and called it the "Lady May."

THE RAPPAREE.

"True for ye, ma'am dear, it is smoking up to the nines, sure enough, but it's by no manner o' manes unwholesome, more particularly at this season, when it's so *could*; it will clear, my lady, in a minute – see, it's moving off now."

"Moving up, you mean," replied the young lady to whom this speech was addressed, and whose eye followed the thick and curling smoke that twisted and twisted, in serpent-like folds, around the blackened rafters of "Mr. Corney Phelan's Original Inn," – so, at least, the dwelling was designated by the painted board that had once graced it, but now played the part of door to a dilapidated pig-sty. Again, another volume folded down the chimney, for so the orifice was termed, under which the good-tempered and rosy Nelly Clarey was endeavouring to kindle a fire, with wet boughs and crumbling turf. The maid of the inn knelt before the unmanageable combustibles, fanning the flickering flame with her apron, or puffing it with her breath; the bellows, it is true, lay at her side, but it was bereft of nose and handle. "Poor thing," she said, compassionately, "it wasn't in it's nature to last for ever; and sure, master's grandmother bought it as good as thirty years ago, at the fair of Clonmel,[397] as a curiosity, more nor anything else, as I heard say."

"Are you sure," interrogated the young lady, after patiently submitting to be smoked-dried for many minutes – "are you sure that the flue is clear?"

"Is it clear, my lady! Why, then, bad cess to me for not thinking of that before! – sure I've good right to remember thim devils o' crows making their nesteens in the chimbley; and it's only when the likes o' you and yer honourable father stop at the inn, that we light a fire in this place at all."

She took up the wasting candle, that was stuck in a potato in lieu of a candlestick, and, placing a bare but well formed foot on a projecting embrasure[398] near the basement, dexterously catching the huge beam that crossed the chimney with her disengaged hand, swung herself half up the yawning cavern, without apparently experiencing any inconvenience from the dense atmosphere. After investigating for some time, "Paddy Dooley! – Paddy Dooley!" she exclaimed, "come here, like a good boy, wid the pitchfork, till we make way for the smoke."

"I can't, Nelly, honey," replied Mister Paddy, from a shed that was erected close to the "*parlour*" window, "a'n't I striving to fix a bit of a manger, that his honour's horses may eat their hay, and beautiful oats, dacently, what they're accustomed to – but Larry can go."

"Larry, avourneen!" said Nelly, in a coaxing tone, "do lend us a hand here wid the pitchfork."

"It's quare manners of ye, Nelly – a dacent girl like ye, to be asking a gentleman like me for his hand (Larry it must be understood, was the *bocher* and wit of the establishment), and I trying for the dear life to rason wid this ould lady, and make her keep in the sty; she's nosed a hole through the beautiful sign."

"Bad luck to ye both!" ejaculated Ellen, angrily; "I'll tell the masther, so I will," she added, jumping on the clay floor, her appearance not at all improved by her ascent. "Masther, dear, here's the boys and the crows, after botherin' me; will ye tell them to help me down with the nest? – the lady's shivering alive with the could, and not a sparkle of fire to keep it from her heart."

"Don't *you* be after botherin' *me*, Nelly," replied the host; "but I ax pardon for my unmannerliness," he continued, coming into the room – his pipe stuck firmly between his teeth, and his rotund person stooping, in a bowing attitude, to Miss Dartforth – "sure I'll move it myself, with all the veins o' my heart, to pleasure the lady at any time! – Give us the loan of the pitchfork, Larry."

"To tell God's truth, master, it's broke, and the smith – bad luck to him! – forgot to call for it, and little Paddeen forgot to lave it – but here's the shovel 'll do as well, and better too, for it's as good as a broom, seeing it's so neatly split at the broad end." "The master" took the shovel, not angrily, as an English master would have done, at such neglect; but taking for granted that a shovel would do as well as a pitchfork, or a broom, or anything else, "when it came asy to hand," and perfectly well satisfied with Larry's ingenuity. He poked, and poked, up the chimney, while Ellen stood looking on at his exertions, her head upturned, her ample mouth open, displaying her white teeth to great advantage. Presently, down came such an accumulation of soot, dried sticks, clay, and disagreeables, that Nelly placed her hands on her eyes, and ran into the kitchen, exclaiming "that she was blinded for life;" while the young lady, half suffocated, followed her example, and left "mine host of the public" to arrange his crows' nests according to his fancy. The kitchen of an Irish inn (not an inferior place of public accommodation – but what would be termed in England a "posting-house"), at the period of which I treat, would now be considered as a more befitting shelter for a tribe of Zingari,[399] than for Christian travellers; it was a room of large dimensions, and high elevation, with an earthen floor worn into many inequalities, and an enormous hole in the roof, directly over where the fire was placed, through which the smoke escaped, after hanging, as it were, in fantastic draperies around the discoloured apartment. A massive bar stood out from the wall, against, or nearly against, which the fire was lighted, and from it were suspended sundry crooks and nondescript chains, fitting for the support of iron pots and such cooking vessels as were put into requisition, when "quality" stopped, either from necessity or for refreshment, in the wild and mountainous district where resided Mr. Corney Phelan; indeed, the house was frequented more by farmers' drovers endeavouring to conduct wild mountain sheep to the markets of Waterford, or even Dublin (and I have now in my possession some old family memoranda, which state the price paid for such animals, at that time, to have been two shillings and sixpence per head), and persons in that sphere of life, than by such gentry as Mr. Dartforth, who travelled in his own carriage, and with a suitable number of attendants; he was a rich landed proprietor, a justice of the peace, and M.P. for the county town. It may be readily supposed that the arrival of persons of rank was a matter of importance, and that some preparations were made in the "parlour," as it was called, while the worthy magistrate occupied himself in inspecting the accommodation provided for his horses in the outhouses. The animals had undergone much fatigue, for the gentleman and his daughter had journeyed from Dublin; and when he drew near the dwellings of some of his principal tenants, he had called upon them, as "gale day" was passed, to collect his rents. The roads leading to those dwellings had, in many instances, been rendered heavy and nearly impassable by the rains; the horses were almost foundered; and, although within a few miles of home, it was found impossible to proceed without giving them some hours' rest. Miss Dartforth, with the cheerfulness and good-nature so charming in females of every age, accommodated herself to circumstances, took off her hat, and, having in vain sought, with the ken of a laughing blue eye, for what a woman, however old and ugly, would fain see in every room – a looking glass – shook back her clustering tresses, which twined in wild luxuriance over her graceful form; then partially unclasping a silver-laced riding habit, she made her way amid five or six barelegged "helpers," some dozens of various-sized pigs, fowl, and collies, to a three-legged seat near the fire, close to a petted white calf, that had established itself very quietly on a "lock of straw," in the most comfortable portion of the apartment. She then commenced leisurely investigating the whims and oddities of the assembly; and the smiles that occasionally separated her full rich lips, showed she was an amused spectator of the *mélange*.[400] Everything appeared in confusion; the landlady, whose mob cap was trimmed with full and deep lace of no particularly distinguishable colour, bustled about in a loose bed-gown of striped cotton, beneath which a scarlet petticoat, of Dutch dimensions, stuck forth; she was the only female in the establishment who luxuriated in shoes and stockings – the former were confined on the instep by rich silver buckles; and, though she occasionally sat with much state behind a soiled deal board, which presented a varied assortment of drinking measures, and was garnished at either end by kegs of whisky, yet did she keep a necessary, and not silent, *surveillance* over the movements of the various groups. Some idea of her conversation or more properly speaking, her observations (for she never waited for a reply), may be gathered from the following: –

"Miss Dartforth, my lady! – (Mary Murphy, will ye never finish picking the few feathers off that bird?) – my lady, I humbly ask yer pardon on account of the smoke, and – (Nelly Clarey, Nelly Clarey, may-be it's myself won't pay you off for your villany; don't tell me of the crows; what do I give you housemaid's wages for, but to look after my best sitting-rooms?) – Miss Dartforth, ma'am, is that baste (the calf I mane) disagreeable to ye? – it's a pet, ye see, on account of its being white – quite white, Miss, every hair – and lucky – Billy Thompson, ye little, dirty spalpeen! will ye have done draining the glasses into yer well of a mouth! – it's kind, father, for ye to be afther the whisky, yet I'll trouble ye to keep yer distance from my counter – Corney Phelan, it 'ud be only manners in ye to take the dooden out o' yer teeth, and the lady to the fore; I remember when ye'd take it out before *me* – why not? – the day ye married me, dacency and dacent blood entered yer barrack of a house, and made it what it is, the most creditable inn in the country – Peggy Kelly, ye're a handy girl, jump up, astore, on the rafters, and cut a respectable piece of bacon off the best end of the flitch – asy – asy! – mind the hole in the wall, where the black hen is sitting – there, just look in, for I'm thinking the chickens ought to be out to-morrow or next day – Larry, ye stricken devil! have ye nothin' to do, that ye stand chuck[401] in the door-way? – are ye takin' pattern by yer master's idleness – he that does nothin' from mornin' till night but drink whisky, smoke, sleep – sleep, smoke, and drink whisky? – Oh! but the heart within me is breakin' fairly with the trouble – bad cess to ye all! – there's the pratees boilin' mad! and the beef! – I'll rid the place of the whole clan of ye – for it's head, hands, and eyes I am to the entire house – ye crew!" &c. &c. – And the eloquent, burly lady sprang, with the awkward velocity of a steam-carriage, towards the fire-place, oversetting everything in her way, to ascertain how culinary affairs were proceeding in two large iron vessels, round which the witches in Macbeth might have danced with perfect glee – so deep, and dark, and fitting did they seem for all the purposes of incantation.

Much amused, the young lady patted the calf, which looked into her face with the unmeaning innocence of expression that characterizes the animal; and, as she stooped to conceal the smiles excited by Mistress Corney Phelan's anger, the loosened tresses fell over her brow and eyes; their re-adjustment occupied a few moments – but when she looked up she saw a woman seated opposite to her, whom she certainly had not before noticed, and who she thought it very strange should have escaped her observation; her dress bespoke the mendicant, and she eagerly stretched her bony and muscular hands over the blazing turf fire; her frame appeared chilled by the cold of a keen October evening that was fast closing – for her cloak remained fastened, and even the hood, that perfectly concealed her features, was unremoved: Miss Dartforth could not help remarking that the cloak was much longer than is usually worn by Irish beggars, and the foot which projected from beneath its ample folds was covered by a substantial brogue. Once, and once only, the fugitive, but expressive, glance of a wild, bright eye met hers, and the idea that *somewhere* she had before encountered a similar look possessed her imagination. While she was endeavouring to remember the *where* and the *when*, her father entered, attended by one or two of his servants, and accompanied by a relative who, according to the miserably dependant feeling that, I regret to say, is not yet banished from my country, played clerk, toady, whipper-in,[402] understrapper,[403] or what you please, to his patron, who afforded him bed, board, washing, clothes, and shooting; kindly requiring, in return, that he should act as affidavit man on all occasions (particularly when he recorded wonderful stories), and laugh invariably at his jests: – "Time out of mind such duties wait dependance." The justice was a free-hearted man, frank and violent, good-natured and obstinate, a talker of patriotism, a practiser of tyranny, and fonder of his pretty daughter, Norah Dartforth, than of his hounds, his hunters, or even his landed interest. It was, however, a well-known and accredited tale that he had broken his wife's heart by his frequent fits of violence; or, more properly speaking, he had frightened her out of the world while in the prime of youth, and delicate, lily-like loveliness; he then took an oath, which, I believe, he religiously kept, that he would never get into a rage with his daughter. This, nevertheless, did not prevent his getting into passions with others, and, indeed, his life, as must always be the case where anger is indulged in, was a round of sins and repentances. The county report went to say that there was one error he more sorrowed over than the rest: –

Sometime after his marriage, disappointed in not being blessed with an heir to his estate, he adopted a boy of singular talent and beauty, whose parents, humble and industrious cotters,[404] died of malignant fever, near his avenue-gate; this boy he cherished with all a father's love and tenderness, and even the birth of a daughter, after the lapse of many years, did not appear to diminish the affection he entertained for the interesting youth. Unfortunately, over-indulgence nurtured a proud and daring spirit, which, by different management, could have been tamed to the gentle and ennobling duties of life. The boy grew in beauty, and increased in talent; but he also became imperious and overbearing: even if Mr. Dartforth and his gentle lady were inclined to make allowances for his wayward fancies and insolent actions, the very humblest serf on his domain was loud in complaints of the *parvenu's*[405] tyranny; and the worthy man, who had obstinately persisted in a new-fangled idea, which he had imbibed from some of the French authors of the period – that the human mind was of itself perfection, and that there were no impulses given that needed restraint – persevered in his "system," as he called it, until the impetuous James brought himself under the

strong arm of the law, by an open act of violence, directed against one of his protector's brother magistrates, which, but for the interposition of powerful friends,
would have banished him the country. It would have been better, perhaps, had
the law been suffered, at that time, to take its course. He returned home with an
insulted, but unsubdued, spirit, and the remonstrances of his well-meaning, but
ill-judging friend, were heard with visible symptoms of impatience. The voice of
reproof sounded harshly on the ear that, for eighteen summers, had listened to
nothing but the honied accents of praise. In an evil hour, when both were heated
with that noxious spirit – of which I cannot sufficiently express my detestation,
having too often witnessed its baneful and pernicious effects – words terminated
in blows; Mr. Dartforth struck his *protegé*, and the other, whose tiger spirit could
ill brook such an insult, hurled his almost-father to the earth. It is but too probable that murder would have terminated the disgraceful scene, had not Norah,
roused from her light and innocent slumbers by the fearful noise of the unnatural combat, rushed between them, and, in an instant, her soft, but energetic voice
awoke the intemperate youth to a sense of his crime and ingratitude; the remembrance of the insult inflicted, was effaced by a sense of the evil he had done,
and he humbled himself, even to the dust, at Mr. Dartforth's feet. Then was the
moment, when his heart and feelings could have been caught on the rebound,
but the wrathful and intoxicated man cursed the stripling in the madness of his
rage – it was a deep, a bitter, an irrecallable curse – that made the maiden's warm
blood run cold in her veins, and withered the heart of the unfortunate victim
of intemperate passion. Pale, trembling with varied emotion, he crouched, for
a moment, beneath the ban – then rising, as the young wolf-hound from his
lair, without a word, a groan, or a tear – without even an adieu to her who had,
regardless of her own interest, often palliated his faults – he left, for ever, the
halls that had sheltered his childhood.

Great as James's faults certainly were, it was said that Mr. Dartforth secretly
blamed himself for the result; but even Norah was interdicted from mentioning the name of the once favoured boy, who, it was believed, had quitted the
country for some far distant land. There were, however, many who asserted that,
after Patrick James had left Mr. Dartforth, "his honour had never been rightly his
own man;" and, indeed, it was evident to all that his temper and habits had not
improved since his *protegé* had absconded.

As the magistrate seated himself on a chair, which the bustling landlady offi-
ciously presented him, next to his gentle and affectionate child – "his heart's
darling," as he termed her, in the warm language of Irish phraseology, that daughter thought she had never seen her father's cheek so pale, or his eye so rayless.

"Dear father!" she exclaimed, pressing her left cheek to his, "sit at the opposite side, I will move with you – you are chilled, but there you will be quite
shielded from the draught of the door."

"Make way for yer betthers, honey!" screamed the landlady in the ear of the mendicant, who did not seem inclined to relinquish her seat to "the gentry;" a very unusual thing in Ireland, where so much outward homage is rendered to the aristocracy. "Good woman," interposed Miss Dartforth, coming up to her, and placing her hand gently on her shoulder, "will you oblige me by exchanging seats, as my father suffers by the draught from which your cloak protects you?"

The beggar rose, and leaning, as if from excessive weakness or fatigue, on her staff, crossed over to the other side, at the same time muttering some faint words, which neither father nor daughter could comprehend.

"Is the woman deaf and dumb?" inquired Mr. Dartforth, angry, perhaps, at her tardiness of motion.

"She's as good – just then as good as the one and t'other," replied the *bocher*, coming forward, dexterously managing so as to make his crutch supply the place of his lost leg. "She's an afflicted crathur – God presarve us! – but harmless, and's under a vow never to let the hood fall off her head, in rain or sunshine – heat or cold – night or day: and, what's more, never to lay side on a bed for the next seven years. Oh! there's a power o' holiness about her, plaze yer honour."

"I suppose she has committed some dreadful crime, for which the religion you believe in requires such atonement?"

"Crime! the crathur! – bless ye, no; she's as innocent o' crime, or passion, or anything o' that sort, as yer honour. Och! no – the poor thing's heart aches for the sins o' the world, and she wishes to ease 'em."

"A female crying philosopher!" observed Mr. Dartforth to his daughter.

"And yet there is something that, under other circumstances, would be called philosophy, about it," replied Norah; "how often is it that situation and influence command the homage which, at first sight, appears paid to the virtue, not the person!"

"Miss Norry, you are growing too wise for me," said the male toady, who was called, by his associates, "Swallow-all Dick;" by his superiors, "Dick;" and by his inferiors (meaning those who honestly worked for their living), "*Mister* Dick." He stood, with his hands in his pockets, before the fire, to the manifest inconvenience of all engaged in preparing the anticipated meal.

"What a wonder that is, to be sure!" muttered Lame Larry, "as if you were one who could shoe the goslins, catch a weasel asleep, or split a sunbame."[406]

"Has there been much news stirring lately – I mean during my absence?" inquired Mr. Dartforth, addressing Larry, who certainly was the most intelligent person of "the Original Inn."

"Only a few more of Freney's[407] tricks playing here, and there, and everywhere, plaze yer honour."

"The rascal! – has any one yet discovered who he is, or where he came from?"

"Lord, no, sir! – a body might as well hunt and catch a leprechawn[408] as him; did yer honour hear how he sarved the judge and jury, at the ferry o' Mount Garrett? Well, ye see, there was a lot of fire-arms he wanted to get over; and the boatman tould him as how he daren't let him pass, in rason that the judge was going to cross in the coorse of the day, and his people were keepin' the boat. 'Is that all?' says Freney, says he – the blue eye dancin' out of his head wid scorn at the little wit o' the boatman; and he goes his way. Well, jist as the judge, and all the law and the justice in the country – (yer honour's glory was out of it at the same time, ye know, so it didn't take up much room) – the law and the justice all packed tight and comfortable in the boat, as need be – up comes a poor blind ould crathur of a man – seemingly as dark as dungeon, leadin' a baste, with a load o' brooms on his back. 'Och, my misery!' says the ould crathur – setting up a pulhalew[409] that 'ud reach from this to Bantry, – 'and it's I'll be too late, God help me! and miss the market.' Well, yer honour, for once a judge listened to marcy – and a poor man the pleader. 'Come, honest friend,' says he, 'we'll make room for you, and yer baste can swim over.' 'God mark ye to glory,' says the ould man, 'but what'll I do with my brooms?' – 'Lay 'em in the bottom of the boat,' says the judge; and they all got over comfortable together. Well, when they reached the other side, sure as life there was a whole troop of the red-coats, waiting to cross the contrary way. 'What are ye after?' says the judge. 'Plase yer lordship,' replied the sargent, 'we've just heard that the daring rascal, Freney, is over the water, with fire-arms, and combustibles, and contrivances enough to blow up ould Ireland, and murder it intirely; and that he wants to get to this side, and waylay and destroy every mother's son at the 'sizes;[410] so we're going to stop him.' 'God bless ye for that same!' said the ould crathur of a man, setting his brooms on his baste at the same time; 'it was only yesterday that the rapparee took every fardin' I had in the world – and only left me these few screeds o' clothes; and if he's let go on that way, neither gentle nor simple will be alive in the country this day three months.' 'Could ye describe him?' says the judge. 'He's a good portly man, to my seeing,' made answer the ould crathur. 'Middling-sized – middling-sized,' repeated the sargent, stepping into the boat; 'I'd know him ten miles off, if the devil himself set him a maskin.'[411] The ould man gave a chuck of a laugh, and off wid him, after making his obadience, mannerly, to the great gentlemen – and the boat and the soldiers towed away for the other side; and the judge and grandees gothered[412] themselves up, quite stylish-like, on the horses that were waitin' for them – and, by the time they were settled, from the top almost of the hill that ye mind is so overgrown with osiers,[413] and all kinds of creepin' bushy herbs, came a loud, wild laugh – and they looked up, one and all – and sure enough, there was a sight to frighten the tories![414] – every plant seemed grown into a livin' man, with a musket on his arm, by way of a shoulder-knot; and 'Freney's brooms are the brooms that 'll sweep clean!' shouted one fellow. 'Our brave little commander for ever!' roared another; and then Freney himself stepped upon the ancient grey rock at the top of all, and wavin' his hat, with the air of a raale nobleman, he bowed to the company below. 'I'll find an opportunity of returnin' yer lordship's civility; and you or yours shall never be harmed by me or mine,' says he; 'and I hope you won't forget Freney and the ferry o' Mount Garrett.' Well, before ye could say 'Cork!' there were the osiers waverin' in the wind, so innocent-like, and the men gone, as a whiff o' smoke; only, as the grandees passed up the bank, wild, cheerful laughter onct or twict broke on their ear. And, may-be, the sargent and his lobsters weren't dancin' mad in the boat with fair spite, jist over the way; and they forced the boatman to tow about, and, somehow or other, as he was turnin', the vessel upset; and such scramblin' and clawin' as they had to get safe ashore – and their ammunition all wet, and their firelocks spoilt: and then they would have it the boatman did it a-purpose, and swore they'd baygnot[415] him; the poor fellow was frightened – why not? – and got away out of their reach, just in time to save his life.

"But that's nothin' to the escape he had, not long since, when he hid in a hay-rick, and seven soldiers passed him, and every one *prodded* the rick with their baygnots; and, every time they did, it went into him; for all that sorra a stir did he stir, only stud it out like a Trojan."

"He has had a great many escapes by flood and field, papa; I feel quite interested for him; he is, I have heard, brave and generous, and particularly attentive to females," observed Norah.

"Ay, girl! – you are like the rest, of your sweet sex; give a man a character for bravery, and, no matter whether he be brigand, or soldier, or rapparee, you are all ready to defend his cause; and, my life on't, if this Freney, this cut-throat, received womankind recruits, the bushes would be covered with cast-off drapery."

"Dear papa, he is no cut-throat – no single deed of blood is registered against him; and the instances I have heard of his charity, taking from the rich to give to the poor, bestowing, even from his own purse, to clothe the naked, and feed the hungry, have, I confess, interested me in his fate; I do not feel the least afraid of him."

"Nor never need, Miss, my lady," observed the *bocher,* bowing, "I'll answer for it, that James Freney 'ud spill the best drop of his heart's blood for one smile from yer sweet face; sure he's every inch an Irishman."

"You know him, then?" inquired Miss Dartforth, smiling and blushing – for I dare not deny the fact, that all women like a delicately-turned compliment even from a *bocher.*

"I can't say but I've seen him," replied the man, shifting off, at the same time, to the other end of the kitchen. It must not be imagined that this dialogue had proceeded even thus far, without sundry interruptions from worthy Mistress Cornelius Phelan, who was all bustle and anxiety at the impropriety of such visitors dining in the kitchen; "and sure the parlour was cleared, and but little smell o' smoke in it now," &c. &c. Both gentleman and lady, however, persevered in their determination not so enter the "crow's nest," as Norah laughingly called it; and the table was accordingly set in the centre of the kitchen, and covered, if not with elegant, certainly with substantial fare: – boiled fowl, enormous non-descript masses of beef, "neatly boulstered up," to use Mrs. Phelan's term, with fine white cabbage and English carrots; potatoes, of course, were not wanting; and the travellers were too hungry to be fastidious. Miss Dartforth, who never forgot the wants of others, heaped a plate, after the Irish fashion, with meat and potatoes, and, before her own dinner was ended, turned to present it to the men-dicant, but, to her surprise, the woman had disappeared as mysteriously as she had entered! She was about to express her surprise at this circumstance, when Nelly Clarey (who, blooming under a cap which, in some degree, confined her clustering hair, and was ostentatiously garnished with cherry-coloured ribands, stood behind her chair, to the manifest annoyance of Mr. Dartforth's old servant, who always claimed the privilege of waiting personally upon "*his young lady*"), touched her arm, whispering, at the same time, "For God's sake, never heed her."

The October evenings in Ireland, are damp and dreary; nor have they the uniformly clear sunsets, or invigorating atmosphere, which characterize the farewell summer month in England. The weeping skies of Ireland have become almost proverbial; but, even while they weep, they smile – apt emblem of the happily volatile temperament of a people who have suffered much, and suffer still. I learned in early youth to love the quickly closing evenings of autumn, and, at times, delight more in rain than in sunshine. I must, however, resume the thread of my narrative, and mention that, at the distance of about a hundred or a hundred and twenty yards from the hag-yard, which flanked the inn on the north, and protected it from the cold winds, ran a long wall intended origi-nally as a division between the farms of two brothers who had sacrificed their property in litigation, and died at last poor and penniless – the one in a distant land where he had been sent by the offended laws of his country; the other in a jail. The wall was called, by the country people, "the brother's ban," and a good deal of superstitious feeling attached to it. Many of the stones had fallen to the earth, and over them the gay green weeds had triumphed, while others showed dimly in the moonlight, and might have been easily converted, by the magic of imagination, into things of living and mysterious form. A few stunted elms, with here and there a dark poplar, waved gently in the chill, evening air; and although the laugh and wassail[416] sounds of the inn talkers and revellers called to remembrance the proximity of human habitation, yet the undefinable dreariness of the spot was increased, rather than broken, by the shadows of two persons, in earnest conversation, the one passing rapidly backwards and forwards with a firm, undaunted step – the other halting, or rather hopping, after the superior, endeavouring, in vain, to keep pace with him, yet bearing his rapid strides and impatient temper with extraordinary good-humour.

"Fine times, to be sure, they must be wid ye, when ye let a good seven hundred – I dare say goold – hard goold – slip through yer fingers as asy as kiss my hand; the boys 'ill never stand it – how could they?" observed the lame one.

"Not stand it! What the devil do you mean, Hacket – when there is not an ounce of brains among a troop of them? Why, Breen himself dare not – ay – I say *dare not*, dispute my will in anything."

"May-be not; but I know he looked mighty black when I tould him ye meant that ould Huncks to get home scot-free."[417]

"Black! did he? I wish I had seen him. I tell ye, Hacket, his gold, if I touched it, would blister my fingers – it would kindle hell's own fire within my heart. For fifteen years I eat of his bread – and even his own child, that creature whose pure and spotless hand, not two hours since, rested on my shoulder – (it was like a dove seeking repose on a hawk's wing) – even when that child was born, the same shelter, the same smile, was mine. Blessed Virgin!" he continued, striking his forehead violently, "you, a poor dismembered, blighted creature, can understand that you couldn't tear the hand that fed ye."

"It was a pity," replied the *bocher* (for my readers have doubtless discovered that Larry and Hacket are one and the same person), while a cold, sarcastic smile overshadowed the usually good-natured expression of his countenance, "a murderin' pity that ye didn't think of that when ye – ye had the little row." He would have said, "when ye struck him to the earth;" but in the dim light he marked James Freney's eye flashing upon him, and he finished his sentence, modified even as it was, in a trembling voice.

The unhappy young man remained silent for a few moments, while the rapidity of his pace increased. At length Hacket ventured to observe that the gang had lately been very discontented with his liberality – particularly to Lady Duncannon,[418] whose money he had returned, merely because her husband was not with her; and even refused to take her watch, set with diamonds, which they considered robbing them of lawful plunder. "Ay," he said, mournfully, "it is ever thus; as well might the lordly lion, that I have read of, mate with the baseborn ass, that brays at the moon, as one of gentle breeding assimilate with such a set – but I am a fool to talk thus to you, Hacket – and worse than a fool to have chosen such a life; but the die is cast, and I am a dreaded, degraded outlaw, whose miserable bones will, one of these days, rattle on a gibbet, in the March winds, and scorch there in a July sun – while you – you, Hacket – my poor mother's only relation, will be the sole living thing to shed a tear in remembrance of him who, instead of his own honest name, was called James Freney."

"No such thing," replied the *bocher*, notwithstanding his habits and associations, much moved at feelings which, although he could not enter into, he could sympathize with, simply because they affected one whom he sincerely loved, not merely for the sake of kith and kin, but from mingled and undefined sensations. "No such thing, you'll live and make a fortune, and get the pardon. Sure, you never harm anything to death, and are so complaisant to the ladies, that a woman's mob 'ud save ye, if ever it came to that. Ye may be a lawyer yet; I'm sure ye understand a dale more about it than the half of 'em." The compliment fell unheeded on the ear of the rapparee, who observed:

"You gave my positive instructions to Breen, that all were to pass safe?"

"I did, though I thought it mighty foolish; – for just look here now – the ould justice *owes* ye – sure it's not trusting to seven or eight hundred pounds of his money ye'd be, if ye'd remained wid him? Didn't he breed ye up for his heir? Isn't a promise a debt? – and there can be no harm in taking what's one's own."

"I tell ye what, Hacket, if all the saints, and priests, and bishops, and the blessed Virgin herself, were to absolve me the next minute, I would not – I could not! – There's the share I had out of the Waterford merchants, that troublesome job; why half the plunder now is hid up and down the country, in bog-holes and brier-knocks;[419] but my share they shall have of that, and of any thing else going. A kind commander I have ever been, and mean to remain; but I *will* be their COMMANDER while my brain has strength to frame a resolution, or my finger power to draw a trigger."

"Well – well – yer heart's set upon it, agra! enough said; for, as I live, the ould justice is on the move. I see Nelly Clarey herself, pokin' out with the candle, lookin' for me; and Paddy Dooley, too; and the servin'-men – the overfed, poor porpoises, crawlin' about; – but, Captain, dear, ye'll never be able to get your horse, Beefstakes, out of the back shed, *unknownst,* while them lazy animals are loungin', doin' nothin' at all, at all."

"Too true," replied Freney, evidently much annoyed at this information. "I meant to have been off before them."

"D'ye hear that girl screaming 'Larry' like a skirl-a-white?[420] Choke ye, a'n't I going!" Larry moved several steps towards the farmyard; then, as if remembering something particular, returned, and said, "Mister Captain, I jist wanted to tell ye that I fancied, may-be, ye were throwin' a sheep's-eye after Nelly; now I've always had a mind to that girl myself. Ay, ye may clap a sneer on yer handsome face if ye like; but, though I own to the loss of the limb, I'm no bad fellow to look at when the disguise is off, and a tidy bit of a wooden leg on: there's a time for all things; and I know you'd never think of her as your wife; but I'll tell ye that barefooted lass deserves honourable treatment; and it would be what *I* don't deserve, let alone *her,* to have her head turned for nothin' at all, but, may-be, to make her an open shame before the whole country: so let her alone, and for once take a fool's advice." The *bocher* swung off towards the rude stables, leaving the rapparee, captain of one of the most daring gangs that ever infested the country, in an irritated and melancholy frame of mind. He folded himself up in the long blue cloak that had served to conceal his person at the inn, and ruminated, as he reclined against the mouldering wall, on the uncertainty and waywardness of what he, in his blindness, designated FATE.

> "There is a bitterness in man's reproach,
>> Even when his voice is mildest, and we deem
> That on our heaven-born freedom they encroach,
>> And with their frailties are not what they seem;
> But the soft tones in star, in flower, or stream,
>> O'er the unresisting bosom gently flow,
> Like whispers which some spirit in a dream
>> Brings from her heaven to him she loved below,
> To chide and win his heart from earth, and sin, and woe."[421]

Freney, the robber and the outlaw, felt the reproving voice from "star, and flower, and stream;" and the brief vision of one who, had he conducted himself with common propriety, might have been the cherished and respected wife of his bosom, sent many a bitter pang of self-reproach through his aching heart; – he contrasted what he *was,* with what he could have been; few are there who can bear so miserable a retrospect unmoved.

He had seen Norah Dartforth not an hour before, and the remembrance of her surpassing loveliness pressed upon his imagination, in gentle but firm opposition of the efforts he made to obliterate her image from his memory. Poor Nelly Clarey, whom, with Irish recklessness, he had often jested with, forgetting the impression such conduct might make upon a thoughtless, but not a heartless girl – in his present refined mood now appeared a coarse and vulgar creature; and he felt more angry with for the insinuation he had thrown out about her, than for any other portion of his remonstrance. At length, overcome with contending feelings, he rested his head against one of the huge, white stones I have before mentioned; and, even while he watched the flitting lights in the inn-yard, sleep steeped his senses in forgetfulness.

"Captain, dear, what ails ye?" were the kindly sounds which awoke him to consciousness. "Lord save us! jist at the very minute whin all the wit ye have in the world is most wantin', to find ye sleepin' in this unlucky place, in the could moonlight, and not lookin' a taste like yerself. Rouse, Captain, honey! or those ye wish well to 'll be the worse for it."

The robber eagerly and anxiously inquired what the young woman's words portended.

"Whisht – asy!" exclaimed Nelly, in a low, confidential tone; "sure they think I'm asleep; for ye don't look to me *sensible* that it's close upon eleven; and the mistress's tongue itself is quiet a good hour agone; and the gentry set off afore nine; and there's more hot-foot after them than you'd have a mind to, I'm thinkin'."

"Nelly, for God's sake, come to facts at once, or –"

"I will; sorra a word I ha' said that wasn't as true as gospel – but let me tell it my own way. I heard ye say to Larry (the poor, conceated crature!) that ye wanted most particular to see Breen; well, for sartain sure, the *bocher* tould him so, for he has been skulking about the place all day; but, instead of coming to the fore, I noticed him hidin' and pokin', more like a *grasnogue*[422] than a Christian. Well, ye see, I went out about the stables, jist to cool myself, after the cookin' and the flurry o' dinner, and the quality, and all; and, somehow, my light (though I made a screen for it, with a cabbage-leaf), went out just at the minute I thought o' fodderin' the cow, the craythur, that the boys don't half mind; so, knowin' she doesn't like to be 'woke of a suddent, I went asy to the door, and jist as I was goin' to pull out the kipeen[423] (not that the door's much good, on account of the gap in the wall), I hard Breen in low discourse wid another man, that I'd no knowl-edge of in life; and he went on for to tell him how unreasonable ye war' in regard of takin' a turn out o' the ould gentleman's money; and how he wouldn't listen to no such thing – but purtend to you, whin it was all over, that it was nothin' but a misunderstandin', and down-face the *bocher* that he said one thing, when, to the hearin'of my two ears, the poor thing said the direct contrary."

"The villain! – the double-dealing, mean-spirited villain!" ejaculated Freney.

"Ye may say that," responded Nelly, "but wait awhile till ye know all. 'I'm sartain,' says t'other man, 'that the Captain 'll take to the road after them, by way of purtection, for he has a suspicion over you, when anything like this is stir-rin'; and ye know there's not one o' the boys 'ud disobey the captain.' 'I'm sure he's for the road,' says Breen, 'for Hacket tould me Beefstakes was in the same cow-shed, at the back, as my Slasher; and more betokens, at the right-hand side.' 'And a noble pair o' bastes they are,' remarks t'other; 'but Beefstakes is terrible knowin', and sorra a harm it would be to put a peg to his speed for to-night.' 'What do you mean?' says Breen. 'Bathershin,'[424] makes answer the strange man, 'you don't know – why, just run a nail up the fetlock, – sure it's only an accident, and nobody the wiser."

"The cold-blooded scoundrel!" muttered the Captain between his firmly-set teeth, "the noble horse that has so often saved my life!"

"Well, they coshered, and coshered, so asy, I couldn't make out the words," persisted Nelly, "only the short and the long of it was, that the stranger was to go and lame the beast at once; and, as they couldn't get the animals out while the sarvents were about the house, jist wait till they were gone; and then, takin' the short road to the black gap, wait there for the company. May-be ye think ye have it all yer own way – says I; but better than you have got into the wrong box. So I stole off asy – asy – under shelter of the wall, till I cleared the corner, and then away with me in a whisk to poor Beefstakes. And what do ye think I did? I minded well what had been said, that *your* baste was on the *right* side; so I jist made 'em change places; and, my jewel! afore you could clap yer hands – afore I could make way for myself to get out o' the scrip of a shed, the murderin' black villain comes; and sure it's myself was afeard of the horses' heels, and I *scrudged* up into a mere nothin', right under Beefstakes' legs. And, as if the baste knew the business, he never stirred all the time the fellow was lamin' his own animal. Well, when he thought his job finished, Captain, honey, he skulked off with himself like an exciseman; and, as asy as ever I could, I made the crathurs change places again, like the great parliament lords; and ye may go bail it's little I heeded fodderin' the cow, though she turned her head to me, nataral as a Christian: and, knowin' yer saddle was particular, I changed that too; and God sees I was tremblin' for all the world like a shakin' bog, till I got out o' the place; and the end of it was – I see the gentry off; and Breen wasn't long behind – but he was forced to go asy at first, on account of the road – the short cut, ye know, bein' broke up wid the rain; but, for fear he'd suspect (for the baste must fall lame when he puts any speed upon it), I thought it, most prudent, ye see, jist to lift Beefstakes out o' the shed intirely – and so I led him round to the black thorn to the left, by the gap, in the corner. And now, Captain, 'gra! ye may think as ye plaze – but grim as ye look, all this blessed time, I've done a friendly turn to you and the baste – and –"

"Grim as I look!" repeated Freney, his gallantry and his grateful feelings both rousing to meet the accusation; – "my darling Nelly, I never loved ye half as well as at this moment," he continued, energetically, at the same time imprinting no very gentle salute on her lips. Ellen drew the back of her hand across her mouth, as if to efface the kiss, and then replied:

"Faigs,[425] Captain, I'll not say that's a lie, and yet the love ye talk of isn't deep enough to smother a kitten; I see, as plain as I see the moon in the heavens, that I'm not the sort for you to fix honourable love upon and for the other sort, I'd scorn it, as men scorn the women they bring to shame: I didn't think so *once*, may-be – (the poor girl's voice faltered), but I see this day the *reale* bame o' love from under yer hood, when it *wasn't* at *me* ye looked, and I *felt* the differ; – but never heed it, Captain, aroon!"[426] – and she drew herself up, and laughed a light, bravoing laugh, which any one could hear came from the lip, not the heart, and then half said, half sung, the old stanza: –

> "'While me you thought for to beguile,
> I cared for another all the while;
> And knew, my boy, what ye were at:
> Och! never fear but I spied ye, Pat!
> Wid yer smiles,
> And yer wiles!
> And, by the same rule,
> Ye think every girl ye meet a fool!'"[427]

Freney was too earnest, too occupied, to play the gallant on this occasion; and contented himself with observing, as he hastened towards the spot where his really noble animal pawed the earth, with "proud impatience of ignoble ease:"[428] –

"Well, Nelly, sweethearting out of the question, you have acted the part of a true friend, which, by God's blessing, I will never forget to you or yours. Save ye! my brave lass! The head and the heart of an Irishwoman are always ready when wanting, and, faith, that's more than can be said of the men." He sprang lightly into his saddle, and Beefstakes, as if conscious that his utmost speed was required, used well the freedom of the loosened bridle: horse and rider were soon out of sight.

What the feelings of Nelly Clarey were, must now, for ever remain unknown, even to me, her faithful historian; all I can record of her is, that she repeatedly wiped her eyes with the corner of her apron, and then gazing, only for a moment, upon the spot where he had disappeared, with a deep-drawn sigh retraced her steps to the miserable, almost roofless, apartment, in which her couch was spread, and where she soon sweetly and tranquilly slumbered, as if she had never known sorrow, or revelled in tears.

I know not how it is, but there is a species of – must I call it coquetry? – (I do not mean the regular coquetting system absolutely taught to a young female on her entrance into fashionable life, and which, in nine cases out of ten, from its visible arrangement, is perfectly harmless, and not unfrequently decidedly disgusting) – but a sort of natural witchery, born, I may say, with every genuine Irishwoman, and which, in the cottages, is particularly striking and fascinating. To those who have *not* witnessed it, I fear any description would appear unnatural, simply because unknown; those who *have*, must be heartless if they have not felt, and do not remember, its charm. I cannot think it overstrained to call it the coquetry of innocence, for in it there is neither art nor guile; it plays most bewitchingly in their bright and beaming smiles, when they blush at the remembrance of their earnest and heartfelt laughter; and, though a young Irish girl will seldom look at a stranger, except "out of the corner of her eye," the glance has nothing sinister or suspicious about it, but discourses at the same moment modestly yet frankly; – it, is as apart from French flippancy as from English stiffness, and yet partakes of the gaiety, but not the lightness, of the former, blended with the reserve, without the formality, of the latter.

Freney pursued his course towards the high road, and murmured within himself, in no gentle terms, at the impediments in his way; the by-path was little more than a sheep-trail, and much broken by heavy and continued rains; and, moreover the moon ("pale, inconstant planet") withdrew her light just at the time when our hero required it most. Beefstakes, however, knew his road well, and Freney left him pretty nearly to his own guidance, content with now and then encouraging his speed by some kind word of approbation, or an occasional pressure of his heel against his flank. The road they had taken led almost abruptly to the top of a wild, uncultivated hill, or rather what, in England, would be denominated a mountain; and as the animal was gaining its summit, his master heard, or fancied he heard, the report of a gun or pistol; the horse, too, evidently gave tokens that the well-known sound of fire-arms broke upon his ear, for he snorted, and shook his head, while pressing more eagerly onward.

Freney suddenly checked the rein, and, leaning completely over the neck of the noble animal, seemed as if inhaling whatever sounds the night wind bore up the hill; the pause, though momentary, was long enough for his purpose; he muttered a deep, low curse, too fearful for repetition, and urged the impetuous animal to its utmost speed. It was a noble steed, and cleared every impediment that obstructed its progress, vaulted the highest enclosures, and having attained the summit of the hill, snorted the combat afar off as he dashed in gallant style, down the declivity, with distended nostril and fire-striking foot. Fortunately the moon threw a full and glorious flood of light on their path, so that, even in the distance, Freney distinctly beheld the confirmation of his fears, and the necessity, had it been possible, for redoubled exertion. The ground descended steeply, but unevenly, into a hollow glen, one side of which was skirted by stunted and straggling brushwood, that fringed what was called the carriage road, while the other sloped down to a sort of shingly bottom (the black glen), through which a mountain stream brawled angrily and restlessly on its way. This place had been selected by Breen as the most fitting for his purpose, and at the moment the moon shone forth, the renegade had commenced rifling the carriage of Freney's early friend. The old gentleman's faithful servants had evidently made a desperate, and not a bloodless, resistance; and as the captain of the gang neared the spot, his blood boiled, and his heart throbbed, for in the dim light he beheld Norah Dartforth, with dishevelled tresses, supporting her father in her arms, as she half knelt, half reclined, by the way-side. The group was one that Salvator[429] only could have painted, nor would it have been unworthy of his pencil. The brightness of the clear full-moon, from which the ill-omened, scowling clouds were rapidly receding, leaving her alone and queen-like in the purity of her own heavens – the abrupt and frowning mountain, glowering like a gigantic and malignant spirit over all within its influence – the wild and tangled copsewood that partially shaded, without obscuring, the singular and dissimilar assemblage, that had for its centre the antique and picturesque carriage – while the richly-dressed servants, and the beautiful and interesting attitude of the kneeling girl, finely contrasted with the demoniac appearance of the lawless plunderers. But even my king of painters, had I power to recall him from his repose in that warm and sunny country –

"Where the poet's lip and the painter's hand
Are most divine," – [430]

must have failed in conveying an idea of the *succession* of mingled and warring feelings that were manifested, when Freney, fierce and terrible as the mountain-spirit, his horse covered with foam, his eyes flashing with rage and indignation, plunged in amongst them.

"Villain!" he exclaimed, seizing the wretch Breen by the collar, as a massive pocket-book, large enough for a modern folio, dropped from the false fellow's grasp; while, with his other hand, Freney drew from his belt a large horse pistol – "you are a fit example for all who disobey orders," he continued, with a frightful coolness of tone and manner.

"Mercy and hear me!" entreated the caitiff,[431] falling on his knees; "there is no blood spilt to signify – no harm done:" then, suddenly recollecting himself, he added, "sure I can't understand *why* ye trate me after such a fashion – judgment afore death, in this world, any way."

"Look here, boys," persevered the captain, without loosening his hold, "my orders were given – my orders have been disobeyed, and thus I punish *all* – ay – every mother's son who dares to think and act in opposition to them!" He cocked his pistol and placed its muzzle close to the wretched man's ear, while all who breathlessly beheld the scene appeared paralyzed by the energy and determination of this singular being.

"For God's sake! – as you expect mercy at your dying day! – don't send me out o' the world without cross or prayer! – one – one minute to make my soul! Oh! for the sake of the mother that bore ye, remember another woman's son!" rapidly ejaculated the unfortunate man. His entreaties had little effect, and in another moment, he would have been launched into eternity, had not a small white hand, for the second time that night, rested on Freney's shoulder; and a gentle voice, trembling and faint from agitation, exclaimed, "Forbear!" By degrees, his firm grasp relaxed, the lion melted into the lamb, and the outlaw, who braved the ordinances of man, and who would not have quailed beneath the iron grasp of justice, trembled at that gentle touch.

"I know not – I dread to know," said Miss Dartforth, "by what power you command those men – but I recognize the playmate of my youth; and the child my angel mother fostered will not surely stain his hand with blood."

"Believe me," he replied, earnestly, "that though Patrick James, and James Freney, are one and the same person, I have nothing to do with this night's unfortunate affair. I have not forgotten, Norah – pardon me, Miss Dartforth, I have not forgotten what I owe to your house." He turned abruptly from her, as if afraid to trust himself under her influence. "Rise, ye poor, trembling miscreant! – to the lady you would have plundered you owe your life," he continued, after a moment's pause, addressing Breen, who did not need to have the permission repeated. "And now, my men, help Mr. Dartforth's servants to replace what you would have plundered. Breen, *your* assistance is not required – you hold no communion with my free-hearted boys; not one of them, except yourself, would have dared to disobey me – you and *one other*. All share of booty, for the next three months, I disclaim; there, replace the things, my fine fellows, and I'll count scores with you afterwards."

Freney's utterance and actions were rapid and energetic; his followers did as he commanded, with the air of persons who obey more from habit than inclination. It was, nevertheless, obvious, that Freney was much agitated; not from any dread of revolt amongst his gang, but from the recurrence, at such a moment, of recollections that almost overpowered him. After issuing his brief directions, he walked to where Miss Dartforth had returned to support her father, and hardly answered the question of one of his party, who, having discovered the person I before mentioned, as the family "*toady*," coiled up, or rather, squatting, like the vile reptile, whose name appropriately belongs to his class, under a huge furze-bush, dragged him forth, and held him, after the fashion of a bale of cloth, at either end, while he exclaimed, "Captain, dear! what's to be done wid this parcel? Sure the jontleman 'ud be glad to get rid of it any way; though, I'm thinkin', it's little good is in it, for man or baste."

The old gentleman was evidently labouring under an aberration of mind, brought on by terror, and contending feelings; his every nerve trembled, and it was with great difficulty that his daughter and his own servant supported, or rather carried, him towards the carriage, by that time ready for his reception. He perfectly understood that the young man who tendered his services to assist him forward, and had saved his property, perhaps his life, was the same he had first cherished, and then abandoned; but he did not appear to understand the light in which he stood, as captain of the robbers: he seized his proffered arm with the eagerness of a drowning man, catching at aught that is even symbolic of hope, and looked long and earnestly into his face; at length his pale, dull eyes, filled with unbidden tears, and with a powerful effort he threw himself on the brigand's neck, lifted up his voice, and wept most bitterly. It was a time of trial for all, and, in after years, was often thought of.

Mr. Dartforth was, at length, placed in the carriage, and, in broken accents, he entreated Freney to enter with him. "All shall be yours, James, as before," he murmured – "sure you've saved my life. Norah, you speak for me, he always heeded you." This was more than Freney could bear; – he rushed from his grasp, ordering the coachman to drive on, in a tone of voice not to be disobeyed.

I have heard that Mr. Dartforth never perfectly recovered from the effects of that night's adventure; the consciousness that the youth he had so loved was the rapparee chief, upon whose head a price was set, and who suffered the curse of Ishmael,[432] even in his own land, embittered every hour of his existence; but worse, even than that, was the consciousness that *his* mismanagement had led to such fearful consequences. Even those who suffered from Freney's plunderings, were ready to admit there was that about him, which had it been properly managed, would have rendered him the admiration, not the terror, of his country. And, with this miserable knowledge, the old man descended to his grave, ignorant of that, which a few years of longer life would have informed him – for Freney, in process of time, repented, and became reformed, and finished his days, in peace and quietness, in the town of New Ross.

ANNIE LESLIE.

ANNIE LESLIE was neither a belle nor a beauty – a gentlewoman, nor yet an absolute peasant – "a fortune," nor entirely devoid of dower: – although born upon a farm that adjoined my native village of Bannow, she might almost have been called a flower of many lands; for her mother was a Scot, her father an Englishman; one set of grand-parents Welsh – and it *was* said that the others were (although I never believed it, and always considered it a gossiping story) Italians, or foreigners, "from beyant the salt sea." It was a very charming pastime to trace the different countries in Annie's sweet, expressive countenance. Ill-natured people said she had a red, Scottish head, which I declare to be an absolute story. The maiden's hair was *not* red; it was a bright chestnut, and glowing as a sunbeam – perhaps, in particular lights, it *might* have had a tinge – but, nonsense! it was anything but red: the cheek-bone was, certainly, elevated; yet who ever thought of that, when gazing on the soft cheek, now delicate as the bloom on the early peach – now purely carnationed, as if the eloquent colour longed to eclipse the beauty of the black, lustrous eyes, that were shaded by long, long, eyelashes, delicately turned up at the points, as if anxious to act as conductors to my young friend's merry glances, of which, however, I must confess, she was usually chary enough? Her figure was, unfortunately, "of the Principality,"[433] being somewhat of the shortest; but her fair skin, and small, delicate mouth, told of English descent. Her father was a respectable farmer, who had been induced, by some circumstance or other, to settle in Ireland; and her mother – but what have I to do with either her father or her mother, just now?

The sun fires had faded in the west, and Annie was leaning on the neat green gate that led to her cottage; her eyes wandering down the branching lane, then to the softening sky, and not unfrequently to a little spotted dog, Phillis by name, who sat close to her mistress's feet, looking upwards, and occasionally raising one ear, as if she expected somebody to join their party. It was the full and fragrant season of hay-making, and Annie had borne her part in the cheerful and pleasant toil.

A blue muslin kerchief was sufficiently open to display her well-formed throat; one or two wilful ringlets had escaped from under her straw hat, and twisted themselves into very picturesque, coquettish attitudes, shaded, but not hidden, by the muslin folds; her apron was of bright check; her short cotton gown, pinned in the national three-cornered fashion behind, and her petticoat of scarlet stuff, displayed her small and delicately turned ancle[434] to much advantage. She held a bunch of mixed wild flowers in her hand, and her fingers, naturally addicted to mischief, were dexterously employed in scattering the petals to the breeze, which sported them amongst the long grass.

"Down, Phillis! – down, miss!" said she, at last, to the little dog, who, weary of rest, stood on its hind legs, to kiss her hand; "down, do, ye're always merry when I am sad, and that's not kind of ye." The animal obeyed, and remained very tranquil, until its mistress unconsciously murmured to herself – "Do I really love him?" Again she looked down the lane, and then, after giving a very destructive pull to one of the blossoms of a wild rose, that clothed the hedge in beauty, repeated, somewhat louder, the words, "Do I, indeed, love him?"

"Never say the word twice – ye do, ye little rogue!" replied a voice, that sent an instantaneous gush of crimson over the maiden's cheek – while, from amid a group of fragrant elder-trees, which grew out of the mound that encompassed the cottage, sprang a tall, graceful youth, who advanced towards the blushing maiden.

I am sorry for it, but it is, nevertheless, an incontrovertible fact, that women, young and old – some more, and some less – are all naturally perverse; they cannot, I believe, help it; but their so being, although occasionally very amusing to themselves, is, undoubtedly, very trying to their lovers, whose remonstrances on the subject, since the days of Adam, might as well have been given to the winds.

It so happened that James Mc Cleary was the very person Annie Leslie was thinking about – the one of all others she wished to see; yet the love of tormenting, assisted, perhaps, by a little maiden coquetry, prompted her first to curl her pretty Grecian nose, and then to bestow a hearty cuff on her lover's cheek, as he attempted to salute her hand.

"Keep your distance, sir, and don't make so free!" said the pettish lady.

"Keep my distance, Annie! Not make so free!" echoed James; "an' ye, jist this minute, after talking about loving me!"

"Loving you, indeed! Mister James Mc Cleary, it was yer *betters* I was thinking of, sir; I hope I know myself too well for that."

"My betters, Annie! – what's come over ye? Surely ye haven't forgot that yer father has as good as given his consint; and though yer mother is partial to Andrew Furlong – the tame negur! – jist because he's got a bigger house (sure it's a public and can't be called his own), and a few more guineas than me, and never thinks of his being greyer than his ould grey mare – yet she'll come round; – let me alone to manage the women – (now don't look angry) – and didn't yer own sweet mouth say it, not two hours ago, down by the loch? – and, by the same token, Annie, there's the beautiful curl I cut off with the reaping-hook – that, however ye trate me, shall stay next my heart, as long as it bates – and, oh, Annie!

as ye sat on the mossy stone, I thought I never saw ye look so beautiful – with that very bunch of flowers that ye've been pulling to smithereens, resting on yer lap. And it wasn't altogether what ye said, but what ye looked, that put the life in me: though ye did say – ye know ye did – 'James,' says you, 'I hate Andrew Furlong, that I do, and I'll never marry him as long as grass grows or water runs, that I won't.' Now, sure, Annie, dear, sweet Annie! – sure ye're not going aginst yer conscience, and the word o' true love."

"Sir," interrupted Annie, "I don't like to be found fault with. Andrew Furlong is, what my mother says, a well-to-do, dacent man, staid and steady. I'll trouble ye for my curl, Mister James – clever as ye are at managing the women, may-be ye can't manage me."

James had been very unskilful in his last speech; he ought not to have boasted of his managing powers, but to have put them in practice: the fact, however, was that, though proverbially sober, the fatigue of hay-making, and two or three "noggins" of Irish grog, had, in some degree, bewildered his intellect since Annie's return from the meadow. He looked at her for a moment, drew the long tress of hair out of his bosom, then replaced it, buttoned his waistcoat to the throat, as if determined nothing should tempt it from him, and said, in a subdued voice –

"Annie, Annie Leslie! – like a darlint, don't be so fractious – for your sake – for –"

"My sake, indeed, sir! – My sake! – I'm very much obliged to you, very much, Mister James; but let me tell ye, ye think a dale too much of yerself to be speaking to me after that fashion, and ye *inside* my own gate; if ye were *outside*, I'd tell ye my mind; but I know better manners than to insult any one, at my own door-stone: it's little other people know about dacent breeding, or they'd not abuse people's friends before people's faces, Mister James Mc Cleary."

"I see how it is, Miss Leslie," replied James, really angry: "ye've resolved to sell yerself, for yer board and lodging, to that grate cask of London porter, Andrew Furlong by name, and a booby[435] by nature; but I'll not stay in the place to witness yer parjury – I'll go to sea, or – I'll – "

"Ye may go where ye like," responded the maiden, who now thought herself much aggrieved and injured, "and the sooner the better!" She threw the remains of the faded nosegay from her, and opened the green gate at the same instant – the gate which, not ten minutes before, she had rested on, thinking of James Mc Cleary – thinking that he was the best wrestler, the best hurler, the best dancer, and the most sober lad in the country: – thinking, moreover, that he was as handsome, if not as genteel, as the young 'squire; and wondering if he would always love her as dearly as he did then. Yet, in her perversity, she flung back the gate for the faithful-minded to pass from her cottage, careless of consequences, and, at the moment, really believing that she loved him not. So much for a wilful woman, before she knows the value of earth's greatest treasure – AN HONEST HEART.

"Since it's come to this," said poor James, "any how, bid me good-bye, Annie. – What, not one 'God be wid ye,' to him who will soon be on the salt – salt sea." But Annie looked more angry than before; thinking, while he spoke, that he would come back fast enough to her window next morning, bringing fresh grass for her kid, or food for her young linnets, or perchance, flowers to deck her hair; or (if he luckily met Peggy the fisher) a new blue silk neckerchief as a peace-offering.

"Well, God's blessing be about ye, Annie; and may ye never feel what I do now!" So saying, the young man rushed down the green lane, frighting the wood-pigeons from their repose, and putting to flight the timid hare and tender leveret, who sought their evening meal where the dew fell thickly, and the clover was most luxuriant. There was a fearful reality about the youth's farewell that startled the maiden, obstinate as she was; – her heart beat violently, and the demon of coquetry was overpowered by her naturally affectionate feelings. She called, faintly at first, "James, James, *dear* James;" and poor little Phillis scampered down the lane, as if she comprehended her mistress's wish. Presently, Annie was certain she heard footsteps approaching; her first movement was to spring forward, and her next (alas, for coquetry!) to retire into the parlour, and await the return of her lover; – "what, she wished to be true, love bade her believe;"[436] there she stood, her eyes freed from their tears, and turned from the open window. Presently, the gate was unlatched; in another moment a hand softly pressed her arm, and a deep-drawn sigh broke upon her ear.

"He is very sorry," thought she, "and so am I." She turned round, and beheld the good-humoured, rosy face of mine host of the Public; his yellow bob-wig evenly placed over his grey hair; his Sunday suit well brushed; and his embroidered waistcoat (pea-green ground, with blue roses and scarlet lilies) covering, by its immense lapelles, no very juvenile rotundity of figure. Poor Annie! she was absolutely dumb: had Andrew been a horned owl, she could not have shrunk with more horror from his grasp. Her silence afforded her senior lover an opportunity of uttering, or rather growling forth, his "proposal." "Ye see, Miss Leslie, I see no reason why we two shouldn't be married, because I have more regard for ye, tin to one, than any young fellow could have: for I am a man of exparience, and know wrong from right, and right from wrong – which is all one. Yer father, but more especially yer mother (who has oceans of sense, for a woman), are for me; and, beautiful as ye are, and more beautiful, for sartin, than any girl in the land, yet ye can't know what's good for ye as well as they! And ye shall have a jaunting-car – a bran new jaunting-car of yer own, to go to mass or church, as may suit yer conscience, for I'd be far from putting a chain upon ye, barring one of roses, which 'Cupid waves,' as the song says, 'for all true constant loviers.'[437] Now, Miss, machree, it being all settled – for sure ye're too wise to refuse sich an offer! – here, on my two bare knees, in the moonbames – that Romeyo[438] swore by, in the play I saw when I was as good as own man to an honourable member o' parliament – (it was in this service he learned to make long speeches, on which he prided himself greatly) – do I swear to be to you a kind and faithful husband – and true to you and you alone."

Mr. Andrew sank slowly on his knees, for the sake of comfort resting his elbows on the window-sill, and took forcible possession of Annie's hand, who, angry, mortified, and bewildered, hardly knew in what set terms to vent her displeasure. Just at this crisis, the garden-gate opened; and little Phillis, who, by much suppressed growling, had manifested her wrath at the clumsy courtship of the worthy host, sprang joyously out of the window. Before any alteration could take place in the attitudes of the parties, James Mc Cleary stood before them, boiling with jealousy and rage. "So, Miss Leslie – a very pretty manner you've treated me in! – and it was for that *carcase* (and he pushed his foot against Andrew Furlong), that ye trampled me like the dust; it was because *he* has a few more bits o' dirty bank notes, that he scraped by being a lick-plate to an unworthy mimber, who sould his country to the Union and Lord Castlereagh: but ye'll sup sorrow for it – ye will, Annie Leslie, for yer love is wid me, bad as ye are; yer cheek has blushed, yer eye has brightened, yer heart has bate for me, as it never will for *you*, ye foolish, foolish ould cratur, who thinks the finest – the holiest feeling that God gives us, can be bought with goold! But I am done; as ye have sowed, Annie, so ye may reap. I forgive ye – though my heart – my heart – is torn – almost, almost broken; for I thought ye faithful – I was wound up in ye – ye were the very core of my heart – and now – " The young man pressed his head against a cherry-tree, whose wide-spreading branches overshadowed the cottage. Annie, much affected, rushed into the garden, and took his hand affectionately; he turned upon her a withering look, for the jealous fit was waxing stronger.

"What! do ye want to make more sport of me to please yer *young* and *handsome* lover? Oh! that ever I should throw ye from me?" He flung back her hand, and turned to the gate; but Andrew, the gallant Andrew, thought it behoved him to interfere when his lady-love was treated in such a disdainful manner; and, after having, with his new green silk handkerchief, carefully dusted the knees of his scarlet plush breeches, came forward;

"I take it that that's a cowardly thing for you to do, James Mc Cleary – a cow—"

"What do you say?" vociferated James, whose passion had now found an object to vent itself on – "did you dare call me a coward?" He seized the old man by the throat, and, gripping him as an eagle would a land-tortoise, held him at arm's length: "Look ye, ye fat ould calf, if ye were my equal in age or strength, it isn't talking to ye I'd be; but I'd scorn to illtrate a man of yer years – though I'd give a thousand pounds this minute that ye were young enough for a fair fight, that I might have the glory to break every bone in yer body – but there!" – He flung his weighty captive from him with so much violence, that mine host found himself extended amid a quantity of white-heart cabbages; while poor James sprang amid the elder-trees, which before had been his place of happy conceal-ment, and rushed away.

Annie stood erect under the shadow of the cherry-tree, against which James had rested, and the rays of the clear, full moon, flickering through the foliage, showed that her face was pale and still as marble. In vain did Phillis jump and lick her hand; in vain did Andrew vociferate, in tender accents, from the cabbage-bed where he lay, trying first to turn upon one side, and then on the other – "Will no one take pity on me?" – "Will nobody help me up?" There stood Annie, wonder-ing if the scene was real, and if all the misery she endured could possibly have originated with herself. She might have remained there much longer, had not her father and mother returned from the meadows, where they had been distributing the usual dole of spirits to their barelegged labourers. "Hey, mercy, and what's the matter noo?" exclaimed the old Scotch lady; "why, Annie, ye're clean daft for cer-tain; and, good man Andrew! what has happened to you, that ye're rubbing your clothes with your bit napkin, like a fury? Hey! mercy me, if my beautiful kail[439] isn't perfectly ruined, as if a hail hogshead of yill had been row'd over it! Speak, ye young hizzy!"[440] – and she shook her daughter's arm – "what is the matter?"

"Annie," said her less eloquent father; "tell me all about it, love; how pale you are!" He led his child affectionately into the little parlour, while Andrew, with doleful tone and gesture, related to the "gude-wife" the whole story, as far as he was concerned. The poor girl's feelings were, at length, relieved by a passionate burst of tears; and, sobbing on her father's bosom, she told the truth, and con-fessed it was her love of tormenting that had caused all the mischief.

"I do believe," said the honest Englishman, "all you women are the same. Your mother was nearly as bad in our courting days. James is too hot and too hasty – rapid in word and action; and, knowing him as we do, you were wrong to trifle with him; but there, love, I must, I suppose, go and find him, and make all right again; shall I, Annie?"

"Father!" exclaimed the girl, hiding her face in that safe resting-place, a par-ent's bosom.

"Send old Andrew off, and bring James back to supper – eh?"

"Dear father!"

"And you will not be perverse, but make sweet friends again?"

"Dear, *dear* father!"

The good man set off on his embassy, first warning his wife not to scold Annie; adding, somewhat sternly, he would not permit her to be *sold* to any one. To which speech, had he waited for it, he would doubtless have received a lengthened reply.

As Mr. Leslie proceeded down the lane I have so often mentioned, he encoun-tered a man well known in the country by the *sobriquet*[441] of "Alick the Traveller," who, with his wearied donkey, was in search of a place of rest. Alick was a person of great importance, known to everybody, high and low, rich and poor, in the province of Leinster: he was an amusing, cunning, good-tempered fellow, who visited the gentlemen's houses as a hawker of various fish, particularly oysters, which he procured from the far-famed Wexford beds; and, after disposing of his cargo, he was accustomed to reload his panniers from our cockle-strand of Bannow, which is equally celebrated for that delicate little fish. Neither shoes nor stockings did Alick wear; no, he carried them in his hand, and never put them on, until he got within sight of the *genteel* houses; – "he'd be long sorry to give dacent shoes and stockings such usage: sure his feet were well used to the stones!" His figure was tall and erect; and the long stick of sea-weed, with which he urged poor Dapple's speed, was thrown over his shoulder with the careless air that, in a well-dressed man, would be called elegant. A weather-beaten *chapeau de paille*[442] shaded his rough, but agreeable features; and stuck on one side of it, in the twine which served as a hat-band, were a "cutty pipe," and a few sprigs of beautifully tinted sea-weed and delisk, forming an appropriate, but singular garniture. He was whistling loudly on his way, and cheering his weary companion, occasionally, by kind words of encouragement.

"God save ye, this fine evening, Mr. Leslie; I was just thinking of you, and all yer good family, which I hope is hearty, as well as the woman that owns ye. And I was just saying to myself that, may-be, ye'd let me and the baste stay in the corner to-night, for I've a power o' beautiful fish, and I want to be early among the gentry. But if the mistress likes a taste of news, or a rattling hake – "

"Alick," said Leslie, who knew, by experience, the difficulty of stopping his tongue "when once it was set a going," – "go to the house; and there's a hearty welcome – a good supper and clean straw for ye both. But tell me, have you seen James Mc Cleary this evening?"

"Och! is it James ye're after? There's a beautiful lobster! – let Kenny, Paddy Kenny (may-be ye don't know Paddy, the fishmonger, wid the blue door at the corner of the ould market in Wexford), let Paddy Kenny bate that! –"

"But James McCleary –"

"True for ye, he'll be glad to see ye. Now, Mister Leslie, tell us the truth, did ye ever see sich crabs as them in England? Where 'ud they get them, and they so far from the sea?"

"I want –"

"I humbly ax yer pardon – I saw him jist now cutting off in that way, as straight as a conger eel – I had one t'other day, Mister Leslie (it's as true as that ye're standing there), it weighed –"

"What? – did he go across the fields in that direction?"

"Is it he? – troth, no, I skinned him as nate –"

"Skinned who? – James Mc Cleary?"

"Och, no; the conger."

"Will you tell me in what direction you saw James Mc Cleary go? – the mis-fortune of all Irishmen is, that they answer one question by asking another."

"I don't like ye to be taking the country down, after that fashion, Mister Les-lie; it's bad manners, and I can't see any misfortune about it; and if I did, there's no good in life of making a cry about it; – but there's an illegant cod! – there's a whopper! – there's been no rest or peace with that lump of a fellow all the even-ing – whacking his tail in the face of every fish in the basket; I'll let the misthress have him a bargain if she likes, jist to get rid of him – the tory!"

Leslie at last found that his questions were useless; so he motioned "Alick the Traveller" to his dwelling, and proceeded on his way to James's cottage; – while Alick, gazing after him, half muttered, "There's no standing thim Englishmen; the best of them are so dead like – not a word have they in their head; not the least taste in life for conversation. Catch James! – I hope it didn't turn out bad, though," he continued, in a still lower tone: "what I said a while agone was all out o' innocence, for a bit of fun wid the ould one." He turned, and, for a moment, watched the path taken by Leslie, then proceeded on his way muttering – "'tis very quare though."

At the door of James Mc Cleary's cottage, Leslie encountered the young man's mother. "I was jist going to your place to ask what's come over my boy," said she; "I can't, make him out; he came in, in sich a fluster, about tin minutes agone, and kicked up sich a bobbery in no time: floostered[443] over his clothes in the press, cursed all the women in the world, bid God bless me, and set off, full speed, like a wild deer, across the country."

"Indeed!" exclaimed Leslie.

"I know, Mr. Leslie, that my boy has been keeping company wid your girl; and I have nothing to say agin her; she has a dale o' the lady about her, yet is humble and modest as any lamb: but I think, may-be, they've had a bit of a ruc-tion about some footy[444] thing or other; but men can't bear to be contradicted, though I own it's good for them, and more especially James, who has a dale of his father in him, who I had to manage (God rest his sowl!) like any babby. However, James has too much sense to go far, I'm thinking – only to his aunt's husband's daughter, by the Black-water, fancying, may-be, to bring Annie round; and so I was going to see her, to know the rights of it."

The kind-hearted farmer told her nearly all he knew, with fatherly feel-ing glossing over Annie's pettishness as much as he possibly could. Mrs. Mc Cleary remained firm in her opinion that he had only gone down to the Black-water, and would return the next day. But Leslie's mind foreboded evil. When he arrived at home, he found "Alick the Traveller" comfortably seated in the large chimney-corner – a cheerful turf fire casting its light, sometimes in broad masses, sometimes in brilliant flashes, over the room: the neat, white cloth was laid for supper; and the busy dame was seated opposite the itinerant man of fish, laughing long and loudly at his quaint jokes and merry stories. Annie was looking vacantly from the door that was shut, to the window, through which she could not see; and Phillis was stretched along the comfortable hearth, rousing herself, occasionally, to reprimand the rudeness of a small, white kitten, Annie's particular pet, which obstinately persisted in playing with the long, silky hairs of the spaniel's bushy tail. When Leslie entered, the poor girl's heart beat violently; and the colour rose and faded almost at the same moment. She busied herself about household matters, to escape observation; broke the salt-cellar in endeavouring to force it into the cruet-stand, and verified the old proverb, "spill the salt, and get a scolding,"[445] for the mother did scold, in no measured terms, at the destruction of what the careless hizzy had broken. "Did ye na ken that it had been used for twenty years and mair?" she reiterated; "and did Christian woman ever see sic folly, to force a broad salt, of thick glass, into a place that can na mair than haud a wee bottle? The girl's daft, and that's the end on't." Notwithstanding the jests of Alick, the evening passed heavily: Annie complained of illness, and went soon to bed; and as her father kissed her, at the door of her little chamber, he felt that her cheek was moist and cold. Mrs. Leslie soon followed; and the farmer replenished his long pipe, as Alick added fresh tobacco to his stumpy one. "I'm sorry to see Miss Annie so ill," said the honest hawker, in a kindly tone; "but this time all the girls get tired at the hay-making. Well, it bates all, to think how you farmers can be continted jist wid looking on the sky, and watching the crops, over and over again, in the same place! I might as well lie down and die at onst, as not keep going from place to place. One sees a dale more o' life, and one sees more o' the tricks o' the times. Och, but the world's a fine world, only for the people that's in it! – it's them *spiles* it. – I had something to say to you, Mister Leslie, very partiklar, that I came to the knowledge of quite innocent. Ye mind that Mister Mullager, Maley, as he calls himself for the sake of the *English*, has been playing the puck[446] wid Lord Clifford's[447] tinnants, as might be expected; for his mother was a chimbley sweeper, that had the luck to marry a dacent boy enough, only a little turned three-score; and thin this beautiful scoundrel came into the world, and, betwixt the two, they left him the power and all o' hard, yellow ginnees.[448] Now, he being desperate 'cute, got into my Lord's employ, being only a slip of a boy at the time. Well, lords, to my thinking (barring the ould ancient ones), are only foolish sort of min, any how – I could go bail that my Lord Clifford hadn't a full knowledge box, any way; and so, through one sly turn or other, this fellow bothered him so, and threw dust in his eyes, and wheedled him, that, ye know, at last he comes the gintle-man over us; and tould me, t'other day, that as fine a jacky-dorey[449] as iver ye set yer two good-looking eyes on, was nothing but a fluke[450] – the ignorant baste! Fine food for sharks he'd be; only the cratur that 'ud ate him must be hungry enough – the thief o' the world!"

"What has all this to do with me, Alick?" inquired the Englishman, steadily, while the traveller, incensed at the remembrance of the insult offered to his fish, scattered the burning ashes out of his cutty pipe, to the no small consternation of the crickets – merry things! – who had come on the hearthstone to regale on cold potatoes. "I know," ho continued, "that the agent, or whatever he calls himself, is no friend of mine. When my landlord came to the country, he did me the honour to ask my opinion; I showed him the improvements, that I, as an English farmer, thought might be profitable to the estate; he desired me to give in an estimate of the expense; I did so; but the honest agent, or, more properly speaking, middle-man,[451] had given one in before. His Lordship found that, by my arrangements, the expense was lessened one-half; but Maley persuaded my Lord that his plans were best, and so –"

"Ay," interrupted Alick, "couldn't ye have been content to mind yer farm, and not be putting English plans of improvement into an Irish head, where it's so hard to make them fit? When the devil was civil, and, like a jintleman, held out his paw to ye, why didn't ye make yer bow, and take it? – sure, that had been only manners, let alone sense – don't look so bleared! What, ye don't understand me?" Alick advanced his body slowly forward, rested his elbows on the small table, pressed his face almost close to Leslie's, whose turn it was, now, to lay down his pipe, and slowly said, in a firm, audible whisper, – "Whin Tim Mullager, the curse o' the poor – the thing in man's shape, but widout a heart – met ye one evening, by chance as you thought, at the far corner of the very field ye cut to-day, what tempted ye (for ye mind the time – my Lord thought a dale about yer English notions thin), whin he axed ye, as sweet as new milk, to join him in that very estimate unknownst to my Lord, and said, ye mind, that it might be made convanient to the both o' ye, and a dale more to the same purpose; and, instead of seeming to come in, my jewil! *you* talked something about 'tegrity and honour, which was as hard for *him* to make out as priest's Latin; and walked off as stately as the tower of Hook."

"But I never mentioned a syllable of his falsehood to do him injury," exclaimed the astonished farmer; "I never breathed it, even, to Lord Clifford."

"And more fool you – I ax yer pardon, but more fool you – that was yer time; and it was the time for more than that – it was the time for ye to get, a new laase upon the ould terms, and not to be trusting to lords' promises, which are as asy broken as anybody else's."

"You are a strange fellow, Alick; how did you know anything about my lease? At all events, though it is expired, I am safe enough, for I am sure that even Maley could not wish for a better tenant."

"A better tinant," responded Alick, fairly laughing: "a better tinant! – fait, that's not bad! – What does he care whether ye're a good or a bad tinant *to my Lord?* – doesn't he want – man alive! – to have ye body and sowl? – the rig'lar rint, to be sure, for the master; all fair – the little *dooshure*[452] for himself; the saaling money, if a laase to the fore; and a five-pound note, not amiss as a civility to his bit of a wife; thin the duty-hens, duty-turkeys, duty-geese, duty-pigs; – the spinning and the knitting: – sure, if my Lord or my Lady isn't to the fore, they'll save them the trouble of looking after sich things; and they, ye know, get the cash – that is, as much as the agent chooses to say is their due – and spend it in foreign parts, widout thinking o' the tears and the blood it costs at home. – Och, Mister Leslie! it's no wonder if we'd have the black heart to sich as them!"

Leslie, for the first time in his life, felt a doubt as to the nature of the situation in which he was placed; he looked around upon the fair white walls, so dear, so very dear, to the purest feelings of his heart; every object had a claim on his affections, – even the long wooden peg upon which his great coat hung behind the door, was as valuable to him as if it were of gold.

"I can hardly understand this," said he, at last; "you know I have always been on good terms with my neighbours, yet I have acquired little knowledge in these matters; I have always paid my rent to the moment; and, as my twenty-one years' lease only expired two or three days ago, I have had little opportunity of judging how Irish agents behave on such occasions."

"Don't be running down the country, Mr. Leslie," said Alick, quickly "there's a dale in the differ betwixt the raale gintry, and such *musheroons*[453] as he; but keep a look-out, for he's after no good. The day afore yesterday, whin he behaved so unhandsome to my jacky-dorey – ('twould ha' done yer heart good to look at that beautiful fish), he was walking with another spillogue[454] of a fellow (the gauger, by the same token); and so, as they seemed as thick as two rogues, whispering and nodding, and laying down the law, I thought if I let the baste go on, he'd keep safe to the road; and so, as they walked up one side of the hedge that leads to the hill, I jist streeled[455] up the other, to see, for the honour of ould Ireland, if I could fish out the rogue's maning. Well, to be sure, they settled as how the rint should be doubled on the land that fell, more especially yours, and fines raised, and the gauger's to act as 'turney;'[456] but he said that he knew you'd pay anything rather than lave the house ye settled up yerself; and then t'other said that ('twas the word he spoke), 'the ould Scotch cat' wouldn't let ye spind the money; and then t'other held to it, and said ye must go, for ye set a bad example of indipindence to the neighbours, and a dale more; but the upshot was, that they must get rid o' ye. And now, God be wid ye, and do yer best; and take care of that girl o' yours, and don't let the mistress bother her about that ould man, any more; she's full o' little tricks – may *sense*, not *sorrow*, sober thim, say I; good night, and thank ye kindly; Mr. Leslie, I'm the boy 'll look to ye, and don't think bad o' my saying that to the likes o' you; for ye remember how the swallow brought word to the eagle where the fowler stood. God's blessing be about ye all,

Amin!" And the keen, wandering, good-natured fellow left the house, to share, according to custom, Dapple's couch of clean straw, in the neighbouring shed.

The next morning Leslie's family received a visit from the agent, to the surprise of Annie and her mother, who welcomed him with much civility, while the farmer's naturally independent feelings struggled stoutly with his interests. If there be one thing more than another to admire in the character of English yeomen, it is their steady bearing towards their superiors; they feel that they are free-born men, and they act as such: but an Irish farmer must often play the spaniel[457] to his landlord, and to all that belong to his household, or bear his name; hardly daring to believe himself a man, much less fancy that, from his Maker's hand he came forth a being gifted with quick and high intellect – with a heart to feel, and a head to think, as well as, if not better than, the lord of the soil. But mind, though it may be suppressed, cannot be destroyed; with the Irish peasant, *cunning* frequently takes the place of *boldness*, and he becomes dangerous to his oppressors. Landlords may often thank their own wretched policy for the crimes of their tenantry, when they cease to reside amongst, or even visit them, but leave them to the artful management of ignorant and debased middle-men, who uniformly have but two principles of action – to blindfold their employers, and gain wealth at the expense of proprietor and tenant.

"Yer house is always nate and clane, Mrs. Leslie," said Maley, "and yer farm does ye credit, master; I'm sorry it's out of lase, but my duty to my employer obliges me to tell you, that a new lase, if granted, must be on more advantageous terms to his Lordship. Yer present payments, arable and meadow land together, average something about two pounds five or six per acre."

"Yes," replied Leslie, "always paid to the hour."

"And if it please ye, sir," said the good dame, "when his Lordship was down here, he made us a faithful promise, on the honour of a gentleman, that he'd renew the lease on the same terms, in consideration of the money and pains my husband bestowed on the land."

The agent turned his little grey eye sharply on the honest creature, and gave a grunt, that was less a laugh than a note of preparation for one, observing, "May-be he's lost his memory; for there, Mr. Leslie, is the proposal he ordered me to make (he threw a sheet of folded foolscap on the table), so you may take it or lave it."

He was preparing to quit the cottage, when his eye glanced on a basket of turkey eggs, that Annie had arranged to set under a favourite hen. – "What fine eggs!" he exclaimed; "I'll take two or three to show my wife." And, one after another, he deposited all the poor girl's embryo chickens in his capacious pockets.

Leslie, really aroused by the barefaced impudence of the act, was starting forward to prevent it, when his wife laid her hand on his arm; not that she did not sorrow after the spoil, but she had a point to gain.

"May-be, sir, ye'd joost tell me the Laird's present address; Annie, put it down on that bit paper."

"Tell his address! – anything ye have to say must be to me, good woman. And so ye write, pretty one; I wonder what is the use of taaching such girls as you to write: but ye're up to love-letters before this; ay, ay, ye'll make the best of yer black eyes, my dear!" With this insulting speech the low man in power left the cottage.

Bitter was the anguish felt by that little party. The father sat, his hands supporting his head, his eyes fixed on the exorbitant demand the agent had left upon his table; large tears passed slowly down Annie's cheek; and, if the poor mother suffered less than the others, it was because she talked more.

"Dinna be cast doon, Robert," said she, at last, to her husbaud; "ye hae nae reason, even if he ask sae much money as ye say, as a premium, forbye[458] other matters; why, there are as good farms elsewhere, and landlords that look after their tenants themselves. Oh, that wicked, wicked wretch! – to see him pocket the eggs – and his speech to my poor Annie!"

"My darling girl!" exclaimed the father, pressing his daughter to his bosom, where he held her long and anxiously.

It was almost impossible for Leslie to accede to the terms demanded: four pounds an acre for the farm, a heavy fine, and both duty-work, and duty-provisions, required in abundance."

"Dinna think o't, Robert," repeated the dame; "we'll go elsewhere, and find better treatment. If ye keep it at that rate we shall all starve." But the farmer's heart yearned to every blade of grass that had grown beneath his eye: he hoped to frustrate the intended evil, and yet keep the land. His crops had been prosperous, his cattle healthy; then, his neighbours, when, through Alick's agency, they found how matters stood, had, with the genuine Irish feeling that shines more brightly in adversity than in prosperity, come forward, affectionately tendering their services.

"Sure, the cutting the hay need niver cost ye a brass fardin," said the kind-hearted mower; "I'm half my time idle, and may jist as well be doing something for you as nothing for myself; so don't trouble about it, sir, dear; we like to have ye among us."

Then came "Nelly the Picker," as the spokeswoman of all her sisterhood. "Don't think of laving us, Mrs. Leslie, ma'am, sure every one of us 'll come as usual, but widout fee or reward, excipt the heart love, and do twice as much for that as for the dirty money: and I'll go bail the pratees will be as well picked, and the corn as well reaped, bound, and stacked as iver. Sure, though we didn't much like ye at first, hasn't Miss Annie grown up among us, born as she is on the sod, and a credit to it, too, God be praised!"

These were all very gratifying instances of pure and simple affection: indeed, even Andrew Furlong forgot his somerset[459] in the cabbage-bed, and posted down to the farm with his stocking full of gold and silver coins, of ancient and modern date, which were all at Leslie's service, to pay the premium required by the agent for the renewal of the lease. This last favour, however, the worthy farmer would not even hear of; he, therefore, sold a great part of his stock, and, to the annoyance of the agent, obtained the lease. From this circumstance, he might be said to triumph over the machinations of his enemy, but matters soon changed sadly: the family was as industrious as ever; the same steady persever-ance on the farmer's part; the same bustle and unwearying activity on that of the good dame; and, though poor Annie's cheek was more pale, and her eyes less bright, yet did she unceasingly labour in and out of their small dwelling. Notwithstanding all these exertions, the next season was a bad one; their sheep fell off in the rot, their pigs had the measles, their chickens the pip, and two of their cows died in calf. Never did circumstances, in the little space of six months, undergo so great a change. Leslie's silence amounted almost to sullenness; his wife talked much of their ill-fortune; Annie said nothing; but her step had lost its elasticity, her figure its grace, and her voice seldom trolled[460] the joyous, or even the mournful, songs of her native land in the elder bower, that, before the departure of James Mc Cleary, had rung again and again with merry laughter and music. James never returned after that unfortunate evening; and his mother had only twice heard from him since his absence: his letters were brief – "He had gone," he said, "to sea, to enable him to learn something, and to forget much." His mother and younger brother managed the farm with much skill and atten-tion during his absence. No token, no word of *her* whom he had dotingly loved, appeared in his letters. It was evident that he tried to think of her, as a heartless, jilting woman, unworthy to possess the affections of a sensible man; but there must have been times when the remembrance of her full beauty, of her frank and generous temper, of her many acts of charity (and in these she was never capricious), came upon him; – then the last scene at the cottage was forgotten, and he remembered alone her sweet voice, and sweeter look, in the hay meadow, when he cut off the curling braid of hair, which, doubtless, rested on his bosom in all his wanderings. And then he refreshed his memory by gazing on it, in the clear moonlight, during the night watches, when only the eye of heaven was upon him. Let no one imagine that such love is too refined to throb in a peas-ant's bosom; trust me, it is not. The being who lives amid the beauties of nature, although he may not express, must feel, the elevating, yet gentle influence of herb, and flower, and tree. Many a time have I heard the ploughman suspend his whistle, to listen to that of the melodious blackbird; and well do I remember the beautiful expression of one of my humblest neighbours, when, resting on his hay-fork, he had silently watched the sun as it set over a country glowing in its red and golden light: "It is very grand, yet hard to look upon," said he; "one can almost think it God's holy throne!"

The last letter that reached our sailor-friend contained, amongst others of similar import, the following passage – "Ye'll be sorry to hear, James (though it's nothing to ye now), that times are turned bad with the Leslies; there has been a dale of underhand work by my Lord's agent; and the girl's got a cold, dismal, look. My heart aches for the poor thing; for his mother is set upon her marrying Andrew Furlong, which she has no mind in life to."

Gale-day (as the rent-day is called in Ireland) had come and gone, and much sorrow was in the cottage of Robert Leslie. In the grey twilight he sat in a darkened corner of his little parlour, the very atmosphere of which appeared clouded; the dame stood at the open casement, against which Annie reclined more like a stiffened corpse than a breathing woman. Andrew Furlong was seated also at a table, looking earnestly on the passing scene.

"Haven't ye seen," said the mother, – "haven't ye seen, Annie, the misery that's come upon us, entirely by my advice being no minded? And are ye goin' tamely to see us turned out o' house and hame, when we have na the means of getting anither? I, Annie," she continued, "am a'maist past my labour; ah, my bonny bairn, it was for you we worked – for you we toiled; your faither an' me had but one heart in that; and if the Lord Almighty has pleased to take it frae us, it's na reason why you should forget how ye were still foremost in your parents' love."

Annie answered nothing.

"Speak to her, Robert," said Mrs. Leslie, "she disna mind me noo."

Annie raised her eyes reproachfully to her mother's face. The farmer came forward, – he kissed the marble brow of his pale child, and she rested her head on his shoulder. As he turned towards her, she whispered, "Is all, indeed, as bad as mother says?"

"Even so," was his reply; "unless *something* be done, to-morrow we shall have no home. Annie, it is to shield you I think of this; my delicate, fading flower, how could *you* labour as a hired servant? And – God in his mercy look upon us! – I should not be able to find a roof to shelter my only child!"

"My bairn," again commenced Mrs. Leslie, "sure the mother that gave ye birth can wish for naething sae much as your weel-doing; and sure sic a man as Maister Furlong could na fail to make ye happy. All the goud your faither wants he will gi'e us noo, trusting to his bare word; to-morrow, and it will be too late; – all these things sauld – the sneers of that bitter man – the scorn (for poverty is aye scorned) of a cauld warld – and, may-be, your faither in a lanely prison; eh, child – what could ye do for him then?"

"Mother!" exclaimed the girl, starting, with convulsive motion, from her father's shoulder; "say no more; here – a promise is all he wants to prevent this – here is my hand – give it where you please." She stretched out her arm to its full length – it was rigid as iron. Furlong advanced to take it; and whether Leslie would have permitted such a troth-plight or not, cannot now be ascertained, for the long form of Alick the Traveller stalked abruptly into the room.

"Asy, asy, for God's sake! – put up yer hand, Miss Annie, dear; keep your sate, I beg, Mister Furlong; no rason in life for yer rising; all of ye be asy. Will nobody quiet that woman, for God's sake?" he continued, seeing that the dame was, naturally enough, angry at this intrusion; "first let me say my say, and be off, for sorra a minute have I to waste upon ye. Robert Leslie by name, didn't I, onst upon a time, tell ye truth? – and a sore hearing it was, sure enough. Well thin, I tell it ye again, and if it's not true, why ye may hang me as high as Howth; – don't let your daughter mum herself away after that fashion. Mister Furlong, ye're a kind-hearted man, so ye are, and many a bit an' a sup have ye bestowed upon me and the baste – thank ye kindly for that same – but yarra a much sense ye have, or ye wouldn't be looking after empty nuts:[461] – what the divil would be the good o' the hand o' that cratur, widout her heart? And that ye'll niver have. Mistress Leslie, ma'am, honey, don't be after blowing me up; – now jist think – sure I know that ye left the bonny hills and the sweet-scented broom of Scotland, to marry that Englishman. And ye mind the beautiful song that ye sing, far before any one I ever heard – about loving in youth, and thin climbing the hill, and thin sleeping at the fut of it – John Anderson,[462] ye call it: wouldn't ye rather have yer heart's first love, though he's ould and grey now, than a king upon his throne? Ay, woman, that touches ye! And do ye think *she* hasn't some o' the mother's feel in her? Now, Mister Leslie, don't – don't any of ye make her promise tonight; ye'll bless me for this, even you, Mister Andrew, by to-morrow sunset; promise, Robert Leslie."

"You told me the truth before," said the bewildered man, "and I have no right to doubt you now – I do promise." – Alick strode out of the cottage; Andrew followed, like an enraged turkey-cock, and the family were left again in solitude. The words of the fisherman had affected Mrs. Leslie deeply: she had truly fancied she was seeking her child's happiness; and, perhaps for the first time, she remembered how miserable she would have been with any other husband than "her ain gude-man."

The little family passed the night almost in the very extremity of despair. "Such," said Leslie, afterwards, "as I could not pass again; for the blood now felt as if frozen in my veins – now rushing through them with fearful rapidity – and, as my head rested on my poor wife's shoulder, the throbbing of my bursting temples but echoed the beating of her agitated heart." The early light of morning found Annie in a heavy sleep; and the mid-day sun glowed as brightly as if it illumined the pathway of princes, on three or four ill-looking men, who entered the dwelling of the farmer. Their business was soon commenced – it was a work of heart-sickening desolation. On Annie's pure and simple bed sat one of the officials noting down each article in the apartment. Leslie, his arms folded, his lips compressed, his forehead gathered in heavy wrinkles over his brow, stood firmly in the centre of the room. Mrs. Leslie sat, her face covered with her apron – which was soon saturated by her tears, and poor little Phillis crouched beneath her chair; – Annie clung to her father's arm; her energies were roused as she feelingly appealed to the heartless executors of the law. What increased the wretchedness of the scene was the presence of Mr. Maley, himself, who seemed to exult over the misery of his victims. He was not, however, to have it all his own way; several of the more spirited neighbours assembled, and forgot their own interests in their anxiety for the Leslies. One young fellow entered, waving his shilelah, and swearing, in no measured terms, that "he'd spill the last drop of his heart's blood afore a finger should be laid on a single scrap in the house." The agent's scowl changed into a sneer, as he pointed to the document he held in his hand. This, however, was no argument to satisfy our Irish champion; and, in truth, matters would have taken a serious turn, but for the prompt interference of an old man, who held back the arms of the young hero. The door was crowded by the sympathizing peasantry; some, by tears, and many, by deep and awful execrations, testified their abhorrence of the man "dressed in a little brief author-ity."[463] "Oh!" ejaculated Mrs. Leslie, "oh! that I had never lived to see this day of ruin and disgrace! Oh! Annie, *you* let it come to –"

"Hold, woman!" exclaimed her husband; "remember what we repeated last night to each other; remember how we prayed, when this poor child was sleep-ing, as in the sleep of death; remember how we both bethought of the fair names of our parents – how you told me of the men of your kin who fought for their faith among your native Scottish hills; and my own ancestors, who left their pos-sessions and distant lands for conscience sake! Oh, woman, Janet, remember the words, 'yet have I not seen the righteous forsaken, nor his seed begging bread.'"

Doubtless Mrs. Leslie felt, in their full force, these sweet sounds of consola-tion; – again she hid her face, and wept. It is in the time of affliction that the words of Scripture pour balm upon the wounded spirit; in the world's turmoil they are often unhappily forgotten; but in sorrow they are sought for, even as the hart seeketh for the water-brooks.

The usually placid farmer had scarcely given vent to this extraordinary burst of feeling, when there was a bustle outside the door, which was speedily accounted for. A post-chaise![464] rattling down the lane, and stopping suddenly opposite the little green gate; from off the crazy bar, propped upon two rusty supporters, in front of the creaking vehicle, sprang our old friend, Alick the Traveller: – "Huzza! huzza, boys! Ould Ireland forever! Och! but the bones o' me are in smithereens from the shaking! Huzza for justice! Boys, dear, won't ye give *one* shout for jus-tice? – '*tisn't often it troubles ye.* – Och! stand out o' my way, for I'm dancing mad! Och! – by St. Patrick! – Stand back, ye pack o' bogtrotters,[465] till I see the meeting. Och! – love is the life of a nate. – Och! my heart's as big as a whale!"

While honest Alick was indulging in this and many similar exclamations, capering, snapping his fingers, jumping (to use his own expression) "sky high," and shouting, singing, and swearing, with might and main, two persons had descended from the carriage. One, a tall, slight, gentlemanly man, fashionably enveloped in a fur travelling cloak; the other, a jovial sailor, whose handsome face was expressive of the deepest anxiety and feeling.

The sailor was James Mc Cleary; the gentleman – but I must carry my story decorously onwards.

Poor Annie! she had suffered too much to coquet it again. Whether she fainted or not, I do not recollect; but this I know, that she leaned her weeping face upon James's shoulder, and that the expression of his countenance varied to an almost ludicrous degree: – now beaming with love and tenderness, as he looked upon the maiden – now speaking of "death and destruction" to the crest-fallen agent. The gentleman stood, for a moment, wondering at everybody, and everybody wondering at him. At last in a firm voice, he said, "I stop this proceeding; and I order you (and he fixed a withering glance upon Maley) – I do not recollect your *name*, although I am perfectly acquainted with your *nature* – I order you, sir, to leave this cottage; elsewhere you shall account for your conduct." Maley sank into his native insignificance in an instant; but then impudence, the handmaid of knavery, came to his assistance: pulling down his wig with one hand, and holding his spectacles on his ugly red snub nose with the other, he advanced to where the gentleman stood, and peering up into his face, while the other eyed him as an eagle would a vile carrion crow, inquired, with a quivering lip, that ill assorted with his words' bravery, – "And who the devil are you, sir, who interferes in what doesn't by any manner of means concern you?"

"As you wish to know, sir," replied the gentleman, removing his hat, and looking kindly around on the peasants, "I am brother to your landlord!" Oh, for Wilkie,[466] to paint the serio-comic effect of that little minute! – the look of abashed villany – the glorious feeling that suffused the honest farmer's countenance – the uplifted hands and ejaculations of Mrs. Leslie – the joyous face of Annie, glistening all over with smiles and tears – the hearty, honest shout of the villagers – and even the merry bark of little Phillis; – then Alick, striding up to the *late* man of power, his long back curved into a humiliated bend, his hand and arm fully extended, his right foot a little advanced, while his features varied from the most contemptuous and satirical expression to one of broad and gratified humour, addressed him, with mock reverence: "Mister Maley, sir, will ye allow me (as the gintry say) the pleasure to see ye out; it's your turn now, ould boy, though ye don't know a fluke from a jacky-dorey."

"Sir – my Lord," stammered out the crest-fallen villain, "I don't really know what is meant: I acted for the best – for his Lordship's interest."

"Peace, man!" interrupted the gentleman; "I do not wish to expose you; there is my brother's letter: to-morrow I will see you at his house, where his servants are now preparing for my reception." The man and his minions shrank away as well and as quietly as they could; and the Leslies had now time to wonder how all this change had been brought about; while the neighbours lingered around the door, with a pardonable curiosity, to "see the last of it."

"Ye may thank that gentleman for it all," said James; "besides being brother to the landlord, I had the honour to sarve under him, in as brave a ship as ever stept the sea; and ye mind when matters were going hard here, Alick (God for ever bless him for it!) turned too at the pen, and wrote me every particular, and all about the agent's wickedness, and (may I say it, Annie, *now?*) yer love for me: and how out o' divilment he sent the ould man to make love to you that sorrowful evening – when I went away – and then put me up to catch him; little thinking how the jealousy would drive me mad; well, his honour, the Captain, had no pride in him – "

"Stop, my brave lad, towards *you* I could have had none," exclaimed the generous officer; "where the battle raged the most, *you* were at my side; and when, in boarding the Frenchman, I was almost nailed to the deck, you – you rushed forward, and, amid death and danger, bore me, sadly wounded, in your arms, back to my gallant ship." He extended his hand to the young Irishman who pressed it respectfully to his lips. – "To see the like o' that now," said Alick; "to see him shaking hands with one that's as good as a lord!" – "I held frequent conversations with my brave friend," continued the Captain, "and, at length, he enlightened me as to the treatment my brother's tenants experienced from the agent; I am come down expressly to see justice done to all, who, I regret to find, have suffered from the ill effects of the absentee system. Miss Leslie, I am sorry to lose so good a sailor, but I only increase my number of friends when I resign James Mc Cleary to his rightful commander."

"Och! my dears," exclaimed Alick; "it's as good as a play – a beautiful play: and there's honest Andrew coming over; don't toss him in the cabbage-bed, James, honey, this time. And, James, dear, there's your ould mother running up the lane, – well, ould as she is, she bates Andrew at the step. Och! Miss Annie, don't be looking down after that fashion. And, sir, my Lord, if yer honour plases, ye won't forget the little bit o' ground for the baste."

"Everything I have promised I will perform," said the young man, as he withdrew: an example which I must follow, assuring all who read my story, that, however strange it may appear, Annie made an excellent wife, never flirted the least bit in the world, except with her husband; and practically remembered her father's wise and favourite text – "*I have been young and now am old, yet have I not seen the righteous forsaken, nor his seed begging bread.*"

MASTER BEN.

TALL, and gaunt, and stately, was "Master Ben;" with a thin sprinkling of white, mingled with the slightly-curling brown hair, that shaded a forehead, high, and somewhat narrow. With all my partiality for this very respectable personage, I must confess that his physiognomy was neither handsome nor interesting; yet there was a calm and gentle expression in his pale grey eyes, that told of much kind-heartedness – even to the meanest of God's creatures. His steps were strides: his voice shrill, like a boatswain's whistle; and his learning – prodigious! – the unrivalled dominie[467] of the country, for five miles round, was Master Ben.

Although the cabin of Master Ben was built of the blue shingle, so common along the eastern coast of Ireland, and was perched, like the nest of a pewet,[468] on one of the highest crags in the neighbourhood of Bannow; although the afore-said Master Ben, or (as he was called by the gentry) "Mister Benjamin," had worn a long black coat for a period of fourteen years – in summer, as an open surtout,[469] which flapped heavily in the gay sea breeze – and in winter, firmly secured, by a large wooden pin, round his throat – the dominie was a person of much con-sideration, and more loved than feared, even by the little urchins who often felt the effects of his "system of education." Do not, therefore, for a moment, imag-ine that his was one of the paltry hedge-schools, where all the brats contribute their "sod o' turf," or, "their small trifle o' pratees,"[470] to the schoolmaster's fire or board. No such thing; – though I confess that "Mister Benjamin" would, occa-sionally, accept "a hand of pork," a kreel,[471] or even a kish of turf, or three or four hundred of "white eyes,"[472] or "London ladies,"ᵃ [473] if they were presented, in a proper manner, by the parents of his favourite pupils.

In summer, indeed, he would, occasionally, lead his pupils into the open air, permitting the biggest of them to bring his chair of state; and while the fresh ocean breeze played around them, he would teach them all he knew – and that was not a little; but, usually, he considered his lessons more effectual, when they were learned under his roof: and it was, in truth, a pleasing sight to view his cot-tage assemblage, on a fresh summer morning; – such rosy, laughing, romping things! "The juniors," with their rich curly heads, red cheeks, and bright, danc-ing eyes, seated in tolerably straight lines – many on narrow strips of blackened deal – the remnants, probably, of some shipwrecked vessel – supported at either end by fragments of grey rock; others on portions of the rock itself, that "Master Ben" used to say, "though not very asy to sit upon for the gossoons, were clane, and not much trouble." "The seniors," fine, clever-looking fellows, intent on their sums or copies – either standing at, or leaning on, the blotted "desks," that extended along two sides of the school-room, kitchen, or whatever you may please to call so purely Irish an apartment: the chimney admitted a large portion of storm or sunshine, as might chance; but the low wooden partition, which divided this useful room from the sleeping part of the cabin, at once told that Master Ben's dwelling was of a superior order.

At four, the dominie always dismissed his assembly, and heart-cheering was the joy that succeeded. On the long summer evenings, the merry groups would scramble down the cliffs – which, in many places, overhang the wide-spreading ocean – heedless of danger –

> "And jump, and laugh, and shout, and clap their hands
> In noisy merriment."[474]

The seniors then commenced lobster and crab-hunting, and often showed much dexterity in hooking the gentlemen out of their rocky nests, with a long, crooked stick of elder, which they considered "lucky." The younkers[475] were generally content with shrimping, or knocking the limpits – or, as they call them, the "branyans,"[476] off the rocks; while the wee-wee ones slyly watched the ascent of the razor fish, whose deep den they easily discovered by its tiny mountain of sand.

Even during their hours of amusement, Master Ben was anxious for their welfare; and, enthroned on a high pinnacle, that commanded a boundless view of the wide-spreading sea, with its numerous creeks and bays, he would patiently sit, hour after hour – one eye fixed on some dirty, wise, old book, while the other watched the various schemes and scampings of his quondam[477] pupils – until the fading rays of the setting sun, and the shrill screams of the sea-birds, warned master and scholar of the coming night.

Every one agreed that "Master Ben" was very learned – but how he became so, was what nobody could tell; some said (for there are scandalmongers in every village) that, long ago, Master Ben's father was convicted of treasonable practices, and obliged to fly to "foreign parts" to save his life: his child was the companion of his wanderings, according to this statement. But there was another, far more probable; – that our dominie had been a poor scholar – a class of students, peculiar, I believe, to Ireland, who travel from province to province, with satchels on their backs, containing books, and whatever provisions are given them, and devote their time to study and begging. The poorest peasant will share his last potato with a wandering scholar, and there is always a couch of clean straw prepared for him in the warmest corner of an Irish cabin. Be these surmises true or false, everybody allowed that Master Ben was the most clever schoolmaster between Bannow and Dublin: he would correct even Father Sinnott, "on account o' the bog Latin[478] his reverence used at the altar itself." "His reverence" always took this in good part, laughed at it, but never omitted adding, slyly, "the poor cratur! – he thinks he knows betther than me!" I must say, that the laugh which concluded this sentence was much more joyous than that at the commencement.

The dominie's life passed very smoothly, and with apparent comfort; – strange as it may sound to English ears – comfort. A mild, halfwitted sister, who might be called his shadow – so silently and calmly did she follow his steps, and do all that could be done, to make the only being she loved happy – shared his dwelling. The potatoes, she planted, dug, and picked, with her own hands; milked and tended "Nanny" and "Jenny," two pretty, merry goats, who devoured not only the wild heather and fragrant thyme, which literally cover the sandbanks and hills of Bannow, but made sundry trespasses on the flower-beds at the "great house," and defied pound, tether, and fetter, with the most roguish and provoking impudence. I had almost forgotten – but she small-plaited in a superior and extraordinary manner; and – poor thing! – she was as vain of that qualification as any young lady who rumbles over the keys of a grand piano, and then triumphantly informs the audience that she has played "The Storm."[479]

"Changeful are all the scenes of life,"[480] says somebody or other; and when I was about ten years old, "Master Ben" underwent two very severe trials – trials the poor man had never anticipated; one was teaching, or trying to teach, me the multiplication table – an act no mortal man (or woman either) ever could accomplish; the other was – falling in love. As "Master Ben" was the best arithmetician in the country, he was the person fixed on to instruct me in the most puzzling science – no small compliment I assure you – and he was obliged to arrange, so as to leave his pupils twice a week for two long hours. "Master Ben" rose in estimation surprisingly, when this was known; and, on the strength of it, got two-pence instead of three-halfpence a week from his best scholars; he thought he should also gain credit by his new pupil's progress. How vain are man's imaginings! From the first intimation I received of the intended visits of my tutor, I felt a most lively anticipation of much fun and mischief.

"Now, Miss, dear, don't be full o' yer tricks," said pretty Peggy O'Dell, who had the especial care of my person. "Now, Miss, dear, stand asy – you won't? – well, then, I'll not tell ye the news – no, not a word! Oh, ye're asy now, are ye! Well, then – to-morrow, Frank tells me, Master Ben is to come to tache you the figures; and good rason has Frank to know, for he druv the carriage to Master Ben's own house, and hard the mistress say all about it; and that was the rason ye were left at home, mavourneen, with your own Peggy; becase the ladies wished to keep it all secret like, till they'd tell ye their own selves. Oh, Miss, dear, asy –

asy – till I tie yer sash! – there, now – now you may run off; but stay one little minit – take kindly to the figures. I know you can't abide them now, but I hear they are main useful; and take to it asy – *as quiet as you can*; Master Ben has fine larning, and expicts much credit for tacheing the likes of you. And why not?"

Poor Benjamin! – he certainly did stride to the manor, and into the study, next morning; and in due time, I worked through, that is, I wrote out the questions, and copied the sums, with surprising dexterity, in "numeration," "addition of integers," "compound subtraction," and entered the "single rule of three direct,"[481] with much *éclat*.[482] My book was shown, divested of its blots by my kind master's enduring knife; and even my cousin (the only arithmetician in the family) was compelled to acknowledge that, if I did the sums myself, I was a very good girl indeed. That *if* destroyed my reputation. I had too much honour to tell a story.

What a passion, to be sure, the dominie got into the next day, when informed of my disgrace! I cannot bear to see a long, thin man in a passion, to this very hour; there is nothing on earth like it, except a Lombardy poplar[483] in a storm. However, if poor Master Ben was tormented in the study by me, he was more tormented in the servants' hall by pretty Peggy.

Peggy was exactly a lively Irish coquet: such merry, twinkling, black eyes; such white teeth, which were often exposed by the loud and joyous laugh, that extended her large but well-formed mouth; and such a bounding, lissom figure, always (no small merit in an Irish lassie) neatly, if not tastefully, arrayed. She was an especial favourite with my dear grandmother, who had been her patron from early childhood; and Peggy fully and highly valued herself on this account. Then she could read and write in her own way; wore lace caps, with pink and blue bows; and, as curls were interdicted, braided her raven locks with much care and attention.

The smartest, prettiest girl, at wake or pattern, for ten miles round, was certainly Peggy O'Dell; and many lovers had she; from Thomas Murphy of the Hill (the richest), who had a cow, six pigs, and all requisites to make a woman happy, according to his own account, to Wandering Will (the poorest), who, though not five-and-twenty, had been a jovial sailor, a brave soldier, a capital fiddler, a very excellent cobbler, a good practical surgeon (he had performed several very clever operations as a dentist and bone-setter, I assure you), and, at last, settled as universal assistant in the manor-house; cleaned the carriage and horses with Frank, waited at table with Dennis, helped Martha to carry home the milk, instructed Peter Kean how to train vines in the Portuguese fashion[484] (which foreign treatment had so ill an effect on our poor Irish vines, that, to Wandering Will's eternal disgrace, they withered and died – a circumstance honest Peter never failed to remind him of, whenever he presumed to suggest any alteration in horticultural arrangements), had the exclusive care of the household brewing, and was even detected in assisting old Margaret hunting the round meadow for eggs, which the obstinate lady-fowl preferred hiding among brakes and bushes to depositing, in a proper manner, in the henhouse. Moreover, Will was "the jewil" of all the county during the hunting and shooting season – knew all the fox-earths, and defied the simple cunning of hare and partridge; made love to all the pretty girls in the village; and, as he was handsome, notwithstanding the loss of one of his beautiful eyes, everybody said that no one would refuse William, were he even as poor again as he was – an utter impossibility. The rumour spread, however, that his wandering affections were actually settled into a serious attachment for Peggy; but who Peggy was in love with was another matter. She jested with everybody, and laughed more at Master Ben than at any one else; she was always delighted when an opportunity occurred of playing off droll tricks to his disadvantage; and some of her jokes were so practical, that the housekeeper frequently threatened to inform her mistress of her pranks. Master Ben was always the first to prevent this; and his constant remonstrance – "Mistress Betty, let the innocent cratur alone, she manes no harm; she knows I don't mind her youthful fun – the cratur!" saved Peggy many a reproof.

One morning I had been more than ordinarily inattentive; and my tutor, perplexed, or, as he termed it, fairly bothered," requested to speak to my grandmother; when she granted him audience. He stammered and blundered in such a manner, that it was quite impossible to ascertain what he wanted to speak about; at length out it came – "He had saved a good pinny o' money, and thought it time to settle in life."

"Settle, Mister Benjamin! – why, I always thought you were a settled, sober man. What do you mean?" inquired my grandmother.

"To get married, ma'am;" rousing all his energies to pronounce the fatal sentence."

"Married!" repeated my grandmother; "married! – you, Benjamin Rattin,[485] married at your time of life! – and to whom?"

"I was only eight-and-forty, madam," he replied (drawing himself up), "my last birthday; and, by your lave, I mane to marry Peggy O'Dell."

"Peggy! – you marry Peggy!" She found it impossible to maintain the sober demeanour necessary when such declarations are made. "Mister Benjamin, Peggy is not twenty, gay and giddy as a young fawn; and, I must confess, I should not like her to marry for four or five years. Now, as you certainly cannot wait all that time, I think you ought to think of some one else."

"Your pardon, madam; she is my first, and shall be my last, love. And I know," added the dominie, looking modestly on the carpet, "that she has a tinderness for me."

"What! Peggy a tenderness for you! – poor child! – quite impossible!" said my grandmother; "she never had the tenderness you mean for any living man, I'll answer for it:" and the bell was rung to summon Miss Peggy to the presence.

She entered – blushed and simpered at the first questions put to her: at last my grandmother deliberately asked her, if she had given Mister Ben encouragement at any time – and this she most solemnly denied.

"Oh, you hard-hearted girl you! – did you ever cease laughing from the time I came in till I went out o' the house? – weren't you always smiling at me, and playing your pranks, and – "

"Stop!" said Peggy, at once assuming a grave and serious manner: – "stop; may-be I laughed too much – but I shall cry more, if – (and she fell on her knees at my grandmother's feet) – if ye don't forgive me, mistress, dear – almost the first, sartainly the last, time I shall ever offend you."

"Child, you have not angered me;" replied my grandmother, who saw her emotion with astonishment.

"Oh, yes; but I know best – I have – I have – I know I have! – but I'll never do so more – never – never!" – and she burst into a flood of tears. Poor Master Ben stood aghast.

"Speak," said my grandmother, almost bewildered: "speak, and at once – what have you done?"

"Oh! he over-persuaded me, and said ye'd never consint till it was done; and so we were married, last night, at Judy Ryan's station."[486]

"Married! to whom, in the name of wonder?"

"Oh, Willy – Wandering Willy; but he'll never wander more: he'll be tame and steady, and, to the last day of his life, he'll sarve you and yours; and only forgive me, your poor Peggy, that ye saved from want, and that'll never do the like again – no, never!" The poor girl clasped her hands imploringly, but did not dare to look her mistress in the face. My grandmother rose, and left the room; she was much offended; nor could it be denied that Peggy's conduct was highly improper. The child of her bounty, she had acted with duplicity, and married a man whose unsteady habits promised little for her comfort.

Poor Master Ben! – lovers' sorrows furnish abundant themes for jest and jesters; but they are not the less serious, on that account, to those immediately concerned in *les affaires du cœur*.[487] When he heard the confession that she was truly married, he looked at her for a few minutes, and then quitted the house, determined never to enter it again. Peggy and her husband were dismissed; but a good situation was soon procured for Will, as commander of a small vessel, that traded from Waterford to Bannow, with corn, coal, timber, "and sundries." Contrary to all expectation, he made a kind and affectionate husband.

Winter had nearly passed, and Peggy almost ceased to dread the storms that scatter so many wrecks along our frowning coast. Her little cabin was a neat, cheerful dwelling, in a sheltered nook; and often, during her husband's absence, did she go forth to look out upon the ocean-flood –

"With not a sound beside, except when flew
Aloft the lapwing or the grey curlew;"[488]

and gaze, and watch for his sail on the blue waters. On the occasion to which I refer, he had been long expected home; and many of the rich farmers, who used coal instead of turf, went down to the pier to inquire if the "Pretty Peggy" (so Will called his boat) had come in. The wind was contrary, but, as the weather was fair, no one thought of danger. Soon, the little bark hove in sight, and soon was Peggy at the pier, watching for his figure on deck, or for the waving of hat or handkerchief, the beloved token of recognition: but no such token appeared. The dreadful tale was soon told. Peggy, about to become a mother, was already a widow.

Will had fallen overboard, in endeavouring to secure a rope that had slipped from the side of his vessel; the night was dark, and one deep, heavy splash alone knelled the departure of poor Wandering Willy.

Peggy, forlorn and desolate, suffered the bitter pains of child-birth; and, in a few hours, expired – her heart was broken.

About five years after this melancholy event, I was rambling amongst the tombs and ruins of the venerable church of Bannow. Every stone of that old pile is hallowed to my remembrance; its bleak situation, the barren sand-hills that surround it, and –

"The measured chime, the thundering burst."[489]

of the boundless ocean, always rendered it, in my earliest days, a place of grand and overpowering interest. Even now –

"I miss the voice of waves – the first
That woke my childhood's glee;"[490]

and often think of the rocks, and cliffs, and blue sea, that first led my thoughts "from nature up to nature's God!"[491]

I looked through the high-arched window into the churchyard and observed an elderly man, kneeling on one knee, employed in pulling up the docks and nettles that overshadowed an humble grave, under the south wall. A pale, delicate, little girl quietly and silently watched all he did; and, when no offensive weed remained, carefully scattered over it a large nosegay of fresh flowers, and instructed by the aged man, knelt on the mound, and lisped a simple prayer to the memory of her mother.

It was indeed my old friend, "Master Ben;" the pale child he had long called his – it was the orphan daughter of William and Peggy. His love was not the love of worldlings; despite his outward man it was pure and unsophisticated: it pleased God to give him the heart to be a father to the fatherless. The girl is now the blessing of his old age; and, as he has long since given up his school, he finds much amusement in instructing his adopted child, who, I understand, has already made great progress in his favourite science of numbers.

NORAH CLARY

THE WISE THOUGHT.

She was sitting under the shadow of a fragrant lime tree, that overhung a very ancient well; and, as the water fell into her pitcher, she was mingling with its music the tones of her "Jew's harp," – the only instrument upon which Norah Clary had learned to play. She was a merry maiden of "sweet seventeen;" a rustic belle, as well as a rustic beauty, and a "terrible coquette;" and, as she had what, in Scotland, they call a "tocher," – in England, a "dowry," and in Ireland, a "pretty penny o' money," it is scarcely necessary to state, in addition, that she had – a bachelor. Whether the tune – which was certainly given *in alto*[492] – was, or was not, designed as a summons to her lover, I cannot take upon myself to say; but her lips and fingers had not been long occupied, before her lover was at her side.

"We may as well give it up, Morris Donovan," she said, somewhat abruptly; look, 'twould be as easy to twist the top off the great hill of Howth, as make, father and mother agree about any one thing. They've been playing the rule of contrary these twenty years; and it's not likely they'll take a turn now."

"It's mighty hard, so it is," replied handsome Morris, "that married people can't draw together. Norah, darlint! that wouldn't be the way with us. It's *one* we'd be in heart and sowl, and an example of love and –"

"Folly," interrupted, the maiden, laughing. "Morris, Morris, we've quarrelled a score o' times already; and a bit of a breeze makes life all the pleasanter. Shall I talk about the merry jig I danced with Phil Kennedy, or repeat what Mark Doolen said of me to Mary Grey? – eh, Morris?"

The long black lashes of Norah Clary's bright brown eyes almost touched her low, but delicately pencilled brows, as she looked archly up at her lover – her lip curled with a half-playful, half-malicious smile; but the glance was soon withdrawn, and the maiden's cheek glowed with a deep and eloquent blush, when the young man passed his arm round her waist, and, pushing the curls from her forehead, gazed upon her with a loving, but mournful look.

"Leave joking, now, Norry; God only knows how I love you," he said, in a voice broken by emotion: "I'm yer equal as far as money goes; and no young farmer in the country can tell a better stock to his share than mine; yet I don't pretend to deserve *you*, for all that; only, I can't help saying that, when we love each other (now, don't go to contradict me, Norry, because ye've as good as owned it over and over again), and yer father agreeable, and all, to think that yer mother, just out of *divilment*, should be putting betwixt us for no reason upon earth, only to 'spite' her lawful husband, is what sets me mad entirely, and shows her to be a good-for –"

"Stop, Mister Morris," exclaimed Norah, laying her hand upon his mouth, so as effectually to prevent a sound escaping; "it's *my* mother ye're talking of, and it would be ill-blood, as well as ill-bred, to hear a word said against an own parent. Is that the pattern of yer manners, sir; or did ye ever hear me turn my tongue against one belonging to you?"

"I ask yer pardon, my own Norah," he replied, meekly, as in duty bound; "for the sake of the lamb, we spare the sheep. Why not? – and I'm not going to gainsay but yer mother –"

"The least said's the soonest mended!" again interrupted the impatient girl. "Good even, Morris, and God bless ye; they'll be after missing me within, and it's little mother thinks where I am."

"Norah, above all the girls at wake or pattern, I've been true to you. We have grown together, and since ye were the height of a rose-bush, ye have been dearer to me than anything else on earth. Do, Norah, for the sake of our young heart's love, do think if there's no way to win yer mother over. If ye'd take me without her leave, sure it's nothing I'd care for the loss o' thousands, let alone what ye've got. Dearest Norah, think; since you'll do nothing without her consent, do think – for once be serious, and don't laugh."

It is a fact, universally known and credited in the good barony of Bargy, that Morris Donovan possessed an honest, sincere, and affectionate heart – brave as a lion, and gentle as a dove. He was, moreover, the priest's nephew, – understood Latin as well as the priest himself; and, better even than that, he was the beau – the Magnus Apollo,[493] of the parish; – a fine, noble-looking fellow, that all the girls (from the housekeeper's lovely English neice at Lord Gort's, down to little deaf Bess Mortican, the lame dress-maker) were regularly and desperately in love with: still, I must confess, he was, at times, a little stupid; – not exactly stupid either, but slow of invention, – would *fight* his way out of a thousand scrapes, but could never get *peaceably* out of one. No wonder, then, that, where fighting was out of the question, he was puzzled, and looked to the ready wit of the merry Norah for assistance. It was not very extraordinary that he loved the fairy creature – the sweetest, gayest, of all Irish girls; – light of heart, light of foot, light of eye; – now weeping like a child over a dead chicken, or a plundered nest; then dancing on the top of a hayrick, to the music of her own cheering voice; – now coaxing her termagant[494] mother, and anon comforting her henpecked father. Let no one suppose that I have overdrawn the sketch of my Bannow lass – for, although her native barony is that of Bargy, the two may be considered as wedded and become one. The portraits appended to this story are, at least, veritable, and "from the life."[495] You will encounter such, and such only, in our district – neatly attired, with their white caps, when the day is too warm for bonnets – in short, altogether "well-dressed."

"I'm not going to laugh, Morris," replied the little maid, at last, after a very long pause; "I've got a wise thought in my head for once. His reverence, your uncle, you say, spoke to father – to speak to mother about it? I wonder (and he a priest) that he hadn't more sense! Sure, mother was the man; – but I've got a wise thought. – Good night, dear Morris; good night."

The lass sprang lightly over the fence into her own garden, leaving her lover *perdu*[496] at the other side, without possessing an idea of what her "wise thought" might be. When she entered the kitchen, matters were going on as usual – her mother bustling in style, and as cross "as a bag of weasels."

"Jack Clary," said she, addressing herself to her husband, who sat quietly in the chimney-corner, smoking his *doodeen*, "it's well ye've got a wife who knows what's what! God help me, I've little good of a husband, *barring* the name! Are ye sure Black Nell's in the stable?" The spouse nodded. "The cow and the calf, had they fresh straw?" Another nod. "Bad cess to ye, can't ye use yer tongue, and answer a civil question!" continued the lady.

"My dear," he replied, "sure, one like you has enough talk for ten."

This very just observation was, like most truths, so disagreeable, that a severe storm would have followed, had not Norah stepped up to her father, and whispered in his ear, "I don't think the stable-door *is* fastened." – Mrs. Clary caught the sound, and, in no gentle terms, ordered her husband to attend to the comforts of Black Nell. "I'll go with father myself and see," said Norah. "That's like my own child, always careful," observed the mother, as the father and daughter closed the door.

"Dear father," began Norah, "it isn't altogether about the stable I wanted ye – but – but – the priest said something to ye to-day about – Morris Donovan."

"Yes, darling, and about yerself, my sweet Norry."

"Did ye speak to mother about it?"

"No, darling, she's been so cross all day. Sure, I go through a dale for pace and quietness. If I was like other men, and got drunk and wasted, it might be in rason; but – As to Morris, she was very fond of the boy till she found that *I* liked him; and then, my jewil, she turned like sour milk all in a minute. – I'm afraid even the priest 'll get no good of her."

"Father, dear father," said Norah, "suppose ye were to say nothing about it, good or bad, and just pretend to take a sudden dislike to Morris, and let the priest speak to her himself, she'd come round."

"Out of opposition to me, eh?"

"Yes."

"And let her gain the day, then? – that would be cowardly," replied the farmer, drawing himself up. "No, I won't."

"Father, dear, you don't understand," said the cunning lass: "sure, ye're for Morris; and when we are – that is, if – I mean – suppose – father, you know what I mean," she continued, and luckily the twilight concealed her blushes, – "if that took place, it's *you* that would have yer own way."

"True for ye, Norry, my girl, true for ye; I never thought of that before!" and, pleased with the idea of "tricking" his wife, the old man fairly capered for joy, "But stay a while – stay, asy, asy!" he recommenced; "how am I to manage? Sure the priest himself will be here to-morrow morning early; and he's out upon a station now – so there's no speaking with him; – he's no way quick, either – we'll be bothered entirely if he comes in on a *suddent*."

"Leave it to me, dear father – leave it all to me," exclaimed the animated girl; "only pluck up a spirit, and, whenever Morris's name is mentioned, abuse him – but not with all yer *heart*, father – only from the teeth out."

When they re-entered, the fresh-boiled potatoes sent a warm, curling steam to the very rafters of the lofty kitchen; they were poured out into a large wicker kish, and, on the top of the pile, rested a plate of coarse white salt; noggins of butter-milk were filled on the dresser; and, on a small round table, a cloth was spread, and some delf plates awaited the more delicate repast which the farmer's wife was herself preparing.

"What's for supper, mother?" inquired Norah, as she drew her wheel towards her, and employed her fairy foot in whirling it round.

"Plaguy *snipeens*,"[497] she replied: "bits o'bog chickens, that you've always such a fancy for; – Barney Leary kilt them himself."

"So I did," said Barney, grinning; "and that stick wid a hook, of Morris Donovan's, is the finest thing in the world for knocking 'em down."

"If Morris Donovan's stick touched them, they shan't come here," said the farmer, striking the poor little table such a blow, with his clenched hand, as made not only it, but Mrs. Clary, jump.

"And why so, pray?" asked the dame.

"Because nothing belonging to Morris, let alone Morris himself, shall come into this house," replied Clary; "he's not to my liking any how, and there's no good in his bothering here after what he won't get."

"Excellent!" thought Norah.

"Lord save us!" ejaculated Mrs. Clary, as she placed the grilled snipes on the table, "what's come to the man?" Without heeding his resolution, she was proceeding to distribute the savoury "birdeens,"[498] when, to her astonishment, her usually tame husband threw dish and its contents into the flames; the good woman absolutely stood, for a moment, aghast. The calm, however, was not of long duration. She soon rallied, and commenced hostilities: "How dare you, ye spalpeen, throw away any of God's mate after that fashion, and I to the fore? What do you mane, I say?"

"I mane, that nothing touched by Morris Donovan shall come under this roof; and, if I catch that girl of mine looking at the same side o' she road he walks on, I'll tear the eyes out of her head, and send her to a nunnery!"

"You will! And dare you to say that to my face, to a child o' mine! You will – will ye? – we'll see, my boy! I'll tell ye what, if *I* like, Morris Donovan *shall* come into this house, and, what's more, be master of this house; and that's what *you* never had the heart to be yet, ye poor ould snail!" So saying, Mistress Clary endeavoured to rescue from the fire the hissing remains of the burning snipes. Norah attempted to assist her mother; but Clary, lifting her up, somewhat after the fashion of an eagle raising a golden wren with its claw, fairly put her out of the kitchen. This was the signal for fresh hostilities. Mrs. Clary stormed and stamped; and Mr. Clary persisted in abusing, not only Morris, but Morris's uncle, Father Donovan, until, at last, the farmer's helpmate *swore*, ay, and roundly, too, by cross and saint, that before the next sunset, Norah Clary should be Norah Donovan. I wish you could have seen Norry's eye, dancing with joy and exulta-tion, as it peeped through the latch-hole; – it sparkled more brightly than the richest diamond in our monarch's crown, for it was filled with hope and love.

The next morning, before the sun was fully up, he was throwing his early beams over the glowing cheek of Norah Clary; for her "wise thought" had pros-pered, and she was hastening to the trysting tree,[499] where, "by chance," either morning or evening, she generally met Morris Donovan. I don't know how it is, but the moment the course of true love, "runs smooth,"[500] it becomes very uninteresting, except to the parties concerned. So it is now left for me only to say, that the maiden, after a due and proper time consumed in teazing and tantaliz-ing her intended, told him her saucy plan, and its result. And the lover hastened, upon the wings of love (which I beg my readers clearly to understand are swifter and stronger in Ireland than in any other country), to apprize the priest of the arrangement well knowing that his reverence loved his nephew, and niece that was to be (to say nothing of the wedding supper, and the profits arising there-from), too well, not to aid their merry jest.

What bustle, what preparation, what feasting, what dancing, gave the coun-try folk enough to talk about during the happy Christmas holidays, I cannot now describe. The bride, of course looked lovely, and "sheepish;" and the bride-groom – but bridegrooms are always uninteresting. One fact, however, is worth recording. When Father Donovan concluded the ceremony, before the bridal kiss had passed, Farmer Clary, without any reason that his wife could discover, most indecorously sprang up, seized a shilelah of stout oak, and, whirling it rap-idly over his head, shouted, "Carry me out! by the powers, she's beat! we've won the day! – ould Ireland for ever! Success, boys! she's beat – she's beat!" – The priest, too, seemed vastly to enjoy this extemporaneous effusion, and even the bride laughed outright. Whether the good wife discovered the plot or not, I never heard; but of this I am certain, that the joyous Norah never had reason to repent her "wise thought."

MABEL O'NEIL'S CURSE.

"Where's the good of talking to me of a dance, or any thing of the sort?" said Kathleen Ryley, raising her clear blue eyes to the good-natured countenance of Philip Murphy: "sure ye know my pumps aren't come home – nor, more betokens, won't be till Saturday night; and Saint Patrick himself couldn't cut a step in such brogues as them."

Kate was, in very truth, a frank-hearted, merry girl, with laughing blue eyes, a joyous countenance, and a sweet, love-sounding voice – one whom sorrow had shadowed, but could not cloud. Her father, a respectable farmer, had the misfortune to lose a sensible, industrious wife, when Kathleen was not more than fourteen; leaving him, besides his eldest daughter, five young, troublesome children. Every body pitied Mark Ryley: every body said, "he must marry again; Kate was too young and too giddy to manage such a household." – Everybody, however, was wrong. Mark Ryley did *not* marry again, and Kate *did* manage his household. And, in sooth,[501] it was a beautiful sight – a sight that may be often vainly sought in nobler dwellings – to observe the filial and sisterly tenderness of the simple Irish lass. Kathleen was considered a pretty maiden by all who knew her, and her mother had bestowed extraordinary pains upon her daughter's apparel; but matters changed when the poor woman died; the fine gingham frocks, and Sunday tippets,[502] were cut and manufactured, by Kate's own hands, into holiday dresses for her two little sisters: daily did she send them to the village school, and never permit either to remain at home, to assist her in her labours, which, certainly, were not light. Then her three brothers occasioned her much trouble; such clipping and shaping of jackets – which after all, in fashionable *parlance*,[503] would have been denominated *shapeless* – such patching of shirts, and eternal mending of Sunday stockings! It was at once her pride and pleasure that her father's comforts should be as well cared for as during her mother's lifetime; and, even to the public-house (where it is but justice to state, his visits were seldom made), his daughter's influence extended; for thither would she follow, and so wile him homeward, that the neighbours declared, "of all girls in the world, sweet Kathleen Ryley had the most winning way."

Kathleen did not owe any of her charms to meretricious ornament; her every-day gear was of course striped linsey-woolsey, though its tight-fitting body and short sleeves, it cannot be denied, set off her fine round figure to much advantage; she was seldom guilty of the extravagance of wearing stockings in summer, except on Sundays; but her white muslin kerchief was always delicately clean, neatly mended, and carefully pinned across her bosom. Her light, shining hair – not tortured into curls, but plainly braided to the back of her head, where it was fastened by a small tortoise-shell comb (the only article of finery she possessed, and which, to confess the truth, had been presented to her by no other than Philip Murphy) – she was perhaps, a little vain of.

Philip thought Kate very handsome in her linsey-woolsey gown – very hand-some when washing the face of her troublesome brother, Tom (an obstinate lad of six, lubberly[504] and dirty as any Irish boy need be) – very handsome, when watching to see if her father's pipe wanted lighting, after a hard day's work – or when disrobing him of his "jock coat,"[505] worn only on sabbath or saints' days. Moreover he thought, and no wonder, that she would make a very handsome bride. He had said this, over and over again, both to her and her father; and her father had replied, "that, as they loved each other, and as Philip was well to do in the world, they might be married as soon as they pleased." But the lassie's con-sent was wanting, although his love was the star of her existence.

"When it pleased God (praise be to His holy name, for ever – amen!) to take my poor mother," she would say, in reply to her lover's urgent entreaties for their immediate union – "sure it was all as one as if HE said, 'Katy, machree, be an own mother to them desolate children.' Wait – wait a while, Phil; summer flowers are more plenty than spring ones; the grass will be all the longer, and the blossoms all the sweeter, for a taste o' patience; and Anty will be able to do for my father as well as me, and they'll all have their larning, and the blessing 'll be the more round our own little place, in reason of my having done my duty to the poor orphans."

Such were Kathleen's simple reasons, which, had she been a "high-born ladye," would have called down the applause of an admiring world. As it was, Kate had the approbation of her own conscience, and the increased affection of the heart she so dearly prized – for Philip could not but value more highly the girl who possessed principles so exalted and self-denying.

I must now revert to the humble dialogue with which my story commenced.

"The dickons himself carry all shoemakers, say I!" replied young Murphy; "he might have finished the pumps long enough ago, if he had a mind; to have such nate little feet as them in such vagabone brogueens,[506] sure it's too bad intirely; – but it's always the way, you grudge yerself every dacent tack that goes on your back, let alone yer feet; – well, 'twon't be always so – for, when ye're Mistress Phil Murphy, there shan't be a better dressed girl in the parish, of a small farmer's wife. Any way, you shan't lose the dance, Kate: for 'tisn't more than two miles across the bog to my sister's, and I'll borrow her shoes for ye – and sure she'll be proud to lend 'em. Good bye," he continued, as he left the cottage, "God's blessing be about ye always, my own coushla!"

"He's an honest boy, and a dacent, and, by the same token, a handsome one, too," soliloquized Kathleen, as she peeped through a chink in the cottage wall; then fastening the door, by letting down the latch, and pulling in the latch-string, she began arranging her dress for the dance which the borrowed slippers would enable her to attend. The snowy stockings were carefully drawn on – the white petticoat and open chintz-cotton gown neatly arranged – and her beautiful hair plaited round the tortoise-shell comb, so as to display it to the best advantage: nor will I deny (for my heroine was a true woman) that she gazed upon her own image, as reflected in the cracked looking-glass, with much self-satisfaction. Her meditations were, however, soon interrupted by a smart knock at the cottage entrance, impatiently repeated. "He can't be there yet – let alone back," she thought as she lifted the latch, where, to her no small astonishment, a very different person anxiously waited admittance. A tall, gaunt woman, whose wild and fierce appearance painfully contrasted with the mild beauty of the evening landscape, from which the last beams of the setting sun were gently departing, leaned against the door-post. Her form was partly shrouded in a tattered cloak, which, fastened by a wooden skewer to the throat, wrapped the figure to the knees; a stout leathern belt passed across one shoulder, from which a dirty canvass bag was suspended, containing the dole of meal, potatoes, grits, or whatever the kind-hearted peasantry could spare from their meagre store; her feet were bare – the scanty petticoat reached nearly to the ankles, whose masculine proportions told of extraordinary strength; her skin, eyes, and hair, almost betokened foreign origin, yet her features were remarkable for the shrewd, observant character peculiar to the inhabitants of the south of Ireland; her brow was low and projecting, and her sunken eyes appeared condensed, as it were, into the expression of a deep and malignant hatred towards all the human race – but, when excited by the active passions of rage or revenge, they flashed with the rapidity, and almost the brilliancy, of lightning; her head-tire[507] consisted simply of a kerchief knotted under the chin, which could not be said to confine her dark, matted locks, while it added much to the wildness of her appearance. The peaceable cotters considered Mabel O'Neil as a sort of wild woman, and, in truth, ceded to her the rights of hospitality more in fear than in love; for it was often whispered that, to the lawless, she was not only an adviser, but an accomplice; and many things were said of "Mad Mabel," in her absence, that it would require a good deal of courage even to think of when she was present. Kathleen, contrary to her country's usage, of opening wide the portal when a stranger seeks admittance, still held it, and almost trembled when the woman's eye rested upon her with its usual expression. Without speaking she stretched forth her bony arm, and pushed the door so forcibly, that it swung out of Kate's hand; then she advanced her right foot inside the threshold, and, eyeing the maiden with much bitterness, said:

"And that's yer fine breeding, is it, Katy Ryley? – to stand staring at an aged woman, *outside* the door-cheek![508] – at one whose head is grey – whose feet are sore – whose lips are dry – whose bag is empty – who has neither kin nor friend near, to say 'God save ye!' – nor a stick or a stone to set her mark upon – where she may lay down her bones and die!"

"Come in, Mabel O'Neil, and welcome," responded Kathleen, hesitatingly – "sure, agra, it was only the want of thought."

"Silence!" interrupted Mabel, stalking forward, "silence, girl! – it is too soon for *you* to have a lie on your lip; the time will come – *must* come to you, as well as to yer betters, when it 'll sit as easy there as upon the lip of e'er a lady in the land."

She sat down upon a three-legged stool, near the chimney-corner, and Kathleen filled her a noggin of fresh milk, and presented with it that luxury of Irish life – a piece of white bread. The woman pushed the refreshment from her. "It's not come to that wid Mad Mabel yet," she muttered, in a half-audible voice; "to ate the begrudged bit and drink the begrudged sup."

"Take it, Mabel," persisted the good-hearted Kate, her pity, excited by the worn-out appearance of the wild woman, conquering her fear – "pray do; and I'll get you a *shock*[509] of father's new tobacco, and bathe yer feet, that I see are sore and cut – the crathurs! – Do take it."

I have often thought the music of Orpheus[510] consisted solely in sounds of kindness, addressed to the woodland savages; its power over the animated world is little short of magic. Even that wayward and crime-worn creature could not resist the persuasive gentleness of Kathleen's words. She took the wooden vessel from her hand, and, peering into her face, said, "It's a pity to look upon ye, ye young fool, and to think that, though the lightning may spare ye, the canker won't. I shouldn't have been angry wid yer mother's daughter – who knew me before sin – ay, first sin, then sorrow – black, bitter, stormy sorrow – came over me, and changed me from the light, proud – ay, 'twas the pride that did it – but it's not asy talking of them things."

She paused, and looked moodily on the embers of the turf fire; then finished, at one draught, the milk which Kate had given her, and turned her gaze upon the maiden, who endeavoured, in vain, to arrange the remainder of her village dress under the influence of the woman's ken.

"Did ye never hear," she said, addressing her, after a long silence, – "did ye never hear tell of the countries beyant seas, where a sarpent[511] jist fixes his eye upon an innocent bird, and it trembles – trembles – till it falls into its mouth? Kathleen Ryley, you are now, for all the world, like that bird, and I like that other thing; – but never heed my cronauning. Come here, to my side, and listen. You know 'Squire Johnson – the *justice, as he's called* – and ye have a sort of a regard for the young lady, yer foster-sister – she's a fair flower; but the curse o' the free-hearted is over them, like a thunder-cloud, and a worse curse than *that* even over *him*, and it'll burst this very night. And who *will* escape it, unless *you* bestir yourself, and warn them of their danger! – and it's little time there is for that same. See," and she pointed with her finger to the glowing west, "the sun has sunk this midsummer evening, in red, red glory – but the burning of their house will be as bright before the clock goes twelve this blessed night!"

"Holy Father!" exclaimed the girl, crossing herself devoutly. "Mabel O'Neil, for the sake o' the mercy you expect –"

"I expect mercy!" interrupted the woman, with a fearful laugh, which brought the rumour of her insanity fully to the remembrance of the young Kathleen; "I, the banned, the blighted woman! – yes – this mercy–here!" She threw off her cloak, and bent her almost fleshless figure forward. "Shall I tear away these *skreeds*, and show you the mercy of the scourgings I got in Dublin? Shall I show you the mercy of five stabs in this withered bosom, when I spread wide my arms to save my husband's life? Shall I tell ye of the mercy showed by a heretic justice to my starving childer? – to one – my brave, brave boy – to myself, when I clung by the black ship's side, that was bearing him to the land o' shame, jist to give him my last blessing – their *mercy* knocked me on the head, as if I was a thing of stone! Oh!" she continued, shrieking wildly, and pressing her hands on her temples, "I feel it now; and his last, last look, is ever before me!"

Kathleen's gentle feelings sympathized with the unfortunate creature; and when the paroxysm of her anguish abated, and she saw tears streaming between her fingers, again she spoke to her in gentle tones, mingling her soothing words with entreaties to be informed of the probable fate that awaited Mr. Johnson's house and property.

"Ay, it's for that ye care, and not for me," said the woman, at last, groaning heavily; "if I warn off this burning, 'tis not for the sake o' *mercy*, but because I know the boys are so beset, by the cowardly red-coats, that, before their job 'ud be half done, they'd be powdered down upon,[512] and kilt at once, and, after all, no good done; – and there's one, too, I wish to save from ever feeling what racks me to think upon; but that you can't understand; and moreover, I've a love for the house, that I knew but too well when the present man was nothin' but a bit of an agent to the ancient proprietor. Oh, it would destroy me intirely, to see the ruin of the place in which I spent my innocent days! And often, when my heart's full of what ye'd think could never enter into woman's bosom, I see a glimpse of the white chimleys, or, may-be, the ould turret itself, above the trees; and I cry, and the scalding tears take the venom out o'me; and then I can pray. Child! child! – there are many sorts o' tears; some that come burning from the brain; others that save the heart from bursting!" She paused, and crossed her hands on her bosom; then, resting her eyes on the ground, continued in a subdued tone, – "May-be, I've other reasons, too; only, if a warning could be sent to the 'Squire, the boys would get the wind o' the word, and not attempt it, knowing that he'd be ready for them; and so both one and other 'ud be saved; for the time's past when they could ha' rid the country o' these beggarly Cromelians.[a] [513] And nothin' can be done for a while, any way – I tould 'em this – and more; but I'm ould now, and they never heed me."

"Why didn't ye tell it at the 'Squire's yerself?" interrupted the maiden.

"Do you indeed think me mad?" replied the woman angrily. "D'ye think there's a big tree, or a grey stone, about the place, that, when such things are a-foot, doesn't hide a living watch? And when did ye see the descendant of Irish kings darken, as a beggar, the door of the usurping English?" She stood erect on the cottage floor, and looked around her with mingled pride and wildness.

"How am I to reach the house alive, if it's beset in that way?" said Kathleen, giving utterance to her fears: "I'll jist wait for Phil Murphy, and we'll go together."

The woman laughed a mad laugh. "For Philip Murphy is it? – why he's the ouldest united man[514] of the set! – that's taking a lawyer to guide ye to heaven, sure enough!"

"'Tis false!" retorted Kathleen, her eyes flashing, and her cheek crimsoning; "'tis false! Philip Murphy would scorn to be a night-walker.[515] He has no communion with sich ways – I know he hasn't. And I am – "

"A fool!" interrupted Mabel. "I tell you he *has*; and, if he's caught, he'll be hung – and small loss!"

"Ye're a bad woman, Mabel O'Neil, and I don't care for your wicked looks a bit now; but I'll make a liar of ye – that I will! – to slander a dacent boy after such fashion! I'll go, this minute, to 'Squire Johnson's; and, if any harm happens me – if I'm murdered outright – I'll follow ye night and day, and –"

"That's my thanks for saving the worthless lives o' yer fine friends, and, maybe, of yer bachelor! Ay, go – go; but stop, as ye hope to live and do well; take some eggs in this basket – anything, *as a cloak*; and swear never – but I needn't make you promise – none of ye ever turned *informer*."

Poor Kathleen did as she was desired; resumed the despised brogues; and, without speaking another word, or being able even to arrange her thoughts, took the path she had, with very different feelings, watched her lover pursue, about half an hour before. The hag, who had caused so much consternation, was again re-seated, and rocking herself over the embers of the fire; in a few moments, muttering some words of unknown import, she lit her pipe, and, slowly rising, departed from the cottage in an opposite direction to that which Kathleen had taken.

It would be difficult to describe the various feelings that agitated the bosom of poor Kate, as she thought of Philip, and his uniform correctness of conduct;

and, although she had not the intuitive horror of illegal meetings that an English girl of her age would have possessed, yet she feared for his safety; and the idea of danger to him was more than she could bear. Could she, by any means in her power, prevent his joining the party that night? She knew that, the alarm once given, Mr. Johnson had a sufficient number of partisans in the country to identify, at all events, some of the conspirators, and the beloved of her heart might thus be covered with shame. Should she avoid discovering the plot to the 'Squire's family? She shuddered to think of the dreadful result; and the remembrance of her delicate foster-sister – the hours they had spent together in their infancy, rambling by the silver stream – or, amid the bending grain, seeking the scarlet poppy, and the blue cornflower; – or, in riper years, the numberless times she had climbed the forked trees, to gather, for the lady-playmate, the early blossoming sloe, or the golden laburnum – the look of affectionate thankfulness, with which the prize was received, came again upon her; and she hastened her steps to save one whom she had ever loved.

The ties of fosterage in Ireland, are frequently stronger than those of kindred; the foster-sister or brother remains, through life, the devoted friend – the faithful ally – the obedient servant. In adversity, they shield and succour; and in prosperity, like the humble and affectionate woodbine, what they cannot aid or support, they cling to, and perfume by the odour of devoted tenderness.

"May the Holy Mother direct me!" thought Kate, as she passed into a pathway that led to a continuation of corn-fields, rich in their young greenery; and, as she looked beyond them on the solitary landscape, her eye found nought to rest upon, indicative of human habitation, save a long barn, which had been constructed as a safe place to stow corn in, during rainy weather, before it could be conveniently lodged in the hag-yard. It was a strong building, with a widely-opening gate or door; lonely in its situation, though many a harvest home had been held within its walls. On Kate journeyed, with a firmer step, but an aching heart, until, moving in the distance towards her, she saw a figure, which she instantly recognised as that of her lover.

"Kate, darling!" he exclaimed, bounding forward: "Kate, darling! what brought ye this road? Kate! What ails my colleen? Kathleen ! – why do ye shrink from me, your own Philip?" He passed his arm round her waist, feeling, and almost hearing, the quick throbbings of her heart. She struggled nobly with her agitation, while conflicting ideas rushed through her brain, scorching and rapid as lightning. But soon, with the ready wit of woman, she exclaimed, "Just lead me to that barn-door, and I can sit awhile on the stone that's beside it – I'll soon come round, Phil." – He placed her on the stone; and, when she looked on his kind and anxious countenance, hardly could she imagine that he was linked with those whose thirst was for blood.

"The stone is could, Phil," she said, after a pause.

"Bad manners to me, that didn't think of that afore, Katy, darling! Sure I can get ye a nice clean lock o' straw, off the hurdles[516] inside, to sit upon, if I can only pull this great *kipeen* out of the hasp."

No sooner said than done; the "*kipeen*" was extracted; but, while Philip was making his way to the hurdles, that were at the farthermost end of the building, Kathleen rushed to the door, closed and hasped it, restoring the fastening-stick to its old situation, and hammering it down with all her might. Having ascertained that it was firmly fixed, she flew along her path, almost with the lightness and rapidity of a startled lapwing, leaving Philip Murphy in, what she considered, safe custody, for that night at least. "Thank God!" she exclaimed, as the turrets and chimneys of the old mansion, that Mabel O'Neil had so loved, appeared through the twilight: then, pausing for breath, she raised her clasped hands to heaven, and again repeated, in an earnest tone, "Thank God!" adding, still more fervently, "I *will* save all."

The gable end of the house rested against the ruins of one of those castles of the Elizabethan age, so generally scattered over Ireland; and the chamber window of Caroline Johnson, set, as it were, in the castle wall, overlooked a wild and variegated scene of hill and valley; while one of the most beautiful of Irish rivers bounded, as with a band of molten silver, the distant meadows.

Caroline had often gazed upon this sweet and varying landscape; and a good deal of romance, produced, perhaps, by the surrounding scenery, mingled with her natural character, which, otherwise, would have been more regulated and reserved than that of the generality of her fair countrywomen. She might be considered alone amid the people, such as they were, with whom she associated – a garden flower blossoming unwillingly amongst wild and uncultivated weeds. She was the youngest and the only surviving child of her father's house, and many wondered how so graceful a stem could have sprung from such a root.

The long French casement of this fair girl's dwelling, with its white draperies and roseate fringe, but ill accorded with the time-worn stones and mouldering battlements of the old castle; while the roses, which she cultivated in the deep embrasure of the walls, shed their perfume and their beauty over the gigantic ivy and many-coloured lichens. As Kate passed under this favoured window, she looked up, and saw her beloved foster-sister, as usual, busied among her plants. Placing her foot on a slight projection, she seized an overhanging branch, and, after one or two successful springs, performed with all the agility of a free- footed Irish lass, stood, eggs and all, on the rustic balcony, to the no small surprise of her young lady. When a few minutes had elapsed, and Kate's feelings had vented themselves in tears, as quickly as possible she informed her friend of the object of her mission.

"Ye see, Miss Car'line, it's what they want is to murder, burn, and destroy every mother's soul of the whole of ye – and there's no time to be lost; for look – the red flame beams from Knock Mountain,[517] which is as bad as the devil's watchword

– God save us! Whenever *that* fire lights, you may be sure mischief's going on; – and there is a long story about that same mountain, which I'll tell ye some day or other; only now, Miss Car'line, be quick, and away to the master, for there's no time to lose – and the heart within me sinks when I think of the danger."

This sensible advice was soon followed, and arrangements were as quickly made for defence. The house, in common with many in the county Carlow, at the time to which I allude, was well prepared – the men servants were immediately armed, and a half-witted, but cunning and faithful retainer, was despatched secretly to the next police station, to give the necessary information.

Miss Johnson would not, of course, permit Kathleen to hazard a return to her cottage that evening; and, as she often remained with "her young lady," the circumstance was not likely to excite suspicion. She, however, stayed in her foster-sister's room, and employed her fingers, almost mechanically, in telling over the beads that had been her mother's; her thoughts – uncontrollable wanderers – doubtless visiting Philip and her father; and never did Persian worshippers pray more fervently for the presence of their deity, than did both females for the speedy approach of morning.

At length, weak and nervous from watching, Miss Johnson fancied she could sleep. "Can you plait my hair, Kathleen?" she inquired, as the withdrawn band unfastened the long tresses that fell, in rich clusters, over her polished shoulders.

"Sure I can; I always do my own – not that I'd be after comparing them," replied the maiden, as she slipped the rosary on her arm, and prepared to divide the silken hair.

"But I interrupt your prayers."

"Oh, no consequence in life, that, Miss! it's jist a nice employment when I've nothin' particular to do; and a comfort, somehow, to be thinking that, in the *hoight* o' trouble and dismay, the Lord's ear is always open to me, to say nothin' o' the holy saints, and others. Besides," she added, sighing deeply, "I always say my prayers best on the beads of my poor mother (God be good to her!) – when I lay my fingers to them, it's jist as if she was with me herself."

"After all, Kate, you must be a happy girl; you have nothing to trouble you – no world to please, no –"

"Oh, Miss, machree! it's little ye know if ye think that; sure there's my father to plase, and the childer to look after, and –"

"Philip Murphy to look after," added Miss Johnson, glancing at her attendant: who, it may easily be imagined, had not breathed a word, even to her lady, of the barn adventure, or her suspicions concerning Philip. Kate's fingers trembled, and she soon converted what had commenced as a three, into a five, plait; so that, at last, Miss Johnson's patience was exhausted, and she could not avoid saying, "I know you are tangling my hair, Kathleen." As she looked in the glass, that reflected the figures of both, the trifling displeasure she had felt was instantly removed on observing that large tear-drops chased each other down the poor girl's cheeks.

"No coolness between you and your bachelor, I hope, Kathleen?" she added, in her kindest voice.

"Oh, Miss, Miss!" replied Kate, clasping her hands with painful earnestness, "do not ask me; I can say nothin' about him till after the morrow – oh, do not ask me!" She then, without uttering another word, flung herself on her knees, and told over the beads with all possible rapidity, as if haste afforded relief to her overcharged heart. At this moment, the contrast between the two girls, so different in rank and appearance, would have been highly interesting to any painter of feeling and sentiment: – Miss Johnson, part of whose unbraided hair hung negligently around her, pressed her forehead to her hand; and, as her long, pencilled lashes almost rested on the soft roundness of her delicate cheek, the lustre of her clear blue eyes was intercepted by fast-coming tears, that hung like drops of dew on the gossamer webs of morning. She might have reminded one of that exquisite passage in Shelley –

> "She moved upon this earth a shape of brightness,
> A power, that from its objects scarcely drew
> One impulse of her being – in her lightness
> Most like some radiant cloud of morning dew,
> Which wanders through the waste air's pathless blue
> To nourish some far desert:
>
>   * * * * *
>
> Like the bright shade of some immortal dream
> Which walks, when tempest sleeps, the wave of life's dark stream."[518]

How frequently, in a crowded picture-gallery, do we pass, almost without notice, some exquisite gem of art, that, singly, in an unadorned chamber, we should gaze upon with rapture! Woman, to be loved, and valued as she deserves, must be seen and known in solitude – I had almost added, in sorrow. The lily's fragrance is of more value when it blossoms and sheds its perfume in the wilderness, than when only one amid a multitude of flowers.

Another hour had passed, and her slight and graceful figure still reclined on the arm of an old-fashioned, high-backed chair; the full light of a painted glowing lamp fell, in all its brightness and varied hues, upon her beautifully-shaped head; her form was the perfection of symmetry, yet shaped in so fairy a mould that, in their youthful days, Kathleen used to boast she could carry Miss Caroline a mile in one hand, and never knew she was there. Kate's round, red arms, sun-burnt skin, as she knelt with her back to the light – her tight, trim figure, and rustic dress, showed strangely, combined with the apartment and its mistress.

Still she industriously told her beads; and, as her young lady gazed upon her, she pondered many a painful thought on what might be the destiny of both. "Poor girl!" she ejaculated, "I thought that you, at least, would have been happy. So good a daughter; so undyingly attached to one of your own people – to one, too, of a kind and gentle character ! Why is it? (and her fair brow lowered and gloomed, as her thoughts proceeded); – why is it – the feeling that unfolds as womanhood advances, even as the petals of the blushing rose expand to the sun, which at first glows and encourages, but, when the fragrance is extracted, and the canker has entered through their folded leaves, scorches, into a loathed mass of fadedness, what its rays at first had cherished – why is it that it leads to misery, and yet we nourish it within our bosom?" She raised her head, and shook it, as if to dispel such painful feeling; but was again relapsing, as the working of her features plainly showed, into the same train of thought, when a volley of musketry, followed by a shout from the plantations, alarmed both the lady and the peasant; instinctively they clung to each other, when a second, from its proximity, terrified them still more. Kathleen supported Miss Johnson to her bed, and resumed her kneeling position at its side; again, all was silence.

The cool, grey light of morning streamed upon the pale and slumbering lids of the young lady; soon, however, her father's voice called upon her to arise. "It is eight o'clock, Carry, and I am going to have an examination of some prisoners brought in this morning; you have now an opportunity of seeing, in safety, who these rascals are."

She descended to the long, rambling hall, where her father was already seated in due formality; his little rotund person exalted on a high chair of dignity, corresponding with the occasion. Mr. Johnson's eye, in general, bore the expression of calm severity, but, when aroused, indicated fierce and dangerous passion; his mouth was the redeeming feature of his countenance – its formation full, and even tender – and his smile (when it came) sweetness itself. This singular physiognomy, perhaps, led to the following remarks from two gossiping servants, who stood at the lower end of the hall.

"Och! and it's himself that carries the oak-stick[519] between his eyes, any way."

"Hould your whisht, Nilly! – sure it's his honour that bangs the world for the *crame o' sweet smiles*, when he has a mind."

"*Sour crame*, I'm thinkin'," retorted the other; "but how pale the young mistress looks, this morning!" she continued, as Caroline and her humble companion appeared on the stairs. "Well, sure the master has sweetness enough while he has that darlint; no pride in her – see how she puts her fosterer's hand under her arm, as if she was a lady! – why, Katey Ryley is as pale as herself, only her skin is another colour."

From the spot where Miss Johnson stood, when these remarks were made, a group of Irish motley was presented. "The man in authority," seated in the high-backed chair, at the foot of the staircase – a huge table before him, on which was piled a large collection of law-books, in dingy covers. At his right hand, on a low chair (which, being seated thereon, prevented his chin rising much beyond a level with the table), appeared Denny, Dennis, or, *classically* speaking, Dionysius Flannery, the beetle-browed butler and clerk of the house of Johnson – employed in wiping the ink out of his pen on the cuff of his coat, previous to rendering the same fit for service. Long foolscap lay before him; nor must I forget the well thumbed prayer-book, kissed, many a time and oft, by the false and the true. Dionysius was, or, at least, considered himself, a man of learning, having travelled, as a poor scholar, the wilds of the kingdom of Kerry, and officiated as head-master in the hedge-school of Glen-Moyle.[520] He consequently opined that Mr. Johnson had secured a perfect treasure in his person. Towards the centre, the police-sergeant – a tall, lanky fellow, with a shock-head of red, rough hair, and eyes that set at defiance all direct rules – stood a little in advance, ready to swear to the depositions that had been already taken. Farther back, some four or five policemen kept their hands on their arms, notwithstanding that two of the prisoners were firmly manacled. One of these, a slight, trembling old man, stood, so as to shield his face from the observation of "the gentry;" the other absolutely grinned with an appearance of savage good-nature on the proceedings; while the third, whom everybody recognized as "Hurling Moriarty of Ballinla," leaned, with folded arms, against a pillar, now glancing at the magistrate, and then at the crowd, which nearly filled the hall, and extended beyond the opened door to the lawn, and even the plantations in front; it consisted chiefly of men – some with coats – some without; a few females, eager to ascertain the nature of the proceedings, had left their cabins before their hair was snooded, or their cloaks fastened; but the prominent features of the accumulating assembly manifested anxiety and uneasiness, and their murmurs and surmises were, at times, more than half audible; even the countenances of the police, who were scattered amid the throng, expressed the same feeling – the same agitation. Moriarty might have served as the model of an Hercules; his appearance bespoke strength – his bearing, fearlessness – compressed lips – dark and penetrating eyes – the *contour* evincing more than common genius, and – alas! that it should be so! – more than common vice! When his lips parted, they parted in scorn, a movement that was particularly evident as his glance rested on the rotund magistrate. His hat had not been taken off on entering the presence; but when the young lady descended, and took the seat prepared for her, a little behind her father, the covering was instantly removed, and the figure resumed a respectful position.

"Police-sergeant Smith," commenced the justice, "what is the reason that one prisoner, whom, I regret to say, has so often, I understand, appeared elsewhere, under disgraceful circumstances, should be unmanacled?"

"Plaze yer honour," replied the sapient sergeant, "we are always wishful to avoid the shedding of blood; and so, knowing that if this honest man –"

"What do you mean by calling such a scoundrel an honest man in my presence?" interrupted the magistrate, angrily.

"I ax yer honour's pardon; I didn't mean to call any one here an honest man; only ye see in regard of Hurling Morty's always being known to keep his word, either for good or bad; and, says he – I'll give you my honour as a gentleman, says he, that I'll not stir hand or fut, only walk aisy into the hall, if ye don't offer to tie me, says he."

"That wasn't all the rason, though, ye slip o' hazel!" exclaimed the Hurler, casting a scornful look at the poor sergeant; "you *couldn't* tie me – no, nor tin of ye together – though ye trapped me as if I was a fox or a weasel; but I have no fear of coming here, for you can prove nothin' agin me; – and –"

"Sure he murdered me intirely; – me, yer worship !" shouted a little policeman, in the corner, who, by dint of fist and elbows, was trying to make his way through the crowd: "he *hot* me right over the head – I'll swear it, your honour."

"Put that down, my fine penman – that I *hot* him over the head," observed Moriarty, addressing the clerk; "it's down, is it? – *over* the head? Well, now, ye little, miserable, half-starved morsel, that it would be insult even to the trade, such as it is, that owns ye, to call a *tailor* – ye're parjured! He says I *hot* him *over* the head, yer honour; I can prove that it was *on* the head – a fair, firm rap, just to see if it had any brains in it; I'd scorn to hit anything *over* the head!"

The mob enjoyed the jest – the little policeman groaned; while another of the party exclaimed, "Hould yer prate, Barney! – It's asy talking wid ye; – plaze yer worship, he made a fair riddle o' me for the moon to shine through, just wid one stroak of his sledge of a fist."

"Och! and what will I do intirely? – and the sight of my two good-looking eyes as dark as a dungeon, wid the tratement I got from him, and he on his back at t'other side the ring-fence, after we tripped him – the grate monster!" vociferated a third.

"Ye're all a pack of false-swearing Peelers,"[521] exclaimed an old woman; "sure it's himself that wasn't there at all, at all, as I'm ready to prove, if it's truth ye're after, and *not law*, but –"

"Silence in the court, I say!" shouted Dionysius Flannery; "were ye niver before a magistrate, till now, ye unrooly pack? Listen, while I read the deposition to his worship."

The deposition set forth, in quaint Irish phraseology – "that, being aware that seditious organization (of course Miss Johnson had taken care that Kathleen should not be suspected as the informant), and a most horrible plan for burning and murder were meditated, Police-sergeant Smith, with collected

forces, dispersed around Cairn Castle – that, skulking behind the new plantation, they discovered and took prisoner, Moriarty Sullivan – ”

"That's one lie; and the skulking's another!" exclaimed Morty, in a deep, firm
voice; "ye didn't *take* me; ye *snared* me, as ye would a hare!"

"Mighty like a hare ye are!" replied another policeman, whose head was
bound in a stocking: "plaze yer honour's glory, he knocked us clane about like
young goslings, until little Mike Corish and big Kit, and another boy (big Kit's
father, by the same token), got a piece o' the road afore him, and threw a rope
on the ground; and, ye see, he was bating the boys with his pike-handle, and
his baste of a gun (he hadn't time but for one volley yer worship – backwards),
whin we tripped him up, and, before he could say 'Munster,' we had the half of
him – his legs – axing yer pardon – safe, – seeing we twishted and twishted the
cable round it – ”

"Silence!" again vociferated Dionysius, while stifled expressions of – "unfair!"
– "beggarly Peelers!" – "cursed Orangemen!" – "fine boy!" – "more's the pity!" –
and such like, murmured amid the crowd.

"Took prisoners, Moriarty Sullivan," recommenced the clerk, "Phelim Mc
Gunn, and Philip Murphy – ”

"'Tis false!" shrieked Kathleen, rushing from behind Miss Johnson's chair
(where she had hitherto leaned, a mute but most anxious spectator of the proceedings), and confronting the astonished Dinny – "I say, I know 'tis false! Philip
Murphy was not – could not – have been there! I – I myself locked – "Almost
stifled by agitation, she paused for a moment, and then, with firmness, added, "If
you took him, where is he?"

"Here, agra!" squeaked the trembling little old man, "to my sorrow, a coushla – God break hard fortune!" Poor Kathleen staggered towards the crowd
– looked, for a moment, on the namesake of her lover – and a faint laugh sprang
to her lip, as she fell senseless into the arms of those who were nearest to her.

"There's Kate Ryley's own Philip Murphy running like mad!" exclaimed a
neighbour. On the instant, the young man entered the hall, evidently much dis-
composed, and unable to comprehend the proceedings; and as he stood, for a
moment, in the glory of excited and youthful beauty, beside the aged person
who it was now understood, bore the same name, the contrast between the two
turned instantly the quick current of Irish feeling, and a merry burst of laughter
shook the oaken rafters, even while the sounds of execration lingered round the
walls. The attention of the police being momentarily diverted, Philip Murphy,
senior, got rid of his nervous affection, and managed also to get rid, in some
unaccountable way, of the vile bonds which, it is to be suspected, too slightly
restrained his motions. Swift as Robin Hood's own arrow, the *ci-devant*[522] old
man darted through the assembly, which out of pure love of what they considered "fair play," facilitated his escape. Away he flew, amid the applauding and

encouraging cheers of the peasantry, and the yells of the police. "Fire! Dead or alive, bring him back!" shouted the magistrate, descending from his chair of state. "Ye'd better take heels after him yerself," said Moriarty, in a scornful tone, as he looked down upon the worthy 'Squire, who went stumping past him.

"Fetch his honour Pangandrum's boots,[523] can't ye," observed another, "to lengthen his legs a bit?" "Look to these two fellows immediately!" interrupted the enraged justice, while his face bloated and swelled like a turkey-cock angered at the sight of a scarlet cloak. "No need in life for the trouble," replied Moriarty; "I said I wouldn't run, nor I'm not going to *demane* myself. I scorn a lie as much, and may-be more, as e'er a lord in the three kingdoms.[524] Sorra a thing ye can prove agin me, *this* turn, that 'ill keep me in more than three months – though I'd rather it was four; for it's little I can be after these summer evenings, when the nights are so short and so light, and the sun keeps blinking about a dale longer than he ought, if he knew manners." The latter part of this speech was lost upon Mr. Johnson, who had hurried forward to the hall-door, where a wild and singular scene presented itself. The rapidity with which "Phil Murphy, of Tullagh," already recognized as "Swift-footed Phil," a fearless, and, consequently, popular rapparee, proceeded, was even less wonderful than the evenness of his steps; and the sort of flying, swallow-like motion which he kept up, as he bowled along the smooth greensward, and sprang, with the lightness of a bird, over the bounds-ditch that terminated the ancient lawn. While his pursuers were scrambling up and down the tangled enclosure, the culprit made rapid way, first through a clover field, then across the undulating ridges of a potato enclosure, rich in its lilac and orange blossoms. "Fire on him!" again vociferated Mr. Johnson; and the long sandy sergeant took aim, fired, and wounded – not him of the swift foot, but a favourite horse of the 'Squire's, that had strayed, in search of forbidden food, into the enclosure. "Och! may ye iver have the same luck!" exclaimed several peasant-voices at once; while "swift-footed Phil," without lessening his speed, threw up his old white wig, in triumph, and then the *cooleen*[525] of dark hair, released from its confinement, fell, in abundant tresses, over his throat and shoulders. At the bottom of the potato-field ran a narrow but deep stream, a branch of the river I have before alluded to, the depth and rapidity of which had been greatly increased by recent rains. Into it, however, the daring robber plunged, swam like an otter, and, in a few moments, was on the opposite side. "The coble! – the coble!" exclaimed one of the police. They ran towards an old willow, where it was moored, although the thickness of its branches effectually concealed the little boat from their sight, as the leafy screen seemed rooted in the waters. Before they reached it, however, to their utter discomfiture, it glided from its moorings, guided by no other than our old acquaintance, Mabel O'Neil, chanting, as she waved and kissed her hand, with mock solemnity, to the "men at arms," a verse of an old ballad –

> "The boat and the water
>   Were made for the free;
> The gaol and the city
>   Are fitter for ye."[526]

Those who could swim, would not; those who would, could not. Some, who fancied they were competent to the undertaking, got soused and bemired, as a punishment for their temerity, and received the jests of a merciless multitude, including all the barelegged urchins – all the barking and snapping of collies – the taunting of every age and sex, who delighted in beholding the men of law and the men of war outwitted. The beldame[527] floated slowly with the stream, still singing snatches of an old melody, waving her bony arms in wild and fearful attitudes, and intimating, by her gestures, the most perfect contempt for those who failed in their attempts to arrest her progress. "Curse the hag!" muttered Johnson, enraged at all the morning's occurrences, "she's acting in concert with that fellow, and ought to smart for it. Smith, you're a famous shot; couldn't you skim the water, hit the crazy boat, and give the old devil a ducking?" "As easy as kiss my hand, sir," replied the ruffian, calmly arranging his piece for the purpose. As his finger rested on the trigger, one of the peasants struck the gun with his stick, evidently anxious to avert the shot from its intended object.

The movement was unfortunate; for the piece went off, and the old woman, uttering an agonizing scream, nearly fell over the edge of the boat. "Good God!" exclaimed Mr. Johnson, his better feelings, for a moment, triumphing, "you have struck the woman!" Urged now by their naturally kind and active feelings, the peasantry rushed into the water, and soon guided the coble and its helpless freight to the rushy margin of the water; it was sad to see the dark-red stream which trickled down its side, and left a dismal track upon the rippling wave, as they dragged it to the shore."

"I always thought it would end this way," said the dying woman, while speculation faded from her eyes, and the glaze of death appeared beneath their distended lids. "There, boys; the only thing ye can do for Mabel O'Neil now, is to carry her up to the ould castle, and let her draw her last breath within its walls."

Mr. Johnson advanced towards the party who were preparing to obey her directions, though it is impossible to know whether he intended to forbid or to command that those directions should be fulfilled.

She fixed a look of bitter remembrance and scorn on the magistrate; and, slowly elevating her withered hand, beckoned him to come nearer. He did so. She succeeded in raising herself on her elbow, and, with no gentle grasp, drew his head so down that her mouth nearly touched his ear. The word, or words (they could not have been many), that she uttered, sent a fearful shudder through his frame; his lips quivered and grew pale, his eye deadened within its socket, and a change, as extraordinary as it was sudden, passed over his whole countenance.

He uttered no reply; no word escaped him, – he but motioned the people to follow to his house.

As the melancholy group approached the mansion, many who had been left in the vestibule, assembled at the portal, and amongst them, the love-beaming face of Kathleen Ryley was easily distinguished. "I'll be even wid ye yet, Kate, for locking me up; and worse than all, doubting it's among such I'd be," said the lover, fondly: "to keep me kicking my heels, the livelong night, agin that baste of a door, where I might ha' been still, but for the good Christian who gave me my liberty at last; and the rats the crathurs, peepin' and pryin' at me from their holes – mad angry at me spoilin' their supper! Kathleen, astore, wherever there is love, there ought to be full faith – but, whisht, a lanna – och! botheration to me intirely for calling a tear to yer sweet eye, Kate; though, darlint," he added, as the maiden smiled it away, "it made you look more beautiful than ever I see you afore, and that's a bould word. But wait till I catch that *gostering*[528] ould Mabel O'Neil, and I'll pay her off, I'll –"

"Let her alone, if ye're wise, my tight chap," interrupted the deep voice of Hurling Moriarty; for though this conversation had been carried on *sotto voce* between the two lovers, Moriarty caught the last sentence, as he joined the group that had accumulated at the door. The party bearing the wounded woman had now entered the second gate; they had been obliged to return by a longer path than they had taken during the rapparee's escape; and one of the gossiping sister-hood had only time to observe to Philip Murphy, that "he'd better not turn his tongue against Mabel O'Neil, while Morty was to the fore – as people *did* say that he was a son, somehow or other, o' Mabel's own – and it was bad talking ill o' parents under a child's breath," – when Mr. Johnson slowly ascended the hall-steps, followed closely by some three or four who supported the unfortunate woman. Sergeant Smith had taken advantage of the confusion to disappear; he naturally feared the reaction that would take place, in the minds of the peasantry, against the murderer of the being who had so long been looked upon with either fear or sympathy by all classes, and wisely hastened to the police-barracks for a reinforcement. The eagle glance of Hurling Moriarty rested, for a moment, on the ghastly features of his reputed mother, and, in an instant, he was at her side.

With fearful energy he grasped her cold hand, and then they looked into each other's countenances, as only parent and child can look, when the tie – the first, and the dearest – is about to be broken – *and for ever*. In another moment, his ken wandered over the assembly, inquiring of her who had done the deed; and, almost unwittingly, perhaps, her look rested on the magistrate, who had entered the hall, thrown off his hat, and, having covered his burning brow with his hands, remained leaning against one of the oaken supporters of the ancient structure.

It was enough; – a bound, that, for certainty of destruction, could be likened to nothing but the fatal spring with which the young and infuriated tiger fastens on its prey, brought Moriarty to the side of the defenceless gentleman. With both hands he grasped his throat, and so appalled were even Mr. Johnson's own partisans, by the suddenness and violence of the action, that his death would have been certain, had not Mabel O'Neil, with a strong and desperate effort, staggered forward, seized her son's arm, dragged him with her almost to the marble floor, on which she fell, and exclaimed, in a low, but audible voice, "Morty, Morty, as you value yer mother's last *blessing* – as you fear yer mother's *dying* curse, – loose, loose yer hould, I say! – *it is yer father ye would murther!*"

He did, indeed, relax his grasp, and the swollen and discoloured features of the unfortunate Johnson plainly showed that, in a few seconds, Moriarty's forbearance would have been too late. He would have fallen, had not his daughter, attracted to the hall by the crowd and struggle, caught him in her arms, and with Kathleen's aid, supported him to a seat. If a bullet had passed through the young man's brain, he could not have appeared more subdued; – the fires of his eye were quenched, his arms hung powerless in their sockets, and he sank with a deep-drawn groan, on his knees, by his mother's side. "Morty," she said, still more faintly, "ye had no right to have any hand in sich a burning as was intended – I tould ye so, but ye wouldn't heed me; my heart warmed to the ould place, as the limb of ivy, that the lightning blasted on its walls, still clings to the same spot; moreover, I couldn't bear ye to lift a finger against him, who, perjured as he is, is still yer –" father, she would have added, but her son's feelings burst forth. "Do not say the black word again, mother," he exclaimed, furiously; "if *I* am *his* son, what must *you* be?"

"Listen, James Johnson, to that!" said the wretched woman, dragging her body – as a wounded serpent trails its envenomed length along the earth – towards the magistrate's seat: "didn't the sound o' *that* go to yer heart? – the upbraidings of a child to its own parent, when that parent is in the agonies o' death! But, though ye've murdered me, the curse is over ye still!" she continued, the bitter expression of countenance I have before mentioned, returning tenfold, and revenge lighting in her sunken eye, like the red lamp within the sepulchre: "do ye remember it! I'll tell it ye again – the whole – there's life in me yet for the whole of it. In those days, this was yer employer's house, but ye earned his gould, and then he borrowed it, and ye lent him back his own – ye may well turn pale, it's all true. I was his lady's chosen favourite – she tendered me as if I had been a noble child: *you* won me to yer purposes – *you* got me to betray trust; and, when that was done, *you* turned upon *me* – *you* poisoned her heart again' me. In an hour of madness I tould o' your wickedness – I was asked for proofs – I had none – she turned me out – the snow fell – the rained poured – I deserved it all from *her*. – But, under the end wall, where the ivy is still green, and yer daughter tends her flowers – do ye mind *that* meeting, when the boy that scorns to own ye leaped within me – when the feelings of a young mother warmed about my heart? Ye met me *there* – *there* ye spurned and scorned me; and, to save myself from everlasting blight – to save my mother's heart from breaking, I there promised that, as a screen to my sin, I would marry him who since turned a shame to earth, and whose children were born both to that and sorrow. Still they were *my* children, and God in heaven knows what I've suffered for them. Then – then, when I clung to yer knees to bid ye farewell, and when, like a true woman, I could ha' blessed ye, even in my misery – for the thought of yer happiness was ever foremost in my mind – at that moment, ye threw me from ye – ye called me by the name that rings on woman's ear to everlastin', *when she deserves it*; then on the snow I knelt – I cursed ye from my heart's core – my love turned to poison, both for you and myself. I knew the people would call ye fortunate: and I prayed that the riches ye should get, might secure to yer soul damnation – that the higher ye rose, the more should the finger o' scorn point at ye – that ye might be the father o' many honest childer, and that, when they were most bright and beautiful, ye might follow them to their graves, and die a childless man! And didn't I" – as she spoke, the fiend seemed to take possession of her once fine form, and deep and terrible shadows gathered over her discoloured brow – "didn't I travel, unknownst, many a weary mile, to hear the stones clatter on their coffin-lids? And when your innocent son was murthered from spite to his father, weren't the tears, that rolled down yer cheeks like hail-drops, refreshing to *me*, as the May-dew that falls on the summer flower? – and sure, the young craythur that's trembling there, like the blasted meadow-sweet, is dying fast, fast – and so am I –" Her voice sank, and the last words were faint and murmuring, as the breath of a fierce but expiring hurricane.

"Blessed Mary!" exclaimed Kathleen, "will nobody run for Father Delany, that he may make her soul?" – and the kind-hearted girl knelt at her side, and held the crucifix to her separated and ghastly lips. Moriarty, whose bitter feelings could find no utterance, clasped his hands in agony to implore her blessing. Feebly she muttered – they knew not what: then, turning her face to the ground, and, while literally biting the dust, her erring but powerful spirit departed from its dwelling of sin and suffering.

It might be some five or six years after this real and frightful tragedy, that, in a cottage more comfortable than Irish cottages are in general, an interesting peasant group were assembled round a clear turf fire. A young and comely matron was occupied in undressing a fine and beautiful boy, while her husband amused himself in deciphering the contents of a somewhat ancient newspaper; the wife glanced from the babe to her husband, with that sweet expression of proud and satisfied affection that can only rest on the countenance of a happy married woman, when she gazes on earth's greatest blessings – an affectionate husband, and a blooming child. Smilingly she pushed back the little round curls that were just beginning to cluster on her son's fair brow; and, again looking at her husband observed, "Phil, honey, the boy grows mighty like you, I'm thinking – he's yer very *moral* just about the eyes; there, he wants to kiss his own daddy before he goes to sleep! Philip, what ails ye, that ye don't notice the child? – ain't ye well, astore?" Philip Murphy deliberately laid down the paper, took the cherub-boy in his arms, hid his face on its little bosom; and while, with the sweet, untutored affection of infancy, the babe played with the longer and deeper curls of his father's hair, he murmured so earnest, and even eloquent, a prayer, that God would preserve it from sin and shame, that the mother's heart overflowed, and tears of tenderness rolled down her cheeks. As she took the delighted boy from his father's arms, she could not help saying, "That was a mighty fine prayer, Phil, and all out o' yer own head, I'm sure, for neither priest nor minister could make it for ye – clean up from the heart like that; it's a murderin' pity, Phil, ye warn't a priest, for the sarmints[529] would ha' come quite natural to ye."

"Then you should have been a nun, Kate," replied the husband, smilingly, yet not as cheerfully as was his wont; "and that wouldn't have been much to yer taste, would it now?"

"I never thought o' that," said she, laughing.

"Then ye're not so quick-witted as ye were the night ye locked me up in the long barn, ye mind."

"Philip, agra!" replied she, seriously, "I can never abide the thoughts o' that night."

"Nor I, neither," sighed Philip, "only something I've just read on the paper makes me think of it."

"And what would be on the paper, Phil?" inquired Kathleen, anxiously; at the same time rocking herself backwards and forwards, to "*hushow*" the baby to sleep.

"Two things very queer to come together then, Kate: – the death of that bad man, Mr. Johnson – a dale about him that's not thrue – and –"

"Not thrue!" repeated Kathleen; "sure I thought whatever was on a newspaper was as thrue as gospel!"

"Small is yer knowledge, then, my darlint, and so best – I hate a knowing woman; but I tell ye – and I heard it from one who understands it right well – that the half and more o' the papers are made up o' big lies; and sure here's a proof of it – when he that was forced to fly the country (for ye know, after the ripping up Mabel O'Neil, as they called her, made afore us all, and more especially, after the death o' that sweet angel daughter, Miss Car'line, he couldn't stand it at all, at all), is praised up in black and white, 'as a zealous,' – that means useful, you understand – 'a zealous and good magistrate.'" Poor Kathleen threw up her eyes in silent astonishment.

"The begrudged thing never does good," she said, at last; "and what comes over the devil's back –" "True for ye, Kate," exclaimed the husband, who knew the proverb well, and, therefore, I suppose, did not permit his wife to finish it; but the other thing is, that Sergeant Smith, ye mind, who would have been hung for shooting that unfortunate woman, only for the power o' the party, and the bribery o' Mr. Johnson (who certainly had good right to get him off, seeing he instigated him to do it – though every one clears him of knowing, at the time, who Mabel was), was hung at Kilmainim,[530] for murderin' some man or other out in the main ocean – so there's an end to him, any way."

"The Lord preserve us all, and keep us just and honest!" ejaculated Kathleen, crossing herself with one hand, and pressing her child more closely to her bosom with the other; adding, after a pause, "I often heard that 'Squire Johnson ought to have committed Morty to prison, though he was his son, as he was took under arms: that might be law, but there wouldn't be much natur in it."

"I don't know how it was settled," answered the husband: "sure the justices manage the law, and not the law the justices; only Morty went clean off out o' the country, and I was glad of it; it was the only chance he had – for he had some good in him, I've heard; and, though the black drop couldn't but run in his veins, yet trouble and knowledge might get it out, ye know."

"Phil, I want to ask ye," observed Kathleen, after a pause, "as ye're a knowing man, if ye really think it was Mabel's curse that brought all the misery on the 'Squire's family?"

"A curse is a bad thing, Kate, more particklar when it's desarved: but I have heard that a curse made again' the innocent is turned, by the breath of heaven, again' one's self; however, it's ill mindin' sich things, only to keep one's own heart pure: her curse came there, for a sartinty, and it's almost a by-word now – 'As bitter as Mabel O'Neil's curse.' Riches were a curse to him; the higher he got, the more was the finger o' scorn pointed at him, for he hadn't the gentlemanly turn about him; and, though the father o' many childer, he died childless. Temptation is bad; so God keep us from it, or teach us how to overcome it. Howsom'ever, all he got is gone to the bad, long ago – the devil never grants long leases."

"Poor Miss Car'line!" ejaculated Kathleen, "she never rightly recovered that day – though, to be sure, it was a blessed thing that the son was saved from the sin o' the father's blood; the flowers I planted over her grave last May are in blossom again, and it crushes my heart to look at them, for she was a *raal* gentlewoman, one of God's own makin', jist let down from the holy heavens, to show us what angels are; the delight of my heart you war', Miss, avourneen! only, I often think, too sweet and gentle for this world's ways. I'd ha' gone to death for you willingly any day –"

"There, darlint," said Philip, anxious to terminate so painful a reminiscence, "put the boy to bed; and, as it's fine moonlight, we'll take a walk over the field to see yer father." Kathleen passed her hand across her eyes, and prepared to fulfil her husband's wishes (which, by some strange sympathy were generally her own), while he continued, "the poor man's getting ould now, darlint, yet there's none of his childer gladdens his heart like you; and, after all, *the best way to keep off a curse is not to deserve it*."

THE FAIRY OF FORTH.

WE of Wexford, though we have the advantage of our neighbours' mountains, as terminations to our landscape, have but one that we can call our own – the mountain of Forth. I cannot, with all my love for it, style it handsome; though it is, certainly, picturesque – rugged, jagged, rough, and rocky: and I remember when not a single green field, or cultivated plot, was to be seen on its sides. It has undergone changes.

Year after year I have watched patches of oats, potatoes, and even barley, creeping along, and civilizing its sturdy steeps; while, both in sheltered and unsheltered spots, cottages have sprung up – cottages, filled with a bold race of mountain "squatters," who, I hope, may never be dispossessed of the "estates" obtained by their industry.

I have spent some happy, sunny hours on the rocks of my own dear mountain looking round and round, and climbing from crag to crag, to recognise the dwellings that shelter in the valley. There is Johnstown Castle,[531] embedded in its own woods – the gaily-waving flag on its highest tower, intimating that those who "possess the land," are AT HOME, bestowing blessings on all around them! I can see the curling smoke from the trim school-house, and fancy Mr. Shelly's, the good master's face, pale and anxious, lest his pupils' improvement should not keep pace with the wishes of his liberal patroness. There go the mottled deer, in the noble park, scudding right over the mound where that everlasting Oliver Cromwell[532] is said to have reviewed his troops: there, the labourers' cottages, clustered like honeycombs in the thrifty hive. All look happy and cheerful, and are what they appear. The spire of the little church of Rathaspeck[533] is clearly defined by the blue sky; I can see the ruins in the park, and the stream, like a silver thread, where the mill's revolving wheel turns it into mimic foam –

There, and there, and there, are the dwellings of resident landlords, or prosperous landholders, mingled with the venerable castles, which form so distinguished and interesting a feature in the character of the county; – what a fine foreground they form to St. George's Channel[534] – bearing upon its waters the produce of many lands!

Wexford Harbour looks well from this noble eminence; and it is impossible not to regret that the ever-shifting sands form such a barrier to the utility of so beautiful an object. How snugly the Barony of Forth farmers shelter in their comfortable houses! – their barns are spacious, and their hayricks and cornstacks tell of abundance. The Saltee Islands[535] stand fearlessly amid the dashing waves – and the far-off Tower of Hook terminates the sea view.

It is a noble scene; and yet, even as the tiny bird seeks its own nest amid the varied beauties of the grove, so do I seek the white gables and green trees of my childhood's home. Well, I need look no longer; it is but to close my eyes, and now it is before me – all – I can recall the chiming dinner-bell – the dear familiar voices – passed for ever – all – even the old house dog's bay – that roused the echoes of that wild sea-shore!

My own dear home! – What home can ever feel like the sweet home of childhood?

I love the mountain huts, and their hardy occupiers; I love to see them descending into the valleys to their daily labour, and climbing to their homes at night, shouting to each other, or chorusing some wild Irish ditty, while their children leap from crag to crag to meet them. I do not like to hear them sneered at – as they often are – by their lowland rivals. I own they may be a little unpolished – perhaps, fond of having their own way – and I know their manners are more *brusque*[536] than the manners of the men of the plain; they deem themselves independent freeholders – and so they are; and they receive you with warm hospitality in their cottages, if you brave their mountain air, as I have frequently done – to visit them.

Squatters, from every barony in the county, have fixed themselves upon the mountain, and do not relish people of any other county intruding among them: how they existed at first I cannot tell; a family must have made the poor man's individual labour keep them all from starving; but now, every year, I can perceive bit after bit added to their little "properties;" and the eagerness with which they send their children to school, and the interest many of them take in agriculture, lead me to hope that the next generation will be of real value to the country. I am always doubtful as to whether an improvement will be adopted, if it be only practised in a gentleman's domain; the people are apt to say, "It may do for the quality – but not for us;" but the moment one cottager tries a new plan, and it succeeds, his poor neighbours are anxious to adopt it also. "I never would have believed," said John Merry – old John Merry, who is the best dog-breaker, and mountain cottier, in the county – "that the green crop plan[537] was a good one *for the poor*, if I had not seen how well Mr. Pigeon, of the Red-houses, managed it." John Merry is one of the first mountain "settlers." "I'm as good as a grandfather to the mountain," says John, "for I was one of the first that sat down on it – a young man, with a dark-haired wife – and every hair in her head is *white* now."

"It must have been a lonesome place then, John."

"Faix, it was mighty lonesome and quair; and shy the birds and foxes looked at us – as if they thought we'd no right to it – natural enough; and as to the snipes, when they came back after their *divarshun*[538] abroad, ye'd think the wee black eyes would drop out of their heads at seeing the curling smoke, and smelling the burning turf on their own lands! Well, I've often thought what a wonder it was, how the birds in the air found the road in the heavens to wherever they wanted to go; and I have asked every larned gentleman I ever came across, how it was, and never a one of them could tell me; – it's mighty strange," added John, "but somehow, about the growing of a blade of grass, or the flying of a bird – the learned people know as little as a poor man."

John is a regular specimen of a mountaineer – fearless, free, daring, and very superstitious, as all mountaineers are: it would be utterly impossible to invent a story of fairy or spirit beyond his belief. He glories in the mountain, and wonders if the "far-off ones" look as well when you get near them as his own. He says it is a noble thing to have the "main ocean" always before a man's eyes, rowling away at his feet – that it makes him think of Eternity; and as for the dogs, the mountain air and education are the best to strengthen them in wind and limb. He will show you potatoes not larger than walnuts, and tell you that, though they're not big of their age, they're as dry as bread, and the wholesomest that ever grew; and a little patch of green stunted oats will, he assures you, be prime corn before the season's over. John, heaven bless him! makes the best of everything, and looks so cheerful in his coat, which is composed half of tatters, half of patches, that you feel assured the luxuries of life would be thrown away upon him: he will wipe his face after it has been battered by a hail-storm, and smilingly assure you it is "no ways unwholesome." I was told that John "had" a fine "legend" of *the* mountain – *if* he would tell it to me; but that he feared I would laugh at it; promising to keep my countenance, and to listen attentively, I prevailed on him to "show me the *nature* of it." "If your honour will only just walk up some morning, and see the grey rocks that mark the place, and prove there's no deception in it whatever; there's the very stones over the hole, as they were in the ancient times – and if ye remove them rocks, you may find it yourself, though, to be sure, if ye did, you'd meet with present death?"

"Couldn't they be blown up, John?"

"Well, there now, I knew it's laughing at me you'd be," he said, looking seriously displeased.

"Indeed, John, I've not laughed."

"Sure, ma'am, it's all one, if you talk of blowing up; the powder's not made that would blast them rocks," added John.

"Indeed!" I said, gravely; and John, after peering very suspiciously at me, bade me good morning. But I soon found my way to the mountain home – no very easy undertaking, though the path he declared to be both "smooth and whole-some." Seated on a fragment of stone, a few days after, while John leaned on his staff, and every now and then recalled to his side the half puppies, half dogs, that constituted his retinue, John confided to me "The Legend of the Mountain of Forth," which I give in his own language: –

"Long ago," he began, "before that thieving villain of the world, Oliver Cromwell, bombarded Wexford, reviewed his Ironsides[539] in Johnstown-park, or left his ould boots behind him in the town he ill-treated – long before all this, there lived, somewhere up here, a little morsel of a man, with a white head, and a dale in it, by the name of Martin Devereux. White Martin he was called, to distinguish him from every other of the Martins; and they called him so, because his hair was white, you see. Well, White Martin was a cunning hand, entirely, you understand, ma'am, in gathering the *mountain dew*; and whoever wanted it in the valley, used to tip the word to Martin; and be it much, or be it little, they were sure of it – pure and fresh, the *rale* sort, brewed under the moonbeam, that neither sun nor gauger had ever winked at!"

"The gauger!" I repeated.

"Ay, just the gauger! Sure, Queen Elizabeth brought them in first; and, for the matter of that, I've heard my mother say, that 'the ould sarpent in the garden of *A*den was nothing but a gauger in disguise.' Well, Martin Devereux had made a bargain with the good people, what the quality call fairies, who had their bits of stations and divarshuns on the mountain, that he'd not only let them alone, nor suffer mortal eye to look at them, but that he'd give them as much of the moun-tain dew as they'd want for their entertainments, if they'd have an eye to his interests, you understand, and not let any of the wrong sort come upon White Martin's bits of stills, or little hiding-holes; and, to be sure, if the royal family of the good people had fun before they were introduced to Martin, they had ten times the divarshun after, because of the spirits he put into them – the whisky. There was more fun and flirting in the fairy court, than ever was known before."

"And was there no fighting, John?" I inquired.

"See that!" exclaimed John, triumphantly, "I knew how you'd ask that. Well, indeed, my mother said they used to kick up a bobbery now and again, about one thrifle or another; but they were more prudent about it than poor mortals, like ourselves. Now, no one ever did a wiser thing than make friends with the good peo-ple: if you're churning, it's no great matter to leave a drop of cream in the keeler,[540] or a taste of fresh butter on the churn, for the innocent things; and, if you've noth-ing else to leave, why, leave a peeled potato on the hearth-stone, that has never touched salt, and they take the will for the deed; it's the thoughtfulness they look to, and you'll have all the better luck for it. Now you see, ma'am (it's the rale truth I'm telling you), the whole country was fairly riddled with excisemen, and gaugers, and informers, and the like – every little thing that could brew the poor Paddy's delight, was seized throughout the country, except White Martin's: he'd lay down to sleep in the thick of stills, and everything else; the gauger would come and walk over them – ay, may-be, into the whisky – and neither see it nor smell it."

"Oh, John! is that possible?"

"Possible ! Don't I tell your honour what my mother told me, and sure it isn't misdoubting her, or me, you'd be? – it's as thrue as that the sun is now shining on that smoky steam-boat. Oh, then, the sea has never looked the same since they came on it, dirty things – thrue! Well, they'd walk into it, as I tell you, and the deception the good people would put before them, would blind the sight in their ugly eyes, and they'd walk out again, and thrash the informer for misleading them. Ever, and always, after that, the hulabaloo that would be in the poor man's place would delight your ears! – such music! and always they'd have the same piper; and my own great-grandmother was up in the mountain, one night, helping White Martin and his niece, he having a great venture entirely of *the dew*; and, trusting to the power, as well he might, that had freed him from all trouble so long, he drew up his hogshead through a trap-door, at the back of his cabin, and gathered some blankets over it, like a tent, and filled it with poteen, ready to draw off for the neighbours, the vale-boys, that would be up for it before day; and the two, my great-grandmother, and White Martin's niece, got ready some ducks and chickens for the Saturday market; and the whole of them, trusting in the good people, went peaceably to bed, my great-grandmother sleeping with the old man's niece.

"In the thickness of the night, who should knock at the door but the gauger! 'Come in, and welcome,' says a voice, the *very moral* of White Martin's, while he lay shaking like an ague,[541] – 'come in; and thankful we will be to see any good creature, for we're all at the last gasp with the small-pox.' Well, my great-grandmother was like to die with the fright, and the *'cuteness* of the good people, for the gauger was a *beauty*, and would as soon have put his head in a fiery furnace, as into where the small-pox was going. Well, in his hurry to be off, he clattered down the mountain like a troop of wild horses; and then, from behind the hogshead, came such a hurraing and shillooing, that the two girls were mad to steal out to see who it was made the noise: and then, to tempt them more, came the finest of music; and they forgot White Martin's bargain with the good people, and both stole out, and, looking round the hogshead, they saw a responsible looking piper, playing away for the dear life – a little, round-faced fellow, piping like mad; and they could have looked at him all night, only that Martin Devereux pulled them away, whispering about his agreement to let the good people come and go without observation; but the *curosity* of the women had destroyed White Martin's luck, for the piper spied them, and such a hoorishing and whirling as there was, you never heard; and, all of a suddent, a voice says –

'Your bond's out, White Martin –
Your bond's out for sartin.'

"The next night, not content with leaving the good people's allowance, he made them some punch – hot, strong, and sweet; but, no: in the morning sorra a drop was touched, and there stood the hogshead – not one of the vale-boys but broke their appointment! The old man went and sat under his own wall, and, as he sat, who should he see toiling up the mountain, but the same blaguard[542] gauger! 'I'm done now, any way,' he says to himself; 'broke horse and foot, and I'll not stir, to save all the poteen that ever was brewed,' he says; 'I'll deliver myself peaceably to the tender mercies of the law,' he says, 'and that's present death, at the very least,' he says; and so, like some great saint, or martyr, he sticks his dudeen between his teeth, with the determination of an ould Roman, and bruises down his cawbeen over his eyes, settled, as a haro, to his fate. Now the gauger, that was counted such a beauty, was nothing, after all, but a yellow-legged Shelmalier[543] – a sporting fellow: one that would take a bribe with one hand, and betray you with the other – a bould, daring fellow, hiding his wickedness with a brazen face, which half the world mistake for plain dealing; his heart would fit on my thumb-nail; and his conscience – but, as *he* never found out that he had one, I don't see why posterity should bother about it. If the Rogue's March[544] was played at his funeral, it paid him a compliment. Now this gauger had a wife of his own at home, who was, for all the world, like a Buddaugh cow[545] – one that goes about with a board on her forehead, to keep her from destroying the world; and, between the pair of them, the country was ruined intirely.

"Now the Shelmalier was very fond of making love to every girl that would let him; but, above all the girls, the one that hated him most was White Martin's niece; and, while poor ould White Martin had given himself up to his pipe and his prayers: – 'Keep up,' says a voice; 'keep a good heart; though you can't manage the women, I can manage the men!' – and, pushing his hat from over his left eye, who should he see by his side, but his own niece, that frightened the piper, and she dressed up to the nines, smiling like a basket of chips,[546] and beckoning to the Shelmalier to make haste up the mountain!

"'Get in, you huzzy,' says the heart-broken craythur; 'where's your modest bringing-up? – and what's come over you at all?' – and he made a blow at her with vexation.

"'Don't offer to touch me,' she says, waving her arm above him; and, sure enough, White Martin could no more stir from where he was sitting, than the Saltees could move up this ancient ould mountain; – 'come on,' she says to the Shelmalier gauger; – 'come on, and I'll show you every tub he has; come on – darling.'

"Well, the tears rolled down the poor man's face, to think his sister's child should ever be so shameless, but he had no power over himself to speak or move. Well, the Shelmalier came on, grinning and smirking; and, sure enough, she showed him every hole and corner; while poor little White Martin sat shivering and chattering his bits of teeth, until the dudeen he hadn't the power to remove, was crunched into forty pieces.

"'You're a beauty,' he says; 'and, upon my honour, you shall be my second wife; but give me a kiss,' he says, 'on account.'

"'Wait till I've earned it,' makes answer the brazen slut; 'I've only showed you the first gathering of his unlawful practices. You think you've seen a deal; why, that's nothing, yon is his great hiding hole!' and with that she points to the very rocks your honour is sitting under at this minute, only they weren't in the same place, but standing quite silent and grand at either side of a little cave.

"'You don't mean to say,' inquires the gauger, 'that he has more poteen there?'

"'She knows very well!' shouts White Martin, 'that I never was in that cave in all my life, because it's a blessed –'

"'Will you hold your tongue, if you please, good man,' she interrupts, 'and not disgrace your grey hairs with such lies!'

"'Oh!' thought the poor man, 'how deceitful is the world! – My own sister's child, that I reared up as my own, and trusted with all I had in the world, – for whom I was adding one halfpenny to another, and who knew no other father; – to turn on me in my old age!' And the poor old man's tears flowed over his white beard – more for sorrow at the girl's ingratitude, than the ruin of his little property.

"She never heeded his trouble, but walked on with the gauger, until, just by the rocks, there were two or three geese grazing, and they, seeing the gauger – (all living birds and beasts know them by what's called instinct) – took to running, one, one way – another, another, and one flew into the cave. 'Follow her! follow her!' shouts the girl, and so he rushes on, like the March wind, after the goose. 'Well run!' she cries; 'what handsome legs you have!' and he runs the faster. 'Look to the wild goose chase!' she says again. 'Look! look! look!' and, while White Martin could hardly see clear for the blinding tears that gushed from his eyes, he still saw enough to prove that the girl stooped, and, snatching up a 'bouclawn,'[547] that grew at her feet, she waved it in the air, and, as she did, one rock fell over the other, and closed up the cave, as it is closed to this day: – then, turning to White Martin, she waved her hand to him, and he started to his feet, and, as he did, his own *rale* niece stood beside him; and when he looked for her, who had taken her shape, she was gone!"

"And in old times," I inquired, laying my hand upon one of the stones, which, according to Martin, had been so miraculously removed, "was this a cave, or a passage?"

"A passage made by them *tarnation* thieves of the earth, the Danes,[548] up from Ferry Carrig Bridge,[549] under the water; and that was the fun of it; for, when the goose got to the end of the passage, she swam away; but some say the gauger was drowned, others, that he stuck fast, and is to stick fast in it, to the end of the world: and when the *eacho* of the wind and thunder is heard from the bowels of the earth, about here, there are people that will tell you it's the sporting gauger, hunting the wild goose; but I don't believe that myself all out, because," – added John, with the air of a philosopher, who piques himself[550] upon his superior intelligence, – "because it's contrary to reason."

MARY MACGOHARTY'S PETITION.

WHEN first I saw Mary, we resided near London – it may now be some ten years ago (I believe a married lady may "recollect" for a period of ten years, although it is not exactly pleasant to remember for a longer time); she was tall, flat, and bony, exceedingly clean and neat in her dress, and yet attended minutely to the *costume* of her country: her cloth petticoat was always sufficiently short to display her homely worsted stockings; her gown was not spun out to any useless extension, but was met half way by her blue check apron – the "gown-tail"[551] being always pinned in three-corner fashion by a huge corking-pin; her cap was invariably decorated by a narrow lace border "rale thread" (for she abhored counterfeits), and secured on her head by a broad green riband. But Mary's dress, strange as it was, never took off the attention from the expression of her extraordinary face; it was marvellous to look upon; and, had it been formed of cast-iron, could not have been more firm or immovable. Her forehead was high, and projected over large brown eyes, that wandered about unceasingly from corner to corner; her nose – stiff, tightly cased in its parchment skin; cheek-bones – high and projecting; and such a mouth! She talked unceasingly; but the lips moved directly up and down, like those of an eloquent bull-frog, never relaxing into a simper, much less a smile: even when she shed tears (for poor Mary had been acquainted with sorrow), they did not flow like ordinary tears, but came spouting – spouting – from under her firm-set eyelids, and made their way down her sun-burnt cheeks, without exciting a single symptom of sympathy from the surrounding features. She was a good creature, notwithstanding; sincere – I was going to say, to excess. She prided herself upon being a "blunt, honest, God-fearing, and God-serving woman, as any in the three kingdoms, let t'other be who she might," and possessed a clan-like attachment to her employers. I have been frequently struck with the difference between Irish and English servants in this respect; an English servant always endeavours to erect her standard of independence without any reference to her master's name or fame; but Paddys and Shelahs[552] lug in the greatness, the ancient family, the virtues, and the wealth (when they possess any), on all occasions. "Sure, an' Mabby, you may hould your whisht any way," said one servant to another; "what dacency did you ever see? Who did *you* live wid? A taste of an English grocer! – who hadn't a drop of dacent blood in his veins – only *tracle*,[553] why? – the poor spillogue! – but I can lay my hand on my heart, and declare, in truth and honesty, that I always lived wid the best o' good families; and what signifies the trifle o' wages in comparison to the nobility, and the credit? Sure, if we must be slaves, it's a grate comfort to have the rale gintry over us!"

Mary performed her duty as cook in our service admirably, for some time, and was most trustworthy; but, in an evil hour, on a Saint Patrick's day, she obtained leave to visit her son, a soldier in the guards, to make holiday, and faithfully promised to be home by ten o'clock. Ten, eleven – no Mary; at last, with the awful hour of twelve, came – no spirit from the vasty deep, I assure you, but Mary, poor Mary, in the watchman's arms, perfectly – (and I sincerely grieve at being obliged to tell the truth), not ill, not nervous, nor elevated, nor, as the Irish call it, "disguised," but absolutely, stupidly, and irrecoverably, tipsy! What a piece of work there was in the house! – cook was conveyed to bed, and, of course, dismissed the next morning. I was very sorry, I confess; but mamma was never prone to alter her decree, and the duty was done. Mary cried – offered to take an oath against whisky, gin, brandy, rum – anything and everything – if she might only obtain pardon; and, when all was useless, departed in sullen silence, hardly leaving "God be wid ye;" although she afterwards declared "that, barring it would be a most cruel sin, and what no true-born Irish soul ever did, she would lave her curse wid Saint Patrick's day for the rest of its life; for when poor innocent people met to have 'granough,'[554] they forgot themselves, to do honour to the holy saint – why not? though it's a rale pity; and, och! if the mistress herself would just now and thin take only a thimbleful, she would not be so hard upon the poor craturs who are overtaken by the drop."

It was a long time before I heard anything more of poor Mary; summer and winter, and again summer, and again winter, passed, and, at last, I became, from a giddy, laughing girl, a staid, reflective matron, with a tolerable share of cares, and a large portion of happiness of the sweetest kind, springing from a cheerful home, and beloved faces – its dearest ornaments! I had almost forgotten my old friend, her peculiarities, and her Saint Patrick's frolic, when I was, one morning, informed that an Irish woman wanted to speak to me. In a few minutes Mary Macgoharty was ushered in – the very same as ever; even the corking-pin in the back of her gown seemed unmoved; there she stood, looking at me, with her midnight eyes, until, at last, the torrent poured down her wrinkled cheeks.

"And there ye are, God be good to ye! – looking brave and hearty, only a dale fatter; och, it seems quite heart-cheering to see a body with kivered bones these bad times! I'm worn to a 'nottomy[555] wid grief and hardship; and I'd have been often to see ye, before now, only ye're married, and I thought, may-be, the young master wouldn't like to have a thing like me coming about the house; only, ye mind the ould whisky-man, the poor boy what used to bring it, ye know, from

Donovan's, that fetches it over from Cork, pure as any thing, not only quite so strong – *he* can't help that; well, I was strolling about, there, by Hyde Park Corner, and wondering how the people spent their money that lived in them big houses, and a cratur like me often in want of a mouthful o' pratees, let alone bread, when who should I spy coming along – just the morral of the ould thing – but Paddy Dasey; his face as red as a turf fire; and his two bags, one swinging before, and one behind, to hould the whisky jars. Well, ma'am, my dear, he had always the swing, as who should say, 'the street's my own;' and, on account of his being so tall, and the eye he has left always skying[556] – he'd ha' walked over me, only I says, says I, 'Paddy, have ye no sight for an ould countrywoman?' Well, he looks down, and, after a hearty shake by the hand, we walks fair and asy to a sate; and then I tould him how long I'd been out o' place, and the heart trouble I'd met with. Well, he wanted me to take a drop, very civil; but I tould him of the obligation I had taken on myself when I left the best sarvice, the best mistress, and the nicest young lady that ever trod English ground; and he remembered it, too; for he used to come with the whisky to the dear ould master (heaven be his bed – amin!) but, says he, why don't you go see the young mistress? I'll go bail she'll be glad to see ye: and then he spoke very handsome of his honour, yer husband, who, he says, is almost as good as if he was an Irishman like you! – and tould me as how he sometimes bought whisky, and that you had the bit and the sup, kind as ever ye had it whin ye used to taze the life out o' me, by axing me always what o'clock it was, till that scald[557] parrot, mistress's pet, used to begin at four in the morning, 'Mary, what o'clock is it? – Mary, what o'clock is it?' Ah, thin, what's come of the parrot, Miss – ma'am – I ax yer pardon?"

"It's dead, Mary."

"Och, murder! – is she dead? Well, I'll be dead myself soon; stiff as red-herring, and no good in me even for the worms, for sorra a morsel o' flesh is on my bones! I thought I'd just take Paddy Dasey's advice, and tell ye my trouble; and now I'm just come to ye, for God's sake, knowing ye can turn yer hand to the pen at any time; and on account of 'Squire Bromby, who is here now, making speeches in the English Parliament, like ony Trojan as he is – though, for sartin, his father was not that afore him; though that's neither here nor there, as a body may say. Now, on account of the young 'Squire (who isn't the ould, because the ould one's dead – small loss!) – seeing my father (he was a wonderful clear-spoken man, of a poor body, and had powerful larning) lived a matter of five-and-forty years on the 'Squire Bromby's estate (he that's dead, this boy's father) – I being a poor, desolate, lone woman, with no one belonging to me – barring the boy that's in the Life Guards, and had the ill luck (God break hard fortune!) to marry a scrap of an English girl, who had neither family nor fortune, nor a decent tack to her back, and was married in a dab of a borrowed white rag of a *gownd*, not worth a teaster – and he a likely boy (and everybody knows the English girls 'ud give

their eyes – small loss it 'ud be to some of them – for an Irish boy) as ye'd see in
a day's march (ye mind, my first husband was a soldier, and my second, too; I'm
a *Mac*, in earnest, as a body may say; my own name, Mac Manus; my first's name,
Macgoharty; my second's Mac Avoy; – though I go by poor Jim's name, Macgoharty – Mary Macgoharty, at your sarvice – becase I liked him the best; not but
the second was a fine boy, too; but there's nothing goes past first love) – well,
I humbly ax yer pardon, but I always like to tell a thing out of the face at once,
without ony bating about the bush; so, as I was saying, my poor father (God rest
his soul!) lived five-and-forty years to the good on his honour's father's estate,
in pace, plinty, and contintment, and no one could iver say to him, 'black is the
white o' yer eye.' May-be ye mind whin ould 'Squire Bromby was returned for
Tipperary – though it's as much as ye can, for ye weren't born at the time; and
who set up, too, but Jack Johnson? – 'Squire Jack they called him; – though I was
but a girleen at the time, I niver could turn my tongue to say "Squire Jack,' and he
only a bit of a brewer; well, my father (oh! he was down honest) stood up for the
ould gentry; and, seeing he was so main strong, 'Squire Bromby made him one of
the picked men at the election; and, by the same token, the shillalah he had went
whirring through the air like a shuttlecock; now cracking one skull, now another
– now lighting here, now there – spanking about with rale glory; from the beginning to the end, it neither gave, nor had, rest or pace. Well, there niver was such
an election seen before or since; such tearing and murdering; Jack's boys killing
'Squire Bromby's boys, and 'Squire Bromby's boys skivering 'the Jackeens'[558] (as
we called them) like curlews. Well, that wasn't all; but one night (it was either
the second or third day of the election) the ould 'Squire calls my father o' one
side. 'Mister Mac Manus,' says he. 'Don't Mister me,' says my father, 'if you plaze,
because Mister is no part o' my name, yer honour; I'm plain James Mac Manus;'
and my father (he was very proud) stood stiff as an oak of the forest. 'Well, then,'
says the 'Squire, fox-like, 'honest James Mac Manus, my good friend, ye've stood
firm to me for the honour of ould Ireland – a good friend, indeed, have ye been
to me; and it's I won't forget it; but clap yer eye, James, my boy, upon any situation in the three kingdoms, spake but the word, and 'tis yours.' 'Thanks to yer
honour – many thanks to yer honour.' My father was a well-spoken man, but,
innocent-like (he was no ways 'cute), took it all for gospil. Well, my jewel, the
next day they fell to it again, and my father in the thick of it, to be sure, like a
great *giount*,[559] tattering all before him, stronger nor ever; and more betokens,
Jack Johnson (it's only justice to tell the truth) had powers o' money, and made
no bones o' the boys atin' and drinkin' at his expinse; he was a fine portly man,
with a handsome rich nose, and deeshy-dawshy eyes, for all the world like a rat's,
squinkin' and blinkin' under the dickon's own bushy, black winkers – och, so
thundery! And, as the rale ancient 'Squire's tongue wasn't hung asy, and the
other's went upon wires[560] – why, he had the advantage there, too: – and a bitter

ruction[a] it was; all the boys, more or less, had smashed heads, and they tied them up with garters, or stockings, or sugans, or anything the owners came across, to keep the bones together. Why? – but the spirit and the shillalahs held out bravely! And the last day came – as it will upon the best of us some time or other; and, after all, 'Squire Bromby carried it, through thick and thin.

"Well, I'll say that for Jack Johnson – though only a brewer, he bore up like a king – not a taste out o' temper all the time, only as gay as a lark, capering about like a good one. Bromby-park was a good ten mile from the town, and nothing would do my father (for he was parfect mad with the joy), but he put up the boys to draw the new member thim ten miles, like a pack of horses (more like asses, as my mother said), and no bad load either; a heavy lump of a man, good and bad blood – though, to tell God's truth, there was more of that last. Well, away they went, huzzaing and shouting, and got him to the house in less than no time; when, fair and asy, out he steps, makes a bow, and an up-and-down taste of a speech, first swaying on one leg, then on the other, like a bothered goose; and turns into the house, without as much as offering even a drop of smalkum[561] to a mother's son of the whole of thim. Well, after this, all the country called shame on him – the tame negre! and what made it worse, Jack Johnson gave his boys, even after, plinty of entertainment, and said that, if he did lose the election, those who voted for him could not help it, and, consequently, should not suffer for it. After it was all passed, and the people came to their senses again, father thought it was time to put him in mind of his word (mother tould him how it would be), and so he set off, making a dacent appearance, to put the 'Squire in mind of his promise. What d'ye think he said, and he o' horseback, in his scarlet jock, as grand as a Turkey-man?[562] – 'Oh, yer name is James Mac Manus. Well, James, how is the woman that owns you, and the children – all well, ay! Place, indeed – hard things to get – wish I'd a good one myself. Good morning, James – good morning:' and off he rode. Father was so stomached, that he would never go near him again: 'For,' says he, 'though he's a mimber of parliament, he's no gentleman that doesn't value his word; I'm sure I don't know how he came to be such a cankered thing (unless he was changed at nurse), for the breed of the family was always the top of the gentry.' Well, honey, dear, may-be I'm tiring ye too much intirely, but never heed, I'm a'most done; ye see, Lord help us! my father's dead, and the ould 'Squire's dead. I'm in a strange country, and even my boy has no love for the sod, seeing he wasn't born in it, nor never saw the green, green grass, or the clear water, or heard the little birds sing among the beautiful woods, bright and blooming with the hawthorn, and the brier, and the wild crab-tree; it wasn't so with my Annie, my daughter, my only girl, who was born there before my husband took to soldiering; and she was so like him – his very moral; but she's gone – buried near Dunleary,[563] they tell me – and I shall never see her soft blue eye upon me, nor hear her voice, nor – but I ax yer pardon, madam – I ought not to be troubling ye after such a fashion.

"They were pleasant woods that I sported among in my innocent morning; and ye'd hardly think, to look now upon my withered skin, and my dim eye, and my grey hair, that I was once likely, and had the pick of the boys for a husband; but they're both gone from me, and the English daughter-in-law looks could enough upon the old Irish mother-in-law! But, you see, the young 'Squire's got a brave name, and is over here with the commoners – and, I am tould a noble-spirited, true gentleman; so I was just thinking, as ye're handy with the pen, may-be ye'd write him (for me) a taste of a letter, just to put him in mind, ye know, that my father lived upon his father's land, and telling him how poor I am – (an' sure that's true for me! for, bad luck to the tack, I have but what I stand upright in); sure I made this petticoat (and it's a tidy one too) out of the grey cloak I got last winter (winter's a hard time on the poor) was two years, to keep me dacent, and my poor bones from freezing, and never disgraced my country, by being behoulden to man or mortal – only, why the poor has a nataral claim upon estated gintlemin, ye know; and just ax him civilly to give me two or three pounds (he'll never miss it, my darling lady, never), to send me home, where there's old people still I'd be glad to see, more partiklar my bothered sister, who lives nigh where my poor girl lies, jist by Dublin. I've had two warnings for death (they always followed my family), and I know I can't last long; only ye're sinsible, ma'am, nixt to dying in pace wid God and man, there's nothing like laving one's bones among one's own; thin, ye know, it's pleasant not to be among strangers at the resurrection; so I was thinking –"

"In one word, Mary, you want me to write a petition for you to 'Squire Bromby, as you call him?"

"Exactly – och, you've hit it now! – ye were always mighty quick that a way – may God bless ye! – but mind, lady dear, not a word of the past, ye know; it would be bad manners to be putting the dacent, noble young gentleman in mind of his ould foolish father's quare capers."

"Then, Mary, you need not have told me of them."

"Well, now, that bates all; why, how could ye get the understanding of the thing, if I did not tell ye? – sure you must know the rights of the thing, any way, as the ould song says –

    'I do not care for speculation –
    But tell to me the truth at onct,'"[564]

"Well, I dare say, Mary, you were quite right; but now, as you have given me understanding, allow me to commit your ideas to paper."

Poor Mary! I saw her a few days after my scribbling, at her request, the petition she was so anxious about. She was as neat as a bride. New shawl, new bonnet, new petticoat, even a new corking-pin in the gown-tail; for, as the dress was of "stubborn stuff," it needed a strong restraint to keep the corners in proper order. She was very happy, and very grateful to "'Squire Bromby" and me; and, as she seemed only disposed to talk of "Dublin Bay herrings," – "Kerry cows," – "travelling expinses," (which she had fractionally counted up) – "turf," – "pratees," – and "Ould Ireland," I soon made my adieus; faithfully promising, if I visited Erin in the ensuing season, not to forget paying my compliments to her in her sister's cabin; where, she assured me, "their very hearts' blood should be shed to do me and mine sarvice!"

I was enabled to keep my word.

* * * * * *

Oh, but the suburbs of Dublin are miserable! – miserable! – so miserable that, were I to attempt to describe them, your kind hearts would sicken; you would close the page, and not accompany me on my peregrination to the turn which opens direct on the Dunleary road. In the distance, the expanded Bay of Dublin, glittering like molten silver – innumerable vessels sleeping, as it were, upon its glorious waters, all glowing in the rich brightness of the morning sun, formed a background worthy Turner's[565] own gorgeous pencil. Amongst the groups of ragged, but cheerful, peasants, I soon found a guide to conduct me to Mary's dwelling, and gazed upon her little cottage, hardly worthy the name; but, nevertheless, so sweetly situated, that its extreme poverty was atoned for by its picturesque appearance. It was built, literally, on the side of a hill, for part of the eminence formed the back wall of the dwelling; the roof was covered over with lichens and moss, that mingled with the long grass, blossoming brambles, and feathery ragweed, of the overhanging common. As the hill ascended, it was tufted with richly-foliaged trees; and, below the cabin, a clear sparkling stream trickled and murmured quietly along its channel, except where some firm-set stone or saucy brier intercepted its way; and then it grumbled outright, and sent forth a tiny foam, expressive of its anger! The pig had its own proper dwelling, hollowed out of the hill, and, whether he liked it or not, there he was compelled to stay, by an antiquated chair-back, that was placed across the entrance; and through its openings he could only thrust his nose, which, from its extreme length, made me suspect he was an uncivilized Connaught pig. A few fowl of the noble Dorking breed, with magnificent toppings, were wandering about the meadows, and a noisy hen was storming, with might and main, at her duckling progeny, who, heedless of her eloquence, paddled in and out of the streamlet, in perfect safety: it was a calm, and, after all, a pleasing picture. The Irish, when suffering the greatest privations, never lose their elastic spirits, and, even from that lowly hut, came the merry notes of "Planxty Kelly,"[566] although sung by a feeble voice. I wanted to enter unperceived, but a busy cur-dog yelped so loudly, that an aged woman came courtesying to the door – not Mary. I thought I had mistaken the cottage, and was just going to inquire, when I perceived a female figure in the act of dusting the turf ashes off the hearth with her apron; her back was to me; but there was no mistaking the *corking-pin* – there it was in the self-same spot of the pinned-up gown tail!

How delighted she was to see me! – "How ashamed that she had nothing to offer me! – her sister's grand-daughter was jist gone to market with a few eggs – but, sure, Kate Kearney was on the nest, at the far corner, and she'd soon lay, and thin it would be worth atin'! – she was a beautiful hen! Or she wouldn't be a minute whipping the head off one of thim long-legged pullets, the giddy craturs! – small use it was to them! – and grill it like fun in the ashes! Or she would catch the goat for some milk – sure they had grass for a goat; Nanny gave such nice milk – only, bad cess to the cat! there was no keeping a drop in the house for her; they had nothing to kiver it, and she took the pig's share and her own; they wanted to fat him up to pay the rint, which he did regular, except last year, when he (the one that's dead) got the measles, and that was a sad loss to them."

The cabin was very poorly furnished; for the pig, the poultry, eggs, and even the little spinning and knitting the two old women could do, were insufficient to bestow upon them much comfort; and, besides that, they had an orphan relative, who had just sufficient intellect to sell the eggs, and, with true Irish feeling, they shared with her whatever they possessed. Then came the inquiries as to the "ould mistress and the young master," and every living thing she could remember as pertaining to our household. When I bade them good day, Mary hoped I'd let her show me the *short* cut; "a dale pleasanter, although, may-be, a few steps *longer*." As we wended down a narrow glen, carpeted with the short, thick, downy grass, that sheep so much delight to browse upon, I asked Mary if she was happy?

"Happy! – why, middling, God be thanked! middling so; an ould body, like me, has none, nor ought to think o' none, o' that quick joy that sets the heart dancing, and the blood mounting and tearing through the veins like mad.

But the ould have the quiet and the content; the mist moves from their eyes; and they see everything past, and many things to come as they are; they know that the heart's fresh hope will bud, and may-be bloom, but certainly fade; good luck, if it doesn't fade, or be cut off afore it bloom. Sure I'm joyous to see the young things around me dancing like the merry waters, for I know there'll be time enough for the salt, salt tears, with the best of 'em, whether they last long or short; and all I can do, I do – pray that the grate God will keep 'em from sin, and then they never can taste the worst o' sorrow; for bitter is the bed, and hard, o' the black sinner; which, thank God, no one belonging to me ever was; and the priest (God rest his soul!) often said that whin we went to make a clean breast, it's little trouble he had with us; and the hardest pilgrimage my father ever made, was twice to the Lady's Island,[567] and that wasn't for much, in so long a life. When I came over, I thought it only fitting to have a few masses said for the rest of my poor girl's soul! – but the priest (och, he's the good man!) tould me half as much would do as was customary – on account she was such a God-serving girl: – never missed a confession in her life. I'll show ye where she lays; and I've taken an obligation on myself never to pass the grave, without one avy.[568] Whin we turn this knock,[569] we'll come right upon the poor ould churchyard, all so quiet and lonesome by itself! – that's not the way it'll be at the last day! God help me!'

When we "turned the knock" – I was charmed with the old churchyard; it changed completely the style of the landscape – as it stood at the commencement of a long marsh – a little elevated above its level; and the prospect on that side our path was terminated by hills above hills – some slightly wooded – others resting, as it were, against the clear blue sky, huge masses of many-tinted rock. The building must have been one of very ancient structure; what remained was overgrown by ivy, and here and there a solitary tree shadowed the mouldering walls and half-fallen arches; there were few tomb-stones – nought but "green grass mounds," headed by small wooden crosses – some without any inscription – others simply marked thus –

†

I H S[570]

One ponderous relic of ancient days, however, stood in a corner of the churchyard, at which a young man and woman were kneeling.

When Mary had repeated her customary prayer, she rejoined me, observing "she would take longer next time, only she could not bear to keep me waiting in sich a dismal place."

"Mary," I inquired, "can I take any message back to your son, in case his regiment should have returned to London?"

"Oh! God bless ye for that thought! – sure can ye – and my heart was burstin' to ax ye, only I thought, may-be, ye'd think bad of my making so bould. Ye see, ma'am, dear, I thought my sister was better to do in the world; or I'd hardly ha' troubled her, and the times so bad; but my heart bates to see the boy – and I don't want him here, because I know the English girl would be skitting[571] at the poor cabin; and, above all things, ye know, agra, I niver could bear a slur cast upon the country; I don't say but (though I'd be long sorry to let them English hear me) there's a dale more comfort, and eatin', and such as that, among 'em – and they're sturdy, honest, surly sort o' people – no variety in 'em at all – all the one way, all asy going – without much spirit, but a dale o' comfort. Now seeing I got a fresh lease o' my life by breathing such air as this – though I'm ould – yet I find I can't settle myself parfect for death without once more seeing the boy – and seeing London; and so will ye tell him – God bless ye! – that, after this winter, I will have enough to carry me over, an' back, may-be, on account, ye know, of laving my bones in the grey churchyard – near my poor girl; but, if I shouldn't have enough, ma'am, dear, sure you'll be to the fore, and it's little ye'd think o' writing me another *petition!* – I'll engage ye're as nimble at the pen as ever. And if ye see the boy's wife, and she axes any questions, jist put the best face upon it, ma'am, honey, for the honour of ould Ireland! So my blessing be about ye wherever ye go; and the blessing of all the saints, and St. Patrick's at the head of thim! Sure, it's a happy sight to see his beautiful head[572] (the steeple I mean) watching above that sweet, illigint city – that the devil has no power over – the joy of my heart ye are, Dublin agra!"

I bade her adieu, and was proceeding on my way; Mary took my hand, pressed it affectionately to her heart and lips, and the tears showered on it, she could not speak her farewell blessing, but fixed her large eyes on me as I departed, with more expression of feeling than I had ever before witnessed! Poor Mary! – winters and summers have passed, but I have seen her no more! – She needs no more *petitions.*

OLD FRANK.

As long as I can remember, Frank was called – "Old Frank." He was a little, crabbed-looking man, bent nearly double; had a healthy colouring on his cheek, and a few, very few, grey hairs straying over his bald and shrivelled forehead; with a halt in his walk; and was always either singing or coughing; somewhat "cranky" in his temper, and, in his capacity of coachman (which situation he had filled for a period of forty-two years in our family), exercised despotic sway over horses, dogs, and grooms. He was singularly faithful, and strongly attached to his master and mistress, his horses, and myself; indeed, as to the two last, it was a matter of doubt which he loved best; however "snappish" he might have been to others, he was to me, in my childish days, one of the kindest and firmest of friends; no matter how I tormented him – no matter what pranks I played (and they were not a few), "Miss Maria" was always right, and everybody else was wrong. Having lived so long in the family, he was hardly looked upon as a servant, and neither master nor mistress disputed his dictum; indeed, I do not know why they should, for, wherever his authority extended, matters were well managed. The coats of his carriage-horses shone like French satin, and the carriage, an old lumberiug thing of the last century, could not have existed at all under the care of any other coachman. Frank, the carriage, and horses, had grown old together; they were all of a piece, and cut a remarkable appearance, whenever they walked (for that was their most rapid pace) out in the bright, sunshiny summer. But it was not alone in this, his principal situation, that Frank was entitled to, and treated with, respect. All the perfect and all the embryo sportsmen of the neighbourhood came to consult him on every matter connected with dogs and horses; he was famed, all over the county, for educating pointers on the most approved principles, and was permitted to have three or four constantly in training for the neighbouring gentry, who always remunerated him handsomely for his trouble. He had been an excellent sportsman in his youth, and took much pride in boasting that, except his head, all the bones in his body had been broken; indeed, even his head exhibited a sufficient quantity of bumps to puzzle a phrenologist; the old man still loved sporting, and it was owing to this circumstance that Frank and I were such great friends.[a]

I certainly was "a country child;" and to escape from study, and stroll with Frank, Frank's dogs, and Frank's daughter, "my kind and gentle nurse," was one of the greatest of my simple enjoyments. I can hardly tell why, but Bannow, in my remembrance, always seems like fairy-land – its fields so green – its trees so beautiful – its inhabitants so different from any I have elsewhere met!

The aged man used to make it a constant practice to take out a steady old pointer, with a young, untaught, roving, but well-grown puppy; and I believe Joss (the old one) was as much interested in the business of educating the young dog, as Frank himself. Be that as it may, we used all to wander among the green lanes and fields, and, when I was tired, nurse would seat me on an old grey stone, or rustic style, and Frank would lean on his gun, and tell me some of the fairy tales, or legends, with which his memory was so well stored. He had a most confirmed belief in banshees, cluricawns, fairies, and mermaids; and if Mary, who was very superior to the general order of servants, ever presumed to doubt the truth of one of her father's stories, he reproved her in no gentle terms; and no wonder, – he had a mark in his hand, which was actually given by an arrow, shot at him by a fairy queen, one evening, when he was returning home after a quiet carouse at Mr. Talbot's. He could never be prevailed upon to root up large mushrooms (fairy tables), or to pull bulrushes (fairy horses), lest he might offend the good people.

His most favourite walk was across some young plantations, admirable covers for game, to a small hill, thickly wooded at either side, where there was a singularly fine oak, one of whose branches jutted suddenly from the trunk, and formed a rustic seat, which, in childish sportiveness, I used to call my throne. From thence the prospect was very beautiful: the long, white chimneys of my old home sprang, as it were, from amid the trees, that, from this particular point of view, appeared to fringe the ocean's brink; while the many-coloured foliage of the lofty poplar, dark cedar, feathery birch, or magnificent elm, gave richness and variety to the landscape.

But in our own summer-house – a comparatively rude structure, yet which in those days, was, to my mind, the most perfect example of elegance and good taste that was ever erected – how I did love to sit, during the long evenings – nurse's arm around me, to prevent the possibility of any irregular and restless movements terminating in an upset, and listen with delight to Frank's fairies, about whom the good old man so dearly loved to talk, only interrupting his narrative, now and then, by a necessary word of caution to his dogs. Whenever I urged him to tell me a story, he used to shake his head, and say, "Och! Miss, honey, ye'll, may-be, think of ould Frank and his fairies, when ye'll be far from your native land, and my poor smashed bones at rest. But my blessing be about ye," he would add, patriotically, "*never deny your country*."

My favourite story was, "The Stout and Strong of Heart;"[573] and I believe it was Frank's favourite also; for many a time and oft has he repeated it to me, and always have I listened with attention, pleasing the old man, while I was myself delighted. I will give it to my readers, although I fear it will lose much, from the absence of my ancient friend, who, with so much earnestness and native humour, related it.

"There was plenty of mirth, and of everything else, in the little cabin of Jerry Mahony, for his daughter Ellen had just become a bride, and the merry party were beguiling the time while the dinner was in preparation. The blind piper was sitting on the hearth-stone, making beautiful music, and now and again taking a sup of potheen,[574] to the long life of the wedded pair. Jerry himself was listening to all the compliments and good wishes of the neighbours; his wife, Biddy, busily placing all her own and the borrowed delf upon the table, and bustling her maid Peggy with a continual 'Make haste, hurru![575] – 'tis only once in a long life;' while the bride and bridegroom, James and Ellen Deasy, sat in a corner, talking over their future arrangements, and planning ways and means to make themselves happy and comfortable; and, to be sure, the mother of the girl got everything in order. And Ellen was lovely and beautiful enough for a queen, let alone a poor man's wife. But, although she was made much of, by rich and poor, no one thought more of her than Kit Murtough, the blind piper; and good right had he so to do; for she had the pity for him, the poor, sightless creature: – and it was he who made the beautiful music that night; so beautiful was it, that the priest himself could stand it no longer, but capered like a China-man. Well, the next morning, Biddy Mahony went to the foot of the ladder that led to her daughter's room –

"'Ellen, honey,' says she, 'come down, I have some nice tay for ye both.' She waited, and there was no answer; so she went up a few steps, 'James, agra! won't you waken for me?' Still no answer: well she went into the room, and stopped, and said, 'Why then won't either of you spake to yer own mother, that gave birth to one, and a wife to the other? Jemmy, Nelly, dears! – get up and look at the morning that's so smiling and happy.' Still not a word: so she went and pulled the wisp of straw out of the window, and let in the light. She then looked on the bed, patted her child on the cheek, and felt that she was a cold corpse. Her bitter shrieks soon woke the husband; and the neighbours came running in, in crowds; and black grief was in that cabin where, the night before, there had been so much joy. Many suspected that James Deasy, had a hand in his wife's death, and there were some who told him so. But sobs, from the very depth of his heart, were James's only answers. The evening came, and the young bride was laid out for the wake. All was got in readiness for the 'berring,' which, according to custom, was to be on the third day. Now, nobody took the death of poor Ellen more to heart than did Kit the piper, who wandered about the neighbourhood of her dwelling, playing only dismal tunes, until the night before the funeral, when he was sitting, between lights, under the corn-rick that stood in the sheltered corner of Jerry Mahony's field, while the mournful music made the place more melancholy. Suddenly he felt a sudden gush of wind pass by him, and then all was still;

he paused for a while, and again struck up the same tune, the tune that poor Ellen so dearly loved; then the wind came stronger by him, and again he paused; once more he began the air, and the wind beat furiously against him. He now crossed himself, and called on the blessed Virgin, when he heard the voice of the dead bride speak to him, and say, 'Kit Murtough, go to my husband, and tell him not to weep for me, for I am a living woman, but the fairies carried me away. Bid him come here at nightfall, and bring a pail of new milk from the cow; but tell him, be careful not to spill a drop of it, or he'll lose me for ever, but to be STOUT AND STRONG OF HEART; and when he hears the blast rush past him, let him throw it upon me, so that it may drench me all over, but, if he misses me, he'll never see me more.' A joyful man was Kit that minute, and off he posted, and told it, word for word, to the husband, who, to be sure, put but little faith in it, yet the love to the wife made him try. So, to make all sure, he milked the cow himself, without spilling a drop, and off he went to the corn-rick, very much troubled in his mind, with the hope of recovering his bride, the doubts as to the piper's story, and the fear that he should 'miss drenching her, and then lose her for ever.' But James was a bold man, and feared nothing else. So he waited patiently until the first blast of wind passed him. He took up the pail, but his heart misgave him, and he laid it down again. Once more the blast came, and more strongly, but still James Deasy was only half a man. The third time it came furiously upon him; then James was ready, and threw every drop upon the blast, when, all at once, he saw his wife before him, as plainly as when she stood beside the priest; and he clasped his arms about her, while a loud whirling tempest – full of the good people – came all round them. But she was safe from harm, and they returned smiling to her father's cottage.

"No one but a mother can tell Biddy Mahony's joy to see her child come back to her again. And the evening of that day saw happiness returned to Jerry's cottage, where the piper had his old seat, in the chimney-corner, sung many a merry song, and drank a double portion of whisky to the health of the bridegroom and the bride.

"But James Deasy, when he came in, went straight to the coffin, and, in the place of the corpse, he saw a great log of wood, with the shroud upon it. This he quickly put upon the fire, when they heard a loud screech, and the log went up the chimney with a noise like a thunder-storm, that almost shook the roof off the old cabin. The neighbours came running in to know what was the matter; and there they saw James Deasy, and Ellen his wife, sitting in the corner, as if nothing had happened; she looking as beautiful, and he as happy, as when Father Peter blessed them both, a few days before.

"Some months had now passed away, and Ellen was about to become a mother, when she called her husband to her bed-side, and said, 'James, dear, happy have we been, and happy will we still be if you do my bidding; which is, when my little baby is born, put three crosses on its forehead, and three on mine, and don't leave me for a minute, however they may try to wile you away, for the fairies will be after the both of us.' Well, James never left her bedside, but watched her night and day, for fear the fairies should be waiting to take off both the wife and the child; which, when it came, was a glorious boy. But, all at once, James heard a scream outside the door, and a small voice calling 'Ellen Deasy;' he looked round, and saw the latch raised, and the door opening gently, then ran towards it, and pushed it to violently, when, all in a minute, he heard a loud laugh, as if from many persons, and, when he looked on his wife's bed, he saw that both mother and child were dead. James remembered the crosses, and remembered that his wife had warned him to let nothing tempt him from her bed-side. But 'twas too late, they were both gone, and James Deasy was indeed a wretched man.

"They kept poor Ellen and her little one for a long time above the ground, and then they buried them both in the churchyard. But James could not rid himself of the idea that the bodies were not those of his wife and child, so he would not let the priest say mass or anything over them; a thing which brought much shame and scandal upon him. But he had his own reasons for it.

"Now, it happened, one morning, that James Deasy was hoeing his little garden, and thinking, as he did every day, of his poor Ellen, that he had lost nearly a twelvemonth, when his hoe struck against a sod as green as ever was spring leaf, although his spade had been into it many a time, and it had been long covered with black clay. All of a sudden he heard music under it – beautiful and sweet music, such as he had never heard before. He remembered his poor wife's warning, to 'be stout and strong of heart,' so he raised up the sod, and looked down. There he saw, at a depth that seemed many miles underground, a number of little people dancing most merrily; they were all dressed in green leaves, and had fine forms and faces; for, to his great wonder, he could distinguish them plainly, although they were so far off. He thought that one of the little people resembled his dead wife; and he knew it must be her, when he heard her say, 'to the corn-rick at midnight,' while the rest of the fairies repeated her words, 'to the corn-rick at midnight;' and then the music ceased, and the ground appeared the same as it had always been; for James could not discover the green sod he had just raised. The more he thought upon the words, 'to the corn-rick at midnight,' the more he was convinced they had some meaning, and that they were addressed to him. So he waited impatiently till the night came, and went off to the appointed place.[a]

"Now, the green island was well known over all the country as the pet of the fairies. There he waited till he heard the sound of the merry pipes, and saw a long train coming along the path. He stood quite quiet, as if he was minding nothing at all but the road-stones he pretended to be breaking, until the whole of the crowd had passed him; when up from the ground starts James, seizes the last woman of the group, tears off the cloak from the shoulders, signs three crosses on the brow, snatches the child, and does the same to it, when, lo and behold!

his own wife, Ellen Deasy, on her knees before him, and his own beautiful little baby in her arms! The sign of the cross had driven all the fairies away, and, safe and sound, James, and Ellen, and their little one, returned to their cottage, and never more was the life of either disturbed by the good people.

"They are still living in Dumraghodooly,[576] and James is ever and always ready to tell his story over a glass of whisky punch; but no inducement has yet prevailed on Ellen to give any account of her adventures in fairy-land."

"Oh, Miss, don't laugh," Old Frank would invariably add – "it's as true as I'm a sinner, and it's bad to disbelieve the fairies. Sure I was an unbeliever once myself, and this was my punishment – one of their arrows right through the flat o' my hand; I shall carry the mark to my grave. Come, Miss, it's time to go home; – bad luck to the dog! Joss, where's Rover? – Rover! Oh, that young dog wants as much attindance as a Mullenavat pig!"[577]

"How is that, Frank?"

"Why, Miss, the Mullenavat people are Munster, ye know, and quite inferior to the Wexfordians, and depind on the pig to pay the rint, and, on that account, trate him with all the respect possible – why not? – and so they pick out the big pratees for the pig, and ate the little ones themselves; and they give the pig the clane straw, and sleep themselves in the dirty; and they give the pig the candle to go to bed wid, and go to bed themselves in the dark."

"And is that true, Frank?"

"As gospel, Miss; upon my word it is. Here, Rover! – the only way to steady that dog will be to hang him. Rover – Rover!"

Frank delighted in telling stories of the rebellion, but he left it to others to recount what true and faithful service he had rendered his master and mistress in that perilous time; and they were nothing loath to do him ample justice. I have often heard how he buried the best old wine in the asparagus beds, to save it from falling into the hands of the rebels; and how he concealed his favourite horses in the hen and turkey-houses; and how, at the risk of his life, he carried a forged order to General Roche,[578] who commanded the rebel forces in the town of Wexford; which order purported to come from another rebel chief, and demanded the instant freedom of his master, whose life was thus preserved.

It was in the summer of 1798, that my grandfather, who had been, for a few days, in Dublin, on business of importance, embarked with his constant attendant, Frank, on board a small Wexford trading vessel. Intelligence had reached them of the disturbed state of the country; and, as land travelling was unsafe, the "boat" was engaged to convey them direct to the Bay of Bannow.

As they passed Dalkey Isle,[579] and coasted along the beautiful shores of Wicklow, glowing in the full richness of summer, the sea-breeze tempering the fervid heat with its invigorating freshness, my grandfather thought he had never seen the country look so tranquil or so happy; the lowing of cattle, the bleating of sheep, the cooing of the wood-pigeon, even the subdued warblings of the forest birds, were heard on board their light bark; but when the day passed, and the night darkened, unusual fires sparkled on the hills; and, along the shore, lights would blaze for a moment, and then suddenly disappear. The anxiety of both master and servant to arrive at home was intense, and they were much pleased to perceive, through the grey mist of the succeeding morning, the spire of Wexford Church.[580] As the day advanced, Mr. — distinctly saw green flags floating from the masts of the several vessels in the harbour.

"We must sport one too, sir," said Rawson, the Captain of the brig; "if we do not, they will board us." He unfurled his flag immediately, after which, Frank went off deck into the cabin, and slyly took out his master's pistols from his portmanteau; he then (as he subsequently stated), poured a little water into the pans of a fowling-piece, a blunderbuss, and other firearms, that he had perceived lying under some coiled rope and canvass sacks. The fact was, he had ascertained, by overhearing some conversation between the Captain and one of his crew, that Rawson was a United Irishman, and one in no way to be trusted. He then crept on deck, and placed himself beside his master's elbow. My grandfather kept his eye steadily fixed on Rawson's movements; but, to say the truth, if he had been tacking for the bottom of the sea, he could hardly have discovered it, being utterly ignorant of all naval tactics.

The channel into the harbour of Wexford is very narrow; nor was it until the prow of the vessel was passing between the two embankments, Mr. — observed that Rawson, instead of steering for Carnsore Point,[581] was making direct for the town. He instantly sprang at the Captain, who was at the helm, and seized him by the throat; while Frank, nothing loath, presented a pistol to his head, swore vehemently that, if he did not tack about, he would throw him overboard. Rawson, who was a man of great bodily strength, drew a pistol from his bosom; it missed fire; but, at the moment, when my grandfather had overpowered his antagonist, he received a blow on the head from Frank; he was almost stunned, staggered a few paces forward, and fell. At that instant, two or three musket balls whizzed past, and Frank whispered, – "I humbly ax yer honour's pardon, but it was the only way I had left, to make yer honour get out of the way of three blackguards in that boat, who took prime aim, and would have had ye down as clane as a partridge, but for my taste of a knock; the game's up now, but that bit of a blow wouldn't hurt a pointer, sir."

In another instant they were boarded by the rebels, and Mr. — was soon bound hand and foot. He would, most likely, have been piked on the spot, but that the insurgents were, at this period, anxious, if possible, to obtain the sanction and assistance of some of the leading gentlemen of the county. They, therefore, secured him, to prevent the possibility of escape, and Frank was suffered to depart. The poor man arrived at Bannow when it was near midnight, and found my mother and grandmother marking the minutes by their tears. The whole country was in a state of open insurrection; and, although they had hitherto been treated with respect, through the kind interference of the good priest and Captain Andy, yet the uncertain fate of my grandfather, and the continued stories of death and destruction they had heard, kept them in perpetual agitation. Frank's account was not likely to soothe their misery, and they asked each other what was to be done, without receiving consolation from any plan that was suggested. Captain Andy was with his rebel regiment at the mountain of Forth. The priest had gone, it was supposed, to Ross. What plan could be adopted? – "Frank, can you not devise any mode? – "Frank coughed. – "Can nothing be done?" – Frank replied to this question by asking another: "Can ye tell me, madam, if they have taken Grey Bess for the devil's sarvice yet?" – "She was in the stable this morning, with two or three of the old horses." – "Hem! I'm glad of that, I'll jist step out – I wonder they passed her; she's as fine a slug of a mare as there's in the whole county."

The ladies thought Frank's attention to his quadrupeds ill-timed, but he went his way; and, first concealing the carriage-horses in the fowl-houses, mounted Grey Bess, whose strong, well-made limbs merited the encomium he had passed on her, and, without imparting his intention even to his fellow-servants, set off at a brisk trot to the mountain of Forth. Arrived at the encampment, he soon found out his friend Andy, and, in a few moments, they were in close conversation at a little distance from the mass of the people, who were either sleeping, drinking, or singing, in scattered groups over the mountain, canopied by the clear, moonlit sky. "We must get him off, Frank; General Roche is in command – yet I don't know how! Can you write?" – "Is it me?" replied Frank; "not I – can you?" "No; an order from General Keough[582] would do it, but he's for making a bonfire of the town."

"The baste!" exclaimed Frank, "would there be any sin in jist signing his name to a little taste of an order to General Roche, to let him go free on particular business, to be returned when called for? If we had him safe in Bannow, 'twould be asy enough to hide him away in an ould cave, or castle, or cask, or ship him off, like a sack of pratees, to Wales. Where there's a will, there's a way; but he's clane gone if he remains in Wexford. Is Father Mike here?" Andy bent his thumb back to intimate that he was in the camp. "I thought so God be wid ould times! he'll never forget my mistress's attintion to him, and she an Englishwoman, let alone my master's. If ye see a man an' his bit of a wife go past in the morning on Grey Bess, *bathershin*. God be wid ye!" and Frank went off to seek the priest. He was easily found, and soon understood what Frank wanted.

"My simple order would be of no use, Frank, for they think me faithless enough, because I cannot spill blood – blood of the innocent as well as the guilty. General Keough's would do it;" the kind-hearted man paused: "every imprisoned Protestant will, I know, suffer before to-morrow night."

"My poor master, sir, and mistress! – I'll tell ye what, if yer reverence will jist give me the scrapeen of an order, who'll know ye iver wrote it? – and sure it's I that 'ud write it in the crack of a whip, if I knew how. Oh, sir, think of all the good they did the poor Catholicks in the hard winter!"

Father Mike hesitated no longer, drew from his pocket a little inkhorn,[583] and wrote the order on the top of Frank's hat, the moon shining brightly on them at the time.

Away went Frank and Grey Bess into Wexford, and the day had dawned by the time he arrived at the Court-house. He unhesitatingly presented his order, and my grandfather was much delighted to find himself at liberty.

"I wonder the General wrote," said the man who let him out, "for he'll be in Wexford himself in an hour!"

This intelligence alarmed Frank much, and he hurried his master to a dwelling, the fidelity of whose inmates he could depend on; it belonged to his uncle Kit's third daughter, who was married to Mickey Hays, the grocer, at that time Commissary-General to the rebel forces quartered in Wexford. There Frank equipped his master in a good frieze suit, a long coat, straw hat – mounted a bunch of laurel at one side, and a green feather at the other, and presented to him a sturdy pike; he then arrayed his own little person in "his uncle Kit's daughter's" red petticoat and hooded cloak.

"And now," said he, "yer honour will remember that yer name's Pat Kennesey, and that ye're going to the blessed priest's house, and that I'm yer wife – that 'll ride on Grey Bess behind ye."

They arrived safely at Bannow; and my grandfather often said – when the troublesome times were passed, and he jested at the remembrance of by-gone dangers – that, three times within forty-eight hours, Frank saved his life – when he damped the powder – knocked him down – and became his wife.

Honest Frank's services did not go unrewarded; he was suffered to indulge all his little peculiarities, without let or hinderance, and to be as cross as he pleased, without the possibility of a reprimand. Although an ample provision was made for his latter days, he mourned most bitterly our coming over to what he always designated "the could-hearted English country and his affection was so strong, that he would have left his children, to follow us, had he not been (to use his own expression) "past travelling, at eighty-five."

Good old man! I well remember him when the moment of parting arrived, and we were to take our departure for "the great metropolis of nations."[584] He stood foremost of a troop of weeping domestics; his hat held reverentially in his withered hand, while the sleet of a January morning mingled with his grey hairs; tears rolled abundantly down his wrinkled cheeks; we were seated, yet still he held the coach-door open – "God bless you all! – shut the door, Frank," said my dear grandfather, almost as much affected as his faithful servant. Frank still held it, cast a farewell look upon us, and then, turning to a man who was close to him, exclaimed, "You do it, James; I can't close the door that shuts me out for ever from —" the horses went on, and I saw my kind story-teller no more.

I have said that Frank loved his horses; he also loved the old family carriage. And when we left the country, my grandfather presented it to him, thinking of course he would sell it. No such thing. Frank went to live with his daughter, my old nurse, at the village of Duncormuck; and there he erected a spacious shed, under cover of which he deposited his favourite chariot; the poor old man's delight was to wheel it in and out. Until within a few days of his death, he attended to it with the most scrupulous exactness, and invariably got into a passion whenever the propriety of selling it was hinted at.

"Who knows," he would say, "but they may come home of a suddent? – and what a comfort it would be to them to find the ould carriage, and ould Frank, ready for sarvice!" POOR OLD FRANK!

LUKE O'BRIAN.

I WISH, with all my heart, I could adequately describe Luke; I have often requested him to sit for his picture, and, if he had done so, I think I should have had it engraved for the benefit of the English public. Luke, however, has, what he calls, "a mortal objection to his face being in print." Therefore, good reader, you can never have an accurate idea of the subject of my story. He was, when I first knew him, about two-and-twenty; in height, six feet four inches: slight, and muscular; and the too visible size of his bones renders him not unworthy of his gigantic nomenclature. His countenance is nondescript – appertaining to no particular nation, yet possessing, it may be said, the deformities of all: – an Austrian mouth, French complexion, Highland hair (of the deepest tint), small pepper-and-salt coloured eyes, that constantly regard each other with sympathetic affection, and a nose elevated and depressed in open defiance of the line of beauty, are the most striking objects in his strange physiognomy; – in common justice, I must add, that his face is remarkably long, pale, and much disfigured by a cut he received from a "hurley"[585] in his boyhood, which carried away his left eye-brow, and a small portion of his cheek; this mark, Luke, who is an acknowledged wag, terms "his beauty-spot."

It was a drizzling, damp evening, in the month of November, when the aforementioned Luke O'Brian, grasping his shillalah in his enormous hand, passed through the beautifully situated town of Enniscorthy; – glancing, as he could do, without inconvenience, one eye towards Vinegar-hill,[586] and the other towards the noble ruins of "the Castle,"[587] he proceeded on his way, intending to reach Wexford that night. Although Luke was a tall, stout, brave boy, he would rather have been anywhere than just where he was: with a dreary road before him, and no one to speak to, the huge rocks looked frowning enough, to a lonely traveller, in the deepening twilight, on one side of the way; and, on the other, rolled the dark blue waters of the Slaney. Luke had been serving writs in a distant part of the country; he was not a native of the county of Wexford, though selected for the performance of this, by no means safe, task, by an attorney, who shall be nameless. He had wandered away from the right road, when he fancied he heard steps behind him; his merry whistle sank into a kind of hiss, and his long legs trembled somewhat, as he strode forward; he soon ascertained that his pursuers were two in number, and, from their trot-like walk, justly concluded that they were short, stout men; nevertheless, they soon overtook Luke; long-shanked though he was, he had no chance of out-striding them.

"May-be you've walked far this bleak night?" they inquired.

"May-be I have," replied Luke.

"May-be ye're going far on?"

"May-be so."

"How dim the ould stones look in the grey light!" observed one of the persevering travellers.

"So they do."

"They say they're mighty unlucky," continued one of the men.

Our hero summoned courage, and replied, firmly, "Nothing's unlucky to a stout heart."

"Say you so, my boy?" exclaimed the younger one: "then here goes!" and the click of a pistol, that was instantly presented at Luke's breast, sounded very disagreeably through the dark night. His arms were instantly pinioned, with almost supernatural strength, by the fellow-robber, and he was drawn back into a sort of fosse, or deep dike, that skirted the path. He shouted loudly for assistance, but was told, very coolly, to "hould his whisht." "Do ye think that people have nothin' to do but to walk the road, to look for young chaps in distress? Hould yer whisht, I say! By the powers! if ye don't, I'll —"

"Stop," said the elder; "as ye value yer mother's curse or blessing! – don't ye remember what she said not two hours agone?"

"Can't he give up what he has got?" retorted the younger; "does he think I'm a fool, to feel the cash in his pocket, and lave it there? I'll tell ye what," he continued; "give it up, and ye shall meet wid genteel tratement; it's good to have to do wid gintlemen, in our trade. But look ye, my lad; I've a mother dying of starvation: food hasn't crossed her lips for more than two days; and we're all hunted like wild animals, from house and home. So, if ye've a mother of yer own, *give* us the means of saving her life."

"In troth," replied Luke, "I never had either father or mother, that I know of. But there, – I'm only a poor lone boy. Sure ye wouldn't take all I have in the world to depind on?"

"Not *all* ye have," responded the elder of the men, with a bitter groan; "we couldn't take *all* ye have, for ye have a good name, may-be, and *that* is what *we* can never have again." They rifled the contents of his leather-bag; which the younger was about to pocket, when the elder interposed.

"It's only five one-pounders,[588] and a few bits of silver. And is this all ye have, for the many times you've been a'most kilt, sarving the law, to be sure? Well, the half of it will do our turn: keep the rest. We'd be long sorry to take all he had from any fatherless boy." The young man grumblingly returned half the money; and Luke, with that natural cheerfulness of feeling, the almost peculiar characteristic of the Irish, felt as if he had gained, not as if he had lost anything. Still he was sadly perplexed; – he had wandered considerably from the main road, and, in endeavouring to regain it, grappled amid what appeared an interminable wilderness of over-grown fern, sharp, stinging furze, and low broom-wood – the most intricate thing in the world to escape from, as the frequent cuttings it receives from the broom-gatherers make it very spreading in its under branches; then the turf-holes, and the various inequalities of the ground – now up, now down: not a star twinkling in the firmament – not a light to tell of human habitation in any direction; the rain pouring unceasingly, and the wind blowing, as Luke afterwards declared, "in whatever direction he turned, always in his face." At length he had almost resolved to sit down quietly upon a rock, and wait the morning dawn, when, in what appeared a high mound of clay, at a short distance, he perceived a little ray of light; he well knew that, in Ireland, wherever there is a roof, there is a resting-place for the poorest traveller; and, guided by the flickering spark, he soon arrived at what could hardly be called a human dwelling. It was, literally speaking, a large excavation in the earth; two boards, nailed together, closed the aperture through which the wretched inhabitants entered, and a hole in the clayey roof served the double purpose of chimney and window. For a moment he rested outside the threshold; and, between the intermediate blasts, the low murmurings of a female voice, in earnest prayer, could be distinctly heard. He pushed aside the unprotecting door; and, stretched on the cold, wet floor, with scarcely sufficient straw to keep her wasted limbs from the earth, covered by the remains of a tattered cloak, he saw the apparently dying form of an elderly woman. The miserable rush-candle, that had guided him to the hovel, was stuck in a scooped potato; her head was supported by a bundle of rags; a broken tea-cup, and an equally mutilated plate, both without either food or liquid, were within reach of the skeleton hands that were fervently clasped together. Through the opening in the roof, the rain fell in torrents, forming sundry pools around the fireless hearth; and no article of furniture of any kind was visible in the miserable dwelling-place – the last earthly home of the departing spirit. As Luke entered, she endeavoured to turn her head towards him, but appeared unable, and barely articulated, "Is that you, Tom, honey?"

Luke returned the usual friendly salutation of "God save all here!" and advanced towards her. The look of her fast-glazing eye fixed steadily upon the young man, and he has often said, "the freezing of that look will never leave his heart." I have seen him shudder at the remembrance. Slowly she pushed back the grey, yet clustering, hair, from her clammy brow, and gazed upon him long and fixedly. "Don't be frightened, agra!" said he, at last; "I've lost my way, and, maybe, ye'd jist let me wait here awhile, till the storm goes by; and, may-be, also, ye'd fancy a bit of what I've got in my pocket (he pulled out the fragments of some wheaten bread); or a drop of this would bring the life to yer heart, astore." She grasped the food he offered, with all the frightful eagerness of famine; but, when she endeavoured to swallow, it almost caused suffocation. Luke took a little of the rain-water in a broken cup, and mixing with it a small portion of whisky, knelt, and gently supporting her head poured it down her throat. She appeared somewhat revived; and, placing her long, bony fingers on his arm, whispered: –

"God reward ye! – God reward ye! – may God keep ye from bitter sin! – there's nothin' to offer ye, nor no fire to dry ye! – but take the wet tacks[589] off, they'll give ye yer death o' could."

Luke obeyed her bidding, and, in a few moments, the dying woman turned towards him another long and piercing look. "Can ye spare me a taste more of that cordial, honey?" she inquired. Luke again knelt, in the same position as before, and she drank with avidity of what he offered. As he was about withdrawing his arm, her eye fixed upon a mark that had been engraved upon his wrist, by a species of tattooing, which the Irish, particularly along the sea-coast, frequently use. It was of a deep blue, and he had no recollection when or how it had been impressed. She grasped his hand with fearful violence, and her energies seemed at once awakened. She tried to articulate; but, although her eyes sparkled, and she sat upright on her bed of straw, yet she could not utter a single sound. "Is it the maning of that mark, ye want to make out? Why, thin, it's just myself that can't tell ye, because, ye see, I don't know: I'm sorry for it, agra! but it can't be helped; only I often think that, may-be, it will be the manes of my finding out who owns me, which, at present, I don't know from Adam. Sorra a one ever laid claim to me, only poor Peg O'Brian, of Cranaby Lane, Cork; who, found me, as a new-year's gift, the first day of January, one thousand eight hundred and seven, outside –"

A scream, loud and piercing, interrupted Luke; and, at the same instant, the withered arms of the poor woman strained him, with a strong grasp, to her bosom. "I haven't an hour to live, boy!" she exclaimed, at last; "and, oh! for the sake of the mercy you expect hereafter, do not throw from ye the poor sinful dying mother, that bore ye; – don't, don't – for, oh! my child! – I'm still – though banned and starving – I'm still your mother!"

Luke was much affected: he had argued himself into the belief that he was a son of one of the nobles of the land; and that, some day or other, he would, according to his own phrase, "turn out a lord, or, at the laste, a gentleman;" and it would have been difficult to analyze the nature of the contending feelings that agitated him. Pity, deep and affectionate pity, for her who had just declared herself his parent, was, however, the predominant one; and he returned her embrace with warmth and sincerity.

"I must tell you all I can," she continued, in a broken voice; "but first, let me ask ye, have ye been honest in yer dealings with rich and poor? Have ye kept from the temptation of gould! – Och; but it's the yellow and the bitter curse! – that leads – but tell me, tell me! – are ye honest?"

"God knows," he replied, "I never took to the value of a traneen from man or mortal; and, what's more, many a gentleman's son would be glad to take up with the *karacter* of poor Luke."

"Heaven be thanked for these words!" ejaculated the unfortunate creature; "for, in the deep of misfortune, the best of comfort is come to me – may the Lord be praised! When I dared to strive (sinner that I am) to pray even one word, it was, that *you* might be honest. All belonging to me are bad, – bad. My children – all, all but you, banned, cursed, – but brought up as they were! – sure, the kittens of the wild cat must seek the young bird's nest! – even now, to bring me food, my husband, and my other born son, are – no not murder! – they swore that they wouldn't take life."

The horrid truth flashed upon the young man's mind, that he had encountered his father and brother; and he explained that he had met them, and told also of their generous conduct towards him.

"Thank God! – but that man is not your father," she said: "listen for one minute. I married a man I hated, for money; but my wild, fierce passions could not bear it – I broke his heart; – you were born after his death – I loved you – but no matter – I loved also a wild and wandering man. He was handsome to look upon, and he promised to make an honest woman of me, if I got rid of you. God had a hand in ye for good, though you needn't thank me for it. So I left ye in a strange place, first setting my mark on ye; and after, whenever I could, I found out that ye were like an own child to poor Peg. But the love of gould followed us both; and, at last, the man was transported.[590] It is quare how my love for him held out; but it did. I followed sin, that I might be sent where he was; and, sure enough, I found him in that land which it's a shame to mintion. Still we longed to get back to ould Ireland; and, though we returned too soon, yet we meant to do well; but the informers got scent of him, and again we were forced to fly. I became a sorrowful mother to many children; and some of them I followed to the gallows-tree: and, at last, my heart turned to iron, and all sins seemed one but, if a wretch like me can say so – I heard, and I read among some loose leaves (for I had my share of larning once), that came from a house they wracked one night, that there was a hope even for us! And I tould *thim* of it, but they laughed at me; and, even when my heart feels burst and burning, I think upon thim, and strive to pray."

With a trembling hand she drew, from under the straw, some torn leaves of the Bible.

"I cannot see to lay them properly," she said; 'but this half I give to you, and these I will leave here; they will find them when I am dead. And God can bless them – may-be, to salvation."

Luke took the pages, while the tears flowed abundantly down his cheeks.

"And now," said she, "*go*. I would not have them know ye for the world; they would want ye to be like them. Go – go – I shall see them; for they can only get food at night for me, like the wild bastes. One thing more: – in Wexford," and she accurately described the street and house, "you will find Father —; tell him *all*, and *where* I am. Though none of us are of this country, he knows me well – he will come; and then you may know where they lay my poor bones, and, may-be, ye'd say one prayer for the soul of yer sinful mother."

The unfortunate woman had only a little ray of light afforded her to point the true path to a happy eternity; but to Luke it was granted, at a future period, to know and profit by the words of the Gospel of peace. That night he hastened to find the priest, who was a kind and benevolent man, and hastened to his duty: his mother died before the next sunset. He has been long settled, where his early occupation is unknown; and has often rejoiced in the hope that the dead may be received, even at the eleventh hour; and prayed that he may continue in the right way!

INDEPENDENCE.

"INDEPENDENCE!" – it is the word of all others, that Irish – men, women, and children – least understand; and the calmness, or rather indifference, with which they submit to dependence, bitter and miserable as it is, must be a source of deep regret to all who "love the land," or who feel anxious to uphold the dignity of human kind. Let us select a few cases, in different grades, from a single village – such as are abundant in every neighbourhood.

Shane Thurlow, for example, "as dacent a boy," and Shane's wife, as "clane-skinned a girl," as any in the world. There is Shane, an active, handsome-looking fellow, leaning over the half door of his cottage, kicking a hole in the wall with his brogue, and picking up all the large gravel within his reach, wherewith to pelt those useful Irish scavengers, the ducks. Let us speak to him.

"Good morrow, Shane!"

"Och! the bright bames of heaven on ye every day! – and kindly welcome, my lady! – and won't ye step in and rest? – it's powerful hot, and a beautiful summer, sure – the Lord be praised!"

Thank you, Shane. I thought you were going to cut the hay-field today; if a heavy shower come, it will be spoiled; it has been fit for the scythe these two days."

"Sure, it's all owing to that thief o' the world, Tom Parrell, my lady. Didn't he promise me the loan of his scythe? – and by the same token, I was to pay him for it; and, *depinding* on that, I didn't buy one – what I've been threatening to do for the last two years."

"But why don't you go to Carrick and purchase one?"

"To Carrick! Och, 'tis a good step to Carrick, and my toes are on the ground (saving your presence), for I *depinded* on Tim Jarvis to tell Andy Cappler, the brogue-maker, to do my shoes; and – bad luck to him, the spalpeen! – he forgot it."

"Where's your pretty wife, Shane?"

"She's in all the woe o' the world, ma'am dear; and she puts the blame of it on me, though I'm not in fault this time, any how: the child's taken the small pock; and she *depinded* on me to tell the doctor to cut it for the cow-pock, and I *depinded* on Kitty Cackle, the limmer, to tell the doctor's own man, and thought she would not forget it, becase the boy's her bachelor – but out o' sight, out o' mind – the never a word she tould him about it, and the babby has got it nataral, and the woman's in heart trouble (to say nothing o' myself) – and it the first, and all."

"I am very sorry, indeed, for you have got a much better wife than most men."

"That's a true word, my lady – only she's fidgetty-like, sometimes; and says I don't hit the nail on the head quick enough; and she takes a dale more trouble than she need about many a thing."

"I do not think I ever saw Ellen's wheel without flax before, Shane!"

"Bad cess to the wheel! – I got it this morning about that, too – I *depinded* on John Williams to bring the flax from O'Flaharty's this day week, and he forgot it; and she says I ought to have brought it myself, and I close to the spot: but where's the good, says I, sure he'll bring it next time."

"I suppose, Shane, you will soon move into the new cottage, at Clurn Hill. I passed it to-day, and it looked so cheerful; and, when you get there, you must take Ellen's advice, and *depend* solely on yourself."

"Och, ma'am dear, don't mintion it! – it's that makes me so down in the mouth, this very minit. Sure I saw that born blackguard, Jack Waddy, and he comes in here, quite innocent-like – 'Shane, you've an eye to 'Squire's new lodge?' says he. 'May-be I have,' says I. 'I'm yer man,' says he. 'How so?' says I. 'Sure I'm as good as married to my lady's maid,' said he; 'and I'll spake to the 'Squire for you, my own self.' 'The blessing be about ye,' says I, quite grateful – and we took a strong sup on the strength of it: and, *depending* on him, I thought all safe; – and what d'ye think, my lady? Why, himself stalks into the place – talked the 'Squire over, to be sure – and, without so much as by yer lave, sates himself and his new wife on the laase in the house; and I may go whistle."

"I was a great pity, Shane, that you didn't go yourself to Mr. Clurn."

"That's a true word for ye, ma'am dear; but it's hard if a poor man can't have a frind to DEPIND on."

"James Doyle, General Dealer," and a neat good looking shop it was – double fronted – its multifarious contents, doubtless very amusing. Mr. Doyle was a sleek, civil little man as any in the county, and much respected; he would have been rich also, were it not that he was, unfortunately, a widower, with five daughters. If you had seen his well-stored counters and shelves, and the extraordinary crowd that assembled in his shop, you would have felt certain that everything was to be had within – pins, ribands, knives, scissors, tobacco-pipes, candles, mousetraps, tea, soap, sugars, tape, thread, cotton, flax, wool, paper, pens, ink, snuff and snuff-boxes, beads, salt herrings, cheese, butter, muslins (such beauties), calicoes (like cambric), linens (better than lawn), twine, ropes, slates, halters, stuffs, eggs, bridles, stockings, turf, delisk, pepper, mustard, vinegar, knitting-needles, books – namely the "Reading made Easy,"[591] "Life of Freney, and his many wonderful escapes, showing how, after his being a most famous Robber, he lived and died a good Catholic Christian in the beautiful and celebrated town of Ross, in the ancient county of Wexford,"[592] "Valentine and Orson,"[593] "Seven Champions of Christendom,"[594] and such like – which books, by the way, turn the heads of half our little girls and boys. The village shop would have vended its finery to greater advantage, if there had been no direct communication with Wexford; for it must be confessed that some of the pretty lasses took it into their heads to be dissatisfied with the goods at the big shop, and absolutely sent for their Sunday elegancies to the county town; but, nevertheless, James Doyle would have made a fortune, if his five daughters had been willing to assist him in his business. Had you seen them, they would not have appeared like the industrious children of an English tradesman, who invariably think it their duty to make every effort for the well-doing of their family, and exert themselves, either at home or abroad, to procure "Independence." Could the slatternly appearance of the five Misses Doyle, or their tawdry finery, designate any beings in the world except the daughters of an ill-regulated Irish shopkeeper? I say ill-regulated, because truly, all are not so; very far from it. Their mother died when they were young, and their father unadvisedly sent them to one of those hot-beds of pride and mischief, a "fifteen-pound" boarding-school[595] in a garrison town, where they learnt to work tent-stitch,[596] and despise trade. When they returned, honest Doyle saw he could not expect anything from them in the way of usefulness, and not possessing much of that uncommon quality, miscalled *common* sense, he was contented to support them in idleness, hoping that their pretty faces might catch the unwary.

"And sure," said Miss Sally, the first-born, to Miss Stacy, the second hope of the family – "haven't we had six months a-piece at Miss Brick's own school? – can't our father affoord us a clear hundred each, down in yellow guineas? – hasn't he got a thousand, may-be more, at the very laste pinny, in Wexford Bank? – and if he, with such a power o' money, demanes himself by keeping a paltry shop, instead of living like a gentleman upon his property, and cutting a dash to get us dacent husbands, not bog-trotters, there's no rason in life why we should attind to it. I hope we have a better spirit, all of us, than to do the likes of that, indeed!"

And so the five Misses Doyle chose the handsomest "prints" in the shop for their own special use; loitered the mornings *en papillote*,[597] lounging up the street, or down the street, or staring out of the window, their shoes slipshod, and the torn-out strings replaced by pins, that invariably made one rent while they secured another; – and, in the evenings, excited the stare of the silly, and the contempt of the wise, by their over-dressed but ill-arranged persons, parading in trumpery finery and French curls. Then they were perpetually quarrelling, although their tastes on matrimonial points were very similar; and if a young farmer, or, more delightful still, a "boy" from Wexford or Waterford, put up at the village – mercy bless us all! What a full cry! Such a set! – five to one!

Take a specimen of the quarrels of the five rivals in love.

"Little good, Babby, there is in your trying to make anything dacent of that head of yours, as long as it's so bright and carroty." "It's no sich thing as carroty, Stacy, and, for the matter of that, look at yer own nose. Sure no one in life would think it worth their while to be afther a pug dog." "It's good fun to hear the pair o' ye argufying about beauty – beauty, indeed!" interrupted Miss Sally, tossing her head, and eyeing her really very pretty person in the cracked looking-glass. "Oh, to be sure, you think yourself wonderful handsome!" exclaimed two of the girls at once. "I never could see any beauty in curds and whey," continued she of the elevated nose. "Ye little go-by-the-ground, keep out of my way," said the tallest sister. Johanna, to the shortest, Cicely; "ye keep as much bother about yer dress, as if ye were a passable size." "Hould yer tongue, ye long gawky," retorted the little one, "there's no use in your dressing at the stranger boy – he's not a grenadier!"[598]

Poor Doyle! Miss Sally ran off with a walking gentleman,[599] who refused to marry her unless her portion was made three hundred pounds. "Oh," said the father, "the pride of my heart she was, but it is bad to *depind* upon beauty!" True, Doyle, or upon anything – except well-regulated industry. If he would come into partnership, he might be useful, but the *gentleman* disdained trade. The poor father mortgaged part of his property, paid the money, and Sally was married; but, in less than a year, was returned on his hands, with the addition of a helpless infant, the scorn of her unfeeling sisters. Stacy was the next to heap sorrow on the old man's head; she, to use her own expression, "met with a misfortune," for she *depended* on "the boy's" honour; but her sin was too degrading to allow of her continuing in the house. Cicely married – honestly married, a daring, dashing smuggler, who, *depending* on his former good fortune, dared an exploit in the contraband trade, which would have banished him for ever from the country, had not Doyle again mortgaged his property to save him; the young man's good name was gone, however, and he lived *depending* on his father-in-law, who now began to suffer seriously from pecuniary embarrassment. Johanna married what was called well, that is, the young man was a gentleman farmer, too proud to look after his own affairs; he *depended* upon "his right-hand man," or the goodness of the times, or anything but his own exertions, for his success – speculated, failed, prevailed on his unfortunate relative to bail him, and, in open defiance of truth and honesty, fled to America.

Then, indeed, the wail and the woe resounded in that house where peace and comfort, and happiness, might have dwelt; and the old man's bed was the cold jail floor, and the family were scattered, and branded with sin and shame, and all for want of INDEPENDENT feelings.

The Honourable Mister Augustus Headerton, who once lived in yonder villa, was the youngest of eleven children, and, consequently, the junior brother of the noble Lord of Headerton, nephew of the Honourable Justice Cleaveland, nephew of Admiral Barrymore,[600] K.C.B., &c. &c. &c.; and cousin, first, second, third, fourth, fifth, sixth or seventh remove – to half the honourables and dishonourables in the country.

When the old Earl died, he left four Chancery suits, and a nominal estate, to the heir apparent, to whom he also bequeathed his three younger brothers and sisters, who had only small annuities from their mother's fortune, being assured that (to use his own words) "he might *depend* on him, for the honour of the family, to provide for them handsomely." And so he did (in his own estimation); – his lady sisters "had the run of the house," and Mr. Augustus Headerton had the run of the stables, the use of hunters and dogs, and was universally acknowledged to possess a "proper spirit," because he spent three times more than his income. "He bates the world and all, for beauty, in a hunting jacket!" exclaimed the groom. "He flies a gate beyant any living sowl I iver see; and his tally-ho! my jewel – 'twould do yer heart good to hear his tally-ho!" said my Lord's huntsman. "He's a generous jentleman as any in the kingdom – I'll say that for him, any day in the year," echoed the coachman. "He's admired more nor any jintleman that walks Steven's-green[601] in a month o' Sundays, I'll go bail," continued Miss Jenny Roe, the ladies' maid.

"Choose a profession!" Oh, no! – impossible! But the Honourable Mr. Augustus Headerton chose a wife, and threw all his relations, including Lord Headerton, the Honourable Justice Cleaveland, Admiral Barrymore, K.C.B., and his cousins to the fiftieth remove, into strong convulsions, or little fits. She, the lady, had sixty thousand pounds; that, of course, they could not object to. She had eloped with the Honourable Mister Augustus Headerton; – mere youthful indiscretion. She was little and ugly; – that only concerned her husband. She was proud and extravagant; – these were lady-like failings. She was ignorant and stupid; – her sisters-in-law would have pardoned that. She was vulgar; – that was awkward. Her father was a carcass butcher in Cole's-lane Market![602] – death and destruction!

It could never be forgiven! – the cut direct was unanimously agreed on, and the little lady turned up her little nose in disdain, as her handsome barouche[603] rolled past the lumbering carriage of the Right Honourable Lord Headerton. She pursuaded her husband to purchase that beautiful villa, in view of the family domain, that she might have more frequent opportunities of bringing, as she elegantly expressed it, "the proud beggars to their trumps;[604] – and why not? – money's money, all the world over." The Honourable Mister Augustus *depended* on his agent for the purchase, and some two thousand and odd pounds were consequently paid, or said to have been paid, for it, more than its value. And then commenced the general warfare; full purse and empty head – *versus,* no purse and old nobility. They had the satisfaction of ruining each other: in due course of time, the full purse was emptied by devouring duns,[605] and the old nobility suffered by its connexion with vulgarity.

"I want to know, Honourable Mister Augustus Headerton," (the lady always gave the full name when addressing her husband; she used to say it was all she got for her money) – "I want to know, Honourable Mister Augustus Headerton, the reason why the music-master's lessons, given to the Misses Headerton (they were blessed with seven sweet pledges of affection), have not been paid for? I desired the steward to see to it, and you know I *depend* on him to settle these matters."

The Honourable Mrs. Augustus Headerton rang the bell – "Send Martin up."

"Mister Martin," the lady began, "what is the reason that Mr. Langi's account has not been paid!"

"My master, ma'am, knows that I have been anxious for him to look over the accounts; the goings-out are so very great, and the comings-in, as far as I know – " the Honourable Mister Augustus Headerton spilt some of the whisky-punch he was drinking, over a splendid hearth-rug, which drew the lady's attention from what would have been an unpleasant *eclaircissement.*[606]

"I cannot understand why difficulties should arise. I am certain I brought a fortune large enough for all extravagance," was the lady's constant remark, when expenditure was mentioned. Years pass over the heads of the young – and they grow old; and over the heads of fools – but they never grow wise.

The Honourable Mister and Mistress Augustus Headerton were examples of this truth; their children grew up around them – but could derive no support from the parent root. The mother *depended* on governesses and masters for the education of her girls – and on their beauty, connexions, or accomplishments, to procure them husbands. The father did not deem the labours of study fit occupation for the sons of an ancient house: – "*Depend* upon it," he would say, "they'll all do well with my connexions – they will be able to command what they please." The Honourable Mistress Augustus could not now boast of a full purse, for they had long been living on the memory of their once ample fortune.

The Honourable Mister Augustus Headerton died, in the forty-fifth year of his age, of inflammation, caught in an old limekiln, where he was concealed, to avoid an arrest for the sum of one hundred and eighty guineas, for Black Nell, the famous filly (who won the cup on the Curragh of Kildare) – purchased in his name, but without his knowledge, by his second son, the pride of the family – commonly called Dashing Dick.

All I know further of the Honourable Mistress Augustus Headerton is, that –

"She played at cards, and died."

Miss Georgiana – the beauty, and greatest fool of the family, who *depended* on her face as a fortune, did get a husband, – an old, rich, West India planter,[607] and eloped, six months after marriage, with an officer of dragoons.

Miss Celestina was really clever and accomplished. "Use her abilities for her own support!" Oh, no! – not for worlds! Too proud to work, but not too proud to beg, she *depended* on her relations, and played toady to all who would have her.

Miss Louisa – not clever; but, in all other respects, ditto – ditto.

Miss Charlotte was always very romantic; refused a respectable banker with indignation, and married her uncle's footman – for love.

Having sketched the female part of the family, I will tell you what I remember of the gentlemen.

"The Emperor," as Mr. Augustus was called, from his stately manner and dignified deportment, aided by as much self-esteem as could well be contained in a human body, *depended,* without any "compunctious visitings of conscience," on the venison, claret, and champagne of his friends, and thought all the time he did them honour – and thus he passed his life.

"Dashing Dick" was the opposite of the Emperor; sung a good song – told a good story – and gloried in making ladies blush. He *depended* on his cousin Colonel Bloomfield's[608] procuring him a commission in his regiment, and cheated tailors, hosiers, glovers, coach-makers, and even lawyers, with impunity. Happily for the world at large, Dashing Dick broke his neck in a steeple-chase, on a stolen horse, which he might have been hanged for purloining, had he lived a day longer.

Ferdinand was the *bonne-bouche*[609] of the family: they used to call him "the Parson!" Excellent Ferdinand! – he *depended* on his own exertions; and, if ever the name of Headerton rises in the scale of moral or intellectual superiority, it will be owing to the steady and virtuous efforts of Mister Ferdinand Headerton, merchant, in the good city of B—; for he possesses, in perfection, "the glorious privilege of being INDEPENDENT."

BLACK DENNIS.

"WELL!" exclaimed Michael Leahy, as he entered his cottage – "well! the Lord be praised! – I've seen a powerful deal of happiness this day, one way or the other. Above, at the big house, the mistress was giving out the medicine, and food, with her own two blessed hands, to half the parish; there she was, at the closet window, slaving herself for the poor – that's Christianity!" He proceeded to shake the snow from his "big coat," and hang it up. "It's a powdering night of snow, as ever came out of the heavens; but, any how, we have a roof to shelter us, thank God! – to say nothin' o' the sod o' turf, and the boiling pratees; and the master gave me a good quarter o' tobaccy; so now, Norry, lay by your spinning, and let's have our bit o' supper."

"With all the joy in life, Mick – and thank God, too, that my husband comes home, when his work is done, to his wife and childer."

Mick Leahy looked affectionately at his wife – and well he might. She was clean and industrious – cheerful and contented: the mud walls of her cabin were whitewashed; a glass window, small, but unbroken, looked out on a little garden, stocked with potatoes and cabbages, and hedged with furze. No labourer in the country had thicker stockings than Mick Leahy – they were his wife's knitting; no whiter shirts were on the town-land than Mick Leahy's – and they were all of his wife's spinning. No finer children knelt to receive the priest's blessing on a summer Sunday, than Mick Leahy's; and proud were father and mother of them.

"God help all poor travellers! – it's blake and bitther weather," continued Mick, as he lit his pipe, and took his seat on the settle, under the wide chimney, after he had finished his supper: "I wish some unfortunate cratur had a share of the chimbly-corner, for there'll be neither hedge nor ditch to be seen by morning, if it snows on in this way."

"It does my heart good to see little Mary bless herself when she lays her head down for the night," said Norah, coming out of their only bed room – which was always in neat order. "And then, Lanty has the Ave-Mary and all, so pat; – och! Mick, honey, 'tis sweet to look at childer – and very sweet to look at one's own childer; but it's bitter to think that, one day, may-be, they may come to sin and shame."

"No child of mine, Norah," said the father, proudly, "shall ever come to sin or shame."

"Whisht, Mick, whisht!" said the meek mother; "we are all born to sin, you know – but God keep away shame! – all we can do is to pray for, and show them a good patthern."

"Then, that's true, and spoken sinsible, like my own Norry," replied the father; "and the blessing o' God will always be about you and yours, at any rate. What! – agin to the wheel! Well, ye're never idle – I'll say that for ye."

Bur, bur – went the wheel, and the turf sparkled; still the storm increased, and shook the little cabin, that seemed almost beneath its vengeance.

"Was there any signs of fire-light in the place on the far moor, as ye passed it?" inquired Norah.

"None, that I see," replied the husband.

"Do you know, Mick, I never could make them people out; there's the three of 'em live upon nothin' at all – that I can think of; they never beg – they never work. Lanty met the child, this morning, picking bits o' sticks near the moor-hedge, and he tould him his daddy was dying, and his mammy not much better; so Lanty brought him home, and I gave him plenty to ate, and as many pratees as he could carry away, and a morsel o' white bread; and, to be sure, he ate, the cratur, as if he was starved; but was so shy and wild – like a young fox-cub – that I could get nothin' out of him."

"Of all the men I ever see, in my born days, that man has the black-heart look. The wicked one – Heaven bless us! – set his mark[610] between his two eyes, or he never did it to anybody yet."

"Hush, Mick! – is that the wind shaking the windy, or a knock of the door?"

The knock was distinctly repeated, and Mick inquired who was there? A female voice requested admission, and, on his opening the door, a tall woman, enveloped in a long blue cloak, entered; when in the cottage, she threw back the hood that had quite covered her face; it might once have been handsome, but want and misery had obliterated its beauty, and given an almost maniac expression to eyes both dark and deep; the hair was partly confined by a checked kerchief; and the outline of the figure would have been worthy the pencil of Salvator.

"Ye don't know me, and so much the betther; but I am wife to him that's dying on the far moor; and I want you, Mick Leahy, to go to Father Connor, and ask him, for the love of God, to come to the departing sinner, and – if he can – give him some comfort."

"Sit down," said Norry, kindly; shrinking, nevertheless, from her visitor. "'Tis an awful night, and a long step to his reverence's; but Mick will do a good turn for any poor sinner: yet I wonder ye didn't call to himself, and ye passed close by his gate coming here."

"Me call on the priest!" half screamed the woman; "me, the cast away! – the thing that's shunned as soon as seen! – Me! – but do not look so at me, Norry Leahy! – do not. Ye were kind enough, this morning, to my starving boy; ye sent food to my miserable cabin! Do not – do not! Now, when he is dying! Bad as he is, Norry, he is still my husband."

"Asy, asy," said Mick; "I do not care who he is! Sure, we're all sinners, and God is good: he may get betther."

"No, no, I do not wish him that; he has nothing to live for: the ban[611] is on him; and, if he was known, even here, he would be torn in pieces."

Mick and Norah exchanged glances, and slowly did the former take his long coat off the peg; and wistfully did poor Norah look at her husband, for the woman's wildness had quite overpowered her; yet, to refuse going for a priest, was what no Irishman ever did, and she thought it was her husband's duty; her fears, for a moment, conquered her resolution, when he was in the act of opening the door; and, laying her hand gently on the woman's cloak, she said, with a quivering lip –

"And won't ye tell us yer name; and Mick going to do yer bidding?"

"Ye will have it, Norry Leahy," replied she, almost fiercely – "Anne Dennis! – my husband was called Black Dennis, the informer!"

Norah staggered back, and Mick withdrew his hand from the latch.

"Ye will *not* go, then?" said the unfortunate creature; "and because he's a sinner, ye think he should be left to die like a dog in a ditch; and you, Norry, you shrink from me; and what power have I to harm ye? – look!" She threw back her cloak; a worn jacket and petticoat hardly shrouded so perfectly skeleton a form, that poor Norah looked on her with pity and astonishment. "Look! – and say, if I have power to harm! – I have hardly strength enough to hold *his* dying head off the cold earth."

"I'll go, in the name o' mercy," said Mick, "though it's little he deserves a good turn from any one, even on his death-bed."

Norah was horrified at her husband's visiting one who had brought sorrow to so many dwellings; but he was gone, and she was left, in her cottage solitude, to brood over what she had just heard and seen. "Black Dennis" had been a United Irishman, and one of the most violent order – the projector of more burnings, murders, and robberies, than any chief of them all; and when, at last, he found that he could no longer carry on the system of rebellion and plunder, into which he had drawn so many unfortunate victims, he turned king's evidence; many were the men either transported or executed on his statements – all less guilty than himself. No wonder, then, that Black Dennis was regarded with peculiar sentiments of abhorrence, and that, wherever he went, he was a banned man! His wife had shared his plunder, and exulted in his deeds, when he was a bold rapparee; but, when he became a cold-blooded informer, she spurned both him and his wealth, and left him to his wanderings. He went abroad, but his ill-got gold wasted and wasted; and he returned to his native country, "to lave his bones," as he said, "among his own people."

His wife had been no less miserable than himself; and, when her wretched husband made his appearance at her poor door, she felt relieved at beholding the only being who could truly appreciate her varied sufferings: his money was gone – he was dying a lingering death; and her still woman's heart yearned towards its early affection. They could not remain in the village where she and her boy resided: because, there, Black Dennis would soon have been recognized; so she sold a few articles of furniture and clothing she possessed, and went away with her husband, that he might die in peace on "the far moor." Her anxiety to procure for him the rites of the church in his last moments, overcame her repugnance to discovery; and a sort of holy fear prevented her going to the priest herself: the kindness shown by the Leahys to her child, induced her to confide in them; and silently, but thankfully, she accompanied Mick to Mr. Connor's house.

The good priest went with his guides to the hut where the informer lay. It was, in truth, meet dwelling for such a man: "the far moor" showed an extensive waste of snow, with but one tree to break its white surface: and the hovel rested against its immense trunk, which, having escaped the axe and the tempest, stripped even of its bark by time, threw far and wide its knotted and distorted limbs, as if in mockery of the whirlwind and the storm.

The sands of life were nearly run. Black Dennis lay extended on some straw, scarcely covered by portions of tattered clothing, and his head rested on the knees of his boy; he moved it quickly as they entered, and pressed a little wooden cross to his lips: the priest poured a cordial down his throat, and, for a few moments, he revived.

"That man need not go," said he, seeing Mick about to take his departure, in order that the sinful man might confess; "I have nothing to tell but what all the world knows; nothing to say, except that my heart is – hell! Oh! will your reverence tell me," – and he raised his head from the child's lap – "if there is hope for me, the murderer, the burner, the rebel, the INFORMER?" – Madly his glaring eyes watched for a reply.

"There is hope for all," replied Father Connor, "through God's mercy."

The head fell back, the eye fixed, the lip quiveringly uttered "Hope," and Black Dennis was no more.

The unfortunate widow shed no tears, but knelt and gazed on him who had known so much sin, and endured so much sorrow: the child clung around its mother's neck, and wept bitterly. Leahy endeavoured to rouse her from her stupor, but in vain. "I cannot leave her in this way; and the poor boy – he's innocent any way; and that's not 'Black Dennis' now, but only a lump o' dust! Yer reverence, what am I to do?"

The priest stooped down, and endeavoured to disengage the child from the parent; this aroused her. "My boy! – my boy!" and the tears flowed from eyes to which they had long been strangers. "Ye'll put him in holy ground, Father?" said she, looking at the priest. "Ye'll not deny even an informer Christian burial? I know *'twould be a bad example* to bury him by daylight; but, by night, what would hinder?"

"Yes," replied Mr. Connor, "to morrow-night, I will see that duty properly performed; and now I can only commend you to the mercy of God."

The grey morning dawned on Leahy and his good Norah, tracing their path to the hut on the far moor. "It would be a sin," said the latter, "to bear spite and hatred to a senseless corpse; and, bad as the woman was, she left him when he turned informer." During the day, the priest procured a rude coffin, and, with the assistance of one of his own people, by the light of the waning moon, that shed her cold rays over the snow-clad country, in a corner of the old churchyard – far from any other grave – the body of Black Dennis was deposited.

No inducement could prevail on the unfortunate woman to forsake the grave: she sat on it, wrapped in her long blue cloak, and suffered her boy to be led away by the priest to his own dwelling – for the amiable man could not bear to leave a child of six years old exposed on so inclement a night.

When the morning came, the woman was not seen; the boy went crying from the churchyard to the hut, but could nowhere find his mother. He grew up in Mr. Connor's house, a solitary, but not a friendless, being – a melancholy, gentle youth, whose intellects appeared to have suffered from the recollection of early misery: he was, nevertheless, tractable and obedient, and devotedly attached to his benefactor.

It was long unknown what became of the widow. Some said she was dead – others, that she was employed in unceasing pilgrimage and penance. Although the death of Black Dennis was almost forgotten, no one cared to rebuild the hut on the far moor; and even the village children, when seeking heath-bells and buttercups, avoided the shadow of the "Informer's Tree."

The youth, who was always called "Father Connor's Ned," often visited the cheerful Norah and her husband, and seemed particularly fond of every inhabitant of their happy cottage. Mick Leahy used to lament that the boy was an "innocent;"[612] but Norry would reply, "So best, Mick, for ye see, by being weak, he escapes being wicked; and it was natural to suppose he'd be one or t'other, seeing he came from a bad stock."

Mick, and his wife and family, had been laughing over the embers of the fire, one evening, telling tales, and singing old ballads; poor Ned, who formed one of the party, was even more silent than usual, when he suddenly started up, and, pointing to the window, exclaimed, "Did you see that?"

"There, 'tis passed now," he continued, wildly. "Norry, if ever there was a banshee, that's one; and it is not the first time, nor the second either, that I've seen it, wid its large grey eyes fixed on me, so death-like; but I don't think I iver see it more than once in the same year."

"A shadow certainly passed the windy, I'll take my bible oath," said Mick. He went out, and to his astonishment, no person was visible. "God save us all!" said he, re-entering his cabin, "it's very quare."

Soon after, the simple boy returned home; but the first news the Leahys heard, next morning, was, that, on the cold door-stone of the priest's house, an aged corpse was found – the worn and wasted corpse of Anne Dennis!

The wretched wanderer had, it was afterwards ascertained, been an occasional visitor to the neighbourhood: anxious, doubtless, to look upon her child, yet careful to avoid discovery, and feeling most probably, that her last hour was come, she had that night laid her down at the door of the house that had sheltered the only being she loved, and expired. They buried her quietly, near her husband. The long grass, and the broad-leaved dock, wave over them in the chill blast of the winter evening; and, sometimes, poor harmless Ned, is seen to stand and look, with tearful eyes, upon his parents' grave.

GERALDINE

GERALDINE.

WHERE my distinguished countryman, Mr. Maclise, obtained the original of this portrait, I cannot tell; but it brought to my mind an incident that occurred to me a few summers ago, when visiting Honfleur. It is impossible to conceive anything more beautiful, either in situation or interior, than the simple chapel of our "Lady of Grace," that crowns the cliffs, where sailors and their wives offer their prayers, and pay their vows. I found a number of my countrymen and women at Honfleur; and was much struck with the appearance of one in particular, who climbed the hill leading to the chapel, every morning, and remained there during the day. The servant who accompanied, or, rather, followed her, never revealed her surname; she spoke of her, and to her, as "Miss Geraldine," and threw into this name of lofty sound as great a quantity of Irish unsophisticated brogue, as the three syllables could express. It was very pleasant to me to hear the tones of my own country in a foreign land, and still more pleasing to observe the attention, amounting to positive devotion, which the good-tempered, broad-featured woman bestowed upon the fair devotee.

"Devotee!" – I do not know exactly why I should call her so, except from the fact of her perpetually climbing that most picturesque and winding road, leading to the chapel, and kneeling before the pretty shrine of the Madonna, for hours together: her attitude was one of perfect devotion; one small hand held the rosary, the other shaded her face; the cloak appeared abandoned to its own drapery – her hair fell, as you see, in the most *dégagé*[613] undress; and it was not until you approached the fair saint that you perceived her eyes were anything but quiet – they rambled from corner to corner of their fringed pent houses, with an observant, rather than coquetish, expression; certainly, with anything but the devoted one which her attitude would lead you to expect. She appeared thinking of, and expecting, some one who did not come. Her step, in the morning, seemed buoyant with hope – but, in the evening, she hung her head, and descended to an obscure lodging in the town, as if weighed down by disappointment. Meeting her so frequently, and feeling deeply interested in one so beautiful, it was impossible not to evince a portion of that feeling, restrained as it must be, by the fear of offending its object; at last, however, we exchanged brief greetings; and she would, when I visited the chapel, rise from before the Madonna, and point out some particular offering for my sympathy or admiration; but our acquaintance gained no further ground: she spoke but few words, and their tone conveyed the idea that she was not in the least interested in what she said; her words were with you, but not her thoughts – they were away; but where? With her deserted country, or forsaken parents, or absent brothers, or – that is ever the uppermost thought on such occasions – a wandering lover? Her attendant seldom entered the chapel, but would sit outside, under the magnificent Cross[614] which casts its protecting shadow over the waters. I can imagine nothing more cheering to the spirits of a French sailor, than the sight of that Cross, as he returns, after wrestling with the spirits of the deep, to his native country.

The attendant was naturally communicative; and anxious to impress me with a notion of Miss Geraldine's sanctity and greatness "in her own country;" but, with all her national garrulity, she guarded well her young lady's secret, whatever it was.

"It's hard, so it is," she said, one evening, just as the sun was about to set: – "it's mighty hard to have nothing to do but sit here, looking over the sea, or taking account of the *voteens*[615] that come up to pray for the return of those that, may-be, have left their bones to the mermaids, long ago; but I don't care, it's the love and duty I owe my *fosterer;* for, although she's a lady, as any one may see, and I'm – just what I am, and nothing more or less, we were both reared on the same milk; both slept on the same bosom – that's cold, colder than them stones, now; if it wasn't – it's in dear Ireland we'd be still;" and tears poured from her large grey eyes, but were quickly suppressed. "Oh, it's mighty grand," as I say to Miss Geraldine, "to come to foreign parts; – but where's the country like our own, – the country that has the nature in it – the welcome that comes from the heart, – the farewell that bursts from the eyes? Oh, my! and she in there, all day; and, when she comes out, it's more dead than alive she'll be! If you had seen her a year ago, when her beautiful face was ever in motion – like the sunbeams on the sea – and when she'd lay down, and uprise with a song upon her lips, that, like two real lovers never parted but to meet in smiles! Oh, my! the spirit's prayed out of her – so it is."

"Not quite," I said, and I remembered the inquiring expression of her wandering eyes.

"Oh!" answered the ready Irish woman – "if she prays she watches too, – she must – though that's neither here nor there. There's fine religion in this country, and nothing to go against it; and yet I wish we were back in ould Ireland once more: but, let her go where she will, I'll never part her. I promised the dying on the death-bed, I never would – with her liking, or without it; and, as the ould verse says,

'By a promise to the dead,
Through the world you may be led;'[616]

and that's thrue, and why not? – it's a promise you can't be absolved from, only by a priest, and his reverence would not like being troubled about such a thing, at all. The sight's wore out of my eyes, and the feet off my legs, and the *laugh from my heart,* just with following her; but I don't care for that; – when her vow's out, we'll have peace, may-be."

"But what is her vow to you?"

The large grey eyes dilated, until they looked half as large again as usual, while she repeated, "Is it to me, ma'am? sure I *tould* you, dear, she was Miss Geraldine, my own young lady, away from her people, and country; – and the promise! Ah, then, sure now, I've just *tould* you of my promise to them that loved her; and little thought it's in this outlandish country she'd be, where they are so ignorant that they have no English; though it's a God-fearing country, for all that. 'What is her vow to me,' avick! Ah, were you ever in Ireland at all, to ask that, and she my fosterer – besides? 'Her vow to me,' the jewil! the heavens above knows – more than my own – ten times; may-be I won't follow her through the earth – my soul's delight!"

"But, suppose she was to become very poor," I said.

"She'd want me all the more," replied Irish fidelity. "Besides," she added, laughingly, "it is not easy to frighten any one with poverty, who has lived all her life, for seven days out of the week, upon potatoes and milk, I don't care for any hardship that would come upon myself; but I'd lay down my life to save *her,* the darling of my heart, from any harm. May the Lord put all heavy trouble past her! Sure I pray for that on my bended knees, night and morning, as well as all day long: she's had her cross, and, in time, will have her crown. I left my country, and him I loved better than any country, to follow her; and, if she's here to-day, she may be gone to-morrow: – there she is now, as white as a snow-drop – so, good evening, ma'am; and God be with you!"

About ten days after this, we had nearly achieved the summit of our favourite walk, and only paused to look back upon the town, when a gentleman passed us, with steps, it would seem, more eager than his strength permitted; his dress was more foreign than French – decidedly not belonging to the British Isles. We did not see his face, which was turned away. When we arrived on the hill – there, in her old place, sat the faithful Irishwoman, looking over the sea; and by some instinct, turning her head to scrutinize every one who set foot upon the natural platform on which the chapel stands and the cross is planted: her recognition was a broad smile, a closing of her hands, and a motion of her head – and then, as we approached, she rose. We had not, however, exchanged a word, when a faint scream sent her flying to the chapel. We followed, to see the fair devotee weeping and sobbing, like a child, on the shoulder of the stranger we had passed on the hill.

The next morning they had quitted Honfleur – some said, in a ship sailing for Mexico – others declared, for Sydney. The old woman of the house protested the stranger to be Miss Geraldine's brother – for he was so like her; and the brown-skinned, black-eyed daughter observed, that husbands were sometimes like their wives. There was no doubt that the servant still followed her lady's fortunes – faithful and devoted to the last.

CAPTAIN ANDY.

"Good day, Master Andy; you have a prosperous time of it; plenty of water to work the mill, and plenty of corn to grind. Well, Captain, after all, peace is better than war."

Andy glanced, from under his white hat, one of those undefinable looks of quiet humour, perhaps the peculiar characteristic of an Irish peasant. He made no reply, but elevated his right shoulder, and drew his left hand across the lower part of his face, as if seeking to conceal its expression; "Yer honour wouldn't be going to Taghmon this fine morning?"

"No, Captain."

"Well, now, Mr. Collins, dear, may I make so bould just to beg that you'd lave off calling me Captain; and give me my own dacent name – Andy, as yer honour used before the 'Ruction,'[617] and sure the peaceable time has lasted long enough to make ye forget it?"

"So, Captain (I beg your pardon), Andy – the peaceable times have lasted too long, you think."

"I ax yer honour's pardon, I said no sich a thing. May-be, if it was said it would be nothin' but the truth; but that's neither here nor there, and no business o' mine. The government's a good government – may-be, ay – may-be, no – and the king, God bless him!" – and he lifted his hat reverently from his head – "the king's a good king!"

"Ay, ay, I remember your famous flag, made out of the green silk curtain, and garnished with real laurel leaves, mounted on the top of a sapling ash, the motto, 'God bless the king, but curse his advisers!'"

"Well, yer honour has a mighty quare way, I must say, of repating gone-by things, and tazing a person, quite useless like."

The gentleman who had been amusing himself at the poor miller's expense, now assumed a more serious look and manner, and, placing his hand on his shoulder with kind familiarity –

"Andrew," said he, "when I speak seriously of by-gone days – of times of terror and bloodshed, there is one feeling that absorbs every other – gratitude to the noble little Captain of the Bannow corps, who, when one of my own tenants declared, 'it was the duty of every man in the division to spill Protestant blood, until the United men could stand in it knee-deep,' rushed forward, and baring his bosom, as he stood before me, called to his men to strike *there,* for that not a hair of my head should fall while he had arms to use in my defence."

The miller turned away for a moment, and then, taking off his hat, extended his broad hand to the gentleman, making sundry scrapes, and divers indescribable gestures.

"May I make so bould as to ax yer honour to walk in, and ate or drink something? and, besides, I had a little matther o' my own that I wanted to spake to ye about: and, sure, ye need never think of what ye've jist mintioned; for, if it hadn't been for yer good word, thim children o' mine would have had no father. I was ready enough to die for the cause like a man, dacently; but, to be hung, jist for nothing, like a dog, was another thing. It 'll niver come to that wid me now, God be praised! To be sure, we all have our own notions; but I'll not meddle or make any more, in sich matters; for all the boys wanted to be commanders and gentlemen at once, and wouldn't be said or led by their betthers. But I ax pardon for talking, and ye standing outside the mill-house, when the woman, and the fire, and all's widin, that 'ud rejoice to see yer two feet on the harth-stone, even if it were of pure gould."

"Oh, then, kindly welcome, sir! Jenny, set a chair for the gintleman; arrah, bother, not that one wid the three legs! (Tim, is that the patthern o' yer manners, to stand gnawing yer thumb there; where's yer bow? Mabby, set down the grawl, can't ye, and make yer curtshy.) – Sure it's proud we're of the honour," continued bustling Mrs. Andy, "and grateful; and what will yer honour take? (Tim have done picking the bread.) – A cruddy⁶¹⁸ egg and a rasher, or some hot cake and frish butter, yer honour, as frish as the day, made wid my own hands. Jenny, quiet that child, will ye? Oh, Mabby, Mabby, run for the dear life; there's the ould pig – bad cess to her! – and all the bonneens,* through the cabbages. I humbly beg yer honour's pardon (courtesying), but, may-be, yer honour would just taste –"

"Will ye hould yer whisht, Biddy?" interrupted the Captain, stepping from the inner room, carrying a stone jar, and a long green bottle; "she has a tongue in her head, sir, and likes to use it," he continued, placing both jar and bottle on the table; "but here's something fit for a mornin'ᵃ for Saint Patrick himself, and yer honour must taste it – raale Innishown; or, if ye're too delicate (striking the jar), the likes of this isn't in e'er a cellar in the county." He filled a glass, and presented it to Mr. Collins, who looked at, tasted, and finally drank it off.

"It came from foreign parts, sir, as a little testimonial from one whose last gift it will be."

"Indeed, Andy! pity such cordials should be *last* gifts."

* Young pigs

"True for ye, sir. Tim, make yer bow to the gintleman, and take yer 'Voster'ᵃ ⁶¹⁹ out under the sunny hedge, and yer slate, my man, and do two sums in fractions, for practice. Jenny, woman, lift out your wheel, and see that yer brother minds the sums."

"Don't ye see she's getting out the white cloth, for a snackᵇ for his honour? I wish ye'd let the girl alone; or, any way, lave her do *my* bidding," continued the wife; "ye've no earthly dacency in ye, or ye'd ha' tould me his honour was coming in, and then I could have got something proper, not trusting to rashers and eggs, and yer outlandish drops;" and the angry dame, angry because she could not pay "his honour" sufficient attention, bustled about more than ever.

"The devil's in the woman! But – save us all! – they can't help it," muttered Andrew; "may-be, while she's doing the eggs, yer honour would walk out, and look at the new spokes in the mill-wheel, and the little things I've been trying at; thank God, we've no middle-men in this parish, but resident landlords, who give every earthly encouragement to the improving tenant, and never rise the rint because the ground looks well; only a kind word, and every praise in life, and encourage ye wid odd presents: a wheel, a bale o' flax, or a lock o' wool to the girls; a new plough or harrow, or some fine seed potatoes to the boys; and that's the true rason why the parish o' Bannow is the flower o' the country."*

The neighbouring fields looked indeed, beautiful; and the bright greenery extended, at either side, around the mill-stream; here and there, a gnarled oak, or a gay thorn tree, added interest to the landscape; while the sweet, waving willows, rooting themselves in the very depth of the rippling water, which, dancing between their trunks, and sparkling through their weeping foliage, formed a picture as calmly beautiful as even fruitful and merry England could supply. Andrew, from some cause or other, forgot the "new spokes" when he reached the mill-house with Mr. Collins, and peered behind the piled sacks, to ascertain that no one was in the small square room, which contained flour bags and piles of fresh grain, a long form, and sundry winnowing sheets, flails, and sifters.

"I have got something particular to say to yer honour, but couldn't for the woman; but I'll boult her out (fastening the door). Sure I'm king o' the castle here, any way. Oh! don't lane against thim bags, sir; there's no getting the white out o' the English cloth, at all, at all. Sure the binch – (I wish yer honour was on the raale binch, and it's then we'd have justice!) – the binch'll do the turn." And Andy pulled off his wig, dusted with it the form, or, as he called it, "binch," replaced the powdered "bob" over his own black hair, crossed his feet,

---

* This statement holds good to the letter. It is a common occurrence for the tenants of Mr. Boyce – even those who have no leases – to make him their banker; exhibiting to him the profits they make out of the land, not only with justifiable pride, but with perfect confidence that the more they make, the better pleased their landlord will be, and without the remotest dread that their increased prosperity will be a cause of rising the rent.

gave the wig a settling pull, folded his arms, and, leaning against the door-post, commenced the disclosure of his secret, in a confidential under-tone: –

"Yer honour remimbers ould times, I'm thinking?" – Mr. Collins smiled.

"And the Bannow corps?" – Another smile.

"Well; I know yer honour's sinsible that, though the boys would have me head thim, yet I nivir thought they'd have turned to the religion, and murdered the innocent craturs o' Protestants for nothin', or, as God's my judge, I'd have let thim all go to Botany,[620] afore I'd any hand in it; but that's all gone and past, and nei-ther here nor there. Well; whin once I was in, I thought it right to behave myself properly. But there were bloody sins o' both sides, as nataral; – burnings and mas-sacres – and all bad; and time was, whin I couldn't, for the life o' me, tell which was worst; only the poor Catholics had no arms, but the bits o' pikes, for the most part, to make fight wid. Och! it was bitter bad! Well, yer honour remimbers Thomas Jarratt, the farmer, who lived on the hill-side, far from kith or kin; a lone man, wid one son, a wild chap – yet kindly; fierce – but gentle-like at times, and a generous boy; striking handsome, and prouder than many more rich and power-ful nor himself. Well, he always had his own way; the poor father doted down on him; and, for many a day, he was the white-headed boy o' the whole country.

"Now, sir, dear, call another to mind. Ould James Corish, though suspected o' being a black Protestant (I ax pardon, but that was what they were called), was well counted by all his neighbours; he had seen a dale o' years, and there were not many happier; for his prosperity had lasted for more than half a hundred, and appeared sartin to continue for the remainder o' his days. He had had a joy-ful fireside o' childer; but they were all gone excipt two: Mary, the eldest – so larned, so wise, and so charming; and James, a fine, gay boy, rising seventeen; thoughtless – but all are thoughtless, sir, before they mix in the world, to drink of its bitterness, or be marked by its corruption. It used to do my heart good, of a Sunday, to see that family passing on to their own church. The ould man, his silver hair falling over his shoulders; his two childer, the one, wid her dark long curls half hid under her straw hat, and her short scarlet petticoat, that set off the white stockings and slight ankles; the other looking so cheerful, his light blue eyes jumping out of his head wid innocent joy. Well, sir, young Thomas Jar-ratt cast an eye upon the colleen, and, as he was no ways a strict Catholic, ould Corish thought, may-be, he might answer for Mary, as he was well to do in the world: and though he didn't get any grate encouragement – to say grate – yet, for all that, he went in and out, and the two boys were very much together, and no one dare look at Mary, on account o' young Tom. Yer honour remimbers the militia regiments;[621] well, young Corish was drawed to go in thim."

"I do. I remember it well," replied Mr. Collins; "I was there the evening he went to join the Wexford militia.[622] 'God bless you, my only boy!' sobbed the poor father; it's like spilling one's own blood, to fight against one's neighbours;

but, God bless you, boy; do your duty, as your father did before you; only remember, a Protestant soldier need not be an Orangeman.' Mary neither spoke nor wept; but she pushed the curling locks from off her brother's brow, and mournfully gazed upon it; and when, laughing at her fears, he affectionately kissed her cheek, still she looked sad; and long and anxiously did her eyes follow him, until his form was lost in the twilight mist, as he ascended the mountain of Forth."

"Poor cratur! – poor cratur!" sighed the miller; "well, sir, you know I was over-persuaded to join the boys, and we used to have little meetings in this very room, and I didn't care to let the wife know anything of it, at first; but she found it out, somehow or other (the women are very 'cute), and was all aginst it: but she comed over a bit at the thought of my being a captain, and she, to be sure, a captain's lady; well, we hid a good many pikeheads in the grain, and sint more to the boys o' Watherford, into the very town, though it was under martial law at the time: but we hid them among brooms, and in sacks o' flour, and what not. The wife, one day, had crossed the Scar, to give a small sack o' barley-male to one at the other side, and who should she meet this side, and she comin' back, but young Thomas Jarratt. 'Good morrow, Mistress Andy,' says he. 'Good morrow kindly,' says she. 'May-be,' says he, 'ye won't tell a body where ye've been.' To be sure she up with the lie at once. 'That won't do for me,' says he; 'I know what ye're after, and good rason, too, for I'm sworn in; and, by the same token, the pass-word into your own millhouse is – green boy.' Well, she was struck quite comical, for she thought of his father's white head, and of the poor lad's own rosy cheek; but, above all, of sweet Mary Corish. 'Oh, Thomas!' says she, 'sure it wasn't my man that united ye; oh! think of yer old father, and the black-eyed girl that loves ye.' Och! the laugh he gave was heart-scalding. 'No,' says he, 'yer husband would call me a boy; and as to Mary, some one has come betwixt us, and she believes me bad, and ye know I wouldn't desave her,' and away he goes like a shot. For sartin, sorry I was whin I hard it, but it was too true; Mary soon got the wind o' the word, and it was too late – he wouldn't lade nor drive; and it was one of the *Scarroges* that drew him in, for which the same man niver had luck nor grace – for the boy was too young intirely to be brought into sich hardship. Well, I needn't tell about thim times. Thomas flourished the green flag, and did it bravely; but, in the battle of 'The Rocks,'[623] it was his fate to cut down the brother of poor Mary. James Corish, however, wasn't much hurt, and, wid others, was carried to the barn of Scullabogue.[624] I had little power, excipt in my own regiment, and I couldn't help the mischief. Yer honour knows, better nor me, what that cratur, Mary, wint through."

"I remember, as if it were but yesterday," said Mr. Collins; "poor old James fled with Mary to Ross, but the knowledge of her brother's danger came like a blight to her young heart, and long and eager were her inquiries as to the fate of the Wexford militia. A report reached her, that her brother was a prisoner in the barn of Scullabogue, and that the barn was to be set on fire that night or the next."

"I don't like to hear tell of that barn, at all, at all; but I should like to larn from yer honour how she made her way from Ross to Scullabogue; you were in the town at the time, so ye have a good right to know all about it."

"True, Andy; but what has that to do with your secret?"

"Och! more nor yer honour guesses, any way. I remember her at the barn, but the cratur niver tould me how she got there."

"Poor thing! – she wrapped her blue mantle around her, and, with a blanched cheek, but a resolute eye and firm step, she passed the Ross sentries; the shades of night were thickening, yet the intrepid girl pursued her noiseless way towards the prison, or, perhaps, the grave of her brother. When some distance from Ross, she heard the trampling of horses; they drew nearer and nearer, and, for the first time, the necessity of avoiding the high road occurred to her. She concealed herself behind some furze, and, as they passed, their suppressed voices and dis-ordered dress informed her to what party they belonged. She next trod her path across the country, over the matted common, and through the swampy moor; nor did her steps fail her, until within a mile or two of Scullabogue."

"Poor colleen!" said the miller.

"The grey mist of morning had succeeded the night, and the thrush and blackbird were hailing the dawning day, as Mary sank down, exhausted, on the greensward. 'Merciful heaven!' she exclaimed, 'I am near – very near, yet I cannot reach it!' and she clasped her hands in silent, yet bitter agony. At this moment she saw a horse quietly grazing upon the common, and, with a desper-ate effort, rushed towards the spot, unfastened her cloak, and girthed it round the animal, like a pillion – sprang on its back – and, having previously converted the ribands of her hat into a bridle, at a fearless and quick pace she gained the main road, encountered the rebel outposts, passed them, by naming your name, and, at length, halted opposite the barn-door."

"Well, I mind it now, sir, as if but yesterday," interrupted Andy; "she looked like a banshee, in the early light; her black hair streaming over her shoulders, and her eyes darting fire, as she flung herself off the panting baste. The officer over the door was – Thomas Jarratt."

"'And you, Thomas,' said she, quite distracted-like, 'you here, a commander! – you know me well! The fire blazed for ye, the roof sheltered ye, the welcome smiled for ye in my father's house, since we were both childer. I have left my ould father, Thomas, and have come all alone, to ask these men my brother's life, or to tell them I will die with him!'"

"'You are mad, Mary,' he answered: 'neither the Captain nor I could save him if we would: you, Mary, I can save; but as for James – there is too much Orange blood in the corps already.' That was the word he spoke. She fell on her knees, clenched her hands, and, in a deep, smothering voice, sobbed out, 'Let me see him, then; let me see James once – only once more!'"

"The young man, without making answer, rushed into the barn, and, in a moment, returned, from crowds of famishing, death-doomed craturs, with James Corish. James thought they had brought him forth to the death, and he tried to draw up his fainting, bleeding, shadow-like body, to meet it as a man; but when he saw his dear sister Mary, he would have sunk to the earth, had she not sprung to his side."

"'Now, mark me, boys!' cried she, as, half turning from her brother, she kept him up with one arm, – 'now, mark me! – the man that forces him from me, shall first tear the limbs from my body. And if there be one amongst ye who denies a sister's claim to her dying brother, let him bury his pike in my heart, or burn me wid him.'"

"She flung him on the nearest horse, and mounting behind, guided the animal's bridle. The last sound of the galloping, and the last sight of her streaming black hair, were long gone, before hand or foot was moved; they stood like stocks and stones, even in the time of destruction, wondering at woman's love.* 'Fire the barn!' was the next sound I hard, and that from Thomas Jarratt's own mouth. I seized his arm. 'What do you mane?' said I. 'Fire the barn!' he repeated, stamping, and hell's own fire flashing, like lightning, from his blood-red eyes. 'Isn't he half murdered by this hand?' he muttered to himself; 'and isn't she whole murdered, or worse? – for I know that, in twinty-four hours, she'll be either mad or dead. United Irishmen!' he screamed out, waving his green flag, 'the soldiers are in Ross.' And, sticking his pike into a bresneugh,ᵃ which some devils had lit, he rushed towards the door. I saw it was all over, so I shouted to the Bannow boys to close around their Captain; and, sure enough, out o' my two hundred and odd, there weren't five that didn't march home that day to their own cabins. Och! but the crackling, and the shrieks, and the yells, as we hurried on!"

The old miller covered his face with his hands, and pressed his rough fingers against his eyeballs, as if to destroy such horrid recollections.

"Poor Mary! – she gained Ross in safety," said Mr. Collins, "and her father rejoiced much. James soon recovered; but we all know the wretched Thomas was right. When she arose from that fearful brain fever, her reason was perfectly gone. You are all kind to her, very kind. She seems more happy wandering about your mill, and gathering flowers for your children, than in her brother's farmhouse. I remember well old Jarratt's funeral. His son was killed; but, I believe, his body was never found."

"He was *not* killed, sir," replied the miller, looking earnestly at Mr. Collins. "Many a night after, he slept in this very room."

"Here, Andy! – what, here? – and you knew it?"

---

* The circumstance here recorded is strictly true. I have seen my heroic countrywoman, Mary Corish, often–but never without grief. The effort was too much for her mind, and her reason sank under it.

"Yer honour may say that, when it was myself put him in it."

"But, Andy, your own life was not then safe from the king's troops. How could you commit such a very imprudent action (to call it by no harsher term,) as to harbour a proscribed man, when a rich price was set upon his body, dead or alive? And such a wretch too! I am perfectly astonished!"

"No need in life for that last, sir. As to my own head, it was but loosely on my shoulders then – sure enough; – as to the prudence, it's not the character of the counthry; – as to the price set upon his head, none o' my breed, seed, or genera-tion, were iver informers (my curse on the black word!) or iver will be, plase the Almighty. And as to his being a wretch – we are all bad enough, and to spare. But, had he murdered my own brother, and, after, come – ay, with the very blood upon his hands – and thrown himself upon my marcy – I'm a true-born Irish-man, sir, who niver refused purtection, when wanted, to saint or sinner. But the fair and beautiful boy, to see him, and he dressed like an ould woman pilgrim; his cheek hollow, his eye dead, so worn; and no life in him, but bitter sorrow, and heavy tears for sin. We kept him here, unknownst, as good as five weeks, and then shipped him off beyant seas far enough."

"But the money, Andy – how did you get money to fit him out?"

"Is it the money? – his father's land was canted[a] and, to be sure, he couldn't touch a pinny, and he banned: but I'll tell ye who gave some of it – young James Corish. I knew the good drop was in him, and so I tould him all about it; and, says he, 'There have been many examples made of the misfortunate, misguided people, Andy,' says he; 'and if he did hew me down, why, 'twas in battle, and I'd ha' done the same to him; but the drink and the bad company made him mad: any way, he took me out o' the barn; and, more than all, sure *they* loved each other; and, more than all to the back o' that, doesn't the blessed word o' God tell us to love our enemies, and to do good to thim that ill use us? Sure, that's the true religion, Andy; and Catholic or Protestant can't turn their tongues to betther than the words o' the gospel o' pace;' and, without more to do, he gives me twinty hard guineas, and a small bible, and I gave Thomas the bible on the sly; and, one way or other, we sint him clane out o' the land."

"And did you never hear of the unfortunate young man since?" inquired Mr. Collins.

"Did I not? – sure it was he sint me over the cordial ye tasted; and, more than all, sure he's come over himself, in the strange brig that's at the new quay."

"Good God!" said Mr. Collins, starting up; "he'll be hung as certainly as he lands."

"Och! no danger in life o' that," replied Andy, quietly.

"You're mad – absolutely mad!"

"I ax yer honour's pardon, I'm not mad; and sure it's nat'ral for him to wish to lave his bones in his own land."

"Leave his bones on a gibbet!" exclaimed the gentleman, greatly agitated.

"I wanted particular to spake to yer honour about it, as he is to land tonight, under the ould church, and Father Mike is to be there, and Friar Madden, and not more than one or two others, excipt the poor boy that brought him over." "As sure as he lands," said Mr. Collins, "he will be in the body of Wexford Jail in twelve hours."

"Well, that's comical, too," replied Andy, quietly, – "sind a dead body to Waxford Jail!"

Mr. Collins looked perplexed.

"Yer honour's not sinsible, I see; sure it's the dead body o' what was Thomas Jarratt that's come over; and, by the same token, a letther (the priest has it), written – (he had a dale o' schooling) – jist before the breath left him; and he prays us to lay his body in Bannow Church, as near the ould windy as convanient, without disturbing any one's rest; and, on account he doesn't wish a wake, he begs us, if we want him to have pace, to put him in the ground at twelve o' the night, by the light of four torches. I can't see the use of the four, barring he took it from the little hymn –

> 'Matthew, Mark, Luke, and John,
> God bless the bed that I lie on.'[625]

"But it's hard telling dead men's fancies; be that as it may, the letther's a fine letther – as good as a sarmint; and he sint a handsome compliment to his reverence, but nothing said about masses; and he sint forty guineas to James Corish, and remimbered Mary; and more to myself than iver he got from me; but, says he, 'I can pay the living, but what do the dead ask of me?' And the boy that came over wid him (an ould comarade), that was forced to fly, for a bit of a scrape, nothing killin' bad, only a bit of a mistake, where a chap was done for, without any malice – only all a mistake; well, he tould me, though all worldly matthers prospered, his soul troubled him night and day, but he used to read the bible at times (sure it's the word o' God), and sob, and pray; and he wasted, while his goods increased; but where's the use o' my delaying yer honour now? I only want to ax ye if there's anything contrary to law, in landing and burying the poor ashes to-night?"

"Nothing that I know of, certainly."

"But is yer honour sartin sure about it? Becase, if there was any earthly doubt, I'd not go aginst the law now, the least bit, for the price o' the 'varsal world; and sure I'd go to the grave any time, night or day, to keep the cratur asy, only, if it's aginst the law –"

"I assure you, Andy, it is not," replied Mr. Collins; "and if you will allow me, I should like to be there myself; it is wild and singular, and Father Mike will not object, I dare say."

"Och! yer honour's kind and good."

It was agreed that they should meet at twelve that night. Mr. Collins, of course, partook of Mrs. Andy's hospitality, and, exchanging kindly greetings with the honest miller's family, turned his steps homeward.

It was nearly midnight when Mr. Collins gained the cliffs that overhang the little harbour of Bannow; the moon was emerging from some light, fleecy clouds, that shaded, without obscuring, her brightness, and, as she mounted higher in the heavens, her beams formed a silvery line on the calm waters, that were fleetly crossed by a small boat: at the prow stood a tall, slight figure, enveloped in a cloak, and, on the strand, four or five men were grouped, in earnest conversation. The path Mr. Collins had to descend was unusually steep, and various portions of fallen cliff made it difficult, if not dangerous. As he passed along, he thought the shadow of a human form crossed his way; but the improbability of such an event, and the flickering light, made him forget the circumstance, even before he joined the priest and Andy on the beach. No word was spoken, but hands were silently grasped in hands, and they prepared to assist in the landing of the coffin; it was large, covered with black cloth, and on the lid – "Thomas Jarratt, aged 42," was inscribed. The simple procession quickly formed. The priest and friar lighted each a torch; the young man who brought the body over, still shrouded in his cloak, supported the head of the coffin; Andy and another bore the feet; and the remaining torches, and Mr. Collins, brought up the singular procession. As they slowly ascended, the torches threw a wild, red light over the mounds of cliff, fringed with sea moss and wild flowers, fragments of dark rock, and tangled furze, which the hardened soil appeared incapable of nourishing. When they had nearly arrived at the highest point, Mr. Collins distinctly saw the passing shadow he before imagined he had observed, fade, as it were, behind a broken mass, composed of earth and rock; at the same moment, all the party perceived it; the priest commanded a halt, and murmured an Ave Mary.

"What was it?" whispered one.

"Lord presarve us! – it's lucky they're wid us; no blight can come where the priests do be," replied Andy.

Without further hinderance, they crossed the grassy plain that extends between the ruined church and the cliffs, and entered the long aisle, where no more –

"The pealing anthem swells the notes of praise."[626]

If there be a solitude like unto that of the sepulchre, it is the solitude of ruins. In mountain loneliness you may image an unpeopled world, fresh from God's own hand – pure, bright, and beautiful, as the new-born sun: but a moss-grown ruin speaks powerfully, in its loneliness, of gone-by days – of bleached and marrowless bones.

All was silent as the hollow grave which yawned at their feet. The innocent birds, that nestled among the wall-flowers and ivy, frightened at the unusual light, screamed and fluttered in their leafy dwellings. The moon shone brightly through the large window, as the bearers rested the coffin on the loose earth.

"He requested," said Father Mike, addressing Mr. Collins, "that his body should be placed in the ground without so much as a prayer for the repose of his soul – that was heathenish; yet his other words were those of a penitent and a Christian."

The coffin was deposited in its narrow home; and Andy held the torch over the grave, to ascertain that all had been properly managed.

The priest, the friar, and Mr. Collins, stood fixed in silent prayer, and the passing night-breeze shook the withered leaves from the dark overhanging ivy. Each individual was surrounded by the urns and tombs of his ancestors; nay, more, by those of relatives, who, in the bud or blossom of life, had passed away, and were no more seen; and it was not to be wondered at, that the silent power of death, and the everlasting doom of eternity, pressed heavily on the hearts of them all at that midnight hour. At this very moment, a dark shadow obscured the cold moonbeams that streamed from the window; a piercing shriek echoed along the broken walls; and, even while their eyes were fixed on a female, who stood, with streaming hair and extended arms, on the large window-frame – she sprang from the elevation, with unerring bound, into the open grave, and the echo was again awakened by the fearful sound made by her feet upon the coffin-lid.

"Heaven and earth!" exclaimed Andy, as he raised the light, "it's Mary Corish!"

She seized the torch from the astonished miller, lowered it, so as to read the inscription, which she distinctly repeated, and fell, without farther motion, on the coffin of him she had loved, even in madness. They raised her tenderly, out of the grave, but the pulses of life were slackening, and the film of approaching death was stealing over the wild brightness of her eyes.

"She is passing," said Mr. Collins, chafing her damp temples as he spoke; "poor Mad Mary!"

"I am not mad," she murmured, and her utterance was very feeble – "not mad now; I was so, and ye all pitied me; God bless ye! I know you – and you – and you – and I know him – that's – " with a last effort she turned towards the grave, looked into it, and expired.

No one could ever discover how she was apprized of the intended funeral; but as she was always wandering about the sea-shore, it was supposed she had overheard some of the conversation that had occurred on the subject.

Poor Mary! – the innocent children who gather ocean-weed and many-tinted shells on the strand of Bannow, when they see the white sea-bird seeking its lodging in the clefted rock, after the sun has set, and the grey mist is rising, as if to shield the repose of nature, softly and fearfully whisper to each other, that it is time to return to their homes, for that Mad Mary's ghost will be flitting around the aged church of Bannow.

GOOD SPIRITS AND BAD.

WHEN I wrote the stories of which this volume is composed, in common with every other writer concerning Ireland, I had frequent occasion to notice the habitual intemperance of a people naturally excitable. This, more than all their other failings, rendered them liable to misrepresentation: – "an Irishman drunk, and an Irishman sober," were two distinct beings; but the stranger had little time to inquire into the causes, when he witnessed the effects. And though many efforts have been made to change the bad spirit for the good – though Professor Edgar,[627] in Belfast, the Rev. George Carr, in New Ross,[628] and some excellent men in Cork, had made strenuous exertions to establish Temperance Societies, nothing comparatively had been done to influence the Roman Catholic population. What the Rev. Mr. Mathew has wrought – his untiring perseverance, his disinterested efforts for the regeneration of his countrymen, his labouring unceasingly through evil report, which was, at last, silenced by the overwhelming good that became apparent throughout the country – I need not here record. During the last two years, the difficulty has been, not to find an Irishman sober, but an Irishman intoxicated: the change is wonderful, and must be seen to be believed.[a] I trust the good may be permanent, and see every reason to think that such will be the case. A person who had not visited Ireland for some years, would not know the country again; indeed, I hardly knew the people myself, some of whom I used to lecture after my own fashion; and you may lecture Paddy for ever, without running the risk of an unpleasant answer: he is the most ready of all people in the world to *listen* to advice – he will agree to the letter with you in everything you state. "Bedad, ma'am, I know that – I often thought so." – "Ah, then, see that now! – Sure it was always the way, and a cruel bad habit, leaving us worse than it found us, and that's no asy matter." – "Oh, indeed, it's as clear as print, and as thrue as gospel!" but you did not carry your point a bit the sooner for all this acquiescence: the next day, the next hour, you might have chanced to meet the same Paddy in the most senseless state of intoxication. Alas! it was very, very sad! How different now! Paddy's coat – though not according to English notions of comfort – is a wonderful improvement upon my old acquaintance; his eye is clear; the yellow palor of inebriety has given place to the colour of a healthy state of existence; and his step is firm, as of a man newly escaped from slavery. I have heard many, not conversant with the country, wonder that, in consequence of the spread of temperance, the children are not now all well clothed, and the cabins furnished. They ought to remember, that the pay of an Irish labourer, at *most,* is but six shillings a week; that what he drank formerly took the absolute *food,* the potato and milk, from his children, who now are able to have sufficient of this humble fare; but a much longer period must elapse before the little that can be spared, shows to the eye accustomed to the luxuries of a higher station: – a cup and saucer, a plate, a piggin,[629] a new stool, a potato-basket – are valuable additions to the humble cottage, yet are hardly noticed by the casual visitor, who sees the misery that is, but forgets that which has been. It is not a little curious to observe, how opinions alter with the times. I remember, when it was considered a positive extravagance in the wife of even a decent tradesman to take a cup of tea; though the gentry, who condemned her, would not hesitate to order her husband a glass of raw alcohol, when he brought home his work. Indeed, the habit of giving *the evil spirit* to every person who called on business, was, when I was a child, so common, that neglecting to do so was considered a breach of hospitality.

There was a very excellent person in Bannow – a woman whom I never think of but with pleasure; my grandmother used to employ her in her capacity of dressmaker and needlewoman, for, I should think, pretty nearly six months out of the twelve. She plied her needle in my nursery; and I have sat for hours on my little chair, by her side, looking into her beautiful face, and listening with intense pleasure, to the legends she used to tell, and the exquisite ballads she used to sing, with the most untiring patience, for my amusement. Poor Mrs. Bow! She little thought how she was storing my mind with the richest treasures. She had been nearly brought up in Graige House, and nothing could surpass her affection for all who dwelt within its walls. Her manners and mind were superior to her station; and yet, strangely enough, she had married a man – a smith – a good and clever workman, as remarkable for personal ugliness, as she was for personal beauty; and in proportion as her temper was sweet, his was sour. But this was not all; Mr. Bow had a most decided affection for whisky, raw – or whisky-punch – it was never "too hot nor too heavy" for him; and if his temper was cranky when sober, it was worse than cranky when, after his hard day's work, he issued from his forge a tipsy Vulcan,[630] overthrowing, in his homeward progress, all who stood in his way. This was a heavy trial to his poor wife, who, in proportion as she was proud of her husband's uprightness and integrity, so was she grieved at his fits of intoxication. "If," she would exclaim – "if he would only take to the tea, I'd die happy." Now Mrs. Bow had a dog, a very pretty black spaniel, called Diver – a creature of extraordinary sagacity, and one of the first, as well as firmest, advocates of Temperance: he might, had he lived long enough, been the favourite dog of Father Mathew, and been worthy of such a distinction.

Diver hated "the bad spirit," as his mistress always called whisky, with his entire heart. He would never accept a caress from a hand that had the odour thereof; and the sound of drunken revelry excited him to the bristling of hair, and gnashing of teeth. When his master returned home, in the full possession of his senses, Diver would manifest the greatest joy; but when he staggered into the room, Diver would retreat under a chair, gather his lips from off his white and glistening teeth, and look both distressed and angry. His master was perfectly aware of this, and did not fail to bestow on his wife's favourite, sundry epithets of dislike and contempt. Now this antipathy to the smell of whisky could, perhaps, be accounted for: the dog had, probably, been ill-used by persons under the influence of intoxication; but the remarkable part of his canine character was – his attachment to the teapot. Although every one declared "it was a shame for Mrs. Bow to take to the tea, every evening like a lady, and her husband, honest man, content with nothing but a glass of whisky;" still, she persevered in the almost hopeless hope of winning her spouse to partake of the exhilarating, yet harmless, beverage; in this desire Diver apparently concurred. His mistress had only to show him the teapot to set him bounding and skipping about the room with delight; he would whirl round, wag his tail, and finally dart forward in search of his master, whom he would endeavour, by every possible means in his power, to induce to return with him. The smith well knew what he wanted; and, at last, took pleasure in displaying his sagacity to his neighbours, making them accompany him home, because then, indeed, the animal's joy knew no bounds. To see his master and mistress seated at the tea-table, was the summit of his delight; he would stretch himself along the ground, and howl with pleasure. Poor Diver did not live long enough to witness the triumph of "teatotalism;" but he succeeded in making his master fond of tea. I hope this anecdote of the first "teatotallers" of my acquaintance, will not be considered "out of place." Happily those who sneered at the impossibility of Irishmen becoming *sober* members of society, are convinced that Irish perseverance is worthy of respect, not ridicule. The marvel to me is, not that some few have broken "the pledge,"[631] but that so many have kept it. It must be remembered, that it was the Irishman's *sole* luxury.

> "Surely it is my father and mother,
> My Sunday coat – I have no other;"[632]

was the "refrain" of one of the many songs he had heard from his youth up. "His father liked a drop, honest man, took it off and on, and sure if it did harm, it was to no one but himself," was what he had often heard. His uncles were fine, free-hearted fellows, that "shared a drop with their neighbours." His cousins "took their glass like men." "The piper never played up hearty, till he had his eye glazed with the whisky." "The priest was a fine man, entirely, after his reverence had the second tumbler." His landlord, the next object of his veneration, "was fond of his hot tumbler, and always a good hand to order it to a poor man, wet or dry." No entertainment was given without whisky – no bargain concluded until the libation to the evil spirit was poured forth: no account was ever taken of the horrors produced by intoxication. "Ah, sure, he couldn't help it – he wasn't himself when he struck the blow – bad luck to it for whisky, it does a deal of harm: but *what can a poor man do?* – sure it's the only comfort he has – the only thing that puts the throuble past him; it takes the feel of sorrow from his heart, and the sight of starvation from before his eyes."

And yet – the Irishman has had the moral courage to relinquish, and the moral firmness to adhere to the determination of giving up, as I have said, his *only luxury* – and that, without any of the complaining we, of a better class, should make if we abandoned one of the scores that we indulge in.

I look upon this triumph with great admiration. It is impossible not to respect those who make great sacrifices from a desire to do right; and I am sure what has been effected, in the way of self-denial, by the Irish, in this matter, proves, that they have not only energy, but perseverance, for anything they undertake. – *This* fact should be borne in mind by all whose duty and interest it is, to see that such fine qualities are *well directed.*

I must illustrate my text of "Good Spirits and Bad," by one or two stories: –

"What I'm thinking of, Nelly, darlin'," – said Roney Maher to his poor pale wife – "what I'm thinking of, is – what a pity we were not bred and born in this Temperance Society, for then we could follow it, you know, as a thing of course, without any trouble!"

"But – "

"Whisht, Nelly, you've one great fault, avorneen – you're always talking, dear, and won't listen to me. What I was saying is, that, if we were brought up to the coffee, instead of the whisky, we'd have been natural members of the Temperance Society: as it is now, agrah! why it's meat, drink, and clothing, as a man may say!"

He paused, and Nelly thought – though, in his present state, she had too much tenderness to tell her husband so – that whisky was a very bad paymaster.

"You're no judge, Ellen," he continued, interpreting her thoughts, "for you never took to it; and, if I had my time to begin over again, I never would either; but it's too late to change now – all – too late!"

"I've heard many a wise man say, that *it's never too late* to mend," observed Ellen.

"Yah!" he exclaimed, almost fiercely, – "who ever said that was a fool!"

"It was the priest himself, then, Roney, never a one else; and sure you wouldn't call him that!"

"If I did mend," he observed, "no one would take my word for it."

"Ay, dear – but deeds, not words;" and, having said more than was usual for her, in the way of reproof, Ellen retreated to watch its effect.

Roney Maher was a fine, likely boy, when he married Ellen; but when this little dialogue took place, he was sitting over the embers of a turf fire, a pale, emaciated man, though in the prime of life – a torn handkerchief bound round his temples, and his favourite shillalah, that he had greased and seasoned in the chimney, and tended *with more care than his children,* lay broken by his side. He attempted to snatch it up while his wife retreated, but his arm fell powerless, and he uttered a groan so full of pain, that, in a moment, she returned, and, with tearful eyes, inquired "if it was so bad entirely as that?"

"It's worse," he answered, while the large drops that stood upon his brow, proved how much he suffered.

"It's worse – the arm I mean – than I thought; I'm *done* for a week, or maybe, a fortnight – and, Nelly, the pain in my arm is nothing to the weight about my heart – now, don't be talking, for I can't stand it. If I *can't* work next week, nor this, and we without money or credit – what – what?" The unfortunate man glanced at his wife and children – he could not finish the sentence. He had only returned, the previous night, from having "been out upon a spree," as it is called; spending his money, wasting his health, losing his employment – not thinking of those innocent children whom God had given him to protect; and only returning to the abode, which his propensity had rendered one of squalid wretchedness, because he had been disabled in a disgraceful riot.

When sober, Roney's impulses were all good: but he was as easily, perhaps more easily, led away by the bad than the good; in the present instance, he continued talking, because he dared not think, and it is a fearful thing for a man to dread his own thoughts. It was a painful picture, to look upon this well-educated man – he *had* been an excellent tradesman – he *had* been respected – he *had* been comfortable; he felt lost, degraded, in pain and sorrow, and yet he would not confess it. Once or twice he attempted to sing snatches of those foolish or bad songs, which entice to intoxication, but the words "stuck in his throat;" in truth, he was too ill, either to think or act, – ashamed of the past, yet endeavouring, in vain, to convince himself, that he had no right to be ashamed.

It was evening: the children crept round the fire, where their mother endeavoured to heat half-a-dozen cold potatoes for their supper – looking, with hungry eyes, upon the scanty feast. "Daddy's too bad entirely to eat tonight," whispered the second boy to his eldest brother, while his little thin blue lips trembled, half with cold, half with hunger; "*and so we'll have his share as well as our own!*" and the little shivering group devoured the potatoes, in imagination, over and over again – poking them with their lean fingers, and telling their "mammy" they were *hot* enough; – shocking that want should have taught them to calculate on their parent's illness as a source of rejoicing!

"Nelly," said her husband, at last – "Nelly, I wish I had a drop of something to warm me."

"Mrs. Kinsalla said she would give me a bowl of strong coffee for you – if you would take it."

What drunkard does not blaspheme?

Roney swore; and, though his lips were parched with fever, and his head throbbed, declared he must have just "one little thimble-full to raise his heart." It was in vain that Ellen remonstrated and entreated. He did not attempt violence, but he obliged his eldest boy to beg the "thimble-full?" and, before morning, the wretched man was tossing about in all the heat and irritation of decided fever. One must have witnessed what fever is, when accompanied by such misery, to understand its terrors. It was wonderful how he was supported through it – indeed, his ravings, when, after a long, dreary time, the fever subsided, were more torturing to poor Nelly, than the working of his delirium had been.

"If," he would exclaim – "if it wasn't *too late,* I'd take the pledge they talk about, the first minute I rise my head from the straw; but where's the good of it now? – what can I save now? – nothing – it's too late!"

"It's never too late," Ellen would whisper. "It's never too late," she would repeat; and, as if it were a mocking echo, her husband's voice would sigh – "Too late! – too late!"

Indeed, any who looked upon the fearful wreck of what had been the fine, manly form of Roney Maher – stretched upon a bed of straw, with hardly any covering – saw his two rooms, now utterly destitute of every article of furniture – heard his children begging in the streets for a morsel of food – and observed how the utmost industry of his poor wife could hardly keep the rags together that shrouded her bent form – any one almost, who saw these things, would be inclined to repeat the words, which have, unfortunately, but too often knelled over the grave of good feelings and good intentions – "Too late! – too late!" Many would have imagined that not only had the demon habit, which had gained so frightful an ascendancy over poor Roney, banished all chance of ref-ormation, but that there was no escape from such intense poverty. – I wish, with all my heart, that such persons would, instead of sitting down with so helpless and dangerous a companion as despair, resolve upon two things; first of all, to trust in, and pray to God; secondly, to combat what they foolishly call fate – to fight bravely, and in a good cause; and sure am I, that those who do, will, sooner or later, achieve a victory!

It is never too late to abandon a bad habit, and adopt a good one. In every town of Ireland, Temperance has now its members, and these members are so thoroughly acquainted with the blessings of this admirable system, from feeling its advantages, that they are full of zeal in the cause, and, with true Irish generos-ity, eager to enlist their friends and neighbours – that they, too, may partake of the comforts which spring from Temperance. The Irishman is not selfish: he is as ready to share his cup of coffee, as he used to be to share his glass of whisky.

One of these generous members was the Mrs. Kinsalla, whose offer of the bowl of coffee had been rejected by Roney the night his fever commenced: she was herself a poor widow, or, according to the touching and expressive phraseology of Ireland, "a *lone* woman;" and, though she had so little to bestow, that many would call it nothing, she gave it, with that good will which rendered it "twice blest:" then she stirred up others to give; and often had she kept watch with her wretched neighbour – Ellen, never omitting those words of gentle kindness and instruction, which, perhaps, at the time, may seem to have been spoken in vain; but not so: for we must bear in mind that, even in the *good ground,* the seed will not spring the moment it is sown. Those who would effect a great moral revolution, must have patience: those who, in their families, seek to reform a beloved object whom they love, despite his or her errors; or to reclaim a backslider, and teach that the ways of peace are the ways of loving-kindness and religion, must have patience; they must be assured that it is *never too late,* as all *do* think, whose trust in God is founded in the belief of His mercy and forgiveness.

Roney had been an industrious, and a good workman, once; and Mrs. Kinsalla had often thought, before the establishment of the Temperance Society, what a blessing it would be, if there were any means of making him an "affidavit man;"[633] but, as she said, "there were so many ways of avoiding an oath, when a man's heart was set to break it, not to keep it, that she could hardly tell what to say about it."

Such poverty as Roney's must either die beneath its infliction, or rise above it. He was now able to sit in the sun at his cabin-door. His neighbour, Mrs. Kinsalla, had prevailed on a good lady to employ Ellen, in the place of a servant who was ill; and had lent her clothes, that she might be able to appear decently "at the big house." Every night she was permitted to bring her husband a little broth, or some bread and meat; and the poor fellow was regaining his health, though his arms still continued weak. Their dwelling, however, remained without any article of furniture: although the rain used to pour through the roof, and the only fire was made from the scanty "bresnaugh"[a][634] the children gathered from the road-side, they had sufficient food; and, though the lady expected all she employed to work hard, she paid them well, and caused Ellen's poor forlorn heart to leap with joy by the gift of a blanket, and a very old suit of clothes for her husband. And here let me observe that wherever man and wife continue to exist together, there is hope amounting almost to certainty, of better times, if one stems the torrent of vice or mismanagement. If *both* go wrong, woe, woe, to their children! – but how often is the husband rendered, as it were, the salvation of the wife, and the wife, of the husband!

"I have seen yer old master to-day, Roney," said the widow Kinsalla to her neighbour, "and he was asking after you."

"I'm obliged to him," was the reply.

"And he said he was sorry to see your children in the street, Roney, honey."

"So am I – but you know he was so angry with me for that last *scrimage*,[635] that he declared I should never do another stroke of work for him;" and he added, "that was a cruel saying for him, to lay out starvation for me and mine, because I was not worse than the rest; sure, as I said to Nelly, poor thing, and she spending her strength, and striving for me – 'Nelly,' says I, 'where's the good of it, bringing me out of the shades of death, to send me begging along the road! – let me die easy where I am!'"

"Well, but the master will take you back, Roney – on one condition."

The blood mounted to the poor man's face – and then he became faint, and leaned back against the wall. Three times had he been dismissed from his employment for drunkenness, and his master had never been known to receive a man back after three dismissals. Mrs. Kinsalla gave him a cup of water, and then continued – "The master told me, himself, he'd take you back, Roney, *on one condition*."

"I'll give my oath against the whisky – barring – " he began.

"There need be no swearing – but there *must* be no *barring*. I'll tell you the rights of it – if you'll listen to me in earnest," said the widow. "The master you see, called all his men together, and set down fair before them, the state they were in from the indulgence in spirits. He drew a picture, Roney, a young man in his prime, full of life, with a fair character; his young wife by his side; his child on his knee; earning from fifteen to eighteen shillings or a pound a week; able to have his Sunday dinner in comfort; well to do, in every way; at first he drinks, maybe, a glass with a friend – *and that leads to another,* and another, until work is neglected, home is abandoned, a quarrelsome spirit grows out of the high spirit which is no shame – and, in a very short time, you lose all trace of the man in the degraded drunkard. Poverty wraps her rags around him; pallid want, loathsome disease, a jail, and a bedless death, close the scene. 'But,' said the master, 'this is not all; the sneer and the reproach have gone over the world against us, and an Irishman is held up as a degraded man – as a half-civilized savage, to be spurned, and laughed at – because – "

"I know," groaned Roney – "because he makes himself a reproach. Mrs. Kinsalla, I knew you were a well-reared and a well-learned woman, but you give that to the life: it's all true."

"He spoke," she continued, "of those amongst his own workmen, who had fallen by intoxication; he said, if poverty had slain its thousands, whisky had slain its tens of thousands; poverty did not always lead to drunkenness, but drunkenness always led to poverty; he spoke of you, my poor man, as being one whom he had respected."

"Did he say that, indeed?"

"He did – "

"God bless him for *that,* any way. I thought him a hard man; but God bless him for remembering old times."

"And then he said how you had fallen – "

"The world knows *that,* without his telling it," interrupted Roney.

"It does, agra! – but listen! He told of *one* who was as low as you are now, and lower, for the Lord took from him the young wife, who died, broken-hearted, in the sight of his eyes; and yet it was not *too late* for him to be restored, and able to lead others from the way that led him to destruction.

"He touched the hearts of them all; he laid before them how, if they looked back to what they had done when sober, and what they had done when the contrary, they would see the *difference;* and then, my dear, he showed them other things; he laid it down as plain as print, how all the badness that has been done in the country, sprang out of the whisky – the faction-fights, flying in the face of that God who tells us to love each other – the oaths, black and bitter, dividing Irishmen, who ought to be united in all things that lead to the peace and honour of their country, into parties; staining hands with blood, that would have gone, spotless, to honourable graves, but for its excitement.

"Then he said how the foes of Ireland would sneer and scorn, if she became a backslider from Temperance; and how her friends would rejoice, if the people kept true to their pledge; – how every man could prove himself a patriot, a *rale* patriot, by showing to the world, an Irishman, steadfast, sober, and industrious, with a cooler head, and warmer heart than ever beat in any but an Irishman's bosom! – He showed, you see, *how Temperance was the heart's core of ould Ireland's glory,* and said a deal more than I can repeat about her peace, and verdure, and prosperity; and then he drew out a picture of a reformed man – his home, with all the little bits of things comfortable about him; his smiling wife – his innocent babies; and, knowing him so well, Roney, I made my courtesy – and, 'sir,' says I, 'if you please, will that come about to every one who becomes a true *member* of the Total Abstinence Society?' 'I'll go bail for it,' says he, 'though surely you don't want it; I never saw *you* overtaken, Mrs. Kinsalla.' 'God forbid, and thank your honour,' says I; 'but you want every one to be a member?' says I. 'From my heart, for his own good, and the honour of old Ireland, I do,' he says.

"'Then, sir,' I went on, ' there's Roney Maher, sir – and if he takes and is true to the pledge, sir – ,' and I watched to see if the good-humoured twist was on his mouth, 'he'll be fit for work next week, sir; and the *evil spirit* is out of him so long now, and – ' 'That's enough,' be says, 'bring him here to-morrow, when all who wish to remain in my employ will take the resolution, and I'll try him again.'"

Ellen had entered, unperceived by her husband, and flung herself on her knees by his side.

The appeal was unnecessary; sorrow softens men's hearts; he pressed her to his bosom, while tears coursed each other down the furrows of his pallid cheeks.

"Ellen, mavourneen! – Ellen, aroon!" he whispered – "Nelly, agra! a coushla machree! – you were right – '*It is never too late.*'"

* * * * * *

Nineteen months have elapsed since Roney, trusting not in his own strength, entered on a new course of life. Having learned to distrust himself he was certain to triumph.

You could hardly believe that the Roney Maher of the past, and the Roney Maher of the present, are the same; the pale, shivering, sullen, and red-eyed drunkard changed by the blessing – the one blessing which every human being can make his own – the blessing of Temperance: changed – I repeat it most joyfully – into a hale and happy, open and clear-eyed man; his voice steady; his step firm; working from Monday morning until Saturday night; the source of humble, but certain, comfort to his family; standing before God, and his country, in the dignity of manhood, undebased by vice.

It is Sunday; his wife has taken her two eldest children to early mass, that she may return in time to prepare his dinner; the little lads, stout, clean, and ruddy-faced, are watching to call to their mother, so that she may know the moment he, her reformed husband, appears in sight. What there is in the cottage betokens care, and that sort of Irish comfort which is easily satisfied; there is, moreover, a cloth on the table; a cunning-looking dog is eyeing the steam of something more savoury than mere potatoes, which ascends the chimney; and the assured calmness of Ellen's face proves that her heart is at ease. The boys are the same that, hardly two years ago, were compelled, by cruel starvation, to exult – poor children! that their father's being too ill to eat, insured them another potato.

"Hurroo, mammy – there's daddy!" exclaimed the eldest.

"Oh! mammy, his new beaver shines grand in the sun!" shouts his brother; "and there's widdy Kinsalla along with him, but he's carrying little Nancy; now he lets her down, and the darling is running, for he's taken off her Sunday shoes to ease her *dawshy* feet; and, oh! mammy honey, there's the master himself shaking hands with father before the people!" This triumphant announcement brought Ellen to the door; she shaded her eyes from the sun with her hand, and, having seen what made her heart beat very rapidly in her faithful and gentle bosom, she wiped them, more than once, with the corner of her apron. "What ails ye, mammy, honey? – sure there's no trouble over you now!" said the eldest boy, climbing to her neck, and pouting his lips, not blue, but cherry-red, to meet his mother's kiss.

"I hope daddy will be very hungry," he continued, "and Mrs. Kinsalla, for even if the schoolmaster came in, we've enough *dinner* for them all."

"Say – thank God, my child," said Ellen. "Thank God," repeated the boy. "And shall I say what, you do be always saying as well?" "What's that, *alanna?*" "Thank God and the Temperance! – ah! and something else," "What?" inquired his mother. "What? – why, *that it's never too late.*"

The friends of Temperance have so great a dread of the people taking what are called, "Temperance Cordials," that I am induced to illustrate the subject by relating an incident – in the humble but fervent hope of its being useful in preventing persons from laying down *one* bad habit, only to take up another.

"Well," said Andrew Furlong to James Lacey, "that ginger cordial, of all things I ever tasted, is the nicest and warmest. It's beautiful stuff; and so cheap."

"What good does it do ye, Andrew? and what want have you of it?" inquired James Lacey.

"What good does it do me!" repeated Andrew, rubbing his forehead, in a manner that showed he was perplexed by the question, "why, no great good, to be sure, and I can't say I've any want of it; for since I became a member of the 'Total Abstinence Society,'[636] I've lost the megrim[637] in my head, and the weakness I used to have about my heart. I'm as strong and hearty in myself as any one can be, God be praised! And sure, James, neither of us could turn out in such a coat as *this*, this time twelvemonth."

"And that's true," replied James; "but we must remember that, if leaving off whisky enables us to show a good habit, taking to 'ginger cordial,' or anything of that kind, will soon wear a hole in it."

"You are always fond of your fun. How can you prove that?"

"Easy enough," said James. "Intoxication was the worst part of a whisky-drinking habit; but it was not the only bad part – it spent TIME, and it spent what well-managed time always gives, MONEY. Now, though they do say – mind, I'm not quite *sure* about it, for they *may* put things in it they don't own to, and your eyes look brighter, and your cheek more flushed, than if you had been drinking nothing stronger than milk or water – but they *do* say that ginger cordials, and all kinds of cordials, do not intoxicate. I will grant this; but you cannot deny that they waste both time and money."

"Oh, bother!" exclaimed Andrew, "I only went with two or three other boys to have a glass, and I don't think we spent more than half an hour. There's no great harm in laying out a penny or two-pence that way, now and again."

"*Half* an hour even, breaks a day," said James, "and, what is worse, it unsettles the mind for work; and we ought to be very careful of any return to the *old habit*, that has destroyed many of us, body and soul, and made the name of an Irishman a bye-word and a reproach, instead of a glory and an honour. A penny, Andrew, *breaks the silver shilling into coppers;* and two-pence will buy half a stone of potatoes – that's a consideration. If we don't manage to keep things comfortable at home, the women won't have the heart to mend the coat. Not," added James, with a sly smile, "that I can deny having taken to TEMPERANCE CORDIALS myself."

"You!" shouted Andrew, "*you!* a pretty fellow you are to be blaming me, and forced to confess you have taken to them yourself; but I suppose they'll wear no hole in *your* coat? Oh, no, *you* are such a good manager!"

"Indeed," answered James, "I *was* anything but a good manager, eighteen months ago: as you well know, I was in rags, never at my work of a Monday, and seldom on a Tuesday. My poor wife, my gentle, patient Mary, often bore hard words, and, though she will not own it, I fear still harder blows, when I had driven away my senses. My children were pale, half-starved, naked creatures, disputing a potato with the pig my wife tried to keep to pay the rent, well knowing I would never do it. Now – –"

"But the cordial, my boy!" interrupted Andrew, "the cordial! – sure I believe every word of what you've been telling me is as true as gospel; ain't there hundreds, ay, thousands, at this moment, on Ireland's blessed ground, that can tell the same story? But the cordial! – and to think of your never owning it before: is it ginger, or aniseed, or peppermint?"

"None of these – and yet it's the *rale* thing, my boy."

"Well, then," persisted Andrew, "let's have a drop of it; you're not going, I'm sure, to drink by yourself – *and as I've broke the afternoon –*"

A heavy shadow passed over James's face, for he saw that there must have been something hotter than ginger in the "*Temperance* Cordial," as it is falsely called, that Andrew had taken; else he would have endeavoured to redeem lost time, not to waste more; and he thought how much better the REAL Temperance Cordial was, that, instead of exciting the brain, only warms the heart.

"No," he replied, after a pause, "I must go and finish what I was about; but this evening, at seven o'clock, meet me at the end of our lane, and then I'll be very happy of your company."

Andrew was sorely puzzled to discover what James's cordial could be, and was forced to confess to himself, he hoped it would be different from what he had taken that afternoon, which certainly made him feel confused and inactive.

At the appointed hour the friends met in the lane.

"Which way do we go?" inquired Andrew.

"Home," was James's brief reply.

"Oh, you *take* it at home," said Andrew.

"I *make* it at home," answered James.

"Well," observed Andrew, "that's very good of the woman *that owns ye*. Now, mine takes on so about a drop of anything, that she's as hard almost on the cordials as she used to be on the whisky."

"My Mary helps to make mine," observed James.

"And do you bottle it, or keep it on draught?" inquired Andrew, very much interested in the "cordial" question.

James laughed very heartily at this, and answered –

"Oh, I keep mine on draught – always on draught; there's nothing like having plenty of a good thing, so I keep mine always on draught:" and then James laughed again, and heartily.

James's cottage door was open, and, as they approached it, they saw a good deal of what was going forward within. A square table, placed in the centre of the little kitchen, was covered by a clean white cloth – knives, forks, and plates for the whole family, were ranged upon it in excellent order; the teapot stood, triumphant, in the centre, – the hearth had been swept, the house was clean, the children rosy, well dressed, and all doing something. "Mary," whom her husband had characterized as "the patient," was busy and bustling, in the very act of adding to the tea, which was steaming on the table, with the substantial accompaniments of fried eggs and bacon, and a large dish of potatoes. When the children saw their father, they ran to meet him with a great shout, and clung around to tell him all they had done that day. The eldest girl declared she had achieved the heel of a stocking; one boy wanted his father to come and see how straight he had planted the cabbages; while another avowed his proficiency in addition, and volunteered to do a sum instanter upon a slate he had just cleaned. Happiness in a cottage seems always more real than it does in a gorgeous dwelling. It is not wasted in large rooms – it is concentrated – a great deal of love in a small space – a great, *great* deal of joy and hope within narrow walls, and compressed, as it were, by a low roof. Is it not a blessed thing that the most moderate means become enlarged by the affections? – that the love of a peasant, within his sphere, is as deep, as fervent, as true, as lasting, as sweet, as the love of a prince? – that all our best and purest affections will grow and expand in the poorest *worldly* soil? – and that we need not be rich to be happy? James felt all this, and more, when he entered his cottage, and was thankful to God who had opened his eyes, and taught him what a number of this world's gifts were within his humble reach, to be enjoyed without sin. He stood – a poor but happy father – within the sacred temple of his home; and Andrew had the warm heart of an Irishman beating in his bosom, and consequently, shared his joy.

"I told you," said James, "I had the *true Temperance Cordial* at home. Do you not see it in the simple prosperity by which, owing to the blessings of temperance, I am surrounded? Do you not see it in the rosy cheeks of my children – in the smiling eyes of my wife? Did I not say truly that she helped to make it? Is not this a true cordial?" he continued, while his own eyes glistened with manly tears; "is not the prosperity of this cottage a *true Temperance Cordial?* – and is it not *always on draught,* flowing from an ever-filling fountain? Am I not right, Andrew; and will you not forthwith take my receipt, and make it for yourself? You will never wish for any other: it is warmer than ginger, and sweeter than aniseed. I am sure you will agree with me, that a loving wife, in the enjoyment of the humble comforts which an industrious, *sober* husband can bestow, smiling, healthy, well-clad children, and a clean cabin, where the fear of God banishes all other fears, make

THE TRUE TEMPERANCE CORDIAL."

EDITORIAL NOTES

Sketches of Irish Character

1. *absentee*: Land seized and granted to English settlers during the sixteenth and seventeenth centuries was rented out to the dispossessed at unconscionable rents, resulting in a pattern of abuse that was detrimental to the development of the country. English landlords, many of whom chose not to live in Ireland but to remain in England, neglected the upkeep of their estates in Ireland and did not care about the welfare of their tenantry. Unscrupulous agents, often native Irish, exacerbated the problem by deceiving both landlord and their own people for pecuniary gain. Rack-renting was rife and even tenants who could afford to make improvements to their cottages or land were discouraged from so doing as they would incur even higher rent which, if unpaid, resulted in eviction. Hall seeks to highlight in her story the injustice of the 'absentee system'. Interestingly, she also supports the Union which perpetuates it.

2. *Baronies of Bargy and Forth*: Bargy and Forth are two of the ten county divisions of Wexford, the other baronies being Gorey, Scarawalsh, Ballaghkeen North, Ballaghkeen South, Bantry, Shelmalier East and Shelmalier West. Each barony is a group of Civil Parishes dating from the Norman Invasion of 1169 and based on the territories submitted by the Gaelic chiefs. The Yola language was spoken in Forth and Bargy until the nineteenth century and was indicative of the independent and distinctive nature of the early Norman settlers.

3. *Whose deep blue eyes ... seem colour'd by its skies*: Baron G. G. Byron, 'Childe Harold's Pilgrimage; Canto IV', *The Works of Lord Byron in Six Volumes*, 6 vols (London: J. Murray, 1827), vol. 2, verse CXVII, p. 117, l. 28.

4. *brogue*: a stout shoe, from the Irish *bróg* or *barróg*, speech impediment. There is a view that the Irish people used to speak English unintelligibly (as a result of linguistic contamination from Irish syntax and vocabulary), as though they had a shoe on their tongue; cf. A. Breval, '*The Play Is the Plot*' in *Spoken English in Ireland 1600–1740*, (Dublin: Cadenus Press and Dolmen Press, 1979), p. 158: 'ARRAH, is not the Brogue upon [your] Tongue' (T. Patrick Dolan (ed.), *Dictionary of Hiberno-English* (Dublin: Gill & Macmillan, 1998), hereafter *DH-E*).

5. *setting hens*: domestic hens bred to brood.

6. *marking*: the art or practice of embroidering fabric with initials or other devices (*Oxford English Dictionary*, hereafter *OED*).

7. *pip*: respiratory disease in poultry characterized by a white scale or horny patch on the tip of the tongue which prevents a bird from feeding (*OED*).

8. *pumps*: shoes.

9. *nondescript*: lacking distinguishing features; dull, drab *(OED)*.

10. *Colleen Rue*: translation of an ancient Irish ballad, 'An Cailín Ruadh', 'The Red (Haired) Girl'.

11. *wisha*: indeed; well *(DH-E)*.

12. *jewil*: jewel.

13. *agra*: from Irish *grá*, love; also *agradh, agraw, a ghra*: term of endearment used by an older person to somebody of either sex *(DH-E)*.

14. *'cute*: abbreviation of *acute*.

15. *no ho*: 'ho' was formerly an exclamation ordering the cessation of an action. 'There was no ho with him' means that he was not to be restrained *(OED)*.

16. *avourneen*: variant of *avoorneen*. Term of endearment from Irish *a mhuirnín*. 'Don't be long away, avoorneen ...': William Carleton, 'Denis O'Shaughnessy Going to Maynooth' (*Six Irish Tales, Newly Selected* ed. by Anthony Cronin (London: New English Library, 1962), p. 115) *(DH-E)*.

17. *thief o' the world*: great thief. See 'Dr Joyce and the Anglo-Irish Dialect' in *The Spectator* (2 August 1890), p. 23.

18. *acoushla*: also *acoolsha* and *acushla (machree)*. Term of endearment: my heart's dear one; from Irish, *a chuisle mo chroí* (lit. pulse of my heart) *(DH-E)*.

19. *residenther*: an old inhabitant, from English dialect: 'Residents – families of old standing in the countryside – are old *residenters*; others are *runners*' (Liam Ua Broin, *A South-west Dublin Glossary*, notes by J. J. Hogan (Dublin: n. p., 1944), p. 180); a non-literary source *(DH-E)*.

20. *spencer*: 'Spencer'; named for George John Spencer, 2nd Earl Spencer (1758–1834), Viscount Althrop and Home Secretary 1806–7, the Spencer was, from 1790, a woollen tail-coat without the tails. The design of this short, double-breasted man's jacket became that of the mess jacket and in Regency fashion was adopted by women and worn as a cardigan or fitted short jacket to complement an empire-line dress.

21. *bobbery*: a noisy commotion or disturbance. Also 'bobberree' and, according to Sir Henry Yule (1820–89), distinguished linguist and historical geographer, an Anglo-Indian representation of Hindi '*Bāp re!* O father!', a common exclamation of surprise or grief *(OED)*.

22. *wroth*: angry, irate.

23. *cluricawn*: *clurican*; a fairy. T. Butler, *A Parish and Its People* (Wellington Bridge: Grantstown Priory, 1985), p. 219.

24. *gramachree*: from the Irish *grá mo chroí*, my darling. Lit. love of my heart *(DH-E)*.

25. *tower of Hook*: 800-year-old lighthouse built by Strongbow's son-in-law, William Marshall (see, n. 306).

26. *gomersal*: Hall's form of *gomeral*; a fool, blockhead, half-wit; from Irish *gamal*, simpleton *(DH-E)*.

27. *keen at her berrin'*: make a lament at the burial.

28. *spalpeen*: from the Irish *spailpín*; an agricultural labourer who travelled about the country at certain seasons seeking work and who sometimes got into scrapes; hence figuratively a rascal or good-for-nothing, a scamp *(DH-E)*.

29. *Father Mike*: Hall based her character 'Father Mike' on Fr Edward Murphy (pastor in Carrig from 1793–1830), or 'Fr Ned' as he was known locally, parish priest of Bannow with chapels at Carrig and Ballymitty; he ministered to his parishioners during the troubled period of the rebellion. Educated in Paris, he was a friend to both Protestant and Catholic, ensuring no blood was spilled in the parish, writing 'protection' over the gate

of Graige House and notes in French to the family telling them to fear not, but to put their trust in God. See T. C. Butler, *A Parish and its People: History of Carrig-on-Bannow Parish* (Wellingtonbridge: Grantstown Priory, 1985), pp. 88–91.

30. *cloak*: the ubiquitous garment worn by Irish peasant women. Full length and made of wool, it protected against the elements. It had a capacious hood with a drawstring. Ritchie records that 'when an Irish girl travels ... she wears a cloak, generally blue, which is, perhaps, the only national dress extant in her country'. He notes that 'in almost every country there are minute modifications in the garment. In the times of chivalry, the Knights were accustomed to wear their ponderous furs, even in summer; and, in like name, the Irish girl, when she is rich enough to possess a cloak, continues to wear it in the dog days'. See L. Ritchie, *Ireland Picturesque & Romantic* (London: Longman, Rees, Orme, Brown, Green and Longman, 1838), p. 77.

31. *belting*: surrounding or encircling (*OED*).

32. *fetch*: 'In Ireland, a Fetch is the supernatural fac-simile of some individual, which comes to insure to its original, a happy longevity, or immediate dissolution: if seen in the morning the one event is predicted; if in the evening, the other'. This description of a 'fetch' in *OED* is given by J. Banim and M. Banim, *Tales, by the O'Hara Family; Containing Crohoore of the Bill-hook. The fetches, and John Doe* (London: W. Simpkin & R. Marshall, 1825). Thus, when Peggy suggests that she may have seen Lily's fetch by moonlight, the implication is sinister.

33. *mavourneen*: a term of endearment, 'my dear one'; from the Irish *no mhuirnín* (*DH-E*).

34. *free rovers*: pirates or smugglers.

35. *natural*: a person having a low learning ability or intellectual capacity; a person born with impaired intelligence. Archaic Hiberno-English (*OED*).

36. *pig wanted ringing*: refers to the practice of putting a metal ring through pigs' noses to prevent them from digging up the ground with their snouts.

37. *troth*: indeed, truly (*DH-E*).

38. *vagabone mill*: roving or straying; not subject to restraint or control. In this case, the latter applies as a term of abuse used by Mrs Cassidy (*OED*).

39. *onct*: once.

40. *resave*: receive.

41. *lanna*: child; from the Irish *leanbh*.

42. *colloguing*: to collogue is to conspire, chat confidentially. The origin is obscure; cf. Latin *colloquor, v.,* to talk together, and Modern English *colleague*. S. O'Casey, 'Juno and the Paycock', *Three Plays*, (Basingstoke: Macmillan, 1973), l. 25: 'Juno: D'ye mean to tell me that the pair of YOUS wasn't collogin' together here when me back was turned?' (*DH-E*).

43. *smithereens*: small broken fragments; little pieces. From Irish *smidiríní* (plural of *smidirín,* diminutive of *smiodar,* fragment). *OED* thinks the word may have originated from *smithers*, meaning fragments, plus the anglo-Irish suffix '*-een*', but Hogan states that *smithereens* is first recorded in 1825, earlier than *smithers*. J. J. Hogan, *The English Language in Ireland* (Dublin: Educational Company of Ireland, 1927), p. 115 (*H-ED*).

44. *skiver*: verb from 'skewer', an implement used in thatching.

45. *Lady-day*: a day on which the Virgin Mary is honoured in religious festivals; now only 25 March, the feast of the Annunciation. It is also the first of the traditional quarter days, fixed by custom as marking off the quarters of the year and on which tenancies began and ended, servants were hired and the payment of rent fell due (*OED*).

46. *vasty deep*: Shakespeare, *Henry IV, Part I*, III.i.52.

47. *houseleek*: any of various perennial plants constituting the genus *Semervivum*; most likely here to be the Common Houseleek, *S. Tectorum*, with pink flowers and a thick stem of leaves, formerly planted on the roofs of house as protection against lightning.
48. *sould the pass*: In Ireland, to 'sell the pass' was to betray one's countrymen (considered a heinous act) by giving information to the authorities (*OED*).
49. *red-coats*: British soldiers, so named for their coats of madder red.
50. *potteen*: 'poteen' or 'potheen'; from Irish *poitín*, little pot. Also home-made (illicit) spirits, once distilled from potatoes in a little pot (hence the name), as distinct from 'parliamentary' whiskey, on which duty had been paid (*DH-E*).
51. *brave*: meaning 'fine' in the locality of Forth and Bargy. See Butler, *A Parish and Its People*, p. 218.
52. *lannan*: child; colloquial form of the Irish *leanbh*.
53. *Giant's Causeway*: one of the wonders of the natural world, the Giant's Causeway, near Bushmills, Co. Antrim, Northern Ireland comprises a vast range of basaltic columns, enormous in size. They rise to a height of 636 feet and the interlocking pillars were originally formed due to ancient volcanic action. According to legend, the causeway was built by Fionn mac Cumhaill in order to meet Benandonner, a Scottish giant, who has issued a challenge to Fionn from across the Northern Channel. Columns of similar basalt are to be found across the water at Fingal's Cave on the island of Staffa, in the Inner Hebrides. The Giant's Causeway became a much-frequented tourist destination in the nineteenth century. The Irish artist Susanna Drury (1698?–1770) painted two views of the Causeway in gouache on vellum which were the first ever accurate depictions of the site. This pair of landscapes won the £25 premium of the Dublin Society in 1740 and were subsequently engraved in London (1743–4) by François Vivarès, landscape engraver. These engravings provided the French geologist Nicholas Demarest (1725–1815) with evidence to support his 'Vulcanist' theory of the origin of the basalt, against the current 'Neptunist' theory held by the German geologist Abraham Gottlob Werner (1749–1817). Consequently, Drury's landscape paintings of The Giant's Causeway became landmarks both in Irish topography and in European scientific illustration. A forensic and interestingly detailed description of The Giant's Causeway and the legends surrounding the area is provided by the Halls themselves in their own work, *Ireland: Its Scenery, Character &c*, 3 vols (London: Jeremiah How, 1846), vol. 3, pp. 138–76.
54. *widout knowing B from a bull's fut*: 'without knowing B from a bull's foot'; being entirely illiterate (OED).
55. *go bail for ye*: to go bail, colloquial, 'I will be bound', I am certain (*OED*).
56. *rattling* [*Jimmy*]: splendid or fine.
57. *gumption:* spirited initiative, shrewdness (*OED*).
58. *bocher*: although the *OED* gives the meaning 'butcher', in Ireland the word 'bocher' meant 'lame man'. See Mrs. S. C. Hall, 'The Bocher of Red-Gap Lane', in *The New Monthly Magazine and Literary Journal, Part the Second*, no. clxxiii, vol. XLIV, ed. by T. Campbell, S. C. Hall, E. B. Lytton, T. E. Hook, T. Hood and W. H. Ainsworth (London: H. Colburn), p. 81, where Hall glosses the word 'bocher' from her title as 'a lame man'. Butler, however, gives 'bocher' as the Irish *bachach* and the meaning 'applied to a beggar-man' (Butler, *A Parish and Its People*, p. 219).
59. *peep-o'-day boy*: member of a Protestant agrarian organization, the Peep o' Day Boys. They were active in the north of Ireland *c.* 1784–95 and clashed with the Roman Catholic Defenders. Their name supposedly arose from their practice of breaking into the houses of their Roman Catholic opponents at daybreak in search of arms (*OED*). See

S. J. Connolly, *Divided Kingdom: Ireland 1630–1800* (Oxford University Press, 2008), pp. 453–5.

60. *Sir Boyle Roche's bird*: Sir Boyle Roche, 1st Baronet (October 1736–June 1807), was remembered for the language of his speeches, which were riddled with metaphor. He was best known for excusing an absence in Parliament thus: 'Mr. Speaker, it is impossible I could have been in two places at once, unless I were a bird'. This quotation was referenced by A. Bierce, *The Devil's Dictionary* (Cleveland, OH: WPC, 1911), p. 354 in his definition of 'ubiquity'. However, Roche was not uttering a malapropism here, he was quoting, and quoting correctly. The line appears in Jevon's play *The Devil of a Wife*:

    Wife: I cannot be in two places at once.

    Husband (Rowland): Surely no, unless thou wert a bird.

    Thomas Jevon, *The Devil of a Wife: or, a Comical Transformation* (1686).

61. *bachelor*: an unmarried man of marriageable age (*OED*). In Edgeworth as in Hall, however, it indicates a sweetheart; as in '"No, he's her bachelor," said an old woman ... "Her bachelor?" "That is, her sweetheart..."'. M. Edgeworth, 'The Absentee', *Works of Maria Edgeworth, Complete in Thirteen Volumes*, 13 vols (Boston, MA: Samuel H. Parker, 1826), vol. 6, p. 371.

62. *revolving sweet and bitter thoughts*: evidence in this quotation of Hall's close attention to the work of Maria Edgeworth. Although not identified elsewhere, this exact phrase is given in quotation in M. Edgeworth, 'The Absentee', *Tales and Novels, in eighteen volumes, containing Tales of Fashionable Life*, 18 vols (London: Baldwin and Cradock, 1832), vol. 4, pp. xi, 218.

63. *quilled*: to quill fabric was to form fabric into narrow pleats or folds, resembling quills (*OED*).

64. *get up fine linen*: to dress it and make it ready for wearing.

65. *card*: to prepare wool or tow for spinning by combing out impurities and parting and straightening the fibres with a card (*OED*).

66. *cram fowl*: to stuff fowl.

67. *noggins*: 'noggin', also 'naggin'; a small mug or drinking vessel; 'a wooden vessel made of tiny staves, one of which is longer than the others and forms the handle' (*DH-E*).

68. *I ranged through Asia ... the siege of Paris*: Hall has taken these lines from the anonymous verse and old Irish ballad 'The Colleen Rue', which is the English rendering of 'An Cailín Ruadh', 'The Red (Haired) Girl' (see also n. 10). Gerald Griffin (1803–40), Irish novelist, playwright and poet, made use of 'An Cailín Ruadh' in his novel *The Collegians* (1829). His comic character Lowry Looby sings a few verses of the ballad while waiting to visit Eily O'Connor. However, the words of the ballad are delivered in colloquial pronunciation, which Petrie believes is revelatory of the peasant mind and demonstrates the attempt to express thoughts in an unfamiliar, recently acquired language.

69. *sorra*: sorrow. Used to express absence or an emphatic negative. Hogan (*The English Language in Ireland*) notes *sorrow* as a mild imprecation and emphatic negative in mediaeval English, and it survives in Scotland and Ireland (*DH-E*).

70. *mumming*: to mum is to make an inarticulate sound with closed lips, especially as an indication of inability or unwillingness to speak (*OED*).

71. *hould your whisht*: 'hold your whist', meaning 'hush!' or 'be quiet'; see the Irish folk song 'The Old Woman of Wexford': 'Yerra hold your whist old woman, sure I can't see you at all'. Possibly derived from the Irish *éist*, 'listen' (*DH-E*).

72. *omathawn*: English-Irish variant of the Irish *amadán*; a fool, buffoon, stupid person (*DH-E*). Elsewhere, relating the tale of St Kevin and the 'sarpint' (*Handbooks for Ireland:*

Dublin and Wicklow (London: Virtue, Hall & Virtue, 1853), p. 137), the Halls say: 'So wid that, the omathawn crawls into the trunk, having the ind of his tail outside'.

73. *grawl*: child (*DH-E*).

74. *hushowed*: hushed; imitative of the sound made; to quieten a child, baby or animal with soothing noises. See Hall's story 'The Drowned Fisherman', *The Amulet* (London: Frederick Westley and A. H. Davis, 1836), p. 54: 'the babby went off to sleep without an *hushow*!'

75. *tester*: a coin, from *teston* or *testoon*. In England a shilling of Henry VII, Henry VIII and Edward VI. Subsequently a colloquial or slang term for a sixpence. Originally the French name of a silver coin struck at Milan; in Italian, *testone*. In 1543 it was equal to 12d., but it sank in value to 6d. 'Pistol: Tester I'll have in pouch when though shalt lack, base Phrygian Turk!' Shakespeare, *Merry Wives of Windsor*, I.iii.81–2.

76. *massy*: massive. Of metal, solid and weighty; not hollow, plated or alloyed. Sheridan, *School for Scandal* (1780), III.iii.41.

77. *pigeon's craw*: also 'buffont'; late Georgian style when a gauze scarf or large starched kerchief was used to fill in the neckline of a décolleté gown and worn puffed out in 'pouter pigeon' style. See E. J. Jewandowski, *The Complete Costume Dictionary* (Plymouth: Scarecrow Press, 2011), p. 41

78. *stuff*: material for making garments; woven material of any kind, though usually coarse wool or linen, not silk. In this period it was associated with the lower orders: 'A coarse sort of stuff used by the common people', G. P. R. James, *Robber*, 2 vols (New York: Harper & Brothers, 1838), vol. 1, p. 14.

79. *lobster's claw*: lobster claws were used as 'teething-rings'. John Ruddy records that 'The Claws [of lobsters and crabs] are sometimes hung about children's necks as Coral, to rub their gums in breeding their teeth'; J. Ruddy, *An Essay Towards a Natural History of the Country of Dublin* ... (Dublin: pr. for W. Sleator, 1772), pp. 371–2.

80. *national hood*: 'the national hood' refers to the hooded cloak worn by Irish women (see also n. 29). The Halls provide a detailed description in Hall, Mr and Mrs S. C., *Ireland, its Scenery, Character, &c.*, new edn, 3 vols (London: Virtue, n. d.), vol. 2, p. 272. The description is interesting not only for the detail it supplies, but for an insight into an English perspective of the Irish peasantry: 'The Irish cloak forms very graceful drapery; the material falls well, and folds well. It is usually large enough to envelop the whole person; and the hood is frequently drawn forward to shield the face of the wearer from sun, rain, or wind. Yet we would fain see its general use dispensed with. A female in the lower ranks of life cares but little for the other portions of her dress if she has "a good cloak;" and certainly her ordinary appearance would be more thought of, if the huge "cover-slut" were not always at hand to hide dilapidation in her other garments'. They go on to recommend that the cloak be replaced by the tartan shawl seen in Rosstrevor in the north, which would provide almost as much warmth 'at about a fourth of the cost' and 'is *easily washed* – a great consideration in all matters of peasant clothing'.

81. sporting squireens: a petty squire with pretensions; from English 'squire' and Irish diminutive suffix 'een' (*DH-E*). 'A squireen, or buckeen in Ireland, is a certain biped, given to top-boots and corduroys, who makes himself conspicuous at fairs and races, in the vain hope that he may be taken for the son of the "masther" at the "big house," or some other great man', J. W. Carleton (ed.), 'Bee's Wing, Characters of "the Field"', *The Sporting Review*, August 1846, pp. 114–19.

82. *sand blind*: half blind, dim-sighted (*OED*).

83. *kitling*: a young cat, or kitten (*OED*).

84. *Reginald's Tower*: Built in Waterford city as a defence tower in the thirteenth century, it is the oldest urban civic building in Ireland. With a chequered history, the fall of the tower heralded the fall of the city when attacked by the Anglo-Normans in 1170. Its name derives from the Hiberno-Norse Ragnall Mac Guillemaire, who was imprisoned in the tower by the Anglo-Normans. Aoife, daughter of Dermot MacMurrough, King of Leinster, met the Anglo-Norman Strongbow (see n. 300) at the tower and they were later married. King John visited in 1210 and had coins minted. Richard II visited in 1394 and 1399 when, on 27 July, he left the tower as King of England and Wales, shortly thereafter to be captured by Henry of Bolinbroke, the future Henry VI, and forced to abdicate.

85. *asthore*: *a stór*; Irish, from *stór*, treasure; darling, my dear, my love (*DH-E*).

86. *flaggers*: the 'flag' or 'iris'; one of various endogenous plants with a bladed or ensiform leaf; from the French, 'flagiere'. Although earlier applied to any reed or rush, here with mention of 'blossoms' the yellow or blue iris is indicated (*OED*). They favour moist or sedgy places. A mention by Samuel Lover, 1797–1868, is the earliest record of this Anglo-Irish dialect word in *OED*. 'It's banks sedgy, thickly grown with flaggers and bul-rushes' (S. Lover, *Handy Andy*, (London: H. Lea, 1842), p. xv.

87. *fairy flax*: *linum catharticum*; a herb with small white flowers and wiry stems which could be used to make string or fibre for spinning. Also a mild purgative, used on the Scottish island of Colonsay until recent times as such. So named as it was said that the fairies used the stems to weave their diminutive clothing. See G. Hatfield, *Hatfield's Herbal* (London: Penguin, 2009).

88. *the quality*: term used to describe the upper echelons of society, but carries derogatory implications.

89. *gaberlunzie*: a strolling beggar or mendicant (OED). The word is Scottish in origin and was used by Sir W. Scott; Hall's adoption of the word perhaps evidences her familiarity with his works.

90. *Bedad!*: 'by dad' or 'by God'. An Irish asseveration (*OED*).

91. *clamping turf*: stacking sods of cut turf into compact heaps or mounds to allow drying.

92. like Hagar and Abraham in the picture: See n. 409. The 'picture' referred to here may perhaps be a print popular in the 1800s, entitled 'Abraham giving up the Handmaid' by Sir Robert Strange (1721–92), after Guercino (1591–1666) which is mentioned in the February edition of *The Art-Union* (London: Art-Union Office, 1840) p. 29 with regard to an auction of the proofs and early impressions of the work of Sir Robert Strange. The Art-Union was a monthly magazine edited by Carter Hall.

93. *Read-a-made-aisy*: 'Reader-made-easy'; colloquial reference to a primer used in the hedge schools, *The Imperial Spelling Book or Reading Made Easy* (Dublin, n. p., n. d.). See A. McManus, *The Irish Hedge School and Its Books* (Dublin: Four Courts Press, 2002), pp. 112–16.

94. *haro*: hero.

95. *Naro*: Nero Claudius Caesar Augustus Germanicus (AD 37–68), who became fifth emperor of Rome in AD 54 at the age of 17. His legacy was one marked by tyranny and brutality, with matricide, murder and vengeful persecution of members of the Christian sect a mere indication of his misdeeds. Today he is often associated with the apocryphal tale that he fiddled while Rome burned.

96. *Queen Elizabeth*: Elizabeth I (1533–1603), Queen of England and Ireland, only child of Henry VIII (1491–1547) and Anne Boleyn (*c.* 1500–36). She never visited Ireland, though governing the country was a thorn in her side. The ubiquitous fear of invasion from Spain via Ireland was lived out in the unsuccessful Desmond rebellions and Siege of

Smerwick in Munster, which were followed by the plantation of that province. Through her characterization of Master Ben in this episode and his particular selection of 'tyrants', Hall presents what Protestant families like the Carrs feared: the sewing of the seeds of sedition and rebellion in the minds of the young through their lessons from hedge-school masters.

97. *Oliver Crummel*: Oliver Cromwell (1599–1658) was made Lord Protector of England, Scotland and Ireland on 16 December 1653. In politics he had always taken a strong line against Irish rebels. Zealous in his Puritan faith, he was driven by a desire to eliminate royalist sympathizers in Ireland and destroy the Confederation of Kilkenny. His name became synonymous with ruthless cruelty, particularly in Wexford and Drogheda, towns which were witness to the mass slaughter of rebels and civilians alike on a scale hitherto unseen. Cromwell's pretext was revenge for the massacre of Protestants during the 1641 rebellion. Frequent mention by Hall's characters of 'Cromwell' and 'Cromwellians' – those settlers who were given Irish land and settled in Ireland – attests to the deep and anguished mark he made on the country's collective imagination.

98. *Enniscorthy*: town in Co. Wexford; Enniscorthy castle was occupied by the de Prender-gast and other Anglo-Norman families from 1190 to the 1400s. Enniscorthy was still a village when captured by Cromwell and his army in 1649, he having crossed the river Slaney and taken the diocesan centre of Ferns on his progress to Wexford. Enniscorthy was incorporated by James I and until the Union sent two members to the Irish Parliament.

99. *Bray*: Once a quiet fishing village, in the eighteenth century Bray became a bustling sea-side resort due to its popularity with the leisured classes of Dublin, who favoured it as an escape from the city. Situated on the Dargle river in north Co. Wicklow, in mediaeval times Bray was on the border of the Pale, that area under the jurisdiction of the English crown from Dublin Castle.

100. *castle of Coolhull*: dating from the sixteenth century, the castle tower has the later addition of a two-storey fortified hall. The building was possibly converted from a church to a secular fortification. See P. Harrison, *Castles of God: Fortified Religious Buildings of the World* (Woodbridge: Boydell & Brewer, 2004), p. 36.

101. *an excellent thing in a woman*: paraphrases Shakespeare, 'Her voice was ever soft, gentle and low; an excellent thing in a woman', *King Lear*, V.iii.270–1.'

102. *pattern*: patron or saint's day, also called 'patron' and commonly 'pattern' in Ireland. On such a day there is a gathering around a holy well or place consecrated to a saint for prayer and other devotional practices. 'We went up to the pattern to say a few prayers ... and the walk did us good as well'. J. Joyce, *Finnegan's Wake* (Harmondsworth: Penguin, 1969), p. 402 (*DH-E*).

103. *gometry staircase*: 'geometry' staircase; Hiberno-English. An example of such is the Dean's Stair or Geometric Stair in St Paul's Cathedral, London. Wren's stone spiral of 1705 rises around a cylindrical void, the treads supported only by the wall end, the whole appearing to be magically suspended though arranged on geometric principles.

104. *Kilkaven and Duncormuck*: Kilcavan was named for the fifth-century monk Cavan, who founded a monastery at Ardcavan and was one of the first to preach the gospel to parts of Hy Kinsella. Duncormuck is a village close to Kilmore Quay on the river Muck.

105. *Rosinante*: the name for a worn-out horse, or nag; from the Spanish *rocín*, horse, and *ante*, before. Punningly given to Don Quixote's horse in the book of the same name by Miguel de Cervantes and alluding to the animal's former status as a workhorse (*OED*).

106. *caparisons*: caparison; a cloth or covering spread over the saddle of a horse, often gaily ornamented, or the dress of a person; in this case the word refers to both Rosinante the horse and his owner.

107. *cawbeen*: an old cap or hat, from the Irish *cáibín*.

108. *scratch wig*: a small, short wig; Hall's description of the old schoolmaster's scratch wig indicates both the versatility of the item and her acute attention to Edgeworth's writing: 'He wore a rough scratch wig, originally of a light drab colour; and not only did he, like Miss Edgeworth's old steward in "Castle Rackrent," dust his own or a favoured visitor's seat therewith, but he used no other pen-wiper, and the hair bore testimony of having made acquaintance with both red and black ink'. Hall, *Ireland, its Scenery, Character, &c.*, vol. 1, p. 265.

109. *doodeen*: Hiberno-English, also 'dudeen', from the diminutive of the Irish *dúid*, stump, *dúidín*; a short-stemmed clay pipe, often smoked by women (*DH-E*).

110. *bandboxes*: lightweight cylindrical boxes used to hold small articles of apparel. Originally made to hold the 'bands' or ruffs of the seventeenth century (*OED*).

111. *pole screens*: tapestries attached to a brass or wooden stem on a tripod base. These fire-screens were chiefly used in the period to protect women's complexions.

112. *village Public*: the village public house.

113. *meal-a-murder*: variant of 'míle murder'; uproar, trouble, a violent outbreak, ructions; from Irish *míle*, a thousand, and English 'murder' (*DH-E*).

114. *tall and straight as a popilar tree*: 'tall and straight as a poplar tree'; old song not identified, although the line crops up regularly in the period and again in Halls' *Ireland, its Scenery, Character, &c.* (London: Jeremiah How, 1843), vol. 3, p. 470.

115. *Curnol Piggot's [hounds]*: Hall refers to William Pemberton-Pigott of Slevoy Castle, Taghmon, Co. Wexford. Born on 3 January 1773, he was Lieutenant Colonel of the Wexford Regiment for nearly fifty years, having joined as an ensign in 1796. He was also Justice of the Peace and was appointed High Sheriff of Wexford in 1794. He held the mastership of the Wexford Hunt Club for many years until about 1847. See G. H. Bassett, 'Hunting, Coursing, Racing, Boating, Angling, Athletic sports, Cricket and Lawn Tennis', *Bassett's Wexford Guide and Directory 1885* (Dublin: Sealy, Bryers & Walker, 1885), p. 19.

116. *balsams*: a flowering plant of the genus *impatiens*; '*impatiens balsamina*' is an ornamental garden flower producing variegated double blooms (*OED*).

117. *netting-silk*: Silk thread was favoured over linen, wool or cotton in this ancient handicraft for the making of small items, gloves, doilies and purses; netting produced an open-meshed fabric which was knotted or woven at regular intervals.

118. *The gardener prunes ... to grow its own way*: Hall also uses this phrase in 'Mary Clavery's Story', *Bradshaw's Manchester Journal*, (Manchester: n. p., 1841), vol. 1, p. 292. No reference has been found elsewhere despite the biblical tone.

119. *by the same token*: moreover or furthermore.

120. *negur*: negro.

121. *gale day*: from Middle English 'gavel', rent (*DH-E*); traditionally 1 May and 1 November when tenant farmers paid their half-yearly rents to landlords.

122. *blackguard*: a man who behaves in a disgraceful or contemptible way; a ruffian, rogue or scoundrel. The unruly menials in a household or camp followers in charge of the pots and pans were called 'blackguards'. Origin uncertain, but may lie in a type of snuff called Irish Blackguard, originally an abusive name given to a shop boy in a Dublin snuff merchant's

by the owner because he made a mistake in the preparation of some snuff, but which subsequently became successful and was known by the name of its creator (*DH-E*).

123. *vamps*: that part of stockings or hose which covers the foot and ankle (*OED*).

124. *listed*: enlisted.

125. *the three graces*: In Greek mythology, the three graces were the daughters of Zeus and companions to the Muses. Usually represented in art as three young women unclothed, with wreaths of myrtle in their hair and holding hands to dance in a circle, they are Thalia goddess of festive celebrations and luxurious banquets, Euphrosyne, goddess of good cheer, mirth and merriment and Aglaia, goddess of beauty, adornment, splendour and glory.

126. *great*: 'fine' or 'splendid', a meaning frequently used.

127. *Chancery suits*: attendance at the court of Chancery, the highest court of judicature next to the House of Lords. In Ireland, the Court of Chancery was distinct from but analogous in character to the English court (*OED*).

128. *Term*: the session of a law court during such a period; the court in session (*OED*).

129. *a filthy pebble in the wheel of justice*: Mrs Hall also uses this 'quotation' in *A Week at Killarney* (London: Virtue, 1850), p. 205. In the latter case, the 'proverb' (origin not known) again seems to indicate an obstacle which hinders correct or honourable action.

130. *The Divil Sir Jimmy ... may ye niver come back*: not identified. Also appears in Mrs S. C. Hall, 'The Bannow Postman', *Tales of Irish Life and Character* (London: T. N. Foulis), p. 59.

131. sobriquet: epithet or nickname (French).

132. *Eau de Luce*: 'water of Luce' (French). A medicinal preparation of alcohol, ammonia and oil of amber, used in India as an antidote to snakebites, and in England as smelling salts (*OED*).

133. *the Curragh*: Carter Hall gives us a contemporary description: 'Within a short distance of the town is the far-famed Curragh of Kildare, the principal race-ground in Ireland. It is a fine undulating down, about six miles in length and two in breadth, and is unequalled, perhaps, in the world, for exceeding softness and elasticity of the turf: the verdure of which is "evergreen," and the occasional irregularities of which are very attractive to the eye. The land is the property of the crown, and includes above 6000 acres, where numerous flocks of sheep find rich and abundant pasture'. (S. C. Hall and Mrs. S. C. Hall, *Ireland, its Scenery, Character, &c.*, new edn, 3 vols (London: Virtue, n. d.), vol. 2, pp. 258–9.

134. '*sdeath*: a euphemistic abbreviation of 'God's death' used in oaths and asseverations (*OED*).

135. *seem to be ... and mountains all of gold*: These lines are taken from a poem by C. Hall, 'The Clouds', *The Amulet; or Christian and Literary Remembrancer* (London: Baynes & Wightman, 1828), p. 242. This is the third edition of *The Amulet*, a publication of deep religious inflection of which Carter Hall was publisher. Mrs. Hall is, in some sense, publicizing her husband's literary offering.

136. *Mant*: a toothless mouth or space where teeth have fallen out (*DH-E*).

137. *gown-piece*: a length of fabric suitable to be made into a dress. Thomas Hardy, *The Return of the Native*, 3 vols (London: Smith, Elder & Co., 1878), vol. 2, p. 195: 'Among the cups on the long table ... lay an open parcel of light drapery – the gown-piece, as it was called – which was to be raffled'.

138. *Anty the darlint ... her Paddy's pride*: not identified.

139. *Colleen das Crutheen Amo*: an English phonetic rendering of the Irish title 'An Cailín Deas Crúite na nBó', 'The Young Girl Milking the Cows', a love song or ballad attributed to Thomas Moore (1770–1852). The singer is a youth who, on hearing a young maid singing as she milked her cow, falls under her spell. He declares he would rather live without riches than without her. She prefers 'to live single and airy' and he pleads once more for her consent, having warned that time (and her beauty) will pass all too quickly. The tone of the penultimate verse is in stark contrast with the lyrical romance of the rest:

> An old maid is like an old almanac,
> Quite useless when once out of date;
> If her ware is not sold in the morning
> At noon it must fall to low rate.
> The fragrance of May is soon over,
> The rose loses its beauty, you know;
> All bloom is consumed in October,
> Sweet Cailín deas crúite na mbó.

140. *jilty*: 'jilty', is not recorded in *OED*. Hall's usage perhaps indicates local dialect accommodation of the noun/verb 'jilt'/'to jilt' to adjectival usage. Anty tells Grey Lambert here that she would not deceive after holding out hopes of love to Patrick Lambert; she claims not to be one who would cast off a lover capriciously.

141. *wedding of Ballyporeen*: Ballyporeen, 'Béal Átha Póirín', is a village near the town of Cahir, Co. Tipperary. The author of this comic song is unknown. See Anon., *Oliver's New Selection of Comic Songs; or, Momus's Budget* (Edinburgh: pr. Oliver, 1806), pp. 67–70. The first and final verses (of eleven) give a flavour of this variant of a broadside ballad:

> Descend ye chaste Nine to a true Irish Bard
> You're old maids to be sure, but he sends you a card,
> To beg you assist a poor musical elf,
> With a song ready made, he'll compose it himself,
> About maids, boys, a priest, and a weddin[g],
> With a croud you could scarce thrust your head in,
> A supper, good cheer, and a bedding,
> Which happen'd at Ballyporeen.
> Now Patrick the bridegroom, and Oonagh the bride,
> Let the harp of old Ireland be sounded with pride,
> And to all the brave guests, young or old, grey or green,
> Drunk or sober, that jigg'd it at Ballyporeen.
> And when Cupid shall lend you his wherry,
> To trip o'er the conjugal ferry,
> I wish you may be half so merry,
> As we were at Ballyporeen.

142. *Ude's nor Kitchener's sauces*: Hall refers to two contemporary lions of the culinary world. Louis-Eustache Ude (d. 1846) was a celebrated cook who worked at the court of Louis XVI. The saying 'coquus nascitur non fit', 'a cook is born, not made', is attributed to him and he wrote of his belief that 'sauces are the soul of cooking' in L.-E. Ude, *The French Cook*, facs. edn of 1828 (New York: n. p., 1978). His glory years were as chef at Crockford's, the gaming club established in St James's in 1828 (*ODNB*). Hall also refers to William Kitchiner (1850–1916), epicure and *soi-disant* medical doctor, who spent his substantial inheritance on the arts he enjoyed: music, gastronomy and optics. His book *The Cook's Oracle* (1817) ran to many editions and was an acknowledged source

for Mrs Beeton. His piquant 'Wow-wow sauce' was enjoyed in an age of boiled mutton and roasts and the recipe appears in Anon., *Enquire Within upon Everything* (London: Houlston, 1856), p. 311 (*ODNB*).

143. *hag-yard*: a stackyard or 'haggard' where hay is kept.

144. *worsted*: items [such as stockings] made from well-twisted yarn spun of long-staple wool combed to lay the fibres parallel (*OED*).

145. *suggan*: from the Irish *súgán*, a rope made by twisting straw or hay (used to tie hay-cocks) (*DH-E*).

146. *lock of straw*: a bundle of straw, a 'lock' being a quantity of something (*DH-E*).

147. *sowkins*: a mild oath; from the word sag, to cut. *Translations of the Philological Society, 1899–1902* (London: Kegan Paul, Trübner & Co., 1902), p. 95.

148. *cant*: auction to dispose of goods; from the Irish *ceant* (*OED*).

149. flahulagh: also 'flahoolagh'. From the Irish *flaithiúlach*, generous. Often used ironically: 'he was very flahoolagh with his chequebook, wasn't he?', James Joyce, *Ulysses* (Harmondsworth: Penguin, 1969), pp. 309. In this case the word emphasizes robust health.

150. *high in air*: Hall seems to have borrowed the phrase from Washington Irving (1783–1859), who describes a similar mountain scene in W. Irving, *Rip Van Winkle* (Philadelphia, PA: David McKay, [1819] 1921), p. 48.

151. *our Lady of Grace*: a title given to the Blessed Virgin Mary.

152. *to come like truth … like dreams*: rephrased quotation from 'Childe Harold's Pilgrimage' by Byron, who wrote:

> I saw or dream'd of such, – but let them go –
> They came like truth, and disappear'd like dreams;
> And whatsoe'er they were – are now not so.

See Byron, 'Childe Harold's Pilgrimage', vol. 2, verse VIII, p. 11, l. 2.

153. *nuns in France and Flanders*: In the sixteenth century, during the reigns of Henry VIII (1509–47) and Elizabeth I (1558–1603), thirty convents in Ireland were closed and many of the nuns fled to the Continent or remained in hiding. Following the Dissolution of the Monasteries under Henry VIII (1536–41), girls from well-born Catholic families who wished to follow a religious vocation joined or formed communities in Europe. In 1608, Mary Ward had established a monastery for girls as the Order of St. Clare at Gravelines, on the border of Spanish territory in Flanders. Irish nuns joined them in 1642, intending to return home when persecution ceased. The Irish Dominicans became established in Lisbon in 1639 and the Benedictines at Ypres in 1665. Frequently supported by Catholic royals and aristocrats, the nuns had contact with male relatives studying in the Irish Colleges throughout Europe, from Louvain and Douai to Salamanca and Rome.

154. *the unbidden guests* …: Hall is evoking Shakespeare: 'unbidden guests/ Are often welcomest when they are gone', *Henry VI, Part I*, II,ii,55–6.

155. *Trinity*: Trinity College, Dublin, founded in 1592 as Queen Elizabeth's College of the University of Dublin. 'I could hardly afford to take a tram into Dublin, never mind the cost of transporting myself into Trinity'; H. Leonard, *Out After Dark*, (Harmondsworth: Penguin, 1990), p. 57 (*DH-E*).

156. *esprit fort*: free thinker or libertine (French).

157. *The Glorious Memory*: Traditional Orange toast which loyal Irish Protestants raised to the memory of William III (King Billy), champion of the Protestant cause in the Jacobite (or Williamite) wars and victor at the Battle of the Boyne in 1690.

158. *Orangeman*: a member of the Orange Order, formerly the Orange Association, who defends Protestant political principles and the union of Great Britain and Northern Ireland (*OED*). The association was founded in 1795 and the Halls are quoted in the *OED* as stating that in 1836 there were between 120,000 and 140,000 Orangemen in England (*OED*).

159. *the castle*: Dublin Castle. Built on an early Danish Viking fortress, the castle functioned variously for 700 years as prison, treasury and seat of English colonial power. In 1800 the Union of Great Britain and Ireland saw the end of the castle as the seat of policy-making, which devolved to Westminster.

160. *seguidilla*: an old Castillian folksong or courtship dance using springy steps and foot taps in three-quarter time. With many regional variants, it is danced with a proud bearing.

161. *Sweet olive groves* ...: not identified.

162. *I know no blessing* ...: not identified.

163. *the good cause*: 'at length the good cause triumphs', a motto of the Orange Order.

164. *nevvy*: nephew.

165. *doubt*: use of the word 'doubt' here means 'certain' or 'sure'. See Butler, *A Parish and its People*, p. 218.

166. *bogle*: a phantom causing fright, a goblin, bogy or spectre of the night, undefined creature of superstitious dread. 'I played at bogle about the bush wi' them', Sir W. Scott, *Waverley; or, 'Tis Sixty Years Since*, 5th edn, 3 vols, (Edinburgh: A. Constable, 1815), vol. 3, ch. 23, p. 354. (*OED*).

167. *It's face was black as Briant coal ... that puffed out fire and Brimstane*: This quotation is taken from a poem by The Ettrick Shepherd, *nom de plume* of James Hogg (bap. 1770–1835), poet and novelist:

> The Bogle
>
> A Song
>
> I met a bogle late yestreen,
>
> As gaun to see my dearie,
>
> Wi crokkit tail, an' waulin een,
>
> And wow but I was eiry:
>
> Its face was black as Bryant coal,
>
> Its nose was o', the whunstane;
>
> Its mou' was like a borel hole,
>
> That puffed out fire an' brimstone.

A 'bogle' is a ghost, from Middle English *bugge*; 'Whinstone', used in quarrying, is any dark-coloured rock, such as basalt or chert. See *The Edinburgh Literary Journal: or, Weekly Register of Criticism and Belles Lettres*, no. 112 (1 January 1831), p. 171.

168. *banshees, cluricauns*: 'banshee', Irish *bean sí*, a woman of the spirit world, a female spirit whose wailing presages death in a family (*DH-E*). 'Cluricaun', also 'cluricawn', 'clooricaun' and Irish *clurican*, a fairy (Butler, *A Parish and its People*, p. 219).

169. *merryman*: jester (*OED*).

170. *read-a-me-daisy*: *The Imperial Spelling Book, or Reading Made Easy*; see n. 82.

171. *cochering*: feasting; also the practice or custom, claimed as a right by Irish chiefs, of quartering themselves upon their dependants or tenants (*OED*).

172. *qui vive*: on the alert or on the lookout (French). Literally 'who should live?' a sentinel's challenge to discover to which party the person challenged belongs, to which the answer should be '*vive le roi!*' (*OED*).

173. *pippin*: a young foolish or naïve person (derogatory here) (*OED*).

174. *fore'nent*: also 'fornent', meaning 'in front of', 'facing', 'right opposite to', 'over against'. 'No more NOR the genteels fornent ye'; M. Banim, *The Boyne Water, by the O'Hara Family* (Dublin: J. Duffy, 1865), p. 119 (*DH-E*).

175. *neagre*: negro.

176. *rouleaus*: from *rouleaux* or 'little rolls'; especially a stack of coins put up in paper or fabric (French) (*OED*).

177. *olive groves of Spain*: not identified.

178. *sudden and quick ...*: Shakespeare, *As You Like It*, II.vii.150.

179. *Sorrow and guilt ... their purpose on them*: W. Howitt, Epigram to 'The Forest Minstrel', *The Forest Minstrel & Other Poems*, by W. and M. Howitt (London: Baldwin, Cradock, and Joy, 1823), p. 21.

180. *keener*: from the Irish *caoine*, meaning 'wail'; a professional mourner at a funeral or wake (*DH-E*). See Hall, *Ireland, its Scenery & Character*, vol 1, pp. 221–36.

181. *coquette*: a flirt or woman who trifles with the affections of men (*OED*).

182. *corking-pin*: a pin of a large size formerly used to attach a woman's headdress to a cork mould.

183. *Emeralder*: from the Emerald Isle, Ireland. In the United States of America, one of fifty-five recorded mildly offensive nicknames for the Irish. See I. Allen Lewis, *The Language of Ethnic Conflict* (New York: Columbia University Press, 1983).

184. *mealy*: purple russet potatoes with thick skins, a high starch content and low in moisture and sugar; the opposite of waxy (red, or new) potatoes.

185. *that bates Bannaher*: 'that beat Banagher', a phrase expressing something as extraordinary or all-surpassing. The rejoinder to the phrase is 'and Banagher beats the devil'. There are several explanations for the origin of the phrase, but the most likely describes Banagher, a town of strategic importance in King's County, now Co. Offaly, on the river Shannon as having gained infamy as a corrupt pocket borough. The *OED* records the first use of the phrase in W. Carleton, *Traits and Stories of the Irish Peasantry*, 3 vols., (Dublin: W. Curry Jr, 1830), vol. 1, p. 50.

186. *bawn*: Irish *bábhún*, an enclosure for cattle; a yard; a paddock for cattle; the green space in front of a house (*DH-E*).

187. *the very moral*: colloquial phrase meaning 'the very model, or likeness, of' (*OED*).

188. *French curls*: Soon after 1745 'French curls made their first appearance in Paris &c. They looked like eggs strung in order on a wire, and tied around the head'. In addition, 'the English made [the curls] in false hair from a notion of cleanliness'. See *The Mirror of Literature, Amusement and Instruction*, (London: J. Limbird, 1838), vol. XXX, p. 450. In *Jane Eyre*, Mrs. Brocklehurst's entrance wearing a 'false front of French curls' is a wry commentary on Mr. Brocklehurst's earlier fulminations, equating curled hair with a lack of modesty and evangelical virtue. See C. Bell [Charlotte Brontë], *Jane Eyre: An Autobiography* (London: W. Nicholson, 1847), p. 55.

189. *Dunbrody Abbey*: established in 1182 at Campile, Co. Wexford, when Herve de Montmorency, who accompanied Strongbow (see n. 300) on his invasion of Leinster, gifted the land to the monks of Buildwas Abbey in Shropshire. The monastery was finally set up under the Cistercian mother house in Dublin, St Mary's, and confirmed by Pope Lucius III under the name of 'Portus St. Mariae', 'harbour of St. Mary', taking account of the proviso that the abbey be a place of refuge. A Cistercian monastery established in the thirteenth century, it was dissolved by Henry VIII in 1536, plundered and burnt down, and today lies in ruins.

190. *Seven Castles of Clonmines*: a group of ruins on the banks of the river Scar, described in 1684 as comprising four or five castles, an old church called St Nicholas and a monastery called St Augustine. The belfries of the church and abbey were thought to have been viewed as warlike towers, hence the totality of the buildings came to be called 'the seven castles of Clonmines'. See Hall, *Ireland, its Scenery, Character &c.,* vol. 2, p. 152.

191. *Scar*: the Scar of Bannow river. The word *scar* (or *skar*) means 'rock' or 'rocky promontory' and is of Danish or Viking origin. The Scar of Bannow is formed at the confluence of the Coragh and the Owenduff (in Irish, the 'Abha-dubh' or Blackwater) below Clonmines. It forms the boundary between the baronies of Shelburne and Shelmalier. See Butler, *A Parish and its People*, p. 59.

192. *mere Irish*: of a people; unmixed, from the Latin *merus* meaning 'pure'.

193. *carder*: one who combs out or cards wool in preparation for spinning or weaving (*OED*).

194. *wirrasthrew*: also 'wirrasthru', alas, from Irish *a Mhuire, is trua*, 'Mary [i.e. the Virgin Mary] 'tis pity' ['trua'] (*DH-E*). *DH-E* gives 'trua' as 'true', but 'pity' is correct.

195. *North*: the north of Ireland; around Belfast particularly, mills for spinning flax for the linen trade abounded. The weather in the northern province suited the crop and seventeenth-century Huguenot refugees brought with them expertise in weaving.

196. *crap*: the husk of grain; chaff (*OED*).

197. *Och hone*: from the Irish *ochón*, cry of lamentation; 'alas' (*DH-E*).

198. *The Niverlands*: The Netherlands.

199. *bla'gardly*: blackguardly; behaving dishonourably or contemptibly.

200. *gridiron*: a metal frame with parallel bars and supports used to broil meat or fish over a fire (*OED*).

201. *griskin*: the lean portion of a loin of a bacon pig (*OED*).

202. *upon the ledge*: To leave a crop 'on the ledge' is to leave it unstacked in order that the grain may mature and harden. See E. Murphy and M. Doyle, *Irish Farmer's and Gardener's Magazine and Register of Rural Affairs* (Dublin: W. Curry Jr, 1834), vol. 1, Nov. 1833– Dec. 1834, p. 587.

203. *dernier ressort*: as a last resort (French).

204. *Barcelona*: a kerchief or neckerchief of twilled silk worn around the neck or head (*OED*).

205. *go-by-the-ground*: a dwarf; or, that which creeps along the ground (*OED*).

206. *lantin' puff*: 'lantern puff', a hurry. T. Wright, *Dictionary of Obsolete and Provincial English* (London: H. Bohn, 1857), p. 621.

207. c'est le premier pas qui coûte: 'It is the first step that costs' (French).

208. but the woman triumphed: See the poem Anon., 'A Lady Faust: An Allegory', *Otago Witness*, 1004: 25 (25 February 1871), p. 1.

209. *there was naebody by*: This phrase occurs in a book about the Scottish Protestant martyr George Wishart (1513–46). See D. Alcock, *The Dark Year of Dundee: A Tale of the Scottish Reformation* (London: T. Nelson, 1867), p. 305.

210. *flitch*: a side of bacon, salted and cured (*OED*).

211. *meed*: recompense for labour or service (*OED*).

212. *the cry of the country*: from *posse comitatus* (Latin), 'power of the county'. It was codified in section 8 of the Sheriff's Act of 1887 that 'every person should be ready at the command of the sheriff and at "the cry of the country" to arrest a felon'.

213. *deuce*: the personification of mischief or evil; the devil (*OED*).

214. *tyke*: a dog, usually a low-bred or coarse dog; a mongrel (*OED*).

215. *barefoot to Jericho, to serve me or mine*: 'Jericho' is used colloquially for a place far distant and out of the way (*OED*). 'I'd go from this to Jericho to oblige so handsome a gentleman

as yer honour', Mrs. S. C. Hall, *Marian; or, A Young Maid's Fortunes,* 2 vols (New York: Harper, 1840), p. 47.

216. *Otter's Hole*: a cave on the seashore, north of the quarry at Herrylock and beside the mill-stone quarry. Carved into the red sandstone of Otter's Hole are the names of former residents and stonemasons who temporarily used the cave: 'Fardy', 'Tweedy' and 'Breen'. See B. Colfer, *The Hook Peninsula: Wexford* (Cork: Cork University Press, 2004), p. 217.

217. *Duncannon*: Duncannon Fort. Situated on a promontory in Waterford Harbour, in 1588 this castle was earmarked for conversion to a fort under Elizabeth I to protect from possible attack by the Spanish Armada, although work did not begin until 1590. The fort was of strategic importance throughout a history of conflict and siege; it was taken by Cromwell in 1650. Following the rebellion of 1798 prisoners were detained there before being sent for trial to Geneva Barracks. Occupied by the British army throughout the nineteenth century, it is preserved today as an Elizabethan artillery fort.

218. *Waterford Chronicle*: Ramsay's *Waterford Chronicle* was serving local readers in 1766, with a second series issued in 1769 at a cost of a shilling a quarter. 1778 saw a larger publication of four columns; in 1800, the price was four pence.

219. *Irish Herculaneum*: Bannow today comprises the village of Carrig-on-Bannow, or Carrig. In Norman times there was a substantial town or borough on the island of Bannow. The channel which separated this island from the mainland silted up over the years and the island now forms part of the mainland. The old town was dubbed the 'Irish Herculaneum' after the ancient Roman town which was inundated following the eruption of Mount Vesuvius in AD 79. From the *Cromwellian Valuation Returns* (1654) may be read a list of the streets of the old town: High St, New St, Little St, Our Lady's St, Lackey St, Weaver St, St Mary's St, Toolick St and Ivory St. Sir Robert Leigh of Rosegarland, writing in 1684, reports: 'The town of Banno is now quite ruined, there being nothing there but the ruins of the old church and of several stone houses and ancient streets of some few cabins – yet it sends two burgesses to serve in parliament still'. See Butler, *A Parish and its People*, pp. 37–8.

220. *Graige House*: The ancestral home of George Carr (d. 1824) and reported to be one of the oldest in the parish of Bannow. Hall lived there with her mother and grandmother, having moved there from Dublin on the death of her father *c.* 1800. When Hall was 15, they moved to London. George Carr was held in affection locally, to such a degree that he and his household were spared in the rising of 1798.

221. *maiden hair*: 'maiden hair fern', *adiantum*.

222. *two Keeroes*: situated off Ballymadder Point on the Hook Peninsula near Cullenstown, two islets, surrounded by dangerous rocky reefs, now called the Keeragh Islands. A ruin on the larger island is what remains of a shelter built in 1800 for the survivors of shipwrecks.

223. *ould French*: 'old French'; Hall here refers to Walter French, renowned for his apparent longevity. A gravestone in the churchyard at Bannow was noted by a commercial traveller and reported in *The Irish Times*: 'Erected by Peter French to the memory of his parents. Here lieth the body of Walter French his grandfather who departed this life 14th January 1701 aged 140'. A report in 'Past Times' in *The Irish Times*, 10 March 1930, surmises that 'headstone hunters long before my time have noted this stone and researched the man's origin and believe his age to be correct'.

224. *HOSPITALITY – no formality* ...: Words from the song 'In the land of potatoes O!', set to the tune of 'Morgan Rattler'. The verse runs:

    Hospitality,

> No formality
> There you ever see,
> The free and the easy
> Would so amaze ye
> You'd this is all crazy
> For dull we never be!

The song is attributed to Robert Mc Owen, father of Lady Morgan, by T. Crofton Croker, *Popular Songs of Ireland* (London: G. Routledge, 1886), pp. 57–9.

225. *Barrytown*: Barrystown Castle. The name originates with Robert de Barry, who landed in Bannow in 1169 from the island of Barry in Glamorganshire. In 1641 the estate was forfeit under the Cromwellian settlement and granted to Nicholas King in 1655 for his military service. The estate came down through the family to Jonas King, who lived there with his mother. Mrs Hall writes with affection about visits to the Kings and Barrystown House in Mrs S. C. Hall, *Grandmama's Pockets* (Edinburgh: Chambers, 1849), pp. 31–3. Jonas King died in 1877, the house having burned down in suspicious circumstances shortly before his demise (Butler, *A People and its Parish*, pp. 47–8).

226. *fowling-pieces*: a light gun for shooting wild fowl.

227. *Mr Barry*: Hall's fictional representation of Jonas King (d. 1877) of Barrystown House.

228. *Blenheim*: a breed of spaniel (King Charles); named by John Churchill, Duke of Marlborough; named for his estate in honour of his victory at the battle of Blenheim (*OED*).

229. Angola cat: 'Angola' is a corruption of 'Angora'; Angora being a town in Asia minor which gave its name to a species of goat with fine silky hair. In 1854 E. C. Gaskell mentioned acquiring a cat with long hair; 'It is called an Angola or Persian cat' (*OED*).

230. *the family canvas*: Hall evokes a scene in R. B. Sheridan, *School for Scandal* (1773), V.iii.72–3, in which a sham auction of family portraits is held:

> Sir Oliver: Sir Peter, do you know, the rogue bargained with me for all his ancestors; sold me judges and generals by the foot and maiden aunts as cheap as broken china.
>
> Charles Surface: To be sure, Sir Oliver, I did make a little free with the family canvas, that's the truth on't.

231. *what-not*: derived from French étagère, an article of furniture with slender uprights supporting a series of shelves for holding, displaying china, curiosities, ornaments or 'what not' (*OED*).

232. *Ottomans*: 'ottoman'; a low upholstered seat or bench, without back or arms, serving as a box with seat hinged to form a lid.

233. *lappet cap*: a small cap with decorative folds and pendant streamers (*OED*).

234. *gigs*: light two-wheeled one-horse carriages (*OED*).

235. suicide[s]: a particularly lofty gig, considered dangerous, hence the name. See R. Straus, *Carriages & Coaches: their History & Evolution* (London: M. Secker, 1912), p. 214.

236. *jaunting-cars*: light two-wheeled vehicles, popular in Ireland, carrying passengers back to back or facing, with a driver's seat in front (*OED*). S. C. Hall says that 'between the years 1839 and 1844, I posted on the ... nearly obsolete "jaunting-car" – six thousand miles', S. C. Hall, *Retrospect of a Long Life: From 1815 to 1883* (New York: Appleton, 1883). p. 476.

237. *jazey*: 'jasey'; humorous or familiar word for a wig, especially one made of worsted (*OED*).

238. *Yarrow*: erect herbaceous perennial plant, *achillea millefolium*.

239. *bad cess*: 'bad luck'; may be a contraction by apheresis of 'success' (*DH-E*).

240. *gauger*: an exciseman (*OED*).

241. *weeders*: 'weeder'; a person employed to remove weeds from the gardens of the rich.

242. *gossoons*: 'gossoon', from the Irish *garsún*, 'boy'; also 'gas', a stem or stripling; possibly from the French *garçon*. It is fancifully suggested that the French root of this word may indicate the practice of Anglo-Norman gentry calling their Irish serving-boys 'garçon' (*DH-E*).

243. *china rose*: the Monthly Rose, *Rosa indica*, and the Red Rose, *Rosa semperflorens*, with their many varieties (*OED*).

244. *blue*: bluestocking.

245. *japanning*: the art of producing a highly varnished surface on wood, metal or other hard substance, sometimes of one colour only, but more commonly figured or ornamented (*OED*).

246. cavatina[s]: a short song of simple character, 'frequently applied to a smooth melodious air, forming part of a great schema or movement' (*OED*).

247. *nautilus*: free-swimming cephalopod with short tentacles and a smooth coiled shell lined with mother-of-pearl (*OED*).

248. *storming Gibraltar*: Hall may be alluding here to the Great Siege of Gibraltar (1799), when Spain and France made an unsuccessful attempt to gain control of the territory.

249. *long-tailed family*: family with many children.

250. *ullagone*: from the Irish *olagón*, a cry of lamentation, wail or funeral lament; of imitative origin (*OED*).

251. *fine-plaiting*: the making of hats and baskets from plaited straw; a skill taught to girls.

252. *curricle*: a light two-wheeled chaise, usually drawn by a pair of horses running abreast (*OED*).

253. *Vale of Avoca*: beauty spot in County Wicklow, known as the 'Meeting of the Waters', where the rivers Avonbeg and Avonmore join to become the Avoca.

254. *Moore*: Thomas Moore (1779–1852), poet; born at 12 Aungier St, Dublin on 28 May. He was a visitor to the Halls's home where he sang one of his famed Irish melodies: 'As a beam o'er the face of the waters may glow'. Appalled by the poor attendance at Moore's centenary memorial on 28 May, 1879, Mr and Mrs Hall had marble tablets erected over the door of his Dublin birthplace (Hall, *Retrospect of a Long Life*, pp. 354, 357). The lines referred to are from Moore's melody:

> 'The Meeting of the Waters'*
> There is not in the wide world a valley so sweet
> As that vale in whose bosom the bright waters meet;†
> Oh! The last rays of feeling and life must depart
> Ere the bloom of that valley shall fade from my ear.
>
> Yet it *was* not that Nature had shed o'er the scene
> Her purest of crystal and brightest of green;
> 'Twas *not* her soft magic of streamlet or hill,
> Oh! No – it was something more exquisite still.
> 'Twas that friends, the beloved of my bosom, were near,
> Who made every dear scene of enchantment more dear,
> And who felt how the best charms of Nature improve
> When we see them reflected from looks that we love.
>
> Sweet vale of Avoca! How calm could I rest
> In thy bosom of shade, with the friends I love best,

> Where the storms that we fell in this cold world should cease,
> And our hearts, like thy waters, be mingled in peace.

* "'The Meeting of the Waters" forms a part of that beautiful scenery which lies between Rathdrum and Arklow, in the county of Wicklow, and these lines ere suggested by a visit to this romantic spot in the summer of the year 1807'.

† The rivers Avon and Avoca.

T. Moore, *The Poetical Works of Thomas Moore*, ed. by W. M. Rossetti (London: Ward, Lock, n. d.), pp. 339–40.

255. *Florian['s]*: Jean-Pierre Claris de Florian, 1755–94, French poet and writer.

256. *Le Rossignol et le Prince*: 'The Nightingale and the Prince', a fable by the French poet Florian in which a young prince is charmed by the song of a nightingale and wishes to capture it to replace the sparrows in his court which give him no pleasure. See Rev. C. Yeld (ed.), *Florian's Fables: With Philological and Explanatory Notes, Exercises, Dialogues, and Vocabulary* (London: Macmillan, 1888), p. 111.

257. *Les sots savent ... il faut l'aller trouver*: the final lines of Florian's fable 'Le Rossignol et le Prince'. Translated from the French, they mean that 'stupid people know how to get centre stage; true worth must be sought' (Yeld, *Florian's Fables*, p. 111).

258. *melting as a lover's prayer*: recurring line from 'An Ode in Praise of Music, 1703' by John Hughes (1677–1720). See S. Johnson (ed.), *The Works of the English Poets with Prefaces Biographical and Critical* 58 vols (London: n. p., 1779), vol. 22, p. 143.

259. *Proteus*: god of the sea and rivers in Greek mythology.

260. *Mars*: god of war in Roman mythology.

261. *Dr. Townsend's lectures*: Hall's description here of a 'Dr. Townsend' reveals that she may have had in mind one Dionysius Lardner (1793–1859), a professor, writer, lecturer and popularizer of science. He delivered to the Dublin Royal Society a series of lectures published in 1828 as 'Lectures on a Steam Engine'. Something of a parvenu, he was socially ambitious, inviting women from the aristocracy to his lectures, while remaining on the perimeter of serious science.

262. *fresh through a thousand pipes* ...: E. Darwin, 'The Economy of Vegetation', *The Botanic Garden: A Poem in Two Parts. Part I. Containing the economy of vegetation. Part II. The loves of the plants. With philosophical notes.* Canto I, p. 17, ll.272–3.

263. *Rosacynth*: not identified.

264. *papilionaceous*: of or relating to butterflies (*OED*).

265. *hortus siccus*: 'dry garden' (Latin). An arranged collection of dried botanical specimens; a herbarium (*OED*).

266. *loves of the angels*: 'The Loves of the Angels', allegorical poem by T. Moore based on the Eastern story of Harut and Marut and the Rabbinical fiction of the loves of Uzziel and Shāmachazai; T. Moore, *The Poetical Works of Thomas* Moore (Boston: Phillips Sampson, 1856). Moore recalls in the preface that in June 1823, payment of £1,000 for the poem saved him from pecuniary embarrassment while living in Paris (pp. 527–51).

267. *conversazioni*: in Italy in the 1800s, the name for an evening assembly for conversation, social recreation and amusement. Later introduced to England and applied to the private assembly known as an 'at home'. From the close of the eighteenth century, applies to assemblies of an intellectual character, in connection with literature, art or science (*OED*).

268. *blue stockings*: 'Bluestockings'. The Bluestocking Circle was founded in the 1750s in London by Elizabeth Vesey, Frances Boscawen and Elizabeth Montagu, well-heeled hostesses who developed a new kind of informal sociability and intellectual community among

women who believed that stimulating intellectual conversation and tea-drinking should replace such popular pursuits as card-playing, dancing and indulging in strong drink. See E. Eger and L. Peltz, *Brilliant Women: 18ᵗʰ-Century Bluestockings* (London: National Portrait Gallery, 2008).

269. *blue milk*: milk from which the cream had been removed. See J. Donnelly Jr, *The Irish Agrarian Rebellion of 1821–24* (Madison, WI: University of Wisconsin Press, 2009).

270. *becomes a Goth, a Vandal* ...: Hall's character Miss Spinner here alludes to Hannah More's poem 'The Bas Bleu: or, Conversation' (1786), in which reference to Vandals and 'Gothic night' indicates the barbarism the Bluestockings perceived as prevalent in society and sought to reform through a renewed integrity and intellectual conversation:

> Long was society o'er-run
> By Whist, that desolating Hun;
> Long did Quadrille despotic sit,
> That Vandal of colloquial wit;
> And Conversation's setting light
> Lay half-obscur'd in Gothic night.

271. *pucker*: bad humour. Dialect (English) 'poke' or 'pocket', the notion being that of forming purse-like gatherings in the face (*OED*).

272. *trumpery biscuits*: 'rubbishy'; appearing to be better than they are (*OED*).

273. *eau sucres*: *eau sucrée*, 'sugar water' (French). Sugar mixed with water was popular in the nineteenth century and many claims were made for its beneficial effects. For a discussion of the introduction of *eau sucrée* and its uses, see J. Brillat-Savarin, *The Physiology of Taste* (Kansas City, MI: Andrews McMeel, 2012).

274. *electrifying machine*: apparatus used to electrify. From the seventeenth century electrification was used in many areas; medically, it was a fashionable treatment for various ills: aches, pains, insomnia, even blindness (see note in *OED*).

275. *inquisition at Goa*: Inquisition, in the church of Rome, is a tribunal, in several Roman Catholic countries, erected by the popes for the examination and punishment of heretics. It was founded in the twelfth century by Pope Innocent. The Office of Portuguese Inquisition acted in Portuguese India and in the rest of the Portuguese Empire in Asia. Established in 1550, and briefly closed down between 1774 and 1778, it brought many thousands of people to trial and execution, punishing apostate new Christians who were suspected of reverting to their former religions. It was abolished in 1812. See M. Dellon, *An Account of the Inquisition at Goa, in India* (Pittsburgh, PA: R. Patterson and Lambdin, 1819).

276. *Pope's willow*: The species was introduced to England in the 1700s and a willow tree was reputedly planted by Alexander Pope (1688–1744) in the garden of his villa in Twickenham. Cuttings were sent all over the world and the tree gained iconic status. Catherine the Great is said to have planted a slip in her own garden in St Petersburg and J. W. M. Turner wrote a verse about the tree. Various legends about Pope's willow having its origins in a basket of figs brought from Smyrna or arriving via Babylon are examined and refuted in T. Meehan, *Meehan's Monthly: A Magazine of Horticulture, Botany and kindred subjects*, (Philadelphia, PA: T. Meehan, 1895), vol. 5, p. 991.

277. Digitus de Sancto Pietro: (Latin) 'The pointing out with the finger (or toe) of Saint Peter'. (Hall wrote here 'Digit de Sancto Pietro'). The Protestant aversion to – and Catholic reverence for – the veneration of relics of the saints is treated humorously here. A statue of St Peter, in St Peter's basilica in Rome (attributed to Arnolfo di Cambio, 1245–1302), depicts the saint with one hand raised in blessing and the other holding

the keys of the kingdom of heaven. St Peter's right foot protrudes over the marble plinth, within reach of pilgrims who since mediaeval times have touched the bronze and worn away the outline of the toes.

278. *vulgo*: 'commonly' or 'popularly' (Latin).

279. *eau-de-luce*: 'eau-de-Luce'; a medicinal preparation of alcohol, ammonia, and oil of amber, used in India as an antidote to snake-bites, and in England sometimes as smelling salts (*OED*).

280. *[eau] de Millefleurs*: a perfume distilled from flowers of different kinds (*OED*).

281. *[eau] de Cologne*: a perfume consisting of alcohol and various essential oils, originally (and still very largely) made at Cologne (*OED*).

282. *Janus*: ancient Italian deity, doorkeeper of heaven, represented with two faces, the second on the back of his head. The doors of the temple in the Roman forum were always open in time of war and shut in time of peace. Hall refers to Janus to indicate the hypocritical nature of Thomas Dorrington.

283. *I have been young ... begging their bread*: Hall paraphrases a verse from the bible: 'I have been young and now am old; yet have I not seen the righteous forsaken, nor their seed begging bread' (Psalms 37:25).

284. *Blackwood*: *Blackwood's Magazine*, 1817–1980: a conservative publication founded by William Blackwood which became popular for its barbed critiques and satirical commentaries. William Maginn, with whom S. C. Hall had fallen out in their younger days in Cork, was one of its mercurial and highly gifted writers. It was ideologically opposed to the rival Whig magazine *Edinburgh Review* and remained in the Blackwood family throughout its long publication history.

285. dénouement: 'unravelling' (French). The final unravelling of the complications of a plot in a drama, or novel; the final solution of a complication or difficulty (*OED*).

286. *distrained*: constrained or forced a person by the seizure and detention of goods to pay money owed or to punish by such seizure and detention the non-performance of such obligation (*OED*).

287. *grate mass*: 'great Mass'; from French *grand-messe*; High Mass is celebrated with a deacon and sub-deacon with incense and music (*OED*).

288. *mock*: pretending (*OED*).

289. *shiver*: to break or split into fragments; to splinter (*OED*).

290. *Heaven doth with us ... as if she had them not*: Hall misquotes from Shakespeare, *Measure for Measure*, I.i.33–6:

> Heaven doth with us, as we with torches do;
> Not light them for ourselves; for if our virtues
> Did not go forth of us 'twere all alike
> As if we had them not.

291. *suite*: retinue or train of attendants.

292. à la pastorelle: (French); variant of 'pastourelle' and here meaning 'in the style of a shepherdess'; from 'pastourelle', a medieval lyric whose theme is love for a shepherdess (*OED*).

293. *tow*: flax, hemp or jute prepared by some process of scutching (*OED*).

294. *deeshy-dawshy*: tiny or insignificant. The first use is in 1825 by T. C. Croker, who records that the three original diminutives are 'tiny', 'dony' and the Scottish 'wee'. From these and by use of the termination 'shy' come 'deeshy', 'doshy' and 'weeny' (*OED*).

295. *Rakes of Mallow*: a lively song and polka which originated in Scotland in 1780. It celebrates the rackety lifestyle of the dissolute youths of Mallow, a town in Co. Cork.

296. *heart's-ease*: wild pansy, *viola tricolor*, which has small white or cream flowers with purple and yellow markings (*OED*).
297. *quizzing-glass*: a single eyeglass with or without an attached handle; a monocle (*OED*).
298. *horseback*: 'a horseback-rider'.
299. *achora*: *a chora, a chara*; Irish term of endearment, 'my friend' (*DH-E*).
300. *May-dew*: 'The English women, and Gentlewomen in Ireland, as in England, did use in the beginning of the summer to gather good store of dew, to keep it by them all the year after for several good uses both of physick and otherwise'. The May-dew was believed to improve the complexion. Hall refers to the 'May-dew before it falls ...'. Boate emphasizes this aspect of gathering the dew, by going 'before sun-rising into a green field, and there either with their hands strike off the dew from the tops of the herbs into a dish, or else throwing clean linen cloths upon the ground, take off the dew from the herbs into them, and afterwards wring it out into dishes until they have got a sufficient quantity of dew according to their intentions'. G. Boate, *Ireland's Natural History. Being a true and ample description of its Situation, Greatness, Shape, and Nature; Of its Hills, Woods, Heaths, Bogs; Of its Fruit-full Parts and profitable Grounds, with the severall way of Manuring and Improving the same: With its Heads or Promontories, Harbours, Roades and Bayes; Of its Springs and Fountaines, Brookes, Rivers, Loghs; Of its Metalls, Mineralls, Free stone, Marble, Sea-coal, Turf, and other things that are taken out of the ground. And lastly, of the Nature and temperature of its Air and Season, and what diseases it is free from, or subject unto. Conducing to the Advance-ment of Navigation, Husbandry, and other profitable Arts and Professions* (London: S. Hartlib, 1652), pp. 170–2.
    When Boate wrote this natural history, he had not visited Ireland but worked from reports supplied by his brother and others. It was dedicated to Cromwell and expressed the hope that Ireland would be settled by Adventurers and other Protestants, being written as an enthusiastic description to entice such settlement. Boate and his wife were on the list of Adventurers who financed the suppression of the Irish rebellion of 1641 and in return, Boate's widow was given a thousand acres of land in Co. Tipperary (*ODNB*).
301. *Wellington Bridge*: Also Wellingtonbridge; a village about 5 miles north of Bannow.
302. *chimbly*: chimney (*OED*).
303. *The plough had passed...*: not identified.
304. *let-out*: an entertainment on a large or lavish scale (*OED*).
305. *collution*: collation; a lunch or repast consisting of cold roast meats (*OED*).
306. '*vain show*': Hall refers to the words of poet Edward Young (1683–1765) who wrote in his Satire V 'On Women', 'vain show, and noise intoxicate the brain'. E. Young, *The Poetical Works of Milton, Young, Gray, Beattie, & Collins,* (Philadelphia, PA: J. Grigg, 1836), p. 122.
307. *retrousée*: a nose, turned up (attractively) at the tip (French) (*OED*).
308. *bien foncée*: very dark (French).
309. *à-la-Byron*: in the style worn by Lord Byron, who established a fashion by wearing his shirts open-necked, suggestive of a relaxed and deshabillé manner; this was adopted by Shelley and others. See painting executed in 1814 by Richard Westall (1765–1836), National Portrait Gallery, London.
310. *shilalah*: 'shillelagh'; a cudgel, from the Irish *sail*, willow, and *éille*, from *iall*, meaning thong or strap. A seasoned oak or blackthorn stick about two and a half feet in length, it was often used in the days of faction fights. The word has never been naturalized and is only used as an Irishism. The word is associated with the village of Shillelagh, Co. Wicklow. See *DH-E*, p. 238.

311. *cuckoo-bells*: bluebells, also know as Auld Man's Bells and Wilde Hyacinth. The name of the bluebell in Welsh is *clychau'r gog*, 'cuckoo-bell', so named as they flower in spring when the cuckoo may first be heard. See M. Raine, *Nature of Snowdonia* (Caernarfon: Pesda, 2010), p. 72. In his poem 'Light of Love', John Payne (1842–1916) wrote:

> ... Was there, where fawns came down to drink
> At eventide: and on the brink
> The nodding cuckoo-bells did blink.

J. Payne, *New Poems* (London: Newman, 1880), p. 147, ll.4–7.

312. *Robin-run-the-hedge*: *galium aparine*, 'goosegrass' or 'cleavers'. A spreading plant that attaches itself to others with small hooked hairs. See R. Lynd, *The Pleasures of Ignorance* (Fairfield: 1st World, 2004), p. 71.

313. *milch white cow*: a white cow yielding milk or in milk (*OED*).

314. *bar'ny*: barony.

315. *tasselled gentil*: 'tassel-gentle'; a male falcon (*OED*). The use of quotation marks indicates Hall's imitation of colloquial usage. The words 'tasselled gentil' are used to describe a falcon in a review of the painting 'Old English Hospitality'; G. Cattermole, Review of 'Old English Hospitality', *The Art Union* (London: J. How, 1842), vol. 4, p. 17. The letterpress for this review may well have been written by S. C. Hall as he was editor of the publication. Hall's reference to the young lover Corry evokes Juliet's words on Romeo: 'O for a falconer's voice/ To lure this tassel-gentle back again'. Shakespeare, *Romeo and Juliet*, 2.ii.158–9.

316. *The short passing anger ... sweetest when shake*: Hall paraphrases lines from 'Lalla Rookh' by Moore, *The Poetical Works of Thomas Moore*, pp. 1–144, 126, ll.39–40. In Moore, they run: 'The short, passing anger but seemed to awaken/ New beauty, like flowers that are sweetest when shaken'.

317. *cates*: provisions or victuals bought in and usually more dainty or delicate than those produced at home (*OED*).

318. *Fethard*: 'Fethard-on-Sea'; Hall's description emphasizes the history of invasion of the area as a powerful and constant memory. Fethard is a village situated on the Hook peninsula between Waterford Harbour and Bannow Bay. The district was granted to Hervey de Montmorency following the Anglo-Norman invasion of 1169, who granted the land to Christ Church, Canterbury. The twelfth-century castle with motte and bailey was built on in the fifteenth century by the Bishop of Ferns, who had contested ownership of the land with Canterbury. Occupied until 1922, the castle is now a ruin.

319. *Tintern Abbey*: On his journey to Ireland, the Earl of Pembroke, Richard Marshall, was in danger of shipwreck in Bannow Bay and vowed he would build a monastery should God spare him. He made it safely to land and was as good as his word, gifting nine thousand acres to the Cistercian monks in Monmouthshire. The abbey built was known as Tintern minor or 'de voto' (of the vow) to differentiate it from the mother house, Tintern 'major' in Wales. Following the Dissolution of the Monasteries, in 1575 Tintern and all its lands were granted to Anthony Colclough from Staffordshire, an officer of Henry VIII.

320. *Strongbow*: Richard fitz Gilbert de Clare, second earl of Pembroke, born *c.* 1130, d. 1176/7. Having sent early explorers to land at Bannow Bay in 1169, de Clare, later known as Strongbow, departed Milford Haven in Wales at the invitation of Diarmait Mac Murchada and landed near Waterford with a force of 200 knights and 1,000 men, on 23 August 1170. He took Waterford, although bravely defended, and his marriage to Áoife, Mac Murchada's daughter, which swiftly followed sealed his alliance with the King of Leinster. Strongbow progressed to Dublin, which fell after much slaughter, and

became Lord of Leinster on the death of Mac Murchada in 1171. Strongbow's burgeoning power is said to have precipitated Henry II's expedition to Ireland in 1171 (*ODNB*).

321. *black cabin-boy*: Hall's description highlights complex contemporary views on racial difference. The tension between the expression of fear and superiority echoes the anxieties of the English Protestant ascendancy in Ireland regarding their relationship with the native Irish.

322. *Patlander*: mildly offensive term for an Irish person.

323. *a prophet ... his own land*: Hall paraphrases St Mark's gospel; 'A prophet is not without honour, but in his own country, and among his own kin, and in his own house'. King James, Mark 6:4.

324. outré: unusual or unconventional. From past participle of *outrer*, to push beyond bounds (French).

325. *Mal-a-pert*: 'mal-à-pert', 'malapert'; from French *mal*, 'bad', Middle English *apert*, meaning 'open' or 'frank'; an impudent or saucy person. Sir Toby Belch declares to Sebastian: 'Nay, then I must have an ounce or two of this malapert blood from you'. Shakespeare, *Twelfth Night; or What You Will*, IV.i.36–7.

326. *hindered*: balked or delayed matters.

327. *hoight*: 'height'.

328. guager: in *OED*, a variant of 'guager', an exciseman.

329. happing: 'hap', to cover, comfort or dress. This meaning not given in *OED* (*DH-E*).

330. *Lafont's trim cap*: not identified.

331. céid míle fáilte: Irish for 'a hundred thousand welcomes'.

332. soirées: evening parties, gatherings or social meetings (French).

333. *Cruikshank*: George Cruikshank (1792–1878), graphic artist and illustrator. He produced 'The Outlaw's Burial' for the sketch 'Captain Andy' for Hall. In later life he became attached to the temperance cause, a passion he shared with the Halls. His pencil drawing 'A man lying upon the pavement in a Drunken Stupor' is inscribed 'by George Cruikshank for one of Mrs S. C. Hall's Temperance Tracts'.

334. *Almack's*: Almack's Assembly Rooms, situated on King St, off St James's Street, London, was built in 1764–5 and as a private members' club maintained an exclusive reputation by controlling entry to its weekly Wednesday-night balls. Only influential ladies of the ton were permitted to purchase the ten-guinea voucher which allowed entry for a year. The club was ruled by Lady Patronesses including Lady Castlereagh (1772–1829) and Lady Sefton (1769–1851). See J. Rendall, *The Pursuit of Pleasure: Gender, Space, and Architecture in Regency London* (London: Athlone Press, 2002), pp. 86–8.

335. *losset*: also Irish *losad*; a kneading tray, often square, with a wooden rim, for making cakes or bread (*DH-E*).

336. *thirteen*: the name formerly current in Ireland for a silver shilling, as being worth thirteen pence of Irish copper currency.

337. *clack*: chatter or loquacious talk (*OED*).

338. *swaddling pracher*: 'swaddling preacher'; nickname in Ireland for a Methodist preacher. The name was originally given to John Cennick (1718–55), an evangelical preacher who brought about 'The Great Awakening' of Methodism ahead of John Wesley. Preaching in Dublin on 'the swaddled babe', a misunderstanding led to his being dubbed 'Swaddling John' and the name survived as a derogatory term for members of evangelical sects. See S. Boyle, 'Swaddling John and the Great Awakening', *History Ireland*, 18:5 (September–October 2010), pp. 18–21. (*OED*).

339. *clodhopper*: a clumsy boor or bumpkin.

340. *Rathangan*: small parish in Co. Wexford where Patrick J. McCall (1861–1919) spent summer holidays among musicians and ballad singers. His famous ballad 'Kelly the Boy from Killanne' recalls the exploits of a leader of the United Irishmen John Kelly, immortalized in McCall's song which tells of 'the bold Shelmalier' and of news of the rebellion of 1798 brought to the men of Forth and Bargy.

341. *berring-ground*: burying ground.

342. *entire town under them sand-hills*: Many believed that the old town of Bannow had been buried by sand suddenly blown over it, as in the 'Ireland Herculaneum' theory (see n. 205). See Textual Variants (pp. 449–59) for an article by Rev. Robert Walsh, 'The First Invasion of Ireland with some account of the Irish Herculaneum', which prefaces Mrs S. C. Hall's *Sketches of Irish Character*, 2nd edn, 2 vols (London: Westley and Davis, 1831), pp. 1–20.

343. *the Union*: 'The Union of Great Britain and Ireland'; the rebellion of 1798 highlighted the matter of Irish politics in Parliament at Westminster and William Pitt considered that a legal agreement which would united Great Britain, comprising England and Scotland, with Ireland under the name of the United Kingdom of Great Britain and Ireland would provide a solution to 'the Irish question'. This was enacted legally in both the Irish and English parliaments. The Irish Parliament was abolished and henceforth Ireland would be represented in Parliament at Westminster by 4 spiritual peers, 28 temporal peers and 100 members of the House of Commons. Although strongly opposed in the Irish House, Britain secured the passing of the Act in both Parliaments on 28 March 1800 by the undisguised method of buying votes. The Act was given royal assent on 1 August 1800 and came into effect on 1 January, 1801. Henceforth the monarch would be titled King or Queen of the United Kingdom of Great Britain and Ireland.

344. *Lord Castlereagh*: Robert Stewart, Viscount Castlereagh, 2nd Marquis of Londonderry (1769–1829). Born in Mount Stewart, Co. Down, he held posts as British Foreign Secretary and Chief Secretary for Ireland. Originally the possessor of most liberal views, the excesses of the French revolution altered his perspective on British policy in Ireland to one of extreme conservatism. In 1798 he led the quelling of the rebellion and his strong-arm tactics against the United Irishmen rendered him a despised figure. Pressing forward the passing of the Act of Union, he failed to deliver on promises of concessions to the Catholics. Castlereagh was held in particular contempt in Ireland, more for his deceit than his cruelty. Although government corruption was in play, Castlereagh was deemed responsible for the failure of the British Government to deliver on Catholic emancipation following the passing of the Act of Union which came into effect on 1 January, 1801. ('Act of Union, 2014', *Encyclopædia Britannica Online*, at http://www.britannica.com/EBchecked/topic/614673/Act-of-Union [accessed 29 March 2014].

345. *chirming*: making melodious chatter, like the warbling of birds (*OED*).

346. old régime: from French *ancien régime*; the system of government in France before the revolution of 1789 (*OED*).

347. passée: (French) past one's prime, especially applied to a woman past the period of her greatest beauty.

348. *Colclough*: The Colcloughs, whose origins were in Staffordshire, were a prominent family in Co. Wexford for generations. Sir Anthony Colclough (1520–84) was granted all the lands and estates of the old monastery at Tintern Abbey. Caesar Colclough (1624–84), who served under Cromwell, had land assigned to him in Brandane, Island of Bannow and Ballygow. John Henry Colclough (1769/70–98) was an Irish nationalist, of Ballyteigue Castle, near Kilmore Quay, Co. Wexford. Although an activist in the United

Irishmen, he did not hold office. Sent to Vinegar Hill on 29 May 1798, he did not stay with the insurgents and persuaded the Irish units of Forth and Bargy not to join the rising. Captured on 30 May in Wexford, he fled to the Saltee Islands. Despite his ambivalence about the rebellion, he was arrested on his return, court-martialled for his involvement in the Battle of New Ross and hanged on Wexford Bridge on 28 June 1798.

349. *Dane's Castle*: One of a string of strong towers built by Norman settlers and erected between Bannow and Taghmon along the river Coragh, dividing the baronies of Bargy from Shelmalier and Shelburne. It was built by Sir Reginald Denn in 1290 to a height of fifty feet, with a square tower. Unusual for Irish castles, it had four floors with fireplaces on the third and fourth. From the Denns, the castle passed to Sir Christopher Cheevers in the sixteenth century and in 1668 Nathaniel Boyse was confirmed in this and other lands and properties by Act of Parliament.

350. *wood-quest*: wood pigeon (*OED*).

351. *traneen*: Hiberno-English for *tráithnín*; a blade of grass, a straw, grass tossed in the air to get the direction of the wind; also used disparagingly to indicate something of little or no value (*DH-E*).

352. *the Irish reign of terror*: Hall's use of the phrase 'reign of terror' underscores the Protestant fear of the contagion of revolution from within and without Irish shores. This was heightened by 'La Terreur', the reign of terror so named to describe the period 1793–4 when the Revolutionary government in France decided by decree (5 September 1793) to use 'terror' to strike fear into the enemies of the revolution. During La Terreur, both Paris and the provinces witnessed a wave of executions; 17,000 were officially killed with many languishing in prison who died without trial.

353. *dead as a door-nail*: doornails were used to strengthen or decorate doors for protection or ornamentation. The custom of clenching such large nails – beating back the point of the nail to make it fast – rendered the nail useless for further employment and may be the origin of this saying.

354. *mother-wit*: common sense; native or natural wit (*OED*).

355. *cronauning*: Hiberno-English from the Irish *crónán*; humming, droning, murmuring (*DH-E*).

356. *wiled*: 'beguiled' (*OED*).

357. *Ursulines*: a religious order of nuns, established under the rule of St Augustine in 1572 from a company founded at Brescia in 1557, for the teaching of girls, nursing the sick, and the sanctification of the lives of its members (*OED*).

358. *coble*: a sea fishing boat with a flat bottom, square stern and rudder extending 4 or 5 feet below the bottom, rowed with three pairs of oars and furnished with a lug-sail (*OED*).

359. *gad-fly*: the popular name of a fly which bites and goads cattle, especially a fly of the genus *Tabanus* or *Œstrus* (*OED*).

360. *impenetrable stuff*: Hall's casual allusion here to Hamlet's words underscores her narratorial 'address' to an English audience 'over the heads' of her characters in the sketch. In the play, Hamlet addresses Polonius: 'I took thee for thy better ... and let me wring your heart; for so I shall,/ If it be made of penetrable stuff'. Shakespeare, *Hamlet, Prince of Denmark*, III.iv.31–6.

361. *delisk*: also 'dillisk', a burgundy-coloured edible seaweed with divided fronds; dulse.

362. *Herculean*: like Hercules, especially in strength, courage or labours; prodigiously powerful or vigorous. Hercules is the celebrated hero of Greek and Roman mythology whose strength enabled him to perform twelve extraordinary tasks or 'labours' imposed upon him by Hera.

363. *Bag-an-bun*: Baganbun is a headland of about thirty acres in south county Wexford. It is a place of historical import, being the site where the first Normans stepped ashore on Irish soil. In May 1169 Robert Fitzstephen, Governor of Cardigan Castle in Wales, and Harvey de Monte Marisco disembarked here from their vessels, the *Bagg* and the *Bunn*. This event is recounted in Rev. Robert Walsh's article 'The First Invasion of Ireland – see n. 341 and Textual Variants, pp. 449–59.

364. teams: a 'teem' is a downpour of rain and the phrase 'it's teeming with rain' is still in use in Ireland.

365. *musha*: also *maise, mhuise*; indeed; well, well; is that so? (*DH-E*).

366. *dancing the hays*: performing winding or serpentine movement, a 'hay' being a country dance having such a form; in the nature of a reel (*OED*).

367. *Innishown*: Inishowen, whisky, illicit; from the Irish *Inis Eoghan*, 'the island of Eoghan', a peninsula in Co. Donegal bounded by the saltwater lakes of Lough Foyle and Lough Swilly. The area was famed for the illicit distillation of *poitín*, known as 'Mountain Dew', which was prized over legal whisky. See B. Bonner, 'Illicit Distillation in Inishowen' in *Our Inis Eoghain Heritage* (Ballycastle: n. p., 1972) and Anon., *Notes on a Journey in the North of Ireland, in the summer of 1827: To Which is Added, a Brief Account of the Siege of Londonderry, in 1689* (London: Baldwin, Cradock, Simpkin, Marshall, 1828), p. 14.

368. *Henry the Second*: the first King of England to set foot in Ireland when he arrived in Waterford with a large force on 18 October 1171, to regain authority following the preceding invasion by Norman knights in 1169. The earlier contingent came at the request of Diarmuid MacMurchada, deposed king of Leinster, landing near Bannow in 1169. So, Hall here refers to those who came over with or after Henry II in 1171.

369. sotto voce: in a subdued or low voice (Italian).

370. unencumbered *property*: property which was not hindered by or subject to a mortgage.

371. *hourisht*: tar isteach, 'come in'; addressed to pigs when feeding them. T. Butler, *A Parish and its People*, p. 220.

372. *praskeen*: an apron of rough material, or sacking, worn when sowing, picking or carrying potatoes. From the Irish *práiscín* (*DH-E*).

373. *kish*: a wicker container or pannier. From the Irish *cis*. 'Bring in a kishful of spuds for the dinner', Brigid Clerkin, Meath: non-literary source (*DH-E*).

374. *sheebeen*: also 'shebeen'; an unlicensed liquor-house; from the Irish *síbín* (*DH-E*).

375. *the pratees are laughing*: the most favoured potatoes were a floury variety which burst open when cooked. The metaphor here equated the split skin to a smile on the 'face' of the potato.

376. *pathern*: pattern.

377. *Moll Row, Darby Kelly, St Patrick's Day*: popular jigs and tunes. 'Moll Row' was a slip jig called 'Maire Rua', 'Red Mary'. For the humorous lyrics of 'Darby Kelly', see T. Dibdin, *The Last Lays of the Last of the Three Dibdins* (London: Harding & King, 1833), p. 144.

378. *skreeds*: torn strips of textile material. 'He has been sometimes seen going about with hardly a screed to cover him'. T. Crofton Croker, *Fairy Legends and Traditions of the South of Ireland*, 3 vols (London: J. Murray, 1825), vol. 1, p. 162 (*OED*).

379. *gumshogue*: nonsense.

380. *dickons*: 'the deuce!' or 'the devil!'; an interjectional exclamation expressing astonishment, impatience or irritation (*OED*).

381. *Mountain of Forth*: 'Sliabh Fothart', 'Mount Fothart'; 'mountain' is a misnomer as this is a hill rather than a mountain, being 237 metres in height. It lies a few kilometres south

west of Wexford town, commanding views of the town, Rosslare harbour and the Saltee Islands.

382. *We'll down wid ... wherever they're seen*: not identified.

383. *water-guard*: a body of men employed by the Custom House to watch ships in order to prevent smuggling (*OED*).

384. *bounds-ditch*: a long narrow excavation dug in the ground to indicate a limit or boundary (*OED*).

385. *threading*: treading.

386. *Milesian*: Led by Míl Espáine, the Milesians, of Spanish descent, were, according to legend and believed by some antiquarians, invaders who arrived in Ireland around the time of King David. See R. A. S. Macalister (ed. and trans.), *Lebor Gabála Érenn: Book of the Taking of Ireland*, Parts 1–5 (Dublin: Irish Texts Society, 1941).

387. *croppy*: derogatory soubriquet for members of an agrarian rebel organization who cropped their hair to acknowledge their 'anti-Whig' or anti-aristocratic ideals. Anyone with cropped hair was immediately assumed to belong to the Society of United Irishmen who supported ideals of the French revolutionaries.

388. *white-boy*: The 'Whiteboys' were members of an agrarian rebel organization which originated in Co. Tipperary (1761). They were so called for the white smocks they wore. In protest against punitive taxation and tithes, they committed arson and other criminal acts. Laws were drawn up in the 1760s and 1780s to hand down the death penalty for such activities.

389. *rapparee*: a robber, cut-purse or outlaw, from the Irish *rapiare*, meaning 'half-pike'. Rapparees were a mobile force in support of the Jacobites within Williamite territory in the late 1600s.

390. *fair of Bannynasloe*: 'fair of Ballinasloe'; this was known as the 'Great Cattle Fair', where livestock reared in Connaught were sold for fattening in the eastern counties. It was held in October and was reputed to be one of the largest in Ireland. See Maria Edgeworth's letter of 8 March 1834 to M. Pakenham Edgeworth Esq., in which she mentions being held up on a journey due to the vast number of sheep being driven from the fair. A. J. C. Hare (ed.), *The Life And Letters of Maria Edgeworth*, 2 vols (London: Edward Arnold, 1894), vol. 2.

391. *gilloure*: galore.

392. *Maclise*: Daniel Maclise (1806–70) was born in Cork to Scots Presbyterian parents. Having left Ireland for London in 1827, he entered the Royal Academy Schools of Art and in 1840 was elected R.A. Encouraged in his career by S. C. Hall, editor of *The Art Journal*, his fame rests on his monumental narrative subjects, particularly 'The Meeting of Wellington and Blücher after the Battle of Waterloo' and 'The Death of Nelson' for the Royal Gallery of Westminster. His portrait of Mrs Hall as a young woman hangs in Chertsey Museum (*DNB*).

393. *withered and wild in their attire* ... Shakespeare, *Macbeth*, I.iii,l.41.

394. *forms*: long rectangular school-room benches (*DH-E*).

395. *Covering the buckle*: the name of a jig. Also a display of agility known as 'cover the buckle' when a dancing master took to the floor to demonstrate his skill. The rapidity of motion with which he crossed his feet seemed to cover the large buckles always worn by a dancing master. S. Mackenzie, *Bits of Blarney* (New York: Redfield, 1855; eBook edn 2013).

396. *Candlemas*: 2 February. Christian feast of the Presentation of the Child Jesus in the Temple and also the Purification of Mary forty days after the birth of Jesus. Traditionally candles for use in the coming year were blessed on this day.

397. *Clonmel*: Overlooked by the Comeragh mountains and Slievenamon, Clonmel, 'Cluain Meala' or 'Honey Vale', is situated on the river Suir and is the county town of south Tipperary. The fourteenth-century walls of the town attest to its Anglo-Norman origins when William de Burgh, one of Henry II's barons, was granted lands in the Suir valley in 1185. A strong resistance was made to Cromwell's attack on the town, in the Siege of Clonmel in 1650.

398. *embrasure*: a slanting or bevelling in the outward sides of an opening to a wall, window or door. From French *embraser* to widen, obs. (*OED*)

399. *Zingari*: 'gypsies'; from *gli zingari*, meaning 'the gypsies' (Italian) (*OED*).

400. mélange: mixture or hotchpotch (French).

401. *chuck*: 'also' (*DH-E*).

402. *whipper-in*: a huntsman's assistant who keeps the hounds from straying by driving them back with the whip to the main body of the pack (*OED*).

403. *understrapper*: a subordinate agent or assistant (*OED*).

404. *cotters*: peasant farmers.

405. parvenus: upstarts or social climbers (*OED*).

406. *split a sunbame*: the 'most intelligent' Hacket, alias Larry the bocher, refers here to a famous moment in scientific discovery. It was Sir Isaac Newton (1642–1727) who first 'split a sunbeam' into its various colours by use of a prism. Cartesian and atomist philosophers thought light to be homogenous until Newton demonstrated his theory that light, as it comes from the sun, is a mixture of rays that differ in the sensations of colour they cause. Newton's successful experiment which 'split a sunbeam' overturned a tradition upheld for more than two thousand years in Western science and philosophy (ODNB).

407. *Freney's tricks*: James Freney born c. 1719, Inistioge, Co. Kilkenny and died New Ross, Co. Wexford in 1788. An infamous highwayman, robber and adventurer, he was described by his contemporary John Edward Walsh as 'mean-looking fellow, pitted with the smallpox and blind of an eye … he was a coarse, vulgar, treacherous villain, much of the highwayman and nothing of the hero'. Nonetheless, he was revered by many who viewed him as an Irish Robin Hood. Over five years his gang terrorized the countryside and his exploits are immortalized in his autobiographical account, 'Himself', *The Life and Adventures of James Freney, commonly called Captain Freney: from the time of his first entering on the highway, in Ireland, to the time of his surrender, being a series of five years remarkable adventures* (Dublin: pr. for S. Powell, 1754).

408. *leprechawn*: variant of 'leprechaun', from the Irish *leipreachán*, a dwarflike sprite; an industrious fairy seen at dusk or by moonlight mending a shoe (*DH-E*).

409. *pulhalew*: not identified, but suggests 'hullaballoo'.

410. 'sizes: assizes.

411. a *maskin*: 'a-maskin'', masquerading.

412. *gothered*: gathered.

413. *osiers*: willow trees.

414. *tories*: members or supporters of the Irish Conservative Party.

415. *baygnot*: bayonet.

416. *wassail*: drinking and revelry.

417. *Huncks*: Hall may refer here to Sir Fulk Huncks, also 'Hunkes' and 'Hunks', a personal friend of Charles I. He raised a regiment of 2,000 foot and 600 horse, landing at Dublin in June 1642. He also served at Drogheda. His brother Henry was a Royalist colonel and Hercules (d. 1660) was a parliamentarian colonel and regicide.

418. *Lady Duncannon*: Henrietta Frances Ponsonby (née Spencer), countess of Bessborough (1761–1821), was born in Wimbledon to John Spencer, first Earl Spencer (1734–83), and Margaret Georgiana Spencer (née Poyntz, 1737–1814). Intelligent and witty, she was attracted to Whig politics. Having married Lord Duncannon, she was drawn into a hedonistic lifestyle of gambling, affairs, extravagance and debt. In 1793, on his father's death, her husband became 3rd Earl Bessborough (Irish Peerage) and they took over the estates at Bessborough, Co. Kildare. He was, however, an absentee landlord, selling the pictures from the house in 1801. Their imprudent neglect of Pilldown, in south Killkenny, led Thomas Creevy to comment: 'In 1808, he and Lady Bessborough came a tour to the lakes of Killarney and having taken their own house in their way, either going or coming, they were so pleased with it as to stay here a *week* ... and once more in 1812 ... they were here for a month ... so from 1757 to 1825, 68 years, the family were (here) five weeks and two days. My dears, it is absenteeism on the part of the landlords, and the havoc that middlemen make with their property, that plays the very devil'. See A. P. W. Malcomson, *The Pursuit of the Heiress: Aristocratic Marriage in Ireland 1740–1840* (Belfast: Ulster Historical Foundation, 2006).

419. *brier-knocks*: hillocks formed by overgrown briers; from the Irish *cnoc*, hill.

420. *skirl-a-white*: a 'skirl' is a Scottish or northern English dialect word for a shriek or scream. Possibly Hall's use of 'skirl-a-white' refers to the cry of a seagull or other white and raucous bird.

421. *There is a bitterness ... from earth, and sin, and woe*: lines from J. J. Callinan, 'The Recluse of Inchydony', *Gems of the Cork Poets Comprising the Complete Works of Callinan, Condon, Casey, Fitzgerald, & Cody* (Cork: Barter, *c.* 1883), ll. 55–63. Jeremiah Joseph Callinan was admired by Hall, who quotes a verse from another of his poems, 'Gougane Barra', in Hall, *Ireland: its Scenery, Character, &*, vol. 1, p. 116. This poem, written in the year of his death in Lisbon, also evinces Callinan's great love of the scenery of his native county. Thus 'his grave was made, not by the "calm Avonbuee", in accordance with his fervent prayer, but by the banks of the Tagus –'.

422. grasnogue: grasnog; partially explained by T. Butler in *A Parish and its People*, p. 220, with the phrase 'more like a grasnogue than a Christian'.

423. *kipeen*: a small hurling-stick; a stick used to secure the hasp on a door. See p. XXX of this volume.

424. *Bathershin*: 'never mind' in Hiberno-English. See Mrs S. C. Hall, 'The Groves of Blarney' in *Lights and Shadows of Irish Life*, 3 vols (London: H. Colburn, 1838), p. 87. 'Bathershin' is given as equivalent in meaning to 'nabauchlish', Hiberno-English for *na bach leis* 'don't bother about it'.

425. *Faigs*: faith! An exclamation of surprise. See *A Scots Dialect Dictionary*, compiled by A. Warrack (London: W & R Chambers, 1911), p. 162.

426. *aroon*: term of endearment from the Irish *a rún*, 'dear one', 'loved one'.

427. While me you thought ... every girl ye meet a fool: not identified.

428. *proud impatience ...*: not identified.

429. *Salvator*: Salvator Rosa (1615–73), Italian artist famous for his paintings of wild landscapes, hermits and bandits. Much admired by Hall, who refers to him as 'my king of painters'. See Hall, *Sketches,* third revsd edn, p. 244.

430. *Where the poet's lip ... are most divine*: L. E. Landon, *The Improvisatrice and Other Poems* (London: Hurst Robinson, 1825), p. 1, ll. 1–3.

431. *caitiff*: captive or prisoner (*OED*).

432. *the curse of Ishmael*: Ishmael was the son of Abraham by the slave-girl Hagar. Later, when Abraham was a hundred years old and Sarah also aged, Isaac was born to them; but the Covenant was made with Isaac rather than Ishmael and he and Hagar were turned out to roam in the wilderness of Beersheba and destined not to inherit his father's house. See Genesis, 16:9–12.

433. *of the Principality*: the Principality of Wales, 1216–1536. Hall regards Annie's short stature to be consequent to her Welsh ancestry.

434. *ancle*: ankle.

435. *booby*: a dull, heavy, stupid fellow (*OED*).

436. *what she wished ...*: not identified.

437. *Cupid waves ... for all true constant loviers*: not identified.

438. *moonbames that Romeyo swore by*: Hall refers here to *Romeo and Juliet*, II.ii.107–8, wherein Romeo swears his love to Juliet: 'Lady, by yonder blessed moon I swear, That tips with silver all these fruit-tree tops'.

439. *kail*: kale.

440. *hizzy*: 'hussy', originally a phonetic reduction of 'housewife'; here, a badly behaved, pert or mischievous girl (*OED*).

441. *soubriquet*: nickname, sometimes humorous, even uncomplimentary and usually given by another (French).

442. *chapeau de paille*: straw hat (French).

443. *floostered*: fussed over.

444. *footy*: paltry, worthless, little and insignificant (*OED*).

445. *spill the salt ...*: the notion of salt-spilling as an omen and that ill should follow is an ancient superstition. Evidence from the fifteenth century may be seen in 'Il Cenacolo', 'The Last Supper' (1495–98), a mural painted in the refectory of the convent of Santa Maria della Grazie, Milan by Leonardo da Vinci (1452–1519), in which Judas Iscariot appears to knock over a salt cellar. This has been interpreted as symbolically indicating Christ's betrayal by his apostle.

446. *playing the puck*: 'The Pouke or Phooka, as the word is pronounced means ... the evil one. "Playing the puck" a common Anglo-Irish phrase, is equivalent to 'playing the divil.' The commentators on Shakespeare derived the beautiful and frolicksome Puck of the Midsummer Nights' Dream from the mischievous Pouke – Vide Drayton's Nymphidia. 'Crofton Croker's Legends', *The Dublin Penny Journal*, 125:3 (22 November 1834), p. 162.

447. *Lord Clifford*: Hall possibly refers here to William Cavendish (1748–1811), fifth Duke of Devonshire, 7th Baron Clifford. On 3 October 1764, following the death of his father, he inherited vast estates in England and Ireland which included Lismore Castle, Co. Waterford.

448. *ginnees*: 'guineas'; a guinea is an English gold coin, not minted since 1813. It was first struck in 1663 with the nominal value of 20 shillings, but from 1717 until its disappearance circulated as legal tender at the rate of 21 shillings (*OED*).

449. *jacky-dorey*: John Dory fish or St Pierre or Peter's fish.

450. *fluke*: a flat fish, especially the common flounder, *Pleuronedes Flesus* (*OED*).

451. *middle-man*: During the 17th century, England confiscated more that 3 million acres of land and one of the ways in which this land was managed was known as the 'middle-man system' whereby an intermediary was appointed by the English landowner large tracts of land were let on a long lease, which the middleman then sub-let to the Irish peasantry. Cecil Woodham-Smith states that 'this "middleman system" produced mis-

ery; the landlord rid himself of responsibility and assured himself of a regular income, but the tenants were handed over to exploitation' (p. 22). The prime motive of largely absentee landlords was profit and the middlemen were seen as parasites on the poor. The land was sub-divided into smaller and smaller parcels until the patch allocated was not large enough to support a poor Catholic farmer and his family. For a discussion of the system, see C. Woodham-Smith, *The Great Hunger: Ireland 1845–9* (London: Hamish Hamilton, 1962), pp. 15–24.

452. *dooshure*: from *douceur*, a conciliatory gift, pleasantness (French), previously from *dulcis*, sweetness (Latin).

453. *musheroons*: 'mushrooms'. The 'mushroom gentry' was a term applied to the *nouveau riche*; they were regarded as upstarts, people of low social stature who displayed their new-found wealth in vulgar display. The mushroom grows quickly and is largely composed of air, hence the metaphor.

454. spillogue: *spilleog*; an untidy person (Butler, *A Parish and its People*, p. 220).

455. *streeled*: verb from *straoil*, an untidy person; to walk in an untidy way, dragging along the way.

456. *turney*: attorney.

457. *play the spaniel*: '[to] fawn'; Hall alludes to Shakespeare: *King Henry VIII*, V.iii.150–1; 'To me you cannot reach, you play the spaniel, and think with wagging of your tongue to win me'.

458. *forbye*: hard by or near (*OED*).

459. *somerset*: somersault (*OED*).

460. *trolled*: sang a song with a chorus or round (*OED*).

461. *empty nuts*: evokes the Gaelic proverb 'Cha'n ann air chnothan falamh a tha fud eile': 'It is not from empty nuts all this comes'. D. Macintosh, *Collection of Gaelic Proverbs, and Familiar Phrases Based On Macintosh's Collection* (Edinburgh: Donaldson, Creech, Elliot and Sibbald, 1785).

462. *John Anderson*: Robert Burns (1759–96), Scottish poet and lyricist, wrote 'John Anderson, My Jo':

> John Anderson, my jo, John,
> When we were first acquent;
> Your locks were like the raven,
> Your bonie brow was brent;
> But now your brow is beld, John,
> Your locks are like the snaw;
> But blessings on your frosty pow,
> John Anderson, my jo.
>
> John Anderson, my jo, John,
> We clamb the hill thegither;
> And mony a cantie day, John,
> We've had wi' ane anither:
> Now we maun totter down, John,
> And hand, in hand we'll go,
> And sleep thegither at the foot
> John Anderson, my jo.

See J. Daverio, *Robert Schumann; Herald of a 'New Poetic Age'* (Oxford: Oxford University Press, 1997), pp. 400–1 for a discussion of Schumann's adaption of Burns' lyric poem.

463. *Dressed in a little brief authority ...* Shakespeare, *Measure for Measure*, II.ii.118.

464. *post-chaise*: a fast carriage designed to carry passengers and mail for long distances travelling between 'posts' or 'stations' along the route. Painted yellow, with four wheels and a closed body, it held two to four persons, the driver riding postilion on the near horse of one of the pairs. Fresh horses were provided at the coaching posts, or inns.

465. *bogtrotters*: persons with awkward manners, originally used of Irish people in general, due to the proliferation of bogs in rural Ireland and the difficulty of walking on the tufted ground of bogland (*DH-E*). More commonly, from the 1700s, a pejorative term to describe a person of Irish birth or descent.

466. *Wilkie*: Hall refers to the artist David Wilkie (1785–1841), born in Fife, Scotland. He was a personal friend of the Halls and painter of historical, genre and portrait works, whom S. C. Hall dubbed 'honest, earnest, faithful and true' and worthy of the universal respect his reputation earned. Wilkie died on 1 June 1841 on board *S.S. Oriental* and was buried at sea near Malta. S.C. Hall, *A Book of Memories of Great Men and Women of the Age* (London: Virtue, n. d.), p. 480.

467. *dominie*: schoolmaster or pedagogue (*OED*).

468. *pewet*: 'peewit', the lapwing, *vanellus vanellus*. Imitative of the sound the bird makes (*OED*).

469. *surtout*: a man's great-coat or overcoat, from French *sur*, above, and *tout*, everything (*OED*).

470. *sod o' turf ... small trifle o' prates*: the hedge-school master was sometimes paid in kind with turf, butter, vegetables or fowl. His assistance was often required on other matters, when a letter needed to be drafted, a will written or a lease drawn up, and he would be paid for his assistance in comestibles or fuel. Hall, however, is keen to state that Master Ben is a step above the kind of teacher who was always reimbursed for his services in this way.

471. *kreel*: 'creel'; a wicker basket for transporting turf, often in pairs placed on each side of an ass's back (*DH-E*).

472. *white eyes*: White Eyes is a variety of potato listed among those cultivated in Galway. H. Sutton, *A Statistical & Agricultural Survey of the County of Galway* (Dublin: Dublin University Press, 1824), p. 353.

473. *London Ladies*: a variety of potato mentioned in eighteenth-century verse:

> Nor do I want a few good beds
> Of driest wholesome *English reds,*
> With London Ladies and White Eyes,
> And *high-cawls* of a monstrous size;
> These by no means could neglect,
> The very name deserves respect ...

C. Ó'Gráda, *Black '47 and Beyond; The Great Irish Famine in History, Economy and Memory* (Princeton, NJ: Princeton University Press, 1999).

474. *and jump ... in noisy merriment*: not identified.

475. *younkers*: youngsters (*OED*).

476. *branyans*: 'limpets'; a gasteropod mollusc with an open tent-shaped shell, found adhering to its resting place on rocks (*OED*).

477. *quondam*: 'former' (Latin).

478. *bog Latin*: a spurious form of Latin. It was used by tinkers as a secret language to protect themselves; also known as 'Tinker's Cant' or 'The Ould Thing'.

479. *The Storm*: Likely to be Ludwig von Beethoven's Sonata N.17 in D minor op.31 No.1, 'The Tempest', composed in 1801/02. It was not named by Beethoven, but became associated with Shakespeare's play of the same name.

480. *changeful are all the scenes of life*: not identified.

481. *single rule of three direct*: mathematical formula which teaches that if you have three out of four numbers, the fourth will bear the same proportion to the third as the second does to the first.

482. éclat: brilliancy, to dazzling effect (French) (*OED*).

483. *Lombardy poplar*: a species that grows straight and tall; *populus nigra*; brought from northern Italy in the seventeenth century.

484. *Portuguese fashion*: the Portuguese method of training vines was using the *latada* (trellis), raising them high off the ground.

485. *Benjamin Rattin*: Hall's character 'Benjamin Rattin' was in life one Benjamin Radford, who was a hedge schoolmaster in Cullenstown, with thirty-seven pupils in 1826 and earned a meagre £5 a year. See Butler, *A Parish and its People*, p.103.

486. *Judy Ryan's station*: 'station' being a visit by a parish priest on a weekday to say Mass (*OED*).

487. les affaires du coeur: 'matters of the heart', 'love affairs' (French).

488. *with not a sound beside ... or the grey curlew*: lines from G. Crabbe's poem in G. Crabbe, 'Tales of the Hall', *Tales of the Hall*, 2 vols (London, J. P. Murray, 1819), vol. 1, p. 82, ll. 3–4.

489. *the measured chime ...*: quotation from F. Hemans, 'Where is the Sea? Song of a Greek Islander in Exile', *Poems by Felicia Hemans*, 2 vols (Boston, MA: Perkins, Marvin, Russell, Odiorne, 1833), vol. 2, pp. 243–56.

490. *I miss the voice ... my childhood's glee*: lines from Ibid., p. 243, ll. 5–6 which are paraphrased by Hall. The lines by Hemans read:

> I miss that voice of waves, which first
> Awoke my childhood's glee ...

491. *From nature up to nature's God*: Hall quotes from Rev. Robert Montgomery, 'A Landscape of Domestic Life', *Luther: The Spirit of the Reformation*, 3rd edn (London: Francis Baisler, 1863), pp. 188–98, 197, ll. 8–9. 'And not from nature *up* to nature's God/ But *down* from nature's God – look nature through'.

492. *in alto*: 'high-pitched'; relating to a voice occupying the range between soprano and tenor; from Italian *alto*, a high voice in polyphonic music.

493. *Magnus Apollo*: 'great Apollo' (Latin). A god of the sun and prophecy in Greek mythology and patron of musicians, physicians and poets.

494. *termagant*: boisterous, overbearing or quarrelsome (*OED*).

495. *from the life*: Hall evokes the French phrase *d'après nature* to explain that she has 'drawn' aspects of her characters from people she has known.

496. perdu: 'lost', 'concealed' (French).

497. *plaguy snipeens*: 'plaguey'; originally relating to bubonic plague or other diseases, but here meaning 'vexatious' or 'annoying'. 'Snipeens' are little snipe, with the use of the Irish diminutive 'een' (*OED*).

498. *birdeens*: little birds, with the Irish diminutive 'een'.

499. *trysting tree*: a tree where people engage to meet, for romantic or other assignations.

500. *runs smooth*: Shakespeare. Hall evokes *A Midsummer Night's Dream*: 'The course of true love never did run smooth', I.i.134.

501. *in sooth:* in truth (*OED*).

502. *tippets*: 'tippet'; a wool or fur covering for shoulders with hanging ends; also a long narrow slip of cloth hanging from a dress or hood and sometimes loose as a scarf (*OED*).

503. parlance: way of speaking; from French *parler*, 'to speak' (*OED*).

504. *lubberly*: coarse of figure and dull of intellect (*OED*).

505. *jock coat*: often made of frieze, a long great-coat, with sleeves, a hood or cape and a broad belt which fastened around the waist. Worn by both sexes, it was for a period fashionable with the upper ranks.

506. *brogueens*: 'little shoe', from 'brogue', 'shoe', and the Irish diminutive 'een'. A brogue is a stout shoe often made of untanned leather (*OED, DH-E*).

507. *head-tire*: 'head attire'; any headgear or an ornament worn on the head (*OED*).

508. *door-cheek*: one of the side-posts of a door (*OED*).

509. shock: a bunch or heap; here referring to 'tobacco', but the word was probably in use in Bannow to refer to a group of sheaves of grain placed upright and supporting each other to permit drying and ripening (*OED*).

510. *Orpheus*: In Greek mythology, Orpheus, son of a Thracian prince, inherited from his mother the gift of music which had the power to charm the beasts; often depicted holding a lyre, he attempted to recover his wife Euridice from Hades.

511. *sarpent*: serpent.

512. *powdered down upon*: reduced to powder (*OED*).

513. *Cromelians*: 'Cromwellians'. Settlers in Ireland at the 'Cromwellian Settlement' of 1652 or their descendants (*OED*).

514. *united man*: a member of the Society of United Irishmen, a liberal political organization originally formed to promote union between Catholics and Protestants, but which eventually became a separatist secular society. Inspired by revolutions in America and France, Wolfe Tone (1763–98) along with James Napper Tandy (1737–1803) and Thomas Paliser Russell (1767–1803) were founders of the society. Although aid was enlisted from France, it did not arrive and the rebellion of 1798, launched by the United Irishmen in order to end British monarchical rule and found a sovereign state, foundered.

515. *night-walker*: a nocturnal miscreant (*OED*).

516. *hurdles*: a portable rectangular frame, originally having horizontal bars interwoven or wattled with withes of hazel or willow; used chiefly to form temporary fences and sheep pens (*OED*).

517. *Knock Mountain*: not identified, but from the context, in Co. Carlow.

518. *She moved upon this earth* ...: A poem in twelve cantos by Percy Bysshe Shelley (1792–1822) originally called 'Laon and Cythna', which proved controversial and was edited and reissued in 1817 as 'The Revolt of Islam'. Hall compares her character Miss Caroline to Shelley's description of Cythna in Canto II, xxiii. Hall omits the lines 'she did seem/ Beside me, gathering beauty as she grew' from the verse; they follow 'To nourish some far desert ... '. For analysis of 'Laon and Cythna' and the controversy regarding the subject of Shelley's possible treatment of incest in the poem, see K. Everest and G. Matthews, *The Poems of Shelley 1817–1819* (Harlow, UK: Pearson, 2000), pp. 10–261.

519. *carries the oak-stick between his eyes*: the shillelagh was also called an 'oak-stick', so Hall indicates that Mr. Johnson had an angry or threatening look.

520. *hedge school*: a school held by a hedge-side or in the open air, as was once common in Ireland (*OED*). See W. Carlton, 'The Hedge School', *Traits and Stories of the Irish Peasantry*, 2 vols (Dublin: W. Curry Jr, 1830), vol. 2, pp. 109–210. Carleton gives a more accurate appreciation of a hedge-school education ('What was Plato himself but a hedge

schoolmaster?' p. 198) than that in the *OED*, which defines the hedge school as a 'low-class school'.

521. *Peelers*: Sir Robert Peel, 2nd Baronet (1788–1850), while serving as Chief Secretary in Dublin in 1817, proposed the foundation of a police force, members of which became known as Peelers or 'Bobbies'.

522. ci-devant: from before (French).

523. *Pangandrum's boots*: dialect for 'Panjandrum's boots'. This refers to a nonsense piece written by Samuel Foote (1720–77), dramatist and actor, in order to test the memory of actor Charles Macklin (1699–1797), and is quoted in Edgeworth, 'Harry and Lucy, Concluded', *Works of Maria Edgeworth*, vol. 13, pp. 160–1.

524. *the three kingdoms*: England, Scotland and Ireland. In 1603 when James VI of Scotland came to the English throne, these countries were firmly styled 'the three kingdoms'.

525. cooleen: English rendering from Irish *cúl*, meaning the back of something; by extension the head and a length of hair, qualified by the Irish diminutive '-een'.

526. *The boat and the water …*: not identified.

527. *beldame*: an older woman; a hag or virago (*OED*).

528. *gostering*: gossiping; from 'goster', empty talk or a gossipy person (*DH-E*).

529. *sarmints*: sermons.

530. *Kilmainim*: colloquial shorthand for Kilmainham Gaol, Kilmainham, Dublin; built in 1796, it was where the leaders of Irish rebellions during the eighteenth and nineteenth centuries were imprisoned.

531. *Johnstown Castle*: built by the Esmond family who came from Lincolnshire following the Anglo-Norman invasion of 1169. It is said that Cromwell reviewed his troops on the lawn after having stayed overnight at the castle. The family was expelled by Cromwell in the 1600s and it came to the Grogan family by marriage. Cornelius Grogan (*c*. 1738–98) was hanged in the rebellion of 1798; in 1810 the Grogans regained the demesne.

532. *Oliver Cromwell*: see n. 86.

533. *Rathaspect*: village in the barony of Forth, Co. Wexford, close to Wexford town and between Forth Mountain and Wexford Haven.

534. *St. George's Channel*: situated between the coasts of Wexford and Pembrokeshire, south of the Irish Sea and north of the Celtic Sea.

535. *the Saltee Islands*: Great and Little Saltee Islands in the barony of Bargy, off the coast of Kilmore parish. Little Saltee is joined to the larger island by a shingle ridge called St Patrick's bridge. During the rebellion of 1798, Harvey Bagenal, commander-in-chief of the United Irishmen, and John Henry Colclough, a general of the rebel forces (see n. 327), fled to the islands, seeking refuge in a cave. They were later captured and hanged in Wexford.

536. brusque: curt or abrupt to the point of rudeness (*OED*).

537. *green crop plan*: not identified.

538. divarshun: diversion.

539. *Ironsides*: Oliver Cromwell's troopers were named 'Ironsides', reflecting his own nickname of 'Ironside' given him by Prince Rupert following the English Civil War battle of Marston Moor on 2 July 1644, where Cromwell's cavalry forces were deemed strong and impenetrable.

540. *keeler*: also *ciléar*: a shallow wooden tub with iron hoops, about one and a half feet high, used to contain the day's milk; a butter tub (*OED*).

541. *ague*: a fit or spell of shaking or shivering induced by either disease or fear (*OED*).

542. *blaguard*: blackguard.

543. *Shelmalier*: both a barony of Co. Wexford, comprising East and West Shelmalier, and the men of the area who hunted wild fowl, fished, then took up arms in the rebellions of 1798. See M. McGuckian, *Shelmalier* (Oldcastle: Gallery Books, 1998).

544. *Rogue's March*: military slang for a tune played by a military band to accompany the expulsion of an offender from a regiment (*OED*).

545. *Buddaugh cow*: buddogh, also bodagh, buddaugh; a clumsy fellow, an unintelligent person. In J. Swift, *A Dialogue in Hibernian Stile by A and B, and Irish Eloquence*, ed. by Alan Bliss (Dublin: Cadenus Press, 1977), p. 164: 'A. what kind of a man is your neighbour squire Dolt? B. why, a meer buddaugh' (*DH-E*).

546. *basket of chips*: a basket made of thin wooden strips, 'chips' here being wood hewed by the carpenter in the course of his work (*OED*).

547. *bouclawn*: ragwort.

548. *Danes*: natives of Denmark or, in older usage, including all the Northmen who invaded Ireland and England. Brian Boru was killed following a victory at the Battle of Clontarf in 1014, when the Danes were routed by the men of the provinces under his leadership.

549. *Ferry Carrig bridge*: This bridge over the Slaney was built by Lemuel Cox (1736–1806) of Malden, Massachusetts in 1795. Prior to this he built the Foyle bridge in Derry and went on to build more at New Ross, Enniscorthy and Portumna.

550. *piques himself*: credits himself; awards himself a 'pique', a score of thirty ahead of one's opponent in a card game (*OED*).

551. *gown-tail*: a rectangular length of fabric attached to the back of a woman's dress. Decorative when pinned up with a corking pin, it proved useful for wiping away tears, covering the head in a shower of rain or even concealing stolen goods.

552. *Paddys and Shelahs*: 'Patrick' and 'Sheila'. The ubiquity of these Irish names led to their adoption as derogatory soubriquets abroad for all Irish men and women. Mass emigration of a largely poor and uneducated Irish population from the eighteenth century onwards led to a perception of the Irish male as 'coarse and drunken'. Coughlan and Hughes note that following the transportation of thousands of Irish to the penal colony of Australia, 'all women (not just Irish) came to be known as Sheilas'. G. Coughlan and M. Hughes, *Irish Language and Culture* (London: Lonely Planet, 2007), p. 12.

553. tracle: treacle.

554. *granough*: cereal; from the Irish word 'granach'.

555. *'nottomy*: 'notomy'; a skeleton or an emaciated person (*OED*).

556. *skying*: to strike a ball high into the air; in this case, 'skying' means that Dacey's good eye always seemed to be thrown, or looking skyward.

557. *scald*: affected with the 'scall'; scabby (*OED*).

558. *Jackeens*: a self-assertive Dubliner with pro-British leanings. Jack was the nickname of the stereotypical Englishman in *The History of John Bull*, a collection of pamphlets by John Arbuthnot, 1712. With the Irish diminutive added, it becomes 'Jackeen'. Also attributed to derivation from the small Union Jacks (or Jackeens)

559. *giount*: giant.

560. *went upon wires*: treaded carefully, as on a tightrope (figurative).

561. *smalkum*: small beer. Hall gives this meaning of the word in a footnote to the Second Series of *Sketches*, 1831, p. 360. Not in *OED*.

562. *Turkey-man*: Turk.

563. *Dunleary*: once a small fishing village near Dublin, but since 1930 named Dun Laoghaire, or 'fort of Laoghaire'. S. C. Hall mentions 'Kingstown, formerly Dunleary, which received its modern name in honour of His Majesty George the Fourth, who took

shipboard here on leaving Ireland in 1821'. Hall, *Ireland, its Scenery & Character*, vol. 2, p. 294.

564. *I do not care ... tell to me the truth at onct*: not identified.

565. *Turner['s]*: Joseph Mallord William Turner (1775–1851), Romantic landscape painter. Hall evokes Turner's skill at capturing morning sunlight on water in his seascapes, such as 'Sun Rising Through Vapour' (1807).

566. *Planxty Kelly*: old folk tune composed by Ireland's famous blind harper Turlough O'Carolan (1670–1738), who was born in Nobber, Co. Meath.

567. *Lady's Island*: 'Our Lady's Island' or 'Cluain-na-mBan', 'the meadow of the women', is a village in Co. Wexford, near Rosslare, where St Abban founded a Christian community in the seventh century. It has long been a place of pilgrimage. The 'island' itself comprises about thirty acres, sits in a tidal lake and is connected to the shore by a man-made causeway. Lady's Island, or in ecclesiastical records, 'St. Mary of the Island', in the Barony of Forth extends to an area no larger than three three hundred and eighty acres. 'There are few parts of Ireland in which there are so many monuments of the English invasion of 1170, and still fewer, so indistinctly described. This may perhaps be owing to its being the settlement of the first colony from Britain, generally known by the name of Anglo-Saxon'. For an illuminating historical account of this area, written within a few years of Hall's first edition of *Sketches*, see 'The Lady's Island in 1833', *Dublin Penny Journal*, 30:1 (10 January 1833), pp. 233–4, on p. 233.

568. *avy*: colloquial word for 'Ave'; 'Ave Maria' or 'Hail Mary', devotional Catholic, prayer requesting the intercession of Our Lady, but also prayed by other Christians.

569. *knock*: 'hill' or 'hillock' (*OED*).

570. *I H S*: I. H. S. is a monogram in Western Christianity for the name of 'Jesus', denoting the first three letters of the Greek alphabet: *iota* (I), *eta* (H), *sigma* (S). It was first used in English in the fourteenth century.

571. *skitting*: from 'skit', a vain wanton woman, 'skitting' here perhaps means behaving like the same (*OED*).

572. *St. Patrick's ... his beautiful head*: St Patrick's Cathedral, the largest in Ireland. The present building was erected in 1220.

573. *The Stout and Strong of Heart*: Old Frank seems to be familiar with and have recited to Hall in her childhood a very ancient story. Lucius Annaeus Seneca, b. 1 BC in Cordoba, Spain, said in 'On the Natural Fear of Death', Letter XXXII, 'The whip cracks, the sword flashes. Ah now, Aeneas, thou must needs be stout/ And strong of heart!'

574. *potheen*: see n. 46. Mrs Hall's friend Maria Edgeworth wrote in *Tales of Fashionable Life* (London: J. Johnson, 1812), p. 160: 'potsheen, plase your honour: – because it's the little whiskey that's made in the private still or pot, and *sheen* because it's a fond word for whatsoever we'd like, and for what we have little of, and would make much of' (*OED*).

575. *hurru*: variant of 'hur(r)oosh'; to drive with the cry of 'hur(r)oosh', 'hurrish'.

576. *Dumraghodooly*: not identified.

577. *Mullenavat pig*: a 'pampered pig'; Mullinavat was a village in Co. Kilkenny where it is said the pig was so important to the economy that it was better treated than its owners: 'I thought of the happy pigs of Mullinavat, who have the clean straw to lie upon, while their lords and masters put up with the dirty, – who eat that Irish luxury, a *maley* potato, while their mistresses are content with the damp ones, and who go to bed by candlelight, while the family sit in the dark'. Hall, *Lights and Shadows of Irish Life*, vol. 2, p. 6.

578. *General Roche*: Reverend Philip Roche, a Roman Catholic priest who was born at Monasootagh, took part in the rebellion of 1798, joining the rebels, who elected him

commander of the encampment near New Ross. Despite his skill at deploying troops, the rebel forces were driven to retreat from Vinegar Hill. Following their surrender, Fr. Roche was set upon, tried and hanged on Wexford Bridge on 25 June 1798, where his body was thrown into the river Slaney.

579. *Dalkey Isle*: Dalkey Isle is at the south-eastern extremity of Dublin Bay, with Howth bounding the north east. This oval, rocky island of twenty-nine acres is uninhabited, save for a herd of goats and a seal colony. The ruins of the eleventh-century church to St. Begnet remain, as does the Martello tower, which differs from all others in Ireland, having an entrance at the top of the structure. This tower, built in the early 1800s as a fortress against Napoleonic invasion, is reputed to be the site of an earlier structure which provided shelter for those trying to escape bubonic plague in 1575.

580. *Wexford Church*: not identified.

581. *Carnsore Point*: Headland on the south-eastern corner of Co. Wexford with Our Lady's Island Lake and Tacumshin Lake inland.

582. *General Keogh*: Matthew Keugh (*c.* 1744–98). Following a career in the British army in which he served in America and rose to the rank of Captain-Lieutenant, he was residing in Wexford during the rebellion. He was appointed Military Governor of the town when the rebels took Wexford, but, having failed to prevent a mob murder of loyalists, was captured, tried and hanged on 25 June 1798 and his body thrown into the river Slaney, meeting the same fate as General Roche. See n. 552. Prior to this despatch, his remains were desecrated; he was decapitated and his head displayed on a pike before the court house in Wexford. See F. Plowden, *An Historical Review of the State of Ireland: From the Invasion of that Country Under Henry II to Its Union with Great Britain on the First of January 1801*, 2 vols, (London: T. Egerton, 1803), vol. 2, pp. 762–7.

583. *inkhorn*: a small portable vessel, formerly make of horn for holding writing-ink (*OED*).

584. *great metropolis of nations*: Hall here refers to London; the term was much in use regarding the city. When laying a pier stone for the new railway bridge over the river Medway for the Manchester to Stockport railway, George Watson Buck made a speech in which he declared that this was a bridge on which would flow 'a mighty stream of wealth from this manufacturing metropolis to London, the metropolis of nations'. J. Herapath, *The Railway Magazine and Annals of Science*, New Series, 5 vols (London: Wyld & Son, 1839), vol. 5, p. 355.

585. *hurley*: a 'hurling stick' used to play hurling or hurley, a fast game similar to hockey. It is of ancient origin, played especially in Ireland and the diaspora. The hurley, or *camán* in Irish, is used to hit the *sliotar*, a hard ball made of cork covered with sewn leather, similar in size to a baseball.

586. *Vinegar-hill*: Vinegar Hill, 15 miles north of Wexford town, near Enniscorthy, was the scene of the 'Battle of Vinegar Hill', which took place on 21 June 1798, during which the United Irishmen were attacked at their rebel headquarters and suffered grievous losses.

587. *the Castle*: Dublin Castle. Built on an early Viking fortress, for 700 years Dublin Castle, near Dame St, Dublin, functioned as a prison, treasury, fortress, law court and the seat of English Government administration until the Act of Union. In 1800, the Union of Great Britain and Ireland saw the end of Dublin Castle as the centre of policy-making, which was devolved to Westminster.

588. *one-pounders*: a one-pound note or coin (*OED*).

589. *tacks*: 'tack'; a stitch of clothes, a shred. This use of 'tack' is peculiar to Hiberno-English (*DH-E*).

590. *transported*: In April 1791 the first ship left Ireland for the penal colony in New South Wales, Australia; previously convicts were transported to North America, but this ceased with the end of the War of Independence. Between 1791 and 1853, 26,500 Irish were transported to New South Wales, often for minor offences of theft, but also for treason and sedition. Following the rebellion of 1798, shiploads of the defeated were transported. Prisoners from the south of Ireland were held at the city gaol in Cork.

591. *Reading made Easy*: see n. 82.

592. *Life of Freney*...: see n. 383.

593. *Valentine and Orson*: A medieval romance associated with the Carolingian Cycle based on a lost original *chanson des geste*. It tells the tale of twin brothers who were abandoned in woods at birth, Valentine raised as a knight and Orson reared in a bear's den. The earliest English version is by H. Watson, *The Historye of the Two Valyannte Brethren; Valentyne and Orson*, (n. p.: William Copland, *c.* 1550).

594. *Seven Champions of Christendom*: *The Famous History of the Seven Champions of Christendom* was written by Richard Johnson (1573–1659). 'The Seven Champions' of the title are St George of England; St Denis of France; St James of Spain; St Anthony of Italy; St Andrew of Scotland; St Patrick of Ireland and St David of Wales. Originally published in 1576, this version was printed in London for R. Scot ... in 1687, being the copy owned by Dr Samuel Johnson.

595. *'fifteen-pound' boarding school*: boarding-schools where the emphasis was on preparing girls for the marriage market rather than learning. 'Accomplishments' were confined to such pursuits as needlework, drawing, dance, French and Italian. 'Fifteen-pound' refers to the annual fee charged by such establishments.

596. *tent-stitch*: also called 'petit point', parallel embroidery stitches worked diagonally across the intersections of the threads (*OED*).

597. en papillote: from *papillon*, butterfly (French), a 'curl-paper'; a small triangular piece of paper used to enclose and hold a piece of damp hair which has been wound into a curl (*OED*).

598. *grenadier*: a member of the Grenadier Guards, the first regiment of Household Cavalry (*OED*).

599. *walking gentleman*: usually a male actor playing a small part with few lines; here, more likely to be a man who has either no need or no desire for an occupation, but who styles himself an esquire (*OED*).

600. *Honourable Justice Cleaveland ... Admiral Barrymore*: not identified.

601. *Steven's-green*: 'St. Stephen's Green'; a Dublin landmark, this park was opened to the public on 27 July 1880. Rectangular in shape, comprising twenty-two acres, the landscaping was designed by William Sheppard. Prior to development, this marshy ground had been used to graze cattle. Following enclosure by Dublin Corporation, the surrounding land was sold for building and Georgian houses replaced the older buildings. The Green then became a popular place of recreation for the well-born of the city.

602. *Cole's-lane market*: Cole's Lane was a street in north Dublin city between Denmark St and Moore St. The area was famous for its boisterous and lively market traders, with shops and outdoor stalls selling fruit, vegetables and second-hand clothes to the poorer class who occupied the tenement buildings close by. Hall's comments humorously express the way in which the gentry considered shopkeepers and traders, particularly from such an area, to be completely beyond the pale when it came to matrimony.

603. *barouche*: a barouche was a four-wheeled carriage with a forward seat for the driver, an adjustable half-hood and seats inside for two couples facing each other (*OED*).

604. *to their trumps*: to bring someone to their last expedient (*OED*).

605. *devouring duns*: a 'dun' is an importunate creditor or an agent employed to collect a debt. The word originated with one 'Joe Dunn', a bailiff of Lincoln. It became part of a proverb, as, when a debt was unpaid, it was asked: 'Why don't you Dun him?' – i.e., 'why don't you send Dun to arrest him?' (*OED*).

606. éclairissement: 'enlightening'; a clarification or enlightening explanation of something hitherto obscure (French) (*OED*).

607. *West India planter*: an owner or manager of a large estate in the British colonies of the Caribbean.

608. *Colonel Bloomfield*['s]: Col. Hon. Sir Benjamin Bloomfield (1768–1846) from Newport, Co. Tipperary. During the rebellion of 1798 he commanded the British, while Captain Crawford had charge of the Irish corps of artillery at the battle of Vinegar Hill, near Enniscorthy, on 21 June 1798. He was Private Secretary to the Sovereign, George IV, from 1817–22. His remains were interred at Borrisnafarney Parish Church, near Moneygall, Co. Offaly (*ODNB*).

609. bonne-bouche: *bonne-bouche* (French) is regarded as 'the best, saved to the end which leaves a good taste in the mouth', so Hall uses the metaphor to describe Ferdinand as the last, or youngest and 'sweetest' child of the family.

610. *the wicked one ... set his mark*: The devil is said to brand or claw his initiates to seal their obedience permanently to his will.

611. *the ban*: members of the United Irishmen who turned King's evidence were considered traitors and treated with abhorrence, being banished from their community.

612. *innocent*: a simpleton or half-wit (*OED*).

613. *dégagé*: relaxed, unconstrained (French) (*OED*).

614. *Cross*: Hall refers to a large crucifix which stands on the hill of Côte-de-Grace near Honfleur. The shrine was popular with pilgrims and tourists in the nineteenth century, who offered prayers for men at sea. It is depicted by the artist Jean-Baptiste Corot (1796–1875) in 'Calvary on the Côte de Grace', *c.* 1830 (Metropolitan Museum of Art, New York), and shows its commanding position on the hillside near to the church of Notre-Dame-de-Grace, which was built between 1600 and 1615.

615. voteens: zealously pious people (*DH-E*).

616. *By a promise ... you may be led*: not identified.

617. *Ruction*: from the Irish *ruchtacht*, 'rumbling' or 'disturbance'. The Insurrection of 1798, when the United Irishmen rose against British rule in Ireland, was known as 'The Ruction'.

618. *cruddy*: curd-like or coagulated; from 'curdy' (*OED*).

619. *voster*: abbreviated title of the popular educational book *Arithmetick in whole and broken numbers digested after a new method and chiefly adapted to the trade of Ireland...* by Elias Voster (Dublin: W. Jones, 1793).

620. *Botany*: Botany Bay in New South Wales, former penal convict settlement; named by Captain Cook for the variety of plants collected there by the botanists who accompanied him on his first voyage. See J. Dimant and C. Humphries (eds), *Banks' Florilegium*, 35 vols (London: British Museum, 1980–90). 'Botany Bay' became a generic term for the destination of convicts sentenced to transportation from the late eighteenth century, even though this particular bay was not used for convicts. See A. G. L. Shaw, *Convicts and the Colonies* (Dublin: Irish Historical Press, 1998).

621. *militia regiments*: These regiments of part-time local forces were an integral part of the establishment and were called up regularly to respond to perceived threats from the

enemy within or without. The Irish militia was first formed into county regiments in 1661 by the Lord Lieutenant of Ireland, James Butler, 1st Duke of Ormonde (1610–88). Whereas Catholics had been excluded from the right to bear arms, the outbreak of war with France in 1793 and a shortage of soldiers prompted Parliament to pass a law removing the prohibition on Catholics and they became subject to enlistment for military service in the same way as Protestants.

622. The Wexford militia was formed in 1661 when part-time Irish militia defence forces of the British army were given county titles. In 1756 this force comprised Protestants only and its strength was 2,001 men.

623. *The Rocks*: site of the victory of the United Irishmen at the Battle of Three Rocks on 29 May 1798, when British artillery columns marching to reinforce the town of Wexford were ambushed and defeated at this site on the eastern end of Forth Mountain where the ground receded.

624. Scullabogue: Infamous atrocity of the rebellion of 1798, when on 5 June, hundreds of non-combatants, mainly Protestant, were massacred. On 13 May 1798, the rebels requisitioned the home of Francis King, on whose land near Carrigbyrne the barn of Scullabogue was sited. This thatched barn, thirty-four feet long, fifteen feet wide and twelve feet high, was used to imprison 230 men, women and children. It was under guard by 300 rebels, one commander being Andy Colfer (Hall's character 'Captain Andy'), when news came of rebel defeat at New Ross. The infuriated men arriving from New Ross overpowered the guards and fired the barn. Hall's fictional account varies from that of historians. See R. Musgrave, *Rebellions in Ireland* (Dublin: n. p., 1802); T. Dunne, *Rebellions: Memoir, Memory and 1798* (Dublin: Lilliput, 2004), c. 13, pp. 247–64.

625. *Matthew, Mark ... that I lie on*: a prayer recited for protection against evil spirits, usually by children at bedtime. Of many variations up to the twentieth century, a common version known as the White Paternoster runs:

> There are four corners on my bed,
> There are four angels overhead,
> Matthew, Mark, Luke and John,
> Bless the bed that I lie on. (*OED*)

626. *the pealing anthem ...*: quotation from 'Elegy in a Country Churchyard' by Thomas Gray. See H. Reed (ed.), *The Poetical Works of Thomas Gray* (Philadelphia, PA: H. Carey Baird, 1851), pp. 145–50, on p. 146.

627. *Professor Edgar*: John Edgar (1798–1866), Presbyterian minister born at Kilkine in Co. Down. He was a leading advocate in Ireland of the temperance movement, although he refused on biblical grounds to support teetotalism (*ODNB*).

628. *Rev. George Carr*: curate of New Ross, Co. Wexford, who set up the first Temperance Society in Europe to address the ills of intemperance in his own town. As with Edgar, he did not advocate teetotalism (*Wexford Independent*, 1 March 1902).

629. *piggin*: the origin of 'piggin' is obscure, thought to be the source of the Irish 'pigín'; a small pail or tub, wooden dish or basin, smaller than a noggin (*DH-E*).

630. *Vulcan*: in Roman mythology, the god of fire and of metal-working, the son of Jupiter and Juno, and the husband of Venus (*OED*).

631. *the pledge*: the pledge is a solemn undertaking to abstain from alcohol, known colloquially as 'taking the pledge'. Fr Theobald Mathew (1790–1856), a Capuchin friar from Thomastown, Co. Tipperary, inaugurated the Pioneer Total Abstinence Association in response to pervasive drunkenness among the population, the chief cause of faction fights and other ills. His association was an immediate success, with many thousands

signing up in the first ten months. The pledge taken was: 'I promise to abstain from all intoxicating drinks, except used medicinally and by order of a medical man, and to discountenance the cause and practice of intemperance'. There followed the blessing; 'God give you strength to keep your resolution!' (Hall, *Ireland, its Scenery, Character, &c.,* vol. 1, p. 291). Mr and Mrs Hall were fervent supporters of the temperance movement, knew Fr. Mathew personally and supported him in his successful crusade.

632. *Surely it is my father.... I have no other*: quoted by Carter Hall in *Retrospect of a Long Life*. He recalls the many songs that encouraged intemperance: 'Whisky was "mate, drink, and clothing ... my outside coat, I have no other" ... in short ... whisky was the panacea that cured all the evils flesh is heir to ... ' (Hall, *Retrospect*, p. 287).

633. *affidavit man*: a person hired to give false witness, especially in a court of law; a person who commits perjury for payment (*OED*).

634. bresnaugh: Hall herself provides a footnote in 'The Whiteboy', *Fraser's Magazine for Town & Country*, 15 (Jan–June 1837), p. 710: 'Bresnagh [alternative spelling], a bundle of sticks, or brushwood, intended for fuel'. The word also appears as 'brestnaugh' in *The New Monthly Magazine and Literary Journal*, 44:173 (1835), p. 83, where Hall footnotes the meaning as a 'bundle of sticks'.

635. scrimage: 'scrimmage'; a skirmish or noisy contention or tussle (*OED*).

636. *Total Abstinence Society*: This society was founded in 1838 by Theobald Mathew, a Capuchin Friar and temperance campaigner. Born at Thomastown Castle, Co. Tipperary in October, 1790, he trained for the priesthood at Maynooth, before joining the Franciscan order. While ministering to the poor in Cork, a city famed for its many distilleries, Fr Mathew recognized the social misery and evil caused by widespread drunkenness. He took up the cause already begun by earlier temperance campaigners, including Rev. George Carr of new Ross, a close relative of Mrs. Hall. Those who joined the association took 'the pledge'; a promise to abstain from alcohol. Due to his efforts, Carter Hall was of the opinion that 'what was formerly a glory is now a degradation' and that Theobald Mathew, who died at Queenstown, Cork in December 1856 was a 'Martyr as well as the Apostle of Temperance'. See Carter Hall's recollection of Theobald Mathew in *A Book of Memories of Great Men and Women of the Age*, Second Edition (London, Virtue, 1877), pp.412–15.

637. *megrim*: from the Irish *méigrim*, headache, migraine, vertigo or mild tinnitus (*DH-E*).

SILENT CORRECTIONS

p. 16, l. 30,	and if] as if
p. 19, l. 5,	clssed] closed
p. 24, l. 31,	fidgetty] fidgety
p. 28, l. 36,	see raved] she raved
p. 32, l. 13,	aid] laid
p. 39, l. 13,	"Its quite true] "It's quite true
p. 39, l. 27,	employments] employments!
p. 39, l. 32,	tried] tired
p. 54, l. 10,	tos tarve] to starve
p. 60, l. 35,	the/the] the
p. 67, l. 23,	oft he] of the]
p. 91, l. 30,	earest] earnest
p. 106, l. 29,	o'money] o' money
p. 108, l. 26,	redied] readied
p. 109, l. 6,	insure] ensure
p. 109, l. 39,	stifly] stiffly
p. 114, l. 21,	blessin'it] blessin' it
p. 139, l. 21,	bonny] bony
p. 141, l. 16,	remote antiquit ,] remote antiquity,
p. 145, l. 3,	i] in
p. 149, l. 32,	Raymnnd's] Raymond's
p. 152, l. 22–3,	Hyde Park Cork] Hyde Park Corner
p. 156, l. 29,	a fear me] I fear me
p. 158, l. 21,	*Digit*] *Digitus*
p. 159, l. 2–3,	Millefleures] Millefleurs
p. 175, l. 24,	whose knows anything] who knows anything
p. 177, l. 33,	lookso] look so
p. 177, l. 38,	dosen't] doesn't
p. 178, l. 2,	jewel,"] jewel."
p. 179, l. 28,	broken"] broken."
p. 185, l. 30,	cabin] cabin –
p. 186, l. 38,	*cèad mile fàilte*] *cèad mile fàilte*
p. 187, l. 21,	wont lend] won't lend
p. 196, l. 5,	throught hesky] through the sky
p. 200, l. 3,	theerrors] the errors
p. 200, l. 3,	catholicism] Catholicism

p. 200, l. 11,	kidly] kindly
p. 206, l. 38,	but sat] but sat,
p. 213, l. 6,	sleep] asleep
p. 214, l. 10,	rest his elbow] rests his elbow
p. 214, l. 30,	exists] exists,
p. 215, l. 28,	cabin.'] cabin."
p. 224, l. 5,	honour,(bowing] honour, (bowing
p. 231, l. 38,	shewas] she was
p. 241, l. 34,	spit] split
p. 251, l. 31,	queen like] queen-like
p. 252, l. 14,	looseni ngh is] loosening his
p. 252, l. 35,	fogrotten] forgotten
p. 255, l. 9,	declaret o] declare to
p. 259, l. 36,	griping] gripping
p. 266, l. 37,	girls embryo chickens] girl's embryo chickens
p. 269, l. 22,	Anuie] Annie
p. 281, l. 24,	God!] God!"
p. 281, l. 27,	wall] wall.
p. 285, l. 17,	sposo] spouse
p. 291, l. 38,	present,] present.
p. 298, l. 24,	stream.'] stream."
p. 301, l. 25,	be] he
p. 303, l. 16,	itself,] itself.
p. 312, l. 4,	houses] houses!
p. 313, l. 15,	far off-ones] far-off ones
p. 313, l. 34,	theybe blown up] they be blown up
p. 317, l. 33,	did one] did, one
p. 324, l. 33,	ony] any
p. 325, l. 1,	corking pin] corking-pin
p. 327, l. 36,	study] sturdy
p. 346, l. 37,	lawn,)] lawn),
p. 348, l. 2,	a carroty] and carroty
p. 355, l. 17,	wont] won't
p. 361, l. 21,	*degagé*] *dégagé*
p. 370, l. 22,	sbe saw a horse] she saw a horse
p. 370, l. 31,	Thomas Jarratt.] Thomas Jarratt."
p. 370, l. 37,	"neither the captain] 'neither the captain
p. 370, l. 41,	more!'] more!'"
p. 371, l. 11,	wid him.'] wid him!'"
p. 373, l. 5,	be will be] he will be
p. 388, l. 10,	grouud] ground
p. 388, l. 22,	o' clock] o'clock
p. 388, l. 27,	lane,] lane.
p. 388, l. 36,	draught!"] draught?"

TEXTUAL VARIANTS

The complex and detailed nature of the textual variants and the number of editions featured here has necessitated the subdivision of this section into individual editions, ordered chronologically. Where different variants for the same word or phrase occur across multiple editions, cross references have been included.

Mrs S. C. Hall, *Sketches of Irish Character*, 1st edn, 2 vols (London: Frederick Westley & A. H. Davis, 1829).

Sketches of Irish Character was first published in 1829 in London, by Frederick Westley & A. H. Davis, in two small volumes without illustration. The eleven sketches which comprised this first series were:

Volume One: 'Lilly O'Brien', 'Kelly the Piper', 'Captain Andy', 'Independence', 'Black Dennis' and 'Old Frank'.

Volume Two: 'The Bannow Postman', 'Father Mike', 'Master Ben', 'Hospitality' and 'Peter the Prophet'.

Hall had already published three of her sketches: 'Master Ben'; Black Dennis' and 'Independence' in *The Spirit and Manners of the Age: A Christian and Literary Miscellany, New Series*, 2 vols (London: Westley and Davis, 1829) – a periodical strongly of Christian and Evangelical bent, edited by her husband Carter Hall.

The sketches tell of the lives of the local people of Bannow, County Wexford, where Mrs Hall spent her childhood and they take as their subject the people of the locality, chiefly the peasantry.

The edition contained this Introduction dedicated to Mary Russell Mitford (1787-1855):

Introduction

The *1st edn 1829* contained an Introduction, below, dedicated to Mary Russell Mitford (1787–1855). In her Introduction, Hall inscribes the volumes to Mary Russell Mitford, claiming inspiration from her 'delineations of English character' in *Our Village*. She then praises the advantages of Bannow, 'my native village', but, by emphasising its ancient history and its proximity to 'Bag and Bun', the site of Ireland's first invasion by Strongbow, she evokes memories of a less than peaceful time. She glances off the 'nearly forgotten days' of the Rebellion of 1798 and this mention disturbs any real possibility that the settled and calm world of Mitford may be found in Ireland. Far from being forgotten by the characters in the *Sketches* themselves, there are constant references to the Rebellion and its effects on the inhabitants of Bannow. The Rebellion, as evidenced in the sketches, was fresh and alive to the memory of Hall's own family as she grew up. The years following the writing of the first edition in 1829 was a period of immense social, cultural and political disruption.

The attraction that Bannow's castles and ruins hold for the antiquarian are outlined. This generalised nostalgia for the ancient has the effect of distancing Bannow from the detail of the history that shaped it and its people. Simultaneously Hall evokes a history of transplantation and social turmoil deeply implicated in the architectural ruins referenced. Hall's aim is to introduce Mitford to the inhabitants of the village which are claimed to be little interested, to 'know little and care less' about politics and religious difference. What she actually reveals is a more politically tense scene than apparently intended.

In her inscription, Hall desires to imbue the Irish landscape with the non-threatening qualities of the English picturesque, a genre which arose from a desire to escape the upheavals of industrialisation. However, Hall's sketches are replete with characters whose differences of religion and politics are passionately held and whose lives tell of violence, disruption and displacement. They deny the possibility of Bannow being turned into a type of museum populated by 'pleasant peasants'.

In dedicating *Sketches of Irish Character* to M. R. Mitford, Hall acknowledges that author's influence on her own choice of the sketch genre over the more popular novel. M. R. Mitford, *Our Village: Sketches of Rural Character and Scenery,* 5 vols (London: n. p., 1824–32) was so well received by the public that Hall wished to be associated with her brand of idyllic realism. In her sketches Hall certainly shares some of Mitford's sympathies and demonstrates a similar love of locality. However, Mitford's gentle nostalgia, replete with bucolic scenes from her fictional village of Aberleigh, demonstrate that her ideal is a retreat from the concerns of the wider world into locality. Mitford does not wish to engage with the changes in agricultural society precipitated by the Industrial Revolution and the Napoleonic Wars. Nor is the surface of her stories ruffled by the agrarian unrest in East Anglia in 1822 and the south of England through the 1830s.

It would seem that the critics took Mrs Hall at her own word as expressed in this Introduction and positioned her alongside Mitford. A reviewer writing in *La Belle Assemblée* wrote that, 'since the best of Miss Mitford's, we have seen nothing to equal the sketches that are contained in these volumes.' This reviewer also cemented Hall's opinion of her own work which became the accepted, though inadequate interpretation, stating 'that Mrs Hall has confined herself chiefly to the sunny side of the Irish character.' (Anon., *La Belle Assemblée*, 3rd series (London: J. Bell, 1829), pp. 273–5). Even the *Times* took the lead from Hall's positioning of herself alongside Mitford. The correspondent on 4 August 1829 wrote of the newly published *Sketches of Irish Character* that the work was 'a lively and clever imitation of the ingenious and characteristic volumes called *Village Sketches*, by Miss Mitford, to whom the volumes are very appropriately dedicated.' (*Times*, 13983 (4 August 1829), p. 4, col. B).

INTRODUCTION.

MY DEAR MISS MITFORD,

I can inscribe my Volumes to no one with more pleasure or propriety than to you, from whose vivid delineations of English character, I have derived so much information and enjoyment. Will you, then, accept the tribute of public homage, as well as of private affection?

I am desirous of introducing you to an Irish village – my native village of Bannow – which I must first tell you is situated on the Eastern coast of Ireland, and is justly the pride of the county of Wexford – a county much celebrated in the annals of Old times, and, indeed, unhappily so, in those of more recent, though, I trust, now nearly forgotten days. But let me warn you against the danger of falling into one of two opposite errors – expecting either too little or too much. You are not to behold the people and their dwellings, like those in your own 'sunny Berkshire,' surrounded by all the blessings that independent feelings and well-regulated minds can only give; but if you look for filthy cabins and a miserable peasantry, alike strangers to industry and contentment, you will be equally mistaken. Trust me, you have been often deceived by those who have presented you with broad caricatures, instead of faithful pictures of Ireland and its inhabitants.

I confess, however, that Bannow is a favourable specimen of an Irish village. It is far from any town; the soil is rich; the sea almost surrounds it, and its landlords reside on their estates. Moreover, the people know little, and care less about politics; and the Protestant Clergyman and the Catholic Priest (at least it was so in my time), conceive that each has sufficient employment in attending to the moral and physical wants of his flock. The neighbourhood also affords many attractions to the antiquarian and the lover of wild or beautiful scenery. Several ancient castles, particularly the seven castles of Clonmines, are in its immediate vicinity; the Irish Herculaneum – the old town of Bannow – lies buried in the sands that skirt the coast; and within the distance of a few miles is 'Bag and Bun,' where Strongbow landed on first visiting the country, and where, according to the legend –

'Irelonde was loste and won.'

Allow me, then, to introduce you to the village of Bannow, and to the dwellers therein. I have endeavoured to describe them in the following Sketches; and I trust you will kindly and patiently look them over. They are drawn by a most inexperienced hand; but I have the hope, in which every young artist may be suffered to indulge – of having produced a striking outline, because the model is NATURE! In truth, they have been 'taken from the life;' and I have narrowly and frequently examined every original before I have ventured to give the portrait. I know that your friendly eye, though it may perceive, will not dwell upon, their faults. Of *your* criticism I entertain no dread, –

> 'For you have climbed the mountain top, there sit
> On the calm flourishing head of it;
> And, whilst, with wearied steps, we upwards go,
> See us, and clouds, below.'

But it is with a trembling hand, and a beating heart, that I lay these Volumes before the Public.

I may, however, state, that I was led to publish, rather by accident than design; for having written a few Sketches for a periodical work,* conducted by my husband, and finding that one of them had become too extended for its pages, I was tempted to 'write a Book.'

MY DEAR MISS MITFORD,

VERY AFFECTIONATELY YOUR'S, [sic]

ANNA MARIA HALL

Literary Quotations

In the *1st edn 1829*, Hall placed literary quotations on both the title page and the verso page before each individual sketch:

'Lilly O'Brien'

Title page:

> 'Collecting toys and trifles, for choice matters.'
> Milton

Milton here warns against the reader who, by extracting words out of context becomes 'deep-versed in books and shallow in himself'. See J. Milton, *Paradise Regained*, (London: n. p., 1796), pp. 321–30.

Verso, p. 90:

*   'The Spirit and Manners of the Age', in which three of the shorter Sketches were originally published.

Though he has ta'en a stranger bride,
My love will not depart.
                    Kennedy

These lines are from the poem 'Why Walk I by the Lonely Strand?' by W. Kennedy, *Fitful Fancies* (Edinburgh: Oliver & Boyd, 1827), pp. 166–7. The narrative of the poem bears similarity to that of the sketch 'Lilly O'Brien'. Carter Hall secured a situation for Kennedy as reporter on the *Morning Journal* and declared him 'a man of genius'. S. C. Hall, *A Book of Memories of Great Man and Women of the Age from Personal Acquaintance*, New Edition (London: Virtue, n. d.), p. 249.

'Kelly the Piper'

Verso p. 90:

Here are we met, all merry boys –
All merry boys I trow are we –
And mony a night we've merry been, and mony mae we hope to be!
                    Burns

Hall has altered Burns' poem/song, 'Willie Brew'd A Peck O' Maut', to render it more suitable to the sketch, substituting '*all* merry boys' for *three* merry boys' in two lines, Dr. Currie (ed.), *Poetical Works of Robert Burns, The Ayrshire Bard*, New Edition, (London: Jones & Co., 1826), p. 110.

'Captain Andy'

Verso, p. 130:

Joy has its limits – we but borrow
One hour of mirth, from months of sorrow.
                    Allan Cunningham

A. Cunningham (ed.), 'The Magic Bridle: A Tale', *The Anniversary: or, Poetry and Prose, for MDCCCXXIX* (London: J. Sharpe, 1829), p. 136.

'Independence'

Verso, p. 160:

The glorious privilege
Of being independent.
                    Burns

Lines from R. Burns, 'Epistle to a Young Friend, Mary __, 1786', ed. J. Lockhart, *The Works of Robert Burns: Containing his Life* (New York: Robinson & Franklin, 1839), p. 40, verse VII.

'Black Dennis'

Verso, p. 347:

> Remorse ... she ne'er forsakes us;
> A blood-hound staunch, she tracks our weary step. ...
> We hear her deep-mouthed bay, surmounting all
> Of wrath, and woe, and punishment that bide us.
>
> Coleridge

These lines are *not* by Coleridge, but an altered version of lines by Sir W. Scott, 'Epitaph on Jon o' Ye Girnell' (Francfort O. M: H. L. Brœnner, 1826), verse 8, ll. 1, 2, 7 and 8:

> Remorse – she ne'er forsakes us! –
> A bloodhound staunch – she tracks our rapid step
> We hear her deep-mouthed bay, announcing all
> Of wrath and woe and punishment that bides us.

However the error occurred, it would seem Hall chose the lines to emphasise the remorse of Black Dennis for his treacherous deeds.

'Old Frank'

Verso, p. 188:

> O! good old man: how well in thee appears
>
> The constant service of the antique world,
> When service sweat for duty, not for meed! –
> Thou art not for the fashion of these times.
>
> Shakespeare

These lines are taken from *As You Like It*, II.iii,57–60. Hall here matches Shakespeare's depiction of a faithful servant in the character Adam, with her own family's servant Frank, coachman to her family for forty-two years with whom she spent many childhood hours and whose actions saved her family during the Rebellion of 1798, as recounted in this sketch.

'The Bannow Postman'

Verso, p. 6:

> He comes, the herald of a noisy world.
> ... Messenger of grief
> Perhaps to thousands and of joy to some.
>
> Cowper

Hall's quotes from the poem by W. Cowper, 'The Winter Evening', *The Task: A Poem in Six Books by William Cowper* (Albany, NY: B. D. Packard, 1810), Book IV, ll. 5, 13–14. Had Hall included the following line by Cowper, 'to him indifferent whether grief or joy', the meaning in the quotation would have strayed from a pertinent comparison between Cowper's postman and the Bannow postman as the latter was in no way indifferent to the news be carried to the people of Bannow.

'Father Mike'

Verso, p. 58:

> Sorrow and guilt
> Like two old pilgrims guised, but quick and keen
> Of vision, evermore plod round the world,
> To spy out pleasant spots, and loving hearts,
> And never lack a villain's ready hand
> To work their purpose on them – hear ye me!
> > Mariner's Story

Hall used this quotation in her sketch 'The Last of the Line' in the *3rd revsd edn 1843*; n. 171.

'Master Ben'

Verso, p. 116:

> A village tutor! Say on, I pray you.

This quotation was not identified. It can only be assumed to be of Hall's own invention.

'Hospitality'

Verso, p. 136:

> Hospitality – no formality –
> – There you'll ever see.
> > Old Song

This quotation also appears in the sketch 'Hospitality', in the *3rd revsd edn 1843*; n. 216.

'Peter the Prophet'

Verso, p. 188:

> Light breezes will ruffle the flower sometimes.
> > Moore

This line is from T. Moore, *Lalla Rookh with Select Notes*, New Edition (Exeter: J. & B. Williams, 1837), p. 162, l. 2.

Errata

Errata were recorded on the flyleaf to the *1st edn 1829*:
> Errata in Vol. 11, page 194 for healthy, read heathy
> pages 201,202,203,206, for *father*, read uncle.
> Page 206, for *filthy* read jilty.

Footnotes

Hall used footnotes on a few occasions in this *1st edn 1829* and the importance of these lie in the evidence they provide as to her intended audience. The words footnoted would have been readily understood by an Irish reader, thus her intention to address an exoteric English readership is made plain.

32a gumption] original footnote for 'gumtion': sense, *1st edn 1829. See also* variants for *2nd edn 1831*

32b bocher] original footnote: beggar, *1st edn 1829. See also* variants for *2nd edn 1831, 2nd series 1831*

91a boat] original footnote: The boats used along the Irish Coasts are exceedingly large and deep in the keel; they are very seldom upset, *1st edn 1829*

219a praskeen] original footnote: apron, *1st edn 1829. See also* variants for *2nd edn 1831*

222a nataral] original footnote: fool, *1st edn 1829. See also variants for 2nd edn 1831*

224a minds] original footnote: knows, *1st edn 1829. See also* variants for *2nd edn 1831*

275a London Ladies] original footnote: potatoes held in high esteem, *1st edn 1829.* See also variants for *2nd edn 1831*

323a ruction] original footnote: rebellion, *1st edn 1829*

366a something fit for a mornin'] original footnote: a Dram, *1st edn 1829*

367a voster] original footnote: Voster's arithmetic, *1st edn 1829. See also* variants for *2nd edn 1831*

367b snack] original footnote: A Luncheon, *1st edn 1829. See also* variants for *2nd edn 1831*

383a bresnaugh] original footnote: a Faggott, *1st edn 1829*

372a canted] original footnote: sold, *1st edn 1829. See also* variants for *2nd edn 1831*

Omitted Text

A section of text and some verses by Allan Cunningham from the *1st edn 1829* have been omitted from the *3rd revsd edn 1843*:

329a such great friends] in the *1st edn 1829*, this continued:
> An only child has generally much of its own way, and a country child has very different enjoyments from one of the town. Allan Cunningham says – and who but him could say it so sweetly –
>
> 'Child of the country! on the lawn
> I see thee like the bounding fawn;
> Blithe as the bird which tries its wing,
> The first time on the winds of spring;
> Bright as the sun, when from the cloud

He comes as cocks are crowing loud;
Now running, shouting, mid sun beams,
Now groping trouts in lucid streams;
Now spinning like a mill-wheel round,
Now hunting echo's empty sound,
Now climbing up some old tall tree,
For climbing sake, 'tis sweet to thee,
Or share with thee thy venturous throne.'

333a appointed place] in the *1st edn 1829*, this continued:
   He had not been sitting there long before a blast of wind came by him and he heard a
   voice singing sweetly these words: –

'I lie in the meadow so green
On a spot where the rushes are growing,
Where the footstep of man hath not been,
For the place where I dwell lies between
Two streams that have never ceased flowing.'

The voice ceased but James Deasy knew its sound well, and knew that no other but his
wife could address him in such sweet accents. In a few minutes another blast of wind
rushed by him, and the same voice continued, –

'To-morrow a bride will pass near
The green island, where they have placed me,
Meet her and her twin without fear;
This last is the one you love dear,
I am free, when my love has embraced me.'

James Deasy was struck dumb but he knew there must be something in this mysterious
warning; while he sate musing on the words, he heard the same voice in the distance say, –

'I list their summons e'en now,
O save me, or lose me for ever;
I have told thee the when and the how,
But sign thee the cross on my brow,
And keep me to part again – never.'

Well the morrow came, and, to be sure, James Deasy was on the road to the green island;
a place well known all over the country, as the pet of the fairies.'

Mrs S. C. Hall, *Sketches of Irish Character*, 2nd edn, 2 vols
(London: F. Westley and A. H. Davis, 1831)

Advertisement

The *2nd edn 1831* contains an 'Advertisement to the Second Edition':

ADVERTISEMENT
TO THE SECOND EDITION

The author of the following 'Sketches' cannot neglect the opportunity of expressing her grateful sense of the manner in which her first work has been received
by the public.

Her success has far exceeded her most sanguine expectations. The hazardous,
and sometimes fatal, attempt at authorship has, in her case, been followed by no
feeling of regret, except that her task was not better performed – a feeling which,
she trusts, will incite to renewed and more determined exertion to deserve the
support of those by whose indulgent kindness she has been encouraged.

The only material addition to this volume is an article* from the pen of the
author's valued and esteemed friend, Dr. Walsh, whose accurate description of
the parish of Bannow forms so excellent an auxiliary to her slight Sketches that
she feels it unnecessary to apologise for its introduction.

Additional Article

Also included was an article on Bannow written by the Halls' friend, Rev. Robert
Walsh, author, diplomat and antiquarian. Robert Walsh (1772–1852) was born
in Waterford, graduated from Trinity College Dublin, and became Church of
Ireland curate at Finglas where his interest in archaeology led him to excavate
the Cross of Nethercross, buried since Cromwell's time. There followed spells
as chaplain to the British Embassy at St. Petersburg and Constantinople in
1829. He was appointed to the British Embassy in Rio de Janeiro, Brazil; having qualified as a doctor, he returned to Ireland. Carter Hall claims friendship
with '*four* generations' of the family of Walsh who were all deeply implicated in
colonial affairs and Robert's interest in matters archaeological in Ireland is con-
sonant with the antiquarian interests taken up by many of the Anglo-Irish of this
period. Robert Walsh visited Wexford in the summer of 1826 and his article is
based upon this visit. The reason that Rev. Walsh was intrigued by the possibility
of the existence of the old town of Bannow could be seen as part of a general passion among the Anglo-Irish for antiquarian pursuits. There was an eager market
for the reports by antiquarians such as Walsh. Material was constantly needed
to fill the hungry maw of the periodicals where a demand had been created and
items of Irish interest were lapped up by an English audience anxious to see itself

---

*   Originally published in 'The Amulet'.

more clearly defined in relation to its perplexing colony. Interest flourished in old tales, songs, manuscripts and ruins and this could be attributed to an attempt to by-pass recent political and religious differences within Ireland and between England and Ireland; to revert to a time when a common history could be established. The resulting 'history' would then be accessible to all persuasions and render Ireland fit to take its place as a modern state and part of the Union, as this 'new' history could prove a vehicle for unity across the religious and political spectrum. Perhaps this was an essential move by a class fearful of being banished from their place. The comparison of Bannow with Herculaneum and naming of his article 'The Irish Herculaneum' associated the village with ancient Roman civilization, thus giving Ireland not only a national identity but one that linked it to ancient civilization. Such antiquarian pursuits were all part of a 'civilising offensive' and Walsh was just one among the 'Anglo-Irish gentlemen who investigated the nation's past in a public-spirited effort to improve the state of general knowledge and enhance the nation's standing by elucidating its ancient origins'. (J. Leerssen, *Remembrance and Imagination: Patterns in the Historical and Literary Representation of Ireland in the Nineteenth Century* in Critical Conditions: Field Day Essays and Monographs, 4 (Cork: Cork University Press, 1996), p. 71) Walsh's opinion that the old town of Bannow was inundated in similar manner to Vesuvius in AD 70 have since been refuted by several writers. C. J. Tuomey pointed to Walsh as an example of the kind of antiquarian who wrote in 'an ... exaggerated strain ... [a] highly-wrought specimen of romance' (Anon., 'The Bay and Town of Bannow', *Transactions of the Kilkenny Archaeological Society for the Year 1849, 1850* 5 vols (Dublin: pr. by John O'Daly, 1853), vol. 1, pp. 194–210, on , p. 198). It seems that although an old town did exist, a less romantic explanation of the change that led to its disappearance is that

> in past times a safe harbour [inundation] was brought about in two ways: firstly by the sinking of the land or the rising of the sea level, and, secondly, by the gradual accumulation of sand and gravel deposited by wind and tide within the harbour
> (Butler, *A Parish and its People*, p. 39).

The presence of this article by Rev. Walsh raises the question as to why Hall chose to include it in the *2nd edn 1831*. Rev. Walsh was a relatively well-respected scholar and experienced traveller to exotic regions of the world and his interest in history and archaeology wide-ranging. To have the imprimatur of his theories on the ancient history of Bannow would bestow a certain historical gravitas on Hall's fictional sketches. Importantly, her aim was to focus on the region itself and this article fixes the microscope firmly on Bannow, the place and its history. Presumably, if one accepted Dr Walsh's theories and this version of the history of Bannow as accurate, the same complement would be extended to the sketches, and truth to reality was an important attribute Hall wished to establish with her English readership. Walsh's article also sits well with an antiquarian view which tended to view the past as a 'treasure house of facts and curiosities' rather than assume a historical perspective which would take account of events, disruption and change (See J. Leerssen, *Remembrance and Imagination: Patterns in the Historical and Literary Representation of Ireland in the Nineteenth Century*, in Critical Conditions: Field Day Essays and Monographs, 4 (Cork: Cork University Press, 1996), p. 68). Loeber and Loeber remind us that there are numerous examples of claims to 'factual representations of Irish individuals, life circumstances and Irish settings [which] can be found in a multitude of Irish works of fiction in the nineteenth century' which are not to be taken at face value (See R. Loeber and M. Loeber, *A Guide to Irish Fiction 1650–1900* (Dublin: Four Courts Press), pp. xcviii).

In the sketch 'Lilly O'Brien', Hall appears to lampoon the type of antiquarian the Rev. Walsh exemplifies. The subject of controversy and 'a disputed matter in the neighbourhood' is Mrs Cassidy's Quern':

> Mrs Cassidy will have it that a quern* grinds wheat better than a mill, and produces finer flour; she, therefore, abuses those both of wind and water, and persists in grinding her own corn, as well as in making her own bread. By the bye, this very quern was in great danger some time ago, when an antiquary, who had hunted hill and dale seeking for Danish or Roman relics ... pounced upon it, declared it was a stone bowl of great antiquity, and that Mrs. Cassidy's maiden name, 'Maura O'Brien,' carved on it in Irish characters, proved it to have been used, either by Dane or Roman, in some religious ceremony, or Bacchanalian rite, I cannot take it on myself to say which: – but this I know, that the old gentleman was obstinate; had been accustomed to give large sums for ugly things of every description and thought that Mrs. Cassidy could be induced to yield up her favourite, for three guineas
>
> *   'A kind of hand-mill, still patronized by 'the ancient Irish'
>
> (*2nd edn 1831*, p. 24)

Mrs Cassidy may not be able to tell her Dane from her Roman, but she can spot a bogus provenance when it is bestowed. Leerssen notes 'the tendency to view alien/foreign culture as reflecting older periods in human history', and points out that 'antiquarians had investigated the Irish past and created an image of Gaelic Ireland that was inherently characterised by its pastness; the most genuine and least adulterated form of Gaelic culture was that of the past, before the contamination of the English presence in Ireland (see J. Leerssen, *Remembrance and Imagination: Patterns in the Historical and Literary Representation of Ireland in the Nineteenth Century*, in Critical Conditions: Field Day Essays and Monographs, 4 (Cork: Cork University Press, 1996), p. 49). Although Hall seems to mock antiquarianism here, her inclusion of Rev. Walsh's article was intended to lend historical authenticity and gravitas to her sketches. She also consigns her character Mrs Cassidy to a timeless past. Lilly's aunt 'abuses all mills, both of wind and water and persists in grinding her own corn' with the quern (*2nd edn 1831*, p. 24).

THE FIRST INVASION OF IRELAND,
WITH SOME ACCOUNT OF
'THE IRISH HERCULANEUM.'*

BY THE REV. ROBERT WALSH, LL. D., M. R. I. A.

In the summer of 1826, I paid a visit to the county of Wexford, and took up my residence at the house of William Merchant, Esq., of Kiltra, in the parish of Bannow, which Mrs. Hall has so happily illustrated in her 'Sketches of Irish Character.' As many circumstances render it an object of curiosity, a few local details will be interesting.

Between the harbours of Wexford and Waterford is a tract of fertile land, containing about sixty square miles, called the Baronies of Forth and Bargie. The appellations are significant – Bar is fruitful, Forth is plenty, and Geo the sea;† the names therefore indicate exactly the character of the place, a fertile and plentiful tract on the sea coast. Behind it runs a ridge of mountains, and before it is the sea. So that it is in some measure insulated, and retains much of the primeval and original character of a place cut off from free intercourse with the rest of the country. It moreover lies directly opposite Cardiganshire in Wales; and certain promontories, projecting to the east, approach so near to the contiguous coast as to invite the inhabitants of the other side to come over and visit it. From the earliest periods, therefore, long before the Anglo-Norman invasion, a free intercourse had taken place between the two principalities, and many Irish families settled in Wales, and many Welsh in Ireland. The latter were so numerous, that a large district in the county of Wexford is called Scarla Walsh; and there is a long tract of high land in the neighbouring county of Kilkenny called the Welsh mountains, from the number of families of this name and nation which occupied them, where at this day they form a sept or clan; and as the colonization was gradually effected, by free consent and friendly intercourse, the name of Walsh is held in somewhat more esteem by the peasantry of the country than they attach to others which are not strictly native, because it is not connected with those traditions of rapine and blood which generally distinguished the later foreign settlers during the troubles in Ireland. The language of Wales was also Celtic, and spoken by both people in common; even at this day they are the same, and differ only in some dialectic peculiarities.

In the year 1169, however, this friendly intercourse was interrupted, and the first hostile foot from Wales pressed the soil of Ireland. The occasion was not very creditable to the morality of the invaders. The Normans, having conquered England, were now determined to pass over to Ireland, and only waited for a pre-

---

*   Published in 'The Amulet' for 1830
†   Valencey in Transactions R. I. Academy.

text to effect their purpose. This was soon afforded. Dermod Macmorrogh, the king of Leinster, had looked with a profligate eye on the wife of his neighbour, and seduced her to abandon her husband, and take up her residence in his Castle of Ferns. The circumstance is thus detailed by Maurice Regan.*

'She was a fair and lovely lady, entirely beloved by Dermod. He, by letters and messengers, pursued her love with such fervency, that she sent him word she was ready to obey and yield to his will, and appointed time and place where he should find her. Dermod assembled his lords, entered Leitrim, found the lady, took her away, and returned with joy to Ferns. O'Rourke, full of affliction and wounded pride, addressed himself to O'Connor, king of Connaught, complaining of the wrong and scorn done him by the king of Leinster, and imploring his aid to avenge so great an outrage. O'Connor, moved with honour and compassion, promised him his succour.'

The Irish, it appears, held at this time in high respect the sacred obligation of marriage; for a general spirit of indignation was felt and expressed all over the country, particularly by his own subjects, and Dermod was compelled to abandon his throne. In this distress he applied to Henry II. and the Normans who had recently conquered England, and they readily, and without scruple, undertook to reinstate the adulterer. From this *causa teterrima belli,* the lady has been called the 'Irish Helen.' The Greeks, however, proceeded to punish and not to protect the seducer of their frail beauty.

In the month of May, 1169, Robert Fitzstephen, then Governor of Cardigan Castle, in Wales, accompanied by Harvey de Monte Marisco, collected a force of 30 knights, 60 esquires, and 300 archers, and embarking in two ships, called Bagg and Bunn, according to the tradition of the country, they ran for the nearest headland, and disembarked at a point called at this day Baganbun, from the names of the vessels which brought them over. They were next day joined by Prendergast, with 10 knights, and 200 archers, making in all an army of 600 men. Dermond [*sic*: Dermod] had remained secreted in his Castle of Ferns, waiting the arrival of the strangers; they therefore apprised him of their coming, and in the meantime fortified themselves on the promontory till some expected reinforcements, which

---

* When the Anglo-Normans landed, Regan was secretary to Dermod, and was an actor in, and eye-witness of, the events of the invasion. His work is exceedingly valuable as a document, and curious as a composition. It was written, originally, in Irish, but translated into French verse, by some Norman of his acquaintance. His details are graphic, and his heroes make speeches, so that you become acquainted with events and persons, as with those described by Homer. The cause assigned for the Norman invasion, the abduction of a man's wife, is treated very lightly by the English historians, from Cambrensis down to Hume, Harris says, 'The defection of the nobility could never be brought about, merely from a motive of gallantry with the wife of another prince!' The Irish historians thought otherwise, Regan, with all his partiality for his master and his allies, tells the circumstance like a man of feeling and principle.

he promised to send, should arrive, to assist and guide them. In a short time he was able to dispatch his natural son Donald, with 500 horse; and with this reinforcement they set out from their position to penetrate into the interior of the country. Their direct road would have been through the parish of Bannow, which lay opposite to them; but as they had two deep and rapid channels of the sea to cross, at the mouth of the bay, they were obliged to proceed round the other extremity of it. In their way they were opposed by some Irish, collected hastily at Feathard. Here the first encounter took place between the Anglo-Normans and the Irish; and it is still called by the peasants 'battles-town,' in commemoration of the circumstance. It is further added, by the tradition of the country, that Feathard was a name given to the town built on the spot by the conqueror, who called it 'Fought-hard,' which was, in process of time, corrupted into Feathard.

From hence, ascending the river, which falls into Bannow Bay, he passed through Goffe's Bridge, and so to the town of Wexford. Wexford was originally built by the piratical Danes at a very early period, and called by them 'West, or Wes-fiord,' the western bay. It was rudely fortified, but could not resist the invaders, now reinforced by all Macmorrogh's adherents. It was therefore taken, and Dermod made it a present to Fitzstephen and Fitzgerald, as a reward for their services. Fitzstephen built on the river, not far from it, a castle, on the promontory of a lime-stone rock, and so erected the first Norman fortification ever built in Ireland. This still stands, commanding the navigation of the Slaney, and is a very curious and conspicuous object. It so struck a Catholic barrister, in his way to the assizes of Wexford, that he afterwards declared, as is reported, in a speech at the Association, that 'it ought to be pulled down as a revolting object of Ireland's first degradation.'

This expedition was followed by that of Strongbow, Earl of Chepstow, who has gained the reputation of a conquest which had been achieved by his predecessor, as Americus Vesputius defrauded Columbus of his title to America. Strongbow passed the promontory of Baganbun, and proceeded up the contiguous harbour of Waterford. Waterford was also built by the Danes, and was a place of some strength and trade. It was called by them 'Vader Fiord,' the Father's Harbour, and dedicated to Woden, the Father of Scandinavian deities, of which the present name Waterford is an absurd corruption. On one side of Strongbow stood a tower, erected by the Danes on the Wexford shore; on the other, a church, built by the Irish, on the Waterford. It was necessary to land, but he hesitated on which shore he should disembark to march to Waterford. He enquired the names of the places he saw, and he was informed one was the tower of Hook, and the other the church of Crook. 'Then,' said he, 'shall we advance and take the town by Hook or by Crook?' And hence originated a proverb now in common use. Strongbow took Waterford, where his grim statue, in blue limestone, stands at this day in the front of the Ring Tower, close beside the river. He was followed by Henry II. with a large army, and so the warriors obtained the same footing in Ireland as they had done in England, though it took them a much longer time afterwards to establish it. Henry adopted the example of Dermod; he made Dublin a present to his good citizens of Bristol, and the original of this cool and extraordinary gift of the capital of a kingdom to the traders of a commercial town is still extant in the Record Office of the castle of Dublin.

The prime object of my curiosity, on entering this historic ground, was to visit the spot where the first Norman foot had pressed the shore. It was a conspicuous point from my friend's house, at the extremity of a neck of land; the annexed sketch points out the locality.

I embarked in a small boat, and crossed the narrow but rapid Frith which had stopped Fitzstephen's army. From hence I walked along the sand-hills to the romantic and solitary village of Feathard, where there was no inn; but a man from whom I enquired, directed me to a private house. Here the kind landlady set before me a plentiful breakfast of tea, fish, and eggs, and, what I valued still more, a folio of Irish antiquities, which it was her delight to study. From her I obtained all the directions I wanted, and then proceeded to the object of my search. I enquired, when near the place, from a peasant who was digging potatoes, the nearest path to it. He immediately threw down his spade, and, in the true spirit of Irish courtesy to a stranger, begged to 'go with my honour if agreeable, to shew me the ins and outs of it.' He was full of local information, and I was well pleased to have him for a companion.

The whole headland called Baganbun consists of about thirty acres. It forms a bold projection towards the Welsh coast, and is the only one near Wexford, the shore which extends from it to Carnsore point, near that town, being a flat sand, not safe for shipping to approach. On the side of the greater promontory is a lesser, running from it at right angles, and stretching to the east, about two hundred yards long, and seventy broad; presenting inaccessible cliffs except as its extreme point where it is easily ascended. Outside this is a large, high, insulated rock, which forms a break-water to the surf on the point, and from this several smaller stretch to the shore, just appearing above water, and affording a kind of causeway. Here it was Fitzstephen ran in and moored his ships, protected from the surf by the insular rock, and availing himself of the low ridge to reach the land. The distance of the last rock to the point is considerably wider than the rest, but Fitzstephen, with his heavy armour, sprung across it, and it is called at this day, 'Fitzstephen's Stride.' My companion tried to follow his example, without his encumbrance, and fell into the sea.

Ascending from hence to the esplanade on the summit, he pitched his tent and established his head-quarters. In the middle of the esplanade is still to be seen an oblong hollow space, like the foundation of a house, and as the surface of the soil was never disturbed in this place since the period of his landing, it seems not improbable that such a trace would not be obliterated, and that the use assigned to it by tradition is the true one. His next care was to fortify his situation, to secure him from attack while waiting for Macmorrogh's promised reinforcements; and these hasty fortifications yet remain, evincing that the Normans had attained to no small science in the art of defensive war. On the isthmus which connects the lesser peninsula with the greater, a deep fosse, about seventy yards long, extends from side to side; this was bounded on each edge by high mounds of earth, and in the centre covered by a half-moon bastion, twenty yards in circumference. On each side of the bastion, through the fosse, were the approaches to his camp, by two passages; and a mound of earth connected the bastion with the esplanade. Centinels placed in this half-moon entirely commanded the approaches, and were themselves protected by a rampart which rose around them, and overlooked all the ground in the vicinity. Beyond this, on the neck of the greater promontory, he also sunk a fosse, much more profound and extensive, stretching across the whole breadth, for the space of two hundred and fifty yards. This formed a deep and wide covered way, and was lined with a high mound on either side; that on the outside being defended by another deep fosse. All these remains are very distinct and perfect at the present day, changed only by the growth of vegetable matter, rendering the fosse somewhat more shallow, and the mound less elevated.

But a discovery was made a short time ago, connected with this encampment, which adds considerably to the interest it excites. About five years before my visit, some labourers were throwing up a low hedge round the cliffs to prevent the sheep which graze there from falling over. On turning up the soil, they discovered, about one foot below the surface, the remains of fires at regular intervals on the edge of the precipices. These were supposed to be the watch-fires of the Videttes, which were stationed round the encampment. Some of the freestone flags on which they were made were also found; and as there is no such stone in this part of the country, they must have been brought for that purpose by the strangers. Sundry pieces of bones of sheep and oxen, consumed by the army, were strewed round the fires, particularly cows' teeth, the enamel of which remained perfect, though the osseous parts were decayed: and on the whole promontory fragments of rings and spears were picked up wherever the soil was disturbed. Curious to see some of these remains, I requested my companion to get a shovel and dig for me; he did not require to be asked a second time, but ran off and soon came back with a spade, and began to dig with all his heart, where the first had been discovered; he soon upturned pieces of charcoal and parts of burnt bones, which I brought away with me as memorandums of the first fires ever lighted by the Anglo-Normans on the shores of Ireland.*

---

* Holingshed, in his notes on Geraldus Cambrensis, says of this place, following the traditions of the country, 'There were certain monuments made in memorie thereof, and were named the Banna and the Boenne, which were the names (as common fame is) of the

It is now nearly seven hundred years since that event, and every thing connected with it on this spot is in singular preservation. It is so remote as to be entirely out of the way of intercourse with other places, and seldom trampled on by human feet. The soil, tradition says, was never turned up, and the surface continues at this day as it was then left by the Normans, – it is, and has always been, a sheep-walk. The remains also consist of the most undecaying materials; charred wood and bone are nearly imperishable. The circumstances connected with it are perhaps the most interesting in the history of our country; the first landing of the strangers in this place was of deep importance to England, and still deeper to Ireland. 'Baganbun, where Ireland has lost and won,' is the universal expression of the people of the country, and they consider it an occult and prophetic saying. My companion, when we were leaving the place, asked me, if I had ever heard 'the ould saying about it.' I replied 'yes; but I do not understand how Ireland has won on this spot.' 'Oh!' said he, 'that's to come, they say; sure didn't the boys in the ruction want to fight it out here, entirely?' It is certainly affirmed, that some of the leaders in the Wexford Insurrection in 1798, wished to avail themselves of the feeling it excited. They actually deliberated on retiring to this spot, and bringing on a decisive engagement here, with this powerful prestige strongly impressed on the minds of their followers.

My next visit was to the town of Bannow, which is justly denominated the 'Irish Herculaneum.'

As this was in the more immediate vicinity of his house, my kind host accompanied me. We proceeded to the mouth of the harbour, and entered over a stile into a large enclosure, having the remains of a dilapidated church in the centre. The ground was a low eminence of sand, partly covered with a scanty vegetation, on which some sheep and goats were feeding. It was every where undulated with hillocks, between which were long straight depressions, having an appearance more formal and regular than is usually seen among sand hills. Rising from these was a square mass of hollow masonry, about seven feet high, which, with the exception of the ruined church walls, was the only appearance of the work of man visible around us. After looking about here for some time, I proposed to my friend to proceed to the town of Bannow; when he astonished me by saying, 'You are now in the high-street in the midst of it' In effect so I was. The sands of the shore had risen and swallowed it up as effectually as the ashes and lava of Mount Vesuvius could have done. The hillocks were the houses, the straight depressions were the streets, the dilapidated walls half covered were the high par-

---

two greatest ships in which the English arrived.' There are now no monuments on this spot, except the very striking ones of the encampment. It is evident, however, that the present name of the place, *Baganbun*, has the same origin as that assigned by Holingshed – a corruption of Banna and Boenne.

ish church, and the square tube of masonry was the massive chimney of the town house peeping above the soil, while the rest of the edifice was buried under it.

On more closely inspecting these remains, it was easy to trace the plan of the town, which consisted of several wide streets, crossing one another, and extending generally eighty or a hundred yards before the traces were lost. One of them ran down to the sea at the mouth of the harbour; we followed its traces, and there found what appeared to have been a fine quay at the edge of the water, the remains of which were nearly two hundred yards in length; and higher up was the foundation of a very extensive edifice, evidently some public building. As it was clear that here had existed a large and important town, it was greatly my wish to excavate some part of it in search of antiquities; and a gentleman of the vicinity, who seemed as zealous as myself, promised to assist me with fifty men. He did not keep his word, however, and I made only such discoveries as were possible by my own personal exertions. I cut across one of the hollow ways, and ascertained it was paved beneath the soil, and so had been a street. I dug into one of the mounds, and came to the foundations of walls of masonry, and so was convinced they had been houses. I visited the church, and saw it was a very ancient structure. The windows were not the pointed Gothic, such as were subsequently introduced by the Normans; but Saxon, similar to those of Cormac's chapel, at Cashel, and in that style of architecture known to have existed in Ireland long before the Invasion. I examined the inside, and found it filled with sculptured ornaments, as remarkable for their antiquity as their beauty. Among them was a stone coffin or kistvaen, in the cavity of which was a receptacle for the head and shoulders of the man. Beside it was a baptismal font, of very antique sculpture in relief, – it was that alluded to by Mrs. Hall in her 'Sketches.' In fact, the whole appearance of the place – the impression that we were standing over a once populous city, which yet remained almost entire, with all its busy inhabitants, it might be, buried under our feet, gave to its present silence and solitude an interest greater, perhaps, than is attached to any other remains in the United Kingdoms.

To inquire into its history, and ascertain what was known of its former state, was my next care. It appears to have existed as a place of some note at the time of the Invasion, as it is mentioned both by native and foreign historians.* Sir James Ware says, the name 'Bannow' signifies 'auspicious,' and it induced the Anglo-Normans to land in its vicinity, as a good omen of success. In the Irish Annals of Ennisfallen, the term made use of literally means 'the bay of the pig,' from the multitude of these animals reared there by the Irish, a peculiarity for which the neighbouring county is still distinguished, where they are attended with the greatest care, and increase to an enormous size. It was situated at the mouth of a large inlet of the sea in the barony of Bargie, about twenty-four miles S. of

---

*   Among the native historians who mention it is Maurice Regan; he calls it Bann.

West or [*sic*: of] Wexford. The bay was formerly entered by two deep channels, as appears by a map in the Down Survey in the Record Office, Dublin; and from its favourable situation for trade attained much prosperity. From the quit-rent rolls which I examined at Wexford, it contained among others the following streets, viz.: –

High-street, Weaver-street, St. George-street, Upper-street, St. Toolock's-street, St. Mary's-street, St. Ivory-street, Lady-street, Little-street, &c.

Fair slated houses, horse-mills, gardens, and other indications of a prosperous place, are also mentioned as paying quit-rent.

It had, moreover, a royal charter of incorporation, and sent two members to the Irish Parliament, who were elected by the burgesses or citizens of the town. This last indication of its prosperity continued up to the time of the Union. My friend remembered himself when notice for the election was issued. It was posted on the solitary chimney, as the only representation of the houses of the town. The burgesses were supposed to assemble round it; the members were put into nomination by Lord Ely, and so the forms of election were regularly gone through, and for a series of years two representatives were returned to Parliament from one chimney.

It is not known at what precise time the submersion of this city by the sands took place, but the process by which it was destroyed is still going on in its vicinity. Before it lies a very extensive tract of fine sand, which is continually shifting and changing its place and form. I watched its progress as it rose in little columns, like the sand pillars of African deserts on a small scale. It was driven about by the slightest winds in currents and eddies; wherever it met an obstruction, it formed round it as a nucleus, and in the course of a few hours materially altered the appearance of any particular spot. Not only the town, but the whole harbour, has undergone an extraordinary mutation from this cause. So late as the period of the Down Survey, in 1657, in the map of this district which I examined, the Island of Slade lay opposite to the site of the town, separated from it by a broad channel; and it appears from other authorities that directions were given to mariners how to steer up this channel, so as to clear some rocks which lay in the middle of it. There is now *no* Island of Slade, or *no* navigable channel; the whole was filled up by that process which covered the city: the dangerous rocks are high and dry at a considerable distance inland, and a firm road, over which I passed in a carriage, with several heavy carts, now runs across the harbor –

Puppibus illa prius, patulis nunc hospita plaustris.

The Bay of Bannow abounds with sea fowl, and among them is one which has been the occasion of very extraordinary opinions. It is a bird resembling a wild goose, and is found in abundance in this bay, and also in that of Wexford. It feeds on the tuberous roots of an aquatic grass, which is full of saccharine juice;

and instead of the rank taste of other sea fowl, which feed partly on fish, this bird acquires from its aliment a delicate flavour which renders it highly prized. But the circumstance which long made it an object of the highest curiosity, was an idea that it was not produced in the usual way, from the egg of a similar parent, but that it was the preternatural production of a shell-fish, called a barnacle. This singular absurdity is not to be charged to the Irish; it was first published to the world by Geraldus Cambrensis, who accompanied the early invaders, and saw the bird in this place. It was received with avidity in England, and set down among other *specioso miracula* of the new and barbarous country, where every thing was wild and monstrous. The shell supposed to produce it is frequently found on this coast, adhering to logs of wood and other substances which had remained long in the sea-water; it is attached by a fleshy membrane at one end, and from the other issues a fibrous beard which curls round the shell, and has a distant resemblance to the feathers of a fowl; and on this circumstance the story was founded. So late as the time of Gerard the botanist, this was firmly believed by the naturalists in England. In a folio edition of Gerard's works, in my possession, there is a long account of this prodigious birth, which he prefaces by saying, 'What mine eyes have seen, and mine hands have touched, that I will declare;' and he accompanies his description with a plate, representing one of these birds hanging by its head to a barnacle-shell, as just excluded from it, and dropping into the sea. This fishy origin of the bird rendered it also an object of ecclesiastical controversy. It was disputed with much warmth in England, before the Reformation, that this Irish bird, having a fish for its parent, was not properly flesh, and so it might be eaten with perfect propriety on fast-days; and hence this delicious meat was an allowed luxury, in which many worthy ecclesiastics conscientiously indulged in Lent. One learned man made a syllogism to defend his practice: 'Whatever is naturally born of flesh is flesh, but this bird has no such origin, therefore it is not flesh.' Another retorted on him by the following ingenious position, 'If a man,' said he, 'were disposed to eat part of Adam's thigh, he would not be justified, I imagine, because Adam was not born from a parent of flesh.'* So universal, however, was this belief in the extraordinary origin of this bird, that its supposed parent, the shell-fish, is called by conchologists at this day, *lepas ansifera*, 'the goose-bearing lepas.'

The whole of the district of Bannow, and the neighbouring ones, are covered over with castles, built by the strangers to secure themselves against the attempts of the natives to recover their forfeited land. In the village of Clomines [*sic*: Clonmines],

---

*   Quicquid est caro ex carne commui naturæ cursu gignitur,
Ast talem ortum Bernaculæ non habent
Non sunt igitur Bcrnaculæ carnes.
Stanihurst.
Si quis enim ex primo parentis, carnei quidem licet de carne non nati, femore comedisset, eum a carnium esu non immunem arbitrarer.
Cambrensis.

on the shores of the bay, are seven castles clustered together, forming a very romantic picture.* Many farm-houses are built against the remains of these fortresses of former times, which are converted by the farmers into stables and out-offices. The general appearance, however, of the habitations of the peasantry is singularly neat and comfortable, and indicate a prosperity far exceeding that of any other part of Ireland, with the exception of the county Down, round Belfast; and, as in that county, no beggars are permitted to resort there.

The soil is exceedingly rich, and justifies its Irish appellation. Large tracts of marl are found, but not used; and the ground produces a succession of crops without exhaustion, though never suffered to lie fallow. The only manure is occasionally sea-wrack. The great and favourite crop of the peasantry is beans, so little cultivated in other parts of Ireland. I passed through when they were in flower, and the rich perfume which loaded the air from so extensive a surface of blossoms was almost too strong to endure, and threatened to kill us 'with aromatic pain.' On these blossoms an immense abundance of bees feed, and every farmer has a number of hives in his garden. All the honey consumed in Dublin comes from this neighbourhood. It is brought in great quantities, and is of an excellent quality.

The air is as mild and salubrious as the soil is fertile. Cambrensis spoke of it, in his time, in the highest terms. 'So great,' said he, 'is its clemency, that here is neither the infecting cloud, nor the pestiferous gale, nor the tainting atmosphere. The island needs no physician; you meet no sickly men except the dying; there is no interval between uninterrupted health and parting life.'† In a long series of centuries it has not deteriorated, and the longevity of the inhabitants is particularly remarkable. In Bannow church-yard is the tomb of a man of the name of French, who died at the age of 144. I enquired into the truth of this extraordinary statement, and found it was correctly given, and borne out by the records of his family. Some persons told me they had seen his son, who was likely to exceed his father in length of years. He was killed by accident at the age of 100, and though not in the prime of life at the time, was certainly in the vigour of health.

Among the customs of the people, those of marriage are somewhat peculiar. The friends bring a provision of food of all kinds along with them; the bride sits veiled at a table, unless called out to dance, when one of her bride-maids supplies

---

*　This place was formerly celebrated for its *silver mines*, which were worked before the invasion, and some remains of the shafts may be seen at this day. The *gold mines* of the neighbouring county (Wicklow) were at first supposed to be a recent discovery: but there is evidence that they also were known and worked at a remote period.

†　Aeris tanta elementia ut nec nebula inficiens, nec spiritus hic pestilens, nec aura corrumpens. Medicorum opera parum indiget. Morbidos etiam homines prætor moribundos paucos invenies. Inter sanitatem continuam mortemque supremam nihil fere medium. – Cap. 9. Cambrensis was nominated to the see of Ferus [*sic*: Ferns], by Prince John: Bannow is one of the parishes of this diocese. His description is generally of the salubrity of Ireland, but particularly applies to this place, with which he was best acquainted.

her place; the feasting and dancing are kept up all night, and concluded by cutting an apple into small pieces, and throwing it among the crowd. This practice is not Irish, and was probably introduced by the strangers.

Among their amusements, the 'pathern' is perhaps one of the greatest favourites. It is, in fact, a religious ceremony, paying homage to the 'patron' saint of some particular well or holy spot, and usually commences with prayers, but always ends with dancing, and often with fighting. The most celebrated of these spots is the 'Lady's Island,' between Wexford and Bannow, of which the Virgin Mary is the patron. When I paid it a visit, a number of persons were in procession on their knees. They had commenced at the peninsula which connects it with the main, and were bound to proceed in that posture round the shore, till they arrived at a small shrine, in which was an image of the Virgin, which they were then allowed to kiss. This practice was so universal that the nose and part of the face of the marble bust were actually kissed away.

Notwithstanding the high interest that on many accounts attaches to this district, it is but little known or visited. With the exception of a brief and imperfect notice in the Transactions of the Royal Irish Academy for 1787, by the late General Valancey – who gave more importance to words than things – and copies of it by others, I do not remember to have seen any account of it. Annexed to Valancey's paper, is a vocabulary of words then in use among the people; among them are some which are found in Chaucer, Shakspeare, and Ben Jonson, but are now obsolete in England. They were the phraseology of English settlers at different times, and continued to be spoken in this secluded place, when their use elsewhere had passed away.

Omitted Text

The following text from the *3rd revsd edn* 1843 is omitted from the *2nd edn 1831*:

42a, and the good and kind and generous young lady left them to their 'own company' which it is scarcely necessary for me to say, was not very doleful or wretched; for although the heart of one of the party was too full for words, ample amends was made for her silence by the ever talkative Peggy.] *2nd edn 1831 omit*

42b, O! what a happy group of humble people were assembled in that gay drawing-room! Mrs Cassidy – the desire of her heart gratified, the hope of years realised, the fervent and continual prayer answered – Mrs Cassidy was beyond doubt, the happiest of them all, as she sat with her cheerful grateful face, contemplating her 'two children'.] *2nd edn 1831 omit*

43a, A single tear glistened on his cheek as he pronounced the words that made them man and wife: – it was a tear of which a seraph might not have been ashamed.] *2nd edn 1831 omit*

43b, seeking to abstract herself from household cares and blessings, only that she may render grateful homage to her Creator – sits after evening vespers, with clasped hands and downcast eyes her national hood shading, but not obscuring, the beauty of her pensive face, near yonder cottage, that looks so joyously in the setting sun] *2nd edn 1831 omit*

Additional Notes

Hall's early sketches were highly autobiographical and the notes she added to the *2nd edn 1831* testify to the indelible impression made on her by the Bannow people on whom she based her characters. In this regard, it is interesting to note Hall's development from attempting to directly represent people from the life in her early writing career, to later imaginatively transforming her ideas of people into fictional realisations. Hall recalls a conversation with Maria Edgeworth in which she records that Edgeworth 'was almost angry when she discovered that a sketch I had written on a scene at Killarney was pure invention. Hall endeavoured to convince her [Edgeworth] that to call imagination to the aid of reason, to mingle the ideal with the real, was not only permissible, but laudable.' (C. Hamilton, *Notable Irishwomen*, (Dublin: Sealy, Bryers & Walker, 1904), pp. 136–7).

84a, THE BANNOW POSTMAN.] in the *2nd edn 1831*, p. 294, this continued:

> I cannot avoid stating, in this the *second* edition of my *first* production, that honest John *has* conveyed the tale, in his old capacity, to my native village, and moreover, is particularly angry with me for (as he calls it) 'putting him in print,' a degradation he never expected at my hands. November 23, 1830.

195a, laughing.] in the *2nd edn 1831*, p. 308, this continued:

> To prove that Martin was in this instance correct, I have only to refer my readers to Doctor Walsh's highly interesting article on 'The Irish Herculaneum.' See pages 11–15.

212a, Mike!] in the *2nd edn 1831*, p. 352, Hall placed a footnote here on the death of the priest, Fr. Edmund (Ned) Murphy who, according to Butler, was pastor in Carrig from 1793–1830 – see Butler, *A Parish and its People*, p. 247) – and on whom her character 'Father Mike' was based:

> Since this story was first published, the amiable and excellent man, Father Mike, has been summoned to another and a better world. He had indeed a heart 'open as the day to melting charity;' and his white hair went down with honour to the grave. A few moments before he breathed his last, he beckoned one of his attendants to the bed-side, and whispered 'Give my blessing to all who live, and all who ever have lived, in Bannow!' He was, I believe, in the eighty-first or eighty-second year of his age.

Footnotes

32a   gumption] original footnote for 'gumtion': sense, *2nd edn 1831*
32b   bocher] original footnote: beggar, *2nd edn 1831*
219a praskeen] original footnote: apron, *2nd edn 1831*
222a nataral] original footnote: fool, *2nd edn 1831*
224a minds] original footnote: knows, *2nd edn 1831*
275a London Ladies] original footnote: potatoes held in high esteem, *2nd edn 1931*
366a something fit for a mornin': A portion of spirits drank before breakfast, *2nd edn 1831*
367a voster] original footnote: Voster's arithmetic, *2nd edn 1831*
367b snack] original footnote: A Luncheon, *2nd edn 1831*
371a bresneugh] original footnote: A fagot, *2nd edn 1831*
372a canted] original footnote: sold, *2nd edn 1831*

Mrs S. C. Hall, *Sketches of Irish Character*, 2nd series (London: Frederick Westley & A. H. Davis, 1831)

Additional Dedication

Hall wrote a new dedication to this *2nd series 1831*, inscribing it to Maria Edgeworth (1768–1849). The volume contains thirteen sketches, one of which, 'Irish Settlers in an English Village', was not included in the *3rd revsd edn 1844*. This may have been due to the location of the tale, setting it apart from the others; the story is laid in Petersham, London, not in Bannow. Moreover, some acerbic comments may have been the cause; in his review of the Second Series, William Maginn mocked Alaric Watts, whose rhyme accompanied the story, as a 'poetaster' and, whilst praising other sketches by Hall, dismissed 'Irish Settlers in and English Village' as 'fudge!' (See W. Maginn, *Fraser's Magazine for Town and Country*, IV (August 1831), p. 104).

TO

MISS EDGEWORTH,

A SECOND SERIES OF

SKETCHES OF IRISH CHARACTER

Is Inscribed

AS A TRIBUTE OF GRATITUDE,

RESPECT AND AFFECTION

THE AUTHOR

INTRODUCTION

The Author can have little to say, in sending forth a Second Series of 'Sketches of Irish Character' further than that their publication has resulted from the gratifying manner in which her first work was received by the public. As it has reached a Second Edition, she is led to anticipate favour towards other 'Sketches' – of the same family, it is true, – but distinguished from the former, as more general in their character and not confined to one particular spot.*

But with this volume she feels she will have acted wisely in bidding the subject a dieu.

She cannot however, rest satisfied without expressing most grateful recollections of the encouragement it was her happy fortune to receive, in her humble efforts to accomplish an object always nearest to her heart – that of making Ireland agreeably and advantageously known to England.

April 4, 1831.'

---

* It is proper to state that some of the following 'Sketches' have been already published in periodical works.

Additional Text

In the second series were lines from W. Wordsworth, 'An Evening Walk', *The Poetical Works of William Wordsworth. A New Edition in Four Volumes*, 4 vols (London, Longman, Rees, Orme, Brown, Green, and Longman, 1832), vol. 1, pp. 36–49, 40, 41, ll.98–103, 120–5, although Hall has taken liberties, using 'spots of sparkling water' instead of Wordsworth's 'plots of sparkling water'. The following extract is in the *2nd series 1831*, but was omitted from the *3rd revsd edn 1844*:

> Here, spots of sparkling water tremble bright,
> With thousand, thousand, twinkling points of light;
> There waves, that, hardly weltering, die away,
> Tip their smooth ridges with a softer ray;
> And now, the universal tides repose,
> And, brightly blue, the burnished mirror glows.*

The following unidentified 'Old stanza', featured on p. 152 of the *2nd series 1831*, but was, again, omitted from the *3rd revsd edn 1844*:

> While me you thought for to beguile,
> I cared for another all the while;
> And knew, my boy, what ye were at:
> Och! Never fear but I spied ye, Pat!
> Wid yer smiles,
> And yer wiles!
> And, by the same rule,
> Ye think every girl ye meet is a fool!

Also omitted from the *3rd revsd edn 1844*, is the following text, found on p. 169 of the *2nd series 1831*:

> ... Irish peculiarly susceptible of chivalrous feelings, and to whom a robber is too apt to appear in the light of a hero.
> The library of an English cottager generally consists of his BIBLE, 'The Whole Duty of Man,' perhaps 'Bunyan's Pilgrim's Progress,' a few tracts, and if a young family is springing up, in addition to the necessary school-books, I have found Mrs. Sherwood's, and other cottage tales interspersed with 'The Adventures of Whittington and his Cat' – 'Goody To-shoes' – 'Bluebeard,' and 'The Little Glass Slipper;' the latter all harmless, if not instructive.

---

*   Wordsworth

Difference in Ending and Attitude

Unlike the *3rd revsd edn 1844*, which sees, in the final lines of 'The Rapparee', Freney repent and reform, ending his days in peace and quietness, in the *2nd series 1831*, Hall betrays her fascination with the Romantic aspect of lawlessness, going so far as to recommend, on pp. 165–171, to her English readers the autobiography of the outlaw Freney, giving the work's full publication details. She also includes the dedication written by Freney for their 'amusement'. Having recommended Freney's life story as suitable reading material, she goes on to express anxieties about such books being read by 'the lower order of Irish'. She concludes by comparing favourably the reading material to be found in the library of an 'English cottager' compared with 'the scraps of profane or ridiculous ballads' and lives of highwaymen such as Freney, to be found in an Irish cabin, which she now claims is a 'dangerous volume for youth.'

It is not surprising that these didactic outpourings were expunged from the later *3rd revsd edn 1844*. Hall, or her editor and husband, Carter, must have judged that such open enthusiasm for a rapparee was inappropriate. Indeed, there is a sense of the hand of Carter on many of the alterations. The template for Dickens's character, the unctuous Seth Pecksniff from the novel *Martin Chuzzlewit*, Carter Hall was prone to fanciful flights in speech. Both worked diligently together through their long lives and, through Carter's editing assistance, Anna Maria was free to devote her time to writing. This does, however, present a difficulty in verifying the author of changes in the text.

Additional Footnotes

For the benefit of English readers, Hall used a footnote to clarify how the Irish were keen to differentiate between the 'old Irish' and those adventurers who had followed Cromwell's army to Ireland in 1649 and had benefited from the lands confiscated from the Irish under the Adventurers' Act of 12 August 1652. Lands belonging to Irish and Old English Catholics were declared forfeit in order to repay those who funded the invasion; the Province of Connacht in the west of Ireland and the County of Clare were set aside for the transplantation of the dispossessed. The following footnotes are in the *2nd series 1831*, but were omitted from the *3rd revsd edn 1844*:

294a,   Cromelians] original footnote, *2nd series 1831*: 'Cromwellians'. 'The 'ancient Irish' invariably denominate the more recent settlers 'Cromelains.' A whimsical illustration of this fact occurred within my own knowledge. The following conversation took place, a few months ago, in the streets of Cork, between an English housekeeper and an Irish market woman; –

Good morrow, ma'am I hope ye want a basket this fine morning, ma'am?
I b'lieve I shall.

Why then, long life to you ma'am, I hope you'll take *me*.
I b'lieve you're English ma'am?
Yes.
I thought so, ma'am; *I'm* English too.
Indeed! When did you come over to Ireland?
Oh, ma'am I came over wid Oliver Cromwell, ma'am.'
32b, bocher] original footnote: a lame man, *2nd series 1831*

Additional Article

In this sketch Hall writes in the first person in order to expresses her affection for the bucolic delights of an English village, in this case Petersham, near Richmond. In following events in the life of the Flaherty family who have settled in the area, Hall attempts to blend the 'orange and the green', to explain to the English reader how an Irish family can fit in with life in an English village. However, it doesn't quite come off and she manages to condescend to the Irish settlers while flattering the royal family; something that did not escape William Maginn in his review (W. Maginn, '*Sketches of Irish Character* by Mrs. S. C. Hall', *London Literary Gazette: and Journal of Belles Lettres, Arts, Sciences, &c.*, 640 (25 April 1829), pp. 268–9). His criticism was probably influential in the decision to omit this sketch form the 3rd revsd edn 1844, but it gives an interesting insight into her determination to forge good relations between Irish and English and Hall's belief the Irish could somehow become better if they adopted more orderly 'English' ways.

IRISH SETTLERS IN AN ENGLISH VILLAGE.

'Let poets rave of Arno's stream,
And painters of the winding Rhine,
I will not ask a lovelier dream,
A sweeter scene, fair Thames, than thine,
As 'neath a summer sun's decline
Thou 'wanderest at thine own sweet will,'
Reflecting from thy face divine
The flower-wreathed brow of Richmond-Hill.'
                                                    A.A. Watts

A SWEET poem is that of Mr Alaric Watts, from which the motto is quoted, and beautiful, most beautiful is the scene the poet has so happily described; but if you value nature and nature's charms, you must not be contented with merely gazing from the summit of the far-famed hill, but turning away from the gates of the once royal park, where the humble and virtuous Jeanie Deans is described to have knelt to the queenly Caroline for a sister's pardon, you must descend, not by the road, which leads through that wild and tangled thicket of brambles and hazel bushes toppled over with oak, where, in the soft evening of summer, nightingales sing, and glow-worms sparkle, but down the brown narrow path to the right; *that* will take you direct to the Petersham meadows where the Thames, one wide unruffled mirror of molten silver, as if conscious of its unrivalled beauty, neither murmurs nor sparkles, but reposes in silent magnificence – the pride and glory of this free and noble land! Pursue the fringed footway to the little stile – it will admit you into the grove leading to the humble and simple church; neglect not to cast your eye upwards towards the hill on which you lately stood, and the gay and bustling picture exhibited there is not an unpleasing contrast to the solitude and silence that pervade the scene around you, only interrupted by the merry sound of the distant horn, or the mid-day hum of the half-drowsy insect. Wander onwards to the little village of Petersham, the most pleasing assemblage of wooden and brick buildings in the neighbourhood of London, free alike from poverty and pretension; the high-built and noble dwellings looking what they really are – residences of the good and great – and the sweet modest cottages smiling and coquetting behind clustering roses, and tasselled woodbine, the abodes of an industrious and virtuous peasantry. I cannot tell you how I love that little village; the last time *but one*, that I visited my favourite haunt, (I have my own particular lodging in that place with my old favourite, Mrs Hedworth, who, by the way, is quite civil and good-natured enough to be mistaken for an Irish-woman,) the very last time, *but one*, when, escaping from London and its et-ceteras, I went down to Petersham, taking a new and pleasant book as my travelling companion, and entrusting myself to Butler's inimitable driving, happened to be the 29th of May; the road was all in commotion: houses garnished with oak, and every urchin you met, like a moveable bush, well calculated to puzzle a botanist. – As we approached Richmond, the way became almost choked with carriages, carts, pedestrians, equestrians, donkeys, Savoyards, gipsies, and showmen of various descriptions. – 'What's the reason of all this bustle, Butler?'

Now, the curious reader must know that Butler is a little rotund man, the lower portion of whose face is invisible from being always buried in a green Barcelona handkerchief, so that his voice in general sounds like a muffled drum; on this occasion, however, he put his forefinger to the variegated folds and elongated his neck, replying – 'It's oak-apple day, ma'am – because of king Charles, who you see, was restored; and there's a fair at Ham – and my lady Dysart lets the common as lady of the manor – and all the nobility and gentry will be there.'

I thought I would go there too, as Ham is only a little mile beyond Petersham: and was confirmed in my resolution, by seeing their royal highnesses of Cumberland whirl past our humble vehicle; prince George looking the very picture of anticipated enjoyment.

An English fair, thought I, is a well-conducted place of public amusement: every thing is very orderly and very grand – the shows very superb, the lions, tigers, bears, giants, dwarfs, all wonderful! – the knaves and pickpockets active, silent, and civil; and the gypsies, to my taste, the most interesting of the assembly; but the people have nothing *joyeuse*, nothing animated, about them. They visit the exhibitions, they buy and pay honestly for ginger-bread, ginger-beer, and even join in the mazes of quadrille and country dance, but all this is done in a business-like, mercantile way. It is right and customary for them to assemble; it is right for them to eat, drink, and, I suppose, be merry; but it is a merriment that, in Ireland, would be accounted visible and determined stupidity; a mirthful melancholy-perfume in a charnel-house-flowers on a tomb – all serving but to show that the soul, the spirit, is wanting, and that the heart has no music in it. If this morbid feeling however, lessens enjoyment, it also lessens danger; and I am free to confess that an English fair, although not half so original or delightful, is a thousand times more decorous than an Irish one. No fighting, no party spirit, nobody '*kilt*,' nobody 'murdered.' I was prevented from pursuing the discontented train of thought that accompanied my peregrination, by observing, amongst others of the nobility who crowded to a superb tent arranged as a charity bazaar, the youthful duke and duchess of B— ; they are a pale, delicate-looking couple, polite, gentle in their manners, and devotedly attached to each other. Presently the prince George bustled forward, a noble, bold-faced boy – quite a boy earnest and animated, and evidently delighted with the fairings purchased for his amusement; it is interesting to watch the rigid features of the Duke of Cumberland relax, as his keen cold eye rests upon that royal child; the gray mustache elongates, and tells of the smile beneath; and his voice softens, even to music, when he addresses him. The sturdyism of John Bull struck me very powerfully as the royal party moved to their carriages. Some of the people uncovered; others stood their ground firmly, and neither stirred hat nor inch, as the party proceeded; and but a few shouted – 'God save the Duke!' While the steps of their carriage were putting down, I observed one stiff, immoveable, Englishman, standing perfectly square, bolt upright, his hands in his pockets, his elbows sticking out, to the manifest inconvenience of those who pressed forward to see the royal personages before they departed; you would have imagined the man was rooted to the earth, so firmly did he maintain his ground. 'Take off y'er hat, if ye've any grace in ye!' exclaimed a voice, the tone of which could not be mistaken. 'Take off y'er hat this minute, or I'll be after saving ye the thrubble-tunder and ages! – isn't the son of y'er king, and the brother of y'er king to the fore.' No sooner said than done; a gigantic Irishman stretched forth his hand, and seized the offending hat between his finger and thumb, while the people, thrown off their guard by the expostulation, appearance, and manner of my countryman, laughed, and enjoyed the scene. Not so the burley-bull: he growled, extracted his hands from his pockets, demanded his hat in no gentle terms, talked of English liberty, and of 'hawling' Paddy up to Bow-street for stealing his hat; the crowd prevented their approximating, or, I fear me, the Irish man would have given the *national* reply to the accusation: – 'Is it y'er dirty bit of a hat! – me stale it! – no, nor I'd scorn an exchange with ye, either for sowl, body, or garments, my gay fellow! A purty Englishman ye are, to keep what has no brains in it covered, as if it was full, and the blood royal before ye – y'er hat! By my sowl, ye shall have it an' welcome – when they're gone. Jist look in the face of that darlint young Prence, and see if it 'ill drive any good humour into ye, ye great overgrown black bear! Huzza, for the royal family!' he continued, as the equipage drove off, 'and God bless 'em all!' – adding, in a lower tone, 'it's easier to fault than to mend 'em – like the rest of the world; – and there's y'er hat,' he said, again elevating his voice – 'and, only I'd be sorry to brake the pace, when it isn't, by no manner o' means, the custom o' the country – I'd just give ye a lesson for nothin', to improve y'er manners, and mark ye to grace.'

My Irish readers will expect that a fight occurred after these angry words: no such thing: John Bull pocketed the affront, placed his hands in their old position, and the disputants walked off in opposite directions.

'That's my Lady —'s new gardener,' observed my rural guide, who sees and knows every thing and every body, 'he's an Irishman, as you see by his accent, madam, and has the very finest family of children in the whole neighbourhood – he lives in the lodge; his wife is a very industrious woman, but slamakish; which, of course, is to be expected, considering where they came from: – this is the way; and we can pass Mr. Flaarty's lodge, if you are tired of the fair, and would like to see it.'

It was indeed delightful to get once more into the green lanes, and to hear the noise fade gradually from the ear, until it sounded like the distant humming of the humble-bee. We had not yet gained sight of the lodge, and were discussing various topics of rustic interest, and recent occurrence when 'the rush of racing feet' approached, and three laughing, romping, rosy girls ran past us; and then, ashamed of their wildness, stopped, curtsied, and twisted their hat-strings, while my guide announced them as Ellen, Lucy, and Katey Flaherty, or, as she called it, *Flaarty*. The eldest of the three curtsied still more deeply when she was told that I meditated a visit to the lodge. 'She was sure they would be proud of the honour: and father, mother Mary, Letty, and the duke's gardener, Mr James, would be up in a minute – there they are.'

There they were, most certainly; Flaherty in high spirits, striding forward, and carrying a laughing non-descript, *'flahoolagh'* looking child, in his arms; while his wife and 'Mary,' I suppose, held each the hand of another urchin, just breeched, and triumphing in all the stiffness of corduroy and a well-starched frill.

Last of the numerous family came, loitering and lingering on their way, Letty, and a tall good-tempered looking young man, who employed his cane in decapitating every nettle and noxious weed that disgraced the hedge rows, while his eyes 'discoursed sweet language' to the nymph, who occasionally glanced, or rather darted, bright but modestly-replying looks from under a very pretty cottage bonnet, which shaded her intelligent face.

When Flaherty overtook us, he raised his hat, and displayed a broad and sunny brow, radiant with good-humour, and flushed with his late triumph: and, when all matters were explained, he said,

'Indeed, and I'm proud to see any lady, let alone one of my own country ladies, at the lodge, where, thank God, I can make 'em welcome; – run on, ye three hussies, and get the place in order; – but stop – do *you* go, Mary; sure they litter more than they rid.' Mary, a discreet, English looking young woman, passed meekly forward, and Katey tendered her hand to the newly dressed boy, who seemed pleased at the exchange.

I wish some of my Irish friends could have seen the beautiful garden that fronted the lodge – even at that early season it was redolent of summer flowers. Ice plants sparkled under bell-glasses, and mignionette shed its sweet perfume on the breeze, which shook showers of silver May from a glorious white thorn, that spread its branches far and wide over the gate and path-way. The beautiful vine-leaves that crept even to the red tiles of the dwelling, were still in the light greenery of youth; while monthly roses nodded and blushed all over the rustic porch. Within, indeed, matters were not quite so systematically arranged; every thing was good of its kind, but the *ménage* was not perfect. The clock did not go – the warming-pan was not bright; and moreover, I shrewdly suspect it was used as a slut-hole; for I verily perceived the end of a handkerchief, and the border of a cap peeping from between the openings. In the back windows several panes of glass were wanting – one was stuffed with the crown of a hat, and another with coarse brown paper; – the tea-tray under the parlour table was magnificent! – a scarlet ground with orange parrots, and a purple princess in all the bad taste of Chinese arrangement; but the table had neither been well brushed, nor well dusted – the shepherd and shepherdesses on the chimney, wanted either crooks, or heads, or arms; and the looking-glass was cracked across. These trifles were not noticed by this happy family; and Mrs Flaherty pointed out to me, in the back yard, a standing pool of extraordinary colouring, (at which my humble friend turned up her nose,) and descanted on its merits in duck-rearing. 'It was well enough,' she wisely observed, 'for her husband to have his way in *one thing*, which was the garden – in that she never meddled nor made; but to deny the ducks – the craturs! – a drop of nat'ral drink, or the pig a comfortable wallop in the mud, now and again, when he wanted to cool himself, was what nobody had any right to gainsay – and so she had her own way.'

Next to the worthy master of the house, the persons who interested me most were Letty and her lover – the girl was so pretty, and withal had such a playful archness of expression – now sparkling over, and then withdrawing, from her dimpled face; and the youth was so devoted – so respectful to his choice

– and at the same time somewhat – I cannot call it doubtful, either; perhaps the word melancholy, would better express the impression his looks of subdued tenderness made upon my mind, that I could not avoid expressing to Mr Flaherty – who, when the hour of departure arrived, would walk home behind me to carry a beautiful nosegay he had gathered – my hopes that they might soon be married and happy.

'There's one thing betune them, and I'm sorry for it,' observed the worthy man, 'and that's just the religion – we're Catholics, ma'am, and I'd like we'd keep so; and ever since I've been in this country (twenty years come March), I've been risin' and risin', but there's two things I've never turned my back to,' – (he lifted up his hat reverently from his head as he spoke) – 'my religion and my country – I love 'em both; and, though there's many things I love besides, I love them *best*; however, I'm no bigot – James is a Prospeterian, and indeed I'm thinking the heart of the both's in it for marryin'; and it's hard to get Catholic husbands for seven girls in this country.'

As we were making our adieus, the honest gardener looked wistfully at me for a moment, and enquired in an earnest tone if I had ever been in the county Wexford. He then asked if I had known a person who was my nearest and dearest relative – I replied in the affirmative, and mentioned what my name had been: it was enough – the poor fellow seized my hand – pressed it to his heart – and finally burst into tears. 'Sure I'm a blind devil that didn't mark the likeness; – and the good lady, where is she – may I see her – is she, too, in England? Oh, my God!' he ejaculated, 'not dead!' I shall never forget his change of countenance – the tears of joy were turned to those of sorrow, and the Irish settler wept long and bitterly when he heard of the death of *her* who, I afterwards learned, had been a friend to him and his, in the times of public and private trouble. It would occupy too much time to tell the full tale of his wanderings and sorrow: the son of a respectable farmer, he had been induced to join a set of spirited but mistaken men; and his life would have been sacrificed to the justly-offended laws of his country had it not been for the judicious and kind interference of *her* he so sincerely regretted. Means were furnished for his departure from Ireland – he fled to America, where he was joined by his young and faithful wife – he remained there five years – acquired much practical knowledge of husbandry from a settler, who was skilled in horticultural pursuits. Circumstances, of which the detail was to me highly interesting, removed him to Scotland, where his skill and industry obtained lucrative employment, and finally, through the interest of a member of the house of 'bold Buccleugh,' he was fortunate enough to obtain the situation I have already mentioned. The mingling of feelings of nationality, loyalty, and old affections, formed an extraordinary combination in the mind of this adventurous man; and I regretted that my speedy return would prevent my more closely analysing so interesting a being. 'Said I to myself,' the next time I come down here, I will keep up a very intimate acquaintance with the Flahertys; I shall be able to prosecute my favourite study, and read persons, not books; I shall – but no matter – after remaining some time in Town – last week – only last Tuesday – away we went down to Petersham. Mrs Hedworth, as usual, stood smiling and curtseying at her garden gate, to receive us – fresh flowers garnished the little humble drawing-room, and Mungo (an interesting, and for a cat, intelligent, animal,) elevated her tail in token of welcome. I was in such haste, that I hardly replied to my land-lady's civil enquiries; but I now remember having heard something (by the way, she is dress-maker to all Petersham,) about her having been very busy since my last visit. We bustled out of the back gate down the lane into Lady Dysart's park; and in another moment we were on the strand of the glorious Thames, almost opposite Twickenham, whose church steeple was ringing forth a most merry peal. The water was positively alive with juvenile fish, sparkling and leaping in the river, like diamond stars, full of first existence, and giving the charm of life to the placid waters. The strand opposite presented an animated scene; so animated, that I sat, notwithstanding my anxiety to reach Flaherty's lodge, quietly on the stile to witness the bustle – (I plead guilty to dearly loving a bustle). A wedding-party were embarking in the ferry-boat; and the Charon had mounted a white rose as a bridal favour. I thought there would be no end to the people; the boat was filled almost to sinking – then Tom Tow's large wherry was crammed; and even poor Jack, as he afterwards said, 'manned a boat,' and pushed off with his live cargo.

Married! – Letty Flaherty absolutely married – and in Twickenham church, too, (why were they not married at Petersham, I wonder?) to Mr James. 'My lady heard of it; and his royal highness, who is the best master in the world, took it up,' said my kind-hearted countryman to me, 'and made them a handsome present and they needn't quarrel about the religion, *if the fear of God is in 'em*, each can go their own way – and sure ye'll come home with us; and may-be take share of the wedding dinner, sure ye have a nat'ral right to it. God bless ye.'

We declined the invitation – study character! – that was no time for it – how could it? – when they all looked so uniformly happy; and could think of nothing but weddings, favours, &c. &c.; and the family 'would be busy for a fortnight, any how, settling the young people;' as the 'match came upon them of a suddent, after all.' Notwithstanding that, in the evening Katey and Ellen came to our cottage laden with fruits and flowers; and 'their father,' they said, 'would leave the fishing-tackle ready, if the gentlemen liked fishing, and send better strawberries to-morrow; and, after that week, would be quite at our service,' and a great many pretty civil things, worth a million of what are denominated 'polite attentions,' because they came warm from honest affectionate hearts; – but I was too much pleased in contemplating the lovely appearance of the youthful bride's-maids, simpering amid white satin ribband and book muslin (the taste and fashion of their dresses reflected much credit on Mrs Hedworth,) to attend much to their long speeches.

We returned to London; but when the young couple are quite established, and the usual occupations are resumed at the lodge, I hope to renew my acquaintance with those industrious and interesting IRISH SETTLERS.

MRS S. C. HALL, *Sketches of Irish Character*, 3rd edn (London: How & Parsons, 1842)

This illustrated edition was reprinted in 1844 as the *3rd revsd edn 1844* – the copy-text used in this volume – see Note on the Text, p. xxxi. This *3rd edn 1842* was the first to contain illustrations, and also featured a new introduction:

INTRODUCTION TO THE THIRD EDITION

The Public having required a third Edition of these 'SKETCHES OF IRISH CHARACTER', I have been called upon to prepare it – to revise the stories originally published, and to add several new; and the publishers have given to them the advantage of very beautiful illustrations.

The 'Sketches' chiefly refer to one locality – the parish of Bannow, on the seacoast of the County of Wexford – my native place, where the earlier years of my life were passed. The world has little interest in the personal feelings of a writer; but my readers will, I hope, permit me to say that my first impressions of Ireland were derived from the very favourable circumstances under which I was placed; for, in this neighbourhood, there was, comparatively, none of the poverty, and consequent wretchedness, to be encountered, unhappily, elsewhere. I have so frequently dwelt upon its almost exclusive privileges and peculiar features, in these 'Sketches,' as to render it unnecessary for me to preface them further than by stating they are, in general, accurate, as regards the persons and the scenery; although, no doubt, the happy associations, connected with them, have made both appear brighter, in my eyes, than they may seem to others. It is certain, however, that this district of the County of Wexford is superior to any other part of the south of Ireland. Its landlord is not an absentee; he is surrounded by an attached and prosperous tenantry; the land is naturally rich, and facilities for improving it are many.

The baronies of Bargy and Forth, in the former of which Bannow is situated, are especially fortunate in possessing, to a very remarkable extent, all the moral, social, and natural advantages, which are to be found, although more limited, throughout the County. The inhabitants are, chiefly, descendants of the Anglo-Norman settlers, who, in the reign of the second Henry, invaded and conquered – or, rather subdued – Ireland; and, until very recently, they retained so much of their ancient customs and manners, as actually to speak a language unknown in other districts of the Kingdom.

The ruins of castles are so numerous, that, over a surface of about 40,000 acres, there stand the remains of fifty-nine; and the sites of many more can still be pointed out. The people are to this day, 'a peculiar people,' and retain much of their English character. This is apparent, not alone in the external aspect of the country – in the skilfully farmed fields, the comparatively comfortable cottages, the barns attached to every farmyard, the well-trimmed hedgerows, stocked with other vegetables than potatoes; the peasantry are better clad than we have seen them elsewhere, and have an air of sturdy independence, which they really feel, and to which they are justly entitled, for it is achieved by their own honest industry.

In these 'Sketches' I have aimed at a higher object than mere amusement, – desiring so to picture the Irish character, as to make it more justly appreciated, more rightly estimated, and more respected, in England; at the same time, I have studied – but I trust in a kindly and affectionate spirit – so to notice the errors and faults that prevail most among my countrymen and countrywomen, as to be of some use in inducing a removal of them. There are none powerless to effect good – except those who persuade themselves that attempts to produce it are hopeless. It has been my steady purpose, and zealous wish, to do justice to the many estimable qualities of the Irish peasantry, of whom it has been truly said, 'their virtues are their own; but their vices have been forced upon them.'

With these 'Sketches' I was first introduced to the Public; I have since produced other works, but none into which my heart so completely entered. They gave me, I presume to say, a place in public favour; – it has been my earnest and continued study to retain it.

Within a few years, the property upon which I lived has passed into other hands – those, so near and so dear to me, who, in my time possessed it – I am happy to say, however, INTO GOOD HANDS; for the excellent and accomplished gentleman to whom I have inscribed these 'Sketches,' while he is equally willing, is infinitely more powerful, to advance the moral and social welfare of the people committed to his charge.

Mrs S. C. Hall, *Sketches of Irish Character:*
With Numerous Illustrations by the late Daniel Maclise, R.A.,
John Gilbert, W. Harvey, and G. Cruikshank, 5th edn
(London: John Camden Hotten, c. 1876)

This illustrated *5th edn c.1876* is prefaced by a dedication to Francis Bennoch (1812–90). He was a poet who also ran a successful wholesale silk business in Wood St., London. A much admired friend and correspondent of M. R. Mitford; Carter Hall socialized with Bennoch as fellow members of the Society of

Noviomagus, a confraternity of antiquarians founded in 1828. Once again, Hall seeks to have her work connected in the public mind with that of M. R. Mitford; in this instance, indirectly, by addressing Bennoch, Mitford's close friend and confidant:

DEDICATION

My Dear Sir,

The first series of these 'Sketches' – then crushed into a small volume – was simply an evidence of my desire to do for my native Bannow, what Miss Mitford had done for her 'Village,' and to Miss Mitford, in all the mingled anxiety and pride of young authorship, I dedicated my first fruits.

You – who have been, and are Miss Mitford's attached and zealous friend – who estimated the brightness of her nature and the freshness of her genius, before you had witnessed her suffering and patience, and ministered to her the balm of friendship in these – her later – yet most honoured days – must permit me to inscribe this edition to you, in testimony of my sincere respect and admiration of one, who blends the delicacy of the poet, with the practical wisdom of the man of business, and the benevolence of the Christian.

Your sincere friend,

ANNA MARIA HALL

To Francis Bennoch, Esq.
&c. &c.

Additional Footnotes

16a, spoke the word out o' the face] original footnote: Without consideration, *5th edn c.1876*

16b, held my wisht] original footnote: Held my tongue – kept silence, *5th edn c.1876*

20a, crassing me] original footnote: contradicting, *5th edn c.1876*

41a, a tester] original footnote: a fourpenny bit, *5th edn c.1876*

87a, cant] original footnote: sale, *5th edn c.1876*

105a, ye're sensible] original footnote: you understand, *5th edn c.1876*

229a, And who would be cruel enough ... in the same way?] original footnote: If my accomplished countryman, Mr Maclise, met in the county of Wexford the subject he has so admirably pictured, and which stands at the head of this story, it must have been at Taghmon – Taghmon, cheerless, boisterous, and dirty, even in the days of temperance and whitewash., *5th edn c.1876*

377a, During the past few years ... the change is wonderful, and must be seen to be believed] original footnote: Although, since the above was written, many changes have taken place, and Temperance is not altogether as entirely 'natural' as it was ten years ago, it is quite certain that the beneficial effects of the 'movement' have been great. Throughout Ireland drunkenness is now not an honour but a reproach – of which the drunkard even is ashamed. I have suffered these passages to remain: for beyond question, many of the blessing I anticipated have arisen from the introduction of Temperance., *5th edn c.1876*

Mrs S. C. Hall, *Sketches of Irish Character: With Numerous Illustrations by Maclise, Gilbert, Harvey, and Cruikshank*, 5th revsd edn (London: Chatto and Windus, c. 1876)

This *5th edn c.1876* also contains 'A Rambling Introduction', in which Hall gives free rein to her affection for her native locality and allows her mind to range back over her Bannow childhood and gives an insight into the people who were the inspiration for her characters in the sketches. The piece is revelatory of the deep anxieties that haunted the Anglo-Irish gentry whose memories of the rebellion of 1798 were vivid and carried the unspoken legacy of fear of annihilation.

A RAMBLING INTRODUCTION

TO THE FIFTH EDITION OF
MY FIRST BOOK.

I AM requested to write an Introduction to the Fifth Edition of 'Sketches of Irish Character,' which – although published nearly a quarter of a century ago – still find favour with a public, from whom I have received only indulgent kindness for so many years. Looking clearly back upon my Childhood I seem as if I were contemplating a handful of spring flowers – some wild, some cultivated – which have gone on increasing and blossoming ever since. Although an Author, I am without a grievance! I have had nothing to complain of. The changing seasons still bring me changes of enjoyment – the simple pleasures of my youth have not lost their zest –

> I love the sound of waves – the first
> That woke my childhood's glee,

as fervently as when I sat on the wild rocks of my beloved BANNOW, or gathered sea-shells in those sandy bays – which I shall see no more!

The flowers of my own garden are as bright and as sweet to my senses, as those of which my grandmother was so proud; and though the Firfield grass is not as green, as that which carpeted the meadows of Graige – yet the buttercups of the meadow are as yellow and the daisies as star-like as those which glittered with the cuckoo-sorrel in our old orchard! I feel their association of the past with the present, and enjoy my thoughts. What a blessing it is when even sickness and sorrow are but chronicled by gratitude that they are passed – nay, when happiness is renewed by the remembrance. I look back with freshness and cheerfulness upon sorrows and vexations, which though bitter and hard to endure at the time, seem to me now, as those light clouds, that render earth more pleasant, by veiling sunshine. I can recall two of my country's proverbs which beautifully express my meaning. 'The blackest thorn bears the whitest blossom.' 'The darkest hour is the hour before day.' I relish the return to country life after some twenty 'London seasons,' as a renewal of my youth – yet delight as much as ever when a few days in town brings me once more among those I have long known and loved.

I am turning my introduction into a confession – but so it must be even at the risk of being an egotist. I have enjoyed so many blessings – received so much kindness from strangers as well as friends – been cheered by such sweet household love, that were I to refuse my thankfulness the right of words – I should feel self-convicted of ingratitude to my God and to my fellow creatures. The mercy of GOD has guided me all my days – and I can sing with the Psalmist, 'For thou, Lord, hast made me glad through thy works: and I will rejoice in giving praise for the operations of thy hands.'

So much – perhaps too much – of my present self, and now a few words of old times – to which this book has reference.

I can remember how my voice trembled when, little more than a bride, I ventured to read to my husband the sketch of 'MASTER BEN,' – the very first of those 'Sketches of Irish Character,' – which multiplied so rapidly, and have been so well received – more particularly in America. 'The Lights and Shadows of Irish Life,' 'The Tales of the Irish Peasantry,' even 'The Whiteboy,' are all akin to the 'Sketches' – which, imperfect as they are as *tales*, are more true to actual life than the more varied stories which followed.

In writing the 'Sketches of Irish Character,' I was, as I have said elsewhere, simply anxious to make the sea-side village in which I passed my childhood favourably known to the English – I did not *then* think that I might be useful to my country by endeavouring to correct the failings of its affectionate and generous peasantry: as I have tried to do, for instance, in 'We'll see about it,' 'Take it easy,' and in others of that class. I only, as it were, copied the people whom I had known when my life was young.

My dear mother, anxious that I should become a good arithmetician, had determined that I should understand the 'science of numbers' to perfection. Master Ben, – Schoolmaster of Cullinstown, being considered 'grate intirely at the figures,' was therefore engaged to visit twice a week the 'big house,' which he did, winter and summer, through fair and foul weather, for three years. Many curious specimens of shells and sea-weed – many wild birds tamed for my amusement – many strings of sea-birds' eggs, brought from the Keroe and Saltee Islands – many, many bunches of wild flowers, and curious things gathered when the waves cast back in disdain upon the shore what they had torn from hapless vessels, which they dashed against our cruel rocks – did my old master bring; and much did I learn from him quaintly and strangely of 'ould ancient legends, and natural history, and botany,' and superstitions and bits of garbled history which made me love my country all the more – but as to arithmetic! he certainly led me on to algebra (my mother keeps my books to this hour), but I never could, or did, comprehend any one of the four first rules, which I have often since most grievously regretted. If my improvement was doubted, MASTER BEN showed my books, where sum after sum was noted down with praiseworthy exactness, and I really believe he thought I understood all their mysteries.

I remember thinking that this quaint old schoolmaster ought to be as interesting a person as Miss Mitford's 'Mole Catcher,' and determined to try if I could make him so. 'Master Ben' and John Williams – ('The Bannow Postman') – were the first to inspire me with a literary ambition. As I have said, I well remember reading *that*, my first Sketch, to my husband, glancing from the seamed and blotted page to his young face, then unmarked by the cares and anxieties he has since often felt both for himself and me, and wondering if it were really true that I – *I* could write anything worth being printed and – paid for.

I went on from one Sketch to another, writing chiefly for those pretty Annuals now quite gone by, and grateful to him who cared for, while he corrected, all I did. When a publisher offered me a hundred pounds if I would write a new Sketch, and collect those I had written into one little volume for publication, honestly I told him I thought it too much, though I *did* certainly exult in the 'great fact;' and then how astonished I was to find myself 'famous,' in the generous pages of the 'Literary Gazette,' and occupying two columns of 'The Times!' I can also remember how fearful my husband was that literature – is cares, its claims, and its fame – would unfit me for the duties which every woman is bound to consider only next to those she owes her Maker. I daresay I was a little puffed up at first, but happily for myself, and for those who had near and dear claims upon my love and labour, I very soon held my responsibilities as an author second to my duties as a woman; they *'dove-tailed'* charmingly, and I have ever found the necessary change to domestic from literary care, though sometimes laborious, not only healthful, but pleasant.

I have said the Characters and Sketches in this volume are more decidedly taken from 'the life' than any that followed; as I became more skilled in 'author craft,' I learned how I could better employ my materials, and *combine*, as well as *copy*, grafting invention upon facts, and facts upon invention; but the characters *here* are all portraits, copied with fidelity and earnestness of purpose.

A buoyant yet observant child, without childish companions, I had to seek from the animate and inanimate world interest and amusement, and of these, in and about my old home, there was an abundance – a wild and rocky shore – bays strewn with shells – the old Church of Bannow, with its history and legends – a cultivated domain, gardens fruitful and beautiful – plenty of old castles and abbeys in the neighbourhood, and but few neighbours, except in summer when the bays of Bannow, Cullinstown, and Graige tempted many to put up with the accommodation of our sea-side cottages during the bathing season; but then there was a small library of rich and sound books, and my grandmother's Huguenot descent and extensive reading in her own language, rendered me familiar in childhood with much that was good in the literature of France. I never remember that dear grandmother but in wretched health – her beauty and suffering were the heroism of my childhood, while my gentle, loving mother divided her time between the bed-room of her parent and the school-room of her child; but indeed, the whole district was my 'school-room.'

'Master Ben,' – 'Old Frank,' who had been two and forty years coachman in the family – the old bathing woman, 'Nelly Parell' – my nurse, Mary Redmond – all delighted in imparting their stock of legends and fairy lore to the 'darlint,' who loved to listen as much as they to tell. When my poor grandmother's illness became serious, my mother was more constantly in her chamber, and I had a great deal of leisure. In the early morning returning from my sea bath, up the long walk, lingering amid the old trees, or reading, beside the stream in the domain which encircled an ornamental cottage that was covered with ivy, and formed a very city of refuge for small birds, from the golden crested wren to the overbearing starling – that cottage with its gable, its rustling ivy, its low dark windows, its mossy seats, and grassy banks, and pure limpid stream creeping over the smooth pebbles, after escaping from a cascade, which for years was my ideal of a waterfall, its mysterious arch, composed of the jaw-bone of a whale, which I used to gaze upon with such grave astonishment – that cottage was my paradise! I could hear the ocean rolling in the distance, the refreshing sea breeze passing over fields of clover and banks of roses, was freighted with perfume; the parent birds would fearlessly pick up the crumbs at my feet. I kept my favourite books in a drawer of the rustic dresser. I had a volume of Elegant Extracts, an old edition of the Psalms of David in French, which belonged to some of my grandmother's Huguenot ancestors, and a French Testament; I had an old edition of Shakespeare and Racine, a cherished Robinson Crusoe, Watts' Logic, and Poems, odd volumes of Cowper and of Young; I knew little of Moore, and nothing of Byron, but I knew Quarles and Herbert and Shirley, and Walter Scott's Marmion, and Milton, and often when I closed HIS volume, as the sound of the breakfast bell came through the trees slowly and deliberately, like the measured tread of the old butler Dennis, who pealed it, often have I wondered if hereafter I should meet and *know* that blind man, in heaven. I cannot account for it now, how a child so volatile as I was, so full of energy and motion, could pore for hours over grave earnest books, with as full enjoyment as over poetry, or how my even greater pleasure was to wander to the sand banks, amid which the old church of Bannow is almost entombed, and contemplate the old graves and mouldering records of humanity. I certainly never felt the time hang heavily – never felt it dreary or lonely; my mind seemed full of thoughts, and when aroused to the present, I was as joyful to bound homeward, even before tears, which gathered and fell – I knew not why – were dried. I was often reproved for my dreamy moods, but not by my gentle mother. 'I trust in God,' she would say, 'that she thinks and feels for a purpose; she reads nothing that I do not give her; she receives all her teaching from my lips; she makes acquaintance after her own fancy with God's works by sea and land; and as to the legends, why they belong to her country, though not to mine. I know when she thinks, and I know when she dreams; every key has its minor and major, her spirits and strength would become exhausted but for these rests.' A nervous terror prevented my ever wandering by moonlight; I was content to watch the moonbeams on the sea from my nursery window, and observe the light from the Hook light-house beam out upon the waters; as a child, I was afraid of the moon, and even now the less I see of it the better. I certainly was sufficiently affected by fairy and ghost lore to avoid rambling by moonlight, and to tremble at darkness. It seems to me I must have been a most happy child; I believe the only person I feared was my grandmother's second husband, the only father I ever knew; yet he it was who made me love Milton, and many winter evenings have I sat at his feet while he read aloud to my mother and grandmother grave, staid, books, and I used to look at the great birds on the window curtains, and try to listen even to that awful 'Book of Martyrs,' yet thinking it far pleasanter when they sang catches and trios; for even while 'grand-mamma' was very ill, when her pain lulled, she would sing, and I used to think it cruel to be sent to bed as they were singing – to go into that cold dark hall, all full of shadows – the moon streaming through the fanlight upon the gilt pipes of the old organ, the wind roaring round the house, and setting the old dinner bell ringing at intervals. And then we seldom passed a winter without having two or three shipwrecks on our rocky coast, and once I remember hearing the guns of a distressed vessel, and longing to arouse the house, yet perfectly unable to rush through the darkness, and bewildered by my desire to do something, in a fit of desperation ringing the wrong bell, and rousing every one, which, after all, was fortunate; for away went my dear grandfather and the men servants to the beach. I remember thinking how beautifully the lights and lanterns shone upon the snow, and how grand and mysterious the figures and shadows were, losing all the proper feeling which ought to arise out of a shipwreck, in excitement and enthusiasm, and sitting up all night to prepare comforts for the sailors, who really were, with some few sad exceptions, housed before day-break. It seems strange to confess it, but I felt a sort of triumph in a ship-wreck. I wept by the hour, and for days and nights could neither rest nor sleep; yet a wild feeling of enjoyment mingled with my terror of a wreck. I wrote tales of shipwrecks on my slates, and set sailors' songs to music, and never but then longed to be a boy – only that I might be shipwrecked. How was it that I, who could not cross the hall in the dark without becoming paralysed by terror, had no terror of the stormiest sea that ever cast a helpless ship from the breakers to the rocks? There was a general belief amongst the servants and the cottagers that some day or other 'Miss Marie would either be drowned out of Master's boat, that she was always after, or break her neck off a horse.' Yes, I certainly dearly loved a stormy sea and a wild gallop, and few little girls achieved the age of ten who had more escapes by sea and land. 'It's a great blessing entirely,' said Nelly Parell to my mother, 'it's a wonderful blessing that Miss has a terror of the dark, and no love for the moon – if it wasn't for *that* she'd be down on the beach by night as well as by day, and there would soon be an end of her.' It was simply a return of my old love for the sea that in after years forced me to write 'The Buccaneer.'

Perhaps some of my friends and readers, may feel an interest in seeing the foundation stone of some of my erections – hearing the key note of my small compositions.

The story of 'Father Mike' originated after this fashion:

There was one guest at Graige whose knife and fork was always laid on the Sabbath day – winter and summer made little difference – there it was, and from the side window of the dining room I used to watch for the coming of the Roman Catholic priest of the parish. The good old Father Edward Murphy, had been educated in France, and was almost an ideal picture of the old abbés of past times; it would be impossible *now* to find even a *faint* copy of 'Father Murphy.' Mild and gracious, with all the refinement of the French school, even my stately grandmother, with all her Huguenot feeling, used to say Father Ned had but one fault – he was a Roman Catholic: but he had saved her and hers in the rebellion of '98 from destruction, and when the time of retribution came, and the priests of the county Wexford were under the ban of government, she wrote a letter to a person 'having authority,' representing his care of her and her daughter, and his exertions to save the property and life of her husband, and in due time the Bannow priest was told he had nothing to fear; thus they were bound to each other, and it was curious to see the good breeding with which they watched *themselves* to prevent a word escaping which might wound the religious feelings of the other. Sometimes 'the Master' would indulge a sly jest at the priest's expense, but 'the Mistress' invariably came with her half broken English to the rescue, and thus the Huguenot and the Roman Catholic sat at the same board as friends – fellow-labourers they certainly were for the good of the poor, and in all things appertaining to their advantage they worked together. Dear old Father Murphy was so good to me; I was his pet, and he was never tired of answering my questions, or hearing me repeat the poems I had committed to memory – but if ever those questions broached upon religious matter, he would say – 'Little Marie must ask mamma that.' He was never angry with me but once: and this was how I gave him displeasure. In summer he always read his Breviary for half an hour before dinner, walking round the wilderness – and in winter there was a fire in the little parlour for 'Father Ned,' and there he retired when the dressing bell rang. I had often seen this Breviary in his hand, a large worn book clasped with silver; it was a great mystery to me, and I longed to solve it. When done with it for the time being, he put it into the pocket of his thick blue great coat, which he wore summer and winter, and which dangled over the sides of his white horse, like a guardsman's cloak; this coat always hung in the hall, and at last I took courage, when they were deep in some political question, I crept out of the dining-room and withdrew the book from the pocket, and went into the little parlour, to examine its contents, by the blazing light of Kendal coal.

The volume was illuminated, and I became perfectly absorbed by the prayers and litanies and number of saints, until I unfortunately turned over a page where there was some consecrated wafer. I had never seen or heard of it, I thought it looked very pretty, and might be very nice; I placed a piece between my lips, when suddenly Father Ned's hand fell heavily upon my shoulder, his deep set dark eyes sparkled with indignation, and his cheeks flushed. He snatched the wafer from my lips and called me 'Heretic,' I heard *that* and though he said more, I remembered nothing else. He had left the room to seek his handkerchief and had missed the book.

I was both ashamed and indignant. I told him the truth frankly, and begged his pardon, and I clasped the book and placed it in his hands. His displeasure was short-lived, and my shame and sorrow at having displeased him were sincere, but I wept bitterly at being called 'heretic,' for child as I was, it taught me that between the two faiths 'was a great gulph fixed.'

He was a good, kind, gentle man for all that, and I loved him better than Friar Butler or Friar Doyle, of Danes Castle. They had been educated in Italy, and used to teach me Italian. And Friar Butler, I remember, kept huge greyhounds and hunted hares, and they cultivated flowers to perfection, and I believe educated young men for the priesthood; but they only dined with us at festivals; they used to send my grandmother game, and she sent them hampers of strawberries and peaches; we were rich in peaches; our two 'lions' were a peach tree which once 'had been put in the newspaper,' as having borne and ripened nine hundred peaches; and our myrtle was twenty feet high and fifteen broad! Growing in the open air. What innocent people we all were! We were so proud of our peach tree and myrtle! There was a peach tree in the County Waterford which bore nearly as great a number, and I remember the fact made us all very uneasy and uncomfortable; but the gardener after visiting his rival, rejoiced us with the assurance that the peaches were not in any respect as fine as ours.

I wonder what Rowland Hill, that Emperor of postal arrangements, would have thought of 'The Bannow Postman,' poor John Williams; he was nearly, if not quite the last of his calling. The establishment of a Post-office at Carrick hastened his death (he was not above 80, the Bannow people live to a great age), and I believe all his descendants are gone to America.

The character of Peggy the Fisher, in 'Lilly O'Brien,' was suggested by 'Peg Dunn,' a woman whose height and loud-hailing voice rendered her rather an object of terror to my childhood. She was one of the itinerant 'egg women' who 'travelled the country,' ostensibly to purchase eggs, or wool, or butter, or whatever the cottagers or farmers' wives had to sell; and who become circulating mediums of news, and love, and smuggling – active agents during the periods of public disturbance; always a chatty, amusing class, full of anecdote and legend; enduring great bodily fatigue; a little suspected of want of good faith in their dealings, but certain of the warmest seat in the kitchen, the best bed, and a share of 'whatever was going.' The character was introduced in my little drama of 'The Groves of Blarney;' in which Power performed with the success he always commanded, and Yates made an admirable 'Peggy.'

'The Bannow Boatman,' whose name was not 'Larry Moore,' but Paddy Cahill, was, I must say, a faithful portrait. When *Sketches* was first published, many persons visited the 'Island of Bannow,' and bore testimony to the fidelity of the sketch.

Paddy has long since slept in the church-yard, but I fear there are still many on the 'Island,' who, like poor Paddy, do not 'think of to-morrow.' I have not always given the real names to the real people, for the Irish are not like our transatlantic neighbours, fond of being 'put in a book,' they shrink from such exposures with peculiar sensitiveness.

'Ah, then, Ma'am, dear,' said the girl who is called 'Norah Clary,' and who really had as many 'wise thoughts,' as most persons of her age and sex, 'Ah, then, Ma'am, dear, knowing you all the days of your life, and loving the very ground you walked upon, wasn't it hard entirely of you *to put me in a book* – making a fair show of me all over the world!' Another instance I can call to mind – having a tolerably good Irish cook, I was provoked by her silence – a very unusual fault – I could never get her to answer a question, and when I sent for her she would hold the door in her hand, and after a brief 'yes, ma'am;' or 'No, ma'am;' start off with such evident delight at her escape, that I resolved to know *why* she desired to avoid me.

'Mary,' I said, one morning, 'I want to know why you answer my questions so abruptly. Shut the door – there, let go the handle, and come here – have you any fault to find with your situation?'

'No, ma'am – never a fault at all with the place – Oh, no! God bless you.'

'Then what is the reason that whenever I send for you I can hardly get you to answer my questions? And when I go into the kitchen, you invariably rush into the scullery?'

'It's just nothing particular, ma'am.'

'But there must be a reason for such un-servant-like conduct.'

'No reason in life, ma'am.'

Mary had got back to the door, and regained firm possession of the handle.

'I know you can talk fast enough sometimes, and yet, as I have said before, you will not even answer my questions.'

She made a sudden rush out – then returned – thrust her head through the opening, and exclaimed piteously – 'Ah, then, let me alone, ma'am, dear, you know you'll be putting me in a book!'

They may have a superstition about this, as they have about being weighed and measured; but certainly the *'people'* of Ireland have no ambition to see themselves in print.

I remember, when writing those Sketches to have been strongly imbued with a desire to do justice to the memory of the faithful old servants, whom I may rank amongst my earliest and most devoted friends. 'Old Frank,' the old coachman, who, I believe, loved me, because I loved horses, and often declared that 'every one was born with a *ganious* for something, and Miss Marie with a ganious for horsemanship,' was most devoted in his attachment to every member of the family, in which, as I have said, he had lived forty years. When my mother was yet a young girl, he was anxious for her glory as a horse-woman, as he afterwards became for mine; but she was too timid to mount fearlessly; and he always alluded to this as a misfortune, a thing to be deplored; indeed he considered it a disgrace.

I look back at the dozen or two of old servants and old retainers who belonged to that house, and the house to them, as I do to the legends of past days – there are no such people now – here and there, when wandering amongst my friends, I see an old grey-headed 'follower,' or note the reverential curtsey – and hear, 'God save you kindly, Ma'am;' or 'You're kindly welcome to ould Ireland, madam,' from an aged nurse, or housekeeper; but servants such as those my memory calls before me at this moment, are an extinct race.

Their one single devotion to their employer, and his 'seed, breed, and generation,' – their earnest affection – their championship – suffering no word of disrespect to be uttered against master or mistress, family or friends – not only ready, but anxious to do battle for the glory of those, 'them and all belonging to them war born under' – all this has been dying out, and the late EXODUS has swept the very ashes from the country; and no wonder – the devotion was ill-requited – the people, some five-and-thirty years ago, looked for *no* requital – they were satisfied if not happy in their serfdom – but education and the lightning-like spread of thought and comparison, and calculation, experience, and the newly discovered power of thinking for themselves, have combined with the Encumbered Estates Bill, to overthrow the poetry of devotion towards the ancient families in which they breathed, moved and had their being. The Irish servant now expects his *quid pro quo* quite as much as the English servant; but he has his advantages and disadvantages, all the same as in old times: he is more noisy, more blundering, and untidy, than an English footman; but though without the enthusiastic attachment to his employer, he is more anxious, more zealous, and more physically and spiritually good-natured – he has not *much* respect for the 'honour of the family,' but he has still a *little*, and would rather, if in a tradesman's establishment, conceal the fact from his old mother, or his pretty sweetheart, supposing her to be an Irish girl; but the old self-denying, faithful race are gone, and my young friends may, perhaps, fancy they never existed. Bannow was, as I have so often joyed to repeat, a favoured spot, blessed with resident landlords, and prosperous tenants; the churchyard numbers nearly all among its graves, whose peculiarities are chronicled in these pages; and, except in a few instances, their children have ceased to inherit the land – they are gone to Australia, or Canada, or New Zealand – there are fewer cottages, and sundry new faces and new names.

> We took no note of them,
> But by their loss —

The plough and the harrow have passed over the spot where Graige House once stood, and where my happy childhood was passed.

The Master of Grange – who purchased Graige after the death of my relatives, from the heir at law – an accomplished scholar, a polished gentleman, and amongst the dearest friends of the poet MOORE – he has been called '*home,*' and as yet I believe his stately residence, which took the place of the pretty clergyman's cottage, where Henrietta and Marian and Ellen,* faithfully pictured in 'The Bannow Postman,' lived in my time, has not since been inhabited –

> Old times are changed – old manners gone.

But how bewildering it is to recall the circumstances which, unobserved and imperceptible at first, have gradually revolutionized the whole aspect of Ireland. It was said, when there was no agitation the country would prosper, and as far as the bare land is concerned, there can be no doubt of the prophecy being fulfilled – the *country*, the soil, the hills and valleys, the acres – will prosper, but where are those who were 'to the fore' when the prophecy was uttered? They have taken with them beyond seas, the faith, the habits, and the *prejudices* so long cherished – parting with their native land, sooner than part with *them*.

The Encumbered Estates' Court has swept away the Castle Rackrents, and it is only in the admirable pages of Miss Edgeworth, that 'Thady,' and the unfortunate spendthrift on whom the old man's fidelity was lavished – find a home.

---

* I am almost ashamed thus to chronicle the march of time, but more than *one* of those ladies is absolutely – a grandmamma: I have this excuse to offer – *they married very young*.

Where now could Lady Morgan find an 'O'Donnell,' or a 'Wild Irish girl?' If Banim and Gerald Griffin were still with us, where could they find heroes and heroines! Fortunately, Moore withdrew our melodies from amid the ruins of time, and gifted them with immortality, and Lover has wedded several of our beautiful superstitions to poetry which Moore might have acknowledged without lowering his pinions.

I could identify all my characters – but to do so – I should add a volume – not an Introduction to my 'Sketches of Irish Character.'

My last two visits to Ireland gave me no reading, new or old, of Irish character. What can be seen of Irish character on well-regulated railroads? What wit can be gleaned from erect and taciturn policemen?

It is impossible to say what may be. I should not be surprised to find an outside jaunting car driven by a London cabman. I confess to looking anxiously, and I had almost said hopefully, for even the shadow of a beggar in Sackville Street. They were too numerous at Killarney, but they were not of the 'right sort' – they were beggars of the new régime; they did not ask for 'a little tester, just for the honour of ould Ireland – lady dear;' but for 'sixpence or a shilling, to help pay our passage to Amerikay – sure the sooner we can get away the better; there's nothing here to keep us, if we want to keep flesh on our bones.'

Miles, and miles, and miles we passed in 1852 without meeting one human being! Miles – up hills, down dales, over those bounding leaping rivers – and no creature to greet us with 'God save you, and send you a good journey;' or, 'God be praised for a fine day;' or, 'Take it easy up the hill – may-be the lady would like an air of the fire within there, and the mealy potatoes are just on the boil!'

No smoke from the cottier's evening fires curling up the mountains, or climbing like incense up the blue vault of heaven, until it mingled with the atmosphere. If the deserted cottages had been fairly levelled, and the plough passed over their graves, it would have been paradise in comparison to the bleared and burnt effect of the shattered and roofless walls. More than once I saw the living skeleton of a poor cat, clinging with the instinct of its race to the abandoned dwelling, and staring, unconscious of danger, and incapable of flight, at the carriage as it passed. I daresay, nay, I am sure, the people are better away – better in another land than in the one where those they loved starved and died; but of all the wants the heart aches for, is the want of forms and voices where they once were seen and heard.

Yes! it is better for the landlords to have those people away, and better for the people to be away from the landlords. And in fifty years, or less, those who have moved off in that mighty exodus will have sunk into foreign graves, and their children have become units in the mass of a young and vigorous population – spreading their thousands and tens of thousands over the unmeasured breadths, and lengths, and depths of the new world!

Were I now to kneel upon my grandmother's square grey tomb in Bannow Church, when the moon was rising, the tide flowing gently in, the Hook light flinging its arrows of warning and guidance over the billows, I could easily, in that lonely place, fancy myself *the last woman* – the very last living creature, where once I was surrounded by young life!

Alas! I could now wander from the church, through the moor of Bannow, up the hill of Graige, past the windmill and the forge, and where the cottages stood, and not recognise a single countenance, or hear a single blessing! The children, the few left in the land, to wait until sent for to the new home of their fathers, would regard me as a stranger.

There is the Bay of Graige! – there the Keroe and Saltee Islands – there the Mountain of Forth, with its angry cloud cap – yonder I know are the houses of Grange and Kiltra, and Barristown; and the old castles of Coolhull and Danes are still mouldering away, and over the Scaur are the Seven Castles of Clonmines – and there stretches the Borough or Ballytegue and Cullinstown, and over there –

Bag and Bun,
Where Ireland was lost and won.

And yet they are but names and memories to me now – the old people are all gone – new priests, new ministers, new people!

I look into the valley, where my own home stood so firmly against hurricane and tempest. The wood has marvellously increased. I can remember when much of it was planted. Well do I know where the hospitable home was seated – the long awkward chimneys – the old gable, with its warning bell, the multitude of long narrow windows, the high-backed roof, the in-and-out quaint little courts, the myrtle hedges, the old-fashioned 'flower-knot,' the temple and shell house, and more than all – my darling cottage – all levelled with the earth – all a legend, a tradition – misty as a dream! And, but for ONE– my good and gentle mother – upon whose patient head the snows of eighty years have fallen, but not pressed – I might think all Bannow a mere dream! all a mere dream – but for this dear and sweet reality beside me: still beside me, God be thanked, though five and twenty years have passed since, as an author, I first put 'pen to paper!'

FIRFIELD, ADDLESTONE,
November, 1854.

For Product Safety Concerns and Information please contact our EU
representative GPSR@taylorandfrancis.com
Taylor & Francis Verlag GmbH, Kaufingerstraße 24, 80331 München, Germany